THE WRATH OF LEIA

Ourn produced a small black box from a concealed pocket. "Is a way to send messages to N'zoth—to Nil Spaar. Completely undetectable, untraceable. By what magic, my engineer could not divine. But you have many scientists—they will find out for you."

It was Leia's turn to take a step forward. "Where did you get this?"

"From the viceroy. His ship destroyed mine, you remember—at East Port, the day he left. He promised me restitution, but it was an empty promise—"

"How did you help *him*? By spying for him?"

Ourn swallowed nervously and tried to smile. "Now, Princess—how many secrets does someone like me know? Nothing. Less than nothing. I pretended. I deceived him—"

With a single quick stride, Leia closed the distance between them. "You took my husband away from me," she said, and dropped into a Jedi fighting stance.

"Princess, surely—"

It took only one blow to silence him, one more to bring him to his knees, and one last to send him sprawling, unconscious. Releasing her breath in a satisfied sigh, Leia stood straight and looked to a startled Tarrick.

"Thank you for that," Leia said lightly, flexing her hands in front of her. "I just might be able to sleep a little tonight."

ALSO BY THE AUTHOR

The Trigon Disunity future history:
Emprise (1985)
Enigma (1986)
Empery (1987)

Isaac Asimov's Robot City: Odyssey (1987)
Photon: Thieves of Light (1987)

Alternities (1988)
The Quiet Pools (1990)
Exile (1992)

STAR WARS: The Black Fleet Crisis:
Before the Storm
Shield of Lies
Tyrant's Test

For further information
By mail (please enclose SASE):
P.O. Box 22066, Lansing, MI 48909-2066.
On the World Wide Web:
http://www.sff.net/people/K-Mac

The Black Fleet Crisis
Book Three

♦

Tyrant's Test

♦

Michael P. Kube-McDowell

SPECTRA™

BANTAM BOOKS
NEW YORK TORONTO LONDON SYDNEY AUCKLAND

Tyrant's Test
A Bantam Spectra Book / January 1997

ISBN 0-553-57275-X

Published simultaneously in the United States and Canada

PRINTED IN THE UNITED STATES OF AMERICA

OPM   0 9 8 7 6 5 4 3 2 1

Dedication

For the stalwart crew,
Russ Galen
Tom Dupree
Sue Rostoni
Lynn Bailey

And the bold captain,
George Lucas

Acknowledgments

Writing "The Black Fleet Crisis" has been either the most grueling fun or the most enjoyable marathon of my writing career. Either way, the last seventeen months have been amazingly full—a new home, two new babies (Amanda and Gavin), and more than three hundred thousand new words of fiction.

Though I was on my own in the many long hours I spent with my old friend Qwerty, I couldn't have had those hours, or done nearly as much with them, without the help of a grand conspiracy of allies.

First among them are my immediate family, Gwen Zak and my son Matt, and my *de facto* extended family, Rod Zak and Arlyn Wilson. With unflagging grace and good humor, they pitched in wherever they were needed, doing whatever had to be done to keep the home fires burning and the dragons at bay.

The seasoned professionals of this conspiracy were SCG superagent Russ Galen, Bantam editor Tom Dupree, BDD Audio producer Lynn Bailey, and Lucasfilm's Sue Rostoni. Working their mysterious ways through such arcane media as the fax, the telephone, and E-mail,

they skillfully managed the more far-reaching elements of the master plan.

Then there were the many sympathizers, who—though not formally part of my cell—nevertheless offered their knowledge or services to further our cause. Prominent on that long list are Dan Wallace, Craig Robert Carey, Timothy O'Brien, R. Lee Brown, Michael Armstrong, Jim Macdonald, Daniel Dworkin, Evelyn Cainto, and Mike Stackpole.

Meanwhile, John Vester, Dave Phillips, and Jennifer Hrynik took the point on a fiendishly clever disinformation campaign.

Though security concerns limit my freedom to name names, I also want to acknowledge the aid and comfort I drew from the volunteer flyspeckers in CompuServe's SF Media Two forum (GO SFMEDTWO) and Genie's SF Roundable Three (SFRT3), and from the rascals of RASSM.

I offer my most earnest salute to the chief architect of the Rebellion, George Lucas, without whose inspiration none of us would be here.

Finally, I want to thank the true believers of the cause—Star Wars fans around the globe—for coming along on this journey. Your boundless enthusiasm and vocal support have meant a great deal to me.

—Michael Paul McDowell
August 31, 1996
Okemos, Michigan

Dramatis Personae

On Coruscant, capital of the New Republic:
  Princess Leia Organa Solo, President of the Senate
    and Chief of State of the New Republic
  Alole and Tarrick, aides to Leia
  Admiral Hiram Drayson, chief of Alpha Blue
  General Carlist Rieekan, head of New Republic
    Intelligence
  Brigadier Collomus, operations senior staff
    for NRI
  First Administrator Nanaod Engh, administrative
    director of the New Republic
  Mokka Falanthas, minister of state
  Senator Behn-Kihl-Nahm, chairman of the Defense
    Council and friend and mentor to Leia
  Senator Rattagagech of Elom, chairman of the
    Science and Technology Council
  Senator Doman Beruss of Illodia, chairman of the
    Ministry Council
  Senator Borsk Fey'lya of Kothlis, chairman of the
    Justice Council
  Senator Tig Peramis of Walalla

Belezaboth Ourn, extraordinary consul of the
  Paqwepori

*With the Fifth Battle Group of the New Republic
Defense Fleet, in Farlax Sector:*
  General Etahn A'baht, Fleet commander
  Colonel Corgan, staff tactical officer
  Colonel Mauit'ta, staff intelligence officer
  Captain Morano, commander of the flagship
    Intrepid
  Plat Mallar, sole survivor of the Yevethan raid on
    Polneye

Aboard the Teljkon Vagabond:
  General Lando Calrissian, Fleet liaison to the
    expedition
  Lobot, chief administrator of Cloud City, on
    vacation
  See-Threepio, protocol droid
  Artoo-Detoo, astromech droid

Aboard the yacht Lady Luck, *in pursuit of the Teljkon
Vagabond:*
  Colonel Pakkpekatt, expedition commander, New
    Republic Intelligence
  Captain Bijo Hammax, foray commander
  Pleck and Taisden, NRI technical agents

Aboard the Obroan Institute research vessel Penga
Rift, *at Maltha Obex:*
  Dr. Joto Eckels, senior archaeologist

*On N'zoth, spawnworld of the Yevetha, in Koornacht
Cluster, Farlax Sector:*
  Nil Spaar, viceroy of the Yevethan Protectorate
  Eri Palle, aide to Nil Spaar
  Dar Bille, proctor of the Yevethan flagship
  Tal Fraan, proctor cogent to the viceroy
  General Han Solo, a prisoner

Aboard the skiff Mud Sloth, *en route to J't'p'tan, in the Koornacht Cluster, Farlax Sector*
  Luke Skywalker, a Jedi Master
  Akanah, an adept of the White Current

On Kashyyyk, homeworld of the Wookiees:
  Chewbacca, participating in coming-of-age
    ceremonies for his son Lumpawarrump

Tyrant's Test

Chapter 1

◆

Three levels down from Rwookrrorro and eighteen kilometers northeast along the Rryatt Trail, the Well of the Dead appeared as a solid green wall ahead of Chewbacca and his son Lumpawarrump.

This deep in the wroshyr jungle of Kashyyyk, the tangled web of trunks and branches was ordinarily almost barren. So little light penetrated the dense canopies overhead that any leaves that sprouted quickly withered. Only the gray bridal-veil sucker and the paddle-leafed mock shyr, both parasites, and the ubiquitous kshyy vines decorated the runs and paths.

But neither the bridal-veil nor the mock shyr was abundant enough to block those runs and force the Wookiees to the underside of the web of branches. They—and the creatures that made their homes at that level—could move freely over the top of the tangled maze. Despite the dim light, sightlines of up to five hundred meters were the norm, with the trunks of the wroshyr trees themselves providing the only cover.

It was the Shadow Forest, the realm of the nimble rkkrrkkrl, or trap-spinner, and the slow-moving rroshm, which helped keep the paths clear by grazing on bridal-veil.

The most numerous inhabitants were the tiny barb-tongued needlebugs, whose sucking proboscides could pierce the tough wroshyr bark and draw on the juices within.

The most dangerous inhabitants were the elusive kkekkrrg rro, the five-limbed Shadow Keepers, which preferred to roam the underside and even more strongly preferred the taste of meat. The Shadow Keepers would not attack an adult Wookiee, but long history, now mostly forgotten, had made the kkekkrrg rro the personification of the skulking unseen enemy, and it was the rare Wookiee who would not reach for his weapon on seeing one.

All this and more Chewbacca had shown and explained to his son as they journeyed down from the hunting ground of the Twilight Gardens, a level above. The whole time, memories had swirled around him on the stagnant air. Some were memories of his own journey of ascendance in the company of *his* father, Attichitcuk, of the tests that had earned him the right to wear his baldric, to carry a weapon in city, to choose and confirm his name.

Two hundred years, and the forest is still the same—only I am the father now, not the son. . . .

Chewbacca also vividly remembered the foolish expedition he and Salporin had made to the Shadow Forest in advance of their coming-of-age. Unarmed but for a single ryyyk blade Salporin had pilfered from his eldest brother, Chewbacca and his friend had left the nursery ring and descended into realms forbidden to the children they still were.

They had thought to prepare themselves for the unknown, but managed only to scare themselves with it. Their courage had faded with the failing light, and by the time they reached Shadow Forest, all it took was a skittish trap-spinner to send them fleeing back to the safety of the familiar.

And what we thought we saw filled our nightmares until our tests of ascension finally came—poor Salporin! I only had to wait six days.

If Attitchitcuk knew—then or later—what they had done, he had never let on.

Chewbacca looked at his son appraisingly. He doubted that there were any secret journeys concealed behind those nervous eyes. Years ago, a very young Lumpawarrump had gone alone into the forest near Rwookrrorro in search of wasaka berries and gotten himself lost—a misadventure that had grown much in the retelling, until it became a family fable populated by every monster of the dark depths of both jungle and imagination. But the scare had been real even if the danger had not, and since then his son had been content to stay close to the nursery ring and the home tree.

And Mallatobuck and Attitchitcuk had been content to allow it, to let him be different. Neither, it seemed, had pushed him to take part in the toughening—the unstructured rough-and-tumble play of the nursery ring, where young Wookiees learned their fearlessly headlong fighting style. When Chewbacca had greeted his son with a fierce growling rush, Lumpawarrump had turned from it, yielding as though he were already wounded.

It had been a difficult moment for everyone. But in the aftermath, Chewbacca realized that he was seeing part of the price his son had paid for his absence.

In honoring a life debt to Han Solo, Chewbacca had left his son to be raised by mother and grandfather. He could not fault their love or their care, but something had been missing—something to spark the rrakktorr, the defiant fire, the eager strength that was a Wookiee's heart. Lumpawarrump did not even have a friend like Salporin to test himself against in daily clinches and slap-fights.

The calendar said that it was time. Lumpawarrump had sprung up to adult height. But he had only begun to fill out that tall frame, and it was clear that he did not yet feel the power of his size. It was also not difficult to see that Lumpawarrump was in awe of his famous father, and paralyzingly anxious for his approval. Beyond that, Chewbacca was still trying to take his measure.

His son had talent in his hands. Though he had dragged out the task through nine days, Lumpawarrump had done a skillful job constructing his bowcaster—its weaknesses were the kind that only experience would teach him to correct. And he had shown a steady hand in downing a kroyies with it, the first of the hunting tests.

But the second test, trapping and killing a big-eyed scuttle grazer on level three, had taken even longer and not gone as well. And the test waiting ahead, inside the Well of the Dead, promised to ask more of Lumpy than he was ready to face.

[Explain to me what we see,] he said to his son.

[It is a wound in the forest, where something fell from the sky long ago. It is the bottom of the great pit of Anarrad, which we see from the high lookouts of Rwookrrorro.]

[Why did Kashyyyk not heal the wound?]

[I do not know, Father.]

[Because she needed a home for the katarn. The light falls to the depths and calls forth the young vitality of the wroshyr. The green leaves shelter the daubirds and sustain the sprites and mallakins. The daubirds invite the netcasters, and the mallakins call the grove harriers. And the katarn, the old prince of the forest, comes to the feast.]

[If Kashyyyk has given the katarn this place, why must we hunt them?]

[It is our pact with them, from long ago.]

[I do not understand.]

[Once they hunted us, and the richness of the high forest was theirs for a thousand generations. But their hunting did not destroy us. Nothing of this world is to be squandered, my son. The katarn gave the Wookiee its strength and courage, and allowed the Wookiee to find the rrakktorr. Now we hunt them to repay the gift. Someday it will be their turn again.]

*　　*　　*

The fleet carrier *Venture* loomed ahead of Plat Mallar like a rugged gray island in an endless, empty sea. Snub fighters of the interceptor screen orbited it like hunting birds on the wing.

"Looks awfully good to me," said Ferry Four.

"It's a mirage," said Ferry Six. "They're going to have our heads for losing the commodore."

"Cut the chatter and clean up the formation," said Lieutenant Bos, the ferry flight leader. "*Venture* flight operations, this is Bravo Flight leader. Requesting landing vectors on the ball. I have ten birds ready to roost."

Under ordinary circumstances, the air boss would have handed the squadron over to the landing officer of the active landing bay, who in turn would have activated the landing alignment system's four tracking lasers to guide the fighters in. But all of *Venture*'s landing bays appeared to be locked up tight. "Hold at two thousand meters and stand by, ferry leader."

"What's going on, *Venture*?"

"I have no further information for you at this time. Hold at two thousand meters and stand by."

"Understood. Bravo Flight, it looks like they're not quite ready for us. We're going to parallel the carrier at two thousand meters, single file, landing spacing, until they wave us in."

"Is it just me, or are there guns pointed at us?" Ferry Nine whispered over combat two, the addressable ship-to-ship frequency. "I'm looking right down the quads of an AS battery."

Lifting his eyes from the controls, Plat Mallar studied the flank of the fleet carrier through the recon optics. It did, indeed, seem to him that quite a number of the gun batteries were trained on the ferry flight.

"It might not be about us," Plat whispered back. "We don't know what's been happening out here."

"*Venture* flight ops to Bravo Flight leader. Advise all fighters to shut down engines and thrusters. Recovery will be by tractor."

"Copy," Lieutenant Bos said. "Bravo Flight, you heard the man—turn 'em into rocks."

"Lieutenant, this is Ferry Five—even stationkeeping thrusters?"

"Ferry Five, they're going to reel us in on a line. Don't you know what'll happen if you've got the 'keepers running when the tractor beam grabs on?"

"Yes, sir. Sorry, sir. I just don't understand—why are they doing this, Lieutenant? Why won't they let us land our ships ourselves?"

"Ours not to reason why," Bos said. "Just do as they ask."

"I know why," said Ferry Eight grimly. "They're not sure who's out here in 'em. For all they know, the Yevetha yanked us out during the ambush and put raiders in these cockpits. Think about it."

"Bravo Flight leader, beginning recovery operations now," *Venture* advised. "Request you observe comm silence until further notice."

"Affirmative, *Venture*. Bravo Flight, observe comm silence, effective immediately."

Lieutenant Bos's recon-X was the first to be pulled out of line and towed inside *Venture*'s aftmost landing bay on the invisible line of a tractor beam. Plat Mallar could not see what happened after that—he did not have a good angle on the bay, and the outer doors closed again quickly after Bos's ship disappeared inside. Five minutes later the process was repeated with Lieutenant Grannell and Ferry Two, taken aboard amidships.

Nearly an hour passed before it was Plat Mallar's turn—a long, lonely hour of anxious silence. *They will never forgive us for what we let happen,* Plat thought as his ship began to move. *They will never trust us again.*

The lights in the landing bay were blazing at the levels used for maintenance work and foreign-object scans. After living for nearly two days under combat-cockpit lighting, Plat Mallar was blinded. Before his eyes adjusted, he heard the honk of the rescue alarm and the hiss of the hydraulics as the cockpit canopy began to rise around him.

"Come on down out of there," a commanding voice barked sharply as a boarding ladder clanged against the side of the recon-X.

Squinting against the glare, Plat started to rise, but was hauled back by his unseen umbilicals. He fumbled with the releases, then felt his way over the side and onto the ladder, assisted by a hand that guided his booted foot to the top rung.

By the time he reached the bottom of the ladder, he could see well enough to identify the six helmeted and body-armored troops that surrounded the recon-X. Their blaster rifles remained pointed at him as he stepped down off the ladder and backed away from the ship.

The two security officers who were actually within reach, however, appeared to be unarmed. "Second Lieutenant Plat Mallar reporting. What's going on?" Mallar asked, still trying to blink away the last of the dazzle spots.

"Just stand right there while we take a look at your ID disc," said the nearer of the two officers.

Mallar fished the silver circle out of its special shoulder pocket and held it out to the man who'd spoken.

The major dropped the disc into a portable scanner and studied the display. "What race are you?"

"Grannan."

"That's a new one on me," said the major, handing the disc back to Mallar. "Isn't Granna an Imperial world?"

"I don't know what its current status is, sir," said Mallar. "I was born on Polneye—and I was never much interested in politics."

"Is that so?" The major dismissed four of the troopers with a flick of his fingers. At the same time, the other two shouldered their weapons and moved behind Mallar, one hovering over each shoulder. "Report on ship status."

It was then that Mallar noticed another pilot standing by, a flight helmet tucked under one arm. Behind
him a tech crew waited with an instrument sled. "Engine three gets close to the redline running up to rated
thrust. Other than that, I didn't notice anything."

"Any combat damage?"

"Uh—we were hit by an Interdictor, and then we
took a heavy ion salvo, maybe two, I don't really know.
Everything went out for almost five minutes."

"Any operational gremlins or glitches afterward?"

"No, all the systems seemed to come back all right
once the integrator was stabilized. It should all be in the
flight logs."

"Very well," said the major. "Second Lieutenant
Plat Mallar, I formally accept delivery of recon-X KE-
four-oh-four-oh-nine, pending technical inspection, and
release you from your responsibility for this vessel. Sergeant, escort this pilot to DD-eighteen and remain with
him until the debriefing officer arrives."

"Can I recharge my purifiers first?" Mallar asked,
tapping the rectangular casing on his chest.

The major frowned. "I don't know what that's
about, son. I just know if I were you, I wouldn't be
asking even for small favors right now."

Chewbacca and Lumpawarrump stood together at
the boundary of the Well of the Dead, where the Rryatt
Trail turned away toward Kkkellerr.

[It is time,] Chewbacca said. [Tell me what you
have learned. Tell me the things you must know to hunt
the katarn.]

Lumpawarrump looked nervously at the green
thicket. [Never show him your back, for the katarn will
stalk you. Never flee, for the katarn will overtake you.
Never hasten your hunt, for the katarn will vanish before your eyes.]

[Then how are you to conquer your adversary?]

[You must be patient, and you must be brave,]
Lumpawarrump said, sounding not at all brave. [The

katarn will allow you to follow it until it has taken your measure, and then it will turn and charge.]

[And then?]

[And then you must stand your ground until the katarn's breath is in your face and the scent of its glands is in your nostrils. Your hand must be steady, and you must take it in the center of the chest with your first shot, because your second will find only empty air.]

[You have listened well, and remembered everything I have told you. Now we will see how much of it you have truly learned.]

Lumpawarrump unslung the bowcaster from his shoulder and rubbed the newly polished metal of the stock with his paw. [I will try to make you proud.]

[There is one more thing you must remember: Mind the light. Do not let night find you in the Well of the Dead. The katarn still owns the shadows and the darkness, and even the Wookiee must respect that.]

[How many katarn have you hunted, Father?]

[I have pursued the old prince five times,] Chewbacca said. [Once he escaped me. Three times he fell. And once he gave me this warning that I had been inattentive.] Taking his son by the wrist, Chewbacca made him touch the long double scar ridge hidden by the thick fur on the left side of Chewbacca's chest. [Be attentive, my son.]

Lumpawarrump stared for a moment, then pulled his hand back and began to load the bowcaster. Chewbacca stopped him.

[Why? Am I to go in unarmed?]

[Wait until the moment. If you hunt katarn with your weapon drawn and ready, you will find it too easy to fire the quick shot, the long shot, the startled shot. And then you have given over the advantage. You will never see the old prince that takes you.]

Those words shattered the last of Lumpawarrump's pretense. [Father—I am afraid.]

[Be afraid. But go forward, all the same.]

Lumpawarrump stared, then slowly shouldered the weapon. [Yes, Father.] Turning, his paws found a seam in the green growth and parted it noiselessly. After a moment's hesitation, Lumpawarrump eased himself lightly through the opening and vanished from sight.

Chewbacca waited on the trail for a count of two hundred, then followed his son into the Well of the Dead.

The man who entered compartment DD18 wore a dark green uniform with markings wholly unlike those of *Venture*'s crew or the troops aboard her.

"My name is Colonel Trenn Gant, New Republic Intelligence," he said as Plat Mallar jumped to his feet. "Sit."

Mallar complied. "You must be here to ask me about the attack on the commodore's shuttle."

"No," said Gant. "Actually, we have a pretty good idea of what happened there." The colonel circled the table and Mallar once before sitting down and placing an interview recorder between them. "When did you first learn the nature of the mission?"

"The nature of the mission? You mean the ferry duty, or that we would be escorting *Tampion*?" When Gant showed no sign that he was going to answer, Mallar went on. "I was called to the training commander's office at oh-nine-fifty the day before yesterday, and I was told I had been assigned to a recon-X ferry flight."

"And that was the first you knew of that assignment?"

"Yes—well, no. Admiral Ackbar told me the day before, when we were at the simulator, that there was a chance they might need pilots for a ferry mission. But I didn't know anything else until Captain Logirth called me in. I got the details at the mission briefing, the same as everyone else."

"What details were those?"

"It was a mission briefing," Mallar said, puzzled that Gant would need an explanation. "Ship assignments—the jump vector—the formation we'd be using—the mission schedule—the lift order—the fact that we would be escorting *Tampion,* and that some of us would be returning in the shuttle."

"Is that all?"

"Well—there were some technical details on comm configuration and so forth, yes."

"When did you learn that Commodore Solo would be aboard the shuttle?"

"Not until we were in our ships, ready to lift. Lieutenant Bos recognized the commodore as he was boarding. Before that, all we were told was that the shuttle would be carrying command staff."

Gant nodded. "How much time elapsed between the mission briefing and the cockpit call?"

"Four hours."

"I need for you to account for your whereabouts during that four hours. Don't leave anything out."

"I went right to the simulators and spent two hours doing lifts and formation work. On the way back to the lockers, I stopped for about ten minutes at the Memory Wall, looking at names. I took a five-minute scrubdown, then I crawled into a sleep tube and spent the rest of the time trying to—sleep, that is."

"Who'd you talk to?"

"I hardly talked to anyone. Lieutenant Frekka, my simulator controller. I said a few words to Rags—Lieutenant Ragsall, who flew as Ferry Seven in our group—in pilot country."

"What did you say?"

"I asked him how many of us he thought the Fifth would keep," said Mallar.

"And what did he say to that?"

"He said that in combat, you don't usually lose the mount and get the rider back—that the chances were that with a new fleet they'd need almost as many pilots as they needed fighters."

"Who else did you talk to?"

Mallar shook his head. "The crew chief for my recon-X, the flight leader—that's all I can remember. Major, I was nervous, and when I'm nervous, I don't start a lot of conversations."

"What were you nervous about?"

"About making a mistake. About making people regret giving me a chance."

"Did you talk to anyone off the base?"

"I never left the base."

"What about your comlink?"

"No."

"Are you sure? Shall we look at the comm log?"

"I didn't talk to anyone—wait, I tried to call Admiral Ackbar. But he wasn't available."

"Admiral Ackbar again," Gant said. "Do you have a special relationship of some kind with him?"

"He was my primary flight instructor. And he's my friend."

"You managed to make friends in high places pretty quickly, didn't you?"

"I don't know what you're trying to say. When I woke up in the hospital, Admiral Ackbar was there. Our friendship's been at his initiative—I wouldn't have known who he was to seek him out. I *didn't* know who he was until much later."

"If it's at his initiative, why did you call him?"

"Because I'd just gotten good news, and I didn't have anyone else to share it with who'd understand." Mallar leaned forward, spreading his hands flat on the tabletop. "Look, Major—I know we screwed up, and I know I'm going to be sent back. But every one of us would rather have died than show up here without the commodore."

"Really," said Gant. "My information is that not a single member of your squadron fired a shot."

"We *couldn't*," Mallar said, coming to his feet with enough angry threat in his posture to bring the guard a step forward. "It was just like Polneye all over again. They were *waiting* for us. We were out of it before we knew what was happening. I was hit at least three times in the first five seconds, and I don't think I got the worst of it. But I was pumping my triggers right up to the moment when the last Yevethan ship jumped out—hoping for a green light and a miracle."

Gant's hand shot out and caught Mallar's right wrist, forcing him to turn that hand upward. The movement revealed purple-black bruises across the palm pad and a bloody, scabrous blister covering the last third of the thumb.

Cocking an eyebrow as he released his grip, Major Gant sat back and crossed his arms over his chest. "Yes. They *were* waiting for you—at an intercept point ninety-one light-years outside Koornacht Cluster. They didn't just take a wild shot in the dark. They knew exactly who and what they were aiming at. And that's my problem, pilot. That's my problem with this whole affair."

Mallar relaxed into his chair. "I don't know how the Yevetha found out enough to be there waiting for us. If I had any ideas, I'd have told you when you walked in here, instead of making you sift through the sand. The only thing I know is, it had to come from someone who knew about it before I did—before the pilots did. Tell me if I'm wrong, but I don't think an Interdictor could cross ninety-one light-years in four hours—not on its best day."

"You are correct," Gant said, reaching out and collecting the recorder. Then he slid Mallar's ID disc across the table to him. "Sergeant, take Second Lieutenant Mallar to pilot country and show him how to find the 'fresher and berth forty-D. Mallar, you're restricted to pilot country, comm privileges suspended, until someone cuts new orders for you."

"Yes, sir." Mallar slipped the disc into its pocket as he stood. "Thank you, sir."

"I've done you no favors, Mallar. I'm looking for a traitor. I haven't found him yet."

"Yes, sir," Mallar said, nodding and letting the soldier lead the way toward the hatch.

Gant stood and turned as Mallar passed him. "One other thing."

Mallar stopped short, his heart suddenly pounding. "What, Major?"

"Why do you think the Yevetha left you and the others alive?"

"Sir—at first I thought it was so we could carry the message back, as witnesses."

"And now?"

"Now I think they did it to humiliate us."

"Explain."

"Major, if we'd died out there, or been taken hostage, that would have made us important, too. What they did told us that we aren't even important enough to kill. It's like they understood just how to make us feel small. Futility, Major—that's the message they wanted us to bring back. They showed us they can go where they want to and do what they want to, and there's nothing we can do about it."

"Don't you believe that for a minute, son," Major Gant said firmly. "This isn't over—it's just beginning. We're not going to roll over and surrender to this kind of blackmail. We'll get in our whacks."

"Then I hope someone will get in a few for me," Mallar said, tight-lipped. "Because I think I missed my only chance."

Half a dozen wroshyr leaves moved where there was no breath of air to move them, lifting the width of a hand and then falling again. The movement betrayed Lumpawarrump's position some forty meters east of Chewbacca.

His son was not stalking anything. He was not even moving through the Well of the Dead in search of his prey. To Chewbacca's dismay and disappointment, Lumpawarrump had gone perhaps a hundred timid paces into the thicket, then found himself a hiding place, his back against a wroshyr stump and his body concealed by the heavy, hanging young shoots he gathered around him.

At intervals, Lumpawarrump would peer out from his improvised blind and scan the forest for a few moments as though expecting a katarn to saunter past in full view. Then, seeing nothing, he would retreat back into the false security of his wishful invisibility.

But Chewbacca had had no trouble spotting his son, and neither would any of the Well's predators. And the stump Lumpawarrump was depending on for protection created an enormous blind spot from which a katarn could approach and strike without warning.

Chewbacca knew that his son was in far more danger than he realized, and yet Chewbacca was honorbound not to intervene except to stop a killing blow. All he could do was watch and wait, his bowcaster at the ready, trying not to become so distracted that he made himself a ready target.

To help keep himself alert, Chewbacca kept himself moving. He moved in an irregular arc that had Lumpawarrump's hiding place as its anchor—never drawing too close, never wandering too far away, and never compromising the shot he was constantly visualizing.

Four times Chewbacca saw the wroshyr leaves move, and four times he froze.

Lumpawarrump never saw him.

Chewbacca could tell himself that, even caught in the open, motionless, face averted, a long-furred Wookiee could be taken for another of the stalks and mounds of parasitic jaddyyk moss that dotted the floor of the Well. But even a novice hunter using the simplest blink technique should have noticed that one of the jaddyyk stalks kept changing position. It was a sign of just how terrified Lumpawarrump was, cowering behind his green curtain—which was in turn another hard disappointment for his father.

But although Lumpawarrump had taken no notice, before long Chewbacca knew that something else had. It moved only when Chewbacca moved, and yet somehow managed to draw ever closer. It stayed low in the thick overgrowth and melted into the shadows. When Chewbacca turned to face it, he saw nothing. When he moved toward it, he soon sensed it behind him once more.

With the air in the Well heavy and still, Chewbacca could catch no scent of what was stalking him until it had drawn uncomfortably close. He sniffed the air sharply and breathed a quiet growl. Eight meters away, another Wookiee rose silently from the wroshyr leaves. It was Freyrr, one of Chewbacca's many second cousins, and the lightest-footed stalker in the family.

After a silent exchange scripted in glances and toothy grimaces, Chewbacca and Freyrr came together back-to-back and lowered themselves into the foliage. There the conversation continued in growls so quiet that they could be taken for the groaning of branches.

[Where is Lumpawarrump?] asked Freyrr.

[Gone to cover,] Chewbacca said, tipping his head toward his son's hiding place. [Why are you here? Why do you intrude on my son's *hrrtayyk*?]

[Mallatobuck sent me to find you. There is news that could not wait on your return.]

[What news?]

[It would be better if you left the Well first.]

[My son cannot leave until his test is over.]

[I will stay with him, cousin. Shoran waits for you on the Rryatt Trail, and will tell you all as you return to Rwookrrorro.]

Chewbacca's body went rigid with barely contained fury. [You think to take this duty from me? How can you breathe such shame? Even when the mate of Jiprirr was burned by flame beetles and fell from the Gathering Trail, even when the mate of Grayyshk was confined with yellow-blood malaise and died, they were not recalled from the *hrrtayyk*.]

Freyrr reached back and took a restraining grip on both of Chewbacca's hands. [Mind your voice, cousin.]

The answering growl Chewbacca offered under his breath was all the more menacing for the ease with which he broke Freyrr's grip. [If I do not hear in the next moment what brings you to me, every webweaver, gundark, and katarn within three levels of the Well will hear my voice in the moment after that. Now, what is wrong? Is it Mallatobuck?]

Freyrr sighed his surrender. [No—it is the one to whom you owe your life debt. Han Solo has been taken by the enemies of Princess Leia. He is a prisoner of the Yevetha, somewhere in Koornacht Cluster. The Princess has asked you to come back to Coruscant.]

Only a mouthful of his own forearm kept Chewbacca's howl of distress from escaping his lips.

[You understand now,] Freyrr went on. [You have a duty that goes beyond your duty here. Go. Shoran awaits. He will tell you the rest. I will watch over your son and see him through to the end of his tests. Mallatobuck will see that he understands.]

The decision that loomed before Chewbacca was distasteful, but it was not difficult.

[The *hrrtayyk* can wait until I return,] Chewbacca said, rising to his feet and abandoning his concealment.

Freyrr rose with him. [Chewbacca, I beg you—if your son returns to Rwookrrorro without being able to announce his new name, without being able to wear the baldric Malla has made for him—]

[Better that than for him to return over your shoulder, cousin.]

Freyrr showed a mouthful of teeth. [Do you question my *rrakktorr*?]

[No, cousin. I question his.] Chewbacca called across the Well to Lumpawarrump in a stentorian growl that startled a gathering of scur and rousted a fat-bodied charkarr to flight. Farther away, Chewbacca saw the shiver of leaves that marked a katarn turning away from a hunt.

When Lumpawarrump was slow to appear, Chewbacca repeated the call. [Come to me, first-child. You will sleep this night in the home tree. My honor brother is in peril, and I must go to him.]

Chapter 2

♦

Wincing, Han opened a puffy, purple eye crusted with blood and forced the room to come into focus.

"Barth," he said.

The flight engineer was sitting with his back against the opposite wall, curled up in a ball with his knees drawn up toward his chest and his arms wrapped around them. His face was downturned, his chin against his collarbone, as though he were sleeping—or hiding.

"Barth," Han said again, more distinctly.

This time his cellmate stirred, raising his head and turning his face toward Han. "Commodore," he said in a surprised tone, and scrambled across the rough floor to Han's side. "I don't know how long it's been since they brought you in—hours, at least."

"What's been happening?"

"Nothing, sir. You've been out the whole time. I wasn't sure you were ever going to wake up. Sir, don't take this wrong, but I hope you don't feel as bad as you look."

Han let the flight engineer help him up to a sitting position. "This isn't so bad. I've been beat up by *experts*. The Yevetha are strictly amateurs." Han straightened a leg, grimaced, and leaned back against the wall. "On the other hand, they're amateurs with stamina."

"What do they want with us?"

"They didn't say," Han said. He worked his jaw from side to side experimentally, then sniffed and wrinkled his nose. "Tell me the truth, Barth—is that smell me?"

A faintly embarrassed look crossed Barth's face. "It's all of us, I'm afraid. There's no refresher, or anything resembling one, and no water. I, uh, just picked a corner. But at least it helps mask the smell coming off the captain. And there's something growing on him now—it's covered most of his skin. I can't stand to look at him."

"Don't, then," Han said, looking past the lieutenant at the corpse of Captain Sreas. His face and hands were shadowed by a fine gray down. "Fungal spores, probably. It's a dry world—you can tell from the air, and the Yevetha's skin. A human corpse probably looks like a water hole to the stuff that lives in a place like this."

"I don't want to think about it," Barth said.

"Don't, then," said Han. As he straightened his other leg, pain made him squeeze his eyes shut and grunt. "On the whole, I think I'd rather be beaten up by an expert. Has anyone looked in on us?"

"Not since they brought you in." Barth hesitated, then added, "Commodore, what do you give for our chances?"

"More than I'd give you for our privacy right now," Han said.

Barth twisted his head around, scanning the nearly featureless walls of their prison. The cell had a slitted air vent in the center of the ceiling, a slitted drain in the center of the floor, harsh lights flush in the ceiling corners, and a half-height door armored in riveted plate. "Do you think they're watching us—listening?"

"I would be. *Doko prek anuda ten?*" he asked, hoping Barth knew smuggler cant.

"I'm sorry, I don't understand."

Han switched to Illodian sibilant. *"Stacch isch stralsi?"*

"Sorry, Commodore. I can get by in Bothan, handle a bit of Corporate Sector Contract Standard, and rattle off all nine water curses in Calamari, if that will help. But that's the limit of my linguistic talents." He ducked his head apologetically. "The Fleet Academy dropped its three-language requirement the year I entered."

"Never mind," Han said. "I doubt any of those would stump the Yevetha for long. Let's just assume we have an audience and they're getting most of the jokes. Have they given you any food?"

"No, nothing."

Han nodded thoughtfully. "Well, if that doesn't change, you'll be able to figure out our chances by yourself. Let's take inventory."

The pockets of what remained of the two men's flight suits yielded a flexible comb, the Imperial thousand-credit "Victory Tax" coin Barth carried as a worry-stone, an expired meal card from the Fleet headquarters mess, a pilot's pop-up collapsible cup, and one two-tablet dose of an antiallergen that was on the preflight restricted list. The inventory of jewelry was even shorter—two Fleet service pins with sealed-back attachment mounts, and a fine titanium ankle chain.

"I've seen bigger arsenals," Han said, and nodded toward the corpse. "We'd better see what he has."

Barth blanched. "Couldn't we skip that?"

"They didn't bother to strip him. Maybe they didn't bother to search him, either."

The blaster bolt that had killed Captain Sreas had scooped out a third of his upper chest, leaving behind a cauterized concavity into which the burned edges of the hole in his blouse were fused. The hollow was half filled by the gray down enthusiastically growing on the cadaver.

Gritting his teeth, Han rummaged the pockets and keepaway flaps of the captain's flight suit. He handed his discoveries to Barth, who hung back and tried not to watch.

"How long did you serve with him?" Han asked.

"Four months—nineteen jumps all together."

"Your first assignment?"

"Second. I spent a year with the Third Fleet as a drag pilot on a tender."

Han pulled a Fleet ID from the shoulder pocket and passed it back. "What kind of man was he?"

"All officer," said Barth. "Demanding, but fair. Not much of a talker—I know he had kids, but I don't know their names."

"I know the kind," Han said, then touched his tongue to a comlink power pack. "Dead," he muttered, handing it back. "Did he ever surprise you?"

"He collected glass animals," said Barth. "I wouldn't have expected that. And once he showed me the holo of his wife he always carried with him. It must have been twenty years old. She was sitting on a black-sand beach somewhere wearing nothing but a smile. 'That's the most beautiful woman on this or the next thousand worlds,' he told me. 'I'll never figure out why she fell in love with a dullard like me.' "

"And was she?"

Barth took a moment to consider. "In a way. I guess I'd have to say any man would say so if that smile of hers was aimed at him. I'm still hoping to find someone who looks at me that way."

Han nodded as he gently rolled the corpse onto its back. Then he sat back on his heels. "Well, I can't say that Captain Sreas's worldly possessions are going to have much to say about the outcome," he said. "But hold on to that hope, Lieutenant. You'll see Coruscant again."

By then Barth had retreated from the corpse to the opposite wall. "I don't think so," he said. "I think we're going to die here, too."

Han grimaced as he stood, but erased the pain from his face before he turned toward the young officer. "Lieutenant, our captors went to a lot of trouble to grab us. They're not about to discard us now. And the folks at home aren't going to just write us off. One way or another, our people are going to get us out of here. Until then, we have an obligation to be as difficult and unco-operative as we can manage. You can't let them make you afraid. That just gives them what they want—a way to control you."

"But isn't that what we are—a way for the Yevetha to control the President?"

Han shook his head firmly. "If I thought for a moment that Leia would compromise herself, that she'd compromise the Fleet or the New Republic because of us being prisoners here, I'd find a way to die now, before it could happen."

"Then explain this—if you're right, why should the Yevetha keep us alive once they find out we're not worth anything as bargaining chips?"

"Slatha essach sechel."

"I'm sorry, I don't—"

Han hadn't expected Barth to understand—the reintroduction of Illodian was meant as a reminder. Han pointed at the air vent over his head to underline the reminder, and a light went on in Barth's haunted eyes.

"If your ship was suddenly infested with pests," Han said, "and the first thing the captain did was order you to capture two of them in a jar, would you describe that as taking hostages?"

Pursing his lips, Barth swallowed hard, then shook his head.

"All right, then. From here on out, try to remember where we are, what our purpose is—and that we have an audience, and what *their* purpose is. We had to have this conversation, but I only want to have it once. And some other conversations are going to have to wait for another time and place."

"I know a little nightspot in Imperial City," Barth said. "Good food, sometimes a slava dancer worth overtipping. We'll save 'em for there."

An affable, approving grin creased Han's face. "Done. I'll buy the first round."

The Beruss clan estate in Imperial City was almost large enough to be a city in its own right. Within Exmoor's walls were two parks, one forest, one meadow; a small lake stocked with game fish from Illodia and plied by graceful wind-driven boats; and twenty-one structures, including the hundred-meter-tall Illodia Tower with its external spiral staircase.

Located more than three hundred kilometers southwest of the Palace, the estate was a testament to the long tenure of the Beruss clan on Coruscant. A Beruss had represented Illodia in the Senate for almost as long as there had been a Senate. Doman's first father, first and second uncles, sixth grandfather, and ninth great-grandmother were just part of the long line connecting Exmoor with Coruscant history. Illodia had no royal house, no hereditary rulers, but its oligarchy of five clans had proved longer-lived than many blood dynasties. And the Beruss had survived the various plots, crises, and political tides of Illodia in large part by being content to make Coruscant their home.

Exmoor was likewise a monument to the onetime grandeur of Illodian ambitions. Taxes on Illodia's twenty colonies had paid for the construction, and the skilled hands of colony artisans had decorated and filled the houses named after their worlds. Even the size and spacing of the structures echoed the map of Illodian territories, and each colony house had once borne a brilliant planetary emblem which could be seen only from the lookout lounge at the top of Illodia Tower.

The emblems were gone now, the colony houses largely vacant, the colonies themselves only a memory. When the Emperor had annexed Illodia Sector, he had ordered the colonies "liberated" from the oligarchy's "tyranny"—and then levied assessments on the former colonies that were more than double the taxes imposed by Illodia.

But the old glories were preserved in the approach and facade of the tower itself. The walks were swept and lined with smartly trimmed, bright-leaved plants. The metal and stone gleamed as it had when Bail Organa had brought his young daughter to play in the meadow park with the clan's many children while he and the senator spoke of adult things. And the seventy rooms inside were still a curious mixture of museum and clan commune, with the eleven adults and nearly twenty children who made up Doman's circle sharing and occasionally overwhelming those spaces.

Doman received Leia in a room she had never before been privileged to enter—the clan counsel room on the top level of the tower, where the bonded adults met to discuss and decide family issues. Eleven identical chairs, each bearing the Beruss emblem in silver and blue, were arranged facing each other in a circle. An augmented skylight lit the circle warmly from the center.

Doman's welcoming smile was equally warm. "Little Princess," he said, standing as though he expected her to come to him with a hug and a cheek kiss, as in the old days. "Is there any further news?"

"No," Leia said, entering the circle but coming no farther. "There's been no word from the Yevetha. The viceroy has ignored my messages."

"Perhaps this was not the Yevetha's doing?"

"We now have the flight recorders from several of the recon-X escorts. There's no mistaking the Yevethan thrustship. And Nylykerka has identified the Interdictor they used as the *Imperator,* a ship that was delegated to Black Sword Command. There's really no question about it—this is Nil Spaar's work."

"I see," Doman said, nodding. "In any event, I'm glad you came to see me before the Council sits. It's better that these matters be settled privately."

"I had to come see you," said Leia, settling into a chair a third of the way around the circle from Doman. "I don't understand why you've done this. I feel betrayed—abandoned by someone I thought was my friend, my father's friend."

"Clan Beruss is and always will be the friend of House Organa," said Doman. "That will not change in my lifetime, or yours."

"Then withdraw the summons."

Doman gestured in the air. "I will gladly do so—on your promise that you will not carry the war to N'zoth to rescue a loved one or avenge a casualty. Can you give me that promise?"

"Are you asking me to give Han up? I can't believe that you could call yourself my friend and ask me to do that."

With an easy grace, Doman lowered himself back into his chair. "Two other men suffered the same fate as Han—be it capture or death. Do you care as much for their return as you do for his?"

"What an absurd question," Leia snapped. "Han is my husband, the father of my children. I'm sorry for the others, and I want them all safely returned. But I won't sit here and pretend that they mean as much to me as Han does."

"You need not pretend here," Doman said. "But can you sit in the office of the President of the Senate of the New Republic and pretend so convincingly that nothing you do shatters the illusion? Because unless you're ready to give all three lives equal weight— whether much or none—I do not believe you should sit in that office."

"You don't understand how it is for us," Leia said. "Look at this room—you may have your favorites, but no one spouse is everything to you, the way Han is to me."

"That has always seemed to me a weakness of the way you choose to live," Doman said.

"We can argue that another day," Leia said. "The point is that you can't understand what it would mean to me to lose him."

Shaking his head, Doman settled back into his chair. "Leia, I've watched your kind for nearly a hundred years now, and I've seen the lengths to which passion drives you. A man in love will move mountains to protect the woman who owns his heart. A woman in love will sacrifice all else for the man she has chosen. To us, it seems a grand folly—but I do understand, Leia, or I would not be afraid of your passion for Han."

"Afraid?"

"Afraid that you would sacrifice what does not belong to you—the peace we've struggled toward. The lives of the thousands who would fight at your order, and the millions they might kill. Even the future of the New Republic itself. None of this is beyond human passion, Leia. You know that as well as I."

"Do you think that nothing matters more to me than Han? Do you think I'm that out of control?"

"Dear child, I cannot sit by and trust to reason when reason loses so many battles to passion," Doman said. "Give me the promise I've asked you for, and I will withdraw the summons. I know you'll honor your word."

"You want me to limit my options before I even know why the Yevetha did this," Leia said with the heat of indignation. "You can't ask that of me. It's not time yet to decide how to respond."

"And when do you think that time will come?"

"I haven't even had a chance to go over all the possibilities—Rieekan won't have a report to me for another few hours, and I don't expect to hear any more from A'baht until tonight, after the investigators report from the site of the ambush. Drayson's asked me for thirty hours, and Fleet Intelligence isn't making me any promises at all."

"When do you expect to receive Minister Falanthas's report?"

Leia shot Doman a puzzled look. "What?"

"Don't you intend to involve the minister of state? Or are only *military* options under consideration?"

"Haven't the Yevetha already set the ground rules? Aren't Han, Captain Sreas, and Lieutenant Barth prisoners of war?"

"If they are not already casualties of it—which I pray they are not," said Doman. "But I also pray you remember that every conflict need not be fought to the death, and total war need not follow every outbreak of hostilities."

"So we give them what they want?"

"In the long history of war, far more prisoners have had their freedom bought or bartered than won with arms and noble resolve. There is no shame in compromise." Doman spread his hands wide to embrace the circle of chairs. "This room—this family—is predicated on that idea."

"You lost your colonies and your freedom to Palpatine because of that idea."

"For a time," Doman said. "But here I am, free. Where is Palpatine? Do not let the heat of the moment limit your options."

Leia slumped back in her chair and gazed up at the skylight. "I won't," she said finally. "But I can't let you limit them, either, Doman."

"Leia—"

"We don't know why the Yevetha have done this— to punish me for Doornik Three-nineteen, or in preparation for something still to come." She sat forward, as if about to stand. "But whatever the reason, they'll be watching our response. Don't you think the worst possible sign we could give them is one that says the New Republic has no confidence in its elected leader? Don't you think Nil Spaar will be delighted to see the Senate distracted by infighting?"

"There need not be any infighting," said Doman Beruss. "Step aside until this is over. Let one of us carry the weight. You won't be shut out, I promise you."

"I can't do that." Leia stood and closed half the distance between her and the senator. "Please—on our friendship, on my father's memory—I ask you one last time, Doman, to withdraw the summons. Leave me free to do what needs to be done. Don't make me fight a war on the home front, too."

"I'm sorry, little Princess," Doman said. "There's too much at stake. I have a duty."

"And so do I," Leia said, her eyes clouded with a mixture of anger and regret. "I'll be leaving now, Senator. I have a lot to attend to before the Council session."

"I hope you'll reconsider your position," Doman said, rising from his chair. "I have no wish to embarrass you."

Leia shook her head. "You'll only embarrass yourself, Senator—not least in the eyes of a little girl who once looked on you as family, and Exmoor as a second home."

In the time Chewbacca had been on Kashyyyk, the *Millennium Falcon* had become Rwookrrorro's leading attraction. Its arrival had been a signal event, and its presence on Landing Platform Thyss brought an ongoing stream of visitors from Karryntora, Northaykk, and even the distant Thikkiiana Peninsula. They came despite the fact that all there was for visitors to do was look at the outside of the ship and have a holo taken of themselves standing beside it.

Chewbacca had left the ship in the care of his cousin Dryanta and his cousin Jowdrrl. They had nearly begged him for the honor, and they had taken the responsibility to heart. For Dryanta, a pilot, and Jowdrrl, a ship systems engineer, leaving their homes to live aboard her was an almost unmeasurable privilege.

They had kept the *Falcon* sealed to everyone but themselves and arranged for the platform to be watched around the clock. During the morning and afternoon open-platform periods, either Dryanta or Jowdrrl—and often both—stood watch to see that no one came within arm's reach of the hull.

But there were no visitors on the platform when Chewbacca, Freyrr, Shoran, and a disconsolate Lumpawarrump approached it. Mallatobuck had chased the crowd away without apology and set Dryanta and Jowdrrl to work preparing the *Falcon* for space.

[Lumpy, I need you to go to the home tree,] Mallatobuck said after she greeted the party. [Kriyystak has been preparing a food bundle for your father's ship. See if it's ready, and bring it when it is. Quickly, now.]

He accepted the chore without protest and hurried off.

[You chose to bring him back rather than leave him with Freyrr,] Malla said, turning to Chewbacca.

[It falls on me, not on him. But he was not ready,] said Chewbacca. [Perhaps he will be more ready the next time. Has there been any further news?]

[The grids are silent. The misfortune that has befallen our friend is not yet public knowledge. Ralrracheen has sent a message to the Princess on your behalf, but there has been no reply.]

[And the ship?]

[Jowdrrl will know best,] Malla said, turning and leading the way onto the landing platform. She called out to the ship's custodians, and both came running at her voice.

[Chewbacca, ten thousand apologies. The ship is not quite ready for you,] said Jowdrrl. [I have twenty minutes of work left in the upper gun turret.]

[Explain.]

[I meant it as my gift to Han Solo, in gratitude for your life. I expected to be finished before you returned—]

Chewbacca bared his teeth. [What gift?]

[Cousin, I studied the ship closely while it was in our care. I saw certain weaknesses, and Dryanta helped me devise improvements—]

Chewbacca's grimace grew into a snarl. [Are you telling me that the *Falcon* is not ready because you have been tinkering with it while I was gone, and it is still in pieces?]

[No, cousin, no. Dryanta and I worked all night to finish what we had planned. I need only to test the new systems. If I return to my work now, I will be done by the time you have loaded and received clearance.]

Dispatching her with a growl, Chewbacca turned angrily to Malla. [Did you know of this?]

[Do not turn your fears for Han into fury at your family,] Malla said reprovingly, her snarl matching the intensity of his. [You did not even stop to consider the value of Jowdrrl's gift before rejecting it.]

[She should not have presumed to change anything,] Chewbacca grumbled.

[She is your closest cousin, and all too like you,] Malla said. [How long will it take you to reach Coruscant?]

[I am not going to Coruscant. I can do nothing for Han from there,] Chewbacca said. [He is in Koornacht Cluster, so I must go there.]

[But the Princess asked you to come to Coruscant. Go, listen to her message, it's saved for you on the *Falcon*.]

[If she then asks me to go to Koornacht, I will have lost hours that Han may not have to spare. And if she does not ask me to go there, I must do so anyway, or betray my honor. So I will go there directly.]

[And what will you do there?]

[Whatever is necessary,] he said. [I must go see what Jowdrrl has done. Will you bring me my blaster from the home tree?]

[I will gather what you will need,] Malla said. [Be forgiving of Jowdrrl. She follows the dictates of her honor conscience, just as you do.]

Growling to himself, Chewbacca turned and climbed the *Millennium Falcon*'s boarding ramp with long strides. Malla turned to Freyrr and Shoran. [Come,] she said. [I must speak with you, and there is not much time.]

Grudgingly, Chewbacca was forced to admit that Jowdrrl's modifications to the ship were not only perceptive, but long overdue.

One of the much despised idiosyncrasies of the Corellian YT-1300 stock freighter was the severely restricted field of view from the cockpit. Though the flight crew enjoyed an unobstructed field of view forward and to starboard, visibility aft and to port was virtually nonexistent.

That, plus the extreme offset of the cockpit, made maneuvering or landing a YT-1300 in tight spaces a challenge. Most examples of that model sported five-axis laser-ranging pods as add-ons on the blind side, just forward of the loading port—often installed at the insistence of spooked pilots after a close call with a docking bay wall or another ship. But out of some combination of stubbornness and ego, Han had refused to let Chewbacca install a ranging pod.

"Do you look at your feet when you walk? A real pilot *feels* where his ship is," Han had insisted. "I don't want anyone looking at the *Falcon* and thinking we need that kind of training-school crutch. Give me a meter of clearance and I'll fly this thing anywhere. Do you think Lando could have made that run into the Death Star at Endor if he'd depended on ranging pods?"

But the *Falcon*'s enormous blind spot was an even more serious issue in flight than during landings. That fact was the genesis of the maneuver known to pilots as the Corellian carousel—putting the ship into a slow left-hand roll when making an approach in traffic or maneuvering under fire. Han's addition of a single high-mounted sensor dish to the *Falcon* only accentuated the need to use the carousel routinely, since the dish had an even larger blind spot than the pilot.

Jowdrrl had never flown aboard the *Falcon*, and Chewbacca had never complained about its peculiarities in front of her. But she summed up the problem with one clear, simple truth Chewbacca had not yet managed to impress on his son: [A Wookiee hunter who stands beside a tree hides half the forest from his eyes.]

Jowdrrl's solution was a simple if not obvious one. Everywhere there was an existing viewport—the port and starboard loading hatches, the dorsal and ventral gun turrets—Jowdrrl had covered it with a custom-fitted optical transducer panel.

The output from all four of the nearly transparent sensors was routed to flatscreen displays in the cockpit, giving the pilot the benefit of the familiar views from those four locations. Together, the new sensors eliminated most of the ship's blind spot, leaving only a small area directly aft—an area that was already well scanned by the sensor dish.

In explaining what she had done, Jowdrrl changed from Shyriiwook to the Thykarann dialect, which was much richer in technical vocabulary.

<Something you could do later is pass the signal through the targeting computer—then any object showing relative motion could be highlighted on the flatscreens, the targeting grid, or both,> she told Chewbacca. <And there are better transducers available—dome fisheyes from Melihat and bubble sights from Tana Ire—but mounting them would mean hull work. At least for now you can make use of all your viewports without running all over the ship.>

Chewbacca grunted grudging approval.

[I did not have enough time to work on the other problem,] she said, switching back to Shyriiwook, her tone apologetic.

[Which problem is that?]

[That a Wookiee hunter does not have enough hands to climb and aim at the same time.]

Again, her words showed a surprising awareness of the *Falcon*'s operational realities—in this case, the fact that it was almost invariably undercrewed. The Corellian YT-1300 was officially rated as a four-place freighter for in-system work and an eight-place—four stations, four berths—for interstellar flights.

The cargomaster was expendable, but none of the other three stations was. Even with the cockpit remotes for the gun turrets, it was impossible for two people to simultaneously fly and fight the *Falcon* effectively. The *Falcon* had survived most of its gun battles by fighting just long enough and just well enough to make a break.

[The more mouths at the table, the poorer the feast,] Chewbacca said. [And the silent hunt is best undertaken by a party of two. Still, sometimes four hands are not enough.]

Jowdrrl changed dialect again. <Why have you never installed autotracking fire controllers for the gun turrets?>

<I have told Han for years that we should do so,> Chewbacca said. <But he is too fond of those overbore Dennia quad guns, because they give the *Falcon* surprise punch. The Dennia quads were designed for big-crew Dreadnaughts, however, not for fully automated fire control.>

<As I learned when I looked them up in the Weapons Engineering Guide,> said Jowdrrl. <There is no fast-response ring and ball mount replacement available, and no ready way to adapt the existing mounts for computer control—but I have a few ideas, if I only had more time.> She thumbed one of the eight cables used in the cockpit aiming system. <Did you devise this rig?>

<I did.>

The system Chewbacca had created involved eight motorized cable spools, turning the turret into a mechanical puppet controlled by a joystick in the cockpit.

<It's surprisingly good,> she said. <It gets you most of the way to where you want to be. Did you ever try taking the steering inputs directly from the targeting display, or match-sighting with a scope on the gun itself?>

[I do not have time to talk about what might be done,] Chewbacca said. [But I see from what you have done that I have not given you enough credit for your skill. You have grown while I have been away.]

[Thank you, cousin.] Jowdrrl closed her tool kit and turned to face him. [I hope that that means you will accept me as your partner on the journey you are about to begin.]

[Do not talk foolish talk.]

[I know by what Malla has said that you will face an enemy as fearsome as the webweaver, and more vi-

cious than the gundark. You should not go alone, and
you need not go alone.]

[No,] Chewbacca snarled curtly, turning and clam-
bering down the access ladder to the main deck.

[We are family—the life debt to Han Solo does not
stop with you,] said Jowdrrl, following closely behind.
[And you do not have enough hands. What can you do
alone to help him?]

Chewbacca had reached the cockpit by then and
slipped into the pilot's seat. Turning on the ion coil
preheaters, he began running through the *Falcon*'s
streamlined preflight procedures. [You have three minutes to collect your belongings from the crew quarters
and leave the ship.]

[Aren't you going to talk to Malla before you lift?]
Jowdrrl said, gesturing sideways.

Chewbacca glanced in the direction of Jowdrrl's
gesture. He saw Malla, Shoran, and Dryanta standing
together on the landing platform, looking up at the
cockpit. Dryanta and Shoran were wearing hunting
bandoliers instead of baldrics, and a pair of tough-
shelled tree bags were lying on the ground at their feet.

With a fiercely impatient growl, Chewbacca clambered out of the pilot's seat and half ran to the boarding
ramp.

[What is this?] he demanded over the rising whine
of the *Falcon*'s idlers.

[The rest of your crew,] said Malla.

Shoran grinned brightly and drew himself up to
attention. [The First Wookiee Expeditionary Force, reporting for duty.]

[Malla told us that you're going straight to Koornacht,] said Dryanta. [We can't let you go alone. We're
here to help.]

Chewbacca looked to his wife. [You can't ask them
to risk their lives on my debt.]

[I did not have to ask them,] said Mallatobuck. [I
only had to tell them why you are going and what you
face.]

[It was our idea,] Shoran said, reaching down and

shouldering his well-stuffed bag. [And you can't deny us this hunt without risking betrayal of your debt—if you go alone and fail, you will have no honor.]

Behind Chewbacca, the hiss of injectors and the clicking of compressors told him that Jowdrrl was continuing the *Falcon*'s preflight without his assistance.

[I never wanted any of my family to have to fight again,] said Chewbacca. [I am honor-bound. If I must, I will give my life for my friend. But I will not give yours.]

[My life is not yours to offer,] said Dryanta. [It is mine. And I pledge it to you, my cousin, and to your friend.]

[You cannot refuse us without shaming us, cousin,] added Shoran. [Jowdrrl, too.]

[Go, then, and get aboard,] he said, shooting an annoyed look at his wife. They hastened toward the ship, leaving Chewbacca alone with his Malla. [Your cleverness could cost our family their lives.]

[Or save yours,] Malla said. [I am at peace with my choice.]

Chewbacca seized her in a firm embrace, and they growled with fierce affection into each other's shoulder fur. Then the high whistle of the thrust vents called him toward the ship, telling him that it was ready to lift. But a new voice called him back.

[Father—]

Chewbacca turned and saw Lumpawarrump standing in the wooden arch of the landing platform entryway. He was wearing his bowcaster and carrying the freshly camouflaged tree bag he had taken on his aborted journey of ascendance.

[We will finish your tests when I return,] Chewbacca called.

Lumpawarrump drew closer with tentative steps. [Take me with you. You have already broken with tradition once. I ask you to do so again.]

Malla cried out a protest, but Chewbacca silenced her with a warning gesture as he crossed the platform to where his son stood.

[Why?] Chewbacca demanded. [Why do you ask this?]

[I will be neither child nor adult until you return—I do not belong in the nursery ring or in the council ring,] said Lumpawarrump.

[Are you afraid I will not return?]

[Yes.]

[Then are you not afraid that *you* will not return?]

[I am more afraid to fail than to die,] Lumpawarrump said. [Much is expected from the son of Chewbacca—he cannot be a coward.]

[You need not fear that now. By offering yourself, you have shown your mettle.]

[That is not what they will see. They will say that it was only words, that I knew you would not take me, that I knew Malla would forbid it,] said Lumpawarrump. [They will see that even you did not have faith in me—that Jowdrrl and Shoran and Dryanta were good enough for you, but I was not.]

Chewbacca shook his head. [It is not a matter of faith. I have a full crew. What skills do you bring to this hunt?]

[Everything of you that is in me, and everything that you can teach me,] Lumpawarrump said. [Father, please—I have accepted your long absences, the duties that take you away from us. But I must have a chance to prove my worth to you. I want my baldric and my new name. Give me a chance to earn them beside you, and know that you are proud of me.]

Chewbacca cast a sideways glance at Mallatobuck, who was watching anxiously but keeping her distance. He doubted she could have heard much of the conversation over the noise from the *Falcon*.

[Go,] Chewbacca said, seizing Lumpawarrump by the arm and sending him toward the ship with a push. Malla raised a sharp wail of protest, but Chewbacca moved quickly to block her from reaching their son.

[You can't take him—he's not ready,] Malla insisted.

[If I let you tell him that, if I tell him that, it will

destroy him,] said Chewbacca. [That is why I *must* take him. Now step back and let him see a mother's fierce pride, not her fear.]

Her eyes sad but resigned, Malla cuffed him across the face, and he returned the kiss with equal tenderness and affection. Then he turned and bounded up the boarding ramp while Malla retreated into the growing crowd drawn to the platform by the sound of the *Falcon*'s engines.

Moments later, the ship lifted and wheeled toward the sky.

INTERLUDE I:

Vagabond

The Teljkon vagabond had finally ceased shuddering and groaning around its prisoners. With the starship once again hurtling through hyperspace, at last there was silence.

"Attagirl," Lando said, patting the wall of the chamber in which he and the others floated. "It'll take a lot more than one rusty old escort frigate to run you down."

"But Master Lando, this is terrible, simply terrible," said Threepio, his damaged arm jerking spastically as he gestured animatedly. "That ship could have *rescued* us, and now we've run away from it. We may even have *destroyed* it."

"I hope we did," Lando said. "Trust me on this— any rescue offered by an Imperial warlord in the Core is going to be no rescue worth having. There's probably still a price on my head, maybe on you two droids, too. War hero or war criminal—it's all a matter of your point of view. Chances are we'd find ourselves traded around until we were in the hands of whoever was willing to pay the most for the pleasure of killing us."

"I see what you mean, sir."

Artoo-Detoo burbled a terse comment.

"I'm quite sure he's not interested in your linguistic pretensions, Artoo," Threepio said haughtily. "And neither am I." The droid's tone suddenly changed to a melodramatic melancholy. "Killed or deactivated or disintegrated to atoms, it's all the same to me. Oblivion, the final cessation of awareness—"

Then annoyance suddenly took over Threepio's voice. "Not that it means anything to a random jumble of circuits such as yourself," he added, clanging a golden fist against Artoo's dome. "If you want to do something useful, you might see about fixing those sensors Master Lando placed on the hull. Why you let them be damaged just when we needed them most, I'll never understand."

Artoo's shrill reply needed no translation, even for Lando.

"There's no need to be *rude*," Threepio sniffed.

"If you two keep wasting your power cells on bickering, you'll visit oblivion a lot faster than you were planning on," Lando said, drifting between them. "Artoo, is there any hope for the limpet?"

"I can answer that," said Lobot, who had suddenly busied himself with collecting the parts of his contact suit and climbing back into them. "Just before it ceased transmitting, the sensors measured a monopolar ion density of more than twenty thousand Rahm units. It is a near certainty that the limpet is damaged beyond repair."

"Twenty thousand? Better than I thought. I'd have given you odds that it wouldn't take more than twelve," Lando said. "Well, no matter."

"The primary component of all spectral sensors is Favervil dielectric ribbon," Lobot said. "Dielectric ribbon begins to debond under ion bombardment at a density of fifteen thousand Rahms."

"Is that so," Lando said.

"Master Lando, why didn't the vagabond's shields stop the ion barrage?" Threepio asked.

"Now, that's an interesting question," said Lando.

"The answer might be because there *are* no shields—no ray shields, anyway."

"No shields?" Threepio echoed. "Isn't that unusual—and dangerous?"

"It's unusual—" Lando began.

Lobot interrupted with another encyclopedic answer. "Since the inception of spacecraft licensing under the Registry Office, noncombatant vessels have been required to carry ray shielding generators of at least grade two strength, to protect the crew and passengers from cosmic radiation and stellar flares. More than ninety-six percent of alien ship types in the Registrar's Catalog are known to carry both ray and particle shielding in some form."

Lando looked curiously at his old partner. Before he could give voice to his thoughts, however, Threepio filled the silence with a burst of indignant words.

"Master Lando, this is intolerable. I am certain that Master Luke did not intend for us to be marooned on a vessel with no ray shielding. No wonder my circuits are so sluggish and Artoo has been so peevish. This could have the most serious consequences for us. We simply *must* leave this vessel now."

"That's it," Lando said, snapping his fingers. "That's the reason there's no ray shielding outside. There are no droids, no computers, no electronic devices of any kind on the hull—just organic machines, with organic sensors, and organic repair mechanisms. Different rules. We didn't know because that's the first time we've actually seen the vagabond under fire. *Boldheart* only fired across her bow. Pakkpekatt's task force never fired on her at all. What do you think, Lobot?"

"The issues for biological systems exposed to radiation are rate of damage versus the efficiency of repair, and heat absorption per unit of area versus heat dispersal per unit of area," Lobot said in a flat voice. "The integumentary system of some organisms can provide effective protection for internal structures against charged-particle radiation, and significant protection against the J and C ranges of photonic radiation."

Lando was staring with open concern. "Lobot, *what* is wrong with you?"

"Was there an error in my summation?"

"I'm not talking about your summation—I'm talking about you," Lando said. "Don't take this wrong, old pal, but your conversational style's regressed back to Early Mechanical. You've started nattering like an overeager knowbot. But I can't find *you* anymore—just a wall of data."

Lobot plucked a drifting glove out of midair, avoiding Lando's eyes. "It is possible that I am retreating to the certain and the familiar as a means of reassurance, or in an attempt to enhance my sense of control over my circumstances."

"What kind of answer is that? You sound like a droid running a self-diagnostic," Lando said. "I get the feeling that if your links were up, you wouldn't be talking at all. Come on, partner—what's cracking your glue?"

After a few moments, Lobot stopped fussing with his suit. "I confess I am having difficulty maintaining a positive outlook," he said, his eyes still downcast. "Perhaps you could share with me some of the reasons for your apparent optimism."

"Didn't you feel her wheel around before we jumped into hyperspace? We escaped from the Prakith, and we're headed back to where we *do* have friends. And we now have all the air we need to hang on until they find us," Lando said. "What's more, we're moving through the ship more or less at will, and we've figured out how to operate Qella mechanisms. On top of all that, we're being treated like visitors, not hunted like intruders. Things could be a lot worse."

"Things *are* worse. We're headed for an unknown point within an enormous volume of space in a ship that routinely manages to escape detection for years at a time," said Lobot. "We have no food and limited water, and the droids and the suits are both running low on power. None of the mechanisms we can operate allow us to either control the ship or communicate with it. We're being guided through public spaces and kept out of private spaces—if we're going to get control of the ship, we need to be treated like the owners, not visitors."

"I admit we haven't yet found the doors marked RESTRICTED—AUTHORIZED PERSONNEL ONLY," said Lando. "But we can't be more than two or three compartments away from the bow, according to the map Artoo's been keeping. I say we gather up the gear and keep looking for the control center."

"There is no reason to believe that the control nexus is located in the bow," said Lobot.

Lando peered at Lobot questioningly. "I thought it was you who pointed us in this direction."

"On general probabilities derived from known designs," said Lobot. "But this vessel was not derived from known designs. It was not engineered by starshipwrights working within an established design paradigm. It is unique. And we will never unravel all its secrets, because we are unable to think as the Qella thought."

"One secret at a time will be enough to keep me happy," said Lando. "Why are you so sure the bridge isn't forward?"

"Look at the map. The compartments we've entered over the last few days have gradually been defining a space in the *center* of the ship to which we have no access."

"Then we have to keep going, don't we?" Lando said. "The link between the two zones—the hatch that says SENIOR STAFF ONLY, the key to the executive refresher, the turbolift to the penthouse—could be in the next compartment, or the one after that."

"Or it could be so well hidden that we will never find it. There may not even *be* a link between the two."

"If we have to, we can make one," Lando said, flashing a quick grin. "But right now, it looks like we have a bet to settle. What do you have that's worth anything?"

"Pardon me?"

"If I'm right and you're wrong, I want something out of it," said Lando. "Nothing like a little wager to keep things interesting when the life-or-death stuff gets old. So what are you willing to risk on your opinion that says we die here like trapped rats?"

Lobot stared blankly at Lando. Then his normally expressionless face began to shudder and twitch. His mouth worked, his eyes blinked. Finally he unleashed a stiff, unpracticed bleat that quickly melted down to a stuttering titter. "You're crazy, Lando," he said. "I've been meaning to tell you that for years."

"A first time for everything," Lando said, still startled by a sound he had never before heard—Lobot's laughter. "But you didn't answer my question. Are you in or out?"

Lobot grabbed a drifting boot and threw it across to Lando. "I know you too well to take a wager against you," he said. "Let's go find that control nexus."

"Pardon me, Master Lando—"

Lando was exploring the inner face of a new compartment with his hands while Lobot did the same on the outer face. "What is it, Threepio?"

"There is something that is puzzling me," Threepio said. "Artoo insists that if this ship has no ray shields, there would be no interference with a realspace tracking signal."

"That's right."

"Artoo also insists that even if there were ray shields, they would not interfere with a hypercomm tracking signal."

"That's also right."

"Then can you explain why we have not been sending out a tracking signal each time the ship returns to realspace?"

"Sure. Because we don't have a rescue beacon," Lando said.

"I see," said Threepio. "If it isn't too much trouble,

Master Lando, could you explain how exactly the armada is to locate us?"

"They weren't ever supposed to lose us," Lando said. "Hammax's foray team had orders to go in hard and fast—disable the vagabond before it could clear or break down the interdiction field."

"I see. But you persuaded Colonel Pakkpekatt to let us try to go in gently and slowly."

Lando shrugged. "Something like that."

Lobot raised an eyebrow at the evasion.

"But was no thought given to contingency plans, in the event that the outcome was not as desired?" Threepio persisted. "Surely the possibility of the vagabond escaping came up in your strategy sessions with Colonel Pakkpekatt."

"Of course it did," Lando said. "But a rescue beacon might attract the attention of outsiders. They're designed that way, after all—all frequencies, all receivers. Remember, this was a New Republic Intelligence operation. Getting control of the vagabond was only part of the goal—doing it quietly was the rest. Even Hammax's team didn't have a beacon—just short-range comm units."

"I see—you were forbidden to add a beacon to our equipment."

"No," said Lando. "That was my decision. I figured if we had one, we might use it. I elected to remove the temptation."

"I'm certain I don't understand, Master Lando."

"Well—you don't have all the pieces of the puzzle," Lando said. "Let's just say that my orders and Pakkpekatt's orders don't quite coincide. We didn't have his permission to board this ship, and I didn't intend to hand her over to him—at least not right away."

"Why not?"

"Because she would have disappeared into a black hangar somewhere and never been seen again whole," said Lando. "The NRI has hundreds of people who do nothing but take apart captured alien weapons looking for ideas to steal. The man who sent me out here—call

him the Admiral—had a notion that this ship might be
something more than that, might be something other
than a weapon—and might deserve a better fate. And,
as he usually is, he seems to have been right."

"I see," said Threepio. Artoo chirped briefly,
prompting Threepio to add, "But there seems to have
been some deficiencies in his plan."

Lando shook his head. "The only thing that's gone
wrong with the plan is that I promised him we'd be able
to get control of this ship, and we haven't succeeded in
doing that yet."

"Master Lando, Artoo would like to know if we
have *any* way of signaling the armada."

"Not at light-year distances, no. But remember, I
don't exactly want to be rescued by Pakkpekatt."

"Then how do you intend to signal the man who
sent you out here?"

Lando pursed his lips. "There's a blind-band
hypercomm transmitter on *Lady Luck,* very black
stuff—I have no idea how it works. But the Admiral can
use it to track the ship's movements, locate her anywhere within the transmitter's range—which is a secret,
but I was told it was a very large number."

"But *Lady Luck* is no longer attached to the vagabond," Threepio said. "We saw it cut away from the
airlock. *Lady Luck* may even have been destroyed.
What use is the transmitter to us? No one has any hint
of a clue of an idea where we are. Lobot was right—
we're doomed, doomed to oblivion—"

"Would you plug that leak, *now*?" Lando demanded, his tone dripping annoyance. "I swear before
an honest dealer, you must be the most *tiresome* droid
ever built."

"Oh! How very rude—"

"There you go again," Lando said. Digging a bare
hand into one of the pouch-pockets of his contact suit,
he pulled out a silver cylinder as thick as his thumb and
as long as his palm. "Look," he said. Lando flipped the
cylinder end over end in midair, then snatched it up

cleanly and tucked it safely away. "They'll be able to find us when they need to."

"Why? What are you talking about? What's that thing you're throwing around?"

"The beckon call for *Lady Luck*," Lobot said.

"Did you know about this?"

"Of course."

Threepio cocked his head. "Is that a transmitter? Can we call for help?"

"It transmits the signal that activates the yacht's slave circuits—across hyperspace, too, now, thanks to the Admiral," said Lando. "The slave circuits then bring the ship to me."

"Pardon me, Master Lando, but have you had that device in your possession all this time?"

"That's a stupid question, Threepio—even for a protocol droid."

"I see no reason to respond to simple interrogatives with abuse—"

"Let me save you the trouble of asking any more 'simple interrogatives,' " Lando said. "Yes, I've had it all along, and I haven't used it. The reason I haven't used it is that we don't have control of the vagabond. If I call *Lady Luck* to wherever we stop next, one of two things will happen, neither of which helps us. Either the yacht'll spook the vagabond into running, or the yacht'll provoke the vagabond into firing. And if *Lady Luck* is put out of commission, we're going to be in real trouble. Is that clear?"

"Perfectly clear, Master Lando."

"Good," said Lando. "Then I'm going to get back to what I was doing, and you're going to avoid distracting me. Because we can't go home until we do what we came out here to do, and I'm too tired and hungry to have any patience with a fussy droid. I'd rather blast you into components than listen to you for one more minute. Is *that* clear?"

"As clear as the morning air on Kolos Moon." Threepio tapped Artoo on the dome with his good hand. "Come, Artoo. I believe we're in the way here."

* * *

The bow compartment of the vagabond was at least five times more voluminous than any other that Lando's party had previously discovered. The chamber took the shape of a fat disc standing on edge, with the inner face convex, the outer face five meters away and concave. Counting the one they had entered through, there were eight portals evenly spaced around the rim of the disc. Each of the new portals seemed to be the gateway to another long series of compartments.

"All star routes lead to Imperial City," Lando said. "I don't know if this is the control nexus, but it's something different, that's for sure. And it's pretty clear the Qella didn't want you to miss coming here."

While the droids hovered near the center of the compartment, Lando and Lobot began the now familiar drill of searching its surfaces by hand for contact triggers. But for all the surface area of the compartment, it was unusually unreactive. Lobot found no triggers on the outer face, and Lando only a single trigger on the inner.

That contact brought a pattern of curving, evenly spaced projections curling out from the entire inner face of the chamber. Each blunt-ended L-shaped hook was as thick as Threepio's wrist and as long as Lando's forearm, and the pattern invited the eye to see trapezoids, pinched rectangles, and overlapping wavy-sided triangles.

"What do you think, Lobot? A bridge control panel, Qella-style? They sure say 'grab here' to me," Lando said, hovering near the droids.

Lobot, drifting just over the inner face, reached out and seized hold of one of the projections. There was no response within the chamber and no detectable response from the ship.

"If these are controllers, perhaps they only operate in combination. It would be useful if we knew what the body plan and limb span of the Qella species was," said Lobot, turning toward Lando. "Of course, the size of this chamber would readily allow for more than one operator."

Lando jetted forward. "Isn't this what kids do when you let them sit in the cockpit for the first time— start pushing buttons at random?" He reached for the nearest projection with his left hand, then drew it back. "Artoo, can you spot any writing anywhere on this wall—like what you saw in the airlock when we boarded?"

The droid's silver dome swiveled back and forth for a few seconds. Then Artoo emitted a short squeak that needed no translation.

"Just our luck," said Lando. "We're dealing with a species that never invented the sign."

By then, Lobot was moving across the chamber face by using the projections as handholds. "I don't think these are control devices, Lando," he said. "Or if they are, the controls are locked out. I've touched fourteen different pairs now, and nothing is happening. Even if something was going on elsewhere in the ship, there should be some confirmation here."

"Maybe we're all wrong about this chamber."

"I am more and more convinced by the moment," said Lobot. "I can barely reach from one grip to the next—even if the Qella are larger than we are, it seems inconvenient to scatter controls over such a large area."

"Maybe this is where they hung prisoners, or maidens, or honored sacrifices, like figureheads on the bow."

"I think that unlikely."

With a grin and the faintest puff of thruster gas, Lando began a slow rotation, until he was floating upside down in relation to the others. "You know, Lobot, they look even more like handholds this way—handholds and footrests. I wonder—" He craned his neck back until he could see the outer face of the chamber. "Artoo, how many of the rectangular patterns are there?"

A moment later, Threepio relayed the answer. "Artoo informs me that there are twenty-seven."

"Are there any extra projections that aren't part of those twenty-seven?"

Threepio consulted with Artoo, then reported, "There are none, Master Lando."

"What are you thinking, Lando?" asked Lobot.

Grabbing a projection with his left hand, Lando used that leverage to turn himself so his back was to the inner face, allowing him to reach out and grasp the next projection with his right. His legs were twenty centimeters too short for him to reach the bottom corners of the rectangle. "I'm thinking 'seating capacity, twenty-seven.' Though Wookiees and Elomin would be more comfortable than I am."

"A theater?" Lobot asked, turning himself around as Lando had.

"Maybe. And maybe the show won't begin until the audience is seated. Artoo, Threepio—get on over here and find a place to grab on."

Artoo towed Threepio to the inner face and waited until the protocol droid had grasped a projection with his working hand. Then the little astromech droid took up position beside his counterpart, using a grappling claw to seize hold.

Moments afterward, the chamber was plunged into absolute darkness.

"Lights, Artoo," Lobot said quickly.

"No," said Lando. "Wait. It's their show."

Shortly, all four curious spectators could see a brightening glow opposite them—a glow that seemed much farther away than the outer face of the chamber. As the glow continued to increase, it sharpened and separated into several distinct bright masses. Then, in the span of a few heartbeats, everything before them snapped into vivid, brilliantly lit focus.

Those same hearts skipped a beat at the sight. Human senses insisted that they were no longer inside the vagabond. They were suspended in darkness, looking out upon a beautiful ruddy brown planet painted with sparkling blue oceans and cloaked in a partial veil of lacy white clouds. A brilliant but pale yellow star illuminated the planet's face, which was sculpted by the wandering lines of black mountains and dark green stains spreading outward from the rivercourses. Two moons—the smaller one dusty gray, the larger a startling red—crept along their invisible orbits.

Lando found himself feeling awe, vertigo, and that peculiar panting breathlessness that those who have tasted the cold bite of space are prone to. "Homeworld," he whispered to himself. "The centerpiece exhibit. As though they knew they would never see it again."

"Lando, I feel like I'm spacewalking," said Lobot, also in a whisper. "At least, I think this is what spacewalking would feel like. Is it real?"

"No. It's not quite right—it's more real than reality," Lando said. "But you'd have to have been there yourself to know that the proportions are wrong, that everything's too big and too close together, that the planet's too bright relative to the star, time is compressed, and so on. None of which matters. In every way that matters, it's flawless."

Lobot turned his head toward the droids without taking his eyes off the panorama. "Artoo, what do your sensors tell you about what's before us?"

Even Artoo's long answer seemed respectfully muted.

"Artoo says that the outer face of the chamber is still in place," said Threepio, "but it now has an optical index of absorption below one hundredth of one percent."

"That's as close to perfect transmissivity as any material I know of," Lobot said.

"Do you mean it's not a holo?" Lando asked.

"Master Lando, Artoo says that the star is forty-four meters away. The planet is seventeen meters away."

"It's an orrery," Lobot said. "An enormous shadow-box orrery of the Qella system. I'm very curious about the mechanism—"

Lando was nodding his agreement with Lobot's

conclusion, then interrupted him. "That's enough. I don't want to hear any more chatter right now."

"Why? What is wrong?"

"Nothing," Lando said, drawing and releasing a deep breath. "I may never see another piece of art this beautiful again. I just want to enjoy it for a while before we go on."

The refrigerated cask being loaded into the cargo box of Drayson's landspeeder at the Obroan Institute's Newport landing bay had made the fastest possible journey from Maltha Obex to Coruscant. Even so, Drayson wore his impatience openly on his face as he watched the stevedores maneuver the large coffin-shaped object.

"Excuse me?" someone said at Drayson's elbow. He turned to find a white-haired, sun-bronzed face peering curiously at him.

"Yes?"

"Are you Harkin Dyson? The cargomaster said that the owner was here for the pickup."

"Yes," Drayson said, turning away from the loading. "And you are—"

"Joto Eckels," said the stranger. "I was in charge of the excavation. I just had to see if it was you. I wanted to thank you myself."

"For what, Dr. Eckels?"

"If you hadn't picked up the contract, our trip to Maltha Obex would have been canceled. We might not have been able to recover Kroddok and Josala's bodies for years." He gestured over his shoulder at *Meridian*'s shuttle. "And I want to thank you for agreeing to let me bring them back with me on this run—that was a great kindness to their families."

"Anyone would have done the same," Drayson said.

"We might like to think so, sir, but it's not so. I know that's not why you picked up the contract, but I want you to know how much that opportunity meant to all of us who knew the team. And I want to assure you again that none of this delayed delivery of your material." Eckels nodded toward the cask, now secured in the cargo box.

"I know it didn't," said Drayson, flashing a reassuring smile. "Thank you for your good offices, Dr. Eckels. *Meridian* will return you to Maltha Obex at your convenience—I've already given Captain Wagg his instructions. And please relay my thanks to the rest of your team."

"I will," said Eckels. "And, by the way—based on what I saw before I left, I expect they'll have quite a bit more material recovered and cataloged by the time I rejoin them. There are twelve good, hardworking folks down there, living out of cold camps and logging long days on the digs. You can expect us to return with more than enough to allow us to authenticate those possible Qella artifacts."

"Very good," said Drayson, taking a sidestep toward the cargo speeder.

Eckels moved with him. "I was wondering if it might be possible to get a look at those artifacts, a holo at the very least, before I head back to Maltha Obex."

"Sorry, I don't think that would be possible," Drayson said, smiling politely and trying again to turn away.

"I understand the need for discretion. I just want to point out that it could be very helpful in setting priorities for our remaining time there," Eckels said. "After all, twenty-five days is hardly enough to make a beginning on an entire planet. I can remember expeditions where we spent three months in general survey and site selection before we moved our first pebble."

"Doctor, I understand—and I won't hold you responsible for the handicaps I imposed on you," Drayson said. "Above all else, I'm a realist. I'm quite certain the results will be in line with my expectations."

Drayson moved toward the cargo speeder's door as though to leave, but Eckels moved more quickly and blocked his way. "There's something else I need to speak with you about."

This time Drayson allowed a flash of irritation to cross his face. "What is it?"

"The, uh, material I brought you—" Eckels lowered his voice. "It's clear from the way we found the remains, and the artifacts found with them, that these creatures were sentient."

"Which is as I expected. Did you expect otherwise?"

"Sir, it complicates matters, that's all. If there were survivors, the material would belong to them, of course," Eckels said. "In the absence of survivors, though, the rules and protocols of the Office of Sentient Species apply—material remains must be preserved as found, artifacts may be reconstructed but not restored, and so forth. I'm sure that a collector of your stature is familiar with those requirements—"

"Passingly familiar," Drayson said.

"Well, then, this shouldn't be an issue—for my own conscience's sake, I simply wanted to get your reassurance that the material will be treated with respect," Eckels said. "There are no known survivors at present, but that can change. Look at the Fraii Wys, reappearing nine thousand years after history recorded their supposed extinction. And the last thing any of us want is a situation where survivors appear and find that their ancestors are hanging as decorations in the parlor."

"Is it your purpose to insult me, Dr. Eckels? If so, let me advise you that you're very close to succeeding."

"Please, no, not at all. You must understand, the Institute is very reluctant to let material remains leave our control, and even when we do, we always insist on a right of first examination—"

"Which you've had," Drayson said. "I trust that you took advantage of the travel time to conduct that examination and make whatever holos and scans you ordinarily would."

"Yes. Yes, we did."

"Very well, then," said Drayson, showing a quick

smile. "If it helps, Doctor, let me reassure you that I'm acutely aware of the value of the contents of that cask—and I do not refer only to how much I will have paid for you to retrieve it. It *will* be handled with all possible care. After all, a man spends that kind of money to acquire a treasure, not to squander and destroy one. And the parlor walls are quite full already."

"Yes, of course," said Eckels, bobbing his head. "My apologies if I offended you."

"No offense taken," said Drayson. "Now, if you'll excuse me . . ."

It was a twenty-minute flight north from Newport to the nearest Alpha Blue Technical Services Section, located in the same district where several high-profile senators had their official residences. The unremarkable buildings housing Section 41 were not on the tour routes, however. The small signs bearing the generic and easily forgotten business name INTERMATIC, R.C. accounted for the traffic in and out of the site's two private hangers.

Even before Drayson's speeder had stopped moving, Section 41 staffers were moving toward it with a repulsorlift cargo dolly in tow behind them. As he emerged from behind the controls, he was greeted with smart salutes.

"Admiral."

"At ease, Tomas." Drayson moved to the back of the speeder and helped loosen the tie-downs and guide the dolly under the cask. "Is Dr. Eicroth ready?"

"Lab five," the colonel said. "She's been standing by for the last hour."

"Let's go, then."

Dr. Joi Eicroth greeted Drayson with a professional smile that gave no hint of a relationship that had covered friend, lover, and fellow survivor over a span of thirteen years. But as soon as the cask was safely in place beside the large examination plate, Drayson chased the junior officers away and added a quick kiss to his greeting.

"Scandalous, Admiral. I'm on duty."

"Yes, you are. Let's get it open," he said.

"First things first," she said, pulling a cord that brought two full-body isolation suits descending from the ceiling on their umbilicals. "I have to change into something more comfortable."

It took her the better part of five minutes to don her iso suit, and then the better part of five more to help him into his and seal the lab. But it took almost no time at all to switch off the cask's stabilization system, break the seal, remove the lid, and vacuum away the inert, space-filling foamite that concealed the contents.

Then they stood at opposite ends of the cask, silently looking down at a creature that had died more than a century ago and been buried by its friends on the moving ice of Maltha Obex. Its oval, smooth-skinned body was nearly as wide as the cask. Its slender, double-jointed limbs would not have fit inside it if they had not been neatly folded so that its clumsy-looking three-fingered hands covered its face, and its legs made a neat square-and-X below its body.

"It's no wonder," Eicroth said shaking her head.

"What?"

She moved to the side of the cask. "These limbs must be five or six meters long altogether—and with a cross section not more than six centimeters. A perfectly dreadful adaptation for cold. It's amazing that this one lived long enough to die where it did."

Drayson nodded. "I want the genetic material extracted and sequenced immediately. The general dissection can wait until that's done."

"Understood," she said. "Help me move it up on the plate."

Chapter 3

◆

G eneral A'baht."

"Yes?"

"The gig from the *Yakez* is coming alongside. You asked to be notified."

"Thank you, Lieutenant," Etahn A'baht said without looking up. "See that Commodore Carson is escorted to the flag briefing room immediately."

"Yes, sir."

It was the first of five such vessels expected to rendezvous with the fleet carrier *Intrepid* that morning, and Farley Carson was the first of the task force commanders to be piped aboard for the command briefing. The Star Destroyer *Yakez* was the flagship of the Fourth Fleet's Task Force Apex, and Carson was A'baht's sole friend among the arriving flag officers.

By President Organa Solo's order, the Fifth Fleet had been reinforced by elements drawn from three other New Republic fleets. With the arrival of Task Force Gemstone, all the disparate elements had finally gathered in deep space outside Koornacht Cluster, and the business of forging them into a single command could begin.

That burden was to have fallen on Han Solo, but the Yevethan ambush carried out against the ferry flight and the commodore's shuttle had left the combined fleet without its appointed leader. So far, no replacement had been announced, leaving the chain of command as it had been, with A'baht as senior commander of the forces in Farlax Sector. But Fleet Command had involved itself in the operational details to a degree that sharply limited A'baht's command autonomy, and the selection of a new commodore seemed inevitable.

In the meantime, though, there was work to do.

"General A'baht," said a new voice.

A'baht looked up to see Carson standing in the hatchway wearing a half grin. "Stony," A'baht said, rising from his desk. "I thought I told my aide to deliver you to the briefing room."

"The landing bay officer said the next gig was ten minutes behind me," said Carson, closing the hatch behind him and easing himself into a chair. "I thought I'd take the opportunity to say hello."

Puffing out a breath, A'baht settled back into his chair and thumbed his comlink. "Lieutenant, inform me when the others arrive."

"Yes, sir."

Switching off the unit and setting it on his desk, A'baht sat back and let himself smile. "It's good to see you, Stony."

"And you, Etahn. I hear things have been a little rough."

"I'm glad to have you here," said A'baht. "This is a very green fleet."

"I doubt that your training methods have softened with the years," said Carson. "They'll be all right."

"A leavening of experienced crews and battle-tested ships among them will make them better," said A'baht. "We've trained them hard, but training is not the same as fighting. They got their first taste of that at Doornik Three-nineteen."

"A bitter taste, from what reached us," said Carson. "How did the new ships perform for you?"

"They held up well. The losses we took weren't design-related. A couple of captains learned what not to do next time." A'baht paused, then added gravely, "A couple of crews bought me very expensive lessons that I will probably not have the opportunity to apply."

"You don't think you're going to see home before this is over, do you?"

"No—they won't make any changes now. But when the new commodore arrives, I'll be reduced to a supernumerary—in fact if not in name," said A'baht. "Already I'm little more than a mouthpiece for Fleet Command."

"It's that way sometimes," said Carson, his grin widening. "No one wearing *this* uniform enjoys the latitude of a general in the Dornean navy."

A'baht flashed a brief, knowing smile. "Or enjoys the responsibility. If I had had that from the start—"

"It's not the way Coruscant does things—no matter who's holding the reins, there are always reins," said Carson. "Are you certain they're going to send someone?"

"I think the only thing that's stopped them from sending Ackbar or Nantz to take command is the fear that they, too, might become hostages," said A'baht. "I seem not to have many boosters at headquarters."

"I told you—you should have let them make you an admiral," said Carson. "I'd bet half your trouble with the command staff comes from clinging to your old rank. Headquarters is full of newborn traditionalists, and they can't get it out of their heads that a general should have dirty boots or wings. These lofty quarters"—he raised his hands to take in the utilitarian suite—"are for admirals."

"So you are saying that they offered me the choice of retaining my Dornean navy rank as a false courtesy," said A'baht.

"Oh, I'm sure whoever signed off on the consolidation plan was sincere," said Carson. "Generals are C-one, admirals are C-one—so it's the grade that matters, not the rank, right? But old prejudices die slowly— to say nothing of old rivalries."

"Foolishness," A'baht said disgustedly. "To judge a man by his title—"

At that point, the hatch opened and Lieutenant Zratha poked his head in. "Admiral Tolokus and Commodore Martaff are in the briefing room, sir. The others are on their way up."

"Thank you. We'll be along presently," said A'baht, standing. "Well, Stony, time to don my tarnished title."

Carson was on his feet by then and saluted smartly—to A'baht's surprise. "Sir, if I may say so, I can see no tarnish from here—and neither will the others." He moved a step closer and dropped his voice. "This isn't Imperial City. We know who you are, General—we know that you belong. Just lead the way. You won't need to wonder about whether we're following. They asked me to tell you that, sir."

A'baht showed a quick, tight smile. "Thank you, Stony," he said. "Now let's go roll up our sleeves."

A'baht allowed Carson to go on ahead while he stopped to collect his briefing officers from the staff bullpen. Without consciously intending it, that gave him the opportunity to make an entrance, sweeping into the room with two colonels following in his wake. The five who were waiting there—four commodores and an admiral, from left to right a woman, three men, and a Norak Tull—rose smartly from their seats and saluted.

"At ease," A'baht said, moving toward the center seat. "Let me introduce Colonel Corgan, my staff tactical officer, and Colonel Mauit'ta, my staff intelligence officer. They will have reports for you later in this session." The two officers took chairs flanking A'baht.

The general wasted no time on introductions or other social niceties. "As you already know, you and your task forces have been sent here to reinforce the Fifth Fleet in the effort to contain the Yevetha," he said. "We are no longer here as a symbol, or a warning, or a show of strength, like some sort of War Day parade.

Our mission objectives are threat assessment and containment, and they could grow beyond that at any time.

"We will operate as a single operational unit at double fleet strength, with all ten task forces reporting directly to me through my command staff. Each of your units will retain its current organization, call signs, and command frequencies at the battle group, squadron, and division levels.

"The one exception to that concerns your intelligence assets. All prowlers and ferrets are to be attached to the newly authorized Sixteenth Tactical Recon Group, and will be reporting directly to Colonel Mauit'ta, effective immediately. He will provide you with further details concerning basing and the transfer procedure. Fleetwide tactical reports will come from Colonel Corgan's office. You'll be expected to continue to provide your own local early-warning and fleet defense patrols, using your recon wings and pickets.

"We've taken casualties and can expect to take more, but I will not stand for any commander under me becoming blithe about that fact. We should be prepared to accept every loss by enemy action that is necessary to the success of our mission here—but I will not accept a single casualty due to inattentiveness, incompetence, carelessness, inefficiency, or preventable failures of ships and munitions. Our enemy is smart, strong, and determined, and we're on his turf. I'm asking for the highest possible level of combat readiness at every level of your respective commands.

"While we're on the subject of losses—Colonel Corgan?"

Corgan nodded. "Fleetwide, we are twenty-six combat pilots and eleven support pilots short of our authorized strength," he said. "Those numbers reflect net losses from the Doornik Three-nineteen engagement and the coordinated recon of the Cluster interior.

"Between reserves and resupply from Coruscant, we have rides available—just no riders. One of the down sides of being a new combat division scratch-built to specs is that we had very few experienced pilots banked in nonflying posts, and most of those carry ranks that ordinarily would exclude them from front-line combat units.

"When you return to your commands, please examine your crew and staff rosters with an eye toward locating a minimum of six and a maximum of eight pilots whom you could make available by transfer. We are particularly hurting for experienced recon pilots."

Commodore Poqua leaned forward and rested her folded arms on the table. "Between the expansion to five fleets and the number of Rebellion veterans returning to civilian life, none of us is in a much better position than you are," she said. "I know that up until two years ago, Task Force Gemstone typically had forty or more names in the bank. Now those bank pilots are scattered on forty worlds, making babies and tending gardens and flying commercial shuttles—if they're flying at all."

"We're aware of the effect the drawdown has had throughout the Fleet," said A'baht. "But the need to balance our assets remains. Please submit your transfer lists by fourteen hundred today." He looked to his right. "Colonel Mauit'ta—the Yevethan force assessments."

Mauit'ta slid a datacard across the table to each of the task force commanders in turn. Commodore Grekk 9, the Norak Tull, inserted the card into the input stage on his armored thorax, and Poqua produced a datapad from an inside pocket. The others let their copies remain on the table as finger toys.

"Those datacards contain our complete and most current knowledge about the Yevethan fleet," said Mauit'ta. "That includes recognition holos, sensor profiles, an order of battle and ship inventory, last and best sightings, and preliminary specifications for the hyperspace-capable thrustship design now code-named Fat Man.

"The data we are providing to you is incomplete and in some respects speculative. For example, the order of battle is based primarily on astrographic deployment, since we have no direct information about the combat organization of the Yevethan fleet. But as the General has already noted, one of our jobs right now is to fill in the blanks. We're particularly eager for a chance to make a kill on a Fat Man—right now we don't even have a good sense of what that will take.

"I'll let you review the force assessments in detail with your command staffs, and limit myself to a summary overview. Based on a complete analysis of our contacts with the Yevetha, we are currently estimating their fleet strength at no fewer than ninety-three capital ships, of which at least twenty-nine are Imperial-design vessels and the balance are Fat Men.

"There are at least nineteen occupied and defended worlds, and there may be twenty—Doornik Two-oh-seven hasn't been reconned yet. Eight are defended by a mixed fleet, and we're considering that an indicator that the Yevetha consider those principal targets. Five are League members, and three are former colonies. The other eleven targets are defended by Fat Men only.

"It is possible that the Yevetha have additional vessels cached elsewhere—we hope to start reducing that uncertainty by expanding our surveys of the Cluster. But the biggest question mark—"

Grekk 9 interrupted the briefing at that point. "The Imperial shipyards. Where are the shipyards?"

"Yes, Commodore—you anticipate me. We don't know where they are or what's hiding in them. The probability is that the Yevetha have three operational Imperial shipyards, all of which may be continuing to produce copies of the Imperial ships in their inventory. Four instances of duplicate Star Destroyer ID profiles were recorded during the recon penetration."

Carson spoke up. "Either they're trying to throw us off, or they're duplicating systems without understanding them."

"We have an intelligence source that suggests the latter may be the case," said Mauit'ta. "In any event, locating the shipyards is our number-one intelligence priority. And when located, the shipyards will be designated as primary targets."

"What about the Fat Men?" asked Martaff. "Where are they being built? Given the numbers, we may need to worry more about them."

"The thrustships appear to be built in surface yards, possibly on N'zoth only," said Mauit'ta. "We've located two such yards, and those are designated priority point targets."

"How do you intend to locate the Imperial yards?" asked Grekk 9.

A'baht interrupted at that point. "All of these issues can be addressed at a later time," he said. "The point to impress on your crews is that the Yevetha cannot be taken lightly. Considering only their confirmed assets, they have more than sufficient strength to overwhelm a single task force.

"For that reason, I have ordered that the minimum division for the coming deployment will be two task forces. Token and Bellbright will be paired under Admiral Tolokus. Apex and Summer will combine under Commodore Carson. Gemstone will join Copperleaf, the flag task force, under Commodore Mirx. Are there any questions on that point?"

There were none. Joint task force operations were part of both the training and operational routine, and A'baht had left the natural and familiar pairings in place.

But the order itself underlined how seriously A'baht viewed the Yevetha threat. The commodores of the Fleet's task forces were not accustomed to thinking of their commands as vulnerable. The typical composition of a twenty-one-vessel task force included a Star Destroyer or fleet carrier as flagship, two heavy cruisers and two assault carriers, four escort frigates, and five gunships—a fast, flexible, and formidable aggregation of firepower.

"What *is* our coming deployment?" asked Admiral Tolokus.

"I'm taking the fleet into the boundary systems of the Cluster," said A'baht, turning his solemn and unblinking gaze toward the admiral. "The big parade is over. We're going to make it as hard as we can for the Yevetha to keep track of us, while making it easier for us to keep track of them.

"That includes recon surveys in force, filling the Cluster with as many sensor buoys and probots as we can get, scattering ghost repeaters behind in systems we visit, and sending a squadron to Doornik Eleven-forty-two to look for a shipyard there," he said. "We don't currently have the authority to initiate action against the Yevetha, but we're fully authorized to use all available force if they show up and try to interfere with our operations.

"In short, we're going to stretch the principles of free navigation and legitimate self-defense as far as they'll go," said A'baht. "If our presence persuades the Yevetha to seek a diplomatic solution, that'll be fine with us. But if they insist on war, we have to make certain we're ready to make them regret their choice."

A'baht swept his gaze across the faces opposite him at the briefing table. "That's what I expect from you, and from the ships, officers, and crews under your command. Be prepared to fight when there is no other option—and be prepared to win, because there is no other option."

Luke awoke in *Mud Sloth*'s sleeper with an unaccustomed warmth beside him and an unaccustomed memory hovering close to his thoughts. He stirred, and Akanah melded her body against his again, skin touching skin and coaxing slumbering senses to awaken.

He did not know how to talk about what had passed between them, or what might come of it, but she did not ask that of him. She allowed him to stay in the restful comfort of the circle of their mutual embrace, making no demands, expecting no explanations. He returned that courtesy in kind.

It had been much the same the night before. Loneliness, grief, compassion, and a previously undiscovered hunger for a touch that felt like acceptance had brought them to the brink. But by silent mutual consent, something had been held back. Neither of them had asked for or offered their deepest intimacies. And, unpressured, each had allowed the other to enjoy the novelty of not being alone.

They lay together in the sleeper, awake, aware that the other was awake, and aware that the other was aware. But for a long time, neither of them spoke. Luke barely trusted the privacy of his own thoughts, and didn't dare open himself to reach out for hers.

"Your turn," she murmured at last.

"What?"

"To talk about your father."

For some reason Luke did not fully understand, the familiar inner wall of resistance did not snap into place. "I don't talk about my father," he said, but it was a rote refusal, without conviction.

Even though she must have heard the opening, she did not try to cajole him into a reversal or probe for the exceptions. "I understand," she said, showing a sympathetic smile. Then she turned onto her back, looking up into the holographic galaxy. "It was hard for me."

That small physical retreat was enough to draw Luke out. "It's not as though there's much I could say, anyway," he said, rolling onto his side and propping his head on one hand. "Almost everything I know, everyone seems to know—and almost everything I'd like to know, no one seems to know. I don't remember my father, or my mother, or my sister. I don't remember ever living anywhere but Tatooine."

Akanah nodded understandingly. "Did you ever wonder whether those memories might have been blocked?"

"Blocked? Why?"

"To protect you. Or to protect Leia and Nashira. Young children don't know when they're saying too much or asking the wrong question."

Luke shook his head. "I've deep-probed Leia for unremembered memories of our mother. If there was a block there, I'm sure I'd be able to see it."

"Unless your own block prevented you from recognizing it," she suggested. "Whoever did this might have anticipated that you would have the gifts of the Jedi."

"Ben could have seen that," Luke said uncertainly. "Or Yoda."

"If you wanted, I could—"

"But what possible danger could those memories be to me now?" Luke asked, trampling her offer before she could make it. "No, I think there's a simpler explanation. I think we were just too young. Leia's memories may not even be real. They might be something she invented to fill that empty space you spoke of, so long ago that she can't remember doing it. An imagined memory looks just like a real one."

"And their comfort value is usually very high," Akanah said. "Luke, when did *you* become aware of the empty spaces?"

"I don't know. Much later than Leia did, anyway. Kids say things—you start realizing your family is different." Luke frowned, his eyes focusing somewhere far beyond the bunk. "My uncle and aunt said almost nothing about my father, and even less about my mother."

"Maybe that was to protect you, too."

"Maybe," Luke said. "But I always felt that my uncle disapproved of them, and resented getting stuck with the obligation of raising me. Not my aunt—I think she always wanted children. I don't know why they didn't have any of their own."

"It sounds like she only got her way when it was what he wanted, too."

"I guess that's more true than not," Luke said after a moment's reflection. "But she never complained where I could hear it, or let you know that they'd had a fight and that she'd lost."

"Self-sacrificing," said Akanah. "For the good of the family, for the peace of the household—"

"Owen was a hard man," Luke said. "Hardworking, hard to talk to, hard to know, hard to move. When I picture him, he always looks annoyed."

"I'm all too familiar with the type," said Akanah.

"Your aunt probably didn't dare cross him too often, or too openly."

"She took my side sometimes. But mostly I think she tried to keep us from colliding head-on—especially the last couple of years."

"Was she happy?"

"I used to think so."

"But—"

"I think she deserved better than the way she lived—the way she died." Luke shook his head. "It's been harder to forgive my father for what he did to them than for almost anything else."

"Harder to forgive, or harder to understand?"

Luke answered with a weary smile. "I wish it were harder to understand. But I know how tempting it is to simply bend someone to your will, or break them and push them aside. All of the whims and wishes and wants that we carry around inside—I have the power to fulfill mine. So I find I have to be careful about what I let myself want."

"How do you do that?"

"I have Yoda's example—he led a very simple life, and wanted for very little. My father walked a different road. I try to let him be an example to me, too," said Luke. "The impulse to take control—to impose your will on the universe—has to be resisted. Even with the best of intentions, it leads to tyranny—to Darth Vader reborn."

"Control is a transitory illusion," said Akanah. "The universe bends us to its purposes—we do not bend it to ours."

"That may be so," said Luke. "But in the moment of trying, people suffer horribly and die needlessly. That's why the Jedi exist, Akanah—why we carry weapons and follow a path of power. It's not out of any lust for fighting, or for our own benefit. The Jedi exist to neutralize the power and the will of those who would be tyrants."

"Is that what you were taught, or what you've taught your apprentices?"

"Both. It was one of the First Principles of the *Chu'unthor* academy, and I made it one of the First Principles at the Yavin praexeum."

"And what binds the Jedi to that end?"

"Because it's necessary," said Luke. "There's a moral imperative—the one who can act, must act."

"It would be easier to trust you with the responsibility you seek if so many Jedi hadn't strayed from your high ethic," Akanah said. "Jedi training doesn't seem to prepare a candidate well for the temptations of the dark side. You have lost students, just as your mentors did."

"Yes," said Luke. "I almost lost myself."

"Is it always to be so? Are the temptations beyond resisting?"

"I don't have an answer for that," Luke said, shaking his head. "Is it how Jedi are chosen, how we are taught—a flaw in the candidates, or a flaw in the disciplines—"

"Perhaps there is no flaw," said Akanah. "Perhaps some piece is still missing—something you have not yet rediscovered."

"Perhaps. Or perhaps it will always be a struggle. The dark side is seductive—and very powerful." He hesitated. "I fought Vader with all I had, and still barely escaped with my life. Han saved me at Yavin, Lando saved me at Bespin, and Anakin saved me on the Emperor's Death Star. I never defeated my father. The deepest cut I ever gave him was in refusing to join him." Luke lay back on the sleeper and looked up at the stars. "I think the next deepest was when I forgave him."

The viceroy's personal aide, Eri Palle, ushered Proctor Dar Bille into the blood garden where Tal Fraan and Nil Spaar were already waiting.

Dar Bille offered his neck to his old friend, then accepted Tal Fraan's offer to him.

"*Darama,*" said Dar Bille, "I hear it proclaimed that your breedery gloriously affirms your vigor."

"Fifteen nestings, all full and ripening," said Nil

Spaar. "The scent of it is intoxicating. I had to have my tenders neutered in order that they remember their work."

"Your blood has always been strong, Nil Spaar, going back to when Kei chose you—but it has never been stronger than it is now."

"I would rather have truth than flattery from my old friends," said Nil Spaar. "Those who can remember the glory of our uprising are already too few in number. What news of my flagship?"

"*Pride of Yevetha* is fully ready," said Dar Bille. "The holding chambers for the hostages have been completed, and the hostages are being loaded this very day. What is the prospect for more fighting? Has Jip Toorr reported from Preza?"

"He has," said Nil Spaar. "His report is the reason I called for you. The vermin have not bared their necks or withdrawn. She who claims honor in her own name still defies us. In the last three days, the vermin fleet grew by at least eighty vessels. It has now dispersed into the boundary regions of the All, and our vessels there have lost contact with many of these intruders."

"I am greatly surprised that they value the lives of their own species less than they valued the lives of the other vermin at Preza," said Dar Bille. "Perhaps we do not hold whom we think we hold. Could Tig Peramis have deceived you, in league with the Princess?"

"No," said Nil Spaar. "Han Solo is Leia's mate and consort, and these are relations of great meaning to the vermin."

"Perhaps she does not realize that we hold him," said Tal Fraan. "Perhaps she does not realize that her actions place him at risk. Uncertainty has not made her cautious. Perhaps it is time to show them our hostages."

Nil Spaar made a gesture that said the suggestion was premature. "Tell me what you have learned studying the prisoners."

"They are uncomfortable with blood, even their own weak blood," said Tal Fraan. "The aversion is strong enough to be a distraction, even in challenging moments. Beyond that, they have provided confirmation of suspicions I already held."

"Indulge me and voice them."

"They form alliances as child to parent—one world claiming the protection of a thousand," Tal Fraan said. "They are divided, but they do not see it. They live in the long shadow of their own disharmony, and do not know to seek the light."

"Is that their greatest weakness?"

That was a more dangerous question, and Tal Fraan hesitated before answering. "No," he said. "Their greatest weakness is that they are impure. The strong do not slay the weak, and the weak do not yield their place to the strong. The pale vermin think of self first and kinship last."

"And you find the evidence of this where?"

"It is why eight thousand Imperial slaves still serve us, and why these two prisoners remain in our hands. They fear death more than betrayal," said Tal Fraan. "Any of the Pure would sacrifice himself before letting the warmth of his breath make him a traitor."

"Dar Bille," Nil Spaar said. "Do you agree with my young proctor's appraisal? Are the guildsmen and tenders who serve on my flagship as eager to give themselves up as Tal Fraan declares?"

"It is true of many," said Dar Bille. "But if your young proctor could speak with the late viceroy Kiv Truun, he would know it has never been true of all."

The answer elicited a grunt and grimace of amused delight from the viceroy. "Mark well, Tal Fraan, how the truth is usually a good deal less certain than a willed belief," said Nil Spaar. "Now, tell me—what is the greatest strength of the vermin?"

"It is as with all lesser species," said Tal Fraan, who had anticipated the question. "Their strength is in their numbers. They overwhelm their worlds with their unclean fecundity. You saw yourself how their spawnworld is overrun with their soft, squirming bodies. If they acted in concert, as one kinhold, they could overwhelm us."

"But they do not," said Dar Bille.

"No," said Tal Fraan. "Their great weakness undermines their great strength."

"We will see that they do not learn how to be one kinhold," said Nil Spaar.

"You succeeded most splendidly in that while on Coruscant," said Dar Bille. "But they seem less confused now—and they have not retreated. How shall we answer them?"

Tal Fraan knew that it was the viceroy's question to answer, and he held his tongue. But Nil Spaar turned his way and smiled. "What advice would you offer, Proctor? How shall I make this Leia show me her neck?"

"It is time we showed her our hostages," said Tal Fraan evenly. "And since the pale vermin are uncomfortable with blood, we should find a way to remind them that we are not."

The meeting of the Ruling Council in the matter of Doman Beruss's petition against Princess Leia Organa Solo was delayed two days, then another, then another. No reason was given for any of the postponements. Leia was notified of them by secure messenger—Beruss did not contact her and made no attempt to see her. She suspected that the members of the Council were still divided about how to proceed now that she had rebuffed Doman Beruss's private overtures.

Behn-Kihl-Nahm did come to see her on the third day. But his report was gloomy and his advice unusually terse.

"I cannot count on enough votes to protect you if you refuse to step aside," he said. "But if you accede gracefully, Doman has promised to support me as interim President. Come to the Council and say that your duties are too taxing in this difficult time, that you must be with your family. Ask that I stand in for you until this crisis is past."

"I didn't ask for such help when my children were kidnapped," said Leia frostily. "How will that look?"

"None of this need ever be made public," said Behn-Kihl-Nahm. "Leia, Borsk Fey'lya has been trying to put together four votes for himself. If you appear unreasonable, Rattagagech will turn his support to Fey'lya, who is saying all the right things—and that will give Fey'lya his four votes. You must understand how fragile your position has become."

"There will be no vote at all unless I accept Doman's judgment that I'm unfit to be President," said Leia. "There's no need to select a caretaker if I haven't stepped aside."

"Princess, that option is gone," the chairman said sternly. "All you will accomplish by being stubborn is to force the Ruling Council to report the petition of no confidence to the Senate. And no one can control or predict what will follow. If we are to deal with the Yevetha, there must be stability and continuity."

"Then go back and tell Doman Beruss to put an end to this distraction, Bennie," Leia said. "Because the easiest way to have stability and continuity is for me to stay where I am."

The next morning, Leia received a visit from the tall, slender Rattagagech. He brought with him a balance table and a compartmented canister of colored hemispherical weights—the tools of Elomic physical calculus.

"I have come to analyze with you the logic of your circumstances," said Rattagagech. "It will give you an opportunity to quantify the objective elements in conflict."

"Please don't trouble yourself, Chairman," said Leia.

"It is no trouble—it is a welcome opportunity," said Rattagagech, setting the transparent table on its floating pylon. "I find the old art elegant and the practice of it soothing—it makes me feel very young in the presence of minds that are very old and wise." He sat down before the table, now balanced on its pylon.

"Chairman, I thank you for your concern," said

Leia, stopping him from opening the canister. "But you can't help me."

Rattagagech looked up at her in surprise. Her words verged on an insult to his intellect. "President Solo—Princess Leia—physical calculus is the foundation of logical analysis, and logical analysis is the foundation of Elom civilization. This art raised us from what we were to what we are."

"I respect what the Elomin have accomplished," said Leia. "But physical calculus would have told us rebellion against the Empire was futile. And logical analysis will always sacrifice one life for many, or a few for several, and leave you thinking you've done something noble."

"I must call your attention to the work of Notoganarech, who has demonstrated that a properly weighted table tilts to support of the Rebel Alliance—"

"When you already know the outcome." She shook her head. "I can't let the tilt of the table decide my course. I just don't believe that everything that matters can be quantified for the calculus."

With his indignation undisguised, Rattagagech gathered his tools and left.

Leia had one last visitor from the ranks of the Ruling Council before the day was out. Dall Thara Dru—the senator from Raxxa, chairman of the Senate Commerce Council, and the only female among the seven—had had nothing to say at the last meeting. Behn-Kihl-Nahm's head counts included Dru as a supporter, but that made Leia even more unsure about what to expect from her.

"Thank you so much for making time for me," said Dall Thara Dru as she glided into Leia's office. "This terrible business—I can't imagine! Your life must be completely upside down."

"I appreciate your sympathy—"

"This petition against you is the worst kind of foolishness I can think of. I just came from Chairman Beruss's office, and I'm afraid I found him quite immovable—stubbornly attached to the notion that *you* are the problem. As if it were your fault that there are dead planets all across Koornacht Cluster!"

"I'm grateful for your support—"

"Still and all, I'm afraid that Doman has influenced enough minds to give you a great deal of trouble when the Council meets on the petition. So I've been asking myself, what can be done? How do we reassure the others that you have matters well in hand? And then I realized that the answer is the question no one seems to be asking!"

"Which is—"

"Where is Luke Skywalker?" said Dall Thara Du. "Where are the Jedi Knights?"

"I'm sorry, Senator Dru," said Leia. "I don't understand."

"Why, Skywalker singlehandedly defeated the Emperor. Surely he can handle these Yevetha without any trouble. And if he needs help, he's raised an entire army—at New Republic expense, mind you!—of wizards like himself. Well, no wonder Beruss objects to sending our sons to Koornacht. Why do *we* have to fight this war? Where are our Knights?"

"The Jedi are not the New Republic's army, Senator Dru—or its mercenaries, or its secret weapon," Leia said evenly. "If you're suggesting that I come to the Council and say, in effect, 'Don't worry, my brother will take care of this for me'—"

"Oh, of course," Dru said breezily. "I know that you can't tell the chairmen *exactly* what you have planned. Just let them know that the Jedi are standing with you—that's not too much to say, is it? We're trying to shore up their confidence, after all. And who better to inspire confidence than Luke Skywalker?"

"That *is* too much to say," Leia said. Her tone was frosty, her words blunt. "Chairman Dru, I haven't asked for the help of the Jedi. And neither have they offered it. There are no secret plans to conceal. The New Republic can and will fight its own battles—as will I. And if you're someone who supported my nomination thinking it was a package deal—'Hey, we get Luke

Skywalker for free'—I'm sorry to say that you were mistaken."

There were no more postponements. The next morning, Leia stood in the well of the Council chamber, facing Doman Beruss.

"President Leia Organa Solo, have you read the petition of no confidence offered against you?"

"I have, Chairman." Her voice was steady and strong.

"Do you understand the charges contained therein?"

"I do, Chairman."

"Do you understand the particulars offered in support of the charge?"

"I do, Chairman."

"Do you wish to offer a response to the petition?"

Leia glanced at Behn-Kihl-Nahm, seated to Beruss's right, before answering. "Chairman, I contest the petition in its entirety. I'm shocked and dismayed that it was ever offered."

Behn-Kihl-Nahm slumped back in his chair, weariness causing his features to gray.

"It's not only a personal insult, it's a political mistake," Leia continued. "I have to wonder if the chairman has started taking his counsel from Nil Spaar—because he's the only one who stands to benefit from our infighting."

"There need be no infighting," said Krall Praget. "It's clearly better for all if this matter is resolved quickly and quietly."

"Then ask him to withdraw the petition," Leia said, pointing at Beruss. "This started with him, not with me. It's his fear that's the real issue here."

Beruss said quietly, "The chairman regretfully advises the Council that he cannot in conscience withdraw the petition."

Leia turned her gaze on him. "I don't know why or how Chairman Beruss became infected with the creep-

ing timidity that seems to be on the rise here. But if his
worry is that Princess Leia will lead the New Republic
into a war to rescue her husband, I suggest he's worrying over the wrong question. And I hope the rest of the
Council is about to set him straight."

"Why?" asked Borsk Fey'lya. "How many friends
do you think you have in this room? Do you think that
there's one of us—even your dear Bennie—who hasn't
had doubts about your fitness in recent months? Fire
and idealism may be fine qualities for the leader of a
revolution, but the leader of a great republic needs to be
several degrees cooler and a good deal more canny."

"Point of order, Chairman Beruss—" said Behn-
Kihl-Nahm.

But Beruss, his eyes darkened by disapproval, was
already moving to intervene. "The remarks of Chairman Praget and Chairman Fey'lya are out of order and
will be removed from the record. The floor belongs to
the President for the purposes of her response to the
petition."

"I've said all I have to say," Leia said.

Behn-Kihl-Nahm glanced at something lying out of
sight on the surface in front of Beruss. "Chairman,
point of precedence—"

"Go ahead."

"I would like to offer a compromise that I hope
may satisfy the concerns of all parties," said Behn-Kihl-
Nahm, his eyes warning Leia, *You must help yourself
now.* "If the President will consent to announce that she
is taking a brief personal leave, the Council will name
Chairman Rattagagech to serve as caretaker until she
returns."

It was a judgment call whether Rattagagech or
Fey'lya looked more startled.

"We will give the President time to consider this
proposal," Beruss said. "The debate is suspended. The
vote on the petition is tabled until we meet in three
days."

He rang the crystal, ending the session, before a
startled Fey'lya could speak a word.

Chapter 4

◆

Colonel Bowman Gavin carried the formal title of director of flight personnel, Fifth Fleet Combat Command. But to the more than three thousand pilots and weapons officers of the nearly two hundred squadrons based on the fleet's carriers and Star Destroyers, Gavin was simply fleet air boss.

The fleet air boss had the final say over every "cheeks on the cushions" decision—flight assignments, ratings, transfers, reprimands, and promotions, from the greenest backseater to the squadron leaders and combat wing commanders. His office was off the hot corridor in *Intrepid*'s flag country, fifteen strides from General A'baht at one end and eight strides from the combat operations center at the other.

Despite his high station, Colonel Gavin was a familiar sight on the flight decks and in the hangar bays of the fleet. Approachable and matter-of-fact, he was by his own admission more comfortable with his feet up in pilot country than he was behind his own desk or at A'baht's briefing table. Gavin disliked working from reports alone, and would not promote or pass judgment on a pilot or a junior officer until he had made a personal, firsthand assessment.

The pilots in turn claimed Gavin as one of their

own, and trusted him to give them a fair hearing. They knew that he knew what it was like to sit in the cockpit of a twisting fighter, guns hot and an enemy thundering in from behind. Though Gavin usually chose to wear only the "new sun" campaign bar he had earned as a B-wing pilot at the Battle of Endor, his service history entitled him to wear most of the combat decorations the Alliance and the New Republic had created and conferred.

Administrative chaos had arrived along with the five task forces drawn from the other fleets. Gavin had had to suspend his schedule of informal visits and keep his appointments to a minimum just to keep up with the briefings and reports. It was the closest he had ever come to closing his door to the world since being promoted to flag rank, five years ago.

It didn't take many days for the air in his office to thin to half an atmosphere and the bulkheads of his office to close in to the dimensions of a cell in the brig. But by the time Gavin rebelled and began to plot a temporary escape, the Fifth Fleet had re-formed into double-strength task forces and scattered into the fringes of Koornacht Cluster, taking most of the new arrivals out of ready reach.

But Task Force Gemstone, now attached to the flag task force, offered twenty-two possible destinations for Gavin's getaway. Since a visit to Commodore Poqua's command ship, the carrier *Starpoint,* would only entangle him in more command-level formalities, Gavin skimmed down the list and chose another vessel.

"Roust my pilot and prep my gig," he said, calling down to *Intrepid*'s No. 1 flight deck. "I'm going to pay a visit to *Floren.*"

"Acknowledged, Colonel. We'll notify flight control."

With the fleet on level one alert, even Colonel Gavin was obliged to don combat flight garb when leaving *Intrepid* in a smaller craft. Apart from the time lost climbing into and out of the five-piece high-flexibility pressure suit, Gavin didn't object to the requirement—

and the typically spirited and ribald ready-room chatter usually made that time pass quickly enough.

But at midrotation, the ready room was deserted, and Gavin had to struggle with the waist ring without benefit of a helping hand. It was not until Gavin was in the middle of the helmet-on pressure test that another pilot joined him there—a young alien wearing a purifier pack on his chest and the red emblem of a provisional flight officer on his collar.

Instead of going to one of the lockers, the pilot walked to within two meters of Gavin and stopped, as though waiting for him. When the test rig chimed its approval, Gavin broke the neck seal and removed his helmet.

"Are you looking for someone, son?" Gavin asked, noting the absence of a Fifth Fleet insignia on the pilot's uniform.

The officer saluted belatedly, as though it were an unpracticed reflex. "Are you Colonel Gavin, sir?"

"Guilty as charged. And you are—"

"Plat Mallar, sir. Sir—they told me that you make all the decisions about pilot assignments."

"They?"

"The crew of the gig. And the crew chief told me where I might find you. I'm one of the ferry pilots from Coruscant."

"The escort flight for *Tampion*," Gavin said, nodding. "I know that you were all cleared by Intelligence, but I'm a little surprised to hear anyone's talking to you. Did you ever think they might not be doing you a favor, telling you to come see me?"

"Colonel, you make all the decisions about flight assignments, don't you?"

"Yes."

"Then who else could I see?"

Gavin nodded thoughtfully. "What is this about, then?"

"It's about my orders, sir. There are five of us being sent back to Coruscant on the fleet shuttle, as space is available. We were brought over from *Venture* this morning to wait."

"That's right. What's the problem?"

"Sir, I don't want to be sent back. I can't be. I want to stay and be part of this fight. You have to let me do *something*."

"No, I don't," said Gavin, tucking his helmet under his right arm. "But I'll give you a chance to convince me that I *ought* to. Mind you, though, I signed off on your orders. To be blunt, we do need pilots, but no one wanted you or the others. None of you is experienced enough for the squadron leaders who're shorthanded to take a chance on you."

"If it makes any difference to you, I have another hundred and ninety hours in a TIE interceptor that don't show up on my service record."

"In a TIE?" Gavin raised an eyebrow questioningly. "Give me your ID disc."

The young pilot complied, and Gavin studied the data in a portable reader. When he was finished, he looked up and fixed Mallar with a quizzical look.

"Who *are* you?" he demanded. "I can't figure out what you're doing out here in the first place. You have more hours in sims and fewer hours in a cockpit than anyone I've ever seen in a combat zone."

"I've worked as hard as I can, Colonel, so I could have a chance. I spent every minute my check pilot could spare me flying. I spent every other minute I could training in the simulator. I'll work just as hard here, if you don't send me back."

"Your check pilot, yes," said Gavin, handing the ID disc back. "He seems to have run you through primary training in about a third of the usual time, even though he graded you not much better than passing. What's the missing piece of this picture, Mallar?"

The question seemed to crush Mallar. "I suppose I should have let the admiral put it all in my file, like he wanted to," he said dolefully. "He even wanted to give me a confirmed kill."

"A kill? For what?"

"For the Yevethan fighter I shot down over Polneye, the day the Yevetha destroyed it—the day they killed my family," Mallar said, and shook his head. "I didn't want any special treatment—I wanted to be good enough on my own. Just good enough to do something to help. But I'm not—or you wouldn't be trying to send me back. So all I can do now is beg you, Colonel—don't send me back."

"Offer me an alternative," Gavin said quietly.

"It doesn't matter," Mallar said. "Find something I can do to help. Anything. Find some way that my being here makes it easier for you to hand the Yevetha the same kind of hurt they handed me. That's all I ask. Because what they did to us was wrong. Just let me be a little part of teaching them that lesson. That's the only thing that matters to me now. I'm the only one left—I have to speak for all of them."

Gavin studied him as he spoke, and for a long time after. "Draw a flight suit," he said finally. "Meet me at my gig in ten minutes. We'll talk more on the way to *Floren*."

"Yes, sir. But the shuttle's supposed to leave within the hour—"

"I know," said Gavin, patting Mallar on the shoulder as he moved past him. "I'm afraid you may miss it."

Inbound to Utharis, *Mud Sloth* came out of hyperspace crippled by a data bus power surge that left the port navigation sensors and the navcom unable to talk to each other. The surge had come at the worst possible time, during the cascade in which the hyperdrive systems shut down and the realspace systems reinitialize.

"This is why you should never buy a bargain starship," Luke grumbled as he climbed back out of the service access compartment belowdecks.

"What do you mean?" asked Akanah.

"Just that Verpine cut every corner they could building this thing," Luke said, sliding the access panel back into place. "The power bus can't handle all the systems, so the cascade processor has to juggle them, turning this one off before turning that one on. But for that to work right, the buffer circuits—" He saw her eyes glazing over and stopped. "Anyway, it means we're going to be delayed at Utharis."

"How long?"

"Until it's fixed," Luke said. He secured the last of the access panel hold-downs and looked up at her. "If there's a wrench jockey at Taldaak Station who knows this model better than I do, maybe only a day or two."

"Two days! You said we were going to stop only long enough to top off the consumables and reset the counters."

Luke shrugged. "I'm not any happier about it than you are," he said. "But better this happened now, in-bound to a full-service port, than somewhere in the middle of Farlax."

"I can't bear the thought of any more delay, this close to the end—this close to the Circle."

"I know," Luke said. "But this ship won't go into hyperspace again until she's gone into a service bay." He flashed a wry smile. "At least you'll have plenty of time to pick out that souvenir hat I promised you."

Utharis was in the grip of war fever. Even though Koornacht Cluster was more than two hundred light-years away, Utharis had a border world's heightened sensitivity to matters of interplanetary politics. It was impossible to go anywhere in Taldaak without hearing about the clouds of war gathering over Farlax Sector, and the talk had prompted a quiet but noticeable exodus through Taldaak Station and the planet's other major ports.

The exodus had not yet spread beyond the most affluent, mobile, and well-connected segments of Utharian society, but it had energized conversations everywhere, and intruded on the smooth working of the planet's economic machine.

"Sure, we can take care of you, Stonn," said the

CT
Penguin Group
(USA) Inc., 375 Hudson Street,
York 10014, USA

UK | Ireland | Australia | New Zealand | India | South Africa | China

Ltd., Registered Offices: 80 Strand, London WC2R 0RL, England
ation about the Penguin Group visit penguin.com

by Signet, an imprint of New American Library,
guin Group (USA) Inc.

ay 2013

5   4   3   2   1

ila Kelly, 2013

CT and logo are trademarks of Penguin Group (USA) Inc.

23981-5

nited States of America

TE

fiction. Names, characters, places, and incidents either are the
thor's imagination or are used fictitiously, and any resemblance
s, living or dead, business establishments, events, or locales is
ntal.

does not have any control over and does not assume any
author or third-party Web sites or their content.

Evermore

"Full of exciting twists and turns."   —*Publishers Weekly*

"Lynn Viehl sure knows how to tell a hell of a story."
—Romance Reviews Today

"Another highly satisfying chapter in the Darkyn saga."
—Vampire Genre

Night Lost

"Viehl had me hooked from the first page . . . exceptional. . . .
I definitely recommend this marvelous book."
—Romance Junkies

"Fast-paced and fully packed. You won't regret spending
time in this darkly dangerous and romantic world!"
—*Romantic Times*

Dark Need

"A must read."   —Vampire Genre

Private Demon

"Lynn Viehl's vampire saga began spectacularly in *If Angels
Burn*, and this second novel in the Darkyn series justifies
the great beginning."   —Curled Up with a Good Book

If Angels Burn

"Erotic, darker than sin, and better than good chocolate."
—Holly Lisle

"This exciting vampire romance is action-packed. . . . Lynn
Viehl writes a fascinating paranormal tale."
—The Best Reviews

NIGHTB

LORDS OF T

Lynn V

SIGNET SEL
Published by
Penguin Grou
New York, Ne

USA | Canada

Penguin Book
For more info

First publishe
a division of

First Printing
10 9 8 7

Copyright ©
All rights re
distributed in
participate in
author's righ

SIGNET SE

ISBN 978-0-4

Printed in the

PUBLISHER'
This is a wor
product of th
to actual pe
entirely coin
    The publis
responsibilit

If you purch
is stolen pro
and neither
"stripped bo

A SIGNET S   ALWAYS LE

For my readers,
who make every day of my life
a grand adventure.

Prologue

September 29, 1208
House of Heaven
Jerusalem, the Holy Land

Sunken black eyes peered out of the two-inch view slot in the copper door. "No beggars," a cross voice said in gutter Arabic, spewing into the air the stink of his rotten teeth.

Cristophe pulled back his cowl to reveal his shaven head, and the skin he had darkened with the juice of steeped nut hulls. To distract the eunuch from the light color of his eyes, he held up two pieces of silver.

"Four," the eunuch demanded promptly.

Cristophe shrugged, turned away, and took a step in the direction of another brothel. As he expected, the eunuch threw the bolt and shoved open the door.

Stoop-shouldered by spine disease, a lifetime of beatings, or despair—probably all three—the eunuch twisted his head to one side. "Our women are plump and fragrant, their talents many." He named a variety of sexual acts and services in the monotone of unthinking, repeated recital. "Three."

Cristophe held up the twin silvers again.

"Miserly wretch. For the love of Allah, I take pity on you." The eunuch beckoned, but when he tried to grab the coins from Cristophe's hand, the knight blocked the snatch with a swat. "Not so quick. You pay first."

The scent of frankincense and lung rot touched Cristophe's nose. A thin hand reached out of the shadows behind the eunuch to caress his balled fist. "Leave this to me, Qutaybah. I shall settle with you later."

The eunuch scowled at Cristophe. "He is too big, Afifah, and you too sick."

"He does not come here to make use of me. That work was well done, long ago." The courtesan drew back. "Come."

Cristophe followed her through the narrow passages, ignoring the sounds of rutting all around them as she led him into her private chamber. Fire from the bronze braziers provided the only light, and the resins burning in them masked some of the smell of sickness. The wine table now held a bowl of oily herbs, a bundle of terebinth twigs, and a glass-bowled pipe blackened by the tar of frequent use.

He closed the door behind him and bolted it before he spoke to her in her native Urdu. "Why did you never tell me?"

"Do you care for some dreamsmoke? No?" Afifah went to a pile of cushions by the fire and slowly reclined. As she did, her veil slipped down to reveal her once-beautiful face, now too bony and gaunt for her cosmetics to conceal. "You took your time in coming to me." She coughed into her sleeve, staining it with dark red blood.

She was very near death, he realized. "I could not sprout wings and fly."

"For a time I did not think you would come to me at all." Her lips parted, showing teeth stained yellow-brown from daily use of hashish. "Many nights I beseeched Allah that you would not. That you should already languish in the bowels of some sultan's hell, chained beside your brothers."

"They were my family." Cristophe went to the only window and looked out at the flies swarming in a dark cloud over the open privy pit. "I am a priest now."

"Finally ridding yourself of the concerns of the flesh." Afifah giggled, a raspy parody of the girlish sound. "As you rid yourself of Palestine. Of me."

"I never gave you reason to believe I would stay," he reminded her. "From the beginning you knew what I was."

"Oh, yes. The smith of black souls. The dark hammer of God." Now she sounded sad. "Chiseling away at your own heart of stone." A liquid cough followed the last word, and she covered her mouth with her veil this time, soaking it through.

Cristophe went to her, kneeling beside her to hold her quaking shoulders until the spasm passed. She represented the last of his mortal sins, this ashen flower, who had once been the most beautiful harlot in the city of David. He had imagined himself in love with her, with her clever hands and her silky words.

When she rasped in two breaths, he asked, "Why wait until you were dying to send for me?"

"Why did you leave me?" she countered.

He tucked her head beneath his chin. "I never had anything to offer you but pain and betrayal."

"Then, perhaps. But now you are changed." She used one bony finger to trace the bars of the passion cross on his unmarked tunic. "Doomed, they say, to escape my fate. Does this make you happy? I think not."

He drew back. "If that is why you sent for me, I cannot save you, Afifah. I would but hasten your end."

"We both of us know I am not the one you wish to save now." She tugged off her veil, folding it over and over until she'd hidden the dark, clotted blood staining it. "It will not be long for me, I think. What will you do when you leave here?"

"I shall return to England." He felt her shudder. "I cannot remain here, not as I am."

The kohl lining the crepey skin around her eyes took on a brighter sheen. "And the gift you will take from here? What will you do with it?"

Cristophe shook his head. "I have no family, no holdings. I have given what wealth I had to the order. All I am permitted is my sword and my horse, and those I must surrender once I go into seclusion."

Her thin fingers curled into the laces of his tunic. "You will give my *Sunehri* to them."

She was not making a request. "Yes. That I think the wisest course."

Afifah released him, and clapped her hands twice. When the eunuch hurried in, she said, "Bring my treasure to me."

Qutaybah glared at Cristophe. "For this dog?"

"Not for him," Afifah said. "For his God."

Chapter 1

January 1, 2013
Knights Realm Stronghold
Orlando, Florida

"Stand ready," Harlech, captain of the guard, called out.

His command silenced the three hundred men assembled in the courtyard and sent them into their ranks.

Above the main hall the four gatehouse towers glowed with a torchlit, watchful menace against the night sky. While the thousands of tourists who visited Knights Realm each season believed they had come to a medieval theme park, the castle's occupants were not hired performers. Thrilled by the authenticity of the jousts, melees, and other spectacles of the Dark Ages, no human ever suspected that the people of the Realm were not mortal, or that what they did had never been a show.

Iron sconces bolted to the gray stone walls of the castle cast pools of strange white-blue light over the oiled, packed dirt beneath the men's boots. Harlech preferred the natural scent and warmth of flame, but the modern civilized world had largely abandoned fire in favor of the tamed lightning they called "electricity."

After a century of enduring the yellow light radiated by glass bulbs, Harlech found the merciless glare of the newly installed LED lights particularly annoying. But Americans had lately become obsessed with using as little power as possible—while saving every last tree they could in the bargain. Harlech fully expected mortals would in the next century regress back into a second Dark Age, whence he could happily return to using tallow and wood for light.

At least the important things have not changed. As Harlech scanned the formation, he permitted himself a small amount of pride and satisfaction. While the garrison had given their oath of loyalty to their lady paramount, Suzeraina Jayr mac Byrne, they were all of them his men. He had personally trained each and every warrior, and over time they had become a veritable army of death. While it had been more than a hundred years since war had last been waged on American soil, Harlech took nothing for granted. Centuries of living among mortals had taught him that much, he thought as he walked parallel to the front ranks. Should an invasion land tomorrow on the shores of their adopted country, his warriors were ready to . . .

Harlech halted and peered past a pikeman at a gap in the second line. "Lowell."

The archer standing to the right of the empty space came to attention. "Aye, Captain."

Harlech stepped through the first rank to ensure the

glare of the light had not played a trick on his eyes. "Where is Beaumaris?"

Lowell frowned at the horizon. "Not here, sir."

"So I fathom." Leaning down to eliminate all but an inch of space between their faces added some necessary menace to Harlech's soft murmur. "Where is he?"

Lowell did not blink or twitch a muscle. "I know not his present whereabouts, Captain."

Harlech moved to the man on the left side of the gap. "Ponsworth."

"Sir."

"Your chamber is next to Beaumaris's, and you must walk past his door to report for duty. Is this not so?" The swordsman inclined his head in acknowledgment. "Well? Is he still abed, then?"

Ponsworth's expression remained resolutely bland. "No, Captain."

Harlech smiled. "So you then saw him leave his chamber."

"I . . . I fear upon rising I was much preoccupied with my thoughts, sir." Ponsworth's upper lip twitched. "I passed by his chamber without notice of it or him."

"How convenient for Beaumaris," Harlech said sourly, "that you are such a thinker."

He strode back to the front of the garrison and let the men see his displeasure for a full minute. "Our lady comes tonight to inspect our readiness. I will know where Beaumaris is before she arrives, or every man here will suffer the consequences. Am I understood?"

The men remained at silent attention.

"Rainer." Harlech pointed at the towheaded giant

standing at the end of the trackers' line, and then at the ground. "Come here."

As the garrison's most beloved fool shambled through the ranks to stand before Harlech, he shrugged back his black cloak to reveal a hot pink tunic and glittering blue sequined kilt. Hand-painted smiley faces in matching colors dotted his blue hose and black boots.

"God in heaven." Although like everyone in the Realm Harlech had grown accustomed to Rain's penchant for colorful attire, this latest ensemble reached new heights of outrageousness. "What is this you wear, lad?"

"'Tis my latest fashion statement." The former court jester performed a slightly wobbly pirouette. "I call it 'Don't worry, be happy.'"

Several of the men coughed suddenly, and just as quickly fell silent as their captain gave them a decidedly murderous glance.

Harlech gritted his teeth. "Rainer, where is Beaumaris?"

The big man shrugged. "Not here. Where he is now, I cannot say."

"He bid you *lie* for him?"

Rainer looked puzzled. "Never would Beau ask that of me. He thinks I am too simple to remember such things as falsehoods."

Harlech sighed. "Very well. You—"

"Beau has only ever asked me not to throw knives when I am blindfolded again. Although I assured him the last time was a mistake. In truth I had not aimed for his ribs intentionally, you know." Rain cocked his head. "I wonder, Harlech, if I were to practice in secret until I am much improved with my tossing blades, might Beaumaris be persuaded to change his opinion?"

"I cannot say." Questioning Rain was akin to herding a butterfly, Harlech thought, and just as heartless. "It is best that you have no head for secrets, lad. You may step back in line."

"I can keep a secret, surely." Rain glanced over his shoulder before he added in a whisper, "I told no one that your lady wife and I were the last survivors of Sherwood *jardin*. Well, not counting Nottingham, but he broke my arm six times and then everyone thought him dead. But he never dies, you know, not even after his seneschal near beheaded him. Very unsporting of the villain, I thought."

Harlech shook his head. "Rain, I care not—"

"Oh, neither do I," the fool assured him. "I never warmed to him even when his mother kept him in the dungeons at Sherwood." He frowned. "Why can no one kill him, do you think?"

"Luck, lad. His good, and ours bad."

"There." He swept forth one hand. "There is another secret I have kept, Harlech. 'Twas told to me that Nottingham went to war with mortals to die, but after being blown up and made changeling, *still* he lived." He frowned and scratched the back of his untidy blond mane. "Or perhaps he became a changeling before he exploded. I cannot recall the particular order of it. Either way, you must agree, a messy business and yet—"

"Rainer." Harlech could listen to anything but the jester's babble; another moment of it would drive him mad. "Best you keep the remainder of your secrets to yourself." He glanced pointedly at the main hall. "Ere our lady comes."

"Oh. Yes. Right you are, Captain." Grinning, Rain lumbered toward his place in the back ranks, hesitated, and then went to occupy Beau's spot.

The sound of descending footsteps, one pair light and the other heavy, drifted from the main hall to thump in Harlech's ears. He faced the garrison and barked, "Close ranks."

Rainer occupied Beaumaris's position, which shortened the back line by one man. Quickly Harlech ordered the second and fourth ranks to shift three paces to the left before he turned and stood at attention.

Lady Jayr mac Byrne crossed the courtyard, her form a slender column of bronze leather and moonlight. Sheathed copper daggers rode the sides of her hips; black pearls gleamed from the thick plait of her dark hair. In her left hand she carried a scroll of parchment, but her right remained entwined with one three times its size until she reached the garrison.

Her companion released her hand with visible reluctance, his black cloak swirling around his tree-trunk legs. Even as a mortal Aedan mac Byrne had been a giant among men, as fierce as the savage blue tattoos spiraling over his features, as terrifying as the rare condition from which he suffered. Any act of life-threatening violence caused the big man to temporarily lose his mind and his self-control. The resulting madness that came over Byrne in battle transformed him into a berserker, a machine of death that would kill anyone and anything in his path.

Rising to walk the night as Darkyn had not altered Byrne's monstrous mortal affliction; immortality had simply made him all the more dangerous. Harlech had once seen his former suzerain descend into the killing madness after being stabbed in the back during an assassination attempt by his bastard brother. The Scotsman had not only survived; he had cut down more than a dozen men in a few seconds before using his battle-ax to split his treacherous brother in half.

"Good evening, Captain." Jayr smiled at his respectful bow. "All is well with the garrison?"

Once Harlech tracked down his missing swordsman, and clouted some sense back into his head, it would be. "Aye, my lady."

The shrewd eyes of Jayr's towering companion scanned the ranks. "You've changed the formation."

"Clever," Jayr said before Harlech could reply. "With the lines staggered I can see all of the men's faces. I need not walk the ranks." She lifted a hand to shade her eyes against the glare from the floods. "I cannot say I care for these new lights, however. Who ordered them installed?"

"Accounting, my lady," Harlech said. "They are called 'energy-efficient,' and as such should reduce our power tithes by a fourth."

"Power bills," Jayr corrected, and turned to Byrne. "What do you think, Aedan?"

Byrne turned and squinted at the lights. "Smash the bloody things before our eyeballs commence to sizzle."

Harlech squared his shoulders. "It shall be as you say, Seneschal, but . . ." He paused as he glanced past Jayr's shoulder to see Rainer float up into the air over the heads of the garrison. Since only Beaumaris had the ability to move anything living in such a manner, it seemed his missing warrior had at last reported for duty. ". . . Ah, we might remove them instead and bid the maintenance

crew to install them inside, where the humans work." As
Rain floated back down to his proper place in the back
ranks, Harlech gestured toward the administrative offices. "'Twould save the cost of the bulbs, much shattered
glass, and doubtless mollify accounting."

When Harlech turned back to the garrison, Beaumaris stood between Ponsworth and Lowell as if he'd
never moved from the spot, his eyes fixed on some point
beyond their lady and her seneschal.

"A wise thought. See to it, then, Captain." Jayr stepped
forward and gave the garrison her attention. "Good evening, lads. Now that the winter tournament is over, we
have two weeks left to finish the renovations before the
staff returns from holiday. The council is sending some
prospects to me in hopes of filling our need for a *tresora*
to the *jardin*, so I shall be occupied with these mortals.
You've done well preparing the keep and the grounds
for the spring tourist season. When you have completed
your nightly tasks this fortnight next, your time is your
own." As the men cheered, she held up the scroll she
carried. "Before you hatch plans to search every acre
from here to Valdosta, I would first read you this."

Harlech frowned as Jayr unrolled the parchment and
read the summons from Richard Tremayne. It was the second in as many months from the high lord of the Darkyn,
but the message this time contained only disappointment.
The treasure hunt Tremayne had announced in October
had been called off; the gems he had set the Kyn to find
had been destroyed during a battle with a rogue Kyn in
South Florida. Rule of Ireland, the prize that the high lord
had offered, would be decided by other means.

"I am sorry about the lost opportunity, lads. I would

have been proud to see any one of you made lord paramount." Jayr finished reading and rolled up the summons, handing it to Harlech. "If you would, Captain,
please post this in the commons so the men who are off
duty may read it at their leisure."

"Aye, my lady." He tucked it into his tunic.

Jayr smiled at the men. "Beaumaris, I would have a
word, please. The rest of you are dismissed."

As the other men dispersed and Beau approached,
Harlech quickly inspected his errant warrior. Beau's
clothing did not appear disordered, and he did not detect
the scent of a mortal female on him. The pale cast of his
skin suggested he had not yet fed, and he displayed no
visible wounds. Only his brown hair, which still sported
the golden sun streaks he'd acquired as a mortal, looked
slightly tangled. Harlech met Beau's gaze, and saw nothing but fixed boredom.

Harlech had been Beau's foster brother when they
had been human boys; he knew what that indifferent
flatness meant. *Something troubling has happened.*

"You did not have to hurry back so quickly," Jayr was
saying to Beau. She glanced at Harlech and explained, "I
summoned Beau to my office before sunset. Tremayne
called for him."

Harlech barely managed to keep the shock from his
face. "The high lord wished to speak to Beau directly?
Why?"

"He wouldnae say. But he was no his usual snaky self
about it. 'Bring Beaumaris of York to the phone at once,'
Byrne said. Then he bid us go so they might speak alone."
Byrne regarded Beau. "I never knew you to be one of
Richard's creatures, Beau."

*   *   *

He'd been a fool to report for duty, Beaumaris decided, just as he'd been an idiot earlier to answer the call from the high lord. Now, with three of the Kyn he most respected staring at him as if he'd sprouted a second skull, he could think of a dozen ways he might have prevented this.

All useless to him now. "I gave my oath to you, my lord, and then my lady," Beau said, unable to keep the irony out of his tone. "If I am anyone's creature, it is *yours.*"

"I do not question your loyalty, Beau," Jayr said firmly. "Nor should we leap to any conclusions when Richard is involved. Did the high lord give you leave to tell us what he wanted with you?"

Richard Tremayne had instructed him as to *exactly* what to tell the others. "It seems there is a secret clutch of traitors in our midst. The high lord believes them to be renegade *tresori* who have been turned against us. Already they have attempted to murder several Kyn lords and sentinels, and frame a member of the council for the crimes. Our lord thinks them here now, in our territory, searching for the gems." He glanced at Jayr. "The emeralds were not destroyed by the skirmish in the south, as the high lord would have everyone think. They remain hidden, somewhere in our territory."

Byrne's lips peeled back from his *dents acérées*. "Harlech, cancel the men's leave. We have turncoats to hunt."

Beau shook his head. "Lord Tremayne desires this to be handled discreetly. I am commanded to go and infiltrate a group of mortals being used by the traitors to locate the gems. He bids me persuade them to reveal the

identity of their ringleader, who I am to capture and deliver to him."

"That sounds more like Tremayne," Jayr murmured,
her expression thoughtful. "But why does he command
this of you, Beau?"

The suzeraina trusted him, Beau realized, because she
had no reason not to. No one among his Kyn had any
inkling of how long he had deceived them. For a moment
he wished the earth would sprout a sinkhole to whisk
him to hell.

"I daresay the high lord is aware that Beau knows our
territory better than any member of the *jardin*," Harlech
said before Beau could compose an adequate reply. "He
came here a century before the rest of us." He gave Beau
a hard look. "You were one of the first *jardin* in America,
were you not?"

"Aye." That much was the truth, and might serve as
the reason Tremayne had selected him for this duty. The
high lord had not actually troubled himself to explain his
choice, and as a mere *jardin* warrior Beau could not
question the Kyn's supreme ruler. He still felt a pressing
suspicion as to Tremayne's motives; something in the
tone of the high lord's silky voice had not set well with
him.

"Who is this group of mortals, and how are you to
infiltrate them?" Jayr asked him.

"They are archaeologists from a northern university
who are performing an excavation to the west of the city.
The high lord has arranged a position for me as their
manager." He knew next to nothing about digging in the
dirt for old bones and such, but he could glean some of

the basics from the Internet. "He also directs me to keep close watch over a Dr. Al Stuart, the man in charge of this project. Apparently his knowledge of the Templars puts him in some particular danger."

"So he orders you to skulk about, guard mortals, and spy on traitors, when we could track and kill them in a few hours." Byrne sounded disgusted. "Tremayne has finally gone completely daft. We must call Michael."

"I would rather we not." Jayr put her hand on her lover's forearm. "We have nothing to offer the seigneur but doubts and rumors, and our own suspicions. If we must consult Cyprien on the matter, I wish to present facts and evidence."

"What of this ringleader Beau is to catch?" Harlech asked. "I have no doubt he will snare him, but what is to be done then?"

Jayr faced Beau, her dark eyes intent on his. "I know you are under the high lord's orders, and as such I am loath to ask this of you, but . . . when you find this traitor, will you first bring him to us, that we might question him?"

That she would make it a request instead of an order humbled him all over again. "My lady, my faith is ever with *you*." Beau bowed his head. "You have but to say, and it shall be done."

She touched his shoulder in a rare gesture of affection. "I thank you, Beau." She turned to Byrne. "'Tis likely this traitor is some mortal made unhappy by the Kyn, I think. But if there is more to it, we must know before we turn him over to Tremayne."

"You were never this devious when you were my seneschal," Byrne muttered.

"And if I was, how would you know?" Jayr slipped her arm through his. "Now come. We must ride out and inspect the landscaping. I fear that freeze last night may have finished off the roses at the entry gate."

Harlech said nothing as Jayr and Byrne left for the stables, but once they were out of hearing range, he swore viciously.

Beau dragged his hand through his hair. "You share my sentiments, brother."

"However this is played, no good will come of it." Harlech eyed him. "I know you to be secretive, Beau. Were you once sworn to Sherwood? Is that why Tremayne presses you into his service?"

All the members of Sherwood *jardin* had been executed for conspiring against Richard and slaughtering the innocent and helpless during the *jardin* wars. Only Harlech's wife, Viviana, and Rainer had escaped death and treachery, first by running away from their *jardin*, and then by concealing their origins altogether.

"After I rose to walk the night, I served in the London garrison," Beau said stiffly. "I was sent to the New World to procure property and goods. I liked the life here, so I later petitioned him to be released from my oath, that I might serve Lord Byrne. You may call upon the Seigneur Geoffrey at your leisure to verify my claims."

"Do not take that tone with me, lad," Harlech warned. "You and I were mortal brothers."

"You were the son of the house, and I the orphan whose care was thrust upon it." As soon as he spoke, Beau regretted his words. "Forgive me. Your family, your father, they treated me as their own flesh and blood. I but yearned for what could never be mine."

What would never have been his, had his foster family ever suspected they shared their hearth and home with the son of an English Crusader, and a Saracen whore.

"Think no more of it. I do not envy you this damnable mess." Harlech clapped his hand on his shoulder. "Come. I shall help you gather what you will need for your journey."

Chapter 2

The Jade Palms definitely lived up to its marketing, Alys decided as she walked through the enormous lobby toward the reception desk.

The hotel's facilities occupied acres of what had once been central Florida swampland, now transformed into graceful landscaping embracing an international resort. According to the information package the foundation had sent to her, the hotel offered a multilevel Fitness and Wellness Center, five Olympic-standard pools, two movie theaters, a private river winding through a PGA-scale executive golf course, and various other amusements and amenities. The resort's restaurants, of which there were nine, ranged from a casual Italian bistro to a five-star formal dining room enclosed by glass walls and a skylight in the atrium.

Designed to impress, Alys thought as she glanced up at the lobby's centerpiece, a three-story, stainless-steel sculpture fountain. *Whoever digs it up in a thousand years will probably decide it was a mass burial tomb for*

pilgrims who came to worship the Great God Disney,
Lord of the Kingdom of Mice.

Arriving at the hotel marked the point of no return
for Alys, and while her heart wanted to dance, the enor-
mity of the task ahead kept her excitement and her emotions in check. Over the next thirty days she'd either
make a name for herself by unearthing evidence of her
unorthodox theories or dig a grave for her already-
dubious reputation and fledgling career. She'd talked her
way onto this tightrope of a project, stretching her professional life between triumph and disaster; now she had
to keep a cool head while walking it.

This is what Robert wanted me to do, Alys reminded
herself. Although she'd never spent much time with her
legal guardian, he had provided her with the finest edu-
cation in the world, and the guidance she'd needed to
make something of herself. Out of gratitude she'd always
tried to live up to his expectations. Robert's tragic death
in a car accident hadn't changed that; if anything, she felt
even more determined to prove his faith in her had been
justified.

At the desk, the discreetly suited clerk greeted her
with a shallow smile. "Welcome to the Jade Palms Orlando." He accepted the reservation e-mail she handed
to him as if it were a used tissue. He scanned the page
and looked up at her. "You're with Dr. Stuart's team?"

"Yes." She mirrored the clerk's frown. "Is something
wrong?"

He slid the e-mail across the desk. "No, ma'am. We've
been expecting you." He added another paper.

She thumbed back the bill of her Red Sox baseball

cap before she skimmed the printout, taking in the number of suites and rental cars that had been reserved and sorting them out in her head.

"This is fine, except we won't need this many rooms right now," she advised him. "Two interns had to drop out and I'm not sure when their replacements will be arriving." She wished she could have attracted more graduate students, or one or two of her colleagues, to join the project, but no one had taken it seriously, not even when she had landed the proper funding. The clerk was frowning at her again. "You were informed that we'll be staying here until the end of January, correct?"

"Yes." He looked past her, his eyes moving from one side of the lobby to the other.

She glanced over her shoulder at the mounds of cases, crates, and carryalls the porters were still bringing in from the charter bus.

"We'll be transporting our equipment out to the field tomorrow afternoon, so we'll need to use your storage area only for one day." He didn't seem to be paying attention to her anymore. "Did I forget to give you my credit card?" She began digging through her bag.

The clerk politely cleared his throat. "Ma'am—"

"Here it is." Alys pushed two cards across the counter.

"I'm sorry, but hotel policy requires that . . ." His voice trailed off as he glanced down. "Oh. Pardon me—my error."

Alys filled out the necessary paperwork while the clerk began stacking a pile of electronic swipe cards that served as keys to the hotel rooms. She'd just finished signing the last form when she heard young voices pep-

pering the air, and turned her head to watch a small herd
of college students trudge across the polished black tile
floor.

"I'm here." She waved at them.

The half-dozen interns hurried over to her and
formed a tight, anxious half circle as all of them began to
talk at the same time.

"I'm dying for a hot shower."

"One of those guys knocked over the GPR monitor
case. We should check it out before they try to hide the
damage."

"Some guy is looking for you."

"Like you should talk. Does our grant cover room
service?"

"Are you going out to the site tonight?"

Alys silenced them with a single, two-fingered whistle
that made the desk clerk jump. "Sorry." She scooped up
the key cards to the rooms and began handing them out.
"Charles, you have to share the bath with your room-
mate, which means no two-hour showers, please. Chan,
once you've settled in, bring the GPR to my room; I'll
check it over myself. Brenda, your per diem covers food,
not room service, eating experiences, alcohol, pay-per-
view, massages, manicures, any form of personal grooming, or items from any of the hotel boutiques. Jordan, no
one is going out to the site until tomorrow afternoon,
and that includes me. Paolo, what guy is looking for me?"

"He didn't give a name." The exchange student from
Madrid nodded toward the bar. "He went in there. He's
a big guy. He sounded British, I think."

"You mean that tall, streaky-haired eye-candy man?"
Brenda fluttered her hand over her heart. "He was de-

lish. Seriously. Guy like that makes you want to run for a spoon."

"Do try to curtail your cannibalistic urges," Alys advised, frowning a little as the other interns snickered. "I suggest all of you go to your rooms, unpack, freshen up, call home, order some pizzas—no beer, please, Brenda— and get yourselves organized while you have the time." She picked up her backpack and slung it over her shoulder. "Work hours at the site begin at sunset and end at dawn, so stay up as late as you possibly can before you go to sleep. That will help reset your biorhythms."

"I still think it's beyond weird, that we can excavate the place only at night," Alys heard Brenda say to Charles as they dragged their wheeled cases over to the elevators. "How are we supposed to find anything in the dark, out there in the middle of nowhere? Is she crazy?"

The elevator doors closed before Alys could hear the other intern's response, but she could imagine it. *Why do you think they call her Alys in Wonderland?*

She didn't blame the students; half of them probably weren't planning to list the dig on their CVs. If she didn't find anything to prove her theories, none of them would.

I am not going to fail.

Alys walked over to the bar, and stood just inside the open entryway to inspect the patrons. *A big guy who might sound British.* She saw businessmen with loosened ties and rumpled suits who sat nursing scotch and bourbon at the bar; a few women in cocktail dresses clustered in tight, martini- and margarita-studded constellations around tables so small they resembled stools.

A slight shift in the shadows drew Alys's eyes to one man standing with his shoulders against a back wall.

The crystal chandeliers overhead sketched him with thin slashes of amber light, from the tigereye streaks in his thick sorrel hair to the blunt toes and buckled straps of his dull black boots. His shoulders and chest filled out his leather jacket with enough bulk to make Alys think bodybuilder, but the elegance of his strong hands belonged to a musician, and the long, beautifully muscled stretch of his legs suggested an athlete. He was the tallest and most well-built male in the bar.

Big guy.

He was watching her as well, and set aside a half glass of red wine before he started toward her, moving through the loose maze of tables and patrons without effort or notice of them.

Fascinated now, Alys began mentally compiling an observational construct of facts: *No hesitancy intent gaze unhurried step tailored garments handmade boots red wine negligent grooming physically fit.* The words and their associated images floated in her mind, weaving in and out of one another as she applied her acquired knowledge and her intuition to arrange them together into a cohesive assemblage.

Due to innate short- and long-term memory limits, forming such constructs was beyond most people's capabilities; few had the natural capacity to acquire and retain the bewildering amount of data, much less sort it into multiple paradigms. Alys, however, had possessed the unique talent from birth.

From the connections she failed to make between her observations and her knowledge assemblage base, she concluded that he was not an academic, a hotel employee, or anyone with whom she had prior acquaintance. Nothing about his dress or demeanor indicated anything about him, except that he liked to drink wine.

For her that made him the rarest of men: a complete enigma.

The mystery man didn't stop at a polite distance but walked up to her as if he meant to greet her with a hug. Unused to having her personal space invaded with such nonchalance, Alys took a cautious step back. At the same time a warm pocket of scent followed her, lacing the next breath she took with the piquant but luscious fragrance of burnt sugar and cream.

Delish.

Alys realized her mouth was watering, and swallowed before she asked, "Are you the gentleman looking for Dr. Stuart?"

"I need a word with him, yes." His voice played the words like low notes from a cello, and colored them with a faint accent. "Has he finally got himself here?"

Twenty years melted away as Alys stared at him and heard two different questions. *Do you see that rock, child, the one sticking up from the path? And the old root just before it?*

"Are you feeling unwell?" the man was asking her.

He has a British accent. That's all. Annoyed with herself, Alys shook off the old memory. "I'm sorry; we're rather busy at the moment. You should call the hotel later and make an appointment. Or you could give me your card and I'll have Dr. Stuart call you." In four weeks, when she'd finished the most important work of her career, she silently tacked on.

"I haven't any cards." He bent his head, and his cool breath whispered against her skin as he asked, "What is your name, love?"

Love. He called me love. Alys felt her astonished heart skip a beat before her mind sorted it out. British colloquialism, a term of friendly, casual address.

"My name is Alys." Despite her refusal to help him, the man didn't seem annoyed with her. His stance remained confident, his gaze direct. He'd also managed to eliminate another inch between them without her noticing. If he came any closer, he'd practically be on top of her.

Was he attempting to wheedle information from her by using physical intimidation? She couldn't feel afraid of him, not with that voice. Not with the way it made her feel.

"You've a pretty name, Alys." He stunned her again by lifting his hand and stroking the pad of his thumb along her cheek. "It suits you. Now be a good girl and go fetch Dr. Stuart for me."

The light caress confused her, as most physical contact did. She'd learned that unsolicited touching by males was often a demonstration of sexual interest. Over the years she'd learned to anticipate and avoid some of that. This time, however, it didn't irritate her. In fact she found his unwarranted touching disturbing—and exciting.

Indulgent tone relaxed features gentle physical contact. He seemed to be in a state of amusement. Pairing that with his directive, she concluded that he'd mistaken her for one of the interns.

He thinks I'm a kid.

Well, that was nothing new, and as good as he smelled and as comforting as his voice sounded, he was a stranger.

Alys knew better than anyone what strangers were capable of. "I'm sorry, but I have to go now. It was nice to meet you. Good-bye."

Beaumaris knew some humans were born with the natural ability to resist *l'attrait*, the scent produced by the Kyn that allowed them to influence and control mortals. A few were even immune to it, but those mortals were so rare that he had never before personally encountered one.

Until now.

He watched Alys as she retreated into the lobby, her limbs easy in her loose khaki garments, a thick bunch of her fiery hair bobbing from where she'd pulled it through the back of her cap. She intercepted a porter to speak with him before moving onto the elevators. Not once did she glance back at him again.

To her I am nothing more than a human male in a bar.

Beau had not bothered with mortal females for so long that the annoyance he now felt with this one gave him pause. Like all Kyn, he had indulged himself with human women from time to time, enjoying their welcoming warmth and the fragile sweetness of their passions. None had ever touched his heart, however, and over the centuries the lovers he had taken had become an endless procession of willing lips and caressing hands, the blur of their features fading from his memory even as he slipped out of their beds.

Alys. Even her name intrigued him.

This cheeky wench had been neither willing nor welcoming; perhaps that was what rendered her so singular. Her taste in clothing was nothing short of appalling, but

even her wretchedly fitted garments could not disguise
her charms. Tall and slender as a yearling filly, Alys had
been graced with skin like sunlit snow, the eyes of a fawn,
and the mouth of an enchantress.

Save for that startled look she had given him when
he'd first spoken to her, she'd also shown as much interest in him as she might a potted plant.

Testing the depth of her resistance would please him
to no end, but Beau had to find Stuart. Once she had
disappeared from view, he began making his way along
the bar. None of the men answered to the name or knew
the man he sought. Exasperated, Beau went to the reception desk, and compelled the clerk to give him a key
card to Stuart's room on the seventh floor.

From outside the door to Stuart's room he heard the
sound of the shower, and let himself in. He didn't interrupt the mortal's bath, but used the time to inspect the
man's cases. He carried no weapons, but had filled one
case with electronic gadgetry, and a second with large,
old books. Beau opened one volume to read the title
page, but the words were beyond his understanding.

He tossed the book back into the case, infuriated with
his own anger. As a mortal he had been taught to fight,
not read; in his immortal life shame had compelled him
to hide his ignorance from the other Kyn. When the
Realm had nearly fallen to Byrne's bastard half brother
and his Saracen conspirators, Beau had realized that his
own, long-kept secrets could be revealed someday. A
week after Jayr had been named suzeraina, Beau had
gone into the city to seek a solution.

He soon learned that anyone could enroll in a literacy
class at one of the public libraries; the mortals who

taught them were volunteers who required no payment in return. Even better, most were held after sunset, to benefit those who were obligated to work during the day.

His first teacher, a retired librarian with seeming endless patience, had prevented him from giving up several times that first month. "Reading is like learning another language," Mrs. Decker would say. "You can't expect to be fluent from the start. You must learn, and practice what you learn."

As Darkyn, Beau knew himself to be superior to mortals in almost every way; as a reader he discovered he was painfully slow, and made many mistakes. Mrs. Decker began asking him to stay behind after the class was dismissed to work with her for another half hour.

"You're fighting this too much, my dear," she'd told him after he'd struggled through a line from his primer. "Words are not bombs, ready to explode if you fumble them. Think of them more as gifts, under the Christmas tree, waiting to be unwrapped." Her finger went to the line he'd mangled. "*Sally.* You know that's the name for the little girl in the story. *Blue* is the color of the sky on a summer day. *Ball* is her brother's favorite toy."

Beau nodded, and sounded out the word in the middle of the line. "*Kicks.*" He thought for a moment. "What Sally wants to do to her brother's . . . toy."

Mrs. Decker had chuckled. "Exactly."

Beau heard the shower shut off, and replaced the book in the case. Once he used *l'attrait* to bring the professor under his control, he would interrogate him and learn how much he knew about the renegades, and how best to lure their leader into Beau's hands.

The bathroom door opened, and Alys walked out, her

hands busy tucking a towel around her damp body. Beau was so astonished to see her that at first all he did was stare. She stopped as soon as she saw him, turned, and ran for the door.

Beau reached it before she did and slapped a hand against it to keep it shut. She spun around him, and without thinking, Beau clamped an arm around her waist. "You needn't—"

She kicked back at him, knocking them both off-balance. As they fell forward, Beau brought up his free arm so that it would land on the carpet before her face, and used it to keep most of his weight off her.

"Be still," he said into her arm as she wriggled under him. Her warm, damp body smelled of almond-scented soap over her own fiery scent. She was not afraid, he realized, but furious, and the scent he was shedding was not affecting her in the slightest. "I am not here to hurt you."

Beau lifted up enough to roll her onto her back, but when she struck at his face, he pinned her wrists to the carpet. When he glanced down, he saw that her towel now lay wadded under her. That was what burned through his garments against his cool skin—the bare front of her body.

"I'll fight you," she promised, her voice echoing the trembling of her body, "and whatever you do to me, I *will* hurt you."

"This is a mistake." Beau started to lift himself from her, and then stopped. "I did not come here to assault you, or see you naked, or whatever you are thinking."

"You're on top of me," she snapped. "I'm naked. You have an erection. What am I supposed to think?"

"I do not. . . ." Bloody hell, he was as hard as a club. Softening his voice, he said, "I apologize."

"I'll press charges," she promised. "After I hurt you."

Beau released her wrists, and pushed himself up, turning away as quickly as he could. "Cover yourself now, girl." He could hear her crawling backward and wrapping the towel. "I came to see—"

She tried to get at the door again, and he was obliged to trap her against it.

"This didn't work for you the last time," Beau told her. "We can roll about on the floor again, or you can listen to me and stop trying to run out of here screaming." She instantly opened her mouth and took in a deep breath, forcing him to clamp his hand over her lips. "That was not a suggestion."

She made an angry, muffled sound.

"Listen to me. I can stuff something in your mouth"—Christ Jesus, why had he said that?—"or you can promise me you will not scream by nodding. What's it to be, then?"

Over the edge of his hand, her eyes narrowed, and then she gave a single nod. As soon as he took his hand away, she said, "Would you please get off me?" When he shifted his body away from hers, she ducked under his arm and retreated a safe distance. "Now get out of here or I'll call security."

"I can't. I have business with Dr. Stuart." When she moved toward the phone, he added, "I did check with the front desk. The clerk said that his room number was seven fourteen, and unless they've changed the numbers in the last three minutes, *this* is room seven fourteen."

She picked up the receiver, placing it on her shoulder

before she hitched up the front of the towel. "How did you get in here?"

"You left the door ajar." She wore no ring on her wedding finger, and she didn't behave like a wife. Beau's lust darkened as he imagined her long, graceful body spread beneath some rutting, gray-haired scholar—but surely she was too young for that. "Forgive me, but who are you? The professor's daughter?"

"I didn't leave the door open." Doubt flickered over her features, and her confusion made her seem even younger. "At least I don't think I did." She slowly replaced the receiver. "I'm Dr. Stuart. The *only* Dr. Stuart."

"You can't be." He studied her. "I'm looking for Dr. *Al* Stuart."

"That's me," she insisted. "A. L. Stuart. I use my initials for professional purposes."

Beau dragged a hand through his hair. "You're a woman, and hardly more than a child."

"I'm twenty-six, and I earned my first PhD when I was twenty-one. Excuse me, but I'm uncomfortable talking to you like this." She unzipped a backpack and bent over to rummage through it. "Why did you assume I was a man?"

Beau caught himself admiring the long, elegant lines of her bare legs. "Tremayne told me your name was *Al* Stuart. When we spoke in the bar, you knew I was looking for a man."

"I didn't know who you were or what you wanted, so I was simply being careful." She straightened. "You should have mentioned that you were from the Hylord Foundation."

He inclined his head. "I also happen to be cautious with strangers."

"You mean, when you're not tackling them?" She scooped up a robe from the end of the bed. "I have the preliminary excavation schedule prepared. I was going to fax it to Ireland in the morning." She shrugged into the robe, turning her back to him as she let the towel drop to the floor and tied the belt. "I also plan to file progress reports twice a week, if that's acceptable." She faced him, her features completely composed, but her scent still hot with anger and something more. "Are you with Hylord's local office? Should I e-mail a copy to you?"

Obviously the girl was immune to *l'attrait*, which meant he would have to rely on persuasion. "I have been sent by the—by Hylord—to oversee your project."

That startled a laugh out of her. "*You're* an archaeologist?" When he shook his head, her gaze went from his face to his chest and toes, and then flashed up again. "What other digs have you worked on?"

He couldn't deceive her on that score. "This would be my first."

Her jaw set. "I'm sorry, but I can't have this."

"It's done," he assured her. "I'm yours."

Her scent abruptly cooled. "This project is very problematical. I have a great deal of work to do in a very short amount of time." As even as her tone was, her eyes filled with some strange emotion, as if she regretted the words she spoke. "I can't afford to be distracted by someone like you."

She had no choice in the matter, but still her rejection

rankled. "Why do you believe that I would be a hindrance?" He gestured at the carpet. "Other than the un-
fortunate tackling incident, which, I promise, will not be
repeated."

"In order to make accurate reports to the foundation
on my progress, you'll have to shadow me constantly."
Her lips twisted. "That is the real reason they sent you,
isn't it, Mr. . . . ah . . . ?"

"Beauregard York." He offered the Americanized
name that he used when among mortals. "Do call me
Beau." He gave her his most fetching smile as he lied to
her. "I was not sent here to spy on you, Dr. Stuart."

"Logic dictates no other alternative," she informed
him. "Your foundation has been very generous, but
they've also made several stipulations to ensure secrecy.
This is the first major project I've conducted, making me
unproven in the field. My peers already consider my
theories to be everything from unfounded to ludicrous."

Beau was surprised she could speak so calmly about
it. "What would make them believe that?"

"When the Order of the Knights Templar was dis-
banded by the pope, some were able to escape. According to my research, at least one of them fled Europe for
the Spanish Main, and then sailed from there to Florida.
I believe he came here with a group of Spanish priests
and with them founded a mission to convert the Timucua
natives." She hesitated, tugging at the belt of her robe.
"My colleagues think that is nonsensical, but what they
flatly refuse to accept is my theory as to the Templars'
other motive for coming here."

"You have a second theory?"

She nodded. "Before he left the mission, the Templar

concealed something very old and valuable there. I've never been able to precisely identify the artifact he left behind, but I have a very good idea of what it is. I've also published several articles in trade magazines about it, which is why my colleagues think I'm crazy."

Beau wondered what she would say if she knew a former Templar was standing right in front of her. "Your colleagues sound small-minded."

"They're limited by ego and fear. I'm not, although I do understand the risk I'm taking. Failure on my part will put an end to my career, and the connection to me has the potential to damage the foundation's reputation." Alys watched his face. "So, Mr. York. If you're not here to monitor me, then why would they give someone with no archaeological experience this assignment?"

He grinned. "Oh, to manage things."

"And that." She shook a finger at his face. "That is the other problem I have with you. You're far too attractive. Half of my interns are young, impressionable girls. I don't want them distracted from their work, especially if you decide to tackle one of them."

So she thinks me handsome. Beau had never been especially vain, but her compliment pleased him. "You seem to think I can do nothing but roll about on the floor with women."

She gave him a tight smile. "I can only go by experience."

"Well, Doctor, I don't. And if your young interns are hoping to impress me, perhaps they'll work harder." Someone knocked on the door behind him, and he glanced through the peephole. "There's an Asian lad standing in the hall. He's carrying a very large case."

"One of my interns. I have some equipment to check." She offered him her hand and, when he took it, gave him a brisk handshake. "Thank you for stopping in to meet me, Mr. York, but I really can't use you on the project. Please give my regrets and my regards to Mr. Tremayne."

Chapter 3

Although Jayr usually held meetings with the mortal staff in the expansive area of the reception hall, she preferred to conduct personal interviews in the old armory that Byrne had converted into a study for her.

"I've yet to fathom why you need to acquire a new *tresora* at all," Byrne grumbled as he poured a glass of bloodwine for Jayr. "We've dozens of them about the place. Pick one from our own, and train them to suit you, I say."

"Most of our *tresori* are performers, laborers, or office workers," she reminded him as she accepted the glass. "None of them have any experience with overseeing an entire household or serving the suzerainty. Also, most of them are female."

"Aye, for we've a progressive household, where women are respected and valued." He lifted his glass to toast her. "As well you know, my lady."

"As I do, my lord." She inclined her head. "I might point out that you've also slept with most of them."

He nearly choked. "That was before you confessed

your love for me. Since I've had you, I've naught touched another." He gave her a suspicious look. "Never tell me you are jealous of the house wenches."

"Considering that I once handpicked your bed companions for you, no. I've no quarrel with them." His visible relief made her smile a little. "I am accustomed to working with men, however, and as I am still new to rule, I would prefer a *tresora* with significant household experience."

Being named a lady paramount had made Jayr the first female to rule over a Darkyn *jardin*. Since she had also been the only female seneschal among the Kyn, she had not expected her new position to prove particularly trying. Shortly after being elevated to suzeraina, however, Jayr had discovered she was not, in fact, a nameless orphan, but the bastard daughter of Robin of Locksley.

It had taken a long time for Jayr to accept that stunning revelation, as well as Robin's reasons for never claiming her. Her sense of self-worth had gradually recovered, but there were moments still when Jayr felt as if she were an impostor in her own life.

Here in the study, surrounded by the books and artworks that she and her lover had collected over the centuries, Jayr felt more at ease with her role as suzeraina. She needed that if she was to choose the right candidate to serve her and the Realm as their new chief *tresora*.

The latest aspirant, an Englishman from a very old and venerable *tresoran* family, arrived at the precise time for his interview. After Byrne made the formal introductions, Jayr shook his hand in American fashion and invited him to sit with her beside the fire.

Jayr knew from the file provided by the *tresoran* council that Devan Leeds was single, thirty-two, and the youngest member of an ancient *tresoran* bloodline. Dressed in an immaculate, beautifully tailored navy blue suit, Leeds wore his fair hair very short and neat. Jayr liked the calm directness of his blue eyes; they made his otherwise unremarkable features seem friendlier. His quiet demeanor and economical movements clearly demonstrated that he was accustomed to service.

Leeds had served as an assistant to his father, the chief *tresora* in an Italian stronghold. Such arrangements were common among their most faithful human allies, with fathers training sons in apprentice fashion to take their place after they retired from service. The practice ensured that the Kyn lord would not have to bring a stranger into his household, nor would he have to devote any time to teaching the mortal his personal customs and preferences. *Tresoran* families prided themselves on serving the same lord for centuries; a few had served their masters even before they became immortal.

"I'm flattered that you would take interest in this position and my household," Jayr told him, "but I find myself puzzled as well. Your bloodline is English, and yet your family has served an Italian suzerain for well on five hundred years. After such long and distinguished service, why would you wish to relocate to America?"

"It does sound confusing, doesn't it?" Leeds smiled. "Suzerain Marietto, whom my family has served since he rose to walk the night, was exceedingly fond of his mother. She was an Englishwoman who met and married his father while making a pilgrimage. Even when our lord was mortal, he would hire her countrymen and import them to serve in his household. Every child in my

family has been raised and educated in England specifi-
cally to preserve those qualities he enjoyed so much."

Jayr detected an abrupt change in his scent, one that
indicated he was saddened. Then she realized how he
had referred to his master. *Enjoyed.* "Did something
happen to alter this arrangement?"

"Four years ago the Brethren attacked our stronghold
in the middle of the day." He related the details in spare
but unflinching terms. "They burned everything to the
ground: the villa, the garrison's quarters, the staff's cot-
tages. Our lord and his lady, their warriors, my parents,
and every mortal on the property perished in the flames."

Byrne, who stood behind Jayr, stirred. "Yet you survived."

"I would have died with them, Seneschal, but two
days before the massacre my master sent me on errand
to Rome." His mouth took on a bitter curve. "He wished
to move our entire *jardin* to England, and bade me put
the matter before the council. He wished them to approve the relocation before he petitioned the high lord.
It is ironic. In another month or two, we would have
been safely beyond their reach."

Jayr knew of the Brethren's brutal campaign to drive
the Kyn out of Europe; like the other American suze-
rains, she had offered sanctuary to as many refugee warriors as she could absorb into her *jardin.* She'd never
given much thought to how the horrific attacks impacted
their mortal allies, however. "Such a grievous loss ren-
ders all words inadequate, Mr. Leeds. Please accept my
sympathies."

"You are very gracious, my lady." Leeds bowed his
head. "I count myself fortunate in that I am young

enough to start again, and do what I can to preserve my bloodline. To serve in your household would be a very new experience for me, a chance at a new beginning, if you like."

Jayr was struck by how practical he was; she suspected, like her, he handled his difficulties by working through them. "Some of the *tresori* I have interviewed did not seem comfortable with the thought of making their oath to a lady paramount. How do you feel about the prospect of serving a woman instead of a man?"

"You are the first lady to rule the Kyn, and I imagine all you do is subject to special scrutiny." Now he sounded sympathetic. "It is apparent that you need a well-trained *tresora* who can adapt to this new order of rule. One who has the appropriate standards, who can serve your needs without reservation or prejudice, and who will run your household flawlessly. I believe I am that man, or I would not be here."

"And modest to boot," Byrne muttered.

Jayr frowned at him. "You say our need is apparent, Mr. Leeds, as if there is something wanting."

"Many things, I fear, my lady. This chamber, for example." The *tresora* gestured around him. "I can tell that this was once your armory. Converting it to a study makes it a very welcoming room, but what was done with the weapons that were stored here?"

"I believe my seneschal moved them to our underground storage rooms," Jayr said. "What does it matter where they are?"

"If the keep were suddenly attacked, your men would waste precious time retrieving what they needed for defense from the lower levels." He clasped his hands, bracing his elbows on his knees as he leaned forward. "As I was escorted here, I noted a number of unoccupied rooms which could be used for weapons storage. You should also have caches hidden on every level for the same purpose."

"We are open to the mortal public, lad," Byrne said, sounding peevish. "The Brethren do not skulk about here torching the unwary. They hardly have any presence in America."

"As you say, Seneschal," Leeds agreed, "but now that they have caused so many to flee Europe, I fear they will soon be crossing the Atlantic in pursuit."

Jayr knew Byrne's moods better than anyone; for some reason he had taken an instant dislike to Leeds. She didn't understand why, but she couldn't discuss it with her lover in front of the man. That she didn't share Byrne's odd antipathy made the matter even more complicated. She liked Leeds, who was far more qualified than any of the other candidates, and wanted very much to offer him the position.

"I expect you have much to consider," Leeds said, as if reading her mind. "There is no reason for me to return to Italy immediately, so if it would be agreeable to you, I should like to offer my services as *tresora* on a trial basis. Would a month be sufficient time for you to evaluate my performance? It may help you and your household to decide if I am the right man for the job."

"I think it would." Jayr glanced at Byrne, who was scowling. "This is very generous of you, Mr. Leeds."

"My motives are not entirely unselfish," the *tresora* admitted. "I should like to see if living in America and managing your household will suit me as well."

None of the other candidates had made such an offer, and it would give the man a chance to prove himself. *To me and Byrne.* "That seems quite sensible," Jayr said, and rose to her feet. "Very well, Mr. Leeds. You have your month."

"Thank you, my lady." He stood, giving her a respectful bow before turning to Byrne. "My lord, I know your mortal staff is still on holiday. Could you spare one of your men to show me about the premises?"

"I will give you the tour myself," Jayr said before Aedan could answer. "I am interested to know how our arrangements compare to those in Europe."

"I can tell you that we don't have gift shops or snack cafés." As a knock sounded on the door, Leeds went to it. "Your submersible bridges are enviable as well. Are they operated by hydraulics?"

Harlech eyed the *tresora* before he stepped inside. "Forgive the intrusion, my lady, but the stable master has asked if Lord Byrne would look at one of the mares. She may have the colic."

"No trouble, Captain." Jayr introduced him to Leeds. "Devan will be with us for at least the next month. Please advise the men accordingly."

"Yes, my lady." Harlech nodded to the *tresora*, who followed Jayr out into the corridor.

The phone rang while Alys was in the middle of running a diagnostic on the GPR, and when she ignored it, Chan asked, "Do you want me to get that, Dr. Stuart?"

"Right. Sure." She watched the screen as she thumbed through the troubleshooting manual and studied the potential errors. Without the ground-penetrating radar fully operational, she would be digging blind, and with only four weeks to work, she couldn't afford to guess where she might find some evidence of the fountain.

At least I won't have to dodge him.

Being distracted yet again by the thought of Beauregard York annoyed and pleased Alys; she had no reason to dwell on the man, but the fact that she did illustrated how right she'd been to keep him off her team.

I can stuff something in your mouth. . . .

Attending an all-girls boarding school in Switzerland had effectively sheltered Alys from the opposite sex. Only when she had begun her studies at university did she first encounter the sexual side of social interaction. For a brief time she had even applied herself to study it, although the majority of sexual behaviors among her peers seemed largely a by-product of separation anxieties, self-esteem issues, or stress. She'd watched many of her classmates engage in short-term pseudo-relationships, which they used as cover for the physical liaisons they craved.

She'd also personally experimented with sex herself, several times. It had seemed more attractive than drinking alcohol, a small amount of which she quickly discovered made her violently ill, or the other mind-altering substances her fellow students indulged in, which she avoided because they were illegal. While the mechanics of sex were initially somewhat interesting, the actual pleasures involved were no more exciting or fulfilling to her than a 5K run, or several hours working out at the student gym.

The emotional outpourings and expectations of her partners, on the other hand, had alternately repelled and perplexed her. One of the boys she'd slept with, a computer programming major, had used their first postcoital interlude to profess an undying love for her. He'd also become instantly obnoxious when she refused to verbally reciprocate.

Explaining her opinion on the matter had not improved the situation. "Love is an artificial emotional construct. It provides justification for your pursuit of physical gratification, which you would otherwise consider shameful." She'd been curious about the reason for that, which had prompted her to ask, "Did your parents raise you in an environment with an emphasis on religion?"

"If I wanted to screw a computer, Aly," he'd told her as he'd jerked on his clothes, "I'd have borrowed one from the lab."

After that, Alys had stopped engaging the opposite sex; being found less than a desirable partner had inflicted feelings of inadequacy for which she had no use. Her inability to form emotional bonds with others seemed to be an integral part of her disposition. Since she could no more change who she was than she could have told the computer geek that she loved him, Alys accepted her partner's rejection and moved on.

In the years since she'd left college, Alys had learned to be less analytic and more personable in public. Now around others she kept her thoughts to herself while imitating those social behaviors that allowed her to function successfully within most groups. Until tonight, when Beau York had barged into her room, and knocked her to the floor.

Why can't I stop thinking about him?

It wasn't merely the ghost of his voice, whispering in her head. If the handsome Brit could distract her this much from her work, then his presence at the site would probably reduce her female interns into a pack of fawning little acolytes. Brenda, whose interest in the opposite sex was already a little too well developed, would likely spend the entire four weeks scheming her way into the man's tent.

Something twisted in her middle as Alys imagined finding her student sleeping with Beau. *Is that how he manages things? By seducing coeds?*

"Dr. Stuart?" Chan had to repeat her name two more times before she looked up to see him holding out the receiver. "It's some English guy."

"Again?" She noticed how tired the intern looked, and checked her watch. "Goodness, it's almost dawn, Chan. Go get some sleep. I'll take care of this."

Alys waited until the student left before she spoke into the phone. "Look, Mr. York, I thought I was clear."

"Good evening, Dr. Stuart." The caller was English, but his melodic voice sounded nothing like Beau York's. "This is Richard Tremayne. I do hope I am not disturbing your rest."

"Mr. Tremayne." Alys had never spoken directly to the chairman of the Hylord Foundation, and for a moment she blanked. "Ah, no, I haven't been to bed yet." Why was he calling her? Not to check on the arrangements. "How may I help you?"

"I gather you met my man York earlier this evening," Tremayne said, "and refused to permit him to join your project. May I ask why you found him so objectionable?"

Beau had called Tremayne? That seemed unlikely. How could a project manager have direct access to the foundation's chairman? And why would he?

"Dr. Stuart?"

Alys couldn't very well interrogate Tremayne, nor did she want to cause trouble for Beau. She certainly couldn't tell the chairman of the Hylord Foundation that his employee's voice had shaken her down to her heels.

Be professional. "I have nothing against Mr. York, sir. He seemed like a very congenial and capable person. I simply don't need him." *Or his beautiful body. Or his gorgeous face. Or that stupendous erection.*

Tremayne's voice went flat. "Doctor, you are aware that my foundation has invested close to half a million U.S. dollars in your project."

Of course he'd bring up the money; it was the only power he had over her. "Yes, sir, and I am grateful for the opportunity to—"

"Given the number of charlatans and scoundrels operating under the guise of scientific research," Tremayne continued, as if she hadn't spoken, "I have a keen interest in protecting my investments. York will assure that everything at the site runs smoothly and according to schedule."

Alys had tried to avoid maligning Beau, but now his boss was giving her no choice.

"Mr. Tremayne, you do understand how highly specialized my work is. Mr. York isn't an archaeologist, and he's never worked on any excavation in the past. He will be unfamiliar with the tools and equipment we use as well as the methods we employ during a dig. However gifted he is at resource or personnel management, he has nothing to contribute to the success of this project. I simply can't use him."

"On the contrary, Doctor." Each word he spoke drilled into her ear, as sharp and welcome as a probing ice pick. "Mr. York *will* be a part of your team, and oversee all of your fieldwork, or the foundation will immediately withdraw all funding for the project."

Alys rubbed her aching temple. "Under the circumstances I have no choice but to agree. Please let Mr. York know we'll begin work at the site tomorrow evening."

"Thank you, Doctor. I feel sure you and Mr. York will get on very well, and I look forward to reviewing reports on your progress. Good-bye." The line clicked.

Alys's stomach rolled as she put down the receiver, and the taste of bile in her throat sent her hurrying into the bathroom. After she emptied her stomach into the toilet, she staggered to her feet to rinse out her mouth and wash her face.

She reached behind her neck to unfasten her necklace, which felt like it weighed a ton, and set it on the counter before she glanced at her reflection. Sweat soaked her unruly red hair, plastering the underlying layer to her skull; her face had gone so pale her violet eyes and reddened mouth looked like huge bruises. Her ears still buzzed from the unpleasant sharpness of Tremayne's voice when he'd delivered his final ultimatum. Fortunately the nausea had receded, and after she brushed her teeth, she cautiously drank a half glass of water. She generally had a cast-iron stomach, but the stress of talking to Tremayne had been considerable—almost painful.

Alys saw a glimmer of light reflecting from her eye and leaned closer. The gold ring around the outside of her violet irises seemed larger now, although the mirror might be magnifying it.

"Deal with it," she told her image before she shut off the light and went back to work.

Byrne patted the neck of the sick, weary mare before he said to the stable master, "'Tis not colic giving her the bellyache. More likely she's foraged on buttercups or nightshade. It'll pass, but keep close watch on her tonight, and tell your lads to check the pasture where you last turned her out." He saw his wardrobe keeper hovering just outside the entrance to the stables. "Have them dig up whatever they find, drench the soil, and keep the horses out of there until spring."

As he walked out of the barn, a slim form emerged from the shadows. "You sent for me, Seneschal?" Farlae asked.

"Aye." He glanced at the castle, and felt again the prickle along his backbone that never boded anything good. "We need to talk."

The wardrobe keeper, who as always was dressed in black, wrinkled his nose. "Do we? I hope we need not adjourn to my workrooms for this tête-à-tête."

Byrne sniffed at his sleeve. "You're as priss-nosed as my mother was."

"Knowing how often she wanted you kept chained in the outer ward, I shall take that as a compliment." Farlae inspected him with his strange gaze. While one of the wardrobe keeper's eyes moved normally, and was the color of the sea under a sunny sky, an enormous black mote paralyzed and engulfed the other, making it appear like some bizarre window into the abyss. "But you did not summon me to discuss your lady mother."

"No." He gestured toward the citrus groves. "We'll walk out there."

The frosty wind that accompanied them didn't bother Byrne; winter in Florida was like a balmy Scottish summer. What had chilled his blood was watching his woman warm to that mortal. Leeds had conducted himself with exquisite manners, admirable confidence, and every appropriate protocol. For if he hadn't, Byrne would have seized on it to have the man marched off his land.

No longer my land, he reminded himself. The Realm belonged to his lady now, along with his men, his castle, and his rule, and it was past time for him to accept that.

"We've gone outside the range of any ear, human or Kyn," Farlae mentioned as they made their way down two rows of grapefruit trees. "You are safe to tell me what has your spleen in a knot."

"We've a new *tresora* in the keep. English, from the Leeds bloodline." Byrne described the man to Farlae. "He's to give a month's trial to prove himself as bright and shiny as he looks."

"Leeds." Farlae's expression grew thoughtful. "I thought I knew all the English *tresoran* families, but the name escapes me."

"Aye, but you see, he's English by way of Italy."

The wardrobe keeper halted in his tracks. "He can't be Nottingham's man. Cyprien packed off the few you didn't slaughter to the Orient."

"To hear it told, this one served Marietto. His loyalty is unblemished, and the council has even vouched for him. You know those old bastards. They wouldn't stick out their scrawny necks for just anyone." He reached out and cradled a ripening grapefruit with one hand. "And I have heard of the Leedses myself. 'Tis an old and respected bloodline."

"Then why are we out here inspecting fruit?" Farlae asked.

"It seems he was on errand in Rome during a Brethren stronghold attack. They put to the flames everyone, even Marietto. This one is the only Leeds left alive." Byrne glanced back at the keep. "I dinnae trust sole survivors, Farlae."

"Escaping a horrible death does not automatically warrant suspicion." Farlae's brows drew together. "What is your thinking? That this Leeds betrayed his lord and his mortal kin to the zealots, and now comes here to do the same to the Realm?"

Byrne was not willing to cast that much suspicion on the man, not without proof. "He is here to do something, and the knot in my spleen tells me it has nothing to do with serving my *sygkenis*." He hesitated before he added, "You know of this new group of traitors among the *tresori*, the ones who were hunting those Kyn-maker jewels."

"You mean the Emeralds of Eternity, which were not actually destroyed during the battle in South Florida?" Farlae smiled. "I may have heard a word or two. As for the traitors, they are said to mutilate their Kyn marks, steal our ancient treasures, attack our kind, and commit suicide when cornered."

Which was why Byrne had sent for him: Farlae had spies everywhere. "I should've asked what you *dinnae* know."

Farlae considered that. "Well, I've yet to fathom the motive behind this rebellion. *Tresori* are trained from birth to love and serve us, and we have always cherished them. Those who prove unsuitable are never permitted to know us. There seems little motive for either sort turning traitor."

"As you say. Yet if this Leeds is one of them, come here to bring down our household . . ." Byrne felt wetness on his hand, and saw that he had crushed the fruit to pulp. "Damn me. Four years I've not felt this—not even a twitch—and all my hand wants is a battle-ax. Why this, why now, when I've everything a man could dream?"

"A beast will not sleep when something prods it." Farlae drew a snowy kerchief from his sleeve and handed it to him. "Leeds will have to be shadowed, his rooms searched, his movements tracked. I take it you have not spoken to Jayr about such things."

"She believes his tragedy." He wiped the pulp from his hands. "Aye, she even likes him."

"Then you must keep your distance, Aedan." Farlae nodded toward the jousting field, where Byrne had last descended into the killing madness of his affliction. "Else this mortal sends you in search of your battle-ax, and this dream of yours becomes a nightmare."

Chapter 4

On the table in his chamber Beau rolled out a map of the Central Florida region, on which he had marked the survey site.

"This is where I'll be working with the mortals for the next month," he told Harlech. "The land is undeveloped and deserted. As an additional precaution against attracting attention, the high lord has instructed Dr. Stuart and her team to excavate only at night."

Harlech peered at the symbols on the map. "I've ridden that way a time or two. There's an old Spanish mission, and some sort of Indian settlement near a pond." He glanced up. "How will you feed, and where will you take your rest during the daylight hours?"

"The mission has a large cellar level. I spent some hours last night making it habitable and laying in a concealed supply of bagged blood." Beau rolled up the map. "The high lord has me acting as an overseer so I may remain on-site. I will call in when I can, but it is likely that I shall return before February."

"You've never operated from within a group of mortals," his captain said, "and they are not as oblivious as we would like. Remember not to use ability or your strength, and avoid wounds so they do not see you heal. You must keep to well-ventilated areas whenever possible. What of eating and drinking with them?"

Beau hadn't considered that. "I will find an excuse to be busy when they have their meals."

"Mortals dine three times a day," a sweet voice said, "and will use any excuse to pop corn or roast marshmallows or consume bags of crisps while sitting about a fire swapping ghost stories. They will grow suspicious."

"Never fear, brother." Harlech turned to smile at the red-haired woman looking in on them, and held out his arm. "Viviana has learned a few tricks on how to break bread with them, haven't you, my love?"

"Aye." The skirts of her amber velvet gown swirled as she joined her husband. "Beau, say to the mortals that you have many food allergies and as such you must prepare all of your own meals. You can then arrange this preparation so that you will dine alone. If you must share a table with them, first mix a little of your bagged blood in whatever you put on your plate. At best 'twill hold off the sickness only a few minutes, so eat quickly and then visit the privy at once. If they find you emptying your belly, blame your allergies."

"You might eat with your hands, and belch very loudly," Harlech added. "Whenever Rainer forgets himself and does that during the dining hall performance, the mortals vacate his table at once."

Beau thought of Alys on the floor, her bare body trapped under his. As he did, he felt his cock stir, as it did every time he remembered having her beneath him.

Enough of Alys.

"I've no wish to disgust them." Beau went to his armoire and began selecting the garments he would need.

"Why do you say that?" Viviana asked as she came to help him. "Have they some maiden among them who has caught your eye? Or do they not permit women to do such work?"

"No. In fact the team is led by a woman." He carried his garments over to his cases. "Alys Stuart is her name. Dr. Alys Stuart."

"How interesting." Viviana's brows arched. "What manner of leech digs in the dirt for things forgotten?"

"She is a doctor of archaeology, not medicine." Beau saw the look Harlech's wife gave him. "And yes, Vivi, she is young and lovely and, as far as I know, unattached. Unfortunately she is also immune to *l'attrait*."

Viviana grimaced. "Oh, bad luck. Is there anyone else, perhaps? For if there isn't, I could surely send along one of the household girls to visit you. Several of them are very taken with you, you know."

"Are they?" Beau regarded his captain, who cringed a little. "I thank you, but I think I should be able to bear the burden of an empty bed for a month."

"Well, if you change your mind, you have only to call." She gave his hand a fond pat before she said to her husband, "Harlech, I will be supervising the fittings tonight, so do not expect me before midnight." She kissed his check before she swept out.

"For nigh on five centuries that woman kept from me that she was changed by Nottingham *and* she and Rain were the last of Sherwood *jardin*," Harlech said. "Yet when I confide in *her*, she cannot hold her tongue for five minutes."

As he had lied to Harlech since they were mortals, Beau wondered whether Viviana's offer veiled something more damning. "If you have some doubt of me or this mission, brother, tell me yourself."

"When you were late to assembly, I questioned the men about you. I also asked Rainer." Harlech lifted a hand. "I know, 'twas wrong of me to assume you were at fault. You are the most loyal of men."

A dull fear plumed inside his gut, making it difficult to keep his tone casual. "What was said?"

"You know Rain." Harlech rolled his eyes. "He nattered on about Nottingham and Viviana, and that time one of his trick blades landed in your ribs. I thought I'd go mad listening to him, but then he said something very odd. He claimed that you could not be out wenching, for you had not had a woman in months."

"Is that all?" Beau hid his relief by opening his case. "Well, that explains why your wife wants to fill my bed."

Harlech looked uncomfortable. "'Tis not like you to avoid females, Beau."

"In truth I thought I had tired of them," Beau admitted. "'Twas not until I had Alys under me that I felt the need."

"The woman was immune to your scent, and you still took her to bed?" Harlech grinned. "Small wonder half the garrison envies you."

"I did not take her. 'Twas an accident; we fell together." Beau paced across the room and back again before he regarded Harlech. "I will tell you this: I wanted to have her, right there, even as she was swearing to hurt me if I did. She thought me a brute come to rape her."

"No doubt." Harlech saw his face. "Good God, man, you've never had a mortal female refuse you. That in itself must make this Alys seem like the most alluring Aphrodite ever to walk the earth. So, then. Did you force yourself on her?"

Beau gave him a filthy look. "I may have unseemly thoughts, but never would I violate a woman."

"I never doubted it. I will tell you my great secret, the one that has kept me true and faithful to Viviana all these centuries." Harlech smiled. "I have known any number of fetching wenches, and yes, a few who have thrown themselves at me, begging to see to my pleasure. When this happens, I see them as children too young to know what they are about." His mouth curled. "And then I go and find my wife."

"Alys will not be throwing herself at me," Beau admitted. "She has disliked me from the start."

"She will come to like you, Beau. Everyone does." Harlech clapped a hand on his shoulder. "But likely she is indifferent to you, or her passions run another course. To cool your desire, I suggest you think on some Kyn female you might pursue, and the mortal solely as a sister. A very *young* sister."

A sister, when Beau could not even remember his mother.

"And there is that look on your face again," his captain said. "You've worn it like a mask every day since Byrne's brother attempted to take the Realm. It reminds me of how you were when we were boys."

"'Twas a shock. I should have known those Saracens meant to harm us." *And if I were to tell you the reason for that, you would have my head piked on the castle gates.* "As for women, I see you with Viviana, and our lady with Byrne, and I want the same for myself. A wife, a companion. But there are so few unattached females among our kind that thinking on them in that manner is the same as dreaming."

"I am sorry I have troubled you about it." Harlech grimaced. "Only know that if you are in need of anything from a brother, you have but to find me."

As Harlech helped him pack, Beau's thoughts drifted back to his brief life as a mortal. He remembered almost nothing of his childhood before he had been sent to foster with Harlech's family. The smallest and thinnest of boys, Beau hadn't dared to utter a word to anyone.

Preoccupied with his own training, Harlech had barely noticed Beau until one afternoon in the lists, when some of the older boys had come looking for Beau. That day it had been seven against one, and yet when the tussle ended and the dust had cleared, every squire lay huddled and moaning in the dirt.

Harlech had tethered his mount and walked over to where Beau stood, his battered face tight and his bruised hands fisted, his back pressed against a hay bale. "Well-done. Who taught you to fight?"

Beau spat out some blood, but his eyes never strayed from the boys he had knocked down. "Priests."

"Huh. I shall have to attend church more often." Harlech gave him a measuring look. "Go and wash up. Mother hates to see evidence of our labors at her table."

Beau jerked his chin toward the fallen. "What about them?"

"I expect they'll be too busy now," Harlech said, eliciting new groans from the fallen. To one of them, he said, "Do remind me, Master Thaddius, what is the price for a squire who loses a challenge?"

The older boy hung his head and muttered, "Shoveling out stalls for the stable master."

"Ah, yes." Harlech smiled. "Shit for shit."

"Do you remember Squire Langston?" Beau now asked Harlech as he stowed some extra shirts in his traveling case.

"Thaddius the Thickhead?" Harlech chuckled. "God in heaven, Beau, I have not thought of him in seven lifetimes. Why have you?"

"He died at a tourney in France when he was but twenty," Beau said. "He took a lance through the heart. He couldn't afford the proper armor, but still he rode. I thought it brave of him."

"Stupid, more like," Harlech corrected. "Thaddius was a braggart and a bully who thought himself ever invincible. 'Twas what killed him in the end." He cocked his head. "You were never friends with Thaddius."

"Do you recall the day in the lists, when he and the other squires came to thrash me?" As Harlech nodded, Beau said, "I did not come to the evening meal because I was bloodied and beaten. I went to the stables and shoveled out the stalls with them."

Harlech made an impatient sound. "As angry as they were? They might have smothered you in shit."

"They hated me because I was small and thin and

alone." Beau closed the case and fastened the straps. "I had to show them that I was no different."

"And did you?"

"I took a few more cuffs that night, but none in earnest," Beau admitted. "I have never been one to lead others, Harlech. If not for you, Thaddius might have become my friend and guide. I daresay I would have followed him to France, and died a mortal death as he did."

"But you followed me into the Templars, and off to Crusade, and back to England again." Harlech's expression turned pensive. "Where I, your good friend, gave you the plague that took us both to the grave."

"As well as the immortal life I've lived since we clawed our way out of them." Beau shrugged into the black leather jacket he wore when among mortals. "For a long time I believed we were cursed by God for our sins. But the modern world has changed my thinking, and now I am persuaded to believe it is as Cyprien's leech would have it. We were changed by the strangeness of that plague, not divine condemnation. It was not punishment, but accident."

"You have been thinking too much of late." The captain folded his arms. "So what if it was chance? Would you have rather died on the wrong end of a lance, as Thaddius did? Is that the real reason you've given up wenching? Why you spend so many nights hunting alone? Some manner of atonement?" He peered at him. "Have you taken to excessive praying, or drinking animal blood?"

"No. I have no desire to make myself into a changeling." Beau felt once more the urge to confess to his friend the truth. "Harlech, becoming a Templar was the making of me as a mortal, but being changed to Darkyn was my penance. If Dr. Keller is right, then I must accept that I have done nothing to make amends, not once in these seven hundred years."

"You speak as if you need absolution for some terrible crime, but you have done nothing. Indeed, I have known you to be everything that is loyal and true and good in a man, mortal or Kyn." The captain threw up his hands. "You do yourself injustice without cause. Name a moment when you have not conducted yourself as the most courageous of warriors."

"It does not matter. We must all face a day of reckoning." And if he was right, his would soon be at hand.

Harlech looked puzzled. "Reckoning for what?"

Beau looked out into the darkness toward the east. "All our sins left unforgiven."

Unable to sleep, thanks to the X-rated movie starring Beauregard York that kept playing in her head, Alys went down to the hotel's indoor pool to swim off her frustrations. By dawn she had managed to exhaust herself, which allowed her to sleep until her afternoon wake-up call. It took another hour to rouse her interns and have their equipment loaded into the rental vans they'd be using for transport to and from the site.

Before they left the hotel, Alys coordinated their GPS units, distributed handheld radios, and gave her student drivers strict instructions to stay together. "I don't want anyone accidentally ending up at one of the theme parks."

"Disney is for little kids," Brenda said, sounding huffy. "We were hoping to hit Knights Realm, but they're closed for renovations or something until February."

"I can skip the medieval experience," Charles told her. "Those guys are just a bunch of wimpy RenFaire freaks anyway."

"Might I remind you all? This isn't a vacation." The disappointment on their faces made Alys feel a twinge of regret; they were still kids. "That said, if you're diligent and we finish the project on schedule, I might be persuaded to pay for a celebratory visit to one of the parks for everyone."

"SeaWorld," Chan said instantly.

Brenda shook her head. "Universal is way better."

"The Holy Land Experience." Paolo cringed as the other interns glared at him. "I can't help it. I'm Catholic."

"If the time comes," Alys promised, "we'll take a vote."

Driving her Jeep, Alys led the mini-caravan out of the city, following roads through hundreds of acres of undeveloped land until she reached the turnoff for the survey area. Newly installed fencing made of steel and wire had been tagged every few yards with danger signs warning of high voltage.

"Wow." Brenda, who was riding in the passenger seat, peered at the signs. "Kind of extreme. I guess we won't have to worry about looters."

Electrified fences seemed rather excessive to Alys as well, but obviously Tremayne meant to keep trespassers off the foundation's land at any cost.

She stopped at the entry, where she inputted the access code on the security pad to release the gate's electronic lock. As the final barrier swung inward, the last rim of sunlight vanished, darkening the clear sky to an orange-bordered violet.

The lack of light didn't bother Alys, as she had always been more awake and alert at night. She also liked seeing the stars glittering overhead; that was something she'd missed since leaving Europe.

The sky looks like his eyes.

"What was that, Dr. Stuart?" Brenda asked.

Alys hadn't realized she'd uttered it out loud. "I said that the sky is a nice surprise. We can't see this much of it in the city."

Her intern frowned at her. "Are you okay? You seem a little, um, preoccupied. I mean, even for you."

"I have a great deal on my mind." And there was no room in it for Beau York.

The foundation's property encompassed wide fields, acres of woods, and several small lakes, all of which showed no signs of occupation. Alys liked the sprawling majesty of the black oaks and their long, twisted limbs, made almost elegant by the silvery drapery of Spanish moss. The dirt road on which she drove had been recently leveled and graded, which would make the students' trips back and forth to the site easier.

She spotted a crumbling brick wall illuminated by her headlights and slowed to take in the first sight of the old Spanish mission. Bright lights over the archaic buildings suddenly switched on, making her flinch until she heard the faint rumble of a generator. *Someone is already out here, or Tremayne has the power supply on a timer.* Since there was no sign of any other vehicles, Alys guessed it to be the latter.

At least Beau York hadn't shown up yet. Alys needed time to collect herself and prepare to deal with him.

The preliminary surveys conducted by Hylord's contractor had included a few photos of the mission, but seeing it in person allowed her to appreciate the fine details. The Spanish priests who had arrived here six hundred years ago had evidently taken their time constructing the place, which appeared much larger and more elaborate than some sixteenth-century Franciscan missions on Florida's east coast she had seen in photos.

Four main buildings, all joined by open-sided passageways, made up the compound. In the center stood the mission's church, which featured a two-story tower vestibule and arched windows that might have once held glass panes. Beside it a flat-roofed structure was probably the cloister, where the priests had lived and slept. The other two buildings were smaller, and she guessed they had served as a kitchen and a stable or storage barn.

From all indications the mission had been built as the precursor to the sustained European presence in the area, one that had lasted until the late eighteenth century, when Spain ended two hundred and fifty years of rule over Florida by trading it to the English in exchange for Cuba.

Alys parked in a clearing behind the mission, where she got out and directed her intern drivers to back in so they could easily access the cargo areas.

"Do you think we'll find any dead people out here?" Brenda asked as she went to help with the unloading.

The groans and laughter drew Alys's attention, and she joined the group of students. "If I answer all the questions, then you won't learn anything. Does anyone want to offer an opinion for Brenda?"

"I doubt it," Charles drawled. "The ground's too wet

in this part of the country. That decays the soft tissue right away, and turns any bones left into rice pudding."

"Thank you for that visual, Charles," Alys said. "Human remains can be found almost anywhere humans have lived, but we won't be excavating any we might uncover here. Does anyone know why?"

"Because of chapter eight seventy-two of the Florida Statutes Unmarked Human Burial Law," Chan said. "That makes it illegal to disturb any burial site, and any that we uncover we have to report to both the state and local tribal officials so they can decide on their disposition."

Charles pretended to yawn. "You're such a geek, Chan."

"Bite me, preppy," the Asian shot back.

"Gentlemen." Alys gave them the eye before addressing the rest of the group. "What that means, people, is that any human skeletons or bones are to be left where you find them and reported to me immediately."

Setting up the site would take most of the night, Alys estimated, although some work had already been done. Brush and grasses around the old mission had been neatly trimmed back, and she could see an ancient trail leading into the woods had also been cleared. Thanks to the winter season and its chilly night temperatures, they wouldn't have to combat swarms of biting insects. According to the surveyors, the land hosted only a minimal number of nocturnal predators, none of which was larger than a raccoon.

Alys scanned the site with a deep sense of satisfaction. Hylord's people had relieved her of hours of prep, which would allow her to begin searching for and map-

ping excavation sites as soon as they unloaded and set up
their equipment stations. Her plan was to first use the
ground-penetrating radar to sweep the area around the
mission to identify promising spatial clusters.

Once they had mapped out a grid around the mission,
Alys also intended to visit the nearby Indian village for
any evidence of nonindigenous activity. With only four
weeks to work, however, she wouldn't be able to do
more than perform a quick visual survey.

A grunt escaped her as she heaved a heavy case of
field tools out of the van; a moment later it was pulled
from her hands as the scent of warm caramel whispered
under her nose.

"Allow me, Dr. Stuart."

The sweet, dark fragrance faded from her senses, replaced by the same voice echoing in her memory. *When
he takes hold of your arm, child, jerk yourself to the left,
very quickly.*

"Dr. Stuart?"

Alys swatted at the hair that had fallen into her eyes
to cover her distress. "Mr. York." When she was able to,
she smiled blindly up at Beau's face. "Such a pleasant
surprise. I didn't expect to see you here so soon." She
recalled the absence of any other vehicles. "How did you
get out here?"

"An acquaintance drove the truck that brought me and
the equipment. I switched on the lighting and had a look
around the old church." He hefted the box of tools as if it
were filled with cotton balls. "Where do you want this?"

"Under the long table the interns are setting over
there." She pointed toward Chan and Paolo, and watched
him carry it past a wide-eyed Brenda, who rushed to her.

"Dr. Al, what's the delish guy from the hotel doing here?" the student demanded.

"That's Mr. York, and he works for the foundation that is funding our excavation. Once we've finished unloading, I'll introduce him to everyone." Alys handed her a box of cataloging materials. "This goes in the processing area."

From that point the setup went smoothly and quickly, with Beau moving the bulk of the equipment cases and boxes of supplies, which allowed the interns to begin arranging their work areas. Alys focused on erecting the canopied mesh tent that she and the students would use as an on-site lab. Hammering the support stakes into the cold ground also allowed her to exorcise some of her pent-up annoyance, although the telescopic aluminum poles and the large roll of roofing canvas weren't meant to be assembled by one person.

Before she could call Charles over to help, Beau appeared at her side. "You look as if you could use a helping hand."

"No, what I need is some pepper spray," Alys muttered.

"I have excellent hearing," Beau said casually, "and as I'm certain you really don't wish to temporarily blind me, why don't you tell me how this goes together?"

He had a good sense of humor, Alys thought, feeling a twinge of envy. No one would ever accuse her of the same.

She gave him a brief rundown of how the tent was assembled, and added, "We have to raise the two support poles at the same time, which can be a little awkward. I can have one of the students—" She stopped as he strode over to the opposite side of the canvas and bent to grasp the pole, which he handled without difficulty.

"On three?" he suggested.

Alys nodded, he counted, and together they raised the canopy. Beau appeared to have no problem sinking his pole into the ground, and came over as Alys struggled with her side.

"The ground is still hard from the last freeze." He wrapped one hand around the pole above hers, and she felt the aluminum slide through her fingers as his arm flexed. He stepped back and glanced at the other pole. "Is that even, then?"

"It looks like it." She didn't understand why his effortless show of strength made her feel even more resentful. If anything, it would be good to have a strong, capable man to help the interns with the heavy lifting and other physical work, something she'd always had to handle herself. Sharing the responsibilities with Beau would give her more time to focus on finding the evidence she needed, and for that, she could show a little more gratitude. "Thank you. I appreciate the assistance."

"I think you'll need more of it." He picked up a roll of the enclosure mesh, checked the straps, and eyed the edge of the canvas. "This is used for the walls?"

Alys showed him how to clip the mesh straps to the grommets in the canvas, which he then accomplished in a few minutes. She followed behind him, releasing the ties and securing the edge of the mesh to the ground.

Beau circled around the tent, finding and opening the entry flaps to step inside. "Is this where you'll have your meals?"

"The canopied table over there is our dining area,"

she said, pointing at it. "We use this tent for our lab work." She followed him in. "We'll bring everything we process in here for cleaning, labeling, and cataloging." She touched the inside of the mesh. "This keeps the area reasonably clean and isolated from the rest of the excavation, which prevents any accidental contamination of the finds. You're very handy for someone who has never worked a dig. Are you a camper, or a hunter?"

"A bit of both."

On impulse she asked, "Have you ever been to France?"

"I came to America from England when I was a boy," he said smoothly. "I've not left the States since."

"I see." She felt disappointed, and then, strangely relieved. *It couldn't have been him anyway; he would have been only a boy.* "You should visit it sometime. France, I mean. It's a beautiful country."

"So I've heard." He went to hold back a flap for Chan and Paolo, who carried in one of the long folding worktables. "What do you expect to find out here?"

"Typically Florida sites yield unorganized burial sites, some pottery sherds, refuse pits, shell middens, stone tools." She nodded toward the church. "Spanish priests, like the ones who founded this mission, introduced things like glass beads and forged metals."

"Dr. Al gives a great seminar on coprolite analysis," Chan told Beau. "She's profiled the cultural features of a bunch of villages based solely on accretional deposits."

Alys waited until the boys had left the tent before she said, "My interns are prone to exaggeration. I've only profiled two villages. You don't know what coprolites are, do you?"

He rubbed the back of his neck. "Something you dig out of the ground, I expect."

"They're preserved feces." His expression made her smile. "Don't look so disgusted. We learn a great deal by analyzing human waste and other preserved ecofacts. Latrine pits and garbage dumps help us identify what the inhabitants hunted, the crops they might have planted, the seasonality of their diet, even who in the surrounding region traded with them."

"All that," he said, "from digging through shit?"

"We are what we eat, Mr. York. In a few hundred years some scientist may examine what you left behind in order to know who you were." Alys saw the odd look he gave her. "Do you wonder what his conclusions will be?"

"No." A strange sadness flickered over his features. "I'll take care not to leave anything behind." With that, Beau strode out of the tent.

Chapter 5

Once the equipment had been sorted and the work areas prepared, Beau excused himself from sharing a meal with the team and busied himself by adding fuel to the generators and stowing unneeded packing materials and empty cases inside the church. When he emerged, he found Alys setting up a second, smaller tent to one side of the tower. "What is that used for?"

"Me." She finished knotting a cord through the loop of a ground stake. "The interns will be staying at the hotel in the city, but I have to remain on-site for the duration. This is where I'll be sleeping during the day."

"Not outside, you won't. It's already been seen to." When she stared up at him, he held out his hand. "Come with me."

She pushed herself to her feet. "What's been seen to?"

"Your comfort." He drew back his hand, annoyed with her for avoiding his touch. He could understand such reticence if she had reason for it, but he had spent most of the night trying to anticipate and carry out her wishes, and treat her as Harlech had suggested, like a much younger sister.

"Dr. Stuart?" The buxom, dark-haired intern named Brenda joined them, and gave Beau a meltingly sweet smile before she spoke to Alys. "If you don't have anything else for us to do, we thought we'd head back to the hotel now."

Alys scanned the site before nodding to the girl. "That should do it for tonight. I'll come and see you off."

Beau followed the two females to the vans, where the rest of the interns had congregated.

"Hey, Beau, you need a ride back into town?" Charles asked.

"Thank you, but I've made my own arrangements." He opened the van side door and helped Brenda up inside. "Do be careful on the drive back, then."

She gave him a drowsy smile. "God, I love the way you talk."

"Good night, everyone," Alys added. "You did very well today. Just be sure to report back here tomorrow by sunset."

Once the students had departed, Beau cupped Alys's elbow and steered her toward the cloister. "I've no wish to interfere with how you do your work, but you are not sleeping in that tent."

She looked down at his hand. "I didn't think the matter was up for debate."

"It shouldn't be," he chided her. "You know it is foolish to sleep outside in this weather. You'll catch a fever."

"Bacteria and viruses cause fevers, not weather. I also have a very strong immune system. I'm never sick." She pulled her arm away and peered inside the open doorway. "I also have no way of knowing if these buildings are safe for occupancy."

"They've survived this long without crumbling. Nothing will fall on your head, I promise you." He led her inside and over to the short stairs leading down to the underground vault. He picked up and switched on a battery-powered lantern before he guided her down the steps and handed her the light. "Wait here."

His Kyn eyes allowed him to move easily through the dark to each of the other lanterns he'd placed around the cellar. He heard a soft gasp as he turned on the last of them, and looked back to see Alys's pretty mouth forming an O.

He glanced around at the furnishings he'd arranged, feeling pleased with himself. "So, then. Is it to your liking?"

"My liking?" She met his gaze. "Mr. York, this isn't a cellar. It's an apartment." She moved past him, examining first the beds and then the desk before scanning the rest of the chamber. "There aren't any windows. Of course there aren't. We're underground."

"If it feels too cold for you, I have several space heaters to warm the air." He pointed to the boxes he'd stacked neatly in one corner.

She went over to the adjoining lavatory and ducked her head inside before turning toward him. "My budget doesn't allow for this kind of expense. How am I supposed to pay the rental fees for all this?"

"Hylord has covered the cost." Beau doubted Tremayne would care if he had turned the mission into a restaurant and nightclub, as long as the emeralds were recovered and delivered to him. "We will be living out here for weeks. Proper shelter is a necessity."

She turned around to face him. "We?" Her eyes went to the beds, and then to the cases he'd left by the window. "You mean me."

"You cannot stay here alone, unguarded," he advised her. "You are a woman, and this place is too isolated. If you needed help—"

She produced her mobile. "I'd do what everyone else in trouble does, and call 911."

"Check it," he told her. "You'll find you have little to no reception."

Alys glanced at the display before she shoved it back into her trouser pocket. "It doesn't matter because nothing is going to happen to me. This is private property, surrounded by an electrified fence. My interns will be on-site every night. I'm sure I'm not this safe in my apartment back in Boston."

"You are not in Boston," he said patiently. "You are here, and Hylord wants you comfortable and protected. So during the days, I will be sleeping with you."

Her mouth went tight. "I agreed to let you join my team, Mr. York, not climb into my bed."

"That is why I installed two of them." She refused to use his name, and it was beginning to grate on him. "Stop calling me Mr. York. I told you, my name is Beau."

Her eyes narrowed. "Then why don't you tell me the truth, *Beau*? You got two beds because you thought I was a man. Now that you know I'm not, what will happen? Are we going to push them together?"

The change in her scent tempted Beau to smile—Alys's natural, faintly cinnamon scent practically sizzled and snapped in the air when she was angry—but he managed to keep his expression neutral. "I see no reason for that. You needn't worry, Alys. You will be perfectly safe here, with me."

She started to say something, paused, and then spun on her heel and went back up the steps.

Guessing she wouldn't soon return, Beau closed himself in the lavatory, where he had concealed under the floorboards his cache of bagged blood. The cold ground would keep it from spoiling, but he disliked the thick, chilly taste of the stuff. Still, there was nothing to be done about that.

Aside from Alys and her team, there were no mortals in the area for miles. Even if he were to curtail his feeding and take only every few days the small amount he needed to live, he could not compel Alys, and the thought of making use of her young students turned his stomach.

Once Beau made his way outside, he saw Alys waving toward the two vans driving away from the mission. A glance around the site revealed they were alone, and dawn would arrive within minutes. "They are good workers, your students."

"Wait until tomorrow night, when they begin whining about how sore and exhausted they are." Alys turned and inspected him. "You don't seem tired. You must be in marvelous shape, too. All that work you did today, and I never saw you once break a sweat."

"Perhaps I did, and you were too busy to notice." He surveyed her soiled, wrinkled garments and the faint shadows under her eyes. "You did rather too much yourself, I think. You should leave the heavy work to me."

"I'm accustomed to working alone, and you've taken

on quite enough responsibility." She shouldered a strange-looking silver bag and headed toward the cloister.

Beau lingered behind to switch off the generators and make one last round of the camp. The most expensive, hardest-to-replace equipment had been secured inside the church, the food supplies stored in protective containers and coolers stacked inside a large, animal-proof cage. As he walked the perimeter, he wondered how Alys was faring with the portable shower he'd rigged in the lavatory. She probably disliked it; mortals of this time were not accustomed to bathing with cold water. He should go down and see whether he could warm a ewer for her over the camp stove.

Despite his best efforts Beau could not stop thinking about how she had looked, emerging from the hotel bath, her hair spilling like dark scarlet silk over her bare shoulders, her flesh rosy from the heat of the shower. She should have looked that in his arms, after he gave her pleasure, all shivering delight, her lovely mouth whispering his name—

She doesn't know my name, and when I had her in my arms, she fought me.

Shame crushed his desire, leaving behind only shreds of self-disgust. He would be sleeping in the same chamber with the woman for weeks; he could not seduce her and he would not allow himself to touch her. No, as oblivious to him as Alys was, he would have to think of her as Harlech had said. A girl no older than her students, a young sister, one who neither needed nor wanted anything from him but gentleness and protection.

With that mind-set he made his way downstairs, where he found Alys sitting on the end of one bed and drying her hair with a towel. She had dressed in fitted, cream-colored thermal garments that covered her from throat to ankle, and had stuffed her long feet into bright red fuzzy socks. Her clean skin smelled of some sort of light floral lotion, which didn't completely mask the exciting zing of her scent.

The fact that she was warm enough to shed so much scent did puzzle him. "The water was not too cold, I hope."

"It's winter, Beau. It's freezing." She shook out her hair and smoothed it back. "That's why I didn't use your shower rig."

He frowned. "You have found a hot springs hidden somewhere?"

"In here." She gestured for him to follow her into the lavatory, where she had hung the silver bag she'd carried in. "This is a solar water bag. Have you ever used one?" When he shook his head, she said, "You fill it up and hang it in the sun. In two hours the solar units on the outside convert the sunlight, and that heats the water to a hundred degrees. It's only a little warmer than body temperature, but the chill outside makes it feel hotter."

Beau examined the strange but simple contraption, which sported a temperature gauge strip and a flexible spray-hose attachment. After all the centuries he'd spent bathing in frigid rivers and icy lakes, it seemed almost magical. "How could you make it work at night?"

"I can't, so this morning I put it out on the hotel balcony. It's insulated, so it keeps the water warm for a long time." She touched the bag. "There's enough left for you."

"You saved some of your water, for me." Her kindness left him bewildered.

"Why wouldn't I? If we're going to sleep in the same room, I'd like you to bathe regularly." She handed him a towel and made to leave.

Beau caught her arm, tugging her to him. "You are very kind to someone you dislike. It makes me wonder what you would do for a friend." He kissed her brow in what he hoped was a brotherly fashion. "Thank you."

"I don't dislike you." She lifted her hand as if to touch her forehead, and then dropped it. "You are . . . I'm not . . . I left you some soap over there." She made a quick gesture and quickly retreated.

After Beau had bathed, he wrapped a towel around his hips and looked out into the chamber. Alys had turned out the lights and lay huddled under the coverlet, her face turned toward the wall. Knowing it might embarrass her if he slept naked, as he did at the Realm, Beau pulled on a pair of trousers before he stretched out on the other bed.

Even underground he could feel the rising of the sun, for the day's hours sapped the strength from him wherever he was. He stared up at the weathered stone of the ceiling, on which some priest had scratched the sign of the cross over and over. Although Beau had long ago set aside his faith, and he did not believe in ghosts, from the moment he had stepped foot inside the church, he had felt a presence here. He could not tell whether it was malignant or benevolent, only that it weighed on his senses like a heavy, unseen yoke.

He turned on his side to watch Alys sleep.

Alys walked through the old sanctuary, her feet bare and burning as they crossed the cold planks. Every breath she took seemed to solidify in her lungs, and as she approached the altar, lacy snowflakes drifted down around her. The instant they touched her, they glowed with a strange, intense green light.

She had done this before in her dreams, too many times to count. This time, however, she could see and smell tallow candles burning. The uncertain light flickered over a long row of men in black robes, all on their knees with their hands clasped in prayer. She shifted her gaze to the simple wooden cross suspended from the ceiling, and felt the coldness of its shadow against her face.

"This is silly," she muttered. "I'm not religious. I've never attended church. I don't believe in God. I'm a scientist. I should be dreaming of labs and lecture halls and charcoal-tempered pottery."

"You are not dreaming, daughter."

A tall, broad-shouldered figure came out of the dark, sending a whirlwind of ice crystals around her.

Alys regarded him. His hooded brown robe concealed his features, but his crudely stitched leggings and worn leather boots were embroidered with gold. Heavy leather gloves encased his hands, and brassy golden hair hung long and loose over his shoulders. While the snow was beginning to encrust her shoulders and arms, not a speck touched him or his clothing.

She didn't remember him, but she felt sure she'd seen him before in her dreams. She'd definitely heard his voice before now. "Do I know you?"

"I was the maker of the scroll, and the keeper of the cross, and the savior of the jewels." The priest's voice rasped as if he had a bad case of laryngitis. "It was I who washed them in my blood. You and your mortal family were my army, my guardians, each sworn to protect the secrets of eternity. Now you are last. You will not fail me as your sisters did."

The other priests rose from their prayers and walked in two rows past her, each carrying a smoldering metal sphere. The unpleasant smell of incense and charred metal made Alys feel slightly nauseated, as did the sight of the priests' faces, which were covered in open sores. "You've made an error. My parents are dead, but I was *their* child. Not yours."

"You have the wisdom to protect the mortal world from eternal damnation," the big priest said. "But do you have the heart to do what needs be done? Will you die for love?"

Alys looked down at the blade that appeared in his left hand. Beneath the bloody slush dripping from it she recognized carved bone.

She would not fear a figment of her imagination, not when it spoke with the same voice that had saved her during her childhood. Of course she'd given him that voice, just as she had designed every other part of him.

"You are not real," she told him. "My subconscious has constructed you out of childhood memories and recent encounters to serve as a surreptitious emotional outlet. You represent someone in my waking life, perhaps the chairman of the Hylord Foundation, with whom I have unresolved conflicts. Your questions are therefore irrelevant. I want to wake up now."

"This is your dream, child." The snow grew thicker, changing from a drift to a steady fall as he slipped the bone blade in a sheath on his hip. "You used it to capture me. I could not have made it through on my own. My body no longer remains part of this world for long."

"If you're a ghost," she countered, "how could I capture you? Aside from that fact, I know I'm sleeping. In an unconscious state I'm paralyzed and incapable of any action."

"You are capable of a great deal." He touched her cheek, and his hand felt colder than the snow. "And you have my curse. You never truly sleep, do you, Alys?"

A blizzard roared soundlessly around her, nearly knocking her off her feet. "I'm sorry, but continuing to talk with you is pointless. I'm just talking to myself."

"I will try to help you and the boy if I can," the priest said. "You must watch for my hand."

Knee-deep in a white drift, Alys turned to watch him. "The boy? What boy?"

His form began to change shape, shedding his robe as his chest narrowed and his hair darkened. The ice storm vanished into a curtain of darkness that shrouded Alys.

Go to him, the priest's voice whispered in her ears. *Be with him. He will protect you.*

Alys shuffled toward the bed, where she pulled back the edge of the covers and climbed under them. She smelled something cool and sweet as heavy arms enclosed her, and Beau drew her against his chest. His breath wasn't coming out in white puffs like hers, and his face was dry of the freezing tears streaming down her cheeks. She was shivering so much she could hear her teeth chattering.

She burrowed against him, trying to warm herself, but the frost glazing her skin wouldn't melt.

"Pr-priest," she heard herself stammer. "H-h-el-p-p m-me. . . ."

The big man's eyes opened, and she saw her cold, pinched face reflected in the dark mirrors there.

I will give him to you, the priest murmured in her mind. *His heart can be yours for all eternity. Open your arms to him, my child. Love him as I could not. Give him your blood.*

Alys saw a white, sharp gleam, and when she reached out, it sliced through the tip of her icy finger. She felt Beau's lips move against the little wound, and then the soft, rough caress of his tongue. Her heart began to pound as her fingers and then her hand burned, the snow pelting them beading to warm droplets that slid down to trickle over his chest. The stiffness of her face eased away, and the frozen spikes of her hair drooped and became a dripping veil.

Beneath her his cool body heated as well, his muscles stirring and bunching as he shifted her, settling her on top of him, his big hands stroking her buttocks. Alys straddled him with her thighs and pressed her cheek over his heart, feeling the throb there like a slow, steady hammer.

I want him. His sweet scent rose up in her head, as soothing as the claws of her own lust were vicious. *I have to have him.*

The heat pouring through her raced through her veins, growing brighter and faster with every shallow breath she took. Everywhere their bodies touched, her skin came alive, tight and aching, and she gripped his shoulders, panting as a terrible hunger twisted deep inside her. The smoky sweetness filling her nose made her wonder whether she would spontaneously combust, and burn him alive with her.

She nuzzled his chest, pressing her lips to the hard wall of muscle. *He is mine.*

That is how it can be, she heard the priest say, his voice distant and fading. *All you must do is bring him into your heart. Love him. Give him pleasure. And when you find the fountain, when you drink at last of the waters of forever, you must die for him.*

Something wrenched Alys away from the man, and hurtled her back across the chamber. She slammed back into her own body, shaking as the hunger and heat turned to pain and cold. Once more she lay alone in the darkness, with nothing and no one to call her own.

Rise. Go to him.

Alys's mind cleared of everything but the voice urging her on. She pushed the damp, clinging linens off and swung her legs over the side of the bed.

He is waiting for you. Here.

Her feet scraped against rough wood as she shuffled toward the voice.

Give yourself to him now.

She reached for the coverlet, pulling it back and slipping beneath, her limbs growing leaden as she curled up beside the sleeping man. As she drifted deeper into the blackness, she felt something touch her back, and thought she heard the priest whisper one last time.

My last. My only. My omega.

Chapter 6

The sinking of the sun roused Beau, who should have felt rested, but a heaviness still burdened him. He had spent most of his rest wandering through the nightlands, searching the void for something he had lost, long ago.

Sunehri, the weary, rasping voice of a woman whispered in his heart. *You are going on a journey tonight.*

The words meant nothing to Beau, and yet they weighed on him like a millstone roped round his neck.

This man will protect you. Obey him as you would me.

Beau could see the boy he had been, smiling and sleepy-eyed as he stumbled over to his mother, who caught him in her arms and covered the top of his dark curls with soft kisses.

"*Ammijaan.*" The boy buried his face against her breast, taking one furtive peek at the man.

"*Sunehri.*" She gently lifted his chin, and in Urdu said, "You are going on a journey tonight. This priest is my friend, and he will take you to your father's homeland, that you may know his people." When the boy protested, she touched her fingers to his lips. "Remember, when we talked of this? You promised you would be brave for me." He nodded slowly, and she smiled. "Now, kiss me good-bye."

The boy pressed his lips to her thin cheek, but when she tried to put him aside, he wrapped his arms around her neck. "You come with us, too, *Ammijaan*?"

Beau reached for her as well, but the woman and the boy faded away, leaving him alone with the robed man. *"Aap mhujhe kahan lay kay ja rahe hain?"* he heard himself say as he followed the man to an enormous warhorse. *Where are you taking me?*

"Ghar," the man answered, picking him up and tossing him onto the destrier's back.

Beau frowned as the man swung up on the saddle in front of him, and looked past his shoulder. "The House of Heaven is my home."

"Not anymore, lad."

They rode the horse through the city, and across the desert and into the mountains. Each day the man would stop and set up a nomad's tent so Beau could eat and sleep. Sometimes Beau would wake to see him making chains of tiny links. He made three chains, and on each of them strung . . .

The eye of Yblis.

The tent, the man, and the horse faded from Beau's mind, and the burden pressing on him did the same, lifting and lightening until he felt only a hint of it huddled against his chest: soft, warm, alive.

A single breath told him who the sleeping woman sprawled on top of him was, but Beau couldn't believe it. He lifted his head to see rumpled red hair spread beneath his collarbone. "Alys?"

She answered with a mumble, turning her head and twitching her limbs before going limp again.

Beau touched her back with his hands, intending to gently shake her, but the clammy condition of her thermals gave him pause. Was she sick? Her heartbeat thrummed steadily against his chest, and her breathing seemed regular and clear. Despite the dampness of her garments, they didn't smell of her sweat or anything at all.

Taking care not to jolt her, Beau placed her on her side, climbed over her, and stepped out of the bed. She slept on as he lifted her into his arms and carried her over to her bed.

As Beau lowered her down, he discovered her linens were as damp as her garments. Alarmed now, he rested a hand on her brow. Her skin felt warm, not hot, to the touch. He lifted a corner of her coverlet to his nose, but like her thermals it smelled only of her body scent, not the salt of sweat.

Beau glanced back at his own bed. The dampness of the cellar may have woken her, and in some drowsy confusion she may have mistaken his bed for her own. She had certainly shown no waking desire to share it.

I agreed to let you join my team, Mr. York, not climb into my bed.

Beau drew away from her and took a seat at the desk, swiveling the chair to watch her and think. He did not recall dreaming or waking even once during the day, which was not at all normal for him. The Darkyn did not sleep as mortals did; their rest was more conscious and deliberate, and when they did surrender themselves to the darkness, they often ended up in the nightlands.

Alys's presence had made it difficult for Beau to rest,

but when he had finally drifted off, he had blanked out completely. He could not remember experiencing such an oblivious sleep, in fact, since his days as a mortal.

A faint ache in his head made him rub a hand over his scalp. At the base of his skull he found a new, tender spot that indicated he had been struck there. He eyed Alys's peaceful, innocent face. Had she clubbed him over the head while he slept? Why would she then crawl in bed with him?

"No." As if she'd heard his thinking, Alys sat straight up in the bed, staring at him with wide eyes. "What are you doing?"

"Presently?" He leaned back. "I'm sitting and watching you sleep."

"Oh. Right. We're sleeping together. I mean, we're sharing a room." She fell back against the pillow, and then brought her hands up to touch her sleeves. "Why are my thermals damp?"

"I cannot tell you." Beau regarded her, noting that her confusion seemed genuine. "Did something happen while I slept?"

"How would I know? I was asleep, too. Ouch." She touched the side of her head. "That hurts. Did I fall out of bed?"

Beau rose and went to her, pushing aside her hand to examine the spot on her scalp. "Perhaps you did. You have a bump here."

"Wouldn't I remember that?" Before he could reply, she shook her head. "Never mind. I had an awful nightmare last night. I was thrown across the room, and then I was in bed with you."

She didn't have to say it as if it were the same as being

submerged neck-deep in muck, Beau thought. "Then you do remember something."

"Excuse me?"

"When I awoke"—he nodded across the room—"you *were* in bed with me."

Alys's shoulders stiffened. "That's not funny."

"I am not jest—joking. I woke up and found you on top of me." He knelt down before her. "Let me see your eyes." When she glared at him, he could see that her pupils appeared normal in size. "Do you feel dizzy, or sick?"

"No, I'm fine. Really." Alys glanced over his shoulder. "That part about me being thrown across the room—you couldn't have done that. It's too far. I probably . . ." Her voice trailed off as she went still and closed her eyes. "Oh, God, no. Not now."

"Alys?" He touched her hand. "What is it? Do you recall something?"

"No, but I'm pretty sure I know how I got in your bed." She looked at him. "I must have been sleepwalking. I had a terrible problem with it when I was a child, and I still have episodes once or twice a year. I am so sorry."

He sat back on his haunches. "Why do you apologize to me? You were not awake. You could not know what you were doing."

She cringed a little. "Thanks, but that doesn't make crawling into bed with you any less embarrassing."

Now she thought being in bed with him was humiliating. "When I woke, you seemed quite content to be using my chest as your pillow. I certainly did not mind it."

"You didn't." She gave him a wary glance. "Why not?"

"It seemed to me harmless." *Think of her as a child.* "Something a younger sister might do."

Alys frowned. "Your sister slept in your bed?"

"No; I have no sisters." He was making a hash of this. "I only mean that you should not feel embarrassed. I knew from the moment I woke that it was an innocent thing."

"Yeah, well, it was." She swung her legs over the side of the bed. "And it was probably the nightmare that set it off."

"Unpleasant, was it?"

"I don't know." She thought for a moment. "I was walking through the old church. I saw the missionaries kneeling and praying at the altar. It was so cold, it began to snow." Absently she rubbed her hands over her arms. "That's all I can remember."

Her scent remained clear and sweet; she spoke the truth. Which meant their injuries were the result of Alys's sleepwalking . . . or someone else had come into the chamber while they slept. Beau healed instantly, so whatever had been done to him didn't matter. The thought of someone assaulting Alys, however, made a slow, burning fury ignite inside him. "Do you feel hurt anywhere else?"

"I don't think so." She stood, cautiously stretching out her arms and legs. "I'm a bit stiff, but I think that's from setting up last night." She picked up her watch from the lamp table and strapped it to her wrist. "The interns will be arriving soon. I'd better get dressed."

When she went into the lavatory, Beau pulled on a shirt and his boots before making a complete circuit of the chamber, looking for signs of an intruder. He found no trace of unfamiliar scent in the air, or on anything that might have been used to strike them while they slept. At the same time he felt sure someone else had come inside the chamber.

If the intruder had touched nothing, and had taken the weapon with him . . .

Beau went upstairs and performed a thorough search of the cloister for trace scent. Wherever humans went, they dispersed tiny amounts of their sweat and other body odors into the air. Unless particularly strong, these traces were undetectable to other mortals. The Kyn, however, could pick them up for hours after the human's passage. Because all humans had scents unique to them, the Kyn could also follow the invisible trail to wherever the mortal had gone.

The only scents Beau found inside the cloister were those belonging to Alys and himself. Outside the structure, all he could detect were the faint traces left behind by the interns.

A carefully shielded mortal, or a very controlled Kyn, might have invaded the camp while he and Alys slept, but unless the intruder could levitate, he would have left tracks in the dirt. The only footprints he saw belonged to him, Alys, and her team.

Everything indicated they had slept undisturbed, but Beau didn't believe it. His instincts still insisted that someone had come in the night. Someone who wanted to harm Alys.

Beau's hand itched for his sword. *When I find him, and I will, I will introduce him to his entrails.*

The sound of the cargo vans coming down the dirt

road diverted his attention, and as he walked to meet the students, Alys caught up with him. "Beau, ah, would you mind not telling the interns about what happened last night?"

"They may have seen someone coming this way when they drove out," he said.

"You can ask them if they did, but please don't mention my sleepwalking and getting into bed with you and all that."

She sounded shamed. Beau gritted his teeth. "Why not?"

"I don't have the best reputation," Alys said, surprising him. "With the way that students gossip, it could get back to Hylord and cause you some problems." She sighed. "It would definitely get back to the university."

She was blaming herself for this, and Beau couldn't fathom why. "You did nothing wrong, Alys."

"Your boss and the tenure board won't see it that way." She forced a smile as the interns piled out of the vans and started toward them. "Please. I have to deal with enough people who already think I'm crazy, and I don't want to be responsible for getting you fired." In a louder voice she called out to the students, "I hope everyone got plenty of sleep. We have a full schedule tonight."

The students collectively groaned.

"That's why they call it a working site, people." Alys grinned at them. "The good news is that since you did such a thorough job last night setting up, we can begin the grid layout immediately. Chan, you and I will be operating the GPR. Brenda, Charles, you'll handle marking, and Paolo, you're on mapping. The rest of you can supply the workstations and set up the lab. Any questions?"

Brenda waved one long-nailed hand. "Can Beau—I mean, Mr. York—work with me and Charles?"

Some of the other students chimed in, asking the same, until Alys made a gesture for quiet. "Mr. York has his own work to attend to, and I'd appreciate it if you let him do it. We'll break at ten and three for meals. Anything else?" When no one spoke, she nodded. "Let's get started."

The interns scattered in different directions, and Beau followed Alys as she walked toward the stable. "I've no real work of my own. I would be happy to assist your students."

"Brenda and the other girls only want a chance to flirt with you," she told him. "You should try to avoid giving any one of them too much attention. They develop attachments quickly, and at this age their egos are very fragile."

Beau felt amused and annoyed. "Do you speak from experience?"

"Me? I don't bother with romance." She took out her flashlight and switched it on. "Emotional attachments are time-consuming and unpredictable, and the results are often disappointing. I don't think I'm very good at them, either. Would you carry out that big blue case there?"

Beau retrieved what she wanted. "Matters of the heart are not experiments, Alys."

She considered that. "I'll have to take your word on that. I've never loved or been loved by anyone."

She said it so matter-of-factly that he frowned. "What about your parents, your family?"

"My parents died in a car accident shortly after I was born. I spent my childhood at boarding schools. They were all excellent learning institutions, but growing up in a purely academic environment doesn't encourage much in the way of personal bonding. I liked my schoolmates, and admired my teachers, but they weren't effective substitutes for siblings or parents."

Although she used unfamiliar words, Beau understood what she was saying. During his childhood Harlech's family had been kind to him, and he had responded with steadfast loyalty, but he had never truly felt part of his foster brother's boisterous, happy clan. "Who sent you away to school?"

"My guardian. He knew my parents, and when they were killed, he took care of me." She shouldered a pack. "I didn't see him very often, and he died last year."

"I am sorry for your loss." Beau picked up a second case she wanted before she could lift it. "Why didn't your guardian bring you into his home and foster . . . raise you as his daughter?"

"We never discussed it," she admitted, "but Robert was a bachelor, and he had to travel extensively for his work. Sometimes he sent postcards to me from different countries."

Back in the processing area Alys gave Chan the task of assembling what she called "the trolley" while she set up a monitor screen, computer tower, and wireless transceiver.

To Chan she said, "Mr. York hasn't worked at a site

using ground-penetrating radar. Why don't you explain the system to him?"

"Sure." The intern turned to Beau. "The GPR transmits a signal into the ground, which bounces off subsurface features and objects. The receiver collects the return signals and displays them on the trolley's LCD unit as a graphic. It also transmits them to the computer, where our software processes the time it takes for a signal reflection, and calculates parameters and depth. If the scans are clear, we should be able to construct a 3-D map of the area, which gives us precise coordinates."

"We'll need to use a lower-frequency signal out here," Alys added. "Chan, please calibrate the emitter for two hundred megahertz to start. We'll adjust it after we see the initial test scan."

Beau eyed the trolley unit, which appeared to be little more than a four-wheeled cart. "How deep can the signal travel?"

"With this equipment, depending on the frequency we use, up to a thousand meters," Chan said.

"The saturation of the ground will help." Alys came over to adjust one of the switches on the trolley. "Dry soil doesn't reflect signals very well. When it's saturated, the moisture interfaces with buried objects, retaining or pooling on them, and that acts like a mirror. The more water present, the better the signal and the more details we can see in the reflection data."

Beau studied the equipment as he sorted out what they had told him. "So you push this over the ground, and the echoes of the signal it makes creates a picture of what is beneath the soil. They tell you where you should dig, how deep, and what you will find."

"It doesn't take all the fun out of it," Chan said as he attached the U-shaped push handle to the trolley. "We have to create image maps from the amplitude time-slices and interpret them. Spatial correlation is very objective as well. What we think looks like a Grecian goblet on the screen might turn out to be a big fossilized turd once we excavate."

"A coprolite, you mean," Beau corrected, and winked at Alys.

Jayr rose early from her rest, easing out of Aedan's strong arms to silently dress and slip out of their bedchamber. Keeping the Realm running smoothly always required a great deal of time, and now she had only a few weeks with which to finish the renovations and finalize the arrangements for the new performance schedules. The innumerable details and conflicts involved proved a constant challenge; she felt for every task she accomplished, two more cropped up in its place.

Jayr first paid a visit to the administrative offices to call the Realm's answering service and pick up the inevitable dozens of messages her mortal vendors left for her during the day. This time, however, the operator informed her that the messages had already been relayed to her assistant.

"Would you like me to read them again to you, ma'am?" the woman asked.

She checked the duplicate copy in her message book and saw the messages had been recorded in unfamiliar writing. "That will not be necessary. Thank you."

Once she retrieved the clipboard with her notes on the progress in the different areas under construction,

Jayr retreated to her study, where she found a fire burning in her hearth, a stack of messages sitting on her desk, and a neatly typed page that appeared to be some sort of task schedule. She had barely begun reading it when a knock on the door sounded. "Come in."

"Good evening, my lady." Devan Leeds entered, carrying a bottle of bloodwine and a crystal goblet on a silver tray, which he brought over and served to her. "*Tresora* Burke called earlier to remind you that the lady visitors from Alenfar *jardin* will be arriving tonight. I've readied the reception room, and as they are sisters, I've arranged adjoining chambers for them in the guest quarters. Is that acceptable to you?"

"That sounds very good." Jayr watched him prepare her drink. "Have you been settling in?"

"Quite well, my lady. I took the liberty of checking on the current renovations, which are progressing according to schedule, and placed orders for the props, fabrics, and gift items you wished to obtain for the reopening. The stable master reports the sickly mare has much improved and, as your seneschal suspected, buttercups were the culprit. He promises to eradicate them from the field at once. When convenient, Captain Harlech wishes to have a word about purchasing some new mounts for the jousting performance. I believe he wishes to buy five more from a breeder in the Carolinas." He offered her the wineglass he had filled. "This is a very pleasant Spanish red; I think you'll find it superior to the French label you've been served of late."

Jayr stared at him as she accepted the glass. "Good God, man, have you slept at all today?"

"I have, my lady, thank you." He stepped back and folded his hands behind his back.

Jayr drank from the glass and regarded him. "I am in awe of your efficiency. Have you left anything for me to do?"

"I thought you might want to review the messages from the service, that I might know your wishes and attend to the return calls while you welcome your visitors." He nodded at the typed page. "That is my work plan for the night, but if you need me to do anything else, of course you may change it as you will."

Jayr wasn't sure she dared look at it. "Mr. Leeds— Devan—you likely know better your duties than I ever will. I would ask only that you not exhaust yourself. In two days I believe you've done more work than five men might have in twenty."

"It is good to have some real purpose again," Leeds admitted. "These last months since my master . . . Well, I am happiest when I am busy, my lady, but should I ever prove an annoyance, you have only to say."

"That I think you will never hear from me, sir." She drained the remaining wine from her glass. "I'll review messages with you now, but the return calls can wait until after the Alenfar ladies arrive. I should like you at my side in the reception room."

For the first time a flicker of doubt passed over Leeds's features. "You would? Forgive me; I had assumed that place to be your seneschal's."

"As Byrne refuses to learn proper protocol and quite despises formal receptions, I feel certain that you will do a much better job of it." She picked up the slips. "Now, this call from Disney corporate is likely yet another offer to buy the Realm. Please advise them that my answer has not changed, and that I shall be delighted to sell it to them once hell freezes over."

Farlae slipped onto a viewing balcony, and parted the curtains to look down at the Kyn assembled below. The suzeraina greeted the two just-arrived female visitors differently, shaking the hand of the tall, fair French-woman before embracing the petite, dark American. He knew from his sources in Europe and South Florida that the females were newly turned, the blonde by Korvel, formerly seneschal to Richard Tremayne, and the little brunette by Jamys, son of Thierry Durand. Neither woman had come from the ranks of the Kyndred, or-phaned humans made over with Kyn DNA by the Breth-ren, but he still did not trust them.

If Farlae were to be honest, he trusted no one and nothing. Especially not the smiling mortal standing be-side Jayr.

"What are you doing?" a beloved voice whispered as the scent of warm strawberries teased Farlae's nose. "Spying on our lady? What for?"

"I am not spying. Be silent." He should have expected Rainer would follow him here; when it came to tracking Kyn or mortal, his fool lover had no equal. "Better yet, go back to your poppets."

"They're called puppets, not poppets. What is she do-ing?" Rain tried to peek through the slit in the curtain. "Who are those females? That tall one looks fierce. Do you come here to spy on her?"

Farlae took Rain by the arm and marched him out of

the balcony and into the adjoining corridor. "I have told you about this," he said through gritted teeth. "You cannot tag along after me when I am working."

Rain stuck out his lower lip. "You work in the sewing rooms, where I never go. Except tonight, but I needed more string for my puppets, and you were not there." He hung his head and shuffled his feet. "You were not very attached to that shawl you were making, were you?"

Farlae wanted to tear his hair out. "Rain, I don't give a damn about that bloody shawl, your puppet string, or–"

"My foolishness," Rain finished for him, his eyes sad. "As you have said, many times. But I am not as stupid as you think. I know what you are about here."

He had always managed to keep his lover from knowing about his less scrupulous activities. "I am merely admiring the lady visitors."

"Do not lie to me," Rain said, suddenly looking uncharacteristically fierce. "You watch because you've taken a fancy to that new mortal of Jayr's."

Farlae almost laughed. "Why would I want him when I have you, lad?"

"You do not even deny it." He nodded toward the balcony. "That is why you are there, peeking through the curtain. You have been following him everywhere. You want to do things with him, don't you? Things you've only done with me." His voice rose to a higher pitch. "Things you said you would *only* do with me—"

"Shhhh." Farlae gripped his shoulders to give him a shake. "Must you shout it to the whole of the keep, you idiot?" As he saw the hurt in his lover's eyes, he eased his hold. "I want nothing from that mortal."

"I know I am an idiot," the big man said with great

dignity. "I am very good at it, am I not? But I have never fancied anyone else but you. I love you and only you, even as I know I am going to burn in hell for it for all eternity. If you would allow me, I would shout it to the rafters. But you wish to keep it all secret, so that no one will think less of you."

Was that what he imagined? "Lad, you are mistaken—"

"I am not so much the idiot you think. You never speak of us to anyone and I know why." He jabbed his finger into Farlae's chest. "You are ashamed of me."

Farlae rubbed his head. "It is not my way to natter on about how I feel, especially to others. Christ Jesus, Rain, you ought to know how I feel for you. I bought you out of slavery. I taught you every pleasure you know. I saved you from Sherwood and execution and anything that has tried to harm you these seven hundred years."

"But you do not love me, not as I love you." Rain shrugged off his hands. "You may have the mortal. He is not so handsome, but he is clever, like you. I am sure he will never disgrace you, as I have." He trudged off.

Farlae started after him, swore under his breath, and returned instead to his listening post. When this was over, he decided, he would make it up to his lover. He would take Rainer away with him on a journey. What did the mortals call it? A vacation.

Aye, he would find a patch of woods where they could camp and hunt as they had in the old days, and bathe out in the open, and love each other without fear of being seen or despised.

A look through the curtain allowed Farlae to see Leeds, now dabbing at a large wine stain on the front of his immaculate white shirt. Behind him, Byrne held an empty glass and was trying very hard not to look pleased.

If the *tresora* hadn't been under suspicion, Farlae would have felt pity for him. *Such accidents that will happen every time you try to take Byrne's place beside his lady.*

He heard Leeds excuse himself in order to tidy up, and glanced down to see him retreating from the room. Farlae had to trot out to the corridor and down the back staircase before he could pick up the mortal's scent from a safe distance.

Leeds's trail ended at the door of the nearest unoccupied guest room, and Farlae could hear him moving around inside. Quickly he entered the next chamber and went to the adjoining door, feeling along the surface until he found the plug of wood concealing the peephole, and tugged it out.

Leeds had bolted himself inside the chamber and now stood before a mirror. After rubbing the back of his right hand as if it pained him, he unbuttoned his ruined shirt, frowning at his reflection as he removed a handkerchief and a small container from his trouser pocket.

Farlae watched the mortal shed his stained shirt, his eyes widening as he saw the large black cameo tattoo on his shoulder, and in the mirror the smaller, fainter mark of another over his heart. Leeds used the handkerchief to remove some smudged, flesh-colored paint from the chest mark, revealing it to be strangely done, like a compass. In the center, however, the profile of whatever Kyn lord he had once served had been removed so savagely that all that remained was scar tissue.

Farlae knew exactly what that meant. Byrne had been right. *There is a traitor come to the Realm.*

As he watched the mortal reapply a new layer of cosmetic, Farlae longed to jerk open the door. He could attack Leeds from behind, and snap his neck before the man's black heart beat twice under the mutilated mark. But even as he relished the thought, he knew the mortal would be more valuable alive than dead. If he was lucky, perhaps the seneschal would permit him to interrogate the turncoat. He'd enjoy making the bastard scream for mercy.

Farlae slipped out of the room and made for the reception hall, planning what he would say to have a private word with Byrne. It would have to be some urgent matter that would not alarm Jayr—

Halt.

Farlae's legs buckled, and he fell to his knees as if shoved to them. His nose filled with the stink of burning metal as a strange cloud of glittering gold surrounded him.

This is not your concern, spymaster.

He clasped his hands to the sides of his head as his body went numb and pain crawled through his mind. He could not speak, could hardly think. *Who are you? What do you want with me?*

Peace, brother. We all serve to protect, and protect we must. I would not hurt you.

Rage pulsed inside Farlae. *Fuck you.*

The agony spread through him as he fought the invasion, but the alien presence in his head was too strong, and caused him to fall over and writhe. Just as Farlae thought his head might explode, a strange warmth came over him, as gentle and loving as a mother's caress.

Rise.

Farlae stood.

You will return to your workroom, attend to your duties there, and remember none of this past hour.

A blankness settled over the wardrobe keeper, obliterating everything. A moment later his head cleared, and he eyed his surroundings. He didn't know why he was in the guest wing, and with the work waiting for him, he had no business loitering here.

Farlae smiled to himself as he made his way to his workroom, nodding to his ladies as he passed their worktables. When he went to his loom, he found the shawl he had been weaving in tatters.

"Viviana?" he called out. "Who the devil has been cutting up this shawl?"

Chapter 7

The first week of excavation at the mission went so smoothly that Alys decided she'd give the interns the next weekend off. They'd be ready for a break, and it would also give her two uninterrupted days to solve some problems that had come up since they'd started digging.

One of those problems was sitting with the students now, entertaining them during their last break of the night by telling them another of his stories about life in medieval England.

"No one noticed the smell because no one bathed," Beau was saying. "Villeins often went their entire lives without washing more than their hands and feet."

Brenda's nose wrinkled. "God, they must have been practically black with dirt. And covered in lice."

"Don't forget leprosy," Charles said, tapping the end of his nose. "I've read studies that say as many as one out of ten medieval peasants caught the disease."

"Plague was more common," Beau said, shaking his head when Chan offered him a can of soda. "Sicknesses such as smallpox, cholera, and syphilis ravaged without prejudice. Great ladies who went about in public often had to first veil their faces to conceal the scars, the sores, and the boils. The men, who had no such excuse, grew thick beards and fringes of hair to cover what they could. When they became so disfigured they dared not show their faces in public, they would send their stewards to act on their behalf."

Paolo, the most fastidious member of the team, shuddered. "So much misery, and it could have been prevented with running water and a few bars of soap."

"A quarter of the world died in the fourteenth century," Chan put in, "because they had no rat poison."

"No one in that time knew that the rats could make them sick, or that it was the fleas they carried that caused the Black Death. They were so much a part of everyday life that no one even noticed them. Like bad teeth, which truly was the plague of everyone, rich to wretched. In particular, tooth rot made one queen of England particularly savage. It was said that an inflamed molar drove her to declare war on the Spanish." Beau caught Alys watching them. "But that tale will wait for another time. I think Dr. Stuart has an announcement to make."

Alys watched Beau, who began collecting and stacking the dirty plates for washing. He put his own at the bottom of the pile, but before he did, she saw that once again her project manager had barely touched his food.

"Did you need to say something, Doctor?" Chan asked.

"Yes." She dragged her attention back to her interns. "I'm very pleased with the rate of progress we're making. If we can keep on schedule this week, and finish pro-

cessing and documenting, I'm giving everyone the
weekend off to stay at the hotel, sleep in, and have some
fun in the city."

Instead of cheering or applauding as they normally
would, the students only sat and glanced at one another.

Alys folded her arms. "Don't everyone thank me at
once."

"It's not that we're not grateful, Dr. Stuart," Brenda
said slowly. "A weekend off would be very cool, but you
have to stay at the site, and you shouldn't be out here
alone." She grimaced. "You know. Not with the site being haunted and all."

"Not the ghost again." Alys pressed her fingers briefly
to her temples. "Please. You are too intelligent to believe
in this nonsense."

"What about the shimmering light Paolo saw last
Tuesday night?" Chan asked, nudging the other boy.
"You said it moved, like it was alive, right?"

Paolo looked uneasy. "I saw something shimmering."

"You saw moonlight reflected by the frost on the
brush," Alys said firmly. "The wind picked up, the brush
moved, and that provided the ghostly animated effects."

"What about all the cases that fell over in the stables?" Charles asked. "When we went in to see what
happened, there was no one in there."

"Gravity was in there," Alys assured him. "You stack
too many cases too high, continually shift them by bumping them, and eventually they will tumble over, all on
their own."

"But the ghost tried to push you down the stairs in the
cloister just last night," Brenda insisted. "You could have
been killed."

Alys didn't want to be reminded of her latest brush with disaster. "No one pushed me. I happen to be clumsy, and I tripped over my own feet. Fortunately Mr. York caught me before I fell." She still wasn't sure how he'd done that, but that was a discussion she intended to have privately with her savior. *Stop thinking of him like that.* "As anthropologists and archaeologists, you will encounter a great deal of superstition and ignorance. You will identify it, study it, and use it to better understand civilizations from the past. Don't add to it by believing in fantasies like ghosts. There is always a plausible explanation."

"Okay, maybe the ghost isn't real," Brenda said, "but Beau still needs us."

The other interns nodded, demonstrating another facet of Alys's problem: Her students were now united in their hero worship of Beau. If she let them, they'd follow him around like a pack of affectionate puppies. "I'm sure Mr. York can spare you for a weekend."

"But that's when Beau said he was going to check out the Indian mission," Chan said. "We wanted to go with him." His expression grew uneasy. "He did tell you about it, right?"

"We haven't had a chance to discuss it." Alys had already vetoed this idea the first time it was proposed, and now repeated what she'd told the interns then: "As I mentioned last week, we have to finish the excavations here at the mission before we start surveying the village."

"Why?" Brenda asked. "We could do both, couldn't we? Beau could manage the village site while you continue digging here."

"It's not like we're finding anything useful here at the

mission," Charles tagged on. "The rosaries and prayer books we unearthed are Spanish Dominican. The glass beads left in the dump pit were common trade items. Nothing indicates the Templars came anywhere near the place, assuming they ever . . ." He stopped and squirmed.

"You've gone this far, Charles." Alys rolled her hand. "You might as well say the rest of it."

"Okay." He hunched his shoulders a little before he met her gaze. "Assuming they ever reached America in the first place."

"See? That didn't make my head explode." As the other interns chuckled, Alys sat down at the table. "You are entitled to your opinions, people." She eyed Charles. "Especially when they're the opposite of mine."

Chan nudged Charles. "Yeah, but any other prof would have kicked him off the dig by now."

"I have more training, more experience, and I've definitely read more books than any of you have," Alys said. "All that means is that I'm farther along in my career. Someday most of you will catch up, and some of you will surpass me. Right now there is only one thing I have that gives me a real advantage over all of you."

"Your PhD," Chan said, nodding.

"My patience," she corrected. "Do any of you know exactly how long it took Howard Carter to find King Tutankhamen's tomb?" She waited, but no one answered. "It took him thirty-one years, almost half his life. Here in Florida, Mel Fisher spent nearly two decades searching hundreds of miles of ocean floor for the wreck of the *Atocha*. Dozens of other archaeologists have done the same, with far less illustrious results. The chance at a major discovery might never come along once in your lifetime."

"Maybe I should change my major now," Brenda said, looking depressed.

"I just want you to be realistic," Alys told her. "We're not looking for a tomb or a sunken galleon filled with treasure. We need one item, one single shred of evidence that proves without a doubt that the Knights Templar came to America. And since we have only a month to find it, the odds are excellent that we won't."

"If you know that, if you're sure we won't find anything, then why are we still digging?" Charles countered.

"My research indicates that they *did* come, and not merely to seek sanctuary from persecution." She looked around the table. "I believe the Templars helped build this mission for two purposes: to convert the natives, and to hide something valuable. I can't tell you what it is because the Templars deliberately destroyed every record of it. What I do know is that to find it, we must be diligent."

She didn't have Beau's natural charm, or his colorful communication skills, yet judging by her interns' expressions, she had gotten across her point. They might still have doubts, but none of them were about her.

"It's getting late, and you all look tired, so go on and head back to the hotel. When you come back tomorrow afternoon," she said, pausing to make eye contact with each one of them again, "be ready to work, because I need every one of you. Together we *are* going to find proof that the Templars came to America."

The students nodded, and after gathering their packs

headed off for the vans. Only Charles lingered, his young face pinking as she glanced at him.

"I don't agree with any of your theories," he blurted, and then swallowed. "I never have. It's why I signed up for this project. I wanted to see you fail, so I could tell everyone that I'm smarter than you."

Such youthful arrogance usually annoyed her, but Alys heard something else in his voice, something fearful. "You probably are," she conceded. "No one believes this project will be a success. Well, except me."

"I haven't changed my mind. I don't think the Templars ever made it here from Europe. But after what you said, well, now I'd like to be the one who's wrong." His pinkness darkened to red. "So I want you to know, I'm going to do whatever I can to show you how right you are. And how dumb I am." With a pained smile he hurried off.

Alys felt her eyes sting, and blinked a few times. After years of her being ignored or subjected to scorn by other academics, Charles had offered her something of an accolade.

"That boy," Beau said as he brought the bus bin back to the table, "is coming close to worshipping you."

Beau's observation added to her pleasure before she became irritated with herself for indulging her ego. "Obviously I've made a favorable impression on him, but you're the one they really worship."

"And rightly so." He picked up three forks and began juggling them. "Who among you can scrape a plate or scrub a pot half as well?"

"Oh, it's more than your awesome dish-washing powers," she told him. "How many teenagers do you know who would sacrifice the prospect of a free weekend in the tourist capital of America to help you survey an Indian village?" She watched as he fumbled a fork and it clattered on the table. "That would be the same village that I expressly said we would *not* be surveying until we finished at the mission."

He picked up the rest of the utensils and dumped them into the bus bin. "I was planning to discuss it with you, Alys."

"Of course you were." She watched the students in the vans as they drove out to the road. "I'm sure you would have told me all about it. Afterward."

Beau dropped into the seat beside her. "What harm is there in letting them poke about the village?"

"Frankly I don't care about the village," she said. "I have an issue with you undermining my authority. As I am the archaeologist, and you are not, you should defer to my judgment on these matters. If you disagree with my choices, please feel free to discuss them with me. But don't ignore me."

"Forgive me," he said, surprising her. "It was wrong to disregard your wishes. It won't happen again."

Alys felt a now-familiar surge of exasperation mixed with affection; Beau often unsettled her with such good-natured reactions. Whenever she'd worked on a dig in the past, she'd had to deal with too many egotistical superiors and resentful subordinates. Beau was nothing like that; he went out of his way to make things easier on her. She was beginning to rely on it, and on him. Since she'd only ever been able to depend on herself in the past, it was a novel and oddly comforting situation.

I'm not alone in this. Alys felt her heart melt a little. *He wants me to count on him.*

But could she? Was Beau as sincere as he seemed, or was he simply using his charm to control her?

He touched the side of her arm with his. "You'll feel better if you thump me, you know. Go on. I deserve it."

"I've never struck another person in my life." She'd done far worse, not that she could ever tell him that.

"But you've wanted to." He picked up her hand, which she still held in a tight fist. When she loosened her fingers, he brought them to his mouth for a kiss. "I am grateful for your understanding."

The intimate contact of his lips against her knuckles coupled with his voice and the memory of the nightmare from her childhood combined to completely unnerve her. "It's done. Let's forget it." She pulled her hand away and picked up the carryall. "I'm finished for tonight, too. Would you shut down the generators, please?"

He nodded, and she headed for the cloister.

As she showered, Alys felt less annoyed with Beau and more aggravated with herself. Because he was so willing to shoulder so much responsibility, he was easy to blame for her own shortcomings and frustrations. She hadn't been entirely honest with him or the interns, either. The students' efforts had been remarkable, and they did deserve a weekend for themselves, but Alys also wanted the time to work on her other problem: the flaw in her theory.

Everything had indicated that the treasure was here at the mission. After a week of digging and turning up only the most ordinary and unremarkable artifacts, and finding nothing to indicate the mission was in any sense unusual, she was prepared to admit that she had made a miscalculation.

The most frustrating aspect of all was that she *did* know where the Templars' treasure was; the location had been repeatedly described in dozens of letters and journals belonging to the Spanish priests. She knew it lay deep beneath the earth's surface, and was accessible only by a narrow stone passage. The only entry to it had been carefully concealed to prevent discovery. Some of the priests referred to the location in religious terms, describing stone vaults chiseled by the hammer of God, and sacred waters welling from a source of never-ending life.

Although the descriptions varied, every single one of the mission priests had used the same name to refer to it: the fountain of youth.

The legend of the fountain, which modern texts always paired with Spanish explorer Juan Ponce de León, was usually dismissed as pure myth, no more valid or real than the pool of Bethesda, the philosopher's stone, or any of the other folklore focused on the mystical endowment of eternal youth dating back to the writings of Herodotus in the fifth century BC.

Alys might have rejected the legend of the fountain herself if the timeline and location had been different. But long before Ponce de León had stepped foot on Florida soil for the first time, the mission's priests had entered into a pact to protect the refugee Templars by relocating them to what was then an equally mythic New World.

Down in the cloister, Alys brought her laptop to bed with her, booting it up so she could begin reviewing her notes again. Her most important source, the letters of a priest who had attended the Spanish explorer Pedro

Menéndez de Avilés when he had founded the first enduring colony in Florida at St. Augustine, had provided
her with some clues.

Our master listens too much to his lady's counsel, Father Gonzalo wrote in a letter to his sister. He often
wrote about Menéndez's wife, who had been obsessed
with finding the fountain. *She has urged him to march
against the savages who occupy the land to the west and
south, and capture their leaders, which has outraged the
entire tribe. Yet even under torture, these old men refuse to
reveal the location of the fountain. They will say only that
it was made long ago by white-skinned strangers like us,
and anyone who drinks from it is not restored to youth,
but cursed. So dreadful are their superstitions that several
of the poor wretches used their teeth to open their veins,
so they might bleed to death in silence before they could
be questioned.*

Over time other explorers and missionaries encountered and recorded tales of what the Timucua referred to
as the sacred waters, and from these accounts Alys had
gleaned a few more precious bits of data. The settlement
near the fountain had been abruptly abandoned by the
Timucua at approximately the same time the priests at
the mission had mysteriously vanished. After that, the
natives in the area had become much more aggressive,
vowing to kill anyone who tried to find the legendary
fountain.

By mapping every recorded Indian attack in the region, Alys had been able to narrow down the possible
location of the fountain to within a fifty-mile radius. After reviewing countless geological surveys, she had identified each water feature within the boundaries of her

search area, and further refined her results by eliminating every body of water that was not within walking distance of a native settlement.

That had left her with a dozen potential sites, most of which had been exploited by modern municipalities. And of the three that remained undeveloped, only one had been located near both an Indian village and a Spanish mission.

"You said you were finished with work for the day."

Alys hadn't heard Beau come down the steps—for such a large man he moved with exceptional silence— and when she looked up from the screen, she saw he had left his shirt open to the waist. "Aren't you ever cold?"

"I've lived here for some time," he reminded her. "I imagine I'm used to the weather."

"This region is subtropical, and reports indicate this is the coldest winter on record, so you can't be accustomed to it." Although she rarely consulted with others on her theories, she wanted to discuss her idea with him. "Would you come here and look at this?" She closed the research file and opened the latest version of her site map.

Beau walked over and studied the screen. "What am I seeing?"

"A map of the entire property." She zoomed in and highlighted the location of the mission. "We're here, the Indian village is here, and the spring pond is between them, correct?" When he nodded, she zoomed out. "Every survey on this property dating back to the turn of the century lists a pond as retention or seasonal. It's completely isolated, so this makes sense, but the water in it is fresh, not stagnant. So what's feeding it?"

His eyes shifted as he studied the map. "The source

must be a spring beneath the pool. But what has this to do with finding evidence of the Templars?"

"I believe they hid something in the spring itself. Something they never wanted anyone to find. And whatever it was, it served as the foundation for the legend of the fountain of youth." She closed the laptop and switched it off. "We have to search the bottom of the pond."

"That will be difficult to do in the dark." He regarded her. "You are serious? Alys, that pond is covered with ice."

He was right, of course, but she wasn't planning to stay in the pond long enough to develop hypothermia. "The surface never freezes solid. I'm a good swimmer, and I only need a few minutes."

"A few minutes in water that cold will stop your heart." He took the laptop and set it aside. "You are not going in the pond."

"I don't need your permission." The conversation was turning adversarial, something she had hoped to avoid. "Think about it. It makes perfect sense that they would conceal the treasure underwater. Hardly anyone in their time could swim. They may have even created the pond just for that reason by digging it out and diverting the water to fill it. The feed from a spring would maintain the water level, and the silt on the pond's bottom would conceal the entry point from view."

He didn't look convinced. "You would freeze to death to prove this. What if you are wrong, and the pond is nothing more than a pond?"

"It's not," she insisted. "If it were natural, the Indians would have used it, but we've found no signs of activity

anywhere around the pond. And why didn't the missionaries use it for their water supply, instead of digging that
well we found beside the kitchen?"

He switched off the lanterns. "Natives have all manner of taboos. As for the missionaries, perhaps they
didn't care to walk half a mile carrying filled buckets."

She sat up. "Beau, they were medieval Catholic
priests. They enjoyed suffering so much they invented
self-flagellation. Besides, they had to know the water in
the pond was drinkable. The well would have taken days,
maybe even weeks, to dig." She frowned. "Unless they
dug out the pond after the well, in which case they'd
have to haul water from the nearest river."

He came to stand over her. "You can theorize all you
wish, Alys, but you can't go into that pond. You'll have to
find another way to search it."

"All right. We *are* in Florida, home to most of America's finest marine biology programs. Maybe one of the
local universities has some underwater cameras or robotic gear we can borrow." She watched his shadow retreat to the other bed. "If you're never cold, why do you
wear your clothes to bed?"

"To preserve your modesty, madam." As always he
pushed aside the covers and lay flat on his back. "At
home I don't wear a stitch of anything when I sleep."

"Oh." She turned over onto her back. "Well. Thank
you."

"Good night, Alys."

Alys opened her eyes to the sound of children laughing,
and sat up to see two little mischievous faces peering
over the foot of her bed. "How did you get down here?"

The thin, strawberry blond girl grinned, showing a gap where her front teeth should have been. "*Grand-père* sent us," she said in her lisping French accent.

"He isn't our grandpa," her companion, a tiny brunette with a head full of curls, scolded with a distinctive American voice. Her dark eyes gleamed as she looked at Alys. "He's our great-great-great-great-great-forever-and-ever-great-grandpa."

"I'm sure he is," Alys told them, climbing out of bed. "But you two can't stay here. We're not prepared to look after little girls."

"We want to see the Indian village." The French girl tugged at her hand.

"No, we want to go swimming," the American insisted.

"Children. Please." Alys took hold of their hands and marched them over to the steps. "You need to go home." She hesitated. "Do you know how to get back home from here?"

"We do." The French girl's face grew solemn. "But we can't go away, not yet. You are very close, *ma demi-sœur*. Soon you will find them, and it will be very bad for you."

"Very, very bad," the American intoned.

The blonde nodded toward Beau's bed. "He is last, like you, *Grand-père* says, so he must not fail. You must not let him fail, Alys."

"You know my name."

"We know everything here." The American girl beckoned for Alys to lean down and, when she did, whispered, "He has a secret. We can't tell you what it is because that's not fair, but it makes him sad and lonely. You could make him happy again."

"How?" Alys whispered back.

The brunette's cheeks dimpled. "You know how, silly." She grabbed the French girl's hand, and the two of them skipped up the stairs, vanishing from sight halfway to the top.

"Two ghosts?" Alys sighed and went back to her bed, pushing at the lump under her covers as she tried to get comfortable. The tangle of linens wouldn't budge, so she draped one arm and leg over it and used one end as a pillow.

As awkward and bulky as its shape was, the mound felt very nice against her body. She burrowed against it, smiling as she felt it grow warmer. Just as she was falling back asleep, she felt a caress on her cheek.

The girls again. Alys kept her eyes shut. "I don't believe in ghosts. Go away."

The annoying, nonexistent spirits muttered something as one of them nuzzled the top of her head. The touch didn't feel like it came from a little girl, however.

"I mean it, whoever you are," she warned. "I'll throw you on the floor."

"You can try," a deep voice said.

She opened one eye and saw the pattern of the coverlet fading and smoothing out into a golden brown bulge—but the one on her bed was purple. "Why aren't you violet?"

"I'm not a flower."

Alys lifted her head to see Beau's face, and went very still. "What are you doing in my bed?"

"Let me show you something." He reached out and switched on the lantern nearest to them, and pointed toward the other side of the room.

Alys looked over at her empty bed, the coverlet and sheets in a rumpled pile on the floor, and groaned as she let her head fall against Beau's chest. "Not again."

"I woke up when I heard you talking to the stairs," he informed her. "Then you came over to my bed, flopped on top of me, and here we are."

"I am so sorry." No, if she was honest, she wasn't. Being sprawled on top of him felt good—more than good—and his voice stroked her like a warm silk glove. It made her whole body want to rub itself all over him.

I want to have sex with him.

Alys had never felt such a purely physical impulse, but it didn't frighten her. Neither did Beau. Although he was big and quite strong, he'd always been careful with her while they were working. He would probably be equally as gentle if they were naked. She wanted to be naked with him.

She looked up at him again. "Do you like me?"

He laughed. "Yes, Alys, I like you. I like you very much." He sat up, holding her in his arms. "Any bumps or bruises this time?"

"No, I feel wonderful." She should flutter her eyes at him, or rub her hand on some part of his body, but she wasn't sure which would be more effective. She also didn't want to appear clumsy, not when she wanted to be graceful and alluring for him.

Beau's muscles tightened as he gathered her up in his arms.

He's going to initiate this. Alys felt relieved; for her the first physical overture had always been the most awkward part of sex.

As Beau stepped off the bed and straightened, she

glanced down. "What are you doing?" Could they have sex standing up? Considering the differences in their heights, it seemed unlikely. Unless he held her up in the air.

"I'm putting you back to bed." He carried her over and gently put her down on the mattress before he retrieved and shook out her linens. "Was it another nightmare about the church?"

"No, we were here. The girls and I. There were two little girls." As he draped her sheets and coverlet over her, Alys subsided against the pillows. "No one has ever carried me like that. It's nice."

"I can be a very nice man." He said that oddly, and bent over to kiss her forehead. "Sleep, and try not to walk while you do."

Sleeping was the last thing on her mind, but she pretended to as she listened to him return to his bed. That he hadn't wanted to have sex with her made her stomach feel tight, but she acknowledged that she had misinterpreted his actions and come to an erroneous conclusion.

She wished she hadn't. Beau behaved as if he liked her, and never appeared bored around her. She'd already admitted to herself that she found him very attractive. Hearing his voice made her feel safe, and being in his bed had aroused her. But he hadn't responded to her subtle overtures, and took no initiative of his own.

A thought occurred to her. "Beau, are you still awake?"

He muttered something unintelligible in response.

"Are you married, or emotionally involved with someone?"

He made an odd sound, and then mumbled what sounded like a "No."

With the way Brenda and all the female interns had been ogling him, that didn't seem probable to Alys. "Why not?" Another possibility came to mind, and she sat up. "Are you gay? Is that it?"

The sound of a thud came from his direction. "No, Alys. I'm not married or involved, nor do I chase after other men. What I am is bloody exhausted. Now, good night." He pulled the pillow over his head.

Chapter 8

"Usually we don't have a problem with borrowing equipment from other colleges," Charles said to Beau as he handed him a case of bottled water from the back of the van. "I thought we'd be able to get at least one research submersible on loan. But these other teams got there before us and grabbed everything, even scuba gear and wet suits."

Beau stacked the case with the rest on the hand truck. "You're certain these other archaeologists are working in the area."

"That's what they put in the equipment checkout logs," Charles said. "I Googled the addresses on my phone, and their campsites are only a couple of miles apart, just west of the old village. The American team is so close to the property line they can probably jump the fence. I bet they do so they can spy on us, the assholes."

"Charles." Alys appeared, her expression as stern as her tone. "However much they behave like one, please do not refer to any colleague as a body orifice. They generally dislike it, and someday you may have to work for one of those assholes."

Brenda giggled as she and Chan joined them. "I didn't think you knew how to swear, Dr. Stuart."

Alys gave Beau a narrow look. "Everyone has hidden talents."

"Someone left this at the hotel for you, Dr. Stuart." Chan handed her a sealed gift box stamped with the words PIRATE WORLD. "Maybe it's some complimentary tickets?"

"Too heavy for that." Alys broke the seal and lifted the lid to reveal three large, glittering green gems.

Beau went still.

"Oh, my God. They're gorgeous." Brenda leaned over to look. "Look at how huge they are."

"About thirty carats each." Alys took one out of the box and held it up. "If they were real."

"They're not?"

"They're fakes." She frowned as Beau plucked the emerald out of her hand. "What are you doing?"

"Admiring your gift," he said before he handed it back to her. "Dr. Stuart is right. They're made of glass."

"Thank you for confirming the obvious." Alys emptied the other gems into her palm and looked under the cotton liner. "No card." She glanced at Chan. "You're sure these were left for me?"

He nodded. "At least, that's what the guy at the front desk said."

"That's odd. Maybe it's some sort of park promotional deal. I'll call the hotel later." Alys tucked the box into her backpack, and her eyes shifted briefly to Beau. "Brenda, you and Chan can finish processing the last of the soil samples." After the two interns headed for their workstations, Alys turned to Charles. "Those artifact logs aren't going to update themselves. Get to work."

"Yes, ma'am." The intern made a face at Beau before hurrying off.

"I saw that," Alys called after him before she eyed Beau. "And you. I'd appreciate it if you wouldn't encourage the interns to waste time. We have only seventeen days left to work, and I have to put something in my project summary report other than 'Stood around gossiping with project manager.'"

Beau nodded and frowned as he watched her stalk off. Over the last five days Alys had grown increasingly short-tempered with her students, showing little of her former patience and sometimes snapping at them over the slightest mistake. Beau knew he was the cause, as she'd actively avoided him all week, barely speaking a handful of words to him whenever she couldn't.

He knew why she was so angry with him. Her dark mood had begun one morning a week past, when he'd caught her slipping out of the cloister soon after they'd gone to bed. He'd assumed Alys was sleepwalking again, until he found her setting up her ridiculous little tent beside the church again. She'd insisted she wanted to sleep outside, even as she'd stood shivering in the cold morning wind.

Tired and in no mood for another debate, Beau had settled the argument by picking her up and carrying into the cloister. Once he'd deposited her back in her bed, he'd told her that if he caught her sneaking outside again, he'd burn the bloody tent. She'd turned her back on him in a huff, and the next night had refused to speak to him at all.

Alys's anger wouldn't be so difficult to bear if Beau hadn't been wrestling with his own dark mood. The damned woman hadn't the faintest idea of how lovely she was, how good she smelled, or how sorely she tempted him. When he looked upon her, he didn't see a child, or a young sister. He saw a woman he wanted to touch and breathe in and hold. When he heard her showering in the next room, he drove himself half-mad thinking of her naked and wet. After they retired for the day, he would lie and listen to her breathing, and watch the outline of her breasts lift and fall, his hands clenched against the need to touch them.

No, if anyone should be sleeping in a tent outside, it should be him.

He had not touched her, *would* not touch her. He could not take such a risk. As she had pointed out, they had but seventeen days left to work, and while that now seemed to Beau like an eternity of torment, he could endure it.

Fortunately Charles had given him something else to dwell on besides Alys's myriad allures: the two other archaeological teams that had encamped in the area. One or both of them could be the *tresoran* traitors; using the guise of a dig would allow them to openly search for the emeralds. Once the interns left and Alys went to sleep, he'd have to scout their encampments.

After he put away the supplies Charles had brought, Beau went to check on Alys, following her scent to the mission's kitchen, where she had hung a large map of the site marked with a grid pattern. She was standing before the map when he found her, consulting it as she wrote notes in a small diary.

He cleared his throat. "May I have a word with you?"

Her shoulders tensed, but she didn't look up from her notes. "Go ahead."

"While we were *gossiping*, Charles told me that he was unable to borrow any equipment from the universities." He waited for her to say something, but she only nodded. "I can send a request to the high—to the foundation for the gear you need."

"Fine. Do it."

Beau didn't like talking to the back of her head, and came around her so that he could see her lovely, stubborn face. "You'll need to tell me exactly what you want."

"What do I want?" She tapped the end of her pencil against her bottom lip. "I'd like seventeen weeks—no, make that seventeen months—to continue work here. I'd like a dozen qualified, experienced excavators, artifact handlers, and associate archaeologists who won't act like they're on spring break or treat this project like a glorified Easter egg hunt. You're not writing this down. Do you know how to write? I ask because I've never seen you do it."

"You're right." Beau held up his hands in surrender. "We should talk later."

When he turned away, she darted around him to stand in his way. "Wait. You want answers, and so do I. Why don't we trade? I'll give you an answer for every one you give to me."

He could smell the anger rolling off her skin, and felt his own temper begin to fray. "You want to make a game of it?"

"I want answers. Here." She flipped to a blank page in her notebook. "I'll start making a list of mine for you. I want a small research submersible," she said, writing as she spoke, "with dual remote controls, an onboard camera, probe and collection attachments, and a retracting tether." She looked up at him. "All right. Why have you been following me, and how, exactly, are you locating me when you do?"

"That's two questions." And two answers he couldn't give her.

She began writing again. "I'm adding a wireless video transmitter for the submersible. That's two answers. Your turn."

To keep from snatching the notebook out of her hands and ripping it apart, he shoved his hands into his pockets. "Why do you think I'm following you?"

"I don't think; I know. You followed me into the woods yesterday, and to the palmetto grove the day before, and to the pond the day before that." She gave him a measuring look. "I see. You're not going to tell me the truth. Or you're going to try to charm me into whatever you want me to think. Never mind." She walked toward the kitchen's back entry.

Grimly he held on to his self-control as he followed her. "Alys, you're calling me a liar before I've said a word."

"You're stalling instead of answering, you're avoiding my eyes, and you're hiding your hands." She ducked under some hanging vines and stepped outside. "*That* tells me you're going to lie to me."

"You've told the interns not to go off on their own," he reminded her as he kept pace with her. "So yes, I have been following you, to protect you."

"You didn't see me leave camp when I went to the

grove. You were behind the church, changing that flat tire on the van. You were in the stables helping Chan straighten the handle on the trolley when I walked out to draw some water from the spring." She stopped and glared at him. "And I know you were taking a shower when I went into the woods yesterday. I waited until you did before I left, and I erased my footprints from the trail with a palmetto leaf as I walked. I was very careful."

She was also too bloody perceptive. "This is not a large area, Alys. There are only so many places you can go."

"Don't you patronize me," she snapped. "You know every time I leave the camp, and wherever I go, you find me within a few minutes. Even when I make sure that you can't. So." She gestured at him. "How are you doing it?"

"If I give you this secret, you must never repeat it." When she nodded, he bent down to whisper next to her ear, "I ask the others where you have gone, and they tell me."

She tried to push him away, failed, and nearly fell on her bottom. "You are utterly infuriating."

"I'm not the one covering my tracks," he pointed out.

"But you are hiding something." The fiery note her anger added to her scent abruptly cooled, and her eyes took on a suspicious brightness. "This isn't a game, Beauregard. This is my career, my future. All the work I've done, year after year of study and research and planning, it's all brought me here. I've been given one chance to prove myself, and my time is rapidly running out. What happens to me for the rest of my life will be decided in the next two weeks. I've been trusting you, and maybe that was a huge mistake. If you're here to stop me or discredit me—"

"Alys, no." He reached out to her.

She caught his hand in hers. "Then tell me. Tell me who you are, and why you're here. Please."

Slowly he withdrew his hand from hers, and silently cursed Richard as he repeated the lie. "I am not here to harm you or the project. I was sent only to help. You know who I am."

"No, I don't." She shook her head, backing away from him, and touching her face in surprise as she felt the tear spilling down her cheek. She glanced at her fingers, and then Beau. "I want to, but I don't think I ever will."

Alys fled, and as soon as she was out of sight, Beau turned and rammed his fist into the trunk of an enormous black oak. Bark and wood fragments exploded outward as he swore.

Someone cleared his throat, and Beau turned around to see Chan standing a few feet away. "What do you want?"

"Sex with Brenda," the intern said, his eyes darkening and his voice taking on a dreamy tone. "Sex with Brenda in the back of a brand-new Infiniti. A winning lottery ticket so I can pay off my student loans and take Brenda to Bermuda. A banana split with extra sprinkles. A banana split on Brenda with extra sprinkles. That I eat while someone makes Charles watch."

Beau sighed. "Come here, lad."

The unexpected emotional reaction Alys had during the encounter with Beau left her in a state of confusion and depression. She found that she couldn't concentrate on her work, make useful decisions, or respond to her interns with any degree of coherency. Fortunately Beau joined the students and kept them focused on finishing the last of the processing, allowing Alys to retreat to the lab tent and brood in silence over the unsettling incident. Gradually she came to one undeniable conclusion.

Beau wasn't creating any problems; Beau *was* the problem.

The man was a logician's nightmare. As dirty and taxing as the work they did was, Beau never refused to do any task, even the most menial. He kept busy throughout the night but never sweated or smelled of sweat. Over the past week Alys had yet to observe him stopping for a rest break or showing any signs of tiring. One evening he'd spent five straight hours going back and forth with their largest barrow, wheeling away from the work areas several hundred pounds of dirt, rock, and plant matter.

Beau was incredibly, even suspiciously strong. He constantly carted around packed equipment cases as if they contained nothing but feathers, and had repeatedly hefted huge stones out of the way of the GPR trolley. Alys had later tried to shift one especially large rock herself, and found it to be so heavy she couldn't tip it over, much less lift it. A few nights ago, when she'd tripped on the stairs in the cloister, Beau had caught her from behind and lifted her back onto her feet. He'd saved her from a broken neck with just one hand, pressed to her midsection. Given the angle of her fall and her body weight, Alys knew it should have been impossible.

Then there were his stories about medieval life—supposedly from books he'd read—that included so many strange and unique facts. Alys would have confronted him and accused him of inventing them, but what he told the interns sounded eerily correct to her. She had been studying medieval literature and historical texts since Robert had first told her about the Knights Templar, and yet none of the hundreds of books she'd read contained any of the details he kept producing. Alys had asked him one evening about the texts he'd studied, but despite his excellent memory of their contents, he claimed to have forgotten the titles.

For such a studious soul Beau didn't spend a second studying anything. He had yet to touch a book or one of the computers, and several times she'd caught the interns explaining to him how to use some of the simplest devices. The buzz of Charles's electric razor had made him jump, and when Chan had asked him to work out a measurement on his scientific calculator, Beau had refused, claiming his fingers were too clumsy. Later Alys spotted him sitting alone in the lab tent and playing with the same calculator, turning it over in his hands, eyeing the screen and jabbing the buttons until he accidentally turned it on.

The greatest discrepancy about Beau was his terrible eating habits. Beau had told everyone that he had food-related allergies, so many that he had to prepare his own meals. Most of the time he ate alone in the church or the cloister, but the few times he'd joined her and the interns on their meal breaks, he'd brought almost nothing to eat, and had barely swallowed a mouthful of that. He also refused to drink anything but a little water, and she'd noticed him using the same bottle for the entire day without refilling it. His starvation diet would have caused anyone else to grow weak and dehydrated within a day or two, but Beau showed no ill effects or weight loss whatsoever.

Because Alys knew so little about Beau, every observational construct she had put together about him remained inconclusive and disconnected. While he talked a great deal, he never offered details about himself, his life, or his work for the foundation. A furtive search through his belongings had turned up nothing but clothing and toiletries. The wallet he carried contained a modest amount of cash, a preloaded credit card so new it still had the activation sticker attached, and a driver's license issued one day before Alys had met him at the hotel.

Nothing about Beau fit any theory she formulated so far, which indicated a need for investigation. She simply needed to collect more data about him.

Alys felt a little better when Charles came in to speak to her shortly before midnight. "We're finished with the last grid, Dr. Stuart. Do you need us to do anything else?"

Several forms had to be filled out on each of the artifacts they had recovered, something that would take hours, and Alys needed to begin mapping out and scheduling the work for next week. But she knew how much the students had been looking forward to their free weekend, and she could deal with the paperwork herself.

"Thank you for offering," Alys told him, "but I think that will do it for tonight."

Alys walked with Charles out to where the interns were gathered around Beau and chatting about their plans. Most of the work lights had been switched off, but Beau turned his head and looked in her direction before she came out of the shadows. As Alys said good-bye to the students, she added another item to her mental list: *He can see in the dark.*

Once the vans left, Alys made a circuit of the camp, and was pleased to see that the interns had made an effort to

leave their work areas tidy. She stopped in the galley tent
to retrieve a bottle of water, but found the last case sitting
empty. Annoyed, she picked up a cup from the dishes container and went to the upright metal cooler the interns
kept filled with water from the spring pool. As Alys
reached for the spigot, she smelled a faint, burning metal-
lic scent, and glanced down. An electrical extension cord
snaked along the ground beneath the table.

"Who did this?" Alys crouched down to pull the wire
away, but felt the heat radiating from the broad cable,
and stood up again. She followed the cord around to the
back of the table, where it had been carelessly draped
over the metal handle of the cooler. On closer inspection
she saw some of the protective sheath on the cable had
been cut away, exposing the wires, which lay directly
against the cooler's metal exterior.

Alys backed away, groping until she found a metal
spoon, and then tossed it at the cooler. It bounced off
with a bright flash of sparks, and for a long moment the
lights went dim.

If she had touched the spigot, she would have been
electrocuted.

Alys used a wooden spatula to knock the cable away
from the cooler, and once she disconnected the dangerous cable from the generator extension, she looked
around. Someone had just tried to kill her; the attacker
must have left tracks or some trace behind. The only
thing she spotted out of place was a machete and a pair
of binoculars someone had left on the seat of a chair at
the planning table. She walked over to retrieve them
when she saw Beau's black leather jacket was also
draped over the back of the chair.

Map. Binoculars. Machete. Jacket.

. . . Their campsites are only a couple of miles apart, just west of the old village. . . .

Beau intercepted her at the door to the cloister, his expression carefully bland. "Are you done for the night? I'll shut down the generators."

"Yes, thank you." She covered a phony yawn with her hand. "I'm tired, so I think I'll turn in early."

Alys went downstairs, showered and changed, and got into bed before Beau joined her. She reached out to shut off the lantern near her bed and turned her back on him. Instead of going in to shower, Beau came to loom over her bed.

"Alys, I am sorry that I upset you today," he said, his voice low and gentle. "That was not my intention."

How sincere he sounded for a man planning to sneak out on her. Alys was tempted to tell him about the sabotaged cooler, but that might only make him more determined to do something stupid. "I'm not upset."

His hand touched her shoulder. "You were crying."

"I'm not upset *now*." She feigned a drowsy, somewhat annoyed look as she rolled over to look up at him. "I'm exhausted, and I want to sleep. Can we talk about this tomorrow?"

"Of course. Good night." He retreated into the shower.

Allowing her body to go limp and slowing her breathing was simple enough, and by the time Beau emerged from the shower, Alys felt certain her pretense of sleeping was convincing. She did have to wait for him to leave, but planning how she would follow him kept her mind occupied.

Beau didn't leave immediately, and it was difficult for Alys not to tense when the scent of warm caramel told her that he had come to stand beside her bed.

Does he do this every night? She felt a touch on her cheek; he used the backs of his fingers to give her a gentle caress. *Of course, he's testing me.* She mumbled a few consonants and turned her head away from his touch, hoping that would simulate a natural reaction.

"Don't dream of me, love," he murmured, and then moved away.

Don't dream of him? *Love?* Alys felt like jumping out of bed and kicking him. How could she ever have trusted someone who probably lied to her every time he opened his mouth? She clenched her teeth and waited for the sound of his footsteps on the stairs, and then the sound of the door opening and closing before she opened her eyes and counted silently to thirty.

By now he was out of the cloister, she thought as she pulled back the covers and quickly changed into her darkest clothing.

Cautiously she climbed the steps and tiptoed through the cloister. Once outside, she looked all around and listened before she turned off her flashlight and inspected the ground.

Beau's footprints had left oval tracks through the grass, and led through the center of the site to the village path. Alys grinned and hurried toward the path. The air had grown so cold it stung her nose, but she felt completely exhilarated.

I knew it.

Following the path to the village in the dark proved easier than she'd expected, as Beau had used the machete to clear it ahead of her. Once she reached the open space that led into the village, she paused again, peering through the darkness for any sign of him before stepping out into the open.

Alys hadn't decided what to do when she caught up to him. She could observe more if she concealed herself, and she could also keep an eye on him and make sure he didn't get into any trouble. At the same time she wanted to see the look on his face when he realized she'd followed him. *I wonder how you'll like it, Beauregard.*

To keep from losing him, she needed to make up some time and close the gap between them, so instead of following the longer path around the village, she pushed her way through the tangle of brush and grass in its center. None of the ancient Timucua dwellings had survived the ages, but parts of the clay floors of the main community house, and circles of stones that had once served as its fire pits, remained intact. Since these were hidden by the brush, Alys forced herself to slow down and plant her feet carefully.

A rustle of leaves made her freeze in place and hold her breath, but a subsequent scurrying, retreating sound told her she'd startled something in the brush.

"Another rat, I bet," she muttered, moving away from the brush and through a silvery curtain of Spanish moss laced with dead vines. She had to stop again when a fallen vine caught her right foot, but she shook it off and emerged into an area around the largest of the fire pits that had been recently cleared.

A glimmer of moonlight reflected on something pale in color and moving inside the stones, and for a moment Alys thought of her interns' wild stories about the ghost.

Her mouth hitched as soon as she saw the peculiar way the tendrils of white mist were rolling over the sides of the pit and spreading out in all directions.

"Very funny, you guys," she said, looking down in the direction of the camp.

Ghosts didn't cover the ground with an inch of thick fog, Alys knew as she approached the stones, but exposed dry ice did. The interns must have set this up as some kind of prank on her and Beau —

Dry branches snapped as the ground disappeared from under her feet. Instinctively Alys scrambled backward, trying to find solid footing as the soil collapsed and dragged at her legs. She twisted, clawing desperately at some dead tufts of grass before losing her last handhold and sliding into blackness.

Chapter 9

Beau reached the American encampment first, and took to the trees to inspect the intruders. Although they had pitched their tents within a few feet of the fence surrounding Tremayne's land, they had laid out a grid and begun excavating on the opposite side of the camp. Three men stood talking quietly as they warmed their hands over some brush burning in a barrel; the rest of the companions appeared to be in their tents. He spotted some hand tools, maps, and books arranged neatly on a long table, but saw no weapons, surveillance equipment, or any sign to make him think they had come to do anything other than dig.

He might be able to separate one of the men from the others and compel him to confess any unsavory intentions he might have, but he first wanted a look at the other camp.

Beau couldn't move as quickly as Jayr, whose ability gave her bewildering speed and agility, but his Kyn strength allowed him to reach the second team's camp within a few minutes. As there were no trees in the immediate area, he took to the brush, using it as cover while he employed the binoculars.

No tents for the Europeans—they had parked a dozen large new RVs at the edge of the clearing they were excavating. Mounds of aluminum cases lay neatly stacked under tables of computers, electronic devices, and what appeared to be some manner of radio. A tall, heavily rigged steel frame dangled a long pipe in a vertical position above the ground; he didn't recognize it or its purpose. A portable satellite dish on a trailer sat aimed up at the stars; another held a robotic device mounted with cameras and attached to a coil of shielded cables. Beau suspected the latter was the research submersible Alys had wanted.

She'll be wandering about the Americans' site by now.

Beau had known Alys would follow him, naturally. From the moment she'd produced that phony yawn and announced she was going to bed, he'd been sure of it. Otherwise he wouldn't have bothered with stomping each step to leave visible footprints for her, or using the machete to clear the path.

It was only fair. As unhappy as he'd made her, she needed this little victory, and he hoped it would satisfy her curiosity. He'd also have to make more of an effort to behave more like a mortal. The sharp-eyed little wench had already noticed too much about him, and with her immunity to *l'attrait* he couldn't wipe any of it from her memory.

The Europeans had not bothered with staking out a grid; nor could Beau see any sign of recovered artifacts. Several broad patches of grass had been cleared in the field, but all that had been dug in those spots was single two-foot-wide oval holes. Beau couldn't tell how deep they were, but the breadth of the holes was just a little larger than the submersible.

He shifted the binoculars to inspect the frame and pipe rig a second time; he could just make out the pointed, twisted taper protruding from the end of the shaft. *They're not excavating; they're drilling.*

The entire region lay atop a vast network of underground reservoirs; Beau guessed the Europeans were attempting to tap one and use it to send the submersible onto Tremayne's property and possibly to the spring itself. Which meant Alys's suspicions about the emeralds were dead to rights.

In that moment Beau could have happily invaded the camp, smashed all the equipment, and compelled the entire team to present themselves to the authorities and confess their crimes. Even as his anger billowed up in him, he knew he couldn't do it. If these were the *tresoran* traitors, which he suspected they were, they would likely be immune to *l'attrait*. They'd also have taken the precaution of arming themselves with weapons capable of killing Kyn.

Beau tucked the binoculars in his jacket and checked the time; by now Alys should have caught up to him. He backtracked toward the Americans, breathing in the air deeply to pick up her scent, but even outside the second camp he detected nothing of her presence. She wouldn't have given up so easily, and she couldn't be lost. . . .

Beau backtracked along the trail he'd left for her, first trotting and then racing as he tried to pick up her scent path. He finally found a very faint trace in the air on the east edge of the Indian village, the merest whisper of her.

He concentrated, closing his eyes as he breathed her in. She had been angry—yes, he could taste the peppery heat of that—but there was more, a sharper edge left by a sudden and very different burst of emotion: terror.

Beau followed the scent, pausing only when he picked up the minute particles of the one thing that caused his *dents acérées* to emerge, full and straining, into his mouth: mortal blood.

Alys was bleeding.

Sweeping methodically from one side of the village to the other, Beau searched the ground and called out her name. Toward the heart of the site he saw an unnatural fog wafting over the ground, and spilling into a dark gash in the earth as if it were being sucked in. He made his way to the edge, cursing as Alys's scent rose up to meet him.

"Alys?" He peered into the hole, but it was too deep and dark for even his Kyn vision to penetrate. It wouldn't harm him to jump in, but he might land on top of her. "Stay where you are. I'm fetching some rope."

Beau ran to the camp, grabbing a coil of utility rope, a lantern, and a first aid kit from the supplies stowed in the church. If she was unconscious and the pit very deep, he wouldn't be able to jump out with her, so he grabbed a handful of stretch cords with end clamps that he could use to bind her body to his.

Back in the village he quickly knotted the end of the rope around two tree trunks, and tested his weight on the line before he went back to the edge.

"Alys, I'm here," he called to her. "I'm coming down for you now." He ran the rope through the handle of the first aid kit and the lantern so that both would slide down behind him.

Loose soil rained all around him as he descended, and to prevent another cave-in he tried not to touch the side of the pit. He dropped another twenty feet before his feet touched bottom. Quickly he removed the kit and the lantern, switching on the light.

On the opposite side of the pit Alys lay next to an outcropping of stone, her body nearly buried beneath fallen dirt and broken branches. Beau placed the lantern next to her head, touching the underside of her jaw, where he felt her pulse throbbing strong and regularly. The relief to know that she had survived the fall came over him so strongly that he braced an arm to keep from dropping down alongside her.

"You are supposed to dig the holes, woman, not fall in them." Carefully he brushed the dirt away from her face, which appeared unmarked. Almost at once she began coughing, but he clamped his hands on her shoulders and pinned her in place. "Don't try to move yet, love. I have to check you for broken bones."

Her eyelids fluttered open. "Beau." She frowned at him. "I found a pit trap." Her eyes shifted. "I think I fell in it."

"Yes, actually, you did." He cupped the back of her head, feeling a small bump there but no bleeding. "I have to see if you've broken anything. Can you be a good girl for me while I do?"

"I'm not a child. I only behave like one on occasion." She closed her eyes. "Go ahead."

Beau tested the set of her neck and shoulders, moving his hands down one arm and then the other. The sight of her bleeding palms and broken nails made him feel sick with fear. She'd fallen more than twenty feet; the impact might have broken her back.

"Can you feel this?" He brushed his lips over the knuckles of one hand and the palm of the other.

"Stop kissing me—I'm filthy." She looked past him. "This isn't a pit trap. I'd be impaled on a bunch of spears if it were, it's too deep, and besides that, the Timucua never built them."

Beau began checking her fingers. "Do remind me to thank the natives."

"You can't. The last Timucua Indian died almost two hundred and fifty years ago." She shifted her eyes to the left. "This looks like a borrow pit."

He placed her hands at her sides. "They borrowed it from someone?"

"We call them that because the natives dug them to borrow the dirt for burial mounds," she said. "Which is even odder. There aren't any burials anywhere near here. I think the closest one is in New Smyrna Beach."

"Be still." He pulled away the debris covering her abdomen and right leg. "Does anything hurt?"

"My head is pounding, and something under me is jabbing me." She tried to look down the front of herself. "I can feel my toes." Soil fell away from her sneakers as she wiggled them. "I don't think my legs are broken."

That left checking for the worst. "I'm going to put my hand under you, and feel along your spine."

Her scowl ebbed as fear filled her eyes. "I landed on my back, didn't I?"

"Yes, you did, love. But you just moved your feet, and I suspect you have a spine made of iron." He leaned over and kissed her brow. "Be brave now. Tell me if you feel any pain."

She nodded.

Beau used his ability to lift her body enough to place his hand beneath it. He felt the warm wetness of blood as soon as he touched her back. He felt along her spine for the source, but Alys didn't make a sound until he reached her waist.

"There." She caught her breath. "Something there. It feels like a knife."

He went around the spot and continued until he reached her buttocks. From what he could feel, her bones were intact, which meant he could risk moving her. "I'm going to turn you on your side and have a look. We'll go slowly."

"I can do it." Alys shifted, groaning as she moved onto her left side. "Oh, that really hurts now. Please tell me there aren't any bones sticking out."

Beau lifted the lantern over her, and as soon as the light illuminated her injury, he put it down. "No bones out of place. There's a bit of wood lodged under your skin." He studied it before he reached for the first aid kit. "It hasn't gone in very deep."

"Please." Her voice sounded strained. "Pull it out."

He took a gauze pad from the kit. "Ready?"

"Yes." She muffled a sharp sound as he tugged it free, and then exhaled heavily. "A twig? That was all? It felt more like a log."

Beau tossed the wood aside and quickly bit into his own wrist, opening two puncture wounds that he held over the gash in Alys's skin.

"What's that?"

"Only a little antiseptic." He watched as his Kyn blood sank into the wound, putting an immediate stop to the bleeding. He covered the gash with more gauze, which he taped in place.

"That doesn't sting, but it feels hot." She tried to look over her shoulder. "How did you know I was down here?"

More questions. The wench had nearly died, and she was still asking them. "I heard the ground collapse."

"No, you didn't; that was me falling in. This pit was already here; someone just camouflaged it." She struggled into a sitting position. "I want to stand up."

As he helped her to her feet, Beau glanced at the mound of deadwood around her. "The natives did not do this."

"No." She picked up an oyster shell. "After they dug this pit and did something with the dirt, the Timucua probably used it as a very large garbage can." She gingerly felt the back of her head. "Maybe the kids covered it up as part of a prank."

"They would not do something so vicious." Beau caught her as she staggered, bringing his arms up around her and holding her against him. "I must take you to hospital."

"I can't leave; the terms of the grant were very specific. If I do, Hylord will shut down the project." She looked up at him. "I think I'm all right. Mostly. Are your eyes glowing?"

Beau hadn't fed before leaving to scout the other camps, and expending so much energy as well as using his ability to get to Alys had further depleted him. The scent of her blood had stirred the worst part of him, and if he soon didn't get away from her and feed, his hunger would grow out of control.

"I must leave you here for a little while," he said, holding her at arm's length. "Don't be afraid."

"I'm not the one who's afraid. Your hands are shaking." She tilted her head. "Your voice has changed, and your teeth are different, too."

"You just took a bad fall," he reminded her. "You're shaken from it."

"Not really." She breathed in and smiled as her eyes darkened. "Brenda calls you the Candyman. Do you know why? You smell like caramel. Hot caramel."

She'd fallen again, this time under his sway. Beau knew that even the few mortals who were immune to *l'attrait* could still be affected by it when they were injured or weak. Which made him want to curse God and all the heavens for doing this to him.

"Do you like me," Alys was asking him, "or do you just pretend to because we have to work together?"

"Alys, listen to me. I want you to sit down and wait here." He turned away from her to pick up the lantern and switch it off. "I won't be long."

He reached for the rope, but when he grasped it, the entire length came slithering down, until the other end landed at his feet.

"Do you have to leave me?" she asked. "I don't like being alone down here. Not after someone tried to electrocute us. Can't I climb out with you?"

The fall must have addled her thoughts. "Neither of us will be climbing out of here," he said, his voice sounding harsh. "Someone cut the rope."

"All of the interns are back at the hotel in the city. We're the only ones left out here. Unless it was the ghost, but I don't believe in ghosts." She came up behind him. "Maybe you didn't tie it right."

"No, it was tied well enough." As soon as she touched

his shoulder, Beau moved away from her. "You should sit down."

"Don't worry," she said. "You'll save my life again. Just like you did in France, when I was a little girl."

"You should sit down and rest. Let me help you." When he reached for her, his fingers brushed against her pendant. "What is this?"

"My cross." She tucked in her chin to look at it. "I've had it since I was a baby. Like the omega. I think my parents were religious. And maybe a little weird."

She was still making no sense at all, but neither was the cross she wore. Simply touching it sent an unpleasant tingle through his fingers. Beau was convinced he'd seen it before, and not on Alys. He turned it over in his hand, and saw the glint of a tiny jewel embedded in the center.

The eye of Yblis.

"I've seen you watching me, you know." She tugged the cross from his fingers and bent to turn on the lantern. "Most men don't do that after they talk to me. Either I intimidate them or I don't say what they want to hear."

"You do unsettle me on occasion," Beau said, "but I am not afraid of you, Alys. And you can say anything to me that you like."

"Good." She beamed at him. "Will you have sex with me?"

Whatever antiseptic Beau had used on Alys's back had burned away the pain; now it mellowed into a deep, pleasant warmth that spread through her abdomen and pelvis. She wanted him to hug her again, but he was still staring at her cross. He also hadn't answered her question.

"I said, would you—"

"I heard you the first time, love. No." He moved away from her again until he disappeared into the shadows. "You're not thinking clearly right now."

"I thought you weren't afraid of me." She reached for the stone wall, leaning against it until the pit stopped spinning. "That's strange." She ran her fingers over the surprisingly smooth surface. "This should be clay. With the water table as high as it is here, we should be swimming, too." She turned around until she spotted Beau. "Oh, there you are."

When Alys went to him, he caught her hands and held her away as he looked over her head. "You have to stop this now, love. You're like a sister to me. A young sister. A very young, innocent sister."

"That would be fine, only I'm not your sister." She stretched her arms out to change his angle of leverage, and pressed herself against him. "Remember when you came in my hotel room, and I tripped you, and we fell down together? I was afraid, and really angry, but I liked it, too."

He tried shuffling back, but she followed him until she had him pinned against the stone. "Alys, please."

Pleased she had him cornered, she rested her cheek against his chest. "It was when you rolled me over onto my back, and my towel fell off and I felt you." She shimmied her hips against him, rubbing her belly against the hard length of his penis. "Like this. You were aroused, just like this. I love that I can do that to you."

"I'm a man; you were naked." He lowered his hands, bringing hers down to her sides. "I did not go there to assault you. I've never forced myself on a woman."

"But you thought about it, didn't you?" She looked up at his tight features. "I could see it on your face, and feel it in your touch. Your body was practically shouting how much you wanted me. For a minute, when I thought you were going to spread my legs and push yourself inside me, I wasn't angry. I was excited. I wanted it. I want it now." The pit began to spin again, and Alys sagged against him. "Why am I talking like this? I never talk like this. I feel like I've been drugged."

He muttered some astoundingly foul words before he said, "It's all right, love. I have you."

A moment later he was sitting with his back to the wall of the pit and she was on his lap.

Alys felt bemused. "Is this what they mean by two people having chemistry? I never understood that euphemism. Literally speaking, it makes no sense. What could beakers and Bunsen burners and formulas have to do with sexual attraction?"

"The chemistry is mine, I'm afraid." He tucked her against his shoulder. "You've merely succumbed to it."

"You know, modesty is not one of your shortcomings." She would have felt annoyed with his arrogance if it hadn't seemed so right. "You've been with a lot of women, I guess. I would really like to have sex with you, but I know I'm going to be a disappointment. Just so you're prepared." She started unbuttoning her shirt.

His hand stopped hers. "Alys, you are unlike any woman I've ever known, and yes, there have been many. None of them had your honesty, your simplicity. There is no artifice in you. Your heart is so open and clear and lovely, I think it must be fashioned from crystal."

He was being ridiculous; her heart was made of muscle and arteries and membranes. An organic pumping mechanism, that was all it was, so why did it feel as if it were melting? For once, she knew how to respond in kind, however. "Then please don't break it."

Beau tipped up her face and put his mouth to hers. Alys hadn't indulged in much kissing; the partners she'd taken in college had devoted a desultory effort to fore-play. Beau's mouth tasted cool and wet, and when he touched her tongue with his, it sent a shivery panic through her.

He drew back a little. "You've nothing to fear from me, love. Let me in. Let me show you."

He punctuated his words with light touches of his lips to hers, coaxing them apart for his tongue. His mouth felt warmer now, and not so startling, although other things distracted Alys. Her skin seemed too tight, and she couldn't catch her breath. This close, Beau seemed so much bigger and harder, his body like some smooth, sculpted rock to which she could only cling.

And she was clinging, Alys thought, completely befuddled by the urgency pounding in her chest and the empty ache pulsing between her thighs. She'd never been one to cling or pulse over anyone, and yet here she was, grabbing at him and opening for him and taking each deep, slow kiss as if it was all that mattered.

"Wait." She ducked her head, gasping for breath as she ground her forehead into his shoulder. "I can't think like this. I can't—do this. I don't understand. I feel like I'm coming apart."

"Shhhh." He stroked her arm with a gentle up-and-down motion. "Nothing more will happen. You're tired and hurt, and I shouldn't have touched you at all."

Alys didn't know what to say, but her body reacted by pressing closer against him. "Please," she begged. "Don't stop now. I can handle it. I think."

"It's all right, love. I'll see to it." Beau turned her away from him, holding her loosely around the waist. "Lean back against me, yes, like that."

She glanced down at his hand, which had released the button of her jeans and was opening the zipper. The set of his fingers made her frown. "You have a crooked finger on your left hand."

"Yes, I do."

"Are you going to try to manually stimulate me?" She'd experimented with that, too, but while she'd eventually learned how to bring herself to orgasm, it never felt especially satisfying.

"I'm going to touch you, Alys." His voice whispered against her ear, and the low, rough sound seemed to echo through her, reaching down to intensify the ache. "It's not anything you have to think about. You've only to feel."

She could feel his hands pushing her jeans and panties out of his way, and her thighs trembled as he coaxed them apart. "I'm not very good at having orgasms. Your hand is going to get tired."

"I never weary of touching you." He cupped her, threading his fingers through the curly thatch of her pubic hair, and parted her mons with the edge of his thumb. "Can you feel that?" he murmured as he stroked the inordinate wetness between her folds. "That's your wanting me."

Alys knew the clinical term, but decided she liked his expression better. "That's because I want you." It sur-

prised her how much she did. "I like how you touch me."
A sound came out of her throat as his fingertips moved
lower, pressing in.

"Here?" He drew his hand back, rubbing her own
wetness over her clit. "Or here?"

She had never felt less capable of speech; her throat
tightened, her limbs trembled, and every rational thought
left her head. "Both," she managed to pant out. "Please."

"Since you ask me so nicely." Beau shifted his hand,
working his long fingers into her body while he caressed
the little knot at the top of her sex with his thumb. "I
wish this was my mouth, so I could taste you. And then
my cock, so I could feel you squeeze me as you come.
Another night, Alys, I'll come into your bed and wake
you with my kisses. I'll strip you down until you're naked
for me, and touch every inch of your beautiful skin. I'll
bring pleasures that have no names, delight that you've
never imagined. And when you're wet for me like this,
when you can't bear another moment apart from me, I'll
come into you and fuck you until you scream my name."

Listening to his rough, passionate promises set her imagination on fire; hearing his last threat sent her body out of
control. Alys felt herself clench around his fingers as the
first hot burst exploded inside her, shaking her to her heels
as she lost herself in the heat and sensation. Beau thrust his
fingers deep, his thumbnail grazing her swollen clit as he
caressed her in time with the pulses of her pleasure. She
slipped from one peak only to be hurtled to another, her
heart drumming in her ears, her breath sobbing in her chest.

Beau murmured something as he put his mouth to her
shoulder, and Alys felt something sharp tear through her
shirt.

His teeth grazed her flesh with two sharp points, and she thought he would bite down, but suddenly he wrenched his mouth from her and abruptly put her aside.

Alys propped herself up on one elbow, unable to believe he had shoved her away at such a moment. "Beau?"

"Forgive me, love, I . . ." He stopped and turned his back on her. "Forgive me."

Alys's eyes widened as Beau crouched, and then shot up through the air, disappearing over the edge of the pit. *"Beau."* She scrambled to her feet, wincing as her movements pulled at the wound in her back. "Beau, don't leave me down here."

As she called out his name over and over, the air around her came alive with a soft, shimmering light. Alys's voice died away, and when she tried to move back, her body turned to stone.

He will return for you soon, a deep voice whispered inside her head; a voice that belonged to Beau. As Alys fell to her knees, and then lay down on her side, the light filled her with its golden warmth. *Sleep now, my child.*

Chapter 10

Jayr didn't need another fortnight to decide whether Devan Leeds was the best candidate to serve as her chief *tresora*. Over the last two weeks the man had fit himself seamlessly into her household, and had managed the running of it so skillfully she couldn't imagine the Realm without him.

Only one obstacle remained, and he was sitting by her bedchamber hearth brooding over a half glass of whiskey.

She sat up, swamped as always by the enormous bed she shared with her lover, and looked for her robe. "Why are you drinking that swill?"

"This swill?" Byrne regarded his glass. "I refuse to give it up. Like you, my lady." He rose and came to her, pausing to scoop up her robe from where he'd tossed it on the floor the previous night. "I dinnae know why you insist on wearing garments anyway. I'd chain you naked to this bed if I could."

"You like my touch too much to clap me in manacles." She lifted her face to kiss him, looping one arm around his strong neck as he lifted her from the sheets. "Now tell me what has you resorting to that god-awful liquor."

Byrne carried her over to his big armchair and settled in it, holding her on his lap. "I've to ask you a favor. One you'll not wish to grant me."

She smiled. "Nonsense. You know I would do anything for you."

He kissed the end of her nose. "Send the Englishman back to Italy."

"Anything but that," she said, her smile fading only when she realized he meant it. "You cannot be serious. Aedan, the man has been working like a slave for us."

He picked up his glass again and drained it. "Aye, and so he has." He studied the empty crystal. "A veritable rabbit of efficiency, he is."

"How can you object to him?" she demanded. "He's everything courteous and mannerly; he conducts himself so perfectly I wish he'd take the rest of the mortal staff in hand. He's moved the renovations ahead of schedule by a full week. Every task I've set him has been done perfectly, and when I have no more, he finds work for himself. I vow, Devan hardly sleeps."

"So you're calling him Devan now," he muttered.

Jayr studied his scowl. "You cannot be jealous. Of a mortal? Sweet Jesu." She thrust herself off his lap and strode to the bed, jerking on her robe.

Byrne came up behind her, turning her to face him. "He is a man, and you a beautiful and powerful woman. God's teeth, Jayr. Have you never wondered *why* he labors so long and dearly for you?"

"Could it be that I am the ruler of this territory, and he wishes to earn the highest and most important position for a mortal in my household?" She pretended to think. "No, that cannot be it. You are right; he wants only to crawl in my bed. I wonder how he will get you out of it first."

"There is more to it than lust. He tries too hard. He watches you every second, and not merely to drink in your beauty. Test him." When she started to tell him what she thought of that, he seized her up in his arms and kissed her. "If I am wrong, I will make my apologies and accept him as your *tresora* with all my heart."

Jayr touched her brow to his. "No, you will not."

He sketched his fingers along the side of her face. "Then I willnae look for any excuse to kill him."

Byrne's suspicions plagued Jayr even after they parted, and partially out of embarrassment she skipped her habit of beginning the evening in her study and went instead to attend to her lady visitors.

Christian answered her chamber door with a grin. "My lady Jayr." She bobbed a cheeky curtsy before opening the door wider. "Come on in, we're got *Amélie* on."

"Amélie?" Jayr couldn't place the name, but as soon as she saw Simone sitting in front of the television and watching a subtitled French movie, she felt relieved. "I thought for a moment you had a mortal in here with you."

"I left all my mortals back in Provence," Simone told her. "Fifty-three brothers. They were very unhappy about it, but then, they are also my garrison."

"At least you have guys." Chris offered her a glass of bloodwine. "My garrison is all chicks. Immortal former sex-slave chicks." She winked at Jayr. "Don't worry; I left them back home, too."

"Do not describe them to my garrison, Christian, I beg you." Jayr perched on the arm of one love seat and studied the two women. "Now I can see the resemblance. You have the same smile."

"With only brothers, I always wanted a sister." Simone gave Christian a fond look. "Even one who wishes to steal all of my shoes."

The petite brunette sniffed. "We wear the same size, and you get to shop in Paris."

"While you live in Paradise," Simone countered. *"Literally."*

"To think, you're squabbling like sisters already. I expect you will be great friends." Jayr finished her wine. "When are your lords due to arrive?"

"Tomorrow, we hope." Chris sighed and absently rubbed her temple. "We're already feeling the separation anxiety thing. Massive bond-strain headache here."

"You should know that once their business is done, Lucan promised that he would personally escort Korvel and Jamys here," Simone said, and then glanced at Jayr. "With your permission, of course, my lady."

Like most of the Kyn, Jayr had avoided Lucan while he served as Richard Tremayne's chief executioner. Since coming to America and assuming the suzerainty of South Florida, however, the former assassin had gone to some lengths to establish friendly relations with his neighboring *jardins*. He'd also fought alongside Jayr against a nightmarish enemy, and had proved to be a formidable ally.

"Lord Alenfar knows he has a standing invitation to visit the Realm." Jayr hesitated, not wishing to trouble the women with her own dilemma, but in dire need of feminine advice. "I rarely have the chance to confer with other Kyn women. I wonder if I might trouble you both for your counsel."

Christian exchanged a look with Simone. "We haven't been Kyn that long, but sure. Shoot."

Jayr briefly explained the situation with Devan Leeds. "He is an exemplary *tresora*, and I believe him to be perfectly suited for my household. But for some reason Byrne has taken an unreasonable dislike to him, and wishes him gone. We have argued about it twice now, and tonight he challenged me to test the man."

Simone frowned. "What sort of test?"

"It's a loyalty thing," Chris said. "Kyn lords—and ladies—have to be absolutely sure their mortals will stick to their training and serve them without question under any circumstances, even the most nerve-racking. The only way to know is to deliberately put pressure on them. A lot of heavy, nasty pressure."

The Frenchwoman's expression turned cool. "You intend to physically harm the man, my lady?"

"That is not my want or my thinking." She explained what she thought she had to do, adding, "I do not wish to torment him. But if by some small chance Byrne is right about him, I must alert the council and have him permanently removed from service." Which would destroy Leeds's life all over again.

"Do it." Chris's dark eyes were solemn and direct. "This guy is going to have access and control over practically every part of your life. He's going to be your first line of defense against the mortal world. If he's not a hundred percent, you have to know. So does the council, or you're just going to pass the problem along to another suzerain. You can't be nice or polite about this, my lady. It's too important."

"That is not her worry," Simone said, giving Jayr a shrewd look. "I think she's never done anything like this."

Chris frowned. "Not even with Byrne?"

Jayr shook her head. "I have always served, and it is not in me to be so . . . aggressive."

"Oh, no problem." Chris made a dismissive gesture. "I can walk you through it." She saw how Simone was looking at her. "Not all of us were raised by nuns, sweetie."

"Well, I was," Jayr said, and made them all laugh.

A half hour later Jayr left the women and went to her study, where she found Leeds patiently waiting.

What she was about to do to the mortal made her feel sick, but she would see it through. *I can do this. As Christian said, it is but playacting.* "Hello, Devan."

"My lady." He bowed. "I was about to go in search of you." He watched her secure the door. "Is something wrong?"

"Not at all." Steeling herself, Jayr strode past him, pausing only to switch off the phone on her desk. "I was late rising because of my seneschal. Sometimes he still believes himself lord here." She sat back in her chair and regarded him with what she hoped was an arrogant look. "I had to remind him that this is my *jardin*, and he belongs to me. Like you."

Leeds merely inclined his head. "Would you care to go over the schedule for the evening, my lady?"

"I am weary of schedules and work and business." She picked up the glass of bloodwine he had poured for her, cradling it in her hand but making no move to taste it.

She had to feign boredom, restlessness. "I am in a mood to be entertained." She cringed a little to hear how arrogant she sounded.

"I am not sure what you mean, my lady," Leeds said, frowning slightly. "Do you wish me to summon Rainer?"

"I do not want that fool. He does not even like women, you know." She eyed him. "Are you a lover of men, Devan?"

The *tresora* stiffened. "No, my lady. I am a heterosexual."

"Such cold words you mortals use. I dislike them intensely." She rose and approached him, keeping her gaze locked with his. "No more of them tonight. Say, 'I am a lover of women.'"

He didn't move out of place, not even when she stopped just short of touching him. "I am a lover of women."

"Many women, I think. I can see it in your eyes." Jayr looked him up and down as she might inspect a new horse. "You're stronger than you look as well." She forced herself to lean into him so that only an inch separated their faces. At least the *tresora* had a pleasant scent, or she might not be able to bear what was about to occur. "Take off your jacket."

He blinked once. "My lady?"

"You heard me." She stepped back and circled around him as he removed the garment and draped it over his arm. When she trailed her hand across the back of his shoulders, she felt him flinch. "Very nice indeed. Do you like the look of me, *tresora*?"

"You're a very beautiful woman," he said quietly.

She came around to face him. "Give me your hands."

When he did, she placed them on her waist. Making the man touch her made her think of how it had been with her and Byrne the first time he had kissed her. She'd not been at all prepared for it, and neither would Devan. "Now kiss me."

Leeds's hands tightened before he took them away. "I'm afraid I cannot do that, my lady."

"You needn't fear. No one will see us," she promised, resting her hands on his shoulders. "I've bolted the door. You want to. I can smell the lust on you. Go on, then." She put her lips a whisper away from his. "Give me your mouth."

Leeds took a step back. "I would like nothing better than to please you, my lady," he said carefully, "but you are bonded to your seneschal."

"Byrne? Forget him. He will never know." She touched his face. "I want you to be my mortal lover. When we are alone, I will let you do whatever you wish." She glanced down and felt disappointed when she saw the bulge at his crotch. *Byrne was right about him.* "You like the idea of that, I see."

"I am not made of stone, my lady, and you are everything a man dreams of." He swallowed. "But you already have a lover, and whether he knows what you do or not, I must respect his prior claim on you."

"His claim? Do you forget that I rule here?" she snapped. "You are my servant, and you will serve me as I wish. I want you to pleasure me. *Now.*"

"I have not yet given you my oath," Leeds said. "Even if I had, I would still be permitted the right to refuse. So I must again respectfully decline, my lady."

Jayr no longer had the stomach to keep pressing him,

and the regret in his eyes made her retreat to Byrne's chair by the hearth. "Very well. You may go."

Leeds came and crouched down before her. "Whatever happened between you and Lord Byrne has obviously upset you. Do you wish to talk about it?"

She stared at him. "You would console me, after what I just did to you?"

"You have paid me an enormous compliment." He smiled a little. "And you frightened the wits out of me, but now I think that was your intention all along, wasn't it?"

She groaned and covered her eyes with one hand. "I am a wretched actress."

"I beg to differ. You had me utterly convinced." He sat back on his heels. "At least until you ordered me to kiss you. Kyn ladies who enjoy using mortal males for sex are rather more direct about how their desires should be serviced."

She dropped her hand. "You have served such a lady?"

"I was not the one she used," he said, bowing his head, "but yes."

"Forgive me, Devan." She might as well tell him everything. "It was suggested that you might have some romantic feeling for me. I did not believe it, but . . ."

"You had to be sure." He nodded and stood. "I think this must be my fault. I was raised in a small and very intimate household, and our lord treated me and all the mortals under his rule with great care and concern. Of all that I have lost since the Brethren took my Kyn family from me, it is that affection that I miss most. Perhaps unconsciously I have been seeking the same from you, and I apologize for it."

She reached out and took hold of his hand. "You have it already, Devan. If it still pleases you to serve such an inconstant mistress, I would ask for no one else."

"We have two more weeks to sort this out." He looked uncertain. "Should I speak to Lord Byrne, and explain myself to him?"

"No, let me deal with Aedan. Now that you have passed this damned test of his, he will come round." She stood. "You should have the rest of the night for yourself. Go and spend it doing whatever you please. And thank you for not taking offense."

"You are very kind, my lady." He bowed. "I will not forget this."

Farlae waited until Jayr left the study before he moved the ceiling panel back into place, closing the gap he'd used to watch her with Leeds. Silently he rolled over and stared at the top of the narrow crawl space. He was still holding his dagger, he discovered, which he slipped back into his forearm sheath. He would have to report the incident to Byrne, but that was better than slitting the mortal's throat for daring to touch the suzeraina.

Farlae had known Jayr was putting on a performance from the moment she spoke of Rainer. Their suzeraina had endless affection for the great hulking fool; she alone could tolerate his nonsense better than anyone. She was also excessively protective of him.

Of us both, Farlae had to admit. While most of the warriors pretended not to notice their relationship, and Byrne had merely tolerated it, Jayr had shown her approval openly. Part of the renovations she had ordered was to create new quarters for them both away from the garrison; when construction was finished, they would have their own suite to share.

If Rain ever bothers to speak to me again. Farlae didn't know why his lover had been so pointedly avoiding him, but after the night's work was done, he intended to find out.

He left the crawl space to track the mortal, who had returned to his chambers. Farlae had already searched them several times in hopes of finding proof of his duplicity, but had found nothing but a few dull letters from another *tresora* in service.

Farlae moved past the mortal's chamber and down the hall to the monitoring post he had arranged in one of the unused storage areas. By concealing a pair of video cameras, one in the air vent and another in a wall cache, Farlae was able to see every part of the room on a remote terminal. He sat down before it and switched on the monitor, which brought up twin images from the cameras, which showed the mortal pacing about his room in an agitated fashion, his hands fisted and his expression grim.

"Ah, you were not expecting to be tested, were you, human?" Farlae settled back in his chair. "They are on to you, Devan, as am I."

On the screen Leeds stopped beside the bed, sitting down on it and propping his head in his hands. When he lifted his face a minute later, Farlae saw he was composed again, but then he nearly fell off his chair as the mortal tore open the front of his trousers.

"Well, now." He grinned as Leeds shoved his clothing out of the way and exposed the swollen shaft of his erect cock. "What a lovely lad you have there. Will you give me a show, then?"

As if he heard him, Leeds gripped his shaft with an unsteady hand and began to pump it rhythmically.

Farlae turned on the audio feed, which allowed him to hear what the mortal was muttering.

"—pleasure you," Leeds muttered, his fist stroking up and down his shaft. "Pleasure me first. However I wanted to be fucked."

Perversely aroused by the mortal's crisp, polite voice uttering such obscenities, Farlae reached for the buttons securing his own trousers and released them, easing his rigid penis out of the opening and wrapping the broad head in a handkerchief. "Yes, that's it. Tell me all about it, darling."

"Kiss you, indeed," Leeds murmured, his hand stroking steadily. "I'd have you bound by wrist and ankle, on your knees in front of me. I'd take your pretty hair in my fist and shove my cock in that bloody gorgeous mouth of yours. You'd whimper as I fucked myself in and out of your lips."

Farlae's eyelids drooped as he imagined the same, Leeds on his knees in front of him, his hands chained behind his back, his mouth open and wet. But the mortal's face quickly blurred in his mind, broadening into one dearly loved, as open and unpretentious as a summer's day.

"Jayr," Farlae heard Leeds panting, and squeezed his cock as he answered with, "Rain."

The mortal took only another few minutes to bring himself off, and Farlae followed him, jerking as his body spasmed. He closed his eyes, letting the solitary pleasure ease to a sullen glow as he imagined kissing his seed from

Rain's lips. For all his talk of eventual damnation, his lover was as generous and passionate in bed as he was ridiculous and foolhardy out of it. After so many centuries of being together, Farlae had expected their mutual desire to cool, but if anything, it had grown more intense.

I will tell him that I love him, Farlae thought, *that he is my sygkenis and I will have no other. And if it can be done, I will marry him.*

The slam of a door startled him out of his reverie, and when Farlae glanced at the terminal, he saw Leeds's room was empty again.

"God rot you," he swore as he wiped himself with the handkerchief and buttoned up his trousers. "You'll not spend another night under this roof, you randy little bastard."

Farlae switched off the terminal and left the storage room, tracking the mortal's scent through the corridors and out into the gardens. There he stayed in the shadows as he caught up with Leeds, who moved with purpose toward the potting shed.

Cursing himself for not thinking of searching the grounds, Farlae slipped around to the side window, where he watched Leeds unearth a plastic-wrapped satellite phone from a pot of soil.

Now I have you for certain, you fucking traitor. Farlae watched and listened as the mortal punched in a long string of numbers and began speaking in rapid Italian.

"I believe I have been compromised," Leeds said. "I must move on to the next phase ahead of schedule." As he listened, his shoulders stiffened. "Yes, I will kill her myself. I will contact you as soon as it is done."

Jayr. Farlae drew his dagger, and moved around the shed to wait for Leeds to emerge.

Shortly after midnight Harlech burst into Jayr's study.

"Captain?" She smelled the blood on his hands before she saw it, and jumped to her feet. "How are you injured?"

"It is not my blood, my lady." He glanced over his shoulder. "We've a man down. Would you come, please?"

She hurried out after him, and followed him down to the end of the corridor. Three warriors with blades drawn stood guard as a fourth crouched over a blood-soaked body on the floor.

"One of the household patrols found him here," Harlech told her as Jayr knelt down beside the body. "From the trail he left on the stones, he must have crawled in from the gardens." He produced a dagger. "We found this lodged in his chest."

"You have given him blood?" When Harlech nodded, she leaned over, brushing the hair back from the still face. "Can you hear me?" When he didn't stir, she pressed her hands to his chest, finding no pulse. She concentrated, searching with her Kyn senses for any spark of life left in him, but only when she was about to give up did she find it. "He is still alive. Harlech, we will need a litter to carry him to the infirmary."

"Yes, my lady." He ran off.

A shadow fell across the stone, and Jayr looked up, feeling an intense relief. "Devan, thank God."

"I heard the commotion." He knelt down to look at the wound, which he examined closely. "My lady, this was no accident. This man was stabbed with copper. Who is he?"

"This is Farlae." Despair swamped her as she rested her hand over his silent heart. "He is our wardrobe keeper."

Chapter 11

The smell of honey made Alys frown, as did the warmth enveloping her. The bottom of the pit was cold. She should be freezing.

"You're awake."

She opened her eyes to see Beau standing beside her in the dark, a tray in his hands. "What time is it? Why are you here?"

"It is a little after six, and I sleep here." He reached over and switched on a lantern. "How are you feeling?"

She sat up and rubbed the back of her head where there should have been a bump—and there wasn't. "We're back at the cloister." As he set the tray of tea and food on her lap, she gazed up at him. "I was in the bottom of that borrow pit. You left me there."

"I'm not sure what you mean," he said. "I found you wandering about the native village just after sunrise this morning. You were sleepwalking again."

And he was lying to her. Again. "I was?"

He nodded. "You must have had another nightmare. You were in a pit, you said?"

In the pit where he had done terribly intimate things to her, as he well knew, Alys thought. "Yes, I was." She didn't have to try to sound muddled; she was completely dumbfounded. "I fell into it and you came to rescue me."

He smiled and poured a cup of tea for her. "How did I do that? Was it like that *Raiders* movie you spoke of, with all the snakes?"

"I don't remember any snakes." He was joking about it now. She wanted to hit him. "I saw you jump straight up in the air, and then . . . I must have blacked out." To keep from screaming, she took a sip of the tea, which he'd laced liberally with honey. *To cover the taste of the drugs?* She set down the cup. "It was a very vivid dream."

"It sounds as if it was." He nodded at the tray. "That's the last of the bread and eggs. I'll make a trip into the city for more food supplies."

"I'll go with you." She forced a smile. "I have some things I need to do, too."

After he went to take stock of what they would need, Alys dumped the tea he had made for her down the shower drain, and stuck the food in a self-sealing bag under her mattress. In the process she remembered the back injury she'd sustained, and reached back to feel for the bandage.

She wasn't bandaged or wounded, Alys discovered, and wavered for a moment. She had fallen into a very deep pit and blacked out. Concussions had a way of distorting memories. *Is he telling the truth? Was it all a nightmare?* She felt along her back again, this time more carefully, and felt a faint, irregular scar. She took the hand mirror from her backpack and held it, turning her head and positioning it so she could see the spot. She did have a scar, a brand-new one that had not been there yesterday. Somehow she had healed overnight.

No, he did something to me.

She remembered the strange heat of the antiseptic he'd used on her. If it had actually been antiseptic from the first aid kit, it should have stung; she knew because she'd used it several times herself on the cuts and scrapes she acquired while working the dig. And while she'd never had a problem recovering quickly from any wound, no one could spontaneously heal. . . .

Alys went to the trunk where she kept her books, and searched through them until she found the last birthday gift Robert had sent her, a memoir written by an ex–Catholic priest who among wild fantasies had claimed he'd discovered a second, secret society within the ranks of the Knights Templar. The author, an octogenarian whom the academic community had always dismissed as a madman, had insisted he'd even been attacked by members of the secret sect of Templars, who he claimed were not only immortal but also vampires. He'd prevented them from drinking his blood by hurling holy water at them.

She flipped through the chapters, skimming until she found the section on the evidence the priest had gathered about the sect he referred to as the "dark kyn," and began reading.

Those who are damned for eternity will be comely of appearance, the men strong and handsome, the women delicate and lovely. They exude the precious scent of God's gift of torment, that of flowers, but it is a lie to lure and trap their unsuspecting

victims. They will partake of neither food nor drink
but wine. When brought into the light of heaven
they will shield their eyes and grow agitated; if left
in shelter they will sleep without breath or movement. They have knowledge of the black arts and
wield these against their victims, each with their
own spell to create confusion of the senses and to
enslave with but a few words. Few can resist their
murmurings and touches. They fornicate freely and
respect not the bonds of marriage or betrothal.
Nothing may cut their flesh but copper, which
burns them like fire. They heal from any wound,
but thanks be to God may be dispatched back to
Hell by beheading.

Alys closed the book and sat back against the side of
her bed, building almost helplessly a construct that duplicated the priest's claims: *Strong and handsome. Smells
wonderful. Avoids food. Only awake at night. He has every intern in love with him. He has* me *in love with him.*

She shoved the book back into the trunk and slammed
the lid down. Love wasn't real, and neither were the
imaginings of a disturbed mind. The priest had died
more than a hundred years ago, committing suicide
shortly after the publication of his wretched book. She
could build another, completely logical construct to explain away the similarities. Beau had food allergies. He
was charming. Hylord had insisted they work at night.

Beauregard York was not a vampire.

*Last night I saw him jump out of the pit, just after he
made me orgasm. But before that, he almost bit me.* Alys
reached for her shoulder, and felt a tender spot. With

trembling fingers she pushed back her collar, and saw two shallow scratches surrounded by a fading bruise. Scratches that hadn't been there yesterday. Scratches from two identical sharp objects scraping against her skin . . .

Alys retrieved her laptop and booted it up, watching the stairs as she ran several searches on Google and MapQuest. It would take hours, and if she was wrong, Beau would be furious with her, but nothing else would suffice. And if she was right, she needed incontrovertible proof with which to confront him.

She dressed and prepped her backpack before leaving the cloister, and found Beau stacking equipment cases in the church. "You don't have to do that. We'll only be a few hours."

He gave her an odd look. "It's no trouble. You're ready to leave? Let me get my jacket."

When Beau returned from the cloister, she shouldered her backpack and took out her keys. "We'll take the van; it has more room in the back. Would you like to drive?"

"That would not be wise. The rental agency will have insured only you," he chided. "If you're not feeling well enough to drive, perhaps you should stay here."

"I'm completely recovered, thank you." He had a rational excuse for everything he couldn't do, she thought. Of course he thought she'd never seen the two-week-old driver's license in his wallet. "Let's go."

On the way to the city Beau turned on the radio, scanning the channels until he found the local classical music station. A dark and dramatic cello concerto filled up the silence between them.

"I liked that," he said after the final, stark notes of the piece drifted into silence. "It sounded like a storm brewing."

"Do you know the composer?" She glanced at him. "She's a South Korean with a very memorable name."

"What is it?"

"Unsuk Chin."

"You're jest—joking."

He'd nearly said "jesting" instead of "joking": another of his verbal slips. "You can Google her if you like. What sort of computer do you use at home?"

"Nothing special," he said, turning his head to look at the scenery. "A laptop, like yours."

"Is it Mac, HP, Texas Instruments?" she persisted.

"Texas Instruments."

Who sold their laptop product line to Acer back in 'ninety-seven. Alys was almost beginning to enjoy herself. "So you like vintage tech."

"Like you, I am very fond of old things." He nodded at the windshield. "There is an excellent market on the next block, to the right."

"I thought we'd stop and get something to eat first. Charles told me about this place near here called Hoolihan's. Great food, and live music, too."

"That sounds interesting," Beau said, shifting around to face her. "But you just ate a full meal back at camp."

Alys hoped her stomach wouldn't give her away by growling. "I was thinking about you. You haven't eaten anything yet."

"I did, just before you woke," he said through his teeth. "But I appreciate your concern."

No, you don't. Alys made a turn into the grocery

store's side lot and parked the van. She was tempted to leave the keys in the ignition, but Beau was watching her too closely now.

"We'll need a shopping cart." As she climbed out, she nodded toward a row of them sitting in a return slot several cars down. "Would you mind getting one for me? I need to use the ladies' room. I'll meet you over in the produce section."

She breezed inside the store, heading directly to the restroom sign, glancing back to see Beau pushing a cart in through the doors. As soon as she was out of his sight, she changed direction, walking over several aisles and doubling back. At the end of the aisle she saw a clerk and hurried up to him.

"Excuse me," she said. "Is there another exit other than one at front of this building? There's a man who followed me in from the parking lot, and he's acting a little creepy."

"Sure, you can go out through the liquor store." He pointed to a pair of sliding doors. "They have their own entrance. If this guy's really bothering you, my manager can call the cops."

"No, that's okay. I only need to get away from him." She smiled and hurried toward the sliding doors.

Back outside in the parking lot, Alys ran to the van, fumbling her keys out of her pocket and nearly dropping them twice before she got the engine started. Throwing the van into reverse, she backed out, turning her head to see Beau standing just outside the front entrance.

"Now let's see you follow me, smart guy." She sped off.

Alys drove to the first address she'd written down in her notebook, a busy hotel near the convention center, and parked the van in the visitors' lot. Once she'd locked it up, she hurried over to the long line of taxis waiting by the main lobby.

"Hi," she said to the driver of the first cab she reached. "My rental broke down and I need to get back to my hotel to arrange to have it towed. Can you take me to the Neptune resort?"

"No problem, lady. Hop in."

She climbed in the back and hunched down as far as she could, waiting until they were on the road again before she sat up. "You know, I think it would be better if I go to the place I rented it." She read the address to him from her notebook. "That way I can get a replacement car tonight."

"Whatever you say." The driver made a neat U-turn and headed in the opposite direction.

Once he'd dropped her off at the rental agency, Alys walked past the building out to the bus stop on the corner, where she waited for five tense minutes before the resort shuttle arrived. It was crowded with tourists returning from dinner, so she had to stand, but there were enough people packed around her to effectively block her from the windows.

She got off the resort shuttle at its first stop, taking a second to a satellite hotel, and then a third directly to a theme park, where she rode the tram to the ticket booths.

"You do know that we close in two hours, ma'am," the girl in the booth warned her as she printed out her ticket.

"I know. I can't help myself. I love"—she glanced up at the park's sign—"Pirate World." She paid for the ticket with her credit card. "Are any of your restaurants still serving dinner?"

"The Jolly Roger Grill stays open until the park closes. It's located on the upper deck of the *Flying Dutchman*." She handed Alys a map of the park with the location circled.

"Thank you."

As she walked into the park, Alys couldn't shake the feeling that she was being followed, although she saw no one whenever she turned back to look.

A man jumped out in front of her, making her stumble backward until she saw he was in costume.

"Take your picture with Blackbeard, my pretty?" He lifted the camera hanging around his neck, tugged his fake beard out from under the strap. "It'll only cost ye twenty doubloons."

"I was wrong." Alys went around him. "I hate Pirate World."

An enormous man-made lake formed the center of the park, and held more than a dozen reproduction pirate ships. Some appeared to be stages for live performances, while others housed gift shops, boutiques, and snack bars. Visitors walked back and forth to the vessels across wide wooden bridges labeled on the map as "planks."

"Walking the plank. Of course." Alys stuffed the map into her jacket and started across the bridge that led to the *Flying Dutchman*. High guardrails kept anyone who might have slipped or stumbled from falling into the lake, but the creaking, swaying wood of the bridge made Alys quicken her step.

Two men walking even faster brushed past her, one going to the rail to look over the side. The other slowed and turned around, his dark eyes measuring her as he blocked her path.

"Excuse me." When he didn't move, Alys gestured past him. "I'm going over there."

"You are Dr. Stuart?" he asked, his thick accent mangling her name.

"Yes." She took a step back. "How do you know my name?"

He turned his head and said something in Italian to his companion, who nodded. "Where are the jewels?"

"What jewels? I don't know what you mean. How did you find me here?" Her eyes widened as he produced a gun. "You're going to shoot me? In a theme park?"

"Tell us where the jewels are, and we let you go," he offered.

"I don't have any jewels. All I have"—she fumbled at her neck for her cross—"is this. It's gold, and there's a little gem in it. Here, you can have it." She reached back for the catch.

The other man came at her and seized her by the arm and throat. "Where are they?"

Alys struggled, choking under his brutal grip and then writhing as he thrust her back against the top of the railing.

"Where?" the man shouted, throttling her.

She shook her head, and then brought up her feet and used them to shove him away, pushing herself over the railing. She grabbed at it, desperately trying to hold on, but her fingers slipped and then she was falling.

Dropping into the pit last night had been a quick and petrifying business; falling into the cold, dark water of the lake seemed to take an eternity. Alys felt herself floating, feather-soft, on a cool wind that curled around her, holding her in a gentle embrace. She turned over, wanting to see what had her, and caught her breath as the water rushed up toward her face.

A few inches above its icy surface her body came to a stop and hung there.

She frowned at the distorted reflection of her features, unable to comprehend them. Nothing was holding her up; she hadn't landed on anything. And now she was sliding sideways, parallel to the lake, tugged toward the embankment as if someone was reeling her in like a hooked fish.

Not someone, Alys saw as she turned her head and made out the furious features of the man standing at the lake's edge. *Beau.*

A crowd was heading toward him, led by a group of security guards with flashlights. Beau turned his head to glance at them before he met Alys's gaze. "Hold your breath."

The force pulling at her disappeared, and she plunged into the freezing water. Flailing until she found the bottom with her feet and was able to push herself upright, Alys surfaced. She would have swum toward the bank, but Beau was right there, water streaming from him as he gathered her into his arms and began wading out with her.

Alys looked over at the growing crowd waiting for them, and finally understood. "You couldn't let them see."

"Say nothing," he ordered her. "You're cold and in shock. I will do the talking."

Alys curled up, hiding her face against him. "All right."

By the time he stepped out of the water with her, Alys didn't have to pretend to shiver, although it was difficult to remain silent as Beau spoke to the security guards.

"There were two men up on the walkway," he said as he carried her away from the lake. "They assaulted my wife and threw her over the side into the water. I want them arrested."

"Staff members on the ships saw the entire thing, sir," one of the guards said. "We're trying to find the men now, but they seem to have disappeared."

"They meant to kill her." Beau glared at him. "Try harder."

A short, stout man in a sober business suit appeared with a blanket, and handed it to Beau as he set Alys on her feet. "I'm Louis Taylor, the park manager. On behalf of Pirate World, sir, I would like to apologize for this terrible accident. We will of course refund your tickets entirely."

"You'll do better than that, Mr. Taylor," Beau said. "You have a hotel on the grounds?"

"Three, actually," the manager said. "Uh, the police will be here shortly, and they'll need statements from both of you—"

The air turned darkly sweet as Beau leaned close to him. "My lady needs a hot bath and a place to rest. You will take us to the finest suite you have. Now."

"Of course, sir," Taylor said, almost slurring the words. "This way."

The man led them to a golf cart, which he used to drive them to a large contemporary resort. Less than five minutes later Beau carried Alys into a luxurious guest suite, and took her directly into the bathroom.

He turned on the taps in the big bathtub, testing the water and then turning to her. "Can you undress yourself? I must finish dealing with this fool."

She nodded.

"Call out if you need me." He touched her cheek before he left her.

Alys went to the door and opened it, watching Beau as he issued orders to the park manager, who nodded so often he resembled a life-size bobblehead doll. Beau instructed him to have food and wine delivered to the suite, and issued orders for them not to be disturbed, which didn't seem as outrageous as his final command.

"You will tell the police that we left the park before you were able to obtain our names," Beau told him. "Where are the men who did this to her?"

"Our security team was unable to find them, sir." Taylor sounded heartbroken. "I could go and search the park personally, if you'd like."

"No, they're gone by now." Beau made a dismissive gesture. "That will be all."

Alys backed away from the door and started slowly working her way out of her sodden clothes. She wondered whether she was in shock; she felt completely numb. What Beau had done was contrary to the laws of science, of physics. He possessed some sort of superhuman power that could cancel out gravity. She'd heard of psychics who could make spoons bend and tennis balls roll spontaneously, but over the years nearly all of them had been debunked as tricksters.

This had been no trick, no scam. Nothing on this earth could explain what had happened to her. Nor could

Beau reasonably explain how he'd tracked her to the park, or how he'd compelled Taylor to follow his orders.

He won't have any explanations this time.

Alys should have felt a sense of triumph, but oddly all she wanted to do now was protect him. If Beau's abilities were made public, he would become the most hunted man in the world. That was why he never confided in her or anyone about his powers—he couldn't.

Alys grabbed the complimentary robe hanging from the back of the bathroom door and pulled it on before she stepped out into the suite. Beau had taken off his shirt and was standing at the window looking down, the lamplight gleaming on his bare back. For the first time Alys could see a distinctive tattoo that arced across his spine.

It was the symbol of the body art that made Alys's heart constrict. Someone had tattooed him with the twenty-fourth letter of the Greek alphabet, the universal symbol for the last of anything. She knew every inch of his ink, from the stylized curve enclosing three short, vertical lines to the scrolled embellishments that wove around it like writhing snakes.

Omega. The end.

Chapter 12

"Where did you get that tattoo?"

Beau closed the curtains and turned to Alys, whose face was so pale all her freckles stood out like tiny bruises. "I don't know. I've had it since I was an infant." She still smelled of the park's lake water. "Why haven't you bathed?"

"Your parents tattooed you, didn't they?" When he nodded, her voice began to shake. "And they're dead, and you're an orphan."

"Yes, my parents are dead. I cannot say who gave me the tattoo; likely it was my mother." He started toward her, halting only when she held up her palm. "Alys?"

"You have to see this." She turned around, shrugging off the robe and displaying an omega tattoo identical to his own.

Suddenly he understood. "No."

She pulled the robe back in place and faced him. "My parents are dead. I have violet-brown eyes, like you." She raised her left hand. "A crooked middle finger, like yours. I can do things that other people, normal people, can't

do. Just like you." She covered her face with one hand
and rushed back into the bathroom.

Beau heard her locking herself in and went to the
door. "Calm down, love. It isn't what you think."

"It is *exactly* what I think." She sobbed the words.
"We have the same tattoo, the same eyes, the same hand.
What else could it be?"

He rested his brow against the door. "This was done
to me a very long time ago. You cannot be the child of
my parents. I am sure of it."

"I have to take a bath," she said dully over the sound
of water splashing.

At the same time, someone knocked on the door to
the suite. "We'll talk more after you've bathed." Beau
went to answer the door, and found a waiter with a large
service cart. "What the bloody hell do you want?"

"Mr. Taylor sends this with his compliments," the
waiter said, lifting the linen covering the cart to reveal
plates of food, glasses, and a bottle of wine.

Beau shed enough scent to make the mortal's eyes
darken. "Leave it here. Do not disturb us again. Forget
me."

"Leave. Do not disturb. Forget." The man bobbed his
head and walked back to the elevators.

Beau pushed the cart inside, securing the door and
then pacing the length of the room as he waited for Alys
to emerge from the bath. A short time later she did, the
white robe once more shrouding her slender body.

"They sent food for us." The paleness of her face
made his heart ache. "Come and eat something."

"I'm not hungry." Alys went to the phone. "I'll call
downstairs and get another room."

Beau grabbed the receiver from her hand and slammed it down. "You are not my sister."

"Don't. Please." She turned away from him, hugging herself with her arms as she fled to the opposite side of the suite. "It's horrible that this happened between us, but we didn't know. Now that we do, you can't—you and I can never—"

He seized her with his ability, turning her around and lifting her off her feet as he pulled her through the air to him.

"I was born in the thirteenth century, and when I became a man, I took vows as a Poor Fellow-Soldier of Christ and the Temple of Solomon." When she reached him, he held her suspended in the air before him. "After the Crusades, I came home to England, where I died of plague. Three days later I rose from my grave to live again as a blood-drinker. I have walked the night for seven centuries, love." Gently he lowered her to the floor. "I am all these things, but I am not your brother."

"I want to believe you." Her expression clouded. "I know you have an extraordinary power; you've demonstrated it twice now."

"Three times," he corrected. "I used it to keep you from falling down the steps in the cloister. Why won't you believe the rest of what I've told you?"

"I can't." She clutched at the front of her robe. "You have to understand—I'm a scientist, Beauregard—"

"Beaumaris. My true name is Beaumaris."

"All right." She looked miserable. "Beaumaris, you are an amazing man. You've also been lying to me since we met. As I said, I'm a scientist. I deal in facts, not fantasies. Human beings can't live for centuries. Having the plague doesn't make you rise from the grave or drink blood or give you eternal life. You have a tremendous gift, and I can't explain how you have it, but it doesn't make you an immortal."

She didn't believe him at all. Beau was speechless.

"We can be tested and find out if we're siblings." The wrenching sadness in her voice made it clear that she still thought they were. "Perhaps we're related more distantly; I know cousins sometimes share physical characteristics. The rest of it, well, you don't have to lie to me anymore. I've read about the dark kyn, but they're just stories made up by a mentally ill priest."

She thinks I am lying. Or mad. "You will want proof."

"You can't prove . . . I mean, that's not necessary." She reached out and touched his arm. "I'm sorry. Honestly, I'm not making fun of you. You saved my life tonight. I'll always be grateful."

Grateful. She was bloody grateful. *Not for long.* "Come with me."

Alys didn't resist as he dragged her over to the room service cart. When he picked up the serrated knife from the tray, she reached for it. "Please don't—"

He held out his forearm. "My kind are very hard to hurt, and nearly impossible to kill. Behold." He thrust the knife against his arm. The blade snapped off and fell to the floor. He held up the broken handle. "When we are strong, as I am, steel cannot cut through our flesh."

Doubt flickered for a moment over her face. "Did you use your power to snap the blade?"

He bent down and drew the dagger from the sheath in his boot and handed it to her. "Examine it. Assure yourself it is not a fake."

Alys heaved a sigh before she inspected the blade. "It's a real knife, and the metal looks like copper."

"It is copper, the only metal that can hurt us." Beau took the dagger from her and used it to slash his wrist.

"Oh, my God." Alys grabbed his arm. "What have you done? Are you crazy?"

Beau stopped her from using her robe to stanch the wound. "Watch." After a few moments the blood stopped flowing, and then disappeared as the edges of the slash sealed together. "A mortal cannot heal so fast. Examine it for yourself."

She touched his arm just as the last mark of the wound vanished, and gazed up at him. "I can't explain this, any more than I can substantiate your kinetic power. I wish I could. But it's not proof that you're some kind of immortal vampire who's been alive since the Dark Ages." She touched her shoulder. "Maybe you believe you are, and you behave as if you are, but there are no such things as vampires."

There was nothing left for Beau to do but demonstrate in the most basic way what he was.

He handed her his dagger again. "Prick your finger on the tip. Not deeply, only to draw a drop of blood." When she hesitated, he added, "You said you were grateful to me. I did save your life, Alys. This is what I want in return."

Alys looked sadly at the blade before she pressed her finger to the point. She showed him the drop of blood that welled from the tiny wound. "Anyone can drink blood, Beaumaris. Even me."

He took hold of her wrist, bringing her fingers up to his face and breathing her in. He opened his mouth, tilting his head back so she could see his *dents acérées* stretch out into his mouth.

He lowered his chin. "Can you do that?"

Alys stared at him blankly. "You grew fangs."

"Aye." Now that he had told her all, he saw no reason to mask his natural speech. "The scent of mortal blood sends us into our predatory state. My eyes change as well."

"Your pupils are constricting." She moved closer, her hands cradling his face as she watched. "Like a cat's." She pressed her fingers to his mouth. "May I?"

"Have a care. They're sharper than my blade." Beau parted his lips for her, and stood silent as she traced the shape of his *dents acérées*. The touch sent a new surge of lust through him, and when he groaned, she snatched her hand away. "It does not hurt me." He brought her fingers back to his mouth. "It is a different kind of torment."

She glanced down and up again. "It arouses you."

"Not always. The taste of blood is a pleasure, as is feeding on it, but *you* arouse me." He took her in his arms. "So, then. Have I convinced you at last?"

Slowly Alys nodded. "I don't know what to say to you. You are a vampire. A real, living vampire." She uttered a short laugh. "With food allergies."

"We cannot eat food. Any food," he admitted. "But, Alys, we are *vrykolakas*, not vampires. Sunlight does not turn us to ashes, nor must we sleep in coffins or fear the cross. Like the vampires of folklore we do not age, and we heal instantly from almost any wound, but we are not evil."

She smiled. "You couldn't be evil if you tried."

"There is something more you should know about

me." Beau had never told a living soul about his origins; he'd spent seven lifetimes pretending they didn't exist. But no one had ever loved him before Alys, and she deserved nothing but the truth. "I was born in Jerusalem. The man who sired me came there on Crusade. I never knew him or his name, but I was told he was an Englishman." He had to say this now, this thing that he had never spoken aloud. "He met my mother in a brothel. She was a harlot. A Saracen harlot."

"We call them Muslims now." Her smile faltered. "How did you get to England from Jerusalem?"

"My mother gave me to a Templar. I was only a boy; I didn't understand that she was dying of consumption. He brought me to England and found a family to foster me."

"He didn't tell anyone about your mother," Alys guessed. "And neither did you."

"I didn't speak enough English to say more than 'yes' and 'no.' By the time I did, they believed what the Templar had told them: that my mother was Italian." He held up their hands, her flesh so pale against his. "That explained the color of my skin." He kissed the back of her hand. "I have never told anyone of this . . . but you."

"We all have secrets." Her eyes shimmered with tears. "When my guardian sent me away to school, I realized I wasn't like the other little girls. Their parents came to see them on weekends and holidays, but Robert never visited me. I was so lonely, but I was only seven years old. I didn't understand how busy he was, or even where he was. One Christmas I ran away from school and took a train to Paris. I walked to the address on Robert's checks from there, but it was a church, not a house or a business. The caretaker said he didn't know my guardian. A man drove past me while I was walking back to the station, and offered me a ride. It was raining, and I was wet and cold, so I got into his car. But he didn't take me to the train. He drove off the road into the woods."

Beau could imagine the rest. "You don't have to tell me any more of it, love."

"It's not what you think." She slipped away from him and sat down, staring at her clasped hands. "He told me what happens to little girls who run away—what he was going to do to me. I got out of the car and began walking toward the road. He came after me, but when he grabbed me, he tripped and fell down and he didn't move again. A few hours later the police found me walking on the road toward the train station. They told me the man was dead."

"What killed him?"

She met his gaze. "I did."

Beau's voice grew gentle. "Alys, you can't blame yourself for the death of a man who surely would have killed you. You were a child. It was an accident."

"When the man was saying all those terrible things, I heard another voice. It whispered to me inside my head, and told me to get out of the car." Alys knew how crazy she sounded but pressed on, determined to tell him all of it. "It showed me the rock sticking up from the ground, and the old root stretched across the road. It told me that if I took three steps to the left when the man reached me, that he would catch his foot on the root and fall, and hit his head. I didn't know it would kill him, but no one had bothered to explain death to me yet. I thought he was sleeping."

He came to her, drawing her into his arms and kissing the top of her head. "Perhaps God was looking out for you that day."

"God, if he even exists, doesn't tell runaway seven-year-olds how to kill someone. I didn't know whose voice was inside my head, but I've never forgotten it. And I never heard it again, until two weeks ago, in the bar at the Jade Palms." She looked up at him. "It was your voice, Beaumaris. Twenty years ago, when I ran away from school and was picked up by that monster, you saved me. You were the one I heard in my head. You told me how to kill him."

Beau scooped her up in his arms and carried her into the master bedroom, where he lowered her onto the bed and sat down beside her.

"I wish I had saved you." Beau tucked a piece of her hair behind her ear. "I would have gladly put an end to that monster myself. But I cannot speak to the mind of a mortal; no Kyn has such a gift. Nor was I in France twenty years ago. I never knew you as a child. The voice you heard that day did not come from me. I wish I could explain what happened to you, and why you believed it was me, but I cannot."

Alys put her hand on his. "He sounded exactly like you. Maybe I've convinced myself it was you because you're so good at rescuing me."

"I will never let anyone harm you again. Rest now." He leaned over to kiss her.

Alys looped her arms around his neck, holding him close when he would have drawn back. "You're not jumping out of here this time. I won't let you."

"You know what I am now, and what I can do to you."

Beau pushed aside the robe and traced the marks he had left on her shoulder. "We do not kill mortals; we try to live in peace with you. But we need your blood to survive."

She put her hand over his. "You wanted to feed on me last night. That's why you left me down in the pit. So you wouldn't."

"I cannot bespell you. I would have hurt you." Beau briefly explained how the Kyn used *l'attrait* to lure mortals as well as make feeding on them painless. "Some mortals can resist our influence for a time, but only a very few like you are completely immune to it."

"I'm not that immune." A sudden rush of self-consciousness made her cover her face with her hand. "I'm in love with you."

Beau brought her hand away. "You do not know what you say, Alys. What I did tonight . . . You owe me nothing."

"You saved my life tonight, and for that I am grateful." She leaned closer. "But it's not why I'm in love with you."

"I am not a mortal," he reminded her. "Even if I were, I am no one and nothing to be loved. I was born in a brothel to a whore. My very existence was so repulsive to my father that he never claimed me as his son. I have spent my life like a coward, hiding what I truly am from everyone."

"You aren't hiding it from me now." She took a deep breath and linked her arms around his neck. "You trusted me with the truth. Can't you trust in how I feel about you?"

Beau gave her a desperate look. "You told me that you don't believe in love, Alys."

"Five minutes ago I didn't believe you were one of the dark kyn." She pressed a shy kiss to the corner of his mouth. "I'm flexible. Would you like to find out how much?"

"If I stay," he warned, "it will be much more than a little touching and a few scratches."

"God, I hope so." She reached for the belt of the robe to untie it, and found his hands had already done it for her.

Beau parted the robe's edges by running one hand from her navel to the inner curves of her breasts, which he uncovered with two slow sweeps of his palms. "You should never hide these beauties."

"I sunburn easily, and I'd get arrested for indecent exposure, and oh, my." All the breath left her lungs as he lowered his head and brushed his mouth over her nipples. "What are you doing?"

"Saying hello to your ladies." He stretched out over her, cupping her mounds and watching as her flesh pebbled. "Shy things, they are." He met her gaze. "Like you."

He kept watching her face as he began using his mouth, sucking and licking at her, making the tingle from his touch spread and sink into a deep, swelling ache. His mouth made her nipples gleam, wet and dark pink, while the friction of his tongue sent shocks of excitement jolting through her abdomen that set off slow, deep flutters between her legs. Alys closed her eyes, unable to watch, and opened them again when she couldn't bear not to.

"I want to do that to you," she said, sliding her hands over the wide curves of his shoulders.

"Not yet, love." He moved up to kiss her mouth, his

fingers still exploring her like some delicate treasure, stroking and soothing her breasts, gliding over the curves and hollows of her belly. As Beau put his tongue in her mouth, he moved his hand between her legs, tasting her and penetrating her, and the feel of him at each end of her, pushing in and gliding out, set off a helpless, uncontrollable shaking.

"Not yet," he repeated, rolling onto his back and bringing her on top of him.

Alys wanted to explore him, but as soon as she caressed his nipples, she felt his power wrapping around her, lifting her up from his body, separating her legs and shifting her pelvis toward his parted lips. "You're cheating."

"Yes, I am." He looked up at her. "Open yourself for me. Show me what I've only touched in the dark."

Alys felt her cheeks redden; she'd never put herself on display for any partner. But this was Beau, and she wanted his mouth on any part of her, every part of her. She reached down, embarrassed and thrilled by her own touch as she parted her mons and felt his breath touch her wetness.

He grazed her with his lips, teasing her with little kisses until she groaned and shivered. "Do you want my tongue on you? Do you want to feel it inside?"

"Yes, please." She sounded nothing like herself, her voice low and her breath rushed, and when he covered her with his mouth and the first stroke of his tongue laved over the throbbing knot of her clit, she almost shrieked.

Beau worked at her with his mouth, delicately at first and then harder, his tongue lashing her and then pushing inside her, penetrating and curling and tormenting her. Alys felt herself go liquid as she writhed, so close to the pleasure it seemed to scald her from the inside out.

"Not yet," he said a third time, bringing her down and turning with her again, his big body blotting out the light, his lean hips brushing against the insides of her thighs. He brought her hand down to the thick, rigid length of his penis, wrapping her fingers around him as he rubbed the heavy dome of the head between her folds. She tried to urge him inside, trembling and whimpering, but he still held back.

"Look at me." When she did, he bent his head and pressed his lips once against hers. "You'll never sleep alone again, my beauty."

Alys could feel how much he needed her, his body coiled, his muscles rigid, but when he came into her, it was like being filled with music and laughter and sunlight. He didn't penetrate her; he poured into her, his shaft forging into her clenching wetness so smoothly and sweetly she felt tears of joy spill over her lashes. It felt so perfect, her arms and legs wrapped around him, his penis deep inside her, his mouth kissing the tears from her face, that Alys thought her heart would shatter.

Beau laced his fingers through hers, his eyes glowing a brilliant gold as he looked into her wet eyes. "Now, love."

Everything Alys knew about sex dwindled away as Beau made love to her, his body moving over her, inside her, driving into her with deep, steady rhythm. Something primal and wordless rose inside her, meeting each movement, returning each kiss, and Alys let it take her to him, her pleasure radiating from some nowhere inside herself, where now there was Beau, and he was so much a part of her she couldn't think of herself as Alys anymore. She was with him, surrounding him, caressing him, melting into him.

"Give yourself to me," he murmured against her lips as he went deeper, harder, driving into her now as she cried out his name and let the agonizing delight envelop her. "Yes, love, yes, come to me. Come all over me."

Alys saw the glitter of his fangs, and turned her head, urging his mouth to her flesh. When he pressed a kiss, she curled her fingers into his hair. "Take it. Take all of me."

When his teeth pierced her, she came again, her sex gripping his shaft convulsively, and as he drank from her he filled her, the hard jets of his cool semen flooding her hot sheath.

Beau lifted his mouth from her throat, holding her close and pushing his hand between them. He stroked her softly, playing with her, urging her to another climax before he shifted over onto his side, his hand cupping her bottom so they remained joined.

Alys drooped against him, elated and exhausted, the salt of her tears on her lips, the sound of his heart beating against her cheek. "Do you have another superpower that you forgot to mention to me?"

His chest rumbled with a low laugh. "In this I am just a man, love."

"Hmmm." She lifted her head. "I'll have to do more research." She dropped her head. "In a year or two, when I recover." She closed her eyes.

Chapter 13

Jayr's memory stretched back seven hundred years, to the June when she had run away from the English convent where she had been raised, and traveled to the village of Bannockburn. In search of her parents, she had arrived only a day before King Edward II and his army. Just before the invaders arrived to battle the rebellious Scots, Jayr was promptly dragged out of her room at the inn and shoved into the street.

As the army approached, she went to hammer frantically on every other door she saw, but no one would give her sanctuary. The moment she spoke, they spat and cursed at her; one old boot maker tried to clout her with his gnarled fist. They said ugly things to her in their beautiful language, shouting through tears, glaring through eyes bright with terror. And then the doors would slam, and the heavy bolts inside would fall, and she would trudge on to the next place.

She was an English girl alone in a Scottish town, and in the fields beyond it, her people were killing theirs. There was no haven in these hearts or homes for the likes of her. She could not even buy it, for as soon as word came that the Scots had prevailed over the English, the innkeeper and his wife had taken from her the last of her coin before tossing her out into the street.

Jayr left the town and crossed the marsh, making for the trees. A path of heather sprang up from the ground to guide her steps. It was June; she could spend a night in the woods and not freeze to death. In the morning she would find a church. The priest did not have to know that she had refused to take her vows and fled her convent to search for her parents. For all the poor souls on the battlefield, and the hatred that had sent them to die there, Jayr knew there was still love in the world, and in this place, she would find it. She had only to follow the heather back to the beginning.

"You're very brave."

Jayr whirled around to see a young girl in a dirty frock and pinafore sitting on a tree stump. "Who are you?" Her gaze shifted to the dazzling white creature in the girl's lap. "Where did you find that rabbit?"

"He found me." Carefully the girl placed the snowy animal on the ground. As it bounced away, it left prints made of frost on the grass. "I'm safe, for now. But you're not."

"You're American." Jayr peered at her. "How can you be here? Your country will not exist for another five hundred years."

The girl's eyes shifted up to the rapidly darkening sky. "We're not in Scotland anymore, Dorothy."

Jayr watched as frost spread out from the rabbit's tracks and raced across the ground. The lovely trail of heather wilted, the tiny purple flowers turning icy black.

She looked into the girl's eyes, innocent and jewellike, and recognized their lovely amethyst-gold color. "I know you."

"Not yet." As she spoke, the girl's cheeks flushed. "I am never going to be able to say those words again without blushing. We'll meet soon, my lady. I promise."

I am in the nightlands, and none of this is real. Jayr felt one fear fade and another take its place. "You came to tell me something."

The girl pointed past her at the town. "They thought you were their enemy. You sounded like one, and you looked like one, but you weren't. They didn't know you, or why you came here. Remember that, Jayr. It's the only thing that will save you."

Jayr started after the girl, but without warning, the earth shook beneath her feet, knocking her to the ground as a wide fissure opened. Green light poured out, forming itself into broad towers and solidifying into gray stone. Smoke filled the air as men shouted and arrows flew past Jayr's head.

"My lady." Harlech, his face covered in soot and his garments wet with blood and gore, pulled her up from the ground. "They have cut off the roads and set the moat on fire. They have spiked their rockets with copper—"

They both staggered as multiple explosions landed all around them, gouging huge pits in the ground and showering them with dirt and rock.

"We must flee," he shouted over the din.

Jayr peered through the smoke and saw a line of men dressed in black and carrying automatic weapons advancing toward the castle. "Who are they? Why are they attacking us?"

Byrne came out of the smoke, his limbs and face battered, his eyes filled with blood. "Traitors," he muttered, his voice flat as he lifted his battle-ax. "Die."

Jayr darted in front of Harlech. "Aedan, no."

He dropped his ax and seized her, shaking her until her teeth chattered. "Kill us all kill us all kill us all—"

Jayr drove her fist into his face as hard as she could, her knuckles crunching and her flesh splitting. The burning air stole the breath from her lungs as the smoke wrapped around her, blinding her, smothering her with its whiteness until she struck out again.

"I'm with you, lass." Byrne's hands, now gentle, pulled the cloth away from her face. "You're safe."

Jayr stopped struggling, amazed to find herself tangled in a blanket, and Aedan leaning over her. Behind him, Farlae lay pale and motionless in one of the infirmary beds.

"What in God's name . . ." She stopped as she smelled his blood and saw the condition of his face. "You're not hurt, too?"

"You've deadly aim, even in your sleep." The split in his lower lip disappeared as he pulled her close. "You scared the wits from me, screaming like that."

"I came to sit with Farlae, and I must have dozed off." She eased back and looked around the sickroom. "I was in the nightlands. There was a mortal girl, and a rabbit, and then the Realm was under siege. And you were, ah, not yourself."

"You mean, I went berserk. Glad I am you were but dreaming." He helped her up out of the chair. "Come, you must feed and rest now. Harlech and the men will keep watch over Farlae."

Jayr couldn't shrug off the dread she felt, even when she returned to her chamber with Aedan. She said as much to him, but he didn't seem concerned.

"'Twas but a nightmare, wife." He sat down by the fire to drink his bloodwine. "The Realm is safe, and so are we."

"What if we are not?" Like all Kyn, Jayr understood very little about the nightlands, but she never believed them to be merely a place of dreams. "What if the nightmare was sent to me as some manner of warning?"

"Mortals of this time do not siege castles," he assured her. "Unless you lower the ticket prices. Then they may surround us in hordes."

Annoyance surged inside her. "How can you make light of it?"

"How can you put faith in a fancy?" He went to the armoire they shared and took out one of her riding habits. "Forget it and come here. I will dress you, and we will take the horses for a long run, and forget this foolishness."

He thought she was a fool, did he?

"I think not." She brushed past him and retrieved her leathers. "I need to train."

"You'll burn your hair off again, and I prefer it long." He replaced the habit and turned, scowling when he saw she had used her talent to dress herself in a few seconds. "Jayr."

She went to her weapons case and removed her favorite sparring blade. "Since Harlech is looking after Farlae, I want you to drill the men tonight. Use the back pasture, and have them don full battle armor. Run them through all of the defense formations." When he didn't move, she glared at him. "Do you understand?"

"Aye, I've ears that still work." He folded his arms. "Would you like me to kiss your boots first, my lady?"

"You're my second, Aedan. Try to act like one." She stalked out of their chamber.

None of the men yet occupied the lists, and Jayr was glad of it. She needed to work off this maddening anger, and the fear lurking beneath it, before she did rip off someone's head. She doused herself liberally with water before she chose one of the straw-stuffed practice targets and began working through her forms. With each flash of her blade the effigy sprouted tufted gaps in its burlap, sagging lower and lower until the form toppled from the pole and collapsed at her feet.

Jayr kicked it. "Bloody useless."

"I fear that straw does not present much of a challenge for a blade-arm of your caliber, my lady." Leeds joined her and surveyed the ruined target. "Would you like me to summon one of your warriors?"

"No, they will be drilling tonight." She eyed him. "I am in a mood, Devan. 'Twould be best if you return to the keep."

"If that is your wish, of course, but I thought I might offer my services as a partner." He smiled at her reaction. "I cannot hope to give you much sport, my lady, but I am trained to spar, and I would appreciate the practice."

Jayr had never sparred with a mortal; she was too fast for even Beaumaris, who wielded the deadliest blade in the garrison. Byrne could never spar with anyone for fear of rousing his inner beast. On impulse she nodded, although she suspected he would need a lighter weapon. "You'll want rapiers, then?"

"If I may choose, my lady, I prefer a bastard blade."
He shrugged out of his jacket, draped it over a work-
bench, and rolled up his sleeves as he went to the sword
racks to choose. After going through a brief, economical
series of stretches to loosen his muscles, Leeds returned
and stepped up to the circle.

Jayr took the opposing position, and returned his salute. "You must tell me when you tire."

"If you will tell me when you grow bored." He stepped
into the circle as she did, raising his blade and moving
into the defensive form.

Jayr watched him as they crossed blades several times,
and saw that the *tresora* had not exaggerated his abilities.
"You trained with a Kyn master."

Leeds mirrored her movements. "Lord Marietto did
not separate his *tresori* from his warriors. Every mortal
who served him trained in the lists."

Now Jayr understood the scars, and felt ashamed of
herself for accepting Leeds's offer. "That must have
been painful."

"The Kyn understood we could not heal as they did.
We were never unduly harmed." He easily avoided her
next, halfhearted thrust. "Please don't hold back, my
lady."

"I fear I must." Jayr flashed around him, waiting until
he turned before she went on guard. "Else you would be
fighting a blur."

Leeds nodded, and for the first time attacked, working his jabs from left to right with focused, economical
moves. Jayr felt the surprising weight of his strength as
she parried and was forced to shuffle backward. Sweat
streaked the *tresora*'s face, but he did not relent.

Jayr used her speed to move beyond his reach. "You are tiring—" She stopped as he lunged, and brought up her blade without thinking, slashing his wrist and causing him to drop his weapon. "Damn me."

"It's nothing." He grasped his wrist, and grimaced as blood trickled through his fingers. "The match is yours, my lady."

Jayr drove her blade into the ground and went to him, taking hold of his arm. "Let me see it."

Leeds took away his hand, revealing a gash that nearly went to the bone. "I will pay a visit to the infirmary, and they will set it to rights."

"Stupid of me to react without thinking. I might have lopped off your hand. Forgive me, Devan." Jayr lifted her own wrist to her mouth, biting into it before she held the punctures over his wound. "No, don't move away. This will heal it."

Leeds gave her a strange look. "You would shed your blood for a mortal."

"For an ally, and a friend, yes. I will." On impulse she kissed his cheek.

"Friends, are we, now?"

Jayr looked over Leeds's shoulder to see Byrne standing just outside the circle. "We were sparring, and I was careless and wounded Devan. I'm healing the damage I did."

"Indeed." Byrne made a show of studying the *tresora*. "Yet I see no mark on his face."

"My lord, our lady was simply—"

"She is *my* lady, you fawning little ponce. Not yours." In a blink Byrne had the front of Leeds's shirt in his fist and used it to lift him to eye level. "You've used up your welcome here, English. Pack up your suits and your sniveling and be gone by sunset."

"Aedan. Put him down." For a moment Jayr thought her lover would ignore her, but after a long, ugly moment he lowered Leeds back to the ground. To Devan, she said, "Go inside now, and leave this to me."

The *tresora* smoothed down the front of his shirt with his uninjured hand before he bowed to her. "As you command, my lady." He walked past Byrne as if he were invisible.

"If you mean to persuade me to coddle your mortal pet, save your breath, my lady," Byrne told her. "He's naught but trouble and spite, and I'll not have him on my land another night."

"Your land? Your lady?" Jayr picked up her blade and sheathed it. "You forget, Aedan, you no longer rule here. This is *my jardin*, and you are *my* seneschal. As such, you have no say over my mortal, my territory, or me."

"You are my *sygkenis*, bonded to me. As my woman and my life companion, you are obliged to obey my wishes." He strode a few steps away before turning and coming back to her. "You were kissing him. *Kissing* that mewling bag of blood."

"I slipped while we were sparring, and nearly cut off his hand." She threw out her arms, so infuriated she shouted the rest. *"It meant nothing."*

"To you, aye, I believe that. I'd go mad if I didn't." He bent down to glare into her face. "But I saw the look on his face when you put your mouth on him. The daft prick imagines himself in love with you. Cannae you smell it on him? Or is it a new sport, seeing how oft you can make the sorry little bastard tilt his cods for you?"

Jayr slapped him. The crack of her palm against his face echoed around them, stabbing at her ears, sharp and terrible.

"For love of you, Aedan mac Byrne, I have never looked upon another man, *any* man, human or Kyn. Not since the day I gave my mortal life to save you." She watched the dark pink print of her hand fade from his tattooed cheek. "At first I thought this jealousy of yours amusing, even flattering. You have always been first with me, and I thought no one knew this better than you. But now I see how little you know me, that you would insult my love for you so easily."

He reached out to her. "Jayr—"

"I will not touch you or speak to you or look at you again until you apologize to Devan. Yes, Devan, who is staying on *my* land, and will be joining *my* household, and serving as *my tresora*." She strode off into the keep.

Beau slipped out of bed, leaning over to cover Alys's naked body with the sheets. "Are you sure you want water, and not wine?"

"Alcohol makes me throw up." She gave him a sleepy smile. "I'd rather do other things with my mouth tonight, if you don't mind."

He chuckled and went into the bath to fetch her water. As he filled the drinking glass in the sink, the glitter of gold caught his eye, and he shut off the tap and set the glass on the counter.

The chain of the necklace had been fashioned from very fine, tiny links, each twisted into the shape of an hourglass. From the chain hung a golden cross, as plain as the links were elaborate. The solidness of it felt heavy in Beau's hand as he lifted it and turned it to see the twinkle of the tiny gem set in the cross's center.

Green, like the eye of Yblis, the Evil One. His mother had taught him that. But Beau had ridden with the devil himself, and his eyes had been silver. . . .

The man in the robe rode through night, never stopping until sunrise. Whenever Beau had slumped against him from exhaustion, the man would tie him to his back with the rope-belt from his robe.

When the sky turned from black to gray, the man would find a shaded place, and set up his nomad's tent for Beau to eat and drink and sleep through the long, hot hours of the day. The robed man himself never ate or drank or slept; he would sit and watch the horizon, or he would take out the chains of gold he carried in his pouch. Chains upon which hung the devil's green eyes, captured in gold . . .

Beau closed his hand over Alys's cross as the blurry memory crystallized.

The day had dawned cold, and ice covered the land. When the man found a place for the tent, he had wrapped Beau in his robe, and built a small fire.

"Warm yourself," he told Beau, sitting on the other side of the flames in nothing more than a loincloth. "Soon we will cross the great waters, and then you will be home."

Huddled under the robe, Beau had felt the pouch filled with the devil's eyes against his hip. With frightened fingers he'd ripped it from the pocket within and cast it into the fire.

"What have you done?"

The man's cold voice made Beau's insides shrivel. "They are the eyes of the Yblis, the evil one."

"Foolish boy." The man reached into the fire, and plucked out the smoldering pouch. *"These are gifts I have made for my kin."*

Beau knew how hot the fire burned, and yet no marks did it leave on the man's cold flesh. *"Then you are the devil."*

"Perhaps I am." The man had smiled at him, and held up the three chains. *"I will tell you what these are. My eyes. Those who wear these, my blood kin, will forever be judged by them. If they are worthy, they will be granted special gifts. If they betray me, they will die miserable deaths. And when I grow too weary of this world, one of them shall be changed to take my place."*

Beau didn't understand the man's strange prophecy. *"What will you do to me?"*

"That has already been done." The man reached for his pack, and took out a wooden box. *"I have but to mark you, the last of my mortal seed, my third eye. My omega."*

"Beau?"

He opened his eyes to see Alys in the doorway, and looked down at the cross clutched tightly in his hand. He wanted to go to the nearest window to throw it out into the night, but instead made himself place it back on the counter.

Alys came to wind her arms around his waist. "I hope that ghost didn't follow us here. You look like you've just seen it." She glanced at the cross. "I'm really not religious. I only wear it because my guardian asked me to. Robert was very insistent about it, but I think he was Catholic."

Beau hugged her close. "Did he have gray eyes, your guardian?"

"No, they were brown, I think." She tipped her head back. "Robert is dead, so if the cross bothers you, I don't have to wear it anymore. I never really liked it. Why does it matter what color his eyes were?"

"Alys, I have seen this cross before, when I was a boy. I don't understand everything about it, but with your gift of making sense of things, you may be able to make sense of what I saw." He picked up the glass of water, and saw a flash of green in it as it magnified the glitter of the gem in her cross.

Water. Emeralds. Eternal youth. It seemed in that moment everything was within his grasp. But what did it mean?

Alys broke the spell by taking the glass from him and drinking from it. "Come back to bed and tell me."

It took some time for Beau to relate everything he remembered about the robed man from his childhood, and the journey they had taken from Jerusalem to England.

After describing how he had tried to destroy the crosses, he said, "I cannot remember any more of the journey from there until the day the priests delivered me to my foster family. But I remember my back still burned where the mark is now. I've always assumed my mother gave me the tattoo, but now I think the priest must have done it, that night by the fire, and made me forget."

"Or the trauma of having a man you thought was the devil hurt you made you suppress the memory," she suggested. "You were only a little boy." She shifted around to place a kiss on his spine.

"I have always wondered why the high lord chose me to protect you." He pulled her on top of him so he could stroke the silky line of her back. "We know that we bear the same mark. The cross you wear was made by the priest who took me from Jerusalem. And we have both come here to find the Emeralds of Eternity."

She frowned. "I'm looking for emeralds?"

Beau explained his mission to her. "Tremayne funded your project in hopes that you would find the emeralds for him, and sent me to take them from you when you did. I cannot say why he is so convinced you—or I—would find them."

Alys thought for a moment. "Were you one of the Templars who came there?"

"I was not, love. I never knew of the mission until the high lord gave me orders to join the project." Tremayne would have his head for revealing his schemes to a mortal, but Beau was determined to tell Alys everything. "Cristophe, the Kyn who guarded the emeralds—which I believe to be the same treasure that you seek—was a smith, and a mason. He abandoned the Templars and our kind to join a monastery in Aragon. When the order fell, he fled to the Spanish Main, and then to Florida. He has not been seen in these six hundred years since."

"So I was right." Alys wrapped her arms around herself as she grinned. "I knew it. I *knew* it." She eyed him. "It's possible that Cristophe came here to hide the emeralds. He fits the profile of the unnamed Templar in my research. But why bury them?"

"In my time there were no archaeologists digging up the earth, and none of my kind had yet come to the New World. Perhaps he thought they would be safe." He told her everything he knew about the emeralds, and added, "In truth I cannot say if they are blessed or cursed. What

I can tell you is that almost every mortal who has sought them has died."

Alys shook her head. "Jewels can't kill people. They're simply very pretty rocks. Since he is Kyn, Cristophe is still around, trying to protect their location. Wait." She propped herself up to study his face. "We have the same color eyes, and the same crooked finger. Both are recessive traits. Even if we were born seven hundred years apart, we could still be related."

Beau wrapped his arms around her. "You agreed that you are not my sister."

"No, but I could be one of your mortal descendants. A very distant . . ." She fell silent, and her expression blanked.

Beau cupped her face so he could kiss her mouth. "What do you see in that head of yours?"

"You never knew your father. Your mother sent for the robed man to take you to England. The robed man called you the last of his mortal seed. The crosses. His blood kin. Orphans. The tattoos. The emeralds." She repeated the phrases over and over in a monotone as she stared blindly at him.

Beau could almost hear the thoughts racing through her head. "Yes, love, that's it. Find the connections."

Alys's empty eyes fluttered and then refocused on his face as she smiled. "Out of the fourteen most apparent theoretical constructs, there is only one that maintains complete logical integrity."

He kissed her mouth. "Tell me."

"Cristophe was the robed man, and your biological father. He tattooed you to identify you as the last of his offspring for Tremayne. I am the last descendant of Cristophe's mortal family, and I was tattooed for the same reason. Tremayne identified us by our tattoos and sent us to find the emeralds, probably in hopes that Cristophe would not try to kill us, as we are the end of his immortal and mortal bloodlines. Cristophe is also not finished with us."

"Cristophe is still alive?"

Alys nodded solemnly. "He's the ghost at the mission."

Chapter 14

The sound of a beloved voice tugged at Farlae's ears, luring him out of the haze of pain.

"Harlech said I should talk to you," Rainer was saying. "He is watching me all the time now. If not for his penchant for Viviana, I should be worried."

Farlae was puzzled. The last thing he remembered was going to speak with Jayr about . . . something. Costumes for the spring schedule, probably. With more than five hundred to make, he and his ladies would be cutting and fitting and sewing up until the very last second.

He wouldn't be sewing anything if he couldn't rouse himself from this torpid senselessness. *Why do my bloody ribs feel as if they're on fire?*

"Jayr's new mortal watches me as well," Rainer continued. "He seems kind. I juggled eggs for him, you see, and when one slipped and landed on his shoe, he did not become even a little annoyed with me. If you still mean to have Leeds, I think he would be a good partner for you."

Leeds. The name seemed to twist in Farlae's chest like

a knife, although he couldn't fathom why. *Jayr's mortal. I saw him somewhere . . . through the glass. . . .*

"You must wake up soon, Farlae," Rain muttered. "I do not want you to take Leeds as your partner. I want you to keep me. I do not like sleeping or bathing by myself. I can't even sin by myself. Well, yes, I can. Every man can. And of course I have. But I like it better when you do it. I am more handsome than Leeds."

A soggy sniff dragged Farlae out of his patchwork memories. The feel of his limp hand being lifted and pressed to a wet cheek clawed at his heart.

"Do you hear me? You cannot go away and leave me alone," Rain whispered, his breath soft against Farlae's ear. "You promised you never would. Remember, the first time we were naked together, in that glade by the lake? You told me that immortals never die, so we would never burn in hell for it."

Farlae wanted to turn his head and console his partner, but it remained impaled on the pike of his neck. Neither could he raise his eyelids or make the slightest sound. Only one thing could reduce a Kyn to such a state—copper poisoning—and the amount required to render him so helpless would be a lethal dose. But the pain in his ribs suggested an alternative.

Someone stabbed me in the chest with a copper blade.

Rain's voice changed. "I know what a fool I am, and how often I vex you. If you will but wake, things will be different." He pressed a kiss against the back of Farlae's hand. "I will clear all of the toys out of my chamber. You will never again have to listen my wind-up chattering teeth, or sit upon my cushion that breaks wind, or watch my Monty Python DVDs. I will dress like a true warrior, in armor and leather and those things. You will never have to be ashamed of me again."

The shame was his, Farlae thought as he felt the void dragging at him. His heart had been poisoned long before anyone had taken a copper blade to him, and if not for the endless, sunny love he'd been given, the darkness would have swallowed him whole. He'd been the fool all along, not Rain. He had to live, if only to tell his partner that he would always be proud of him, and grateful that he had saved him from the hell of his own making.

Farlae fought through the sludge of the void, forcing his will through the pain and the emptiness toward Rain's voice. He hesitated only when he smelled another scent clouding his lover's: that of mortal sweat and blood.

He knew that scent. It belonged to the hand that had struck him down.

"How is he?" That was the mortal's voice, the one that came out of his memory in a whisper as loud as a shriek. *You should not have followed me here.*

"He has not awakened yet," Rain said. "Harlech says it will be some time. You are hurt?"

Not by my hand. The mortal had attacked Farlae from behind, thrusting his blade in from the side and skewering him before he could turn.

"It's nothing. I had an accident in the lists." The mortal's voice changed as he added, "Seneschal."

"Tresora." That came from Byrne, and with great reluctance. "I mistook what I saw in the lists. I would ask that you forgive me my harsh words to you."

"There is no need for you to apologize." Leeds sounded contrite. "I was hardly mannerly myself."

Farlae wanted to scream for Byrne to kill the traitor, but all he could force from his lips was a sputter.

"Farlae?" Rain's hands touched his face. "Farlae, can you hear me?"

It took every ounce of his will, and every shred of his strength, to open his eyes. The three men stood all around him, but he focused on the still, pale face of the mortal.

Byrne leaned over, resting a hand on his shoulder. "You took a copper blade to the ribs, lad. That is why you are here. It nearly touched your heart."

Farlae moved his head slightly. "Hmmm."

"What does he say, Byrne?" Rain asked. "And why does he look at Devan like that?"

"Him." Farlae dragged in another breath and nodded once more at the mortal. "'Twas . . . him."

"What he is trying to tell you," Leeds said, almost kindly, "is that I am the one who stabbed him and left him for dead."

Rain lunged across the bed, using his bulk to hold Byrne back as he shouted for the guard. "Please, Aedan, no. You will turn into Death again. I do not like you when you kill. You never wish to stop." He burst into tears.

Byrne stopped trying to fend him off. "Why?" he snarled at Leeds.

The mortal shrugged. "Does it matter now?"

As the guards came in and flanked Leeds, Byrne wrapped his arms around Rain, embracing him like a wounded child.

"There will be no more monsters let loose in the Realm, my lad." To the guards he said, "Take this piece of shit to the dungeons."

*   *   *

Once he had compelled Taylor to forget them, Beau
walked out of the resort to join Alys at the curb. "A pity
we cannot stay another night," he grumbled as he
donned his eyeshades and linked hands with her. "The
manager would have happily seen to our comfort."

"The manager didn't sign for several hundred thousand dollars' worth of equipment, or leave it sitting unguarded for a day." She yawned and leaned her head
against his shoulder. "But the room service was nice. So
was that shower."

"I favored the bed." He'd allowed her precious little
sleep in it, even after the sun had risen, but couldn't stir
himself to feel guilty. "I should have compelled him to
deliver it to the site."

"We'll push ours together." She straightened as a long
dark limousine came to a stop in front of them. "I
thought you called a cab."

"Car service," he corrected, nodding to the driver and
opening the back door for her.

"I've never ridden in a limo." Once inside, Alys had to
inspect everything. "Hylord—I mean, the high lord—
must pay pretty well."

"He pays nothing at all, but no one dares complain."
Beau gave the driver directions to the site before closing
the partition between the seats. "Come here."

Alys perched on his lap, resting her cheek against his
shoulder as she traced the leering skull on the front of
the new T-shirt the manager had given him to wear. "You
never told me how you found me at the park last night.
Can you sense where I go, or something like that?"

"I can track you by your scent when you are on foot."
He smoothed her rumpled hair back from her face. "But

I already knew what you meant to do. Just before we left for the city, when I went back into the cloister to get my jacket, I checked the history on your laptop."

She sat up. "You didn't. You sneak." Her indignant expression eased into a rueful look. "I didn't think you knew how to use a computer."

"I dislike them, but I have learned." Beau tucked her back against him. "I can also drive—I prefer horses, but I have learned to operate any vehicle—and read children's books, and sign my name."

"Why do you read children's books?"

"I could not read at all until a short time ago, when I began taking night classes." Beau told her about his solitary quest to become literate, and added, "Writing is my new challenge. It's not as easy as it looks, and I think I hate cursive more than plague. But such things were not required of me when I was mortal."

"And I taunted you about it." She hugged him. "I'm sorry."

"You are a child of this time. I am not." He kissed the top of her head. "But if you need a sword wielded, or a horse shod, I am your man."

Once the limo dropped them off at the site, Alys waved to the driver and then took Beau's hand. "Damn," she said as they walked past the parking area behind the church. "I forgot I left the van at the convention center. Well, at least we still have the Jeep." She glanced at the camp and frowned. "Did you reset the timers on the generators? They should have come on by now."

Beau breathed in and smelled burnt metal, smoldering plastic, and the scent of several unfamiliar mortals. "Wait here."

He was glad of the darkness when he came upon the GPR trolley, smashed into pieces, and the mounds of equipment that had been destroyed. From the stink, the intruders had doused everything with petrol and set it alight; the camp must have burned all day. Every work-station had been rifled through and toppled; the lab tent lay in shreds. Artifacts, some still in their bags, lay strewn everywhere.

Beau saw the beam of a flashlight, and intercepted Alys as she came around the mission. Immediately he tried to turn her away. "You'll not want to see this, love."

"Please." When he stepped aside, she went to the wrecked trolley, crouching down to touch it before she turned her flashlight over the rest of the encampment. "They torched everything, didn't they?"

"The equipment can be replaced."

"Of course it can, but . . . Oh, no." She stood and dashed off to the cloister.

Beau found her standing beside the empty trunk in their cellar chamber. The mattresses of both beds had been ripped open, all her garments and belongings thrown to the floor.

"My laptop's gone. So are all my discs and books." She bent down to pick up her red cap, turning it over in her hands. "They got my research notes, the reports I wrote for Tremayne, and every other record of the work we've done here. They took everything."

"This is my doing." Beau put aside his own fury and tried to comfort her. "We can begin again. I will call Tremayne, and tell him what has happened."

"Are you going to explain where we were while it was happening? I should never have left." She pushed her hair back from her brow. "I'll have to go back into the city and let the students know. Some of them have other commitments." She gave him a wan look. "Do you think Taylor will let us use that room for another night?"

He bent his head to kiss her. "I'll make sure of it."

Together they collected their garments, which Alys carried up out of the cloister to the Jeep while Beau used the solar shower bag to soak down the still-smoldering equipment. When the last wisp of smoke dissipated, he tossed the bag on top of the pile in disgust.

The danger has only begun, lad.

Beau's head snapped up as a shimmering cloud of golden light appeared a few feet from him. It solidified into the shape of a man who was part flesh, and part light. "Cristophe. Show yourself."

Your lady is about to die.

Beau bunched his hands into fists. "If you go anywhere near her—"

They have already seen to it. Go to her. Save her.

Beau took a step toward him before he remembered what else they had left behind last night. *The Jeep.*

He saw Alys sitting behind the wheel of the Jeep and digging through her backpack. He reached her just as she was putting the key in the ignition.

"I think the battery is—"

He scooped her out of the seat, flinging her over his shoulder as he fled from the vehicle. A moment after he ducked around the stables, the Jeep exploded, sending a huge ball of black smoke and fire into the air.

Alys cringed against him as Beau turned, pressing her against the old brick. He used his body to shield her from the rain of flaming shrapnel, but once it had abated, she wriggled out from under him to look at the fiery ruins.

She turned to him, her eyes shocked. "How did you know there was a bomb in my car?"

"Our mutual relative warned me." Beau took out his satellite phone and began punching the buttons.

"Who are you going to call?" Alys demanded. "Ghostbusters?"

He eyed her. "What?"

"Never mind. It sounded funnier in my head." She pressed a hand to her brow. "Not even shock can make me into a comedienne."

"You may be anything you wish, love, but we cannot stay here." He lifted the phone to his ear. "This is Beaumaris. Send the car back for us. Yes, *now*."

Alys walked over to where she had dropped her backpack, and bent down to collect everything that had fallen out of it. When she straightened, she gave the flaming wreck of the Jeep a helpless glance. "Where can we go?"

"The one place where I know you'll be safe." He switched off the phone. "Home."

Beau wouldn't let go of her, even when the car returned and they were safely on their way, but Alys didn't mind. She'd come within seconds of being blown up with the Jeep; her hands were still shaking.

"Where do you live, anyway?" she asked him, wondering whether he had a house or a condo, and whether she'd put him in danger by staying with him.

" 'Tis not far from here." Beau looked as if he wanted to say more, but turned his head to watch the limo's side mirror, which he'd been doing since they'd left the site.

"Maybe it would be better if we went to a hotel," she suggested. "I don't want whoever did this to come after you and blow up your house."

"They'll not be able to get at my home, love." As the limo slowed, he lowered his window and reached out to input a series of numbers on a security pad.

Alys couldn't see through the dark glass of the partition, so she leaned over him. An artfully painted sign behind the keypad showed two horsemen in armor jousting beneath lettering that read KNIGHTS REALM. "You're taking me to another theme park? Pirate World wasn't enough?"

"The Realm is more than a park." He took her hand in his. "This is where we live."

"We? As in the Darkyn?" She gaped. "There are *more* of you around here?"

He nodded. "Many more."

Another man dressed in a medieval guard's costume walked up to the window and bent down to peer inside. "Beau, what do you here? Harlech said you would not return for another fortnight." The man's eyes shifted, and he grinned. "Hello, pretty thing. What are you called?"

Beau scowled. "Mine."

"As you say." The guard winked at Alys. "If you tire of him, sweeting, ask for Gowain. I love ginger-haired gels."

"Lay a finger on her and I'll gut you." Beau raised the window, shutting out the guard's leer.

"You'll *gut* him?" Alys repeated, fascinated now. "For touching me? Really?"

Beau gave her a narrow look. "Really."

It was as if she'd been transported to her own private fantasyland, Alys thought as the gates opened and the driver moved the car up to the edge of a moat surrounding an enormous castle. She heard the hum of hydraulics as the water parted and a gleaming drawbridge surfaced.

"I can't believe you live in a medieval theme park." She admired the gatehouse towers, and the two armored guards standing at attention in front of them. "How do you keep the tourists from finding out what you are?"

"Mortals are easy to convince; what you see is what you believe." Beau sounded slightly less testy. "Our visitors think they come to a theme park, which permits us to live as we wish."

"And they have no idea." Alys chuckled. "Of course they don't. They think it's all a performance. God, this is brilliant."

In the castle courtyard she saw another group of men leading horses to long, low trenches of water made from hollowed-out logs; each of the men wore a sheathed sword strapped to his shoulder or hip. A pair of ladies in long billowing gowns and wimples curtsied slightly as they passed them, while the warriors bowed. More torches and braziers flamed along the curtain walls and high up on the battlements, where Alys spotted more guards standing watch and moving in pairs on patrol.

She caught her breath as she spotted a towering frame of wood and metal supported by a rolling platform; a long sling hung from a broad beam of wood set at an angle. "Is that a trebuchet?"

"Aye." The car came to a stop in the middle of the courtyard, and Beau helped her out. He looked at the people emerging from the castle. "My lady comes. She is the ruler over all of the Kyn who abide in this region. I must introduce you and explain what has happened."

"Sure." She glanced at the slender girl and the massive warrior approaching them. The man appeared mature, and savage Celtic tattoos covered his face, but the girl looked like a teenager. "Is she your queen?"

"Lady Jayr is our suzeraina. This portion of Florida is her territory, and I serve as one of her defenders." Beau laced his fingers through hers. "Do not be afraid. No one here means you ill."

"Beaumaris." Jayr stopped and regarded him as he bowed. "We were not expecting you this night." Her dark eyes shifted to Alys's face. "'Tis not the best time for overnight visitors."

More warriors poured out of the castle, taking up positions behind Jayr and the tattooed man.

"Forgive me, my lady. I would have sent word ahead, but circumstances forced me to move quickly." He turned to Alys, hesitated, and then faced Jayr again. "This is Dr. Alys Stuart, who works on behalf of the high lord. She is not an overnight visitor. She is my *kyara*."

The men standing behind Jayr reacted by exchanging mutters and staring at Alys as if she'd grown another head.

"You've revealed us to her?" the tattooed man demanded, his harsh words made melodic by his Scottish accent.

Beau nodded. "There was no avoiding it, my lord, but I will vouch for her. She can be trusted."

"So you say, while I've a mortal who trifled with our trust down in the dungeons this moment." The Scotsman came to loom over Alys. "Why should I put faith in your little wench?"

Alys decided cowering would not impress him much.

"Because you look like the last man on earth I'd ever want to trifle with, period?"

He took in a deep breath, and some of the hostility eased away from his fierce features. "Stuart, is it? A good Scots name."

"I've always thought so. Lady Jayr." She went with her instincts and dropped into a somewhat awkward curtsy. "It's an honor to meet you, and I'm sorry to have intruded at an inconvenient time. Someone stole my research, destroyed my camp, and tried to kill me tonight, and Beau—Beaumaris—thought I would be safer here."

"As Byrne mentioned, we've similar troubles." Jayr gestured toward the castle. "Come. We will see to your comfort."

The wonders outside the castle were nothing on what Alys saw inside. As she passed through the oak-plated iron portcullis, Alys was enchanted to see the long, narrow *meurtrières* overhead, as well as a dozen crossbowmen standing ready to fire through them. Inside the hall more guards stood at attention, bowing their heads as Jayr passed, and eyeing Alys with visible suspicion.

Of course, I'm a stranger, and a mortal. Alys wondered whom they had thrown down in their dungeons, and why.

As she followed the suzeraina, Alys passed rooms filled with medieval antiques. While the floors on which they walked were fashioned of slate instead of the expected rush-strewn soil, enormous standing vases filled with heather, tansy, and violets lent their perfume to the chilly interior air.

Alys gulped as they entered a magnificent main hall, where a formal canopied dais occupied a rounded platform of polished granite. Along the walls stood flat, wide rectangles of white marble and carved mahogany trestles, ready to be assembled into tables. Fat tallow candles flicked atop standing, beautifully wrought iron poles; cascades of bowl-shaped oil lamps hung suspended from the vaulted stone ceiling.

No fewer than three giant fireplaces burned, the flames dancing behind brilliantly polished brass screens. Taller, cloth-covered folding screens formed a mazelike concealment at the other end of the hall, and at either side wall hung two wide balconies, the sort of galleries where Alys could imagine musicians playing.

She walked up to the whitewashed stonework and trailed her fingers over it. "This isn't plaster. It's the real thing." She suppressed an excited laugh. "The wall hangings, they look so new."

"They are new. Our ladies are as industrious now as they were in their mortal lives." Beau nodded at the table where Jayr and Byrne stood. "I must relate what has happened at the site. I fear my lady will have questions for you as well."

He meant they would ask about her research, and what she knew about the emeralds. "Trust can't be one-sided."

After they sat down with the suzeraina and her seneschal, and Beau briefed them on the project, he also related a surprising amount of information about the two competing teams that had set up camp near the property.

"The Europeans are far more well equipped than the Americans, and have already begun tunneling into the ground." He turned to Alys. "You studied the geological surveys. Can they reach the spring somehow from underground?"

"If they tap into the aquifer, the submersible may be able to follow water back to the source," she said, "the location of which unfortunately we've never determined exactly. I believe it's under the pond, but I can't know without searching the bottom."

"If they knew, they would not have stolen your research," Jayr put in. "They must have guessed you were close. Destroying your camp and the cowardly attempt to take your life seems reckless. Had you been killed, the authorities would have become involved and, given their proximity, would have definitely detained them for questioning."

"I think not, my lady," Beau said. "The site is too remote to attract public notice. The *tresoran* traitors must know Tremayne purchased the land, and would prevent any mortal involvement or investigation."

"That sounds like Richard." A petite, russet-haired woman came into the room. "Hello, Jayr, Byrne, Cute Guy, Redhead." She came over and hugged the suzeraina. "Sorry to interrupt the fascinating conversation, but I'm on a house call."

"Alex, thank heavens." Jayr rose and glanced at Alys. "Dr. Stuart, would you excuse us? Dr. Keller is needed in the infirmary."

"Another doctor?" Alex's brows arched. "What am I here for, a second opinion?"

"I'm a PhD," Alys said. "Archaeologist."

The shorter woman grinned. "Nice to meet you, Indiana." She turned to Jayr. "Okay, so where's my patient?"

"We'll take this up later, lad," Byrne told Beau, and nodded to Alys before he followed the women out of the hall.

Alys blew out a breath. "Wow. I can't believe I just met the fastest surgeon in the world. She's Darkyn, too. I guess that explains her speed."

"You know of Lady Alexandra?"

"Anyone who subscribes to *Time* magazine does." She smothered a yawn. "Sorry. Lack of sleep, partially your fault."

"You must be exhausted." Beau drew her to her feet. "I'll take you to my chambers."

Chapter 15

On the way to the garrison's quarters, Alys recalled
something Beau had said when they'd arrived, and
how strangely the other men had reacted. "You never
mentioned to me what a *kyara* is. Is that another name
for your mortal allies?"

"Not exactly." He stopped and, after looking around
them, took her hands in his. "Sometimes Kyn warriors
and lords take a mortal into their household to be their
companion. It does not happen very often, as we cannot
bond with mortal females, and unhappily we always out-
live them. But this does not matter to me. You are mine,
and by claiming you as my *kyara*, you will be accorded
every courtesy due my rank."

"So I'm your companion." She frowned. "You mean,
like a girlfriend?"

He kissed her. "A *kyara* is more than that. You are my
mortal wife."

Alys felt her knees buckle, and grabbed his arms. "Excuse me? When did we get *married*?"

"It had to be said." Beau's expression grew shuttered.

"Lady Jayr might turn out any mortal she wishes. As my wife, you have the right to sanctuary here."

Of course, he'd done it to protect her. Alys didn't understand why she felt so disappointed. "I understand."

Beau started to say something and then, as another man walked past them, took her arm. "We'll talk more in my chambers."

When they entered the section of the castle occupied by the garrison, Alys saw a crowd of men lining both sides of the corridor. "They're not going to throw rice at us, are they?"

"This is a Kyn tradition." Beau swept her up in his arms. "Keep your head against my shoulder."

Alys saw why as he started walking down the corridor, and every man drew his sword and held it up to form a canopy of razor-sharp steel. "Oh. This is nice." She hid her face against Beau's shoulder and peeked out now and then to make sure no one was going to start slashing at them.

A tall, stern-faced man with sandy hair stepped in front of Beau at the end of the passage. "Beaumaris." His cool eyes shifted to Alys's face. "So you have finally gone wenching. Was it necessary to bring back a sample of your night's work?"

"Alys, this is Harlech, captain of the garrison, and my foster brother," Beau said. "Captain, this is Dr. Alys Stuart, my *kyara*."

Harlech took a step back. "Your *wife*?"

"Hi, Captain." Alys offered him her brightest smile. "It's nice to meet you."

"Lady Alys." Harlech bowed to her, but when he straightened, he gave Beau a pointed look. "I look forward to hearing your report on the morrow, brother. A *full* report."

"Until then, Captain." Beau carried Alys inside a chamber and, as the men in the corridor began cheering, closed the door.

Alys turned around to take in her new surroundings, which were far more luxurious than she'd expected. In addition to a huge bed, several chairs and tables, and an enormous armoire, Beau's chambers were decorated with heavy, dark purple velvet curtains, several stark paintings of the sea, and a mounted display of some thirty different swords. Soft wool carpets covered the stone floor, and a banked fire glowed in a narrow iron hearth near the bed.

"This looks comfortable." Alys went over to the curtains and looked out one of the tall arched windows at a massive citrus grove. "Do you bring a lot of wenches here?"

"You are the first woman I have ever brought to the Realm." Beau came to stand behind her. "And you are not my wench. You are my wife."

She tried not to stiffen as he put his arms around her waist. "Is that all it takes for a Kyn warrior to marry someone? You just say, 'She's my wife,' and everyone holds up a sword and it's done?"

"We cannot marry as mortals do. Our enemies hide behind the church. We cannot allow any official records to reflect our names or our whereabouts. For us, it must be enough to declare it to each other." Beau turned her around to face him. "Why are you so unhappy with me?"

"I don't know. I've never been a wife." She ran her fingers along the strip of leather that laced the front of his tunic. "That's not true. I always thought that if I ever married someone, I would have a real wedding."

Beau drew her over to one of his big armchairs, and sat down with her on his lap. "What is a real wedding?"

"A traditional ceremony. Not in a church, but somewhere beautiful, maybe outside. I used to buy those wedding magazines and look at the dresses. I definitely wanted to wear a great dress." She looked down at her Pirate World T-shirt and laughed. "That didn't happen. It's silly, I know. I should be grateful to be alive, and to be with you."

"I wish I could give you that wedding," Beau murmured, and kissed her temple. "I would love to see you in such a dress. But for now I must keep you here, and safe."

"I understand." He'd done this to protect her, and she could be gracious about it. "When it's over, do you say, 'She isn't my wife,' and that takes care of the divorce?"

"There will be no divorce, Alys." Beau frowned. "You are my wife, and I am your husband. Whatever happens with the emeralds, and Tremayne, you and I will be together."

Alys stared at him. "But it's not real. You said—"

"I love you." He cradled her face between his hands, kissing the space between her brows, the curve of her cheek, and both corners of her lips before he drew back to regard her with a fierce expression. "And I will have no other woman but you. However you feel for me, in my heart I will be your husband for the rest of my life. Perhaps our way is not how mortals go about it, but marrying means the same to us. More so for us to marry a mortal. Why would you think this not real?"

Alys took a deep breath. "You didn't ask me to marry you, Beau. You didn't even consult me."

"There was no time, and I thought you felt the same. Christ Jesus, I am an idiot." Beau got up from the chair to set her on her feet. "Forget everything that I have said, and everything I have done."

"Everything?" She had some very fond memories from last night. "Do I have to?"

"The worst of it, then." He went down on one knee, and held her hand between his. "I ask you now, Alys Stuart. Will you have me as your husband?"

All her amusement fled. "Some people would say we hardly know each other, but I don't have the luxury of time anymore, do I? Not when I'm in love with an immortal. Maybe the reason I've never been able to emotionally connect with other people is because some part of me was waiting for you to find me."

"I could say the same." Beau kissed the back of her hand.

"Now that I've finally found you, and I could have what other women have . . ." She shook her head. "It's not fair."

"Alys?"

"Don't misunderstand me. I've accepted that I'm not ordinary, and that strange, startling things happen to me on a regular basis. Look at where I'm spending my wedding night." Alys gestured around her. "A fourteenth-century castle. A *working* fourteenth-century castle."

Beau rose to his feet. "But you will never be an ordinary woman."

She nodded. "I've accepted it. I've tried to be a good sport, and see it as an adventure instead of a curse. I think I've coped pretty well, all things considered. I won't complain. There's really only one thing I want you to understand." She pulled the T-shirt up over her head to remove it, holding it in her hands for a moment before offering it to Beau. "This is *not* my wedding dress."

He took the shirt and draped it over the back of a chair.

Alys stripped out of the skull jeans, shaking them out and folding them neatly before placing them with the shirt. "I know we're in terrible danger, and there is no time, and who knows when this will be over? I can wait. But someday, when things stop exploding and all the traitors are vanquished and the dungeons are empty, when this is finished, Beaumaris, I want a real wedding dress. I deserve one."

"So you shall have it." He pulled off his shirt before he took her into his arms. "I never wished I could be human again, until now."

She had to be sure he knew what he was getting into. "I wonder if you've really thought about us. The reality of us. I could die any day in an accident, or from disease. If I do live on, eventually I'll grow old, and you'll have to watch that happen. Whenever my time comes, you'll have to let me go. Can you do that?"

"I would do anything for you," Beau said, and caressed her arm with his hand. "Come, you need to sleep."

"On my wedding night?" Alys shook her head, and drew him over to the big bed. "That's not something I'm willing to wait for." She glanced down at herself. "Besides, you don't have to undress me. I'm already naked. Think of the convenience."

"There is that." Beau reached for the front of his trousers.

"Let me." Alys beat him to it, unfastening the button and sliding down the zipper before she slipped her hand inside. The bulging length of his penis pressed against her palm, deliciously rigid. "You're not sleepy."

"No." He watched her work his trousers down from his hips, and stepped out of them for her. "Not at all."

"Good." She moved around him, running her hands over the hard planes of his muscles. "There are so many things I want to do with you. I hardly know where to start."

"I have some suggestions." Beau caught her by the waist and pulled her against him.

"I liked your first one." She kissed her way across his chest. "When we were in the hotel room."

He buried his hands in her hair. "What was that?"

Alys pushed him onto the bed, and knelt in front of him. "You wanted to keep me quiet." She brought his hand to her lips and pressed a soft kiss against his palm. "But you didn't want to use this, did you?"

Beau's pupils narrowed to slivers. "No."

Alys set his hand aside and brushed her cheek against the upright, straining column of his shaft. "This is what you wanted to put in my mouth."

His thighs tensed under her hands. "Is that what you want now?"

"I admit, I've been thinking about it." Alys looked up at him, holding his gaze as she parted her lips, and let her breath whisper over the satiny plum of his cockhead. "What it would feel like." She brushed her lips over the small slit, collecting the drop of semen there with the tip of her tongue. "What it would taste like." She closed her eyes, savoring him.

A big, unsteady hand cradled the back of her head. "Show me what you wanted, love."

"This." She opened her mouth, enveloping him and sucking lightly as she curled her fingers around his swelling length. Slowly she worked her mouth over him, taking him in, using her tongue to caress and the edge of her teeth to tease. Slowly she let him slide from her lips, relishing his groan when she nearly released him, and then drawing him deeper.

Beau's fingertips caressed her scalp as he guided her, his voice soft and low as he murmured to her. "Your lips are so beautiful on me, love. So warm and wet. I thought of this every time I looked at your mouth. I wanted to see you like this, suckling me, loving me. God in heaven, you feel so good."

Alys reveled in the power it gave her over him, that such a simple thing could make her strong, invulnerable warrior tremble and groan. She released him only once, using her hand to stroke him as she looked up into his half-closed eyes.

"Now show me what you wanted." She released him to lie back on the rug.

Beau came down over her, pressing his body against hers as he pinned her wrists beside her head. "Open your mouth for me." When she did, he rose, straddling her breasts and guiding himself to her mouth. "Take it," he said as he pushed his penis between her lips. "Take all of it. Just like that, yes." He tipped her head so he could forge deeper, his hips stroking faster.

Alys watched his face as he glided in and out of her lips, shaking as he felt every tug of her mouth. She felt his shaft growing even harder, and when she felt the first throb, she dug her nails into his thighs.

Beau hunched over, bracing himself with one hand, his big frame shaking as his seed jetted into her mouth.

Alys drank him in, taking everything he gave her, and when he drew out of her, she smiled. "Yes."

Beau moved down the length of her body, his hand parting her thighs and his fingers finding her slick folds. He bent his head, laving her with his tongue as he worked two fingers into the tight wetness of her sheath, bringing her over so fast and hard Alys cried out.

Beau held her close, lifting her up and stretching out with her on his bed. "Does this mean you'll have me, then?" he asked as he traced the curves of her mouth.

"Oh, you're definitely mine now." She snuggled up against him. "For as long as you want to be."

He kissed her brow. "That would be forever."

Chris knocked on Simone's door, opening it to look in on her sister. "Rise and shine, Frenchy."

A mumble came from the mound of covers on Simone's bed.

"Don't be lazy. The boys are supposed to arrive tonight, remember? You'll be spending plenty of time horizontal."

She walked over to the bed, slowing only when she saw Simone's hand hanging limply over the side. It looked so much like her mother's hand, hanging over the edge of the bathtub in which she'd killed herself, that Chris's stomach turned.

"Simone, wake up." When her sister didn't move, she reached down to pull back the linens, appalled to see that her hand was shaking badly. "Okay, no more all-night movie marathons for you."

Chris slowly uncovered her sister. Simone lay on her side, blankly staring at nothing, her skin an icy white.

"Jesus." Chris rolled her onto her back, crawling onto the bed and kneeling beside her as she felt for a pulse and found none. "No. You are *not* dying on me." She raked her *dents acérées* across her palm and pressed it to Simone's lips.

At first the blood merely trickled out of the other side of the Frenchwoman's mouth, but slowly her lips pursed and covered the wounds. Her skin took on a delicate flush, and her eyes fluttered as she whispered, "Chris."

"It's okay." She bent down. "I'm here. What happened—"

Simone seized her by the throat, rolling over and dragging her from the bed. As Chris tried to free herself, she saw the body of another woman on the floor by the door, her arm outstretched, as if she'd collapsed while trying to crawl toward it.

Simone. Chris clawed at the steely fingers biting into her flesh, trying to scream but unable to make a sound.

The woman strangling her began to grow taller and bulkier, her body radiating a strange dark yellow glow as her features broadened and her hair disappeared.

Chris recognized the dark features of the man trying to choke the life out of her. "Cristophe." She used her Kyn strength to shove him away. "What are you doing?"

"What I and my kin vowed we would do," the smith told her flatly. "Protect the emeralds from the Kyn and the mortal world. Everything I have done has been for that reason. But you and your sister and your lovers have failed to relieve me of my burden. Simone returned to France, and you ran away to the islands with your boy lover. Now there are only two left to save the world. The last of my blood must take my place before it is too late, and I will allow neither of you to interfere."

When he came at her again, Chris used all her strength to slam her fist into the side of his head. He staggered, releasing her, and she jumped to the other side of the bed. "I'm not a mortal anymore. Neither is Simone. Why come after us?"

Cristophe touched the side of his head, where his scalp burned away from a path of light.

A burning sensation made her look down at her hand, where flecks of molten gold were sinking into her skin. "What the hell?"

The smith raised his hand, and one of the tall iron candlesticks flew toward Chris, wrapping itself around her legs before she could evade it. She fell backward, and shrieked as Cristophe used his power over the metal to drag her body across the floor to him.

"You failed me," he repeated. "Now you and your sister will do my bidding."

"I can't believe a mortal did this." Alexandra Keller used her scope to inspect the neat, near-lethal wound in the Kyn male's side. "Judging by your man's condition, the blade came within a millimeter or two of piercing his heart. Did you recover the weapon?"

Jayr went to the storage cabinet and brought a dagger to her. "It was found near his body."

Alex took the blade, sniffing the blood staining it before she held it up and studied the length. "Yeah, this did the dirty work."

"Will he die, Alex?" Jayr asked.

"Doubt it." Absently she set aside the blade and began checking the pulse points on his limbs. "You followed to the letter the instructions I gave you over the phone, which diluted the poison in his blood but didn't send him into thrall. That's half the battle." She combed her fingers through Farlae's matted hair before she nodded and straightened. "He's in the process of shedding the copper. He'll be out of commission for a couple of weeks, but a few more carefully timed transfusions, a decent haircut, and he should make it."

Jayr dropped into the chair beside Farlae's bed and braced her head in her hands. "I cannot thank you enough."

"You're welcome, but it wasn't anything I did." She nodded toward the blade. "The killer mortal wasn't much of a killer. He missed the heart. Or maybe he's a very good killer. He knew exactly where to put the blade, and the correct angle to thrust, but he didn't shove it all the way in. Or he could be bonkers. Who in his right mind would try to kill a Kyn and not finish the job? Where is this guy, anyway?"

"Byrne had him taken to the dungeons." Jayr sighed and dropped her hands. "I have to go now to interrogate him, but I confess, Alex, I never wish to lay eyes on him again."

"You'd rather Byrne do the honors?" Jayr's appalled look made her smile grimly. "Didn't think so. I bet the prisoner is immune to *l'attrait*, too."

"What am I going to do?" Jayr spread her hands. "Leeds came here under false pretenses, and attacked Farlae without provocation. I have to know why."

"This is why I never go for the position of absolute power. Being in charge sucks." Alex took out a chart from her medical case and started making notes on it. "I can talk to the bad man later if you want. I don't do torture, naturally, but I'm his generation and I have an excellent cell-side manner. He might open up to me."

"No, this is my duty. However much it, as you say, sucks." Jayr stood. "Christian and Simone are visiting us, and I know they will wish to see you. When you are finished here, perhaps you'll join us in the main hall?"

"Sure." Alex watched her go before she looked down at her patient. "It's safe now. You can quit pretending to be unconscious." As Farlae did, and revealed the nightmarish flaw in his eye, she made a face. "That's not a very nice birth defect. Are you blind in it?"

"I was, until I changed." His voice rasped with weariness. "So I hear I am to live."

"I guess that's why they made you the spy." She took out her sample kit. "I need to draw some blood and run some tests. Don't give me any grief, and I won't tell Jayr you were eavesdropping."

"You must keep her away from him, my lady." Farlae managed to grab her wrist. "Leeds is a desperate man."

"Take it easy." She pried his hand off and placed it back at her side. "The guy is sitting in a dungeon with every vampire in the place pissed off at him. He's not going anywhere."

"I mean he is desperate for Jayr." Farlae subsided with a groan. "Give me something to get me back on my feet."

"Sadly, I didn't bring a forklift with me." She sat down on the edge of the bed. "Maybe you should tell me what the hell is going on here."

Before Farlae could reply, the door to the infirmary swung open and Jayr came in, followed by two warriors carrying Chris and Simone.

Alex got to her feet. "What happened?"

"We found them on the floor in Simone's chamber. We cannot rouse them." Jayr directed the men to put the women down on two cots. "They show no sign of injury."

Alex went to Chris, checking her pulse and her pupils before doing the same to Simone. "It looks like they're in thrall." She jerked up her head. "You find any unconscious, dying mortals lying around?"

"No. Our human staff remains on holiday," Jayr said. "The only mortal here is Dr. Stuart, and she is with Beaumaris in his chambers."

"Okay." Alex took off her jacket and rolled up her sleeves. "Someone please call my lord and master and let him know I'm going to be here for a while. I could also use some nurses." She met Jayr's gaze. "You'd better go have a word with your traitor, and see if he's somehow responsible for this. Right now."

Beau left Alys in his chambers just before dawn.

"I must go and make my peace with Harlech." He tucked the covers in around her. "Sleep."

Alys smiled as she watched him go, and snuggled down into the sheets that smelled as darkly sweet as her lover. She still couldn't quite believe all this was real; it felt like a dream and any moment she would wake up and find herself back at the site.

I don't have a site anymore. She fell back against the pillows and stared at the interlocking stonework that formed the ceiling. *The project is over.* Somehow she'd have to send word to her team that the dig was closed.

The thought of her career self-destructing no longer frightened her; she'd hardly given her ambitions a single thought since making love with Beau. Not that they had ever been her ambitions—Robert had trained her like a performing chimp. She didn't want to think about her guardian, not here, where her real life was finally beginning. *What will it be like, to be his wife, and spend the rest of my life with him?* She couldn't see the future, but ever since walking into the castle, she'd felt as if she'd finally come home.

A commotion outside the chamber made her climb out of bed and peek out of the door. A group of warriors, visibly angry ones, stood arguing over someone named Leeds.

"I say we go to the dungeons and deal with him now," one thin, stern-faced man snapped. "Whatever he meant to do, I will get it out of him."

"He's mortal, Lasander," another said. "He'll not live long enough to tell you."

"Why should that be a problem for you, Revus?" Lasander demanded. "The coward attacked Farlae from behind, and now he has poisoned the ladies visiting. What more must he do before we put him to the blade?"

"We will take the matter to Harlech," Revus said. "If he gives us leave, Lasander, I'll be happy to stretch the mortal's neck for you."

As the men disappeared down the passage, Alys slipped out of the chamber and quietly went in the op-

posite direction, retracing her steps until she reached the
passage leading back to the main hall. There she hesitated until the scent of warm strawberries enveloped
her, and a towheaded giant dressed in bright pink and
green clothes came out of a side passage.

"Hello," he said, smiling as he approached her.
"You're a mortal."

"Yes. I'm Dr. Alys Stuart." She held out her hand, and
was charmed when he took it and bestowed a decidedly
theatrical kiss on her knuckles. "Beaumaris brought me
here. I needed a safe place to stay."

"I have heard your name spoken. You are the new
kyara everyone talks of. I am Rainer." He bowed. "You
must be the reason that Beau has not gone wenching of
late."

"So everyone knows about this wenching." She'd have
to discuss that with him.

"It is what the men do. I thought it most perverse of
Beau to give it up, but now that I look upon you, I understand." The big man pulled an enormous bunch of flowers out of his pocket and offered them to her. "I like
women. Not in the way Beaumaris does, or used to, but
you are lovely things, and you wear such pretty clothes."

"Thank you." Cautiously Alys accepted the bouquet,
the flowers of which were made of thin silk and collapsing springs. "You're a magician?"

"I am a fool," he said, very seriously.

"Great." Alys was beginning to feel slightly overwhelmed, too. "I was hoping to explore the castle a little
on my own. I hope that's okay."

"You belong to Beau now, so you may do much as you
wish. Do not take the next passage left," Rain advised

her, "for that leads below, to the dungeons. We have a traitor down there, and he is an evil, cunning snake. You will not wish to meet him."

"No, of course not." Alys smiled. "Thank you for warning me."

"You are welcome. I must go now. My lover is very sick and I must talk to him a great deal so that he does not die." He bowed. "Until we meet again, my lady."

Gay medieval vampires, Alys thought as she watched him go. *Well, why not?*

She took the next passage on the left, and the long staircase at the end of it to a deep underground level shrouded in darkness. If she was caught down here, she'd probably end up locked in a cell herself, but something kept pushing her on, as if everything depended on her talking to the assassin.

At the base of the steps she encountered two guards, both of whom eyed her but didn't move or speak.

"I'm just going to say hello to the prisoner." She watched their faces, but they didn't twitch a muscle. "I'm guessing that's okay with you."

"They will not object," a man's voice said from the shadows. "Unless you try to release me, and then they will cut off your head."

Alys touched her neck before she followed the voice to a cell occupied by an average-looking man wearing a bloodstained white shirt and dark trousers.

"Hello." She surveyed the chains manacled to his wrists and ankles. "Did they hurt you?"

"An earlier accident." His chains rattled as he showed her a new, wide pink scar on his wrist. "You're Dr. Stuart, I presume."

"Yes. They said your name is Leeds?" When he nodded, Alys glanced back at the guards and lowered her voice. "Why did you do this to them?"

"Why must you know my reasons?" he countered.

"There are a bunch of very angry men upstairs who want to torture and kill you," she said. "I'd like to persuade them not to."

"That's very kind of you, but you assume I wish to live." He drew back out of the light. "You should not be here."

"I agree." Jayr came to stand beside Alys.

"I'm sorry. I heard some of the men talking, and, well, I really don't know why I'm here." Alys looked at Leeds. "I suppose I thought I could talk to him, one mortal to another."

"That was kind of you." The suzeraina gave the prisoner a disgusted look before she said, "You should return to Beaumaris's quarters now."

Alys glanced at Leeds. "I think he wants you to kill him, my lady. Be careful."

Leeds suddenly shot to his feet, jerking the chains that manacled him to the wall. "Attend to yourself, Dr. Stuart. You are not safe here, and you cannot trust the Kyn. Leave."

"Why?" Alys asked. "What do you think they're going to do to me? They're protecting me."

"You are a mortal, and there is nothing that will keep you safe in this place," Leeds predicted. "Leave now, if you value your life."

With Leeds still shouting after her, Alys fled for the stairs.

Chapter 16

Once Alys had disappeared, Leeds stopped shouting and sat back on the floor of his cell. "She will not go, will she? She smells of Kyn. Of course. That is how he is manipulating her." He spoke as if he was talking to himself.

"I know nothing of your schemes." Anger kept Jayr from looking directly at the *tresora*; she focused on the welds at the base of his cell's bars. "We found Christian and Simone. What did you do to them?"

"Nothing at all."

"Just as you did nothing to Farlae." Jayr clamped down on her temper before she added, "These women are not part of my household. Whatever grudge brought you here to take your vengeance on me has nothing to do with them. Tell me what you used to harm them, and how it may be reversed."

"I did nothing to Christian, Simone, or you."

He was such an accomplished liar that as he spoke, his scent never changed. Jayr knew he would never tell her, not while the women still lived. She would inform him of his fate, then, and leave with dignity. But when she spoke, the words came not from her cool head but from her bruised pride.

"You did nothing to me? You had me trust you, Devan. You convinced me to welcome you into my household, and accept your counsel, and verily believe every falsehood you uttered." She reached out for the bars, and drew back her hand, clenching it into a fist. "You betrayed me in every manner imaginable."

"As you say, my lady." Leeds's chains rattled as he rose and shuffled across the pitted slate to the cell door. "If I may know, when am I to be put to the sword?" When she didn't answer him, he said, "Perhaps you have something else in mind. Do you mean to starve me, or let me rot? Perhaps have the men use me for a target?" Heavy manacles clanked against the bars, and gentle fingertips touched her arm. "You could enrapture me, you know."

"Get off." She spun around, thrusting her arm between the bars to shove him back. "You think yourself so tempting to me. You, who are everything vile and twisted. Rather I would feed on rats for all eternity than let a drop of your blood pass through my lips."

Leeds staggered before he slowly straightened. "I know that, my lady. I know because you are everything that is honorable and true. I think I would kill for you."

"Never say you did this for wanting of me." But she could see it on his face, forlorn with longing. "Have you lost your wits? I am bonded. I belong to Byrne."

He smiled a little. "That was evident from the first moment I beheld you with your seneschal. Do you even know how you look at him, as if he were all the world?

Not even he knows the depth of your love, I suspect. As for me, well, we so often covet that which can never be ours. And I knew I could never have you."

He was toying with her, Jayr thought. Scheming to once more get inside her trust by making such a pathetic excuse. "You never knew me before you came here."

"Also true. I was sent to this place to carry out several unpleasant tasks. I anticipated every danger except you, my lady." He braced his forearm against the bars, his eyes boring into hers. "I am in love with you, Jayr."

She backed away from the cell. "You *are* mad."

"I should have left as soon as your spy found me out, but I could not leave you." He curled his fingers around the bars. "My orders were to kill you. That was why I came to the lists tonight. I meant to run my blade through your heart."

That was why he had taken that final, deadly lunge. "I should have cut off your hand *and* your head."

"But instead you healed me, my lady." He showed her the scar. "I am forever marked now by your blade and your blood. That was why I confessed to stabbing your wardrobe master. I knew I would never leave here. I have nothing left to me but you."

He spoke of her as if she were already his possession; that was how disturbed he was. "You truly believe you have some chance with me."

"On the contrary. I know very well that you will be the end of me. I will go to my death without a murmur." He rested his forehead against the bars. "But no one will ever love you more than I do."

"We're finished." Jayr spun on her heel to make for the stairs.

"My master intends to take the Realm by force," Leeds called out, halting her. "When he comes, and it will be soon, he will slaughter every Kyn here."

She glanced back at him. "Who is this master of yours? Another turncoat, like you? He will be hacked to pieces the moment he sets foot on my land. He and the other traitors like you."

"You cannot put it a stop to it now," he said. "Byrne, your men, they are only hours from dying. But I will not let them have you. Come away with me, tonight, and you will live."

He sounded so desperate, so convincing, that Jayr almost believed him. "You would say anything to be free."

"No." He made a bitter sound. "But I would do anything to save you."

"Make your peace with God, Devan. Jamys and Korvel will soon arrive, and once they have seen what you have done to their ladies, I am sending them to deal with you." She went to the guards. "Go and fetch my seneschal, and have him meet me in the garrison." As one trotted off, she turned to the second guard. "No one else is to see the prisoner, or speak with him."

The guard nodded. "Aye, my lady."

Leeds heard the door to the upper level of the castle slam, and retreated to the shadows. As he'd guessed, Jayr's rejection of him had been quick, unwavering, and absolute. Less certain was her resolve to have him executed before dawn; she would have to set aside the guilt he had instilled in her as well as her own feminine instincts.

Women, even those who were immortal, were nurturers, not killers.

He closed his eyes, tired of the game he'd played too long. Duty had brought him here, but it would be love that destroyed him.

The guard shuffled to the door of his cell and inserted the key in the lock.

Leeds rose to his feet, tensing as he saw the warrior's slack expression, and the glow of gold in his eyes. "So you've come for me."

Did you doubt it, mortal? a voice inside his head asked.

The guard dragged his feet across the cell, and began releasing his manacles.

"I've done my part," Leeds said, rubbing his hands together to restore the circulation. "Where are the jewels?"

Go to the spring. There you will find all that you desire.

Leeds didn't trust the immortal, not since the first time he had spoken to him. "If you're wrong about her, everything will be lost."

She is the last. She is the one. She will not fail me.

To the guard, Leeds said, "I need your clothes."

"This traitor confessed to stabbing Farlae," Harlech told Beau as they walked along the outer ward. "He refuses to say what he used to poison the visiting ladies, but that was his doing as well. As soon as the ladies' lords arrive, the suzeraina will put the traitor in their hands. I expect they will convince him to admit the rest." He made an ugly sound. "I still cannot believe how he deceived us all."

"He has done a terrible thing." Beau felt a hollowness in his chest, and thought of Alys. He wanted to keep her here at the Realm, but he could not stomach the idea of continuing his own deception. "Harlech, there is something I must tell you."

"You do not really mean to take that mortal as your *kyara*, do you?" the captain asked. "She is lovely, and I am certain of her affections for you, but you know how it will go. You cannot give her children. She will age while you do not, and someday leave you to go on living without her."

"What I must say does concern my love for Alys, but not in the manner you think. It is about me, who I am." Beau removed his sword, setting it aside to stand unarmed before his foster brother. "When the Templars brought me to your family, they told you that I was an orphan, the son of an English Crusader and his Italian wife. They gave you my name as Beaumaris of York."

Harlech frowned. "Who told you this?"

"I have always known," Beau admitted. "When I came to your household, I did not say a word for all those months because I could not. Nor could I understand the priests who brought me to you. I did not speak English."

"Of course, you spoke your mother's tongue—"

Beau shook his head. "My mother was not Italian. She was Saracen."

Harlech fell silent.

"By the time I had learned enough English to tell you, I had also been thoroughly schooled on how dearly Saracens were despised. I cannot say why the priests lied to you, but I thought if I spoke the truth—if I told you that I was the bastard son of a Saracen harlot—that you would kill me."

The captain gave him a narrow look. "So you concealed it out of shame."

"You misunderstand me. I loved my mother. I cannot regret being born the son of two enemies. It is not as if I had some choice in the matter." Beau looked into Harlech's eyes. "My shame is that I never confided in you. You have been my brother, and my best friend. That is why you had to be the first I told . . . after Alys."

"So you've confided this to her."

Beau nodded. "I have been afraid of the truth all of my life, and I never meant to tell her, or anyone. I cannot say why I would face it now, except that she makes me want to be a better man." He ducked his head. "I will accept whatever punishment you or Lady Jayr decide I deserve for deceiving you."

"What you deserve is the truth." Harlech lifted his fist, opening it to grip Beau's shoulder. "There is more you do not know, lad. The priests who brought you to my family told us the truth of who you were. They did not name you, or invent an Italian mother to explain away your dark hide. My father and I did. I've always known about your mother."

Beau stared at him. "But . . . all these years, and you said nothing?"

"You were barely out of swaddling when they brought you to us," Harlech reminded him. "You never spoke of it, and in time I told myself that you had forgotten your cradle tongue and your origins. No, truth be told, I had hoped you would never remember. No child should be taken from his mother as you were."

"All my struggles to keep my secret, that was never a secret." Beau sighed and glanced at the garrison's quarters. "Will our comrades be as understanding as you, I wonder?"

"They know you to be a formidable warrior, the best blade in the Realm, and a loyal friend, which is all that matters," the captain said. "I expect your lady Alys feels the same. Unless you now fancy yourself to be Saracen, and intend to go about dressing in robes and speaking your heathen tongue. That may prove somewhat contentious."

"That is not my aim." Beau picked up his sword. "There is another matter I must tell you."

Harlech arched his brows. "Your mother was Saracen, and your lady is a Scot. Never tell me that your grandparents were Huns."

"I cannot say who my grandparents were, but I have kept another thing from you," Beau said, determined to be rid of the last of his secrets. "I have not been going into the city merely to hunt. I have also been taking instruction on how to read, and to write."

"You have been going to school? With mortals?" Harlech chuckled. "Beaumaris the Scholar. Now, that will greatly entertain the lads."

Alys didn't want to tell Beau she'd been caught talking to Jayr's prisoner, and she'd felt light-headed ever since leaving the dungeons. She wandered through the keep, stepping out of sight whenever she saw one of the Kyn, and ended up standing outside the infirmary, unable to decide whether she should go in. It wasn't as if she were really ill; she was probably more upset than anything.

Alexandra Keller opened the door and peered out at her. "Your smell is distracting me, Indiana, so make up your mind." She moved her hand back and forth. "Coming in, or going back to your cute guy?"

Alys still hesitated. "I don't want to bother you, Dr. Keller. I'm okay."

"It's Alex, and you don't look so okay." She took her arm and guided her inside, leading her to an empty cot. "Sit." She pressed two fingers to Alys's wristbone. "Your heart is doing a river dance. Did Cute Guy nibble on you more than once in the last forty-eight?"

"No, he's only, ah, done that once, and not for very long." She glanced at the other three patients, all of whom appeared to be unconscious. "Are they very sick?"

"Spy Guy there has a nasty stab wound, but he's on the mend. Our ladies are in the Kyn version of a coma. Look up; keep your eyes open, please." After she checked Alys's pupils with a penlight, she clicked it off. "Good news. You're not bespelled."

"Beau says I'm immune to that." She kept looking at the two female patients. Tall blonde, petite brunette. "Who are those women?"

"Friends in trouble." Alex stepped back. "Your vitals are on the high side, but nothing too alarming. The dark circles under those gorgeous eyes are turning into luggage, and your scent tells me you're about to drop. Cute Guy needs to give you a couple nights off to sleep." She followed the direction of Alys's gaze. "Something you want to tell me?"

"The blond woman—she's French, isn't she? And the brunette is American."

"Yeah, they are." Alex shifted to block her view. "Would you mind sharing how you knew that?"

"I dreamed of them. They weren't like this—I mean, they were little girls—but I'm sure it was them." Alys knew how ridiculous she sounded, but the doctor wasn't laughing. If anything, she was riveted. "Does it mean something to you?"

"No, but my magic trick is reconstructive surgery, not neurology or psychiatry." Alex slung her stethoscope around her neck. "You, on the other hand, probably know a lot about minerals, am I right?"

"I minored in geology," Alys said. "Most archaeologists do."

"Good, then I'll tell you my bizarre thing." She nodded toward the unconscious women. "I took blood samples from Simone and Chris shortly after they were changed to Darkyn. I also got one from Simone while she was still human. When I put the samples under the scope for the first time, I saw minute crystals in their blood."

"Is there any chance the original samples were accidentally contaminated, or perhaps partially frozen?" When Alex shook her head, Alys grew thoughtful. "The liquid environment of the bloodstream requires absorption of minerals in their electrolyte or ionic form. They'd only crystallize under a few, very specific conditions."

"Like cholesterol forming atherosclerotic plaque in the blood vessels, or Charcot's forming in leukemic blood after death." Alex nodded. "These were different. They were green. And when I checked the samples a few hours later, they were gone."

"Inside the body the liver probably would have filtered out the contaminants; outside the body a chemical or heat source would be required." Alys noted how the doctor had emphasized the color green. "Did you observe the structure of these crystals?"

"Yep." Alex nodded, and picked up a chart, flipping

over the top sheet to make a quick sketch, which she showed to Alys. "They looked like this."

Alys studied the lines. "Cubic. Perfect cleavage in all four directions."

"Is that somehow significant?"

"Only in that I can eliminate one source." She met the doctor's puzzled gaze. "The contaminant in your blood samples didn't come from the emeralds."

Alex drew back, surprised. "How did you know I thought that?"

"That's *my* magic trick." She handed the chart back to her. "Emerald crystals are hexagonal, not cubic like this. Also, when you ran the blood tox screens, you would have detected chromium, which I assume you didn't."

"Right on the money, Indiana." She eyed the chart. "So what the hell is it, and why did it dissolve?"

"Without an intact crystal lattice to study and test, I can only theorize," Alys warned her. "What you saw sounds like an unstable isotope, but behaves like a microorganism, one that spontaneously crystallizes. Which would indicate that it is—"

"Pathogenic." Alex kicked the leg of the empty cot, knocking it sideways. "Goddamn it, not another one."

Alys gave her a sympathetic look. "If you're ever able to collect another sample, I'll be happy to analyze it. What's wrong?"

Alex frowned and rubbed at her temple. "Someone close by is having a bad day."

A guard appeared in the doorway, and before either woman could react, he raised a gun and fired it at Alex.

She looked down at the dart embedded in her chest. "Son of a bitch. Alys, get out of here."

Alys tried to catch her as she sagged, but the guard yanked her back from the doctor, and used a zip tie to bind her wrists behind her back. "Who are you? Why are you doing this?"

Without saying a word the guard produced a roll of heavy-duty packing tape, tearing off a length with his teeth and slapping it over her mouth. Once he dragged her out into the corridor, he shoved her into a large laundry cart and piled linens on top of her.

"If you move or make a sound," Alys heard the guard whisper, "I'll shoot whoever comes near me, and then I'll put one in your head."

Alys felt the nudge of a gun barrel through the cloth behind her head, and stopped moving.

The cart rattled and swayed as her captor pushed it down the corridor. Alys didn't dare move, and when the cart abruptly stopped, she held her breath.

"You, there. Hold," Beau's voice ordered. "Have you encountered a red-haired mortal on your rounds?"

"No, my lord," her captor answered politely. "I haven't seen any women tonight."

"Then tell me," Beau said, "why is her smell on your garments?"

Gunfire made Alys shriek behind her gag, and then her abductor was running with the cart. She was jostled by the twin bumps of the wheels as they crossed a threshold, and the drag as they moved over grass. When the cart came to a stop several minutes later, the linens were yanked away and she was hauled out onto her feet. She looked around wildly, but saw no sign of Beau.

All the life went out of her. *He killed him.*

The intruder held her by the neck as he unlocked the

back of a service van and shoved her toward the hands reaching out. Alys was unceremoniously dumped on her side as the van drove off.

During the fifteen-minute ride that followed, none of the men spoke, not even to one another. Alys couldn't think of Beau lying dead in the passage without wanting to scream, so she focused on her situation. The interior of the van was too dark for her to make out the faces of the two men crouched on either side of her. Both were armed with guns concealed beneath the service uniforms they wore. Whoever the men were, they were probably the same ones who had destroyed her camp and planted the bomb in her Jeep.

They'd wanted her dead; now she was being abducted. *Something has changed.*

The van began to jolt as it drove onto a dirt road, and Alys had to hold her head up to keep it from banging against the floor. By the time the van slowed and coasted to a stop, her neck ached with stiffness, but she welcomed the pain; it was the only thing she could feel besides the ice encasing her heart.

Whoever did this is going to regret it.

The men climbed through the back doors and hauled her out, each one taking hold of her arm as they marched her through a dark grove. Alys saw the dark shapes of tents outlined by firelight but no equipment or other people. The emptiness of the camp indicated whatever work had been done here was finished.

Or taking me was the last job they had to do.

The men marched her to the largest tent and shoved her through the curtain of vinyl strips hanging over it. She promptly tripped and fell to her knees in the dirt.

"Leave us."

The voice made her head snap up, and as the men left, Alys struggled to her feet, turning around as she tried to see who had spoken.

"Hold still." A manicured hand ripped the tape from her mouth. "If you scream, Alys, I'll have you gagged again. Which would be a pity, given how much we have to discuss."

She stumbled back, her eyes widening as a lantern switched on and illuminated his face, and the dazzling white of the suit he wore. Until that moment, she was sure she'd been hallucinating. "You're alive."

"I never died, my dear. I merely had no more reason to act as your guardian." Robert Leeds lowered himself into a folding chair, and gestured to another. "Do sit down before you faint."

Alys stayed on her feet, her mind racing as connections she had never noticed began assembling themselves into a complicated construct. "Why am I here?"

"Your research proved most disappointing, Alys. The treasure is not located beneath the spring pool, or anywhere near it." He took out a cigar and lit it, puffing until the tip glowed orange-red. "You falsified your notes to conceal the fact that you already had the emeralds, didn't you?"

Alys blinked. "You did this because you think I have the treasure?"

"Of course. I sent you here to find the Emeralds of Eternity." He blew out a stream of smoke. "What other reason would I have to waste twenty-six years of my time, a considerable amount of my money and resources, on raising, educating, and guiding an unwanted orphan?"

"You became my guardian so you could train me, and use me." It was almost as brilliant as it was sickening.

"Your mother refused to recognize your potential, or to grant me the access to you that I required." His eyes bored into hers. "I'd hoped to persuade her to marry me, but her unhappy affair with your father left her too emotionally damaged. I had no choice but to kill her and forge the papers granting me guardianship so I could bring you to America and set up your new life."

Alys frowned. "I'm American."

"Your father met your mother while she was an exchange student in Paris, and used her for sex until he grew bored with her. She promptly fled back to Ireland, where you were born eight months later." He smiled. "Not what anyone would call a grand romance. After your father rejected her so cruelly, your mother felt nothing but resentment for you as his child. If not for her religion and her country's antiquated laws, I'm certain she would have opted to abort."

Alys's legs wobbled as she went to the chair across from Robert and sat down. "I don't have the emeralds. I don't know where they are."

"My men watched you pick them up from the ground after the explosion," Robert said. "At which point your Kyn lover whisked you off to the Realm, where no doubt he convinced you to give them to Suzeraina Jayr. Don't look so shocked, my dear. It's what they do best. They feed on us, they work us like slaves, and then, when we are of no further use, they discard us."

His light tone couldn't quite cover the rage and hatred seething behind the words. "Is that what they did to you?"

"My family has served the Kyn since the Dark Ages. Which is to say Lord Marietto bred us like cattle. He had us branded at birth." He rolled up his sleeve, revealing a tattoo that had been partially mutilated. "And brainwashed as well. We believed he adored us, and would do anything for his 'treasures.' But when his lady and I fell in love, I discovered it was all a lie."

Alys pushed away thoughts of Beau. "Did he hurt you?"

"He removed me from my position, stripped me of my rank, and sent me into exile. When I came back for my lady, my parents said she had killed herself the day after I was banished. But I knew the truth." He closed his eyes briefly. "Marietto murdered her and passed it off as a suicide. My family never knew the kind of jealous, murderous bastard they served, but I did. Leora warned me about him when we became lovers. She was terrified of him, and I failed her."

Alys noted the lines of his face, the set of his mouth, and realized why Leeds had seemed so familiar. "The emeralds won't make you immortal, Robert. It's only a legend. If you want to kill this Lord Marietto—"

"Oh, I've already done that." He smiled at her. "One phone call to the Kyn's enemies was all it took. I wished I could have watched him burn, but other matters required my attention."

"I understand." She glanced over her shoulder at the two men standing guard outside the tent. "Building an army of traitors takes some time, doesn't it?"

"I prefer to think of it as freeing my fellow slaves. What the Kyn have never understood about the *tresori* is that we can think for ourselves. After centuries of catering to them, we know exactly what they are. A plague upon the earth, one that has ravaged humanity for far too long." He stood. "A plague that you were born to help me to end."

"I'm not going to help you do anything," Alys told him. "I don't have the emeralds."

"But you do have a photographic memory and excellent drafting skills." Robert picked up the roll of paper and placed it on the table. "Which is why you're going to draw a floor plan of the Realm, and show me precisely where Lady Jayr put the emeralds."

"By now they know you shot Dr. Keller and kidnapped me," Alys said. "Even if I do this, you'll never get your men back inside."

Robert took hold of her arm and pulled her out of the chair, forcing her out of the tent and out into the center of the camp. Once there, he pointed to the road.

Alys saw an endless line of vehicles filling both lanes of the road. There had to be hundreds of them, all driving east toward the Realm.

"As you can see, my army is already on the way," Robert said. "We don't have to sneak into the castle. This time, we're going to take it, and kill them all."

Chapter 17

Clutching his shoulder, Beau hurried out to the service lot, where he saw the taillights of a van as it pulled out onto the road. As it turned to the west, it passed a red Ferrari and a black Porsche entering the access road.

Beau scanned the vehicles left in the lot as the two sports cars parked. Two tall, fair-haired Kyn males climbed out of the Ferrari, while a more youthful-looking warrior got out of the Porsche.

As they approached him, Beau recognized Lucan, and remembered to bow as the suzerain halted in front of him. "Good evening, Lord Alenfar."

"Warrior." The former assassin eyed the front of his tunic. "Are you aware that you are bleeding all over yourself?"

"Aye, my lord. A traitor infiltrated the keep and has taken my woman. I was wounded trying to stop him." Beau glanced back at the castle. "Forgive me; I would escort you inside and summon my lady, but I must go now if I am to recover her."

"Not with that copper slug burning in your flesh." Lucan reached one gloved hand into his jacket and offered the dagger he drew out to the Kyn standing beside him. "I believe you have some experience with this sort of extraction, Korvel."

Beau shook his head. "There is no time. If I do not pursue them now, they will surely kill her—"

"While you will surely drop dead of copper poisoning before you can reach her. I will have it out quickly," Korvel promised. When Beau nodded, he said, "Stand against the wall." He turned to the youthful-looking warrior. "Lord Jamys, hold him, if you would."

Jamys used his arms to brace Beau in place, and Korvel tore aside his shirt before slipping the tip of the dagger into his wound. Beau bit back a howl as white-hot pain sizzled through his joint and down his arm.

"I nearly have it." The Kyn lord deftly worked the slug out of his flesh, and caught it in his palm, tossing it away.

"Here, brother." Jamys bit his palm, and clamped it over the wound.

"I am in your debt." As the pain eased, Beau regarded Lucan. "Might I borrow your vehicle, my lord?"

"And drip your blood all over the hand-sewn leather interior?" The suzerain sniffed. "I think not."

"Oh, for God's sake, Lucan." Korvel looked disgusted. "It's only a car."

"I beg to differ. It is a Ferrari." He glared at his companion. "My *favorite* Ferrari, as it happens."

"Take mine." Jamys pressed his keys into Beau's hand.

"My thanks, Lord Jamys. Suzerain. Lord Korvel." With another hasty bow Beau ran to the Porsche.

Once out on the road, Beau lowered the window to

let the night air stream inside. Being locked up inside the van had effectively cut off Alys's scent, but it was easy enough to pick up and follow the fresh exhaust left from the van's engine. By the time he reached the back roads leading to Tremayne's property, Beau knew where he would find her.

He drove to the site, leaving the Porsche hidden behind the church before he struck out on foot for the Europeans' camp. The dull throbbing in his shoulder hardly registered now, but his fear that he would not reach Alys in time swelled with every yard he ran.

They wouldn't have taken her if they meant to kill her immediately, Beau thought as he vaulted over the fence and made for the Europeans' camp. *They must need her to . . .*

He stopped as the stink of fire and spilled blood and violent death filled his lungs, and listened to the wind before he slowly approached the camp. He found the first body where it had fallen in the brush; the man had been shot in the back while running from the camp.

More bodies appeared as he moved toward the tents: all of them dead, most of them shot. Two had been repeatedly stabbed; one had his throat cut. From the tracks left in the dirt they had been attacked by at least two dozen well-trained killers. All of the team's equipment had been burned, as well as their RVs.

Beau spotted one partially melted bag containing a potsherd, and when he picked it up, he could still make out some of Alys's handwriting on the label. He also caught the scent of the killers, who had gone south, and dropped the bag as he followed their trail.

When he reached the grove of trees concealing the

Americans' camp, he smelled Alys's scent and nearly fell to his knees. She was alive, and very close; he could almost hear the frantic beating of her heart in his ears.

I'm coming, love.

The first explosion came a few moments after Jayr had ordered Harlech to double the patrols.

"Down." Byrne shielded her with his body as stone chips and dust rained over them. A low, deep rumble shook the floor beneath them, swelling to a roar and then dying away,

"That sounded like the forward tower curtain. For once he told the truth." Jayr brushed the debris from her lover's back as he helped her to her feet. "Sound the alarm."

Byrne went over to the square device in the wall that was marked FIRE ALARM and punched through the glass before pulling down the handle inside. Instantly a screeching, repeating wail echoed throughout the castle.

Jayr went to the weapons cache in her cabinet and took out her sword. It was the sight of the battle-ax beside it, however, that gave her pause. "Aedan, if I could spare you this . . ."

"I know you would, lass." His big hand rested on her shoulder. "But you've stopped me before, and you will have need of my affliction now."

She nodded, removing the ax and passing it to him. "Try to hold on to your senses for as long as you can." She reached up to kiss him quickly. "I love you."

He held her hand against his heart. "And I you, wife."

Byrne shouldered his ax and made for the garrison, while Jayr climbed the inner-ward tower to the highest point of the castle, a fortified room lined with monitors projecting every possible view of the keep, along with her communications array. Once inside, Jayr slipped on her headset and studied the screens to survey the damage to the curtain wall.

Beneath the gaping hole in the face of the ashlar, rubble had poured into the moat. Dozens of inflatable rafts propelled by small outboard motors were already crossing the waters and making for the sloped bank. On the opposite bank, two men shouldering a large pipelike device were taking aim at the castle.

Jayr enabled her microphone. "Trebuchet to the opposite bank, fifteen degrees left of tower two, fire at will. Archers, north battlement, commence the hailstorm."

Arrows rained down on the first men attempting to climb the slope of the inner bank, skewering them to the ground. At the same time a massive ball of flame soared across the moat, smashing into the pair with the rocket launcher and setting off an even larger explosion.

Jayr rapidly relayed orders to her defender units as the intruders scattered in all directions. She almost relaxed until she saw the lines of armed men marching out of the groves.

"Aedan, they've a second wave carrying in flamethrowers from the south," she warned her seneschal. "Stable master, release the horses and withdraw to the outer ward."

"Stay aloft, my lady," Byrne's voice rumbled over her earpiece. "We'll attend to these trespassers."

"We've no one faster than me," she reminded him as she scanned the monitors. "They're moving in from all sides now. The Realm is surrounded."

"Then they best buckle on their helmets," Byrne growled before he began issuing orders. "Crossbowmen to the back loops—"

Jayr removed her headset and secured the transmitter before she took out her battle armor from a storage trunk under the console. While she could move faster than the eye could see, she had no illusions about how well her Kyn talent would protect her. She might dodge an arrow, but not a bullet or ground-launched rocket. To survive the night, she would have to be as clever as she was quick.

On her way down to the lower level Jayr heard three voices in the corridor, and flashed the rest of the way to stop in front of Lucan. Her sudden appearance made his two companions start in surprise, but the suzerain merely cocked a brow.

"Someone should really put a bell on you, my lady." He exchanged bows with her. "Perhaps after the mortals have finished playing at siege."

"My apologies for the unseemly reception, and the inconvenience of the attack, my lord." She gestured toward the staircase. "You may take refuge in the loft while we deal with the attack."

"What, and miss all the hacking and dismembering and beheading?" He drew off his gloves. "Please, Jayr. Don't deny me my little amusements."

"What he means to say, my lady," Korvel put in, "is that we would be happy to assist with your defense. He's also summoned his garrison. They should arrive in a few hours."

"Did you have to spoil the surprise?" Lucan demanded.

"Thank you, Captain Korvel. If you would join Harlech in the bailey, he will be glad of your counsel and experience. Lord Durand, your blade will be welcome among my swordsmen at the outer ward." She turned to Lucan. "My lord, thank you for sending for your men. I must inspect the perimeter and assess the traitors' numbers and resources, so if you are willing, I will give you the keep."

"My lady." A glint of respect shone in his cold eyes. "I shall hold it safe until your return."

Jayr used the postern passage to enter the escape tunnel under the castle, and flashed through it until she reached the moat lock. After she sealed herself inside the watertight room, she braced herself and pressed the button to open the outer doors.

Water flooded the chamber, immersing her in seconds. She swam out through the doors, turning long enough to seal them before she kicked her way to the surface.

She came up into the frigid air beneath a low-hanging fringe of branches from the holly Byrne had planted along the very edge of the moat's inner bank to provide concealment. From her position she could see a few boats still floating, their occupants covered with arrows, but the bulk of the rafts had retreated to the outer bank. She glanced up to see the finest of her garrison's snipers still holding position behind the machicolations, each man's weapon poised and ready to fire.

Jayr sank beneath the water and swam across the moat to emerge beneath the platform that connected to the bridges to permit vehicles into the castle courtyard. As soon as the general alarm had been sounded, her men in the barbican towers had locked the bridges at the bottom of the moat; the attackers would not be able to raise them again without access to the tower controls. She crept up the bank, keeping her body close to the earth to avoid being spotted as she listened to the mortals several feet away.

"—that pontoon ready to launch in one hour," a harsh voice ordered. "Move the rocket launchers into position, and have the sharpshooters take out those emergency lights."

Jayr breathed in, appalled by the number of scents she detected. From what she had seen on the monitors, she had guessed the mortals numbered only a few hundred; she smelled close to a thousand or more. The attackers outnumbered her men three to one, and with their sheer numbers and explosives they might breach their defenses before Lucan's garrison could reach the Realm.

We do not die so easily.

She crawled back down to the edge and slipped into the water. A daring idea began to form in her mind as she swam along the entire length of the moat, surfacing every few hundred feet to survey the positions of the mortals. At last she reached the underwater entrance to the lock and used it to reenter the postern tunnel.

She stripped out of her sodden armor, leaving it in the tunnel as she flashed back up into the keep. She found Lucan in the main hall, standing watch on the gallery. "They're preparing a pontoon. They'll use their rockets to cover the launch, which will be in less than an hour." She pulled down from a recess in the wall a large map of the Realm and the land surrounding it.

Lucan jumped down to the floor and joined her. "They're not fools. This time they'll shield the pontoon from your archers. How many are there?"

"A thousand, perhaps more. Once they breach the walls—and they will—we'll be overrun before your men arrive." She glanced at him. "Unless we invite them in first by raising the bridges, and opening the gates."

He scowled at her. "My lady, Kyn do not surrender to mortals, or anyone, for that matter."

"This I know, my lord." She replaced the map. "But who said anything about surrendering?"

Lucan regarded her in silence for several moments before he smiled. "I like you, Jayr. I like you very much."

"Good to know someone's happy." Alexandra Keller leaned against the doorway, her expression dazed. "Me, I've been shot. Every time I come to this fucking place, I get shot. Oops, there go my knees again." She slid down to the floor.

Jayr hurried over with Lucan and helped her to a bench, checking her over before she looked up at the suzerain. "I don't see any blood."

"She doesn't have any," he drawled. "Only ice runs through those veins."

"Shut up, Lucan, before I make you slap yourself. There isn't any blood, Jayr. The bastard tranq'd me." She rested her head against the wall and closed her eyes. "It's wearing off, and I'll be fine. I heard about the siege, and I've got your ladies setting up the infirmary for casualties. Just tell me where you stashed the girls."

Jayr frowned. "I'm sorry; the girls?"

"Simone and Chris? My patients?" Alex looked from

her to Lucan and back again. "You didn't take them out of the infirmary and put them somewhere safer. Great. That means the shooter has them, too."

"Once we take possession of the Realm, I'll be back for you," Robert said as he watched the guard tying Alys to the tent pole. "Then you will show me where the emeralds are hidden."

"I didn't have the emeralds," she repeated wearily. "They're not in the castle. I don't know where they are. What your spies saw were fakes."

Robert crouched down in front of her. "You're being tedious, Alys. If you don't cooperate, I'll give you to my men for a few hours. They know many inventive ways to help jog your memory."

"It won't make any difference what you do to me. I never had the jewels." She closed her eyes, unable to look at his face for another second. "You might as well kill me now."

"You'll die when I say you will, my dear." Robert stood up and walked out with the guard, who took up a position just outside the tent flap.

Alys flexed her cramped, cold fingers, straining again at the plastic tie until it bit into her flesh. Robert would kill her eventually, but he would make her suffer a great deal first, and somehow she had to prepare for that. Or she might try to kill herself before he initiated the torture to come.

Don't be a coward. Beau would want you to keep fighting.

Alys began twisting her wrists against the plastic

again, but while it bruised her, the edges of it were too dull to cut her skin. She couldn't make herself bleed, and blood was the only thing she had that might help her work herself loose.

Blood.

The word triggered Alys's thought matrix, and she turned her focus inward to assemble a loose construct of fragmented facts and theories. The Templar who had come to the mission had been Darkyn. *We need your blood to survive.* All of the Timucua had left their village abruptly, shortly after the Spanish priests had arrived and built the mission. The priests themselves had all disappeared; no bodies were ever found. The borrow pit she'd fallen into had been twenty feet deep. *There aren't any burials anywhere near here.*

What did they do with all that dirt and rock?

Alys imagined herself at the site, and began walking it in her mind. There were no unusual elevations in the ground around the mission or the spring pond. All of Tremayne's property was perfectly flat.

Very funny, you guys.

When she'd stood in the center of the old village, she had looked *down* at the mission. That shouldn't have been possible. It seemed that the natives *had* built a mound — and then they had built their village on top of it.

The construct didn't make sense to her. Mounds were built to serve as tombs, and as such were sacred places of the dead; the Timucua would never have lived on top of one. Some of the mounds found in Florida, however, had not been tombs. Excavation had proved several had been used by many generations of natives as ancient landfills, and were filled only with the discarded shells, bones, and other refuse of their daily lives.

If the natives had attacked and killed the priests, they wouldn't have bothered to honor them by burying their bodies. It was more likely they would have left them to rot, burned them, or even displayed them as proof of their tribe's ferocity.

They constructed the mound, built the village, and then they abandoned it. They fled at the same time the priests disappeared, along with the Templar.

The mission and the village had been flawlessly constructed. They had both survived intact for six centuries. Both had been abandoned. Both had been guarded by the Timucua.

. . . in my time there were no archaeologists digging up the earth.

The Kyn who guarded the treasure you seek was a smith, and a mason.

Mortals are easy to convince; what you see is what you believe.

Those final pieces slipped into place, completing the puzzle. Now all she had left to do was prevent Robert from ever knowing the truth.

"Guard," she called out. "I've changed my mind. I'll tell your boss what he wants to know."

The guard shuffled inside the flap, giving her a strange look.

"He's looking in the wrong place." Alys pushed herself to her feet. "Take me to him."

The guard opened his mouth, closed it, and fell over

onto his face as the man standing behind him stepped over him.

"You can't give the treasure to our enemies, love," Beau said, smiling. "Not after all this."

He's alive. Her heart clenched as she stared at him, almost afraid he would go ghostly on her and shimmer out of sight. But no, he was there, the answer to every wish she would ever make on birthday candles and Christmas mornings and shooting stars.

"Alys?"

"Beau." Something roared in her ears as black spots danced in front of her eyes. "I think I'm going to faint again."

Beau came over to her, cradling her face in his hands as he put his mouth on hers. The gentleness of his kiss made Alys's knees buckle, but he held her up, reaching behind her to snap the plastic tie with a flick of his fingers.

Alys groaned as her aching arms fell to her sides, and dragged them up to rest her numb hands against his chest. "I wasn't going to tell them where the emeralds are. I was going to trick the guard into killing me."

Beau smoothed the hair back from her face. "Do you have such little faith in your husband?"

"No, I thought my husband dead." She swallowed a sob as she huddled against him. "Thank you for being immortal."

"I've never been so glad of it myself." Beau held her tightly, stroking her back with a soothing gesture before he set her at arm's length and examined the bruises on her wrists. "Did they hurt you?"

"I'm all right. They're more interested in getting the jewels, and they believe that I took them to the Realm. They've gone to attack it." As his expression darkened, she put her hand on his arm. "It's okay. I know how to stop them."

"The jewels."

She nodded. "I know where they are."

Chapter 18

"That is excellent news, Dr. Stuart."

They both turned, and Beau bared his fangs at the man standing over the unconscious guard.

Leeds held up his empty hands. "My name is Devan Leeds. I was sent here by the *tresoran* council to recover the jewels, and protect the Kyn." He added something in an archaic language. At the same time, he dug his fingers into the back of his right hand, peeling away what appeared to be the scarred outer layer of his skin. He discarded the prosthesis, and showed Beau his hand, which had been tattooed with an elaborate compass.

Alys felt her lover's tension ebb, and looked up at him. "Is it the mark, or what he said?"

"It is both. Mr. Leeds is a sentinel, one of an elite group who serve the *tresoran* council. They are our most trusted mortal allies." Beau gave the other man a skeptical look. "My lady named you a traitor."

"I was sent by the council to infiltrate the *tresoran* traitors, assess their intentions, and, if possible, recover the Emeralds of Eternity," Leeds said. "They in turn sent me to the Realm to spy on your suzeraina."

"You nearly killed Farlae."

"*Nearly* being the operative word. I'm a sentinel, warrior. You know if I'd wanted him dead, I'd have finished him." Leeds sounded tired. "Dr. Stuart, I owe you an apology. I knew my brother, Robert, was still alive, and that he was the leader of the traitors. I even discovered how he planned to use the emeralds to take his vengeance on the Kyn. But I never knew about you, or what he has done to bring you under his control."

"Robert is your brother." When he nodded, Alys felt a surge of bitterness. "I thought you looked familiar. And thank you for the apology, but that isn't going to bring back my mother."

"Nor will it restore to me the family my brother murdered," he told her. "My parents, my aunts and uncles, my cousins—all of them died at the hands of the Brethren, thanks to Robert's betrayal."

"Is that why they sent you?" Beau asked. "To redeem your bloodline?"

"My bloodline burned to death with my lord Marietto, and I volunteered," Leeds corrected. "I'd hoped to persuade Robert to end this quest for immortality, and to surrender himself and his followers to the council, but the death of his lady cemented his hatred for the Kyn." He looked at Alys. "I know it cannot serve as an excuse for his actions, but my brother is quite insane."

"Aye, and he is a dead man," Beau said flatly.

"By now Lord Alenfar has summoned his men from the south," Leeds said. "You needn't worry, warrior. In a few hours your wish will be granted."

"They may come too late to save my *jardin*," Beau said. "We must do something *now*."

"The three of us can't stop the siege," Alys said. "Not unless we offer Robert what he wants."

Leeds shook his head. "As much as I wish I could save my brother, and end this private war of his, I cannot allow you to give him the emeralds."

Beau studied her face. "But we can use them as a lure, to draw him and his army away from the Realm."

"Especially if he thinks his brother is the one who has them," Alys said. "We don't have to move them. We just need a time-stamped photo of them, one we can send to his mobile. Devan, you'll tell him that you'll give him the jewels in exchange for ending the siege — and you'll have to be convincing."

"As often as I have tried to talk him out of this madness, I believe I can do that." He sighed. "But once we lure him and his men away from the castle, what then? We are still three against an army."

"We put an end to this. Permanently." Alys watched both men's faces. "As soon as we recover the jewels, we destroy them."

Leeds bent to take the gun from the unconscious guard while Beau looped the broken tie around Alys's wrists. "Stay behind her," the *tresora* said, "and keep your head down. If I'm challenged, take your lady and run."

Beau kept his hand on Alys's waist as they walked out of the tent and headed for the car Leeds had stolen from the Realm. Although there were only a handful of guards, they all looked at Leeds, and two moved to intercept them.

"We have orders to keep her here," one of the guards said, resting his hand on his sidearm.

"My brother sent me to bring her to the castle." Leeds sounded bored. "You can call him to confirm, of course, if you want to be held responsible for keeping him waiting."

Fear spiked through the guard's scent as he nodded and quickly retreated.

"Put her in the back," Leeds told Beau before he climbed in behind the wheel. Once they were inside, he started the engine. "I'll have to take the road out and drive until we're out of their sight, and then double back with the lights off. You're sure about the location of the emeralds, Dr. Stuart?"

"Yes." Alys watched the rearview mirror. "You'd better go now, Mr. Leeds. One of those guards is making a call on his mobile."

Leeds drove quickly out of the camp, taking the shortest route across the fields to the road. Just before they reached it, the back window shattered. As more gunfire struck the back of the car, Beau pushed Alys down and covered her with his body. "They know."

"Stay down." Leeds began driving in an evasive pattern until he reached the road, where he shut off the lights and accelerated, racing into the dark until he slowed and eased the vehicle back off the road, pulling beneath a row of trees and shutting off the motor.

"What are you doing?" Beau demanded. "Keep going."

"Wait. My brother's thugs are not that imaginative." Leeds's voice sounded oddly strained.

Beau detected the scent of fresh blood. "You've been wounded."

"Yes, but the round didn't hit anything significant," the *tresora* assured him.

Beau turned to watch the road, and after another minute every vehicle that had been left at the camp sped past them. Only when the last car disappeared from sight did Leeds restart the engine and pull back out onto the road, heading back toward Alys's camp.

Beau helped Alys up and checked her over for new wounds. "We won't have very long to do this, love, and no tools with which to dig. Leeds is wounded."

"We won't need to dig. They're not buried. They're submerged." Alys curled up against him. "The source of the spring isn't under the pond. It's under the village, and I know how to get to it."

Once they reached the mission, Leeds drove the car into the stables and shut off the engine. Beau helped Alys out, and then frowned as he looked at the *tresora*, who still sat behind the wheel. "Come, man. Let me have a look at it."

Leeds grimaced and reached into his shirt pocket, removing his mobile and handing it to Beau. "I won't be accompanying you, I'm afraid. You'll also have to handle the negotiations with Robert."

Beau glanced at the amount of blood smeared on the phone and yanked open the driver's door as Leeds slumped over against it. He eased the man out and placed him on the ground. The moonlight gleamed on the exit wound in the center of his chest.

Leeds opened his eyes to give Alys a rueful look. "Tell

Lady Jayr that everything I said was a lie." He coughed up some blood. "Thank God, that will be the last I tell." He let out a final breath and went still.

Beau checked for a pulse, and then looked up at Alys and shook his head before he gently closed Leeds's eyes.

Alys picked up one of the packing quilts that hadn't burned and draped it over the *tresora*'s body. "Be at peace, Mr. Leeds."

Beau pocketed the mobile and put his arm around her. "Come away now, love."

As they crossed the camp toward the village trail, Alys paused to wipe at her face with her sleeve, and then tugged at Beau's hand.

"Look." She pointed to the ground, which showed two sets of fresh footprints darkening the frosted grass. "Someone just came through here."

Beau breathed in, frowning as he recognized the scents left behind in the air. "They are Kyn, not mortal." He eyed the size and shape of the tracks. "Both of them are women, but unfamiliar to me."

"Simone and Christian." Alys peered ahead. "But how did they get out of the castle, and why would they come here?"

"We will have to ask when we find them." Beau picked her up in his arms. "Hold on to me, love."

He ran with her along the trail until they reached the village, which appeared deserted. When he set Alys down on her feet, she led him to the edge of the borrow pit, and looked down into it. "I can't see the bottom."

"I can." He peered through the shadows and inhaled. "The ladies are not down there, but their scent tells me they were."

"The entrance to the source of the spring is at the bottom." She held out her arms to him. "I need one more ride."

Beau picked her up and jumped into the pit, landing on his feet at the bottom. When he put Alys down, she went over to the stone wall, feeling along it carefully before she stepped back and pointed to a slight outcropping. "There's a depression along the left side."

Beau found the handhold, and used it to pull on the rock. An entire section slid out of the wall, revealing a low entrance to a tunnel. "How did you know this would be here?"

"You told me," she said as she ducked her head and stepped inside. "You said that our mutual relative was a mason."

Beau still didn't understand her. "What has that to do with it?"

"Cristophe didn't come here with the other priests to build a mission, or to convert the natives. There weren't any natives; he simply wanted everyone to think that. The mission and the village were fakes. His version of camouflage." She touched the stone wall of the tunnel. "So he could hide this, and the jewels he left here."

Beau heard the sound of water, and took hold of her hand. "Lead the way."

Alys walked with him along the narrow tunnel, which opened out into a stone cave enclosing a wide pool of water. Instead of being shrouded in darkness, the cave was illuminated by the water, which glowed an eerie green.

Alys caught her breath. "I was wrong about one thing. He didn't take his friends with him."

Beau followed her gaze to the row of skeletons lining the far wall of the cave. Although time had decayed their garments, he could still make out the style of their robes. "The Spanish priests. He must have used them as labor and food, and killed them to protect his secret, and the location of the emeralds."

"I don't think so." Alys walked to the edge of the pool, and knelt there to look into it. "The jewels aren't emeralds, Beau."

"What else can they be?"

"Something much more dangerous," she said. "They've killed almost every human who has come in contact with them or the metal artifacts associated with them. I think short-term exposure to them is what killed the priests who helped Cristophe build this place. If I were to run tests on their remains, we'll find they all died the same way." She regarded the light shimmering in the water. "But I don't think there is any time left for that."

"If the jewels killed the priests, then you are in danger as well." He reached down and tugged her to her feet. "I must take you out of here."

Alys looked past him. "We can't leave."

Chris came hurtling across the stone to sprawl at Beau's feet. Behind her, Simone staggered, shoved forward by the man holding a gun to the back of her head.

"No one is going anywhere," Robert Leeds said pleasantly.

As Beau took a step toward the traitor, Alys gripped his arm. "No. He'll kill her before you can reach him."

"An excellent deduction, my dear." Robert forced

Simone to her knees. "My weapon is indeed loaded with pure copper rounds. One bullet to the brain stem will put a quick end to Ms. Derien's newfound immortality. Warrior, throw your sword to me."

Chris braced herself on her elbows and looked up at Beau and Alys. "Hang on to the blade, big guy. He's not planning to let us out of here alive."

"I'd spare you if I could, Ms. Lang," Robert assured her. "I'd very much like to know how you and your sister accomplished your transition to Kyn without employing the emeralds, and if the same could be done for Alys. I don't see why not; she is your half sister."

"There are *three* of us?" Chris gave Alys a wide-eyed look. "Holy Christ. Did Dad ever keep his pants zipped?"

"Apparently not," Simone murmured.

"Be quiet," Robert snapped. "As I was saying, I'd be delighted to have you as part of my new world order. But I think your loyalties and your lovers would get in my way." To Beau, he said, "Throw your sword to me. Now."

Beau drew his blade, placing it on the stone and sliding it over to the man.

"Pick it up," Robert told Chris. When she did, he took it from her hand and tucked it under his belt.

"You need only me, Father Robere," Simone said. "I am the daughter of Helada. Let the others go, and I will tell you everything you wish to know about the jewels."

"Just as you told your brother Pájaro in France, when he stole the Scroll of Falkonera?" He prodded the back of her head. "My dear girl, you didn't even warn him that simply touching it would kill him."

"These jewels are much more lethal than the scroll or

the cross," Alys warned him. "If you try to remove them, you won't live long enough to die of exposure. You'll also kill everyone within a fifty-mile radius of this place."

Leeds chuckled. "You can't believe in that ridiculous curse. For pity's sake, Alys, you're a scientist."

"That's why you have to listen to me, Robert." Alys nodded toward the glowing water. "That light is being emitted by the energy source contained in the gems. Over the centuries they've been gradually destabilizing, and right now the only thing keeping them safe is the spring itself. If you remove the jewels from the water, and put them together, they will cause an explosion. One that will be equal to dropping a very large and powerful nuclear bomb on this spot."

Leeds looked amused. "You know, you're completely wasted on the academic community. With that imagination, you should be writing novels." He removed a coil of copper cable from his pocket and a pair of wire cutters, and tossed them at her feet. "Bind their wrists and ankles. Tightly, if you please."

Alys looked up at Beau as she looped the cable around his wrists. "I don't know if I was any good at it, but I liked being your wife," she murmured.

"You are my heart." He touched his brow to hers. "This will not separate us, love. Nothing will."

Alys helped Chris up and brought her to sit next to Beau. "Not the greatest end to a vacation. You probably didn't even get to visit Epcot."

"No, damn it, and I wanted to spend a day in Japan." Her half sister closed her eyes. "Jamys is still at the Realm. If this explosion happens the way you say it will, will he . . . ?"

Alys considered lying to her, but knew in her place she would want to know the truth. "If I'm right, it will vaporize everything within a ten-mile radius, and kill every human within a hundred miles."

Chris glanced past her shoulder before her dark eyes shifted to Alys's. "You can't let him do this, Doc. There are over two million people living in the city. God knows how many visitors—"

"Dr. Stuart," Robert called out. "Come here."

Alys took one last look at Beau before she stood and walked to Simone. After binding her wrists and ankles, she dropped the cable and faced her former guardian.

He plucked the wire cutters out of her hand. "What are you waiting for?" He gestured toward the water. "Go in and get the emeralds."

She didn't move. "No."

He came around Simone and pressed the gun to her forehead. "Not afraid to die, are you?" He moved his hand to one side and fired. As Beau swore viciously, Robert smiled. "That was just a little flesh wound to the arm. Next time, I'll aim for his face." When she tried to rush to Beau, Robert caught her by the arm and hurled her into the spring.

The water streamed hot and cold around her, and Alys let it close over her head as she sank to the bottom. Beneath her she made out the large caches, each radiating light from the cracks in the stone. She swam to the first, pushing away the one piece of the capping slate and reaching it.

The jewel should have been hot, but it felt icy in her fingers. She swam up with it, surfacing and holding it up so that Leeds could see it.

He rushed to the edge and stretched out his arm. "Give it to me."

Alys held it just out of his reach. "Cut Simone's ankles loose, release her, and then I'll give it to you." When he swiveled with the gun, she added, "You're right. I lied about what will happen. There won't be any explosion."

Robert's nostrils flared. "Why did you lie?"

"Because the legends are true." She met his gaze. "Once you have all three gems, nothing can ever harm you again. Not even the Darkyn."

He moved back, keeping his eyes on her as he reached for the wire cutters. When he'd sliced through the cable around Simone's ankles, he shoved her toward the entrance to the cave.

"Alys." Simone gave her a desperate look.

"It's all right. Go," she urged before she dove down again. When Simone hurried away, Alys placed the diamond on the stone ledge, and dove back down.

Robert released Christian for the second gem, but when Alys brought up the third, he pulled her from the water.

"Alys." Beau fought his bonds, blood streaming over his hands and feet. "Get your hands off her."

"I'm afraid your little whore has run out of bargaining chips." Robert dragged Alys over, holding her clamped to his side as he kicked Beau over onto his back. After wrestling the last gem from her hand, he threw her down beside Beau. "The other two bitches shouldn't be difficult to track down once I've changed." He cradled the three gems, their eerie green light casting a sickly glow over his harsh features, before he placed them in a pouch, which he hung around his neck.

Alys knew what her guardian would do next, and scrambled on top of Beau, shielding him with her body.

"No." He tried to throw her off, and then went still as she jerked twice. He looked into her widened eyes. "Alys."

More shots erupted, and Beau saw Simone duck behind an outcropping as Leeds returned fire, running as he did to disappear into the second passage.

"Get him," Alys whispered as she collapsed. "Shield . . . jewels . . . somehow . . ."

Chapter 19

Beau eased Alys back into Simone's arms. "Hold on, love." To Simone, he said, "Stay with her."

The Frenchwoman nodded and looked back at her companion. "Christian, give me your jacket."

Beau followed the eerie glow of the water spatter Leeds had left behind through another, narrow passage in the rock. As he emerged on the surface behind the bone pile, he drew his copper dagger. A weapon fired, but the bullet he expected in his heart skimmed his shoulder and buried itself in the bones with an explosion of white splinters.

Leeds stood with his back against a spindly pine, his gun drooping from his blackened hands. "You can do nothing to me, vampire." He coughed, spraying blood from his slack mouth as he slid down the tree's trunk. "I am the one true immortal now."

Beau sheathed his dagger, closing the gap between them and kicking away the weapon Leeds could no longer use. "You're a fool. A dead fool."

"No, you heard her. The legends are true." Leeds

clutched at the hilt of Beau's sword. "Bury me," he pleaded. "I will rise again from my grave to walk the night. I will make you my second. You can have as many . . ." His forehead wrinkled. ". . . women as you . . . like. . . ." He slumped over, convulsing violently before his body went slack.

Beau reached down to pry open the corpse's fist. The emeralds had burned through his flesh to the bone, and now glittered with a strange, rapidly intensifying light.

They're not emeralds.

Vines ripped themselves out of his way as Beau raced back into the tunnel. He found Simone with Alys's head on her lap, and Christian holding her limp hand.

The sight of her, so still, stopped him as nothing else could. "Alys." He knelt beside her body and placed his hand on her cool, damp brow. As he bent to kiss her lips, the shallowness of her breath sent a wave of despair crashing over his heart.

"Beau." Her eyelids lifted a fraction.

"Robert is dead, and I have the gems," he told her quickly. "I will put them back in the spring."

She turned her head from side to side.

"What must I do with them?" He saw her lips move, and bent to put his ear next to them. But she did not speak again, nor did she take another breath. "Alys. *Alys.*"

"Beau." Christian gripped his shoulder, and nodded at the other side of the cave. A shimmer of gold sparkled on the opposite ledge, growing brighter and more dense-looking until it formed itself into a solid figure.

Golden armor covered nearly all of Cristophe's body, and when he spoke, his voice rang like a thousand bells. "I warned you of this, boy."

"You bastard." Beau got to his feet, and strode to the edge of the water. "You and your scheming. You've killed her." He was shouting now. "God damn you. God damn you to hell."

"My strength is almost gone with my body. It took the last of it to come here now. I failed heaven, and your brothers, and the last of my kin." Cristophe closed his eyes, but his lids turned transparent. "Forgive me."

Beau reached out with his talent, seizing what was left of Cristophe's flesh and using it to drag the smith across the water. He held him suspended as he showed him the jewels. "Alys said these will explode, and their power will destroy everything around us for miles. Millions will die. Tell me how to stop it."

"It is too late now," Cristophe said as his head disappeared and reappeared. "Good-bye, my son."

Beau heard Alys's voice in his head. *Shield them.*

With a roar he thrust the gems into the center of Cristophe's body. Pain engulfed his arm as the shimmering light burned into his flesh. He gritted his teeth and held his fist in place until the smith's body began to solidify around his wrist. Spreading his burning fingers, Beau released the gems, and yanked back his arm. Cristophe looked down at the crater in his abdomen, watching as his flesh grew solid and closed over the diamonds. He lifted his face, and the light in his eyes changed from gold to green.

"Into the mouth of the water, my son," Cristophe whispered. "Hurry."

Beau pushed the smith through the air to the back of the cave, and released him just above the source of the spring. Cristophe's form radiated thin beams of green light as he sank beneath the surface.

As the water began to boil, Beau lifted Alys's body into his arms. "Run as fast as you can," he told the other women. "Don't look back. Don't stop for anything."

"We won't make it in time." Simone glanced at Christian, who nodded. "No, I think we will stay here," she said kindly, "with you and our sister."

As the light from the fissure grew brighter, the women flanked him and Alys, encircling them with their arms. Beau blinked back tears of sorrow and gratitude as he pressed a kiss to Simone's brow, and the top of Christian's head, and finally Alys's sweet lips.

The light grew blinding, until it filled his eyes with brilliant emerald, set in shining gold. The air seemed to ripple, once, twice, and then without any sound at all lifted him from his feet, sending him soaring in a fountain of light into the night sky and scattering him among the stars.

"Excuse me. Miss? Excuse me."

Jayr looked up from the body of the dead *tresora* to see a young mortal couple standing by the gate. Both were dressed in shorts and T-shirts, and the male was taking photos of her with a digital camera.

The female smiled. "Sorry to interrupt your performance, but, um, we were hoping to get some tickets for the next show?"

Jayr stood up and surveyed the area. Through the smoke she could see the figures of her warriors and Lucan's moving across the field, checking bodies and collecting weapons. Harlech appeared driving their largest cart and called out for the men to bring the dead.

"God, it looks so real," the young man gushed, snapping away merrily. "What battle are you reenacting? *Hey.*"

Jayr used her strength and ability to pluck the digital camera from his hand and pull it through the fence before he could blink. "We don't allow photographs in the park."

The mortal stared at the gaping hole she had punched through the chain links. "Sure, okay."

She erased the images he had taken of her and the Kyn from the memory card before she handed the camera back to him.

As she turned her back on them, she heard the woman ask, "What about tickets?"

Byrne appeared before Jayr, and yanked her off her feet to hold her tightly against him. Over her head he said, "This was a rehearsal, lass, not a performance." He paused to kiss Jayr soundly on the lips. "We are also in the midst of renovating the Realm, so tickets are not currently on sale. We will be reopening in a few weeks with bigger and better shows, and hope to see you at one of them." He swung Jayr around and began to stride off with her, calling back, "Have a nice day."

She buried her face against his strong neck. "I can no longer be immortal. You just scared the life out of me."

"You should have known better," he chided, setting her down. "'Twas you who insisted I take all those bloody anger management classes on the computer." He brushed the hair back from her face. "Lucan is coming.

Try not to puke when he takes all the credit for our victory."

"I assisted with your ambush, helped you corral the traitors in the keep, and devoted much effort to keeping them busy until my men arrived." Dressed in assassin's black, Lucan walked out of a swirl of smoke. "Thus I *deserve* most of the credit."

"You dinnae even get dirty," Byrne pointed out.

"One of the few benefits of my talent." Lucan held up a bare hand before he took a pair of leather gloves from his jacket and slipped them on. "My garrison will aid with the disposals. Shall we—"

A sudden and enormous flare of bright green from the west interrupted him, and made them all shield their eyes. Although there was no sound from the eruption of light, a moment later the ground trembled beneath their feet.

"What in God's name was that?" Jayr gripped Byrne's hand as the shaking died away.

"It's near where Beau's woman has her encampment." Byrne watched the horizon as the glow spread and settled. "They must have finally found those wretched baubles."

Lucan glanced at him. "Were they using explosives to search for them?"

"However they've done it, it doesnae look good." The big Scotsman flagged one of the warriors passing by them, and gave him orders to assemble a team of trackers. "Have Farlae and Rainer take the lead."

"I will have the lead in my Ferrari," Lucan told him.

"That fancy auto of yours won't take kindly to the

marshland, my lord," Byrne said. "No reason for you to trouble yourself. Leave it to the lads."

"No reason?" The former assassin's voice grew icy. "Christian is still out there somewhere."

Byrne shrugged. "Aye, but you needn't trouble yourself. If she yet lives, they'll find the lass."

Before Jayr could intervene, Lucan reached out, grabbing a handful of Byrne's tunic and using it to jerk the big man closer. "That *lass* is the closest thing to a daughter that I shall ever have. She gave up her mortal life to protect me, Samantha, and my entire *jardin*. So, no, you ignorant behemoth, I will not *leave it to the lads*."

"As you say, my lord." Byrne glanced down at his fist and, when Lucan released him, looked almost pleased. "We've a stable of fast horses. Do you still ride?"

Lucan straightened the line of his sleeve. "Do I still breathe?" He strode off.

"No," Jayr said as Byrne turned to her. "I will not stay behind. Beau and Alys are still missing."

He glanced at Lucan's retreating figure before he said in a softer voice, "Then brace yourself, wife. Whatever caused that light and the ground to quake may not have left anything for us to bring back."

Riding to the old mission took less than an hour, and when they were within a half mile of the site, Jayr began to see the damage wrought by the queerly silently explosion. The trunk of every pine they passed now tilted toward the east; some of the younger saplings lay uprooted where they had toppled. The sound of flapping wings drew her gaze up, where she saw dozens of birds flying away from the site toward the Realm.

Lucan reined in his mount, stopping in front of a

blackened length of metal sticking up from the soil. "This did not sprout here." He leaned closer, and then exchanged a look with Byrne, who rode his mount in front of Jayr's.

"Now that I think on it," her lover said, "you should go back to the stronghold. No doubt Alexandra will need some help with the wounded."

"No doubt." Jayr dismounted and strode over to the half-buried blade. An odd-looking clot of dirt clung to the hilt, one that looked more like a hand with every step she took.

"Jayr." Byrne put himself between her and the blade. "You need not look upon this. Let us see to the rest."

She went around him. "This is Beaumaris's blade." She knelt down in front of it and studied the severed body part still clutching the hilt. "He must have been holding it when the blast occurred."

Byrne helped her up. "Then he died fighting, which is what the lad would have wanted."

"Someone did, but not Beau." Jayr nodded at the burnt hand. "Do you see there, on the third finger?"

Lucan joined them and peered at the appendage. "A ring." He sniffed the air. "From the stink of it, fashioned from copper."

"No mortal could take Beau's blade from him," Byrne insisted.

"No." Jayr gazed at the oak grove, where the setting sun silhouetted the dozens of trees that had been jerked, roots and all, from the earth. "Unless Beau gave it to him. Come." She strode to her horse.

Jayr expected to see nothing but flattened, blackened earth as they drew near the mission, but aside from a missing roof and some scorch marks on the exterior walls, the structure remained largely intact.

Jayr called out for Beau and Alys, but only silence answered her.

"They must have taken shelter in the lower chambers," she told Byrne as they dismounted and secured the horses. "We will begin there."

"My lady." Lucan's quiet voice sent a pang of dread through her. "Your man and his lady are here."

Jayr's steps dragged as she approached the ruin of vines and shattered stone blocking the entry to a cave. Lucan brushed back the rubble to reveal a pair of entwined bodies. Her throat went tight as she saw how Beau held Alys still cradled against him.

More stone shifted, and Lucan stepped back as a slim hand emerged from the debris. The fingers groped the air.

"A little help," a muffled, disgruntled voice said, "would be great."

Lucan reached into the rubble and snatched the girl from it, holding her at arm's length before he jerked her close and embraced her.

"You are an idiot," he muttered against the top of her head. "I am taking you home and locking you in my dungeon for the rest of eternity."

Chris coughed out some dirt. "Hello. You don't have a dungeon."

Lucan began wiping the soil from her cheeks. "Then I shall build one. One riddled with rats and devices of torture and hundreds of video screens that play nothing but reruns of *The Brady Bunch*."

"I'm glad to see you, too, Dad." She rested her cheek against his shoulder.

The sound of vegetation moving and sticks snapping made Jayr scan the area, until a bedraggled figure emerged from the brush.

"I don't know why anyone dreams of flying," Simone said as she joined them, cradling a broken arm. "The landing isn't very pleasant." She looked at the bodies in the rubble. "The traitor murdered the doctor just before the explosion." Her voice softened. "Even after she was gone, your man would not leave her."

"No, I expect he would not." Jayr bent down to remove the gravel away from Alys's peaceful face before she straightened. "We will bury them together."

"As it should be. The lass was his mortal wife," Byrne explained to Lucan.

"Then it is fitting that they died together," the suzerain said as he placed Chris back on her feet. "But I believe you are mistaken on one point." When everyone looked at him, he added, "That female in your man's arms is not human." Lucan nodded at Alys. "Look at her face."

Jayr gazed down and saw that the cuts and abrasions on Alys's skin were slowly shrinking.

"God in heaven." She pushed back Alys's upper lip to reveal two gleaming *dents acérées* emerging from her palate. "She is Kyn." She turned to Byrne. "But yesterday she was mortal. . . . How can this be?"

"The legends say if a mortal is worthy, the emeralds will give them eternal life." Byrne removed a copper dagger from his belt. "'Tis no one more worthy on this earth, I think, than a courageous, warmhearted Scotswoman." He used the blade to slash his wrist, and bent to hold it to Alys's face. "Except perhaps a Scotsman."

"It's all that whiskey you lot drink," Lucan told him. "It pickles your soul."

A strong hand shot out of the debris to seize Byrne's wrist.

"Easy, lad," Byrne said, grinning with delight as Beau glared up at him. "Your lady has made the change. I'm wanting only to help her."

"Mine." With some difficulty Beau freed his other arm, bit into his wrist, and then pressed it to Alys's lips.

At first Beau's blood streamed down the sides of Alys's face, but when Jayr gently used a hand to support her head, she shuddered and swallowed.

Beau had eyes for no one but his beloved, and when she pulled away and opened her eyes, he kissed the traces of blood from her mouth. "Why did you shield me?"

"He would have shot you in the heart." She pressed her hand against his chest. "You couldn't survive that."

"Neither could you."

"But I did, so your conclusion is erroneous." Alys's eyes took on a faint golden glow. "I think you're stuck with me for a while."

"So I am." He kissed her again, and held her tightly. "Thank God."

Chapter 20

"How do I look?" Alys asked, turning around to face her sisters.

"Lovely," Simone said.

"Wrong." Christian turned to the Frenchwoman. "I don't know how they do it in Paris, but in this country the bride traditionally wears white."

"White is not a color. It looks attractive on exactly no one." Green eyes rolled. "So of course it is an American tradition."

"If you two keep arguing," Alys warned, "I'm going to put you both in bridesmaids' time-out." She glanced down at the folds of the soft amethyst velvet skirt. "Besides, I can't wear white. It would be bad luck."

"You see?" Simone patted her shoulder. "That is your French DNA talking, *chérie.*"

"Don't tell me you buy into that whole I'm-not-a-virgin thing," Chris complained. "Beau hasn't been one for, like, seven hundred years."

"No, it's because of Robert." Despite all her guardian had done to her, Alys still felt a twinge of sadness when she thought of him. "The few times I met him, he always wore white."

"He did not do so when he pretended to be Father Robere with me," Simone pointed out. "I only ever saw him in black."

"Yeah, and he dressed like a yuppie when I met him in the Keys," Chris added, her expression darkening. "I knew there was something wrong with that guy; I got a weird vibe from him. I just figured it was the undercover-cop thing. He sent his men after me and Jamys an hour after I met him. I should have known he was the douche bag traitor."

Simone made a hushing sound. "He was the only family Alys has ever known."

"We're her family," Chris countered.

"It's all right. Robert didn't care about me, not like that." Alys picked up the bouquet of lavender roses that Jayr had delivered along with the dress, and wound one of its golden ribbons through her fingers. "When he had me taken from the keep and brought to his camp, Robert told me the truth about what he'd done. How he'd murdered my birth mother in Ireland, smuggled me out of the country, and left me with nannies until I was old enough for boarding school. All those teachers who said I had a natural talent for history and archaeology? They were actually paid by him to train me and push me and make me believe it was my idea. That was how he made me into his 'tool.' Who knows what I might have been if he hadn't stolen me? But his daughter, that was one thing I never was. To him I was nothing but . . . a really smart screwdriver."

"So why aren't we popping open the champagne?"

Chris asked. "The guy took your whole life away from you, and sold out Simone to her psycho adopted brother. I hate him and I'm glad he's dead. And since he used me as sex bait for a mind-controlling immortal pirate, I think I'm allowed."

"That is not what she means," Simone chided, and took hold of Alys's hand. "Robert Leeds was the only father you knew, *chérie*. You cared for the illusion of himself that he created in order to deceive you, not the man he really was. Now that you know it was all lies, and he is gone, perhaps you can begin to let it go."

"Did you forgive your father for everything he did to you?" Alys asked her.

"When I discovered he had not murdered all of my adopted brothers, but had given them new lives . . . on that day, my hatred of Derien ended." She made an elegant gesture. "I can't say if I will ever forgive him, but I do have the man I love, and the brothers I thought I had lost. The Kyn have given me the family I have always wanted. What I hope, what I dream, is that in my happiness, in the love and the life I share with Korvel, that someday I will forget him."

"Yes." That sounded right to Alys. "Beau and I have always been alone. Now we have each other, and our friends, you and Chris. . . . It's everything I ever dreamed of. For that, I owe Derien a lot."

Chris came over and took her other hand. "Well, my sisters, I happen to be petty and selfish, and I wasn't raised by nuns, and he drove my mother insane, so I'm going to keep on hating our dad for a while. Just FYI."

The door to Alys's chamber opened, and Alexandra Keller looked in on them. "We've got a couple hundred vampires crammed in the chapel, a groom who is getting a bit fidgety, and a mortal organist who is becoming so zonked on Kyn pheromones that she's starting to take requests. You ready to clamp on the old ball and chain, Indiana?"

"Very much so." Alys glanced at her companions. "Before we go, I need to have a word with Dr. Keller in private. Would you mind?"

"No problem." Chris linked her arm through Simone's. "Come on, Paris. Let's go find that champagne and think up a cool nickname for me."

"Terrier," Simone suggested. "You are as vicious as one."

When her sisters had left them, Alys set aside the bouquet. "Did Beaumaris tell you what happened to Cristophe?"

"He described how he shoved the emeralds into his dematerializing body, which evidently caused the green mini-mushroom cloud." Alex came over and straightened the lace collar of her gown. "Jayr's men have searched every inch of the springs, the mission, and the other encampments. They didn't recover any remains or traces of him, if that's your worry." She searched Alys's face. "And that's not it."

"Just before I blacked out—no, just before I died," Alys corrected herself, "Cristophe spoke to me. Up here." She tapped the side of her head. "It's funny. All this time I've been thinking Beau was the one who saved me as a child." She briefly described the horrific incident from her childhood, and added, "Cristophe has the same voice as Beau. You can't tell them apart."

Alex nodded. "Why was he bugging you this time?"

"He could see that I was dying, and I was the last mortal Derien, so perhaps he thought it would be safe to let me know," Alys said. "Make one last confession."

"You haven't told anyone yet?" When Alys shook her head, Alex grimaced. "But you want to."

"I'm not sure," she admitted. "Finding out that the guardian that I loved and mourned was still alive, and that he was the maniac who wanted to destroy the Kyn and rule the world . . . It was almost more than I could handle. And he killed my mother to get his hands on me. God. What do I with that?"

"You forget it, and him." The doctor picked up her bouquet. "As for this thing that Cristophe told you, maybe he knew you were going to survive, and trusted you to know what to do with it. Guarding the emeralds for as long as he did gave Cristophe abilities that we'll never understand."

"That's the other thing." Alys glanced at the door. "I mentioned that I minored in geology. When I retrieved the gems from the spring, I got a good look at them, and they match the description of the crystals you found in my sisters' blood samples."

"So they were changed by the emeralds."

Alys shook her head. "Alexandra, they weren't emeralds. They were diamonds."

"Huh?" Alex looked perplexed. "Are you sure? I've never heard of *green* diamonds."

"They turn that color only under certain conditions," Alys said. "Like when they've been irradiated."

"That's an interesting theory, but it wasn't as if you

had time to take samples or run a proper spectral analysis." She studied her fingernails. "Since the jewels were destroyed, I guess we'll really never know."

"We're scientists, Alexandra," Alys reminded her. "Even if we don't have the gems, we can reverse engineer their effect by . . ." Her voice trailed off as she made the final connection. "You've already done that."

"My minor was in genetics, not geology." Alex gave her a narrow look before she huffed out some air. "It was so much easier, being the only scientist. No one knows, Indiana. Not even Michael."

"You can trust me."

"A couple of years ago I stumbled onto it." Alex briefly explained how Robin of Locksley had sacrificed himself to protect the world. "What Rob ingested turned out to be a form of the original Kyn-maker pathogen that had been exposed to radiation at some point—back in the Dark Ages, no one knew about the dangers of uranium exposure—and had mutated into a far more toxic, aggressive strain. The pathogen he already carried in his bloodstream attacked it, and basically they ate each other. He then reverted to a human state."

"But why didn't you formulate a treatment from what you learned from Robin's case?" Alys asked.

"Even if I could collect another sample of the pathogen that turned him mortal, and use it to synthesize a vaccine to force another battle of the mutations, it would require genetic engineering on a scale far beyond anything I can do now," Alex admitted. "At best it would be like me using a sledgehammer to chop up a watermelon. I had to let it go."

"Yet you're still collecting blood samples from the

Kyn, and studying the pathogen." Alys studied Alex's bland expression. "You're waiting for the science to advance."

She lifted her shoulders. "I figure in a hundred years we'll have the means to do it. Then it'll probably take me another century to talk the Darkyn into giving up eternal life. I can't force it on them, Alys. I want *them* to want it."

"But you want to be human again, more than anything."

"I want to be with the man I love just a little bit more," Alex corrected. "For him, I'll wait, but I'm sure you get that." She handed her the bouquet. "Come on. Let's get you hitched before someone gets bored and eats the preacher."

"I do not recall flowers at weddings in our time," Harlech said. "Now, funerals were a different matter. They piled them everywhere; in the chapel, at the cemetery, on the body. . . ."

"That was to cover the smell of rotting flesh." Beaumaris tried not to glance at the back of the chapel again. "Why has she not come? Do you think she has changed her mind?"

"The lady took two bullets in the back for you, brother. She will not desert you now." Harlech's mouth curved as the organist abruptly changed her tune. "As you see."

All of the Kyn stood as Beau turned to see Alys come into the chapel on Byrne's arm. The Scotsman had dressed in his finest plaid and kilt, and wore on his brow the gleaming band of gold and red beryls that Robert the

Brus had bestowed on him after their victory at Bannockburn.

Alys wore a full, lavender-colored veil, but through
the delicate lace Beau could see her lovely eyes shining.
Her lips trembled into a smile as Byrne reached the altar, and offered her hand to Beau.

"Love her for the rest of your days, lad, and you'll be
a lucky man," the Scotsman said, and leaned forward to
murmur the rest. "Hurt her, and you'll be a dead one."

"Aye, my lord." Beau brought Alys's hand to his lips,
and then folded her arm over his as they turned to face
the priest.

"Wait."

Alys and Beau turned to see Farlae struggling to
his feet. Although Rain tried to stop him, he came forward toward the altar, almost dragging the big man
with him.

"Forgive the interruption, but there is something I
must say." As Beau nodded, he turned to address the rest
of the Kyn. "I have been in love with Rainer of Sherwood since the day we met. I purchased him, took him
away, seduced him, and have since been his lover, these
seven hundred years." He scanned the faces staring at
them. "Some of you do not approve, I well know, but it is
not your choice to make for us. And since it is also none
of your bloody business, I beg you keep your narrow-
minded opinions to yourselves."

Rain gaped at him. "Farlae, what are you doing?"

The wardrobe master reached into his pocket, and
produced a large golden ring inlaid with multicolored
stones and one huge sapphire. "I am telling everyone

that I love you, and I wish to marry you." With great difficulty he went down on one knee. "If you will have me."

"Yes. Yes, I will." Rain held out his left hand, and Farlae slid the ring on his finger. "Will we have a wedding, too?"

Farlae nodded. "As soon as I've recovered, lad."

Rain picked up Farlae, kissing him soundly and then setting him back on his feet before he grimaced at Beau. "Sorry, Beaumaris. I had not thought to become engaged in the middle of your wedding. Do go on."

The ceremony was simple, and once they had made their vows to each other before God and all their kind, the priest pronounced them man and wife. Beau gently lifted the veil and smoothed it back from Alys's face before he smiled at her.

"Now you'll never be rid of me, love," he said as he brushed his lips against hers.

Alys pressed her hand to his cheek. "Forever should just about be long enough."

The men of the garrison cheered as Beau lifted Alys off her feet and spun around with her.

From the chapel they went to the main hall, where the visiting Kyn lords and ladies offered formal congratulations to Beau, and Alys was embraced by her sisters and students. Before Alex herded the excited interns off to the banquet table set up for the mortal guests, she caught Alys's arm.

"Korvel and Lucan are over in the gift room having a little chat." She nodded in that direction. "While you have the chance, you might want to take Beau in there and tell the three of them what Cristophe told you. I'm guessing he let you know exactly who he was."

Alys almost choked. "How did you know?"

"Genetics, not geology, remember?" Alex winked.

Coaxing Beau away from the visiting Kyn didn't take much persuasion, although when he saw Korvel and Lucan standing together in the gift room, he gave her a puzzled look. "I thought you wanted a private moment."

"Oh, we'll have plenty of those when we get to Lord Jamys's honeymoon island." Alys closed the door before she led him over to the other men. "I wanted to thank you both for staying for the wedding. I know it was inconvenient, especially for you, Lord Alenfar."

"Miss an opportunity to photograph Byrne in a skirt?" Lucan smiled lazily. "I should never."

"Simone and I never had proper families," Korvel assured her. "We are delighted to have you and Christian as our sisters, and hope you will someday come and visit us in France."

"I would love that." Alys's smile grew uneasy. "And I hope you don't mind adding a few more members to the family. There is something that you don't know. Something Cristophe told me, just before he died."

Beau put an arm around her. "I have admitted to everyone the truth about my mother, love. You needn't worry about it."

"But you don't know . . . I'm not even sure how to say this. Cristophe was your father." She nodded at the other men. "He was also their father. The three of you are half brothers."

Korvel and Lucan said nothing, and Beau hardly knew what to think.

"You were shot just before Cristophe died, love," he

said as kindly as he could. "Perhaps you simply imagined this."

"I think not," Lucan said. His brows arched. "Unless you consider yourself too good to be my sibling?"

"No, my lord." Beau eyed his gloves. "But how could this be? I was born in Jerusalem. You and Lord Korvel are Englishmen."

"I was actually conceived in a slave house in Norway," Korvel said slowly. "Cristophe gave me a vision of it. It seems he was enslaved with my mother, and they became lovers. When she was ransomed by her family, she returned home pregnant with me."

"From what I was shown, he was also my mother's lover," Lucan said. "I was never claimed as son by any man." He eyed Beau. "When he was a Templar, Cristophe spent many years in the Holy Land on Crusade. He must have sired you then."

"He wanted to tell you himself, to claim you as his sons," Alys said sadly, "but he thought you would be safer if he didn't. Especially Beau."

"Richard," Lucan said, and Korvel nodded.

"The smith is dead," Beau said, "and the gems destroyed. We are alive, and together with those we love." He regarded Lucan and Korvel. "What more can we ask?"

Lucan smiled. "Permit me to inform the high lord about the emeralds. Brother." He bowed to Beau, and Alys, and headed back to the reception.

"I wished to make that call," Korvel argued as he followed after the suzerain. "You were merely his assassin. I was his second for seven hundred years."

Beau turned to Alys and took her hands in his. "You have bestowed so much on me. Love, life, your hand in marriage, and now two brothers. What can I possibly give you in return?"

"Oh, I have some ideas." She reached up and kissed him. "Let's start with a dance."

Read on for a preview of Lynn Viehl's

Nightborn

Available now from Signet Select

October 12, 2011
Provence, France

During the day the waitresses at La Théière Verte delivered filling but forgettable meals from the cramped kitchen of the restaurant to the table of any hungry tourist who had wandered in through the old green doors. The owner, Madame Eugenie, prepared all the dishes herself, using the cheapest ingredients and as much garlic as she dared. She considered this blatant desecration of God's bounty an economical measure as well as her patriotic duty.

The tourists, ignorant cretins that they were, never seemed to notice. As long as they were served a plate close to overflowing, they happily handed over their euros.

Only after dark did madame's chef arrive to cook for the villagers who came to dine, and whose standards were French. The local residents could not be appeased by a stew of shredded lapin smothered beneath a *mon-*

tagne of carrots, the blandest of radishes glued by oleo to day-old black bread, or gallons of cheap Spanish wine funneled into empty, French-labeled bottles. If in a moment of madness Eugenie ever dared to serve such swill to her neighbors, they would consider it *their* patriotic duty to lock her and her staff inside the old restaurant before setting fire to the place.

For these reasons madame was not at all pleased when her waitress Marie nudged her and nodded toward a tall, flaxen-haired stranger standing just inside the threshold.

"*Zut*, not a German at this hour. He must have run out of petrol. Unless he is an American." Eugenie almost spit on the last word. To her, the only thing worse than the Berliners were those loud, nosy imbeciles from across the Atlantic, forever thumbing through their phrase books and mangling her native tongue. Or the ones who waddled in, their rotund bodies shiny with sweat and sunscreen, to demand to know whether she served *low-fat* this and *sugar-free* that.

"Whatever he is, he's handsome," Marie said, and shifted to get a better look. "Such a big man, too. Look at those shoulders, and all that hair. It must fall to his waist."

"*Et alors?*" Eugenie gave the girl a hard pinch on the arm. "Forget his hair. Ask if he has a reservation. He will say no, and you will tell him to call for one tomorrow."

Marie rubbed her arm and said in an absent tone, "We do not take reservations, madame."

"Does he know this, you goose?" she hissed, and then saw it was too late. "There, now, because you are lazy and stupid, he is already sitting down. Go and see what he wants. If he asks for the cheeseburger do not tell me. I will choke him with his own hair."

Korvel stopped listening to the conversation between the women behind the bar and checked the interior of the restaurant. Only a third of the tables were occupied, most by couples and some middle-aged men. One delicate fairy of a schoolgirl sat picking at her food while her parents bickered in half whispers. Apart from sending a few uninterested glances in his direction when he had walked in, no one paid any further attention to him.

As transparent as a bloody specter, but not half as interesting.

When the young, smiling waitress approached his table his empty belly clenched, but years of self-denial quickly dispelled the involuntary response. He listened as the girl stammered through a brief recital of the evening specials before he ordered a bottle of a local Bandol and the vegetable soup. The wine would not satisfy his ever-present hunger, and if he attempted to eat the soup he would puke, but they would buy him a half hour of quiet and rest before he continued his journey.

Or I could have the waitress and be gone in five minutes.

He had no time or particular inclination to give his body what it needed: a woman. There had been a time when any woman would do, for no matter how different they were from one another, they all shared the same soft warmth, the same intense fragility. He had thought mortal women as lovely as an endless meadow of flowers.

So it had been until he had fallen in love with Alexandra Keller. The only woman he had ever truly wanted for himself, now gone from his life and forever beyond his reach.

For a time, being caught between his physical needs and his broken heart had produced ungodly urges that had nearly driven Korvel out of his head. Fortunately those, too, were now gone. His will, or what remained of it, permitted him to don a brittle mask each day and carry on with this imitation of life.

God in heaven, he had wearied of this charade, of everyone and everything in it. More than that, he was sick unto death of himself.

"Monsieur?"

Korvel glanced up at madame, who had brought a dark bottle to his table, but seemed more interested in examining him than in pouring the wine. She measured every inch of the hair he kept forgetting to cut, and the garments he had tailored to fit his overlarge frame, which cost more than the average tourist spent on ten vacations. Doubtless she could also name his weight to within five kilos' accuracy.

Her gaze flicked down to dwell with disapproval on the mark that encircled his throat. It resembled a garrote of dark green thorns, and as most mortals did she would assume he had been tattooed. He could not explain that being hanged for weeks in a copper-barbed noose had caused the marks. Copper proved lethal to his kind only when it entered their veins or heart, but its poisonous effects were such that even touching it caused burns. Any extended surface contact with the dark metal left permanent, green scars on immortal flesh; grim reminders, in a sense, of humanity's loathing of their dark Kyn.

He also doubted she would care. *"S'il vous plaît?"* He

gestured at his glass, earning a mild frown from her before she filled it to the rim.

"You are American?" she asked in English as she wiped a dribble from the bottle's neck.

Another reminder of what could never be. "No, madame. I am from England."

"Ah, *les anglais*." She nodded to herself with some satisfaction, and the lines bracketing her mouth softened. "You come with the caravan, *oui*?"

"I am here on business." The business of playing courier for his master, for reasons that had never been adequately explained to him. "Thank you for the wine."

"*Il n'y a pas de quoi*." She bobbed her head and smoothed her hands over the sides of her apron before reluctantly turning away and resuming her post behind the bar. He saw the flicker of confusion that passed over her narrow features before she returned to her task of sorting flatware.

Korvel reached over to open the window a little wider before sampling the glass. Mortals considered Provence a fine-wine void, something the residents likely encouraged to protect their supply of some of the best red and rosé wines in the world. Madame had brought him a Mourvèdre-based red wine with a pleasing amount of spine to it, and Korvel breathed in its tannic perfume while he removed a flask from his jacket. He had to sip some of the wine before discreetly adding a measure of the darker, thicker liquid from the flask to the glass, but his next swallow instantly eliminated the leaden sensation the first swallow had left in his gut.

The mixture of blood and wine went to work, spreading slowly through him to warm his cold flesh and loosen his stiff muscles. It would tide him over until he reached his destination, where he planned to see to his needs once he retrieved his master's property. He took out the small GPS device that had been attached to the car's dashboard to check his current position.

"That no work here, monsieur."

"Indeed." Korvel eyed the plump face of the waitress as she set down a steaming bowl of soup. "Why not?"

"The wind very bad Sunday. The tower, send signal?" When he nodded his understanding, she straightened her hand and then let it fall to mimic something toppling over.

So it seemed the GPS was useless, and the French he spoke hadn't been used in this region for half a millennium or better. He reached out to rest his hand over hers. "Do you know the road to Garbia?"

"Mais oui." Her expression brightened. "Go this way"—she pointed north—"until you reach the second turn. Then go this way." She pointed east, but this time her fingers quivered under his, and her breathing grew fast and uneven. "I come with you. I show you. Madame, she not care."

Korvel eyed the scowl being directed at them from the bar. "Actually I do believe madame will mind."

"You take me. With you?" She released one more button of her blouse, which exposed the sweat beading between her full breasts. "I want go with you."

He knew exactly what she wanted, and carefully removed his hand from hers. "You have been quite helpful," he said as he deliberately shed more of his scent to bring her under his command. "Thank you. You should return to your work now."

The light vanilla fragrance of larkspur enveloped the two of them as *l'attrait* caused the waitress's pupils to dilate.

"Oui." She backed away, bumping her ample hip into the edge of another table. The pain released her from Korvel's control, and she clapped a hand over her giggles as she fled toward the kitchen.

Once he pocketed the GPS, Korvel drank the last of the bloodwine and sat back to let it finish its work on him. While he waited, he checked his mobile for messages. Stefan, the senior lieutenant Korvel had assigned to serve in his place during his absence, had texted him a brief status report before Korvel had left Paris. The men had been drilled, the night patrols assigned, and the high lord had retreated to his study for the night.

All was as it should be, as it would have been if Korvel had never departed. It should have reassured him, but it only made the hollow sensation inside him grow.

Since becoming one of the immortal Darkyn, Korvel had served Richard Tremayne as the high lord's seneschal as well as the captain of his guard. Seven lifetimes he had devoted himself to his duties and honoring the oath he had made to his master. Eight, if one counted his mortal life.

Now it seemed his absence was not even noticed.

"You look sad, monsieur."

The ethereal little girl who had been sitting with the bickering couple slipped into the empty chair beside his. Confusion filled her eyes, as if she weren't quite sure why she was speaking to him.

Korvel knew exactly why the child had come to him. She must have been just on the verge of puberty; his ability to influence female mortals never affected the very young. "I am well, thank you."

"You are a Viking, no?" The girl darted a look over her shoulder. "My *maman* said you look like one, which made my papa very mad. But I think you are more like the beautiful angels."

Korvel glanced around the room and saw he had gained the avid attention of the child's mother and every other female in the place. He'd made a serious error shedding so much scent to influence the waitress, for he had not considered that the cold air outside might have acted as a natural barrier at the ventilation points. His scent saturated the inside air now. If he did not leave at once, all of the women would come over to his table, drawn to him like moths to a burning lantern.

"I must go now and continue my journey." He managed a smile for the little girl. "*Au revoir*, my sweet."

"Take me with you." Tears welled up in her eyes. "Please."

He could not explain to her that what she felt would disappear as soon as he departed, but he would not see her suffer even a few seconds. "What is your name?"

"Tasha."

"Tasha." He touched his hand to the side of her little neck, where the connection of his will to her mind was the strongest. "Go back to your parents. Forget me. Be happy."

"Go. Forget. Happy." She turned like a sleepwalker and shuffled away.

Quickly Korvel took out enough euros to pay for a case of wine and dropped them on the table before he rose to his feet. The habits of many lifetimes compelled him to attend to one final detail: the memories of madame and the waitress, who intercepted him at the door.

As they were both already bespelled, he had only to command them. "You will attend to your work and your patrons. Once I am gone, you will forget me. It will be as if I never came here."

The women spoke in monotone unison. "Attend. Work. Gone."

Korvel left the restaurant, checking the street to ensure it was empty. As the chill of a dark wind streamed against his coat, he turned his head to look back through the front window and saw the waitress taking an order from an older couple. Madame stood once more behind the counter, her expression no longer as sour as it had been when he had walked into the place. For them he no longer existed; he had never existed.

He envied them.

In all the centuries Korvel had lived since rising from his grave to walk the night, he had never considered his own memory to be anything but useful. Indeed, every bit of knowledge he acquired he carefully added to, stockpiling all he knew like weapons. Now he would gladly empty his head of all of it, if it meant he could forget forever what had been. What would never be.

You're supposed to love me.

He had put so much practice into banishing Alexandra Keller's voice from his thoughts that he could silence her in an instant. Her scent, however, still haunted him. But no, what filled his head came on the wind, scoured from acres of blooming lavender. Provençal farmers grew so much of the fragrant herb for the wine and perfume industries that one couldn't drive a mile without passing one of the vivid amethyst fields.

He walked down the deserted street to the spot where he had parked the gleaming black Audi he had rented in Paris. Most of his kind preferred to travel on horseback rather than by automobile, and many refused to learn how to drive, but the demands of serving his master had forced him to make regular use of modern technology. A horse had to be frequently rested, fed, and watered on a long journey; the car required only brief stops for petrol.

As he took out the keys to the vehicle, Korvel stared at them. As the first Kyn ever to be made seneschal, Korvel had set the standard for all the others, one that had yet to be fully matched. He had personally trained every warrior who had ever served in the high lord's garrison, and had taught his methods to the captains of other *jardins* around the world. His unwavering loyalty to the high lord had earned him a spotless reputation as the most trusted and valuable second among all the territories. None would be shocked to learn that he had been sent to France to attend to his master's wishes and retrieve a priceless artifact before it fell into the wrong hands.

To serve Richard again, this time as his errand boy.

Korvel did not succumb to sudden and bizarre urges; nor did he intend to start. He would never turn his back on his duty to walk into the shadows and disappear into the night. Such a thing would violate his oath and break faith with his master, and his honor forbade him to behave in such a cowardly manner.

But oh, how he wished he could.

As he unlocked the car, he could imagine the keys

dropping from his hand to the ground. As he got in and started the engine, the sound of grass brushing against his trousers whispered in his ears. As he tightened his grip on the steering wheel, he could feel on his skin the fearful silence that would fall over the forest creatures as they witnessed his departure from the world of Kyn and man to enter their peaceful realm.

It would be so simple. So uncomplicated. And there, where no one could command him, the loneliness and despair would do their final work.

"Turn around," a muffled voice ordered from his pocket.

Korvel removed the GPS, which he had switched off in the restaurant, and tried it again. The screen displayed his current position as being in the middle of nothing. As he reached to reprogram it, the screen blanked.

He swore softly as he shifted the Audi into drive and executed a three-point turn. The faster he reached Garbia and retrieved the scroll, the sooner he could return to the island, and his duties, and the sanity they preserved.

yard manager of Starway Services. "But it'll be three days before we can even look at it."

"Three days! Never mind—rent me a service bay," Luke said, nodding toward a sign offering that option.

"Sure," said the manager. "Let me check the schedule." His fingers danced over his datapad. "Yes, I should have one available in five or six days."

"Come on, dear—let's go," said Akanah, tugging at Luke's arm. "Someone in this city must know how to treat visitors properly."

"Suit yourself. But you're not going to do any better anywhere else," said the manager.

"And why is that?" Luke asked.

"I had one crew chief and three mechs decide this would be a good time to take a family vacation. Most of the other shops are even more shorthanded," the manager said. "And I had twenty-eight of my regulars call to schedule early annuals or work they'd been putting off. If I weren't keeping a bay open for transients and referrals, you'd be waiting a week."

"Li, dear, I've read about this sort of scam in *Port of Call*," Akanah said. "The yards take kickbacks from the hoteliers for keeping travelers stranded."

Catching the sudden glower in the manager's eyes, Luke patted Akanah's hand patronizingly. "Now, darling, let's not insult the man just because our plans have been upset," Luke said. "Why are you so busy?" he asked the yard manager.

"Because of the war, of course," the manager said.

Akanah's gaze narrowed. "War? What are you talking about?"

"Don't you ever link to the grids? The New Republic and the Duskhan League have been growling and feinting at each other for months."

Akanah turned to Luke. "Did you know about this?"

"I heard something of it on Talos," said Luke. "I didn't want to worry you. It was only rumor then. I guess it's become something more, if people are running the other way."

"You can see Koornacht Cluster in the night sky from here, you know," said the manager. "The idea that a thousand warships are poised to clash somewhere over their heads makes people nervous."

"A thousand warships?" Akanah asked in an awed whisper.

"That's what they're saying." The manager shrugged. "Some of them, anyway. You hear a lot of different stories. So—what are you gonna do?"

"We'll leave our ship with you," said Luke, pushing the registration pad across the counter. "But can you tell me how long it might take *after* you get to it? Do you have a local source for parts?"

"For a Verpine Adventurer?" the manager asked, glancing down at the pad. "Oh, sure. We've got four of them in our scrapyard alone. Call us in three days."

The manager's casual acceptance of war on his doorstep deepened the chill of fear that had come over Akanah on hearing the news. *It's too soon—he's not ready for this,* she thought wildly as she followed Luke out of the depot. *I'm taking him exactly where I don't want him to go—right into the heart of temptation. He's still trying to direct the Current. He's not ready to watch others fight without raising a hand of his own—*

"We can't stay here," she said in a worried whisper when they were outside. "It doesn't feel safe. I don't know what it is, but this place is shadowed."

"I don't see a lot of alternatives," Luke said, leading them back toward the northbound slidewalk. "You need to be able to tell the hyperdrive which way to jump, and *Mud Sloth* can't do that right now."

"I understand that," she said, clinging to his arm. "But we could be here a week or more. Isn't there something else we can do? Can't you buy the parts from him and fix it yourself?"

"Didn't you hear him in there? We're headed into a war zone," said Luke, stopping short. "For all we know about what's happening, J't'p'tan could be one of the battlegrounds. Don't you think it'd be a good thing to be able to count on our hyperdrive?"

She tried desperately to find a fear that would move him. "If we linger here too long, we can count on more Imperial agents finding us. We can't let that happen. We can't let them follow us."

"Even the New Republic can't find us, thanks to your tricks," said Luke. "Look, all we have to do is find a quiet place to stay and play tourist for a few days. Besides, I want to learn more about what's ahead of us—and it may take a while to sort the facts from the rumors."

"Does it matter what's ahead?" she asked. "Would you even consider turning back now? Your mother—my mother—they're almost within reach."

"Not with *Mud Sloth* on crutches, they aren't," said Luke.

"Then we have to get a different ship."

Luke snorted. "How?"

She looked at him in earnest surprise. "Don't you think that with our combined talents we can take almost any ship we want from here?"

"Don't even think about it," Luke said tersely. He scanned about to see if anyone could have heard her, then grabbed her elbow and practically dragged her away from the service center's entrance and onto the slidewalk.

"Yes, we probably could," he said in a sharp whisper as the moving surface whisked them along. "But not without attracting unwanted attention. Do you really want a Utharian patrol boat following us to J't'p'tan? Do you want every ship under New Republic registry alerted to watch for us?"

"I can hide us."

"We're already hidden. All we have to do is wait. You've gotten this close by biding your time until the right time. This is the wrong time to give in to impatience."

"This is the wrong time to delay," said Akanah, still casting about for emotional leverage. "Luke, the darker the clouds, the more important it is for us to move quickly."

"The war's already started," Luke said grimly. "The Yevetha attacked more than a dozen worlds not long after we left Coruscant. We can't arrive before the storm—we can only hope it leaves J't'p'tan untouched."

"Luke, it's not that the Circle is in danger," Akanah pressed. "The danger is that we'll lose touch with them. It's impossible to work when the Current is in chaos. And it's intensely uncomfortable to remain connected when the Current is carrying so much pain. I'm not afraid for them—the Circle is strong. I'm afraid they may already have left J't'p'tan. And any sign they leave for me could be destroyed as easily as Norika's house in Griann was."

"I can ask for another tracking report on *Star Morning,* find out where it went after Vulvarch. That should tell us something about the Circle's plans."

"And what will we chase them in, *Mud Sloth*? You were right, Luke. We can't count on our ship. We should have something faster, more reliable—and we may need room for more than the two of us. Please—we have to leave here now."

"I'm not going to help you steal a starship, Akanah."

Even before he spoke, she realized she had made a mistake. They shared a goal, but he still observed limits on the means he would allow himself to employ in pursuing it. She had committed everything to this quest, while he had a life to return to if it ended in failure. And she had forgotten that difference between them in a moment of selfish anxiety.

"You're right—oh, you're right. I don't know what I was thinking. It's just so hard being this close after so long," she said, hastily troweling over the crack in her facade. "If we don't find them—"

"We'll find them," Luke said.

"I want to believe that with all my heart, and at the same time I'm afraid to, because I don't know if I can bear another disappointment," she said. The tears that glittered in the corners of her eyes were real. "Forgive me. It isn't that I thought you a thief—"

"I know," he said. "It's forgotten."

She smiled gratefully at him and let him draw her into the curl of his arm. "If we must stay here, then at least let's get away from Taldaak," she urged, ending a brief silence. "Let's find some private place safely away from all these eyes. I'll use the time to teach you more of our disciplines."

"First things first," Luke said. "I want to go back to the ship and put out some queries, then see what I can learn here. I want to find out everything I can about what we might find in the Koornacht Cluster—about what our people are up against."

That was the last thing Akanah wanted. Of all the impulses capable of moving Luke's hand toward his lightsaber, she feared the power of his loyalty to his sister most. In frustration, she pulled away from him, moving to the opposite edge of the slidewalk.

"What?" he asked in surprise. "What is it?"

Akanah sensed his confusion and uncertainty and targeted her words there. "I'm just wondering if maybe we've gone as far as we can together," she said. "Maybe it was a mistake to make you part of this. If you don't have the commitment or the trust—"

"Akanah—"

"I have to think about what to do now," she said, and stepped neatly off the slidewalk.

Luke whirled about but did not follow, letting the slidewalk carry him on toward the port. Their gazes locked together for a moment, then she turned away.

Eyes now closed, she studied the Current's flow through and around him, reading its eddies and meanders. There was exasperation there, but a new and still raw worry as well. *Good,* she thought. *Wonder about me. Worry that I'll steal a ship on my own and leave you behind. Then perhaps you won't worry so much about other people's wars or think about joining them. Your place is with me, Luke Skywalker—I still have lessons to teach you.*

* * *

Han had lost track of time. There was no day-and-night cycle in the brightly lit Yevethan prison cell, no regular meals to mark out intervals. Han dozed, exercised, paced, played endless games of hop-stone solitaire on the dusty floor, dozed. His mouth was parched, and his head and empty stomach were possessed by constant aches too sharp now to simply ignore.

In the beginning Barth had joined him in what Han had dubbed the planetary championship of two-handed hop-stone, but both of them were too short-tempered for competitive games now. They had exhausted their repertoires of bawdy jokes, with Barth emerging the uncontested winner for both variety and delivery. In revenge, Han had taught Barth all eighty-six verses of a song that their brains kept singing long after their voices were stilled.

Of late Han had taken to talking to the ceiling, to their unseen jailers. He had peppered his monologues with increasingly savage insults, hoping to provoke a response, any response, that would lead to the cell door opening, that might give them a chance to do something about their circumstances. When he ran out of words, he mentally rehearsed scenarios for overpowering any number of guards up to five.

But all he accomplished was to make both Barth and himself tired of the sound of his voice. By the time the cell door opened, they were so weak from hunger and dehydration that they could barely stand.

One of the three Yevethan guards threw Han a pair of loose-fitting white pants and gestured at Han's uniform. "You will wear what we have given you," he ordered, and tossed another pair of the pajamalike pants to Barth.

Stripping without modesty, they both complied without argument. When the task was finished, the guards prodded them toward the corridor.

There was a Yevethan guard in front of Han, leading the way, and another behind him, with Barth following and the third guard bringing up the rear. It was one of the geometries Han had rehearsed—take out the guard in the middle together, high-low, then turn back-to-back and take on the others—but he weighed the odds against his curiosity about where they were being taken and decided to wait.

But the pants they had been given had been sized for a Yevethan frame—the waist was too low and the legs a handspan too long. Before he had gone half a dozen strides down the corridor, Barth tripped himself on the trailing fabric and went sprawling.

Hearing the noise behind him, Han had only an instant to react. He spun, hands forming into fists, and received a rock-hard Yevethan forearm across his throat for his trouble. Gasping and choking, he fell backward. It was a hard landing, even without the benefit of the first guard stomping his head back against the floor.

"Submit or die," the guard growled.

The sudden pain, and the adrenaline that came with it, had energized Han's body to the point that he was ready to fight the Yevethan who was pinning him down. Then he heard Barth groan in pain, then call out in a raspy, shaky voice, "Don't—don't—it was me, Han, my fault—I fell, that's all, stupid clumsy feet—"

With a will, Han opened his fists and spread his hands wide in surrender. "It's all right, Lieutenant. We'll let 'em off this time, okay?"

The guard looming over Han stepped back. Moving slowly, Han clambered back to his feet. A few meters down the corridor, Barth was doing the same. "You okay?"

"I'm—what are they going to do? Where are they taking us?"

"It's going to be all right," Han said, tugging his pants up at the waist. "Hey, how about this fine Yevethan tailoring?"

Jerking his head to the left, the guard growled, "Enough. *Darama* waits. Walk."

The prisoners were taken to a large chamber with a high domed ceiling decorated with scarlet accents. They were made to sit at either end of a long bench facing a low platform and a large window beyond. Han squinted at the bright light, but savored the warm, fresh breeze entering the chamber with it.

There was one oddity: Lieutenant Barth's wrists were bound to a bar running the length of the bench, low behind their hips. But Han's were not.

Before he could puzzle that out, Viceroy Nil Spaar entered the chamber.

"*Darama,*" Han repeated under his breath.

Nil Spaar was leading an entourage of four. One carried a folding stool, which he set up facing the prisoners' bench. A second carried a tall stand topped by a silver sphere, which he placed a meter to the right of the stool and slightly forward. Those two left when they had shed their burdens.

The two that remained took up positions behind Nil Spaar as he settled on the stool. Han studied their faces, trying to divine what burdens *they* had carried into the room. Advisor? Muscle? Toady? *What does a Yevetha look like when it's nervous? Or do they even get nervous?*

"General Solo," said Nil Spaar, ignoring Barth with both his words and his gaze. "You appear to be the only one who can save thousands more of your kind from dying in shame. I am here to give you that opportunity."

"I don't know what you're talking about."

"You were on your way to take command of the Fifth Fleet when you were captured. You were carrying Princess Leia's orders for the invasion of Yevethan territory."

Han waited, mute.

"Defiance of the sovereignty of the viceroy of the Protectorate makes your life forfeit," Nil Spaar continued. "I have spared you in the hope that you will join me in an act of mercy."

Han cocked his head. "Explain."

"Princess Leia has recklessly sent more ships to threaten us—"

"Good for her."

"—and issued foolish ultimatums. She does not understand us. Perhaps when you do, you can open her eyes."

"Go on."

"Our claim to these stars is natural and ancient. Our eyes have owned them since the beginning of our days. They are alive in our legends. They call to us in our dreams. We draw our strength from the All. The purity of the All inspires us to perfection.

"Our claim to these stars is not a shallow thing of greed, or politics, or ambition. It is not a claim we would ever surrender. We are not like the weaklings you are accustomed to, calculating when to pursue an advantage and when to retreat, believing only in the expediencies of the moment.

"Leia's threats do not move us. We will never give up that which is ours, or share it with those who are not born of the All. If your forces do not withdraw, there will be war—terrible, bloody, unending. We will never yield, General Solo—and none of your soldiers will enjoy my mercy as you have. The fighting will go on until the last of you has been killed or driven out. Do you understand that, General?"

"I think so."

"I hope you do," said Nil Spaar. "I have studied your histories. You have never faced an adversary like us. Your wars are decided by the death of a tenth of a population, a third of an army. Then the defeated surrender their honor and the victors surrender their advantage. This is called being civilized. The Yevetha are not civilized, General. It would be a mistake to deal with us as though we were."

"Thanks for the advice," Han said. "So what do you want from me?"

"Prevent your mate from making that mistake," said Nil Spaar. "Persuade her to recall her fleet. Promise us on the blood of your own children that what is ours now will be ours forever. You will preserve the blood of thousands—and your own as well."

"You'll let us go?" Barth asked, an eager hopefulness coloring his words.

The viceroy did not look away from Han. "You are more useful to me as a witness than as a martyr, General," Nil Spaar said, rising from his stool. "Come—look."

The viceroy led Han to the window, then stepped aside to allow Han an unimpeded view. Squinting, Han looked out on a tumble of buildings and, beyond, a great field of giant silver spheres—*Aramadia*-class thrustships. It was a stunning, numbing sight. The starships were parked so closely together that it was difficult to count them, even though Nil Spaar allowed him to linger at the window.

"What you see is the product of the Nazfar Metalworks Guild," said Nil Spaar softly. "There is such a guild on every world of the Twelve, General. Do you understand? You cannot prevail against us. But you can preserve your children's blood, if you choose to."

Shaking his head, Han turned away from the window. "Why? Why even make the offer, unless you think we might win?"

"Because you would become our obsession, for as many years as it took to destroy you," the viceroy said. "And there are better uses for blood and the labor of our young. I have paid you the compliment of believing the same is true for your kind."

The roar of undampered pulsejets drew Han's attention to a thrustship climbing skyward from the far edge of the array. Torn by conflicting impulses and struggling to focus his thoughts, Han stalled by making his way slowly back to the bench.

"What did you see? What's out there?" Barth asked.

"A fleet of new warships," Han said. "At least a hundred of them."

"Well, there's only one choice, then, isn't there? He's right—stopping the war would be an act of mercy. Now that you know what we'd be up against, you *have* to stop it."

Han's gaze jumped from Barth to Nil Spaar. "Only if I'm willing to forget the blood that's already been spilled," he said. "You didn't see the intelligence reports I saw, Lieutenant—colonies scoured off the face of planets, entire populations exterminated as though they were no more than kitchen pests—"

"Han, please think about this. Do you want the next planet to be Coruscant or Corellia?" Barth pleaded.

Han kept his gaze fixed on Nil Spaar, who was listening impassively. "Do you know that they recorded it all, without even the decency to look away or feel shame? As though they were proud of it—of how efficiently they could murder millions." He shook his head slowly. "No. You can't compromise with an evil as cold as theirs, Lieutenant—not even to spare the lives of our mother's children."

Still Nil Spaar said nothing. But Barth was nearly frantic with fear. "Please, do what he asks. Think of all the casualties, the ships burning—Han, they're going to kill us!"

"Would you rather live as a coward?" Han demanded. "It'll be a tragedy for even one more good pilot to die fighting them. But it'd be something far worse if we turned our backs and walked away—if no one stood up for the millions who are already dead. And I'll be damned if I'll be part of it." His eyes burned into the viceroy's. "You can burn to blazes. I won't help you."

Nil Spaar nodded agreeably and spoke a word in Yevethan. Two guards appeared at the doorway and bound Han to the bar just as Barth had been.

"Please, do something—tell him you've changed your mind—"

"Get a grip on yourself, Lieutenant," Han said grimly. "He doesn't deserve to enjoy this."

The viceroy moved closer, his fighting crests becoming engorged until they seemed to be two crimson slashes from temple to ear. "You vermin wish to teach me a lesson," said Nil Spaar. "I will offer you one in return. You think you have accepted the price in blood for your choice. We will see if that is so."

With a slash of his right claw, Nil Spaar ripped open Barth's bare torso from hip to shoulder, shattering ribs, pulling soft organs from their cavities. Barth's scream, a horrible, inhuman sound of immeasurable agony, was cut short when his lungs were rent by the claw and collapsed with a grisly wheeze.

For too long a moment, the sight held Han transfixed, every detail burning into his memory. Then his stomach heaved, and he turned away, choking on a bitter taste.

"Perhaps you understand us a little better now," Nil Spaar said, stepping back and absently sucking the blood from his claw.

With an effort, Han found his voice. "You bastard."

"Your opinion of me is of no consequence, and never has been," the viceroy said, and looked to one of his aides. "When you are finished here, have him moved to my ship."

"Yes, *darama,*" said the aide. Then he and the others knelt deferentially, almost reverently, as Viceroy Nil Spaar left the chamber.

Han raised his head and forced himself to look at Barth. The white pants were sodden crimson drapes hanging from the flight engineer's legs. The pool of blood and other bodily fluids below him had grown to the point where it was threatening to engulf Han's feet. Something in the spill of organs on Barth's lap was still twitching or pulsing.

I'm sorry, Barth, he thought, working to conceal his anguish as carefully as his fury, determined not to parade either before his audience. *I was wrong about us seeing Coruscant again. I didn't know. I didn't know until now what a monster he is.*

By chance, it fell to Behn-Kihl-Nahm to chair the session at which the vote on Leia was finally taken. He concealed his reluctance behind a well-practiced mask of businesslike duty.

"President Leia Organa Solo, you are called before the Ruling Council of the Senate of the New Republic to answer to a petition of no confidence offered by Chairman Doman Beruss," Behn-Kihl-Nahm said.

Leia stood in the well before the V-shaped table with her fingers laced before her. "I come before you to hear the challenge and respond, as specified in the Common Charter."

The chairman nodded. "The foundation for the petition is given as follows: that your ability to discharge your duties as President of this body is and will continue to be compromised by an irreducible conflict with your interests as wife of General Han Solo, who is presently a prisoner of the Duskhan League, with which we stand on the brink of conflict. Do you have any questions about this charge?"

"No," she said calmly.

"Do you wish to dispute the facts as laid out in section two of the petition?"

"I do not," she said, standing even straighter.

"Do you wish to make a statement in rebuttal of the argument offered in section three?"

"Only that the petitioner has said far more about his fears than he has about my conduct," Leia said with a quick but pointed glance sideways at Beruss. "For whatever reason, Chairman Beruss has prejudged me—and in doing so, he's become the principal disruption to the work of the President's office. I trust that this Council will recognize that fact and put an end to the disruption by rejecting this petition."

"Very well," said Behn-Kihl-Nahm. "Before I call for the vote, the petitioner has asked me to once again offer you an alternative. He is willing to withdraw the petition if you will agree to take a leave of absence until the crisis in Farlax Sector has been resolved and General Solo's return has been secured."

"Not interested," said Leia.

Beruss stirred. "The terms could be worked out so as to leave you with full authority in other areas."

"No, they couldn't," Leia said bluntly. "You can't sit there and start rewriting the Charter to separate President from Commander in Chief from Chief of State. And I wouldn't go along with it if you could."

Quietly defiant, she turned back to where Behn-Kihl-Nahm sat. "Chairman, this body wasn't created to provide an opportunity to blackmail the President behind closed doors. If you think this petition has merit—if you think I'm unfit to do the job I was elected to do—then send the petition on to the Senate. No more delays. Call for the vote."

"Very well," said Behn-Kihl-Nahm. "As the petitioner, Senator Beruss's vote is counted in support. Senator Rattagagech?"

"I support the petition."

"Senator Fey'lya?"

"I share Senator Beruss's concerns and offer him my support."

"Senator Praget?"

"Affirmative."

Praget's vote sealed the outcome, but Leia stood tall and impassive until the last member of the Council had weighed in. The final tally was five to two against her.

"The petition will be reported to the Senate at its next general session," said Behn-Kihl-Nahm, barely holding a rush of angry words in check. "This meeting is adjourned."

When he rang the crystal, he did so with enough force that it cracked—a crack substantial enough to mute its voice but not severe enough to shatter it.

Behn-Kihl-Nahm did not believe in omens, but he handled the crystal carefully as he removed it from the dais and made certain that no one else saw.

INTERLUDE II:

Ambush

"Captain! The intruder's soliton wave has vanished!"

Captain Voba Dokrett struck *Gorath*'s navigator a mighty blow across the back. "Emergency stop! Take us back to realspace! Smartly now—it's your first daughter's life if the enemy isn't under our guns when we exit."

Dokrett spun away from the navigator's station and hunted down the gunnery master with his eyes. "Instruct the blaster batteries to target the intruder fore and aft for weapons, then hole her amidships."

"Sir, shouldn't we disable the intruder first?"

"*Bloodprice*'s ion batteries were ineffective. Dogot went by the book and died. Give the order."

"Yes, sir," said the gunnery master. "All fire stations, attend. Numbers one and three forward, acquire tracking and target bow section. Numbers four and six forward, target aft section. Numbers two and five, rig for hull cutting and stand by."

The gunnery master was barely finished barking the orders when the crossover alarm began to sound and *Gorath* began to shudder and hum.

"A prize share to every officer if we take the intruder intact!" Dokrett cried. "For the glory of Prakith and in service to our beloved governor, Foga Brill, I commit this vessel to the fight before us!"

All around *Gorath*'s bridge, display screens came alive as the cruiser plunged back into the sea of electromagnetic energies that was the sublight universe.

"Captain, there is no sign of *Tobay*," called the sensor master. "If they did not observe the target's soliton change, they will have jumped on ours and overshot the entry."

"How sad for her crew, to lose their prize shares at the ninth hour," Dokrett said. "Range to target!"

"Eight thousand meters."

Grinning broadly, Dokrett clapped his hands on the navigator's shoulders. "Ha! It seems you are a good father after all," he exclaimed.

"Should we wait for *Tobay*, Captain?"

"No!" he barked. "Fire!"

The gunnery master leaned toward his station. "Numbers one and three forward, fire! Numbers four and six forward, fire!"

Almost at once and nearly as one, four of the cruiser's eight primary batteries sent fierce pulses of energy lancing toward the great vessel ahead.

There was no fire, nor any explosions, but Dokrett's telescopic scanner showed plumes of debris scattering from black-edged slashes across both ends of the intruder's hull. "Enough!" Dokrett cried. "To the heart of her, now!"

Moments after the gunnery master relayed the orders, the four active batteries fell silent, and the two batteries standing by opened fire. The ferocious hail of blaster bolts from their muzzles battered a single spot amidships on the giant vessel until another black-edged hole opened there. Then the focus of the blaster bolts spread into a circle, chewing at the edges of the opening until it was twenty meters across.

"Cease fire!" Dokrett shouted. "That should be enough to keep them busy. Gunnery master, enable all batteries for counterfire. Navigation master, bring us up alongside. Boarding parties, to your breaching pods! The prize is nearly ours."

There was no response from the target as *Gorath* closed on it, moving to within a hundred meters of the opening amidships. At that distance, the great bulk of the vessel—more than five times the length and three times the diameter of the Prakith light cruiser—filled every viewscreen and gunner's port.

"Captain!" called the sensor master. "Something odd—at this distance, with a ship that size, the reading from the magnetic anomaly detector should be nearly off the scale. But by the reading I'm getting, I would have said nothing larger than a pinnace was out there."

Dokrett nodded. "Look at the way she burned," he said. "Look at the way she's built. That's not durasteel or matrix armor. Whatever it is, we've never seen its kind before. What do you show for power generation?"

The sensor master waved his hands, frowning in puzzlement. "Field strength is negligible."

"Very well," said Dokrett, much pleased by the answer. "Open the ports. Away all pods."

In the moment between the opening of the ports and the launching of the first breaching pod, something shot out from the intruder and slammed into the hull of *Gorath* with such force that it knocked Dokrett to his knees. Alarms began to sound all over the bridge as the impact of a second projectile again made the cruiser shake from bow to stern.

"Fire! Fire!" Dokrett screamed as he dragged himself to his feet. A few scattered batteries were already engaged, though their efforts seemed undirected. "Gunnery master! Destroy those launchers!"

"We're trying. But the angle—we can't bring the mains to bear from here—"

Movement on the starboard viewer caught Dokrett's eye, and he glimpsed the third projectile as it leaped across the gap between the two ships—it seemed to be ball-shaped, trailing a thick cable extending back to the intruder. *Gorath* groaned under the impact.

"What's happening?" Dokrett demanded. "I want to see what's happening."

"I have something," the sensor master shouted. One pod had cleared its stowage bay, and the relay from its viewers showed that all three projectiles had buried themselves in the cruiser's hull. *Gorath* was now anchored to the vagabond by three slender, undulating tethers at bow, stern, and amidships.

"Navigation!" Dokrett called, wheeling around. "Break us free! Thrusters full! Stand by, main engines!"

At that moment, two more projectiles erupted from two different points along the hull of the intruder. These were slender and spiked, and they drove themselves deep into *Gorath*'s hull.

There was fear in Dokrett's eyes as he started across the deck toward the navigation master. "Full ahead, *now!*" he screamed.

But before the captain had covered half the distance to his beleaguered underling, every bridge station exploded in a shower of sparks. Every metal structure of the ship suddenly became part of the path for an enormously powerful electrical current coursing through the tethers from the alien vessel. The current leaped across isolation blocks and vaporized insulators, vaulted across the open air and skipped over the face of the bulkheads, coursed up the legs of crew members and grounded through their faces and hands. In little more than a second, most of the cruiser's systems were slag.

Just as quickly, most of the crew was dead, and those not yet dead were dying—of massive burns, paralyzed hearts, and scrambled neural systems. On the bridge, the gunnery master and his chair were fused into a single carbonized sculpture. Captain Dokrett was immolated by a lightning spike that used him as a shortcut from a fire-control vent head above his head to the decking under his feet.

By the time the attacking current ceased, small fires were burning in a hundred places throughout the ship, providing the only relief to the darkness that had abruptly fallen inside *Gorath*'s spaces. But when those fires had consumed the available oxygen, the smoke-filled ship became as black, still, and silent as a mausoleum.

The extent of the destruction was not as obvious from the outside. The commander of Pod 5 and his squad of assault troops saw flickering discharges through the open bay doors and scattered viewports, assessed the crushed hull plates at the impact points, noted the gun turrets going cold, spotted the darkening of the outer hull from spot fires within, marked the unbroken static on the command channels. Still, the ship seemed largely intact.

Then the tethers joining the ships suddenly parted close to the intruder's hull, and the pod commander faced a quick and irreversible choice between following his last orders and returning to the cruiser. Loyalty weighed more heavily on him than obedience. As the enormous vessel began to move off, he turned the pod toward *Gorath*. There was one voice raised in protest, but the commander silenced the dissenter with a sharp look.

"The enemy vessel is badly wounded," he said with a savage satisfaction. "See how slowly it moves. *Tobay* is nearby. We will help our brothers on *Gorath*, and then together we will hunt that demon down and destroy it."

When the vagabond returned to realspace after the Prakith encounter, the rumbling entry growl seemed to Lando to have edged closer to a howl. He signaled to the others for silence and then listened attentively to the sounds the vessel was making.

"Is there a problem?" Threepio asked at last.

"I don't know," Lando said. "Get me the database on bioengineered structures and I'll look it up. I don't know if this ship's even susceptible to the kind of fatigue that kills metal ships. Maybe that's why the Qella built her this way—so she could go on forever, indestructible and self-repairing."

"That seems like a reasonable inference," Threepio said.

"Except the mechanisms that do the repairs are just as susceptible to failure, so you need mechanisms that repair the repair mechanisms, and so on. Is everything working as designed? I have no idea."

"Perhaps it was damaged in the attack," said Lobot. "That could account for the altered spectrum of the entry growl."

"How would I know?" exclaimed Lando. "I don't even know something as elementary as what makes her go, what energy source we're tapping when we touch a trigger point. It takes fusion generators to drive a hyperspace engine for a capital vessel—everyone knows that, right? But the radmeter says there are no fusion generators aboard." Lando shook his head. "I'm half ready to throw my hands up and just say it's magic."

"We should learn something in the next few moments," Lobot said. "The last time the vessel jumped to escape capture, it changed course and jumped out less than fifteen minutes later. If the ship is under the direction of rule-based logic, as I believe it is, it should do so again."

"Of course, we were goosing her with a cutting blaster at the time," Lando said wryly. "Wait—quiet."

Straining at first to do so, both men could pick out a buzzing whine that seemed to come from a point several compartments away. As the ship began to shudder rhythmically around them, the sound swiftly grew louder, drowning out the normal background noises of the vessel and acquiring a destructive-sounding rasp.

"What is that?" Lobot asked, the worry in his tone a reflection of the worry on Lando's face. "It sounds like—"

"It sounds like we're under fire again," Lando said grimly.

"Could it be Colonel Pakkpekatt's armada?"

"Not a chance in a billion," Lando said. "Someone must have followed us out from Prakith. Lobot, seal up your suit, fast."

"What about your missing glove?"

"Someone has to operate the portals," Lando said. "That means bare skin. If we lose pressure, I'll make another sample-bag mitten. But I need you functional in case I don't have time or it won't hold. Hurry!"

By the time Lobot had snapped his helmet in place, the chamber's even glow was flickering. As Lando retrieved an unused sample bag from the depleted equipment sled, the chamber illumination failed entirely.

So had Threepio's courage. He had been clinging to the equipment sled while Artoo scanned and cataloged the displays from the center of the chamber, and now his frantic kicking had started the sled tumbling in slow motion. "Artoo! Artoo, come here this instant. Oh, this is ghastly—my circuits and gears can't bear any more. Master Lando, you simply *must* do something. Surely *now* you will signal *Lady Luck*."

"Forget it," Lando said, jetting toward the chamber's forward portal, through which they'd entered a short time before. "What I'm going to do is find out what that noise is all about."

But when he pressed his hand against the portal's trigger, nothing happened. He repeated the motion, then turned toward Lobot. "Did you see a one-way sign?"

Tight-lipped, Lobot shook his head.

It was the same at the other end of the chamber. "We're locked in," Lando announced.

"What does that mean?" Threepio fretted. "You can use your blaster, can't you?"

"Not without knowing if there's atmosphere on the other side, I can't," said Lando.

"This is the limit," Threepio declared. "Master Lando, I *insist* that you bring your yacht here immediately—"

Before the droid could complete his demand, before Lando could voice the rejection that was forming on his tongue, the chamber was filled with a near-deafening wail that was the malignant cousin of the sound they had heard earlier. But the source was much closer this time—no more than one or two bulkheads away.

"Hear the sizzle?" Lando shouted, drifting back from the portal. "That's the sound a blaster bolt makes when it hits a body, burning the fat and making the water boil—but a million times worse than I ever heard before. Someone's slicing this ship to pieces."

By then, Lando had drawn close enough to the tumbling sled for Threepio to release his grip on it and lunge clumsily toward Lando's nearest leg.

"What the—Threepio, what are you doing?" Lando demanded, twisting around to see what had struck him.

Then a new sound made Lando forget about Threepio. It was the muted roar of an explosive decompression—a big rupture, and close by, close enough to make the chamber walls around them ripple visibly in the beams from Artoo's floodlamps.

"Sweet cold starlight—" Lando breathed, slowly shaking his head. "She's in trouble now. We're all in trouble."

"There is no reason to be fearful," Threepio said brightly. "We are safe now."

"Shut up, Threepio. You don't know what you're talking about."

"Please don't worry, Master Lando. No one needs to worry. I have taken care of everything," Threepio declared proudly.

"What?" Looking down, Lando saw Threepio drifting away into the darkness with *Lady Luck*'s beckon call clutched tightly in the hand of his working arm. Lando grabbed at the pouch where the transmitter had been, as though unable to believe what the droid had done.

"Do you know what you've done?" Lando said, his tone low and menacing.

"Why, of course. I have signaled *Lady Luck* to come and rescue us."

"No," Lando said, barely restraining his fury. "You've condemned us. There's something out there big

enough and powerful enough to take on the vagabond
and survive. How long do you think *Lady Luck* will last
after she shows up? You've called a crewless ship into a
combat zone. She's got no way to defend herself. How
did you expect her to get past whatever's out there tearing pieces out of the hull?"

"Oh," said Threepio. "I see."

"Lando—"

"Leave me alone, Lobot," Lando said, his tone un-
derlining the warning. "I'm going to take this pile of
cheap cybernetic junk apart. I'm going to burn his arms
and legs into little pieces so that I'll have something to
throw at the boarding party. Say, how would you like
his backplate to use as a shield?"

"Lando, listen," Lobot insisted. "The firing has
stopped."

Lando swung his head around. "So it has. But
we're not moving. I don't think she's gonna move
again." He looked back at Threepio. "Neither are you."

"Artoo—Artoo, where are you? Master Lando has
gone mad. You must protect me. I don't deserve to die."

"Almost nobody does," Lando said, pulling out the
cutting blaster. "But we die anyway. Be philosophical."

"Lando, wait," said Lobot. "We know this ship.
We have the advantage over anyone coming aboard.
Whatever brings them here can as easily take us back."

"Sure—as prisoners," said Lando. "I've visited
enough prisons, thank you. I don't intend to be captured."

"All right, then," Lobot said. "Let's think about
how to fight them and win. Let's use our advantage.
Forget Threepio. What he did is a distraction, and rag-
ing over it is a waste of time."

With a growl, Lando twisted and pointed the cutting blaster at the forward entry portal. Its beam lit the
chamber briefly and harshly, leaving a meter-wide hole
that did not close.

"She's really hurting," Lando said, shaking his
head. "All right—Lobot, Artoo, let's go. We have to

move quickly." He pointed toward Threepio. "Golden Boy stays here."

"Lando—" Lobot began.

"He'll just slow us down."

"Lando—"

"But if we leave him here, maybe he'll slow *them* down. A diversion. Who knows—maybe they won't even blow him to bits," said Lando. "Come on."

"Where are we going?"

"Chamber twenty-one." Lando jetted toward the hole he had blasted, and the others followed him through.

So did Threepio's plaintive voice. "You can't abandon me here in the dark—Artoo—please—"

Artoo whimpered sympathetically, but he did not turn back.

Nearly five light-years Rimside from the pulsar 2GS-91E20, the powerful external worklights on the under curve of *Lady Luck*'s bow stabbed out into the ebony void toward the target Colonel Pakkpekatt was tracking.

"It's too small by half," said Colonel Hammax, looking up from the displays and out through the viewports, straining to pick out what the NRI deep-contact list called Anomaly 2249.

"Or it is now only half what it was. We will continue," said Pakkpekatt, bobbing his head.

Hammax glanced back down. "Target is now sixty-one thousand meters dead ahead."

"Tell me, Colonel—how is it that a personal yacht has a sensor system that appears to have resolution comparable to a front-line intelligence picket and better range—far superior to that on a cruiser like *Glorious*?"

"Shorter procurement cycle," Hammax said. "He buys what he needs, without having to get the permission of anyone who sits in an office far from the consequences of saying no."

"And what is his need?"

Hammax shrugged. "Considering that this ship mounts only a single low-grade laser cannon, sensors like that might help keep you out of a lot of trouble."

"That does not answer my question," Pakkpekatt said. "Who is this Lando Calrissian? This bridge belongs to a meticulous professional, someone who insists on the best tools and on knowing how to use them. The storage holds belong to a mercenary or a brigand, a man who respects no rule but expediency. The personal quarters belong to a sybarite, a self-indulgent hedonist who surrounds himself with soft pleasures. Which one is Calrissian?"

"I didn't know the baron before he came aboard *Glorious*," Hammax said. "But by reputation, Colonel, he's all three."

"They could not abide each other," Pakkpekatt stated firmly. "Such a man would never be content in any of his pursuits. He would always be drawn elsewhere—the hedonist to purpose, the brigand to security, the perfectionist to impulsiveness, and on. You understand?"

"Humans are contradictory creatures," said Hammax. "Forty thousand meters."

"That I know, Colonel—but can you tell me why they think it a strength?" Pakkpekatt asked.

"I think that's the first of the contradictions," Hammax said with a grin.

"You are no help to me," the Hortek said, annoyed. "Go and wake the others. It is time."

Before *Lady Luck* had closed another five thousand meters on the unknown object tagged by NRI trackers as Anomaly 2249, all four members of the team were at their stations.

On the bridge, Pakkpekatt was handling the piloting duties, Taisden was monitoring the sensor matrix, and Hammax was controlling the laser cannon by means of a lightweight targeting headset. Aft on the enclosed observation deck, Pleck tended the bank of

NRI-issue tracking and holo imagers he and Taisden had installed.

It was becoming a familiar drill, but Pakkpekatt did not allow them to become casual about it. The first five anomalies they had investigated had included a burned-out Modan starfreighter, an abandoned bulk-cargo barge apparently holed by a collision, and a sizable section of an ancient deep-space antenna—all harmless. But they had also found a fully operational Kuat Ranger running with a blacked-out telesponder, which fled at their approach, and a live Ilthani space mine, which Hammax detonated with a precise burst from the yacht's laser cannon.

At three thousand meters, it became clear that Anomaly 2249 was not the Teljkon vagabond or any part of it. The work floods illuminated a metal mesh cylinder some sixty meters long, capped by solid metal spheres fifteen meters across and studded with circular metal fittings. It was slowly turning end over end, rotating around a slightly eccentric center of gravity.

"What in blazes is that?" Hammax asked. "Spaceship? Probe? I don't recognize the configuration."

"Nor do I," said Pakkpekatt. "But I know what it is not." He dragged a datapad toward him and consulted the report provided to him by the keepers of NRI's network of stationary blackball-tracking buoys. "Anomaly ten-thirty-three, near Carconth, is the next highest probability candidate."

"Colonel?"

"Yes, Agent Pleck?"

"Could we give this one a few more minutes—get in to maybe five hundred meters and do a flyaround? I'd like to be able to resolve all the hull detail for the analysts, and there may be markings on the far side."

"I am not interested in performing any extra services for the Analysis Section," Pakkpekatt said curtly, turning *Lady Luck* away from the mystery object and onto a heading for Carconth. "Let them clear their anomalies themselves. Colonel Hammax, retract the cannon pod. Agent Pleck, lock down your imagers. Hyperspace in one minute. This will be a nine-hour jump, so we'll make the watch change now."

Apart from the ugly smell it left hanging in the air, Lando had no qualms about burning a path through the chain of chambers for himself and the others. If the ship survived what was almost certainly more serious damage elsewhere, closing the wounds Lando was making would be no problem—and if the ship was already doomed, the wounds he was making were irrelevant.

But Lobot quickly became uncomfortable watching Lando do it. After only four chambers and four black-edged burnholes, Lobot caught Lando and stayed his hand before he could make the fifth.

"Can't we at least try each portal before we destroy it?" he pleaded.

"Do you have some reason to think the vagabond is recovering?" Lando asked, pulling his arm free and pointing the blaster ahead.

Lobot cringed as the beam burned a hole into the next chamber. "I don't know what's happening," he said. "I do know that we are leaving a trail that will be no challenge to follow, a fact which makes our flight futile. The boarding parties will simply find us in the last chamber."

A new sound reached them as Lando stopped and looked back. It was a series of wet-sounding percussive reports, akin to the sound of a stone falling into soft mud.

"Fluids blowing under pressure," Lando said, craning his neck. "I heard a bad fuel slug pop once, sounded a lot like that." He looked back at Lobot. "Yeah, you're right. We won't be hard to follow. But the darkness helps us, and we don't have to be conveniently waiting for them at the end of the line."

"Is that your whole plan?" Lobot demanded. "Do you think Threepio will have them coming after us so recklessly that we can surprise an entire boarding party with hand tools?"

"My plan is to postpone the confrontation," Lando said. "That's all I have going right now. I'm only thinking about putting some distance between us and whoever's coming in back there."

"Then what about making more than one hole? Make them make a decision. Get them to split up."

"I'd gladly burn some more holes to make it harder for them to follow us, but I don't know what I'd be cutting into," said Lando. "And I sure don't want to increase the odds of burning through into vacuum."

"The topography of the ship does not make any chamber face coterminous with the hull," said Lobot. "When you placed the sensor limpet—"

"We don't know what spaces have been breached by the attack," Lando said. "I could even hit vacuum going straight ahead through the portals. I'm telling you—"

Just then the shoulder joint of Lobot's contact suit bumped gently against the face of the chamber. Moments later, Lando, too, drifted into a solid barrier.

"Ship's moving again," Lando said.

"Just barely moving."

"Changing direction, too."

"Under way, or under tow?"

"No telling from here," Lando said. "But more likely under way—there hasn't been enough time to sweep the ship, and it'd be risky to take her under tow until that was finished. Come on." Lando jetted toward the opening he had made, grabbed the edge, and pulled himself through.

What he saw as he pointed his lights and his blaster at the opposite end of the chamber startled him to speechlessness. The portal was already irising open.

As Lando began to retreat he swiped at his suit controls with his gloved hand, killing the lights. Behind him, Lobot took the cue and did the same. But even after Artoo obeyed the instruction Lobot placed in his language register, the chamber remained faintly lit by the glow from a narrow ring encircling each of its open portals—all six of them.

"Lando—"

"I see, I see," Lando said.

"Lando, those are the STAFF ONLY doors you were talking about. What's going on?"

"I'm not sure." He jetted diagonally to the nearest of the four previously unknown portals for chamber 229 and stole a peek through it.

"What can you see?"

"More of the same, only different," Lando said, heading for the portal to chamber 228. "Check the one behind us."

Both the chamber ahead and the one they had just left were also now showing multiple portals lit by glow-rings. Some of the new portals opened to tiny dead-end chambers, others to narrow cylindrical passageways, still others to the vast interspace Lando had discovered when planting the sensor limpet.

"Any ideas?" Lando asked Lobot.

"Possibly. Rule-based logic must be strictly prioritized, following a conditional decision tree," said Lobot. "The first thing the ship did was to seal all portals, giving the highest priority to containing the damage—a reasonable response to an attack, especially if there was a hull breach. Then, after an inventory of the damage, the next highest priority was given to restoring freedom of movement, perhaps to facilitate repairs."

"Or escape," said Lando. "Are you saying you think this means the attack is over?"

"It doesn't matter," said Lobot. "The ship has thrown all the doors open. We may never have another chance like this." He pointed at the portal below them, leading to the interior. "The heart of the ship is that way."

"Maybe—and for all you know, it's at the other end of a ten-kilometer maze. And if she's on the verge of breaking up, what then?" Lando demanded.

"What else can we do?"

"I have to see how bad the damage is. Give me your left glove."

"Why?"

"Because you won't need it where you're going, and I do need it where I'm going—out to the hull and forward to find out how much damage there is."

"That's pointless. Either it can repair itself or it cannot," said Lobot. "We have to look for the control nexus."

"You can do what you like. I need to know where things stand."

"The *ship* knows," Lobot insisted.

"When you figure out how to talk to her, let me know. Until then, we're both wasting time. The glove, please."

Lobot hesitated, then unlocked the retaining ring and twisted the glove sharply clockwise. He sent it spinning across the chamber toward Lando with more force than necessary.

"Thanks," Lando said, catching it cleanly with his bare hand. "I'll bring it back."

"Is every gambler always sure that the next draw's a winner?" Lobot asked. "If you make it back, you can look for me in here." He jerked a bare thumb in the direction of the portal behind him.

"I'll do that," Lando said, jetting toward a portal on the opposite side of the chamber. "If you want to help me out, you might try blazing your path with the paint stick. The ship might be too busy with other things just now to get around to wiping the marks."

"I will consider it," Lobot said. As soon as Lando disappeared through the opening with a wave, Lobot turned to Artoo-Detoo. "Go get Threepio and bring him here."

Artoo released the equipment grid and dove toward the portal, chirping his relief and approval.

"Don't spare the propellant," Lobot called after him.

Alone, he removed his right glove and his helmet, clipping both to the equipment grid. Bending his neck forward, he reached up with his bare hands and lightly caressed the edges of the Hamarin interface band, his fingertips playing briefly over the attachment release at the back of his head.

The interface had never come off in thirty-four years, not for maintenance upgrades, nor for sleep, nor for vanity. It did more than connect Lobot with a universe of interlinked data resources and control interfaces. The band had become a secondary link between the halves of his own brain, supplementing the corpus callosum so as to allow him to process the tremendous flood of data that pressed in on his awareness. His fingers knew it as part of the familiar and ordinary contours of his head. His mind no longer recognized a boundary between biology and technology; his integrated consciousness bridged both.

Even so, this time, his fingers were exploring the interface as an object apart—and he was wondering what it would be like not to find it there, either with his hands or with his thoughts.

Outside chamber 228, as elsewhere, the inner face of the vagabond's interspace—the open area between what Lando thought of as the ship proper and the outer hull—was covered with hexagonal cells containing sculpted Qella faces. It seemed to Lando that the entire ship must be tiled with them.

As he jetted past the unbroken and unending bas-relief, Lando wondered how many faces there were, and whether each was unique. When he contemplated the numbers, it became almost unthinkable that it was a portrait gallery, that each represented an actual individual—long dead, in all likelihood, and perhaps remembered nowhere else but here.

There must be hundreds of thousands—perhaps millions. I'll have to ask Lobot or Artoo to calculate it, Lando thought. *Who could have made them all? Just gathering and organizing them into this collage would have been a monumental task. How were they made? Are they like the rest of this ship, almost alive?*

The Qella watched with impassive eyes as he

passed, more sanguine about Lando's presence than he
was about theirs.

And why are they here? *All that work, and who
would see them?* The discovery of access portals to the
interspace did not alter Lando's impression of the interspace as a private place. *They gaze outward as if the
outer hull weren't there, as if they're held in trance by
something they see lying beyond, as if they all share the
same thought. Was it infinity? Eternity? Mortality?*

Soon after entering the interspace, Lando discovered that the inner hull and outer hull were connected
by slender stringers. Crisscrossing and arrayed in a con-
tinuous row, they stitched the two hulls together with
an open pattern of diamonds and triangles, like a series
of X's. The smallest openings were large enough for
Lando to pass through easily. Lando suspected that the
stringers encircled the entire inner hull, like the spokes
of a velocipede wheel—a single structure serving as
strut, spacer, and shock mount.

As he continued forward, Lando encountered a second ring of stringers and learned they had another function. For this row was a solid barrier, with membranes
closing the spaces between the strands, sealing off the
next section of interspace. The obstacle drove Lando
back inside the ship at chamber 207.

Forward from that point, the portals leading to the
interspace were still illuminated by glow-rings but
sealed tight. Although none of them would open to
Lando's touch, the center of those he tried to open
transformed into a hexagon of the same transparent
material they had seen in the auditorium. In chamber
after chamber, the viewports allowed him to glimpse the
reason the portals would not open—a gaping slash in
the outer hull that started at chamber 202 and continued forward nearly to the bow.

When Lando peered out into the interspace, he saw
stars.

Even though the giant transparency was opaque,
the best view of the damage was from the auditorium.
Looking through a previously unknown portal, Lando

could see that the attacker had come close to shearing the bow off the vagabond. The burn patterns were familiar and distinctive—the damage was the result of the pulsed output produced by a capital ship's batteries.

This is what we heard, Lando thought, keying the suit's comlink. "Lobot, are you there?"

"Listening."

"I'm in the auditorium," Lando said. "There's a big hole along the starboard side, and everything forward of here is a wreck. The last few pulses punched all the way through her, opening up a smaller hole in the far side. The whole section is sealed—I can't get any closer to the damage without cutting my own door, which I don't need or want to do."

"Is there any indication that the breach is being repaired?"

"It's hard to tell," Lando said. "There's so much hull missing, and I can't get enough light on the closest edges. I'll probably have to wait here a while to know."

"Is there any sign anyone has come aboard?"

"No sign I can see. It's pretty clear they were going after the weapon nodes," Lando said. "Which means they must have seen her fight before, most likely at Prakith."

"Can you see anything of the vessel or vessels that attacked us?"

"Not a hint. From the angle of incidence, I'd say they were well aft of us when this started. Lobot—the orrery is gone."

"No!" Lobot protested. "Gone or inactive?"

"Gone. Destroyed. The whole shadow-box chamber would have been filled with bolt scatter after the initial burn-through. Everything that wasn't swept out in the decompression's been vaporized."

"Perhaps it will regenerate."

"From what? There's nothing out there. No, it looks as if you and I are going to be the last to have seen it."

"That is dismaying," said Lobot.

"No telling from where I am, but I'd guess there are

a few thousand fewer portraits in the gallery, too. Probably came close to losing this chamber."

"How long do you plan to stay and observe?"

Lando glanced at his chronometer. "I'll give it twenty minutes. If I can't see some activity by then, I'll start back. How are you doing? Any sign of trouble there? Where are you now—still in two-twenty-eight?"

"I am fine," said Lobot. "But I do not know how to tell you where I am. I would already be lost if not for Artoo's holomap."

"You've gone into the inner passages?"

"Yes."

"Maybe I should come back now," said Lando. "I've seen most of what I need to. Did you blaze your route?"

"I would rather you did not," Lobot said. "The silence is surprisingly agreeable. I am hearing much more clearly now. That is why I did not blaze my route. That is why I am now going to turn off my comlink."

Lando began an angry protest. "Lobot, what's going on—"

"You said that I should do what I like. That is what I have decided to do."

"Fine, but don't turn off your comlink. What if—"

"I will signal you if I want you," Lobot said. "Until then, I will wish you good judgment, and you can wish us good luck."

That was the end of the conversation. Lando was unable to raise Lobot on any comm channel, not even with an emergency signal.

He's sided with the droids against me, Lando thought, smashing his fist against the face of the chamber in frustration. *Which is just more proof that this ship is making all of us nuts. By the time we get out of here—if we ever do—we're all going to need a mindwipe.*

Turning back toward the portal, Lando pressed the facescreen of his helmet against the transparency and peered into the darkness. The contours of the holes appeared to have changed slightly, as though the holes might be beginning to knit. How far it would go, though, he could not tell. Left untreated, the edges of a cavity wound will heal without regenerating what was destroyed.

Switching off his suit lamps, Lando looked out through the blast hole at the star patterns beyond, seeking a familiar pattern, a recognizable star or distinctive spiral nebula. The odds did not favor him. Even after a lifetime roaming the spacelanes, there was far more unknown than known in a galaxy of a hundred billion stars.

But if there was any way he could, he needed to touch the familiar, and remind himself what it was he was fighting to live long enough to see again.

Lady Luck dropped back into realspace just shy of a light-second from Anomaly 1033 and just more than a light-year from Carconth.

At those distances, the anomaly was invisible except to sensors, but the red supergiant star was still a spectacular sight. Five hundred times as large and a hundred thousand times as bright as the sun Coruscant orbited, Carconth commanded the sky like few other stars. At the peak of its fluctuations, it was the second largest and seventh brightest of the known stars. The Astrographic Survey Institute and its predecessors had been maintaining a supernova watch at Carconth for more than six hundred years.

The chances were that Anomaly 1033 was something left behind by an alien expedition to Carconth. There had been many such, most unrecorded in Old or New Republic records. But Colonel Pakkpekatt and his volunteers would have no chance to find out, and little opportunity to gawk at the galactic spectacle visible off the yacht's port beam.

Within moments of their arrival, *Lady Luck*'s controls went dead under Pakkpekatt's hands. Accelerating as it turned, the yacht veered sharply some sixty degrees to starboard and twenty degrees toward galactic north, pointing its bow in the general direction of Kaa. The displays churned as the autonavigator ran through its calculus and sent the results to the hyperspace motivator.

"What's wrong, Colonel?" Bijo Hammax asked.

"Something has activated a slave circuit," said Pakkpekatt, lifting his hands from the panel and sitting back in the pilot's flight couch. "The yacht is no longer under my control."

"But you're not trying to get control back." The whistle of the yacht's hyperdrive winding up to a jump was now clearly audible to both officers.

"That is correct."

At that moment, Pleck and Taisden joined them on the flight deck. "Colonel—" Pleck began.

Hammax turned his couch toward Pakkpekatt. "Colonel, I don't understand why you're letting us be hijacked."

"It is very difficult to defeat a well-designed slave circuit without doing extensive damage to the vessel," said Pakkpekatt. "They would be of little use if they could be easily overridden."

"But that doesn't explain—"

Taisden shouldered forward past Pleck. "Colonel, I can have the hyperdrive offline in thirty seconds."

"I doubt very much if you can, Agent Taisden. I also doubt very much if you have thirty seconds."

"Let me try."

"No," Pakkpekatt said.

"You think she's going to take us to them," Hammax concluded.

"The most likely person to have installed the slave circuits is also the most likely person to have activated them," said Pakkpekatt. "We will know in"—he glanced down at the nav display—"six hours if that person was General Calrissian."

Seconds later, *Lady Luck* vaulted forward through a tunnel of stars.

*   *   *

"Where are they?" Captain Gegak screamed at the bridge crew of the destroyer *Tobay*. "Where is the target? Where is *Gorath*?"

"There is no sign of either ship, Captain," the sensor master ventured. "I do not detect *Gorath*'s transponder."

"Idiot! Do you think I cannot read a tracking screen?" Gegak bellowed, balling both hands into fists. His rage was indiscriminate and comprehensive, leaving no one on the bridge feeling safe enough to move or speak. "I am betrayed! One of you is in league with Captain Dokrett. Someone has conspired to steal our share of the prize."

Gegak stalked behind the officers at their stations. "Who is the thief? Who is the traitor? Is it you, Frega?" He seized the hair tuft of the navigation master and used it to roughly yank his head backward.

"Captain, I depend on the sensor master. Not five seconds passed from his call before we left hyperspace—"

Sensor Master Nillik rose from his station before Gegak reached it, and retreated before him with hands raised. "I have not betrayed you, Captain. The instruments have betrayed me—"

With a snarl, Gegak lunged forward and closed the gap between them to little more than an arm's length. "And who is responsible for the maintenance of your instruments?"

"I am, Lord Captain—but, I beg you, hear me—"

"I hear only the whining of a traitor."

"This ship is old, twice the age of *Gorath,* and we have had neither the prize money nor the blessings of Foga Brill with which to maintain it. You cannot expect—"

Gegak produced a neural whip from inside a fold of his bright tunic and brandished it in front of him. "I can expect that my officers will not repay the favor I do them with excuses."

"Captain—please!" Nillik now found himself backed against a bulkhead. "To track a ship through hyperspace is difficult even with the most sensitive installations. I was given no time to cool and retune the soliton antenna—I could not hear the target at all. I was barely able to hear *Gorath* above our own compression wave."

"You are only making excuses for your inattentiveness."

"No, Captain—it was not my attentiveness that wavered. The signature was so faint that I lost and reacquired it half a dozen times before the final loss of signal. That was the only reason for my delay. I do not know for certain if those ships left hyperspace behind us or continue on somewhere ahead of us."

Gegak growled and stabbed the neural whip into Nillik's abdomen. The sensor master screamed and collapsed writhing to the floor.

"I should have been informed of your difficulties," the captain said, returning the whip to its pocket. His voice was suddenly tranquil. "You have forgotten the first rule of survival in an autocracy—speak truth to power. I hope the pain will help you learn from your mistake."

Then the captain turned his back on the gasping sensor master. "Point the bow toward Prakith. Make flank speed. Call the second master to the sensing station. We will search back to the point where *Gorath* disappeared from our instruments. And I will hear no more excuses for failure. I have expended all my tolerance on Nillik."

Chapter 5

◆

L uke found it difficult not to step off the slidewalk to pursue Akanah and prolong the argument. The thinly veiled threat she had offered as her parting words, suggesting that she might continue on to J't'p'tan without him, might withdraw her promise to lead him to his mother's people, was not without power.

But that threat was also nakedly manipulative, and his reflexive resentment allowed him both to see the emotional blackmail and to resist it.

It was not that he gave no credence to the threat. Akanah's conduct on Atzerri had made clear that she was perfectly capable of striking out on her own when her interests so dictated. But he had no compromise or concession to offer her. The old, familiar demon of Duty had reentered his consciousness during the conversation with the shipwright, and he could do nothing else until he either answered to his conscience or silenced it.

There was no point in seeking a rapprochement with Akanah until Luke knew his own mind—until he knew if *he* could allow himself to continue the journey.

And for that, he needed information.

After stopping at the port office to authorize Starway Services to move *Mud Sloth* to their work bay,

Luke returned to the skiff. Locking the entry not only against strangers but against Akanah as well, he settled at the flight console and began making queries.

A connection to Utharis GridLink gave him access—at a refreshingly reasonable price—to both New Republic Prime and Coruscant Global archives, as well as to the back numbers of several smaller newsgrids. But the most complete information Luke found came from two local services, *Eye-On-U* and *Taldaak Today!* The Coruscant-based grids were obsessed with Imperial City politics and offered only a cursory—and frequently misleading—overview of the military aspects of the crisis.

"Access *Fleet Watch*," Luke said. The newspacket of the Alliance Veterans Victory Association, *Fleet Watch* was usually current enough and comprehensive enough that many senior staff members at Fleet HQ kept it on their browse lists as a supplement to official sources.

"Requested source is temporarily unavailable," the comm pad reported.

"Why?"

"Access has been voluntarily suspended by the provider. Message available."

"Let's hear it."

The recording contained a familiar face and voice—that of Brigadier Bren Derlin, NRDF, Ret. Derlin and Luke had been thrown together on Hoth, where Derlin had been one of the field commanders at the Rebels' base. Derlin was more of a steadying influence than a leader, but he was a good soldier and a quiet but likable man. Luke had not seen him again until war's end, and since then only once, at the ceremonies when more than a hundred Hoth survivors gathered to dedicate a memorial to the many more who had fallen there.

Now Derlin was commander of the AVVA, an organization with the status of a retirees' club but the ambition to be something more akin to a militia or the Fleet's ready reserve. The recording began with a spiral of unit insignias surrounding the AVVA logo, and a smart salute from a uniformed Derlin.

"Thank you for your inquiry. Due to the current military situation, the AVVA board of governors has placed the membership on a status two alert. For security reasons, access to past and current volumes of *Fleet Watch* has been restricted to members only. Please join us in supporting the soldiers and pilots who are even now risking their lives to guard our freedom."

"How long has that lockout been in effect?" Luke asked the comm pad.

"Nine days."

"I wonder what happened to bring that on," Luke said, scratching his head. "What else do you have? Show me a list."

After another half hour, Luke had satisfied himself that he had all the information he was likely to garner from public news sources. Unfortunately, it was not enough to settle his mind.

He was more reluctant to contact Coruscant directly than he had been the last time he needed information. If a contact watch had been set up for his authorization codes, even querying the impersonal, automated sources might throw him into the middle of a conversation he didn't want to have—with Ackbar, or Behn-Kihl-Nahm, or Han, or possibly even Leia herself.

For the question gnawing at Luke was not whether Leia wanted his help, but whether she needed it. If his presence might mean the difference between triumph and defeat, then he would go to her—as she had come to him in his darkest moment, aboard the clone Emperor's flagship.

Leia had pulled him back from the precipice of the dark power, and joined her power to his to defeat Palpatine. If she had not been willing to sacrifice herself and the child inside her in confronting the reborn Emperor, Luke would never have broken the grip of the dark side—and the history of the intervening years would have been written with the pen of tyranny. He could not have done it alone.

But having seen not only the great strength in her heart but also the Jedi power she could summon, Luke was all the more loath to volunteer himself as a rescuer. He knew that Leia had within her extraordinary resources of will and power—resources she had of late become reluctant to draw upon. Luke thought that he was much of the reason, with both his example and his presence creating disincentives. It was important that she find that strength again.

It seemed to Luke that Leia had neglected, even abandoned, her own training, and that her training of the children had become unbalanced, with the disciplines of warrior and weapon excised as if they were dispensable. Luke had not spoken of it with her, but from what he had seen, it was almost as though Leia hoped to delay, training the children as Jedi clerics rather than as Jedi Knights—as if the path before her, the path he had followed, promised to take her somewhere she did not want to go.

It was her choice to make. Her destiny was no more clear to him than it was to her. But whatever that destiny was, it seemed that she was fighting it rather than following it.

And it was certain she would learn nothing from an errant Knight's well-intentioned but unnecessary rescue—if she would even allow it to happen. Knowing her streak of aristocratic, self-reliant pride, Luke was not at all confident he could count on her to ask for help, even if she needed it—not after the fight they had had the night he left Coruscant.

No, those around her, the others who loved her, would urge Luke to return to her side, no matter what the circumstances. And Leia herself would insist that he stay away, no matter what the circumstances. It was essential that Luke make his own assessment of the situation, that the decision be his alone. And it was better that Luke stay out of sight and out of reach until the decision was made.

Ackbar, especially, would never understand, Luke thought in passing. *He's as devoted to her as a good father to a beloved child—I wonder how clearly she sees it.*

Still, he needed more information—information that could only come from Coruscant. He began by retrieving his registered hypercomm messages from the master archive maintained by the Communications Office.

As a hedge against the vagaries of hyperspace transmission, the archive kept a copy of every registered-recipient message sent out over the New Republic system. Undeliverable messages were held until their intended recipients requested an update—something most people did routinely every time they emerged from hyperspace. But save for those few hours while outbound from Teyr, Luke had been off the system since leaving Yavin 4.

The update took nearly twenty minutes to spill into *Mud Sloth*'s comm bank. As always, there were hundreds of blind messages—love letters and propositions, requests for personal favors, questions from amateur and would-be Jedi, the occasional diatribe from an Imperialist stubbornly resisting the idea that his world had changed.

Luke almost never looked at any of it. The novelty value of blatant proposals had long ago faded, and the one-two punch of praise and begging had worn thin even faster—it was as uncomfortable as being surrounded by a crowd in which everyone wanted to touch him.

The priority queue contained a copy of the message from Streen, which Luke realized he had never viewed and released, and a second message from him time-stamped a day later. But there were no other messages from the twenty or so senders on his priority list—and that was something of a surprise. By and large, he had not announced his hermitage to his friends, so he could only suppose that the word had spread from the few who did know of his self-imposed isolation.

"Show me number one," said Luke.

Streen's face appeared. "Master Luke," he said,

bowing his head slightly. "I received your latest instructions for Artoo and Threepio. But I regret to say that so far, I've been unable to deliver them. Perhaps it slipped your mind that the droids are now with Lando Calrissian? I'll try to locate them and forward your message to them."

"Lando," Luke said, shaking his head in surprise. "What would the droids be doing with him? Show me number two."

Streen's face shifted to the right, and his caftan changed from goldenrod to rust. "Master Luke," he said, bowing his head once more. "I've tried to contact Lando Calrissian by every means available to me, without any success. I not only can't get a message through, I can't find anyone who'll admit to knowing where he or the droids are. It's possible that they're simply in hyperspace somewhere, but I'm guessing that there's more to this, and you probably know more about it than I do. I'm afraid you'd better see to this on your own."

The combination of the two messages left Luke mystified, but he did not devote much time or energy to penetrating the mystery. Apparently Lando had absconded with the two droids, probably in furtherance of some scheme—any deeper understanding would have to wait. The droids' errand had become moot, in any case. If Luke went on with Akanah, he would have all the answers he needed in just a few days.

Luke considered the long list of sources he had tapped the last time, but none seemed promising enough to justify the time and trouble. What he really wanted most was something he had tried for before and been denied—the Fleet Office's daily tactical briefing memorandum. But to get one, he would have to find a military-grade secure-link hypercomm. Or—

"Access Fleet Almanac," he said.

"Ready."

"Reference current location."

"Referencing Taldaak Station, Utharis."

"Identify the nearest Fleet asset in this sector—training center, repair yard, supply base, whatever."

"This access requires a current level blue authorization code."

Luke rattled off his code. "Now give me some good news."

The only New Republic Defense Fleet installation on Utharis was a tiny listening post. The listening post consisted of a three-man office in Taldaak, a four-man maintenance crew flying a work skipboat based at the planet's main geosynchronous station, and a pair of complex antenna arrays located in hundred-year solar-polar orbits.

The highest-ranking officer on orbit was a senior specialist—dirtside, it was a green lieutenant in the first month of a yearlong rotation. The operational continuity of the post came largely from the three civilian employees, all Utharis natives.

It was one of those civilians who Luke encountered first when he entered the security foyer of the listening post's small silo-dome, located adjacent to an abandoned Imperial fighter base, now home only to wild jack-a-dale and black-winged touret. Luke had dressed to the Jedi stereotype, black cape and dangling lightsaber, and allowed the Li Stonn disguise to dissolve as he passed through the concussion hatch.

"I am here to see the post commander," Luke said, resting his palm on the scanner.

The young woman looked up at him with eyes widened by surprise. Her tattooed forehead and cheeks marked her as a follower of the Duality, a popular and benign Tarrack cult founded on the twin principles of joy and service. She looked down at the scanner when it beeped at her, then back up to Luke's face wearing a look of awe on her own.

"You *are* him," she said.

Luke flashed a small smile as he lifted his hand from the scanner. "But I am not here," he said.

"I understand."

"Who is the duty officer?"

"Tomathy—Senior Specialist Manes. Lieutenant Ekand comes on in two hours. But I can call him in early—"

"There's no need," said Luke. "I will speak with Manes. Clear me through, please."

"Yes, of course."

The secure room of the installation accounted for the rest of the volume of the silo—a floor full of instrument stations, a domed ceiling fifteen meters overhead, and two rings of catwalks spaced between to give access to the transceiver arrays.

"I'll be right down," called a voice from above. That was followed by the brisk clatter of shoes descending metal-mesh stairs.

While waiting, Luke sized up the installation. The first thing that struck his eye was that the data system used three black-bodied memory droids for storage. That meant that everything of value, staff and secure data, could be removed from the post in a matter of minutes in a six-place speeder or orbital jumper.

"My goodness," Manes said, his steps slowing as he reached the main level and saw Luke clearly. "My goodness. This is an honor." As an afterthought, he gathered himself for a salute. "Forgive me, sir—I don't know your proper rank—"

"I no longer hold one," said Luke, leaning over one of the data stations.

"Oh—I see. Then I'll confess that I've never met a Jedi. Nothing unusual there, I guess—I don't know anyone who has. Is there a proper form of address—"

"You can call me Luke."

"Of course. Thank you." Manes shook his head. "Forgive me for staring. I'm on my second tour here, and in all that time you're only the second person to come through that door who didn't work here. And to have it be you—" As though suddenly aware of his flustered babbling, Manes cut himself off. "How can I help you, Luke?"

"I need a copy of the current tactical briefing memorandum."

"Of course. You can use the comm pad at my station—right over here—"

"I need you to retrieve it for me," Luke said. "I'm here on a sensitive matter, and I can't have my location revealed."

"Got it," said Manes. "No problem. We get the teebeam twice a day. I'll bring the latest one up for you."

"I need a copy I can take with me." As he spoke, Luke reached out with the Force and gave the senior specialist a gentle nudge.

Manes stared blankly for just a moment. "What am I thinking," he said. "You'll want a copy you can take with you. I'll get a datacard."

"Thank you."

Less than five minutes later, Li Stonn was climbing into his rented speeder, the datacard securely tucked away. But he did not immediately drive away. Sitting at the controls, Luke reached out into the listening post and found its two occupants excitedly discussing their surprise visitor.

The event had given both such inexplicable pleasure that he hated to take those memories away from them, but he had no choice. He had already blocked the machine records of his visit from being written to the logs. Compressing a nerve here, a blood vessel there, Luke brought on a moment of unconscious paralysis, and in that moment swept the memories from their minds.

Akanah had not yet returned to the skiff, nor had the service depot's tow dolly come to claim it. Taking advantage of the privacy, Luke locked himself inside while he reviewed the information on the datacard.

The situation in Koornacht Cluster had escalated to a high level of precariousness. New Republic forces had clashed with a Yevethan fleet at Doornik 319 while trying to enforce a blockade, and dozens of Fleet recon probes had been destroyed on deep penetration missions. Five battle groups of an expanded Fifth Fleet had actually moved into the cluster, and smaller units were actively searching for the former Imperial shipyards. So far the Yevetha had not responded to the intrusions, but it seemed inevitable that they would.

But the real source of concern for Luke was the first confirmation that J't'p'tan—referred to by its catalog name, FAR202019S—had been involved in the fighting. The recon ship sent there had identified a Yevethan thrustship in orbit before being fried; though the probe had completed only thirty-four percent of its ground scan, the destruction of the H'kig commune, estimated at thirteen thousand strong, was listed as "probable."

Balancing that bleak prospect, at least in part, was the report from Doornik 319 that the Yevethan warships were carrying hostages taken from the destroyed colonies. If the Fallanassi had not died on J't'p'tan, they were now prisoners of the Yevetha, aboard one of the more than six hundred ships of the Duskhan League fleet—a fleet that could at any moment be hurled against the New Republic forces challenging Nil Spaar's sovereignty.

Suddenly Luke's journey to Koornacht seemed joined to Leia's crisis at home, and in a way he had not anticipated. If he had a part to play in what was coming, the flow of the Current pointed to J't'p'tan, not Coruscant. Perhaps everything that had happened was part of a larger tapestry he had not yet been able to glimpse. But even without that understanding, he knew that he had to go on, not turn back.

With both his and Akanah's day bags slung over his shoulder, Luke rode the slidewalk back to Starway Services, where the lights and sounds emanating from the covered work bays told him that some of the mech crews were chasing a completion bonus. A few minutes later, depot manager Notha Trome awoke with a start from the nap he was taking on his office floor.

"Li Stonn's ship should be given top priority," he said aloud, as though it were a revelation that had come to him in his sleep. A minute later, he repeated that declaration in front of the yard boss.

"I want half," is all the yard boss said, taking the berth slip and signaling for the tow dolly.

Outside the depot, Luke nodded to himself, satisfied. Then he turned and looked out on the nightscape of Taldaak. It was time to find Akanah. He did not fully understand what her part in these events was, either, but his tumultuous life had taught him to respect what looked like coincidence. For the first time since leaving Coruscant with Akanah, he believed that his destiny and hers were bound together, and that whatever lay ahead on J't'p'tan awaited both of them.

Akanah stood on the dockwalk looking up at a sleek curving hull bearing the name *Jump for Joy* in a flowing royal blue script. It was the best starship in port, at least for Akanah's purposes—a Twomi Skyfire, barely a year old. Six places, the lines of a fighter, and the engines of a racer.

If she was going to leave Utharis—if she was going to leave Luke behind—the means to do so was before her.

She had already been aboard and assured herself that the pilot assist system was the equal of the luxury appointments. Autolanding, autonavigation, crash and collision-avoidance overrides, voice-assisted preflight—despite an advertising campaign heavy on images of danger and adventure, the Skyfire had been designed to make the occasional pilot comfortable at the controls.

More importantly, *Jump for Joy* should be able to outrun any other ship in port, except perhaps the snub fighters belonging to the Utharis Sector Patrol. That kind of speed could be useful in a war zone. Luke had already totted up *Mud Sloth*'s shortcomings in combat, and they were numerous enough to give Akanah pause.

She moved a step to her right and looked down the side of the sprint. *A pretty ship,* she thought, and sighed. *And it would be so easy to take it.*

But leaving now meant abandoning the greater part of her purpose with her goal in sight but not yet achieved. Luke was open to her now—beginning to understand, beginning to change. *More time. All I need now is more time.* If she was there when the next test came, she might see the transformation. Luke was that close—aware of the flow of the Current, almost able to read it, nearly ready to join it—

"It's a beauty, isn't it?" a man said, coming up beside her. He was wiping his hands on a cloth, as though he had been doing some work somewhere out of sight.

Akanah had felt his presence moments before he spoke, but allowed herself to startle girlishly. "Oh! I didn't see you. Yes, it's beautiful—it looks like it's ready to leap into the air at any moment."

Even in the darkness, Akanah could feel the man beaming with pride. "Would you like to see the inside?"

Akanah laughed at him silently, realizing his intent. "I don't think so," she said. "I need to be getting home."

He leaned toward her conspiratorially. "Have you ever had sex in hyperspace?"

This time she could not contain her bubbling laugh of bemusement. "Yes," she said, and melted away into the night.

The skids of the fleet launch kissed the plating of the flight deck so gently that Plat Mallar could scarcely feel the vibration under him.

"Contact," he said, reaching overhead to the auxiliary control panel. "Grapples on. Systems to standby. Shutting down engines."

"All right," said the check pilot. "That's good enough. Come on out, Mallar, and I'll give you your scores."

With a sigh of relief, Mallar released the double harness with a sharp poke of his fingers. Climbing out

of the flight couch, he made his way to the egress hatch
at the back of the simulator's cabin.

He had just flown an imaginary approach and
landing to the number two flight deck of the carrier
Volant, his tenth exercise of that session and his eighteenth of the day. His flight suit was dripping with per-
spiration, his shoulders aching, his feet half numb from
being confined in flight boots that weren't yet broken in.

The launch was the larger of the two boats used for
intrafleet travel and had proven the harder for Plat to
master. A fleet gig was similar in size to an X-wing or
TIE interceptor, and he had had little trouble getting
one in and out of the enclosed space of a combat flight
deck. But a fleet launch was two and a half times longer
and a full meter taller than a gig, and Plat had hit two
simulated E-wings and the flight deck roof three times
before he made the adjustment.

"Like going through adolescence all over again,"
he had muttered to himself after making the cockpit
shake violently for the fourth time.

But the last exercise had felt good to him—good
enough to allow him to enjoy his break. He paused at
the top of the simulator's ladder to remove his helmet,
then swung his leg over and slid down the handrails on
his heels. The check pilot, Lieutenant Gulley, met him at
the bottom.

"Well?"

"You have a nice touch when you're not putting
holes in the bulkheads," Gulley said. "I'm going to
qualify you for the gig now. Come back offshift and
spend a few more hours working the launch, maybe
hitchhike with me or One-Eye on a few runs, and I
should be able to qualify you for the launch soon
enough." He handed Plat his updated identifier disc.

"We're done?"

"You're going on duty," he said. "Get yourself
down to Blue Deck and report to the flight controller.
Your first passenger should be there by the time you
check in."

A grin spread across Plat's face. "Yes, sir," he said, saluting. "Thank you, sir."

Plat jogged through the corridors, helmet tucked under his left arm, until he rounded a corner and brushed against a round-bellied major.

"Is there a combat alert, pilot?"

Coming to a sudden stumbling stop, Plat whirled and saluted. "No, sir."

The dressing-down that followed cost him two minutes but did nothing to dampen his spirits. He showed his ID at the controller's window and collected the enabler key for fleet gig 021, then ran out across the flight deck to where it was berthed. For a long moment, he stood and stared at it unbelievingly.

"Is there a problem?"

Plat whirled, recognizing the voice. "Colonel Gavin. No problem, sir."

"Then let's get going," Gavin said, moving past Plat and twisting the hatch release. "I'm your passenger—and I've got an appointment on board *Polaron*."

With all possible care, Plat ran through the preflight checks and eased G-021 forward to the launch area, then out into space. Picking up *Polaron*'s locator signal, he brought the gig around to the intercept heading and accelerated smoothly to the prescribed velocity.

"This what you wanted, son?" Gavin asked, leaning forward in his couch.

"Yes, sir. Thank you for the chance."

"No gunsights on a fleet gig. Nothing to fire the blood and feed that hunger for revenge."

"I know that, sir," said Plat. "But my being here puts a more experienced pilot in a cockpit that does have gunsights and the firing buttons to go with them. When the time comes, what he does, he'll be doing for me—if you look at it a certain way."

Gavin nodded. "That's right. That's just the way to look at it." He settled back against the acceleration cushions, checked the readout on his command comlink, then glanced out the side viewport at *Intrepid*, rapidly falling away behind them.

"Oh, and there's one other thing worth remembering," the colonel said. "You'll get a lot of cockpit time in this duty—more hours in a single duty shift than most pilots log in a week. Before you know it, you just might find yourself turning into one of those more experienced pilots." Plat heard Gavin's grin as he added, "But save the hammer-eights and counterbreaks for the simulator. I don't want to hear that my gig pilots have been practicing combat maneuvers on intership runs."

Plat Mallar smiled. "I'll remember, Colonel."

Han did not know whether it was a matter of contempt or carelessness, but he was neither blindfolded nor rendered unconscious for the transfer from the dirtside prison to the brig of *Pride of Yevetha*.

All his captors did was bind his wrists to a bar behind his hips and give him an escort composed of two towering Yevethan *nitakka*. Then he was walked through a maze of corridors and chambers to a driveway where a three-wheeled, box-bodied transporter awaited.

From the open viewports of the transporter, he saw every detail of his surroundings and tried to memorize everything he saw—the route that led from the complex where he had been held to the port, the markings on the face of the gate that closed behind them, the design and function of the other vehicles sharing the road, the architecture and arrangement of the buildings they passed.

He also studied the faces and physiques of not only the guards, but the gate proctor, the transporter driver, and any Yevethan pedestrians he could catch a good long look at. With the help of those examples, he made a start at learning to distinguish one Yevetha from another.

At the same time, Han's busy mind assessed the effectiveness of his restraints. The similarity to the bench in the audience room prompted Han to wonder if the method had been designed for Yevethan physiology—it seemed as though the bar would either prevent the murderous dew claw from emerging or render it useless if extended.

But the effectiveness of the bar depended on the prisoner being unable to either pass the bar under his feet or to simply slide a wrist out to one end. Yevethan physiology might not allow for either of those motions, but Han was confident that human physiology—even his less-than-ideally-limber variant—would. He did not immediately test his theory, but he was buoyed by the thought that he could free his hands at any time and—as a bonus—have the bar to use as a weapon.

That happy thought lasted only until they reached the spaceport, where the transport was met by more guards and one of the Yevetha who had been present for Barth's execution. The moment the Yevethan official first saw Han clearly, he barked angry words and cuffed one of the guards sharply across the face. Almost immediately, another guard moved behind Han and wrapped a thick strap around his upper arms, just above the elbows. With it in place, the escape Han had planned was quite impossible.

"An understandable but quite dangerous oversight," the Yevetha said to Han in Basic. His diction was excellent, his delivery almost irritatingly smooth. "The guard detail at the palace is not accustomed to handling human prisoners."

That same Yevetha led the way across the rough pavement of the spaceport apron to where a delta-type Imperial shuttle waited on its skids. Han was surprised to see that the two Yevetha already seated in the cockpit wore no more clothing than any of the others—no pressure suit, not even a helmet. He filed that fact away as he climbed into the spartan cabin.

One guard and the Yevethan official climbed in after him, and Han realized that he was to have a traveling companion. The guard sat beside him on the long portside bench, the official opposite him.

"I am Tal Fraan, proctor cogent to the viceroy."

"I'm sure your mother's very proud of you," Han said. The hatch was secured from outside, and the idling whine of the engines increased sharply. He noted that the engines sounded tight and smooth—much better than the typical Imperial offerings.

Tal Fraan loosed an open-mouth hiss that Han thought might be a laugh. "Tell me, did you enjoy thinking that you might escape?"

Han said nothing and directed his gaze out the viewport as the shuttle began to climb.

"Do you know that we have no prisons?" Tal Fraan said. "In a city of more than one million, on a planet of nearly seven hundred million, there is not a single Yevethan jail, penitentiary, or stockade. We have no need of such things. There is no equivalent in our language for *convict* or *incarcerate*."

"I guess that'd be one of the often overlooked advantages of summary execution," said Han. "Keeps the taxes down."

"So true," said Tal Fraan, with no apparent awareness of Han's ironic tone. "That you choose to sustain those who harm you was a great puzzlement to me for some time."

"It can't have been a complete surprise," said Han. "The place you kept us looked a lot like a prison to me."

"Those you call Imperials made up for this lack of experience on our part," Tal Fraan said. "The cell in which you were kept in the grand palace was built by the overlords during the occupation. And the Imperial starships are well equipped in this regard, as you will see."

"If this is just a goodwill tour, you could save yourself the trouble," Han said. "I've already visited an Imperial detention center."

"Yes, I know," said Tal Fraan. "I have studied your past. I learned a great deal from it. It is how we know how important you are to your people. There are so many stories about you, Han Solo—more than are told of any Yevetha, even the viceroy. I wonder why you permit it." He paused a moment, then continued. "This is also how we knew that Lieutenant Barth was not important. There were no stories of *his* life and heroics. I was not surprised when you let him die."

Han's hot flash of anger overwhelmed any good intentions he had not to be drawn into Tal Fraan's game. "You son of a bitch—you think you understand us, but you haven't the first clue," he snapped. "What you did to Barth *makes* him important to us—just like what you did to those colonists all over the Cluster made them important to us. We're not like you—we *remember* our dead. *That's* why our fleet isn't going away."

Other than a twitch of his forebrow ridges, Tal Fraan showed no outward reaction whatever to Han's outburst. "I have an interesting question for you, Han Solo—do you think that your mate would be willing to fire through your body to kill my master?"

"Is that what this is about? Is that why I'm being moved?" Han looked out at the swiftly darkening sky enveloping the shuttle, at the rich array of bright stars piercing the curtain. "When you can answer that question yourself, Proctor, then you really will understand us as well as you think you do."

"So coy," said Tal Fraan. "Is the answer that distasteful to you?"

"All I'm gonna say is this," Han said, relaxing against the back of the bench and turning a quietly murderous gaze on the Yevetha. "When your last morning arrives—and it'll come sooner than you think—I hope the fates give you a moment to realize that everything that's happened, you brought on yourself."

"You are kind to show such concern for me," Tal Fraan said, nodding and smiling generously. "We will have to talk again. You have been most helpful."

As Han gritted his teeth Tal Fraan peered past him out the viewport at the massive Star Destroyer *Pride of Yevetha,* which had just come into view.

"Such a splendid vessel. The sight of it still inspires my blood," he said with open pride. "You should count yourself honored that the viceroy has allowed you to make it your new home."

*   *   *

From the moment Han knew where he was bound, he had been picturing himself alone in one of the tiny isolation cells of a standard Imperial detention block. A *Super*-class Star Destroyer had six such detention blocks for crew discipline alone, and ten additional high-security blocks for enemy prisoners.

But to Han's surprise, his four-guard escort led him to a different part of the ship, and a different sort of prison. Three of the ship's cargo areas had been designed for the secure transport of large numbers of slaves, refugees, or prisoners of war. Located adjacent to the large landing bays used by the SSD's bulk shuttles, each of the holding areas was equipped with minimal facilities—water taps, ventilation, and food dispensers—considered adequate for up to a thousand people.

The holding area to which Han was taken, number two, was not even remotely that crowded. At a glance, Han guessed that there were no more than a hundred prisoners huddled along the walls or sprawled on the hard deck.

Most took little or no notice of his arrival, but a small group, perhaps twenty strong, formed a large, ragged circle around him as he made his way toward a water tap. More than half a dozen species were represented in the circle, and they looked upon him with a mixture of dull-eyed curiosity and suspicion.

"What world are *you* from?" asked a young woman in a brown fire-scorched caftan. She was either human or Andalese—her tousled hair might have concealed the latter's horn points, and the caftan was shapeless enough to hide the symbiosis grafts.

"Coruscant," said Han. "And you?"

"I was at the Morath pholikite mine number four, on Elcorth."

The others began to crowd closer around him as they recited their own answers.

"Taratan, of the Kubaz, nested at Morning Bell—"

"I am Brakka Barakas, dothmir of New Brigia—"

"Bek nar walae Ithak e Gotoma—"

"Fogg Alait, assigned to Polneye—"

"I am called Noloth by my brothers of the L'at H'kig—"

"My home was Kojash. I am known as Jara ba Nylra—"

"My stars," said Han, turning slowly, hands raised as though to fend them off. "Are there survivors here from *all* the colony worlds?"

"All our homes were attacked by the silver spheres," said the woman who had spoken first. "Are we the only survivors?"

"How much longer will we be here?" asked Noloth.

"Do you think we can go home soon?" asked a slender alien who had not spoken before.

Han swept his gaze across their faces. "I don't know," he said uncomfortably. "I'm just like you are—I don't know what's going on out there."

The days immediately following the presentation to the Senate of a petition of recall against President Leia Organa Solo were full of the kind of moments that made Hiram Drayson despair of leaving the government in the hands of civilians.

Moving quickly in the wake of the Ruling Council's vote, both Fleet Intelligence and New Republic Intelligence had intervened to prevent the news of Han's capture by the Yevetha from being released with the petition. Stripped of its supporting argument by the blue and silver SECURE seals, the petition ought—by all rights—to have foundered on arrival.

But a Ruling Council had never passed such a judgment against a Senate President before, and novelty alone gave the petition an undeserved gravity. And the threat of prosecution for security violations could do nothing to rein in the rumors and leaks that blossomed to fill the information vacuum.

Within twelve hours, Drayson's information filters

had picked up an uncensored copy of Beruss's original complaint, an anonymous interview with one of *Tampion*'s escort pilots, and even a holo that purported to show Jedi "commandos" in training for an imminent rescue mission. When Coruscant Prime led its morning packet with a feature titled "Where Is Han Solo?" and the New Republic Newsgrid answered with "Princess Leia's Personal War," Drayson knew that the battle had been lost.

"You may as well release everything you have concerning Han," Drayson told Ackbar. "At this point, the official silence, the denials, look like admissions that there is something to hide. Leia should be getting a flood of sympathy over Han's situation—but with Borsk Fey'lya leaking everything he can get his hands on, and Doman Beruss appointing himself the champion of the public's right to 'full disclosure,' her stock is dropping almost by the hour."

"I have urged her to that course," said Ackbar. "But she is protecting the children—they still do not know what has happened to their father."

"That can't last much longer."

"She is determined not to burden them with the truth," said Ackbar, shaking his head. "Leia has told them that Han is on a secret mission for her, that they are not to believe anything they hear anywhere else. And Winter is keeping them away from anyone and anything that might contradict Leia's version."

"Children aren't stupid," said Drayson. "Particularly not *those* children. I expect that they already know quite a bit more than she realizes."

"It would not surprise me," said Ackbar. "But until events force her hand, Leia is determined to protect the children from the knowledge that their father is a prisoner of war. And I have personally promised to support that fiction."

Disgruntled, Drayson retired to his private office with the ever-growing catalog of message packets, grid dispatches, comlink captures, and electronic graffiti assembled for him by the Maxwell filters that were riding the planet's busy communication channels. Later that afternoon, reports began to come in from his contacts in the palace complex and Fleet headquarters.

By that time, Drayson had already made a decision about what was needed to change the tone and tenor of the public and political consciousness. His hastily jotted notes to himself read: *Must erase the perception of selfish act—replace with the reality of selfless one. This crisis must have another face.*

Drayson spent the next hour browsing through the personnel records of the casualties of the engagement at Doornik 319. He marked four of them for further consideration—husband-and-wife pilots from the battle cruiser *Liberty,* a female crew chief who died fighting the hangar fire aboard *Venture,* and the Hassarian captain of the ill-fated *Trenchant.*

Each story had a powerful emotional hook. But their effectiveness in deflecting the focus from Leia and Han would be undercut by the fact that, coming so late in the crisis, all four deaths could be as easily blamed on Leia's actions as on Nil Spaar's. The tragedy was obvious; that the Yevetha were to blame was less so.

So Drayson set the casualty records aside and retrieved his data folders concerning the eight destroyed colonies in Koornacht Cluster, including the stasis probes' documentation of the devastation. Assessing the cold realities of emotional kinship, Drayson knew that the most ready identification would be with the humanoid Brigians, the hard-working Morath miners on Elcorth, and the largely human inhabitants of Polneye.

Which, in the end, brought Drayson to the same place his first instincts had said he must go, hours before—to the young Grannan survivor from Polneye, Plat Mallar. It would have been better if Mallar were human, and if Polneye's historical associations were with the Alliance rather than the Empire, but those problems could be dealt with if addressed head on.

The only question remaining was which provider was to receive the benefit of Drayson's gift-wrapped leadline scoop. Over the years, he had cultivated mutually helpful relationships with understanding producers in news organizations of all sizes, but rarely had the material been this hot or the stakes this high. He needed someone who not only would set the proper tone for the copycats hustling to catch up, but who also had the courage to risk a shutdown order, even the seizure of the studio facilities, to break a big story first.

In the end, it came down to an old friend or a young idealist, and Drayson settled on the latter.

"Open message to *The Life Monitor,* blind and secure," he said. "Personal to Cindel Towani. This is your shopping service. I want to alert you to a special offer, limited availability, your signature required. . . ."

The initial release of the sixty-second issue of *The Life Monitor* reached fewer than a hundred thousand subscribers, and Belezaboth Ourn, extraordinary counsel of the Paqwepori, was not among them.

But the lead producer of *Capitol Scavenger* was, and within an hour a licensed crosslink to Towani's feature had appeared in the rolling *CS* queue. That brought Plat Mallar's story to the attention of nearly half a million more viewers, including the senior night producer for *Sunrise* and the Senate correspondent for *Roll Call.*

From there, it was picked up by Coruscant Global and New Republic Prime—both of which gave as small a nod to Cindel Towani as possible, but ran the audio-video portion of her story uncut. By dawn, Mallar's achingly poignant plea on behalf of the inhabitants of Polneye had reached more than forty million ears on Coruscant and ridden the hypercomm trails to eighty thousand other New Republic worlds.

By midday, it had even reached a destitute and dispirited Ourn.

Both the flight crew of the wrecked *Mother's Valkyrie* and his consular staff had long since abandoned him. One by one, they had faced up to the failure and futility of their mission and disappeared, buying cheap passage to Paqwepori on their families' credit or with the proceeds from selling mission supplies and equipment in the no-name market halls. Cathacatin, the licensed breeder-keeper, had been the last to go, slaughtering the few remaining toko birds before he departed rather than see them suffer from neglect.

Ourn's continued presence in the diplomatic hostel was strictly a courtesy, for he no longer had either the status or the resources to command a room, much less an entire cottage. First, *Mother's Valkyrie* was sold for salvage in a lien auction. Then half of the mission's line-of-account was attached by the port authorities as partial payment of the balance of the berthing fees. In the final humiliation, Ourn's appointment was revoked by Ilar Paqwe himself, and the diplomatic account closed.

"You would save your parents from further embarrassment by not returning to the Paqwe dominion," Ourn was advised in the termination notice.

Since that time, Ourn had clung ever more tightly to the frail reed of hope represented by the Yevethan blind-relay transmitter and the promise from Nil Spaar. If only the viceroy could appease his peers on N'zoth and deliver the thrustship as he had agreed he would—not only could Ourn repair his savaged reputation at home, but he would have a hundred generals and five hundred senators begging him for a chance to study the Yevethan vessel.

Ourn clung to that hope against all reason, mining the grids and the gossip in the hostel's courtyards for even the smallest tidbits of information, making himself believe that his next dispatch would be the one by which he would earn the Yevetha's confidence, and his reward.

But when he saw the stories on Plat Mallar's narrow escape from Polneye and Captain Llotta's death at Morning Bell, that hope finally evaporated. There was no escaping the truth—the pretty silver spheres were also deadly warships, and Nil Spaar would never receive permission to deliver one to Belezaboth Ourn.

"If only the peace had held a little longer," he said resignedly in the privacy of his room. "If only the Princess had not been so stubborn. She has cost me everything." He picked up the hypercomm black box and turned it over in his hands. "So perhaps I shall ask *her* for my payment. Perhaps this toy is worth more than the words that have passed through it."

There were a hundred things Leia should have been doing, a thousand better uses for her energy than lining a garden path with brilliant white sasalea blossoms, one fragrant ball—the size of Anakin's fist—to a planting. It was work a droid could do, work the residence's groundskeeper would have gladly seen to in the morning.

But none of those other things she might have been doing that evening had half the appeal of burying her hands in the cool, moist soil, crumbling it between her fingers, cradling each sasalea plant gently into its new home. On a day where nothing she had tackled had yielded to her efforts, it was intensely gratifying to take on a task where every element was under her control— spade and earth, stalk and blossom. Her vision, her time, her labor, her triumph, her satisfaction.

It was a small triumph, a minor transformation of a tiny landscape, but it was balm for her whole being— reassurance that she was, at the end of the day, master of her own world. *If you don't believe that what you do matters, it's awfully hard to get up in the morning.*

"Princess—"

Leia looked up from her work in surprise at the voice. "Tarrick. What are you doing here?"

"There's someone here—back at the gate, actually—who I thought you might want to see. He came to the office early this afternoon sounding like a typical hem-tugger, and we sent him out on the usual off-list runaround. He came back," said Tarrick. "But the second time, he got to the point. We sent him down to see the moles. When Collomus and his people were done talking to him, we all agreed you should hear what he has to say."

Leia stood, brushing the dirt from her hands. "Well—you have me curious. Bring him in."

The visitor was a Paqwe—a short yellow-green alien with a wide carriage and a sway-backed, waddling gait. He was swathed in tattered reception-hall finery and smelled strongly of bitter salts.

"Princess Leia! It is a great honor. I am Belezaboth Ourn, extraordinary counsel of the Paqwepori." Behind him, Tarrick shook his head in a slow, exaggerated fashion. "I am grateful to you for taking the time to see me."

"Yes, yes," she said impatiently. "What do you want?"

"What I want—no, what I can offer. I think that we can help each other, Princess," he said, taking another step forward. "You are having difficult times with a certain party. It's said there'll be war. I may have some information that could be of use to you."

"It's a little late for word games. Be specific—what information?"

"Not information, exactly," Ourn said. "More a *thing*. How you can use it, what you can learn from it—that's for you to discover. But I can put it in your hands and tell you everything I know."

"And this *thing* is—"

Ourn produced a small black box from a concealed pocket. "Is a way to send messages to N'zoth—to Nil Spaar. Completely undetectable, untraceable. By what magic, my engineer could not divine. But you have many scientists—they will find out for you."

It was Leia's turn to take a step forward. "Where did you get this?"

"From the viceroy. His ship destroyed mine, you remember—at East Port, the day he left. He promised me restitution, but it was an empty promise—"

"He gave this box to you *before* he left?"

"Well, yes, of course."

"And you've been in touch with him *since* he left?"

"Only to remind him of his promise—" Ourn stopped, realizing the contradictions. "We had an understanding—he was unfaithful. I will help you now."

"How did you help *him*? By spying for him?"

Ourn swallowed nervously and tried to smile. "Now, Princess—how many secrets does someone like me know? Nothing. Less than nothing. I pretended. I deceived him—"

With a single quick stride, Leia closed the distance between them. "You took my husband away from me," she said, and dropped into a Jedi fighting stance.

"Princess, surely—"

It took only one blow to silence him, one more to bring him to his knees, and one last to send him sprawling, unconscious. Releasing her breath in a satisfied sigh, Leia stood straight and looked to a startled Tarrick.

"Thank you for that," Leia said lightly, flexing her hands in front of her. "I just might be able to sleep a little tonight."

Chapter 6

◆

The spotlight of the next morning's staff strategy session was on the two intelligence chiefs, each of whom had been rudely surprised—and professionally embarrassed—by the previous day's events.

For Admiral Graf, head of Fleet Intelligence, the problem was explaining how the Mallar recording and the holo stills of the destruction at Polneye had escaped Fleet custody. Graf also had to answer for a second, apparently separate, breach of security involving classified data from the battle at Doornik 319.

"There are three authorized copies of the Mallar recording," Graf said. "One here, one in the Fleet system, and one in the hands of the Threat Assessment Office—plus a locked copy in the Fleet archives. We also found two unauthorized copies in private data spaces within the Fleet system and are looking for others."

"Does that mean you have two suspects?" Leia asked.

"No," said Graf. "The thinking right now is that those look like innocent violations. But we're continuing to backtrace the access logs for all six copies. We've already interviewed everyone who had access to the Palace copy—"

"No, you haven't," Leia interrupted.

"Excuse me?"

"You haven't talked to me," she said.

"Well, of course, I presumed that any use you made of this item—"

"How do you know I didn't put a copy on my datapad and take it home? How do you know I didn't make a copy and give it away?"

Graf frowned, flustered. "That seems a very unlikely scenario—"

"Did you talk to Alole? Tarrick? No one can work in my office without high-level clearances."

"We did not," he admitted. "Your office was exempted from the interview list."

"Then let's look outside my office, at the people who just visit. The first administrator?" she asked challengingly. "How about Admiral Ackbar?"

"No."

Leia looked down the table to where Ackbar sat. "Admiral?"

Ackbar placed both hands flat on the table. "It is true that I have taken a special interest in Plat Mallar. I have made no secret of it, except where it might allow Mallar to escape the taint of my favoritism. It is also true, Admiral Graf, that I have in the past urged the President to release the Mallar recording, and I am glad that it has happened, by whatever means."

"No one could question—" Graf began.

"Wait." The admiral craned his neck until he could meet Leia's gaze. "To answer your unspoken question, yes, I have a copy of the recording, in a secure partition at my home. But I give you my word that neither I nor that copy was the source of the leak. I do not know who was responsible."

"I accept your assurances, Admiral," said Leia, turning to Graf. "I don't accept yours. No one is to be exempt from your inquiry."

A chastised Graf said quietly, "Understood, Princess."

For General Carlist Rieekan, head of New Republic Intelligence, the problem was to assess the damage

Ourn had done and prevent a recurrence. The first meant discovering exactly what information he had provided to the Yevetha. The second meant explaining how Ourn had escaped official attention until he turned the black box over and turned himself in.

"Not that it's of any great consequence, Princess, but it looks as though you decked the wrong spy," said Rieekan.

"Why is that?"

"I had seventy people up all night looking into this, and there's no plausible link between Belezaboth Ourn and the interception of *Tampion*," Rieekan said. "He's a nobody, with no connections—a small-time parasitic little sneak all puffed up with air. He simply didn't have an opportunity to acquire and deliver anything at the level of sensitivity of General Solo's appointment or *Tampion*'s flight plan."

"Are you sure about that?"

"Very. Ourn fell apart during the night, started telling the truth as fast as he could blubber it out. He doesn't even know that the general is missing."

"Then there's another Yevethan spy—more highly placed."

"At least one," said Rieekan.

"The viceroy's afternoon callers," said Graf. "Senators Marook, Peramis, and Hodidiji."

"They are all getting a close look," said Rieekan.

"What about the black box?" asked Leia.

"Interesting device," said Rieekan. "Not quite entirely black, but close. We took it into the cold room and opened it in the dark, under vacuum. Good thing we did. The power supply is wired with an oxidation fuse, set to go critical if the box is opened. The yield would probably be about equal to a proton grenade. We took holos and closed it up again, very carefully.

"Then we put it on a dummy transceiver rig, connected the way Ourn showed us. The dummy rig looks like a real transceiver to the device but has only one ten-millionth of the output power needed to actually open a hypercomm channel—just enough for us to record the signal for analysis.

"I just got an update on that before I came in," Rieekan said, looking down at his datapad. "Apparently the box uses a burst-compression algorithm that we haven't quite deciphered yet to hide the signal in the noise. Very efficient." He looked up at Leia. "And distinctively Imperial, according to my senior engineer. Probably hatched right here on Coruscant, back in the days of Section Nineteen and Warthan's wizards."

"Can you use what you've learned about this one to find the others?" Leia asked.

"Possibly. We should be able to catch any new transmissions. We might get lucky and find some old ones hiding in the archived traffic, now that we know what we're looking for," said Rieekan. "But I'd like to suggest another way we might use what we've learned."

"I'm listening."

"We have the tools for a small campaign of disinformation," he said. "We have a working black box and a desperately willing turncoat who'll do most anything we ask. What if we just let him keep talking to the Yevetha?"

Leia nodded thoughtfully. "Do you have any ideas about what we might want to have him say?"

"I have one," Nanaod Engh interjected, drawing attention to his end of the table for the first time. "We don't really know for certain if the Yevetha have General Solo, or—forgive me—if the general is alive. Nil Spaar has ignored every message we've sent him. He hasn't even tried to communicate with us since leaving Coruscant, except through his deeds. Perhaps Ourn can get him to break his silence—"

On his return to *Pride of Yevetha*, Nil Spaar's first concern was to inspect his new breederies. There were three of them, each with forty-eight alcoves. Before the conversion, they had been detention blocks, and they still largely retained that character—the conversion had required surprisingly little renovation.

Picking cells at random, Nil Spaar satisfied himself that each was well suited for the hanging and nurturance of a birth-cask. The walls were plain and clean, the plumbing suitable for feeding lines, and the ventilation fully isolated from the systems for the rest of the ship. There were even individual drains in each alcove for the sacrifices and the rite of emergence.

The new breederies required a new crop of tenders, eighteen in all. After inspecting the new facilities, Nil Spaar had the tenders called together so that he could assess their fitness. Most were experienced hands who had known many successful nestings, but only a few had been neutered.

"Long before all these alcoves have been filled with ripening *mara-nas,* you will begin to feel the power of the breeding magic," the viceroy warned. "The cry of the ancient imperatives of flesh and joy will become a distraction, then a compulsion. You must become immune to this call, lest you betray your solemn duty as custodians of the future."

Nil Spaar gave no thought to giving them the option of withdrawing from his service. Service to the *darama* was an unequaled honor, and service aboard the grand flagship an unprecedented honor. It was unimaginable that any of the tenders would refuse those honors merely to preserve their own poor chance of parenthood. The breeding guildmaster of Giat Nor had made the recommendations and arranged for the affected households to receive replacements—that was all the consideration necessary.

After that, all that was left was to inspect the *marasi* who had been brought aboard to help Nil Spaar fill the new breederies. Chosen from the thousands who had offered themselves, the twenty young females waiting in what had once been detention block F were without exception appealingly supple, pleasingly eager, and understandably anxious.

Nil Spaar found the combination energizing, and

indulged himself, selecting one of the *marasi* for a mating on the spot. By the time they were finished, the *marasi* in the adjoining cells were writhing with need in response to the scents and sounds, and a reinvigorated Nil Spaar took each of them in succession. When the third act was breathlessly complete, he called to the *narada-ti*, who had discreetly removed herself to a distance at which she could pretend not to have heard the passion-cries.

"This one," he said, walking down the corridor, pointing into a cell at one still untouched. "And this one. Bring them to me in my chambers this evening, after the *tolotan* has been read."

"Yes, *darama*," she said, bowing with respect. "When will the others be brought aboard?"

"The next group is expected in twenty days," she said.

"Are there nest-quarters free?"

"Yes, *darama*, both here and in block G."

"Then accelerate the selection," said the viceroy. "Have the next group received as soon as it can be accomplished."

"Yes, *darama*. Only, your senior tender cautioned that the *mara-nas* should be hung at intervals, out of consideration for the timing of the births and the demands on the breedery. Too many too close together—"

"That is not your problem," he said. "Fill the nest-quarters with your best, and keep them filled."

"Yes, *darama*."

Only then did Nil Spaar return to make himself available to Tal Fraan, who had pestered Eri Palle with queries as to the viceroy's schedule and pleas for an early audience. They met in the upper command lounge, a large semicircular compartment high on the forward face of the command tower. The command lounge's double-shielded viewpanes provided a spectacular view of the Star Destroyer's broad eight-kilometer-long spear-point hull.

"Is it not invigorating," Nil Spaar said as Tal Fraan was led in, "to see how much power has passed into the hands of the Blessed? Can any doubt that we are the children of the All, the inheritors of the ancient glory?" He turned away from the viewpanes and accepted Tal Fraan's surrender with a touch. "How far shall that glory carry us, my young disciple? How much shall we claim with our ambition?"

"We are truly the inheritors, *darama*," said Tal Fraan. "But even within the boundaries of the All, our claims have been contested. It would seem that ambition alone cannot measure our destiny."

"Nowhere is there a ship the equal of this one. Nowhere is there blood as powerful as that of the Pure," said Nil Spaar. "They will all yield to us, in time."

"I have come to speak with you of one who still resists," said Tal Fraan. "I have had a new insight into the heart of the pale ones. We must not send them the recording from the viewing hall. It will move them to anger, not to surrender."

Nil Spaar flexed his large hands. "Does my memory deceive me, or was it not you who counseled that we must show Leia our hostages?"

"I did so in error," Tal Fraan said bluntly. "Only fear will give us the result we desire—fear for themselves, for their own safety. Fear for the safety of a hostage can stay a hand, but it will not turn a heart. And when a hostage is harmed, fury replaces fear."

"And from where does this insight come?"

"From the vermin," said Tal Fraan. "I spoke with him aboard the shuttle. I wished to measure his response to the execution of his companion—whether it had served to make him fearful for his own life. I wished to know if the experience had heightened his sensitivity to our concerns or increased his eagerness to be helpful."

"You were disappointed."

"I was alarmed. I am now convinced that if you transmit the recording of the execution, the vermin will never turn away," said Tal Fraan. "My alarm was so great that I ordered that message held until I could speak with you."

"So Vor Duull informed me," said Nil Spaar. "Knowing me well, he wondered at your presumption and came to me for confirmation."

Tal Fraan's face was painted with dismay. "Have I forfeited your trust, *darama*?"

"That remains to be seen, Proctor."

A flicker of relief crossed Tal Fraan's eyes. "Has the message been sent, then?"

"No," said Nil Spaar. "But I am not yet convinced it should not be. When there has been a problem of obedience with the Imperial slaves, the public slaughter of a handful has always been sufficient to guarantee the behavior of the rest."

"There is little spirit in them after so many years," Tal Fraan said. "They were bred for obedience. These others—the vermin queen, her consort, even the pilots we have faced—seem different. They show a foolish stubbornness and a dangerous independence."

"You find them unpredictable, then."

"No, *darama*. I will still risk my own blood on my understanding of them. Showing them the ones we hold will strengthen them, not weaken them. Uncertainty better befriends us."

"And yet there is this," said Nil Spaar. "An hour ago Vor Duull brought to me news of a conversation one of his guildsmen had with Belezaboth Ourn."

"The Paqwe spy? He has given us nothing of value for many weeks."

"Perhaps he has done so now," said Nil Spaar. "The vermin reports that Leia does not believe we hold her consort—that she does not think us capable of such an interception."

"But we allowed there to be witnesses!"

"Then their witness went unheard or unbelieved," said Nil Spaar. "Ourn said she grieves for him but continues on her course unchecked, even in the face of an effort to unseat her. Surely this confirms that your first counsel was correct. We must show our hostage to the vermin queen. That will surely change her tone."

The backs of his hands pressed to his cheeks, Tal Fraan walked the length of the viewpane wall and back before responding. "No, *darama*. I cannot agree. There is nothing in what he says that promises that knowledge of the truth will deter her aggressions. Han Solo answered me with defiance and threat. Surely her fire is of the same temperature as his. You yourself have noted the uncommon closeness of the bond between them. They have risked all for each other—boldly, surrendering nothing. It is in the material you yourself gave me."

Nil Spaar directed his gaze out at the great vessel beneath and before him, noting how the unfiltered light of N'zoth's golden sun made lines and edges gleam like burnished metal.

"Then what course do you now counsel to remove the infection from these stars?" he asked at last.

"We have not managed to make them fear us," said Tal Fraan. "But there are already shadows they will not enter. And the greatest of these is the fear that the horrors of the past will be repeated. The strength of her challengers feeds on this fear. We can confirm their prophecies. We can help them to destroy her."

With more than fifty connected structures and twenty thousand rooms and chambers, the great size and complexity of the Imperial Palace had inspired many stories.

It was said that near the end of construction, eight workers were lost for nearly a month when their comtracker failed. Rumors persisted about a chamber with no doors, sections with a hundred or more rooms that had never been occupied, and the hidden treasure compartment of "the pirate general," Toleph-Sor.

There were at least eleven offices and nine other rooms with their own true stories of murder, plus the grisly tale of Frona Zeffla, who died at her desk and went undiscovered for more than a year. Longtime staffers recalled how the children of Palpatine's aides, given free rein to roam at will, played three-day-long games of "Hunter" in the lifts and corridors.

Though much of the old palace had been damaged or destroyed by the clone Emperor's Force Storm, what survived or had been rebuilt was still easily large enough to either hide in or get lost in. That was a key reason the first administrator had required everyone above the third rank to carry a comlink and to keep it active. Nearly everyone above the third rank required those who served below them to carry them as well.

But Engh's edict did not apply to Leia, whose comlink was typically off as much as it was on. So at the outset of the Yevethan crisis, Alole and Tarrick had conspired with the security teams to make certain that someone with an active comlink was constantly in touch with the President whenever she was in the Palace.

Alole had had the duty that afternoon, but in a busy moment, Leia had slipped away unannounced through her office's second exit. The aide did not discover the President's absence until General Rieekan's red-border alert pushed everything else off the comm displays throughout the suite.

Her first call was to The Sniffer, who should have been standing by at the only entrance to the executive level. "Are you with the President?" Alole asked.

"No, ma'am. She has not left the floor."

Next Alole paged Tarrick, who by then had already heard about the alert. "Have you seen the President?"

"No. She's not with you?" he asked.

"She scampered sometime in the last half hour."

"I'll query the spotters," said Tarrick, referring to their private list of nine offices and seven ministry officials it was Leia's habit to visit. "Have you looked in the cave?"

"I'm on my way there now."

Her feet carried her flying down the back corridor toward the little-used private spaces in the adjacent tower. Mon Mothma had used them as an extension of the President's office, holding private meetings in the small, intimate lounge, taking air and exercise in the sunny garden courtyard. Leia rarely went there—when her office walls closed in on her, the Princess usually preferred to escape the executive level entirely.

But that was where Alole found her—dead asleep on the triangular corner bed in the privacy room. Looking down on Leia's peaceful expression, Alole hesitated to wake her. Leia's fatigue had been obvious to everyone that morning, and this was the first time in many days that she had seen Leia's face unmarked by tension and frown lines.

Then, sighing, Alole reached out and took hold of the golden-green metal post at the nearest point of the triangle. Shaking it gently, she said Leia's name twice, then stepped back.

"Tarrick—she's here," she said quietly into her comlink. "We'll be out in a minute or two. Set up the recording for replay. See if General Rieekan wants to come up."

"I'm on it," Tarrick said. "Admiral Ackbar is on his way over from Fleet."

The distinctively tinny sound of Tarrick's voice as heard through a comlink seemed to be what finally reached through Leia's fatigue and demanded her attention. She sat up with a wordless cry, unfocused eyes, and balled fists.

"It's all right. It's only me, Alole," the aide said, slipping the comlink back into her pocket. "Come—hurry. Nil Spaar is on Channel Eighty-one."

Four of the six people at the conference table with Leia were seeing the viceroy's announcement for the second time. Only one of them ventured to try to prepare her for what she would see.

"If this is an answer to Ourn's message," said Admiral Graf, "the message is that we've been worrying about the wrong thing. Han Solo is no longer important."

"Let me hear it for myself," Leia said, reaching for the controller.

The recording began with something they had not seen before—the emblem of the Duskhan League, a double circle of three-pointed stars on a scarlet background. Then Nil Spaar appeared.

This time, however, he had company. Standing beside him was a human wearing the black uniform of an Imperial Moff.

Graf leaned toward Leia. "Behind them—that's the bridge of a *Super*-class Star Destroyer."

She silenced him with a dismissive wave of her hand.

"I address the strong, proud leaders of the vassal worlds of the New Republic," the viceroy began. "I bring you an announcement, and a warning.

"As I speak, the enormous battle fleet under the command of Princess Leia continues its reckless invasion of Koornacht Cluster—territory that has belonged to the Yevethan people for more than ten thousand years.

"Up until this moment, we have shown great restraint, despite having been attacked in our own home. Against the urging of my military commanders, I have held our own powerful fleet in reserve except where the lives of civilians are in danger. I have done all I can to minimize casualties on both sides. I have given Princess Leia every opportunity to change her course and withdraw her forces.

"I am saddened that she has chosen instead to reinforce them. In recent weeks, she has rejected the wisdom of her advisors and secretly dispatched hundreds more warships to threaten the worlds of the Duskhan League.

"I am saddened, but not surprised. This woman sabotaged a promising negotiation between my people and the New Republic, because peace did not suit her ambitions. She sat across from me and lied about her intentions—and while she lied, her agents spied on us, looking for weakness, planning a war of conquest.

"I know that the good citizens of the New Republic

are even now trying to drive this deceiver from your capital. But she has bought many friends on Coruscant, and others have reason to fear her. It will be a bruising fight, though I hope that honor will ultimately prevail."

"Here comes the good part," Graf whispered to Ackbar.

"But the Yevethan people can no longer await the outcome," said Nil Spaar. "We can no longer risk our future on the hope that Princess Leia will find her conscience and leave us in peace. We must protect ourselves. By refusing our offer of friendship, by threatening our very existence, Leia has forced us to seek friends where we otherwise would not have."

Nil Spaar raised a hand in the direction of the man beside him. "We have invited the Empire to return to Koornacht Cluster as allies—"

"That's—that's completely unbelievable," Leia sputtered. "They *despise* the Empire."

"—I have come to you to announce that the Duskhan League and the Grand Imperial Union have concluded a treaty of mutual assistance. Moff Tragg Brathis is commander of the battle fleet now stationed here."

The uniformed man nodded, Nil Spaar paused, and the holo tracked to the right until the view forward out the bridge viewports confirmed that the vessel was *Super*-class. For a few seconds, at least half a dozen other Star Destroyers were visible as well, flying in formation over the limb of a dusty yellow planet.

Then Nil Spaar moved in to block the view. "You have seen enough now to understand. If the New Republic does not withdraw from our borders—if the President, whoever that might be, does not swiftly acknowledge our just claim to these stars—the combined strength of the League and the Union stands ready. Your actions will determine the course of the future."

The display dissolved to a scarlet curtain, with the Duskhan League emblem appearing again before the screen went black.

"Is that the end of it?" Leia asked.

"That's it."

She pressed a button on the controller and threw it down on the table. "Does anyone here think this is real?"

"I have Asset Tracking working on the recording," said Graf. "Nylykerka should be able to tell us if we've seen those ships before, during the flash recon."

"Will he be able to tell us when they got there and who controls them?" asked Rieekan. "Perhaps this pact is real, and was concluded months ago, in secret."

"Why reveal it now?"

"Why not? Since we already know about the Imperial ships, he has nothing to lose by telling everyone else. And it's obvious what he hopes to gain."

"What do you mean, 'telling everyone else'?" Leia demanded of Rieekan. "Did this go out to the entire system?"

Rieekan raised an eyebrow and looked down the table.

"Yes," admitted the director of the communications agency. "It appeared in the system in a standard diplomatic packet, with the expected coding. There was no reason for the filters to trap it."

"Interesting times are ahead," Ackbar said to himself, shaking his head.

Leia looked disgusted. "Can we at least find out this time where it got *into* the system?"

"We're working on it," the other woman said defensively. "There are more than three hundred thousand authorized entry ports for a low-security channel like Eighty-one."

"Black box on an enabled hypercomm," said Rieekan. "That's all it would take. It doesn't even have to be on Coruscant."

"Excuse me," said Nanaod Engh. Only a few heads turned his way, and he cleared his throat and repeated himself. "Excuse me. This is unimportant. Mere details—trivialities. There is more to this than what happens in this room."

Leia spun her chair sharply toward him. "Go on."

"We are not the intended audience for the viceroy's message," he said, and gestured expansively with his hands. "*They* are. That bolt was aimed at the hearts of our citizens."

"But it is a fraud," Ackbar insisted. "There is no pact. There is no Moff Brathis, no Grand Union, no Imperial fleet. I am certain of it."

"And you may well be right," said Engh. "But that is irrelevant. It doesn't matter if what we saw is the truth or a lie. It doesn't matter what we here believe. General Rieekan, what kind of proof could you offer to refute that image—a black-shirt commander standing with Nil Spaar on an Imperial Star Destroyer?"

"Why, there are many ways to attack it. We have experts in—"

"No, General. You cannot refute that image with words." He looked to Leia. "It does not matter what species they are; people trust what they see. Words alone will not make them believe they were fooled. Out there, they are turning to each other and saying, 'Well, what do you think we ought to do about *this*?' Not 'Do you think it's true?' I don't know what they will decide they feel. I only know that it *is* true, for *them*—the Yevetha have allied with the Empire."

Engh rocked back in his chair. "I think the President's image analysts should see this as soon as possible. And I hope you will finally make time to meet with them yourself, Leia. The days ahead will not be shaped by questions and answers, the lore of experts, the reasoned judgment of earnest beings gathered around tables. Cherished belief, powerful emotion, and the image that plays in the mind in the moment before sleep comes— they will write the story of the days ahead."

Tholatin was uninhabited save for the smugglers' hideaway known as Esau's Ridge, nestled in a deep lateral erosion cut at the base of a towering rock face. The cut was a thousand meters long and up to a hundred meters deep, with a maximum of six meters' clearance in the berthing area under the cantilevered granite ceiling. A warren of smaller artificial tunnels and chambers extended the complex another two hundred meters into the mountain.

It was one of the most private of all the smugglers' sanctuaries, invisible from orbit and well defended against intruders. Even the three landing clearings in the forest that covered the valley floor were concealed, hidden by retractable military-grade camouflage nets with infrared screens.

It was also one of the most exclusive sanctuaries, open only to the elite veterans of the trade, to the well-connected rather than the well-heeled. Or, at least, it once had been. When the *Millennium Falcon* arrived there, Esau's Ridge was more crowded than Chewbacca could remember ever seeing it. Parking clearances in the landing area were down to half a meter, and the floating berth fees were accordingly high.

[Peace did not seem to have hurt the trade,] he growled to the berthing collector as he paid the first day's fee.

"When they are not busy fighting wars, governments amuse themselves by forbidding things," said the collector. "There will always be work for us. Welcome back to the Ridge, Chewbacca. By the way, I threw two of the kids out of here to make room for this trash heap you call a ship."

Chewbacca paid without complaint the expected bribe for that privilege of seniority. [Is Plothis still here?]

"Shot four years ago in a squabble with a customer. Bracha e'Naso took over the business."

[What about Formayj and the brokerage?]

"Same old place," said the collector. "Be sure and look up Armatin the Dread while you're here—he retired and bought the slava bar. He'll be glad to see you if you can catch him sober."

For their own protection, Chewbacca instructed Lumpawarrump and Jowdrrl to stay inside the ship. With Shoran and Dryanta standing guard, the *Falcon* was as safe as it could be in a port of thieves—but Esau's Ridge could be as dangerous as the Shadow Forest for the inexperienced.

Chewbacca had come there for information and for specialized supplies. The former proved more costly than the latter, and the latter came dear enough. e'Naso treated Chewbacca like a celebrity, then tried to overcharge him by half, as though he were some star-eyed pupling who'd never run a picket line.

"It's almost impossible for me to keep these items in stock," e'Naso protested when Chewbacca growled threateningly. "You've seen the berthing line—demand is very high, and replacing my stock will cost me a premium. You want a better price, you get Maniid and the others who run my shipments to take less for their risk."

Another customer, an old Kiffu male browsing through the catalog of bootleg holos, overheard the conversation and intervened. "Haggling with a Wookiee," the customer said, shaking his head. "That shows courage, e'Naso—even Plothis wouldn't have dared it. Have you decided who will inherit the shop?"

Chewbacca showed a toothy grimace, all the more ominous for the hint of a smile it contained.

e'Naso quickly countered his own best offer, cutting the total by twenty percent. When that did not change Chewbacca's expression, he let the Wookiee name his price.

[And you deliver it all to my ship,] he added.

"Of course. Of course."

Outside, Chewbacca paid the Kiffu his third of the savings.

Dealing with Formayj was another matter altogether. The long-lived Yao had not only seen all the tricks, he had gotten in early enough to invent several of them. Besides that, Formayj did not haggle. His memories and his connections, both carefully built up over more than a century of brokering, were his stock in trade. He carefully appraised the worth of each before parting with it.

"Koornacht Cluster," Formayj said, nodding. "Maps, inhabitants, hyperspace routes, ship designs, planetary defenses, sensor grids—very rare. Expensive."

[I will pay your price.]

"Come back two days. Will know more then."

So Chewbacca and the others waited, staying close to the *Falcon* and watching the neighboring ships in the berth line come and go. The arrival of e'Naso's delivery sled brought a welcome interruption to the waiting, and several hours' work studying, testing, and stowing the gear took the edge off their impatience. But by the next morning, Lumpawarrump was bouncing off the bulkheads as though the *Falcon* were a cage.

[How much longer, Father?]

[Long enough for you to take five falls with Jowdrrl in the forward cargo hold.]

[She is busy with the dorsal gun turret again.]

[She is making herself busy—she will make the time if you ask.]

[Could I take some falls with you instead?]

[You already know how to lose—and I must go see other brokers and old friends,] Chewbacca said, ruffling his son's fur roughly. [Stay here. Study the ship, practice your skills of defense and attack—you will need them soon enough.]

A day of drinking in the slava bar, listening to smugglers' bragging and tall tales, ground Chewbacca's own patience thin. When the third fight of the afternoon broke out, he roared to his feet, seized both adversaries, and flung them into opposite corners—for no reason other than that he needed to release the restless tension building up inside.

He returned to Formayj's brokerage the next morning, but the visit claimed little of his day.

"Difficult," said Formayj. "Come back two days."

Two days later, he said the same thing.

On their fifth day in Esau's Ridge, Chewbacca yielded to Lumpawarrump's endless pleading looks and took his son into the sanctuary.

The excursion almost ended as quickly as it began,

when Lumpawarrump took too close an interest in a parked slaver for the liking of its Trandoshan owner.

"Mind your own business!" the owner shouted from atop the ship. An instant later, a blaster bolt singed the flowing fur on Lumpawarrump's right shoulder. "Move along!"

Chewbacca seized his son by the scruff and dragged him away toward the tunnels, waving his bowcaster and exchanging threat-growls and insults with the owner as he did so.

[Did you not listen to me? Curiosity is not rewarded on Esau's Ridge,] he chided Lumpawarrump when they were alone inside. [Watch, but do not be caught looking; listen, but do not be caught overhearing; ask no questions, and question no lies—that is the code honored here.]

Seven days after their arrival, Formayj called Chewbacca to his brokerage. "I show you price first, you decide," he said.

[You would not cheat me,] Chewbacca said. [Show me what you have.]

The price was almost unspeakably high, but the value was there. A smuggler's annotated copy of a Yevethan navigational map—six years old, but priceless even so. An even older Imperial autopsy report on three Yevethan corpses. A recording of Nil Spaar's address to the Senate. A still of a spherical starship with the entryways and gun emplacements overmarked. And the capper: the data and holo files of a New Republic recon pass over Wakiza, complete with an NRI seal.

"So new you can still smell Imperial City on it," said the broker, pointing. "You like?"

[You are the best, Formayj.]

"Of course. That is why they come here." Smiling, he took Chewbacca's payment, then disarmed the erasebot and other daemons that would otherwise have been unleashed by a trigger in the brokerage door. "Now, the other matter."

Chewbacca was already rising to leave at that point, and rumbled questioningly.

"You asked all around the Ridge about Han Solo. Did not ask me, as if I did not know he is a prisoner in Koornacht," said Formayj. "I know where everyone has come from and where everyone is going when they leave. I know why customer wants the information before I sell it to them. At times must even disappoint them because of what I know. You plan a rescue, yes?"

Chewbacca growled his assent.

"You ask where he must be held. Even though you do not come to me, I inquire on my own." Formayj shook his head. "Discouraging. No one knows. There is no prison. His name is not spoken by any who would know, on Coruscant or N'zoth." He reached up and handed Chewbacca another holo card. "Perhaps this helps you. Free—my cost nothing." He gestured toward the viewer. "Go on—see."

It was a recording of Nil Spaar speaking to the members of the New Republic via Channel 81. Time-stamped forty hours ago, it began, "I address the strong, proud leaders of the vassal worlds—"

Formayj pressed another object on Chewbacca, this one a datacard. "Old Imperial Star Destroyer shield codes, sensor jam frequencies, defensive fire patterns— these are readily at hand. No demand. Historical value only," he said. "My service charge will cover." Standing, Formayj offered his hand. "Still like Han, old trickster. Smuggler made good. Deliver greetings to him, if you see him."

Chewbacca hurried back to the ship and played the recording for the others. [My honor brother is Nil Spaar's prize,] he said, and pointed at the blue-black hull of the great starship visible behind the viceroy. [Wherever this enemy is, Han will be.] Then Chewbacca pointed at the planet beyond. [They are there now.]

Twenty minutes later, the *Millennium Falcon* lifted off from Esau's Ridge. Immediately on making orbit, it turned toward Koornacht Cluster and jumped into hyperspace, continuing its solitary journey to N'zoth.

INTERLUDE III:

Derelict

With Artoo guiding him, Lobot had penetrated deep into a realm the structure and purpose of which he was still struggling to understand.

The vagabond's core passages were more akin to the great accumulator conduit in which they had spent their first hours aboard the vessel than they were like the network of chambers in which they had spent the last many days. But the core passages were much narrower than the accumulator conduit. Their cross section was never greater than Lobot's armspan, and often less—especially at the junctions.

And there were many junctions. The passages were cross-connected in a complex web that had not yet revealed its pattern. This web promised to link all parts of the vagabond as a transport or communications system might, but nothing was moving through or along the passages save for Lobot and the droids. None of the ready biological metaphors—vascular tubules, alimentary canals, respiratory ducts, neurological pathways—seemed appropriate.

Lobot wondered if the lack of activity was a symptom of the damage the vagabond had sustained or a sign that he still did not understand the nature of the vessel.

He had to keep reminding himself that though the ship was the product of bioengineering, it was not an organism. It was a biological machine, which was still an unfamiliar paradigm.

Three hundred meters in from chamber 228, the passage had narrowed to the point where Lobot found it necessary to shed his contact suit in order to continue.

"Master Lobot, are you certain that you wish to do this?" Threepio asked in a familiarly anxious tone. "Are you confident that the risk is justified? Given our present circumstances, and the alarming frequency with which warships seem to attack this vessel—"

"I'm certain," Lobot said. "The deeper we go into the core, the more it feels like an obstacle standing between me and the ship. When my shoulders brushed both sides at the same time, it felt like the ship was inviting me to shed the suit. I can't explain this in acceptable terms, but I think I must do this to find what I am looking for."

"I see, sir," said Threepio. "Artoo, are you still monitoring the air in this passage?"

"The air is fine, Threepio," Lobot said, patting the droid on the top of his head. "I am fine. I am simply following a hunch."

"Oh, dear," Threepio fretted.

"What's the matter?"

"Very well, Master Lobot—since you asked, I shall tell you," said Threepio. "If you'll pardon my saying so, sir, Master Lando's influence on your habits of thought is becoming manifest at the worst possible time."

"What influence would that be?"

"Why, his unhealthy psychological dependence on the teleological self-deceptions of a gambler, sir—hunches, lucky streaks, wish fulfillment, feelings of entitlement, and the other trappings of magical thinking," Threepio said. "I have come to regard you as an unusually practical and rational individual—for a human being."

"Thank you," Lobot said. "But what makes you think that Lando ever really gambles?"

"Sir, I have heard Master Han speak of it many times. I believe that Master Lando even considered himself a professional gambler during one period of his life."

"That's true," said Lobot. "And no one hates trusting to chance and fate more than a professional gambler. You've misread Lando all along, Threepio."

"Sir, I do not understand."

"Think about this, then—maybe it will help," said Lobot, discarding the last piece of his contact suit. "When a human being—a *sentient* being—faces a question for which there is no known right answer, a decision for which there's no obvious right choice, he will almost always end up following what *feels* right. The logician will construct one kind of justification, the magician another, but at the moment of choosing, the two are more alike than they are different."

"I see, sir. Thank you. But I do not believe a droid is capable of truly understanding a process that is so fundamentally subjective."

"No?" asked Lobot, raising an eyebrow. "Then tell me, what was going through your circuits when you grabbed that beckon call away from Lando and signaled *Lady Luck*? Were you doing the logical thing, or what you felt was the right thing?"

"I am not entirely certain, sir."

"Good," said Lobot approvingly. "I suggest you think on that a while, too. You may find it has something to do with the questions you asked me in chamber twenty-one. Now, let's get going."

A few hundred twisting meters further, the passages narrowed still tighter, to the point where Lobot could barely wriggle through, and Artoo could not.

"Go back to where we dropped off the grid and my suit and wait for me there," Lobot said. "Artoo, the link I've been using to access your event log and memory registers—can you make it bidirectional, so Lando will know what happened to me if I don't come back? Maybe you could isolate one of my transmit channels."

Artoo chirped reassuringly and relayed his assent over the link.

"Master Lobot, may I say something before you leave?"

"Quickly."

"It is possible that there is no command center as you envision it."

"I don't have anything 'envisioned.'"

"I mean to say that rule-based logic can be encoded very compactly. My own language processors contain the equivalent of more than eight times ten to the twelfth decision trees, all within a space of approximately five cubic centimeters."

"And the giant dewback lizards of Tatooine have a neural cluster smaller than the brain of a newborn human. Yes, I understand your point," Lobot said, looking back at the droids. "But I am not looking for the vagabond's bridge, or its brain. I could easily miss those, or fail to recognize them. I am looking for 'its threshold of awareness, and *it* will know when I have found it."

Lando lingered in the auditorium as long as the question of whether the vagabond could heal its great wounds hung in the balance.

In the beginning, a thin band of new material appeared around the edges of each opening in the hull. The smaller opening forward continued to close, just as Lando had seen demonstrated at the airlock. But for a long time, it seemed as though nothing was happening at the larger wound, as if the process had somehow stalled.

Before giving up, Lando moved to a portal on the other side of the chamber. From there, the beam from his chest lamp revealed that the entire opening had skinned over with what looked like the same sort of transparent material he was peering through.

That discovery held him there, even though it again seemed for the longest time as if nothing was happening. He remembered how when they had first boarded the vagabond, he had been able to see *Lady Luck*'s floodlights through the wall of the airlock.

That should have told me something, he thought. *Like shining a lantern through your hand. I should have been thinking organic right from the first. But we thought the genetic sequence was just some engineer's idea of a clever little code.*

His eyes kept expecting the gossamer transparency to be momentarily transformed into solid bulkhead, just as the transparency in the auditorium went from one state to the other in a matter of seconds. But instead, a lattice of opaque material appeared first, echoing the crisscross pattern he had seen in the stringers in the interspace. Then, finally, each individual section of the lattice began to close over.

That was when Lando tried to leave, feeling as though he had witnessed an exhibition of Qella ingenuity more impressive than the lost orrery.

"Lobot, where are you now?" he called over the suit's comlink, to no reply. "The hull breaches are nearly repaired—I'm heading back. Lobot?" He switched to the secondary comm channel and repeated the call, with the same result.

Returning to the primary channel, he heard a voice he did not expect to hear: "—I would be glad to relay a message to him."

"Threepio, what are you doing on Lobot's comlink? What's going on there?"

"Pardon me, Master Lando, but Master Lobot left his contact suit in our keeping."

"You mean he's gone off by himself? Where is he? Where did he go?"

"He said he was seeking the threshold of awareness," said Threepio. "I'm quite sure I don't know what that means."

"Where are *you*, then? Is Artoo with you?"

"We are somewhere in the vagabond's inner core," said Threepio. "Artoo says that if you return to chamber two-twenty-nine, he can direct you to us from there."

"I'll be there in three minutes."

But Lando had crossed through only two chambers when the portal ahead of him closed as he approached it. Turning, he saw the portal behind him had closed at the same time. Neither would respond to his touch. The portals to the interspace and the core were equally recalcitrant. He was sealed in.

"Threepio, is anything happening there? All of a sudden, the express lanes out here are closed."

The only reply was a burst of white-noise static. Then the ship groaned, deep and long. The chamber shuddered around Lando.

"Blast," Lando said, his eyes searching the boundaries of his prison. "They're back."

The groaning continued, and the shaking grew worse. The glow-rings around the portals dimmed and disappeared. In the darkness, Lando was thrown against the face of the chamber.

She's turning fast this time—the propulsion system, whatever it is, is back online.

"Propulsion—stang! No, please, don't try it," Lando implored the ship. "Not after taking hits like those—"

The vagabond paid him no mind. Moments later, with the roaring growl and violent shaking at a terrifying peak, the vessel twisted realspace until it opened, then fell through infinity's door.

Twenty-seven hours after she had taken custody of the Qella remains, Joi Eicroth hand-delivered a stack of three datacards containing the cadaver's genetic sequences to Admiral Drayson at his home on the north shore of Victory Lake.

Drayson's face was haggard and his greeting embrace distracted. "I expected you to transmit the sequences to me in a secure packet." He rubbed his eyes. "I expected it several hours ago, in fact."

"That was before we knew how extensive the sequences are. It would have taken me nearly as long to encode and transmit the report as it did to fly down here," she said, moving past him into the grand parlor. "And I wouldn't have gotten to see you again."

A tired smile making a bid to reach his lips, Drayson followed her. "You're saying that you found something surprising?"

"Very," she said. "What species was that creature, Hiram? I would love to know more about its ethology and ecological niche."

"I have a small research team looking into that right now," said Drayson. "I hope to be able to share their findings with you soon. What was the surprise? Something about the amount of genetic material?"

She settled in a reclining chair facing the parlor's lakeview transparency. "It's that exactly," she said. "This species has three—at least three—different types of cells that contain genetic material. The ordinary somatic cells have sixty-two chromosomes—"

"That's on the high side, isn't it?" asked Drayson, settling on a small padded bench nearby. "Go on."

"Yes, it is. But that's the smaller part of the whole," she said. "This species has two *other* kinds of genetic material as well, in two different structures located in two different parts of their bodies.

"I call them code capsules, because they're encapsulated in a solid protein coat. There are billions of these capsules in that carcass. I almost mistook them for a massive parasitic infection—that's why I started looking at them in the first place."

"How big are the capsules?"

"Big. About the size of the biggest crystals of silicon dioxide out on your beach," she said. "But the same oval shape as the creature's torso. It took me five hours just to figure out how to extract them from their tubules and break through the protein coat without destroying the contents. The contents turned out to be nearly solid genetic material." She gestured at the datacards. "Your DNA and mine together wouldn't fill one of those. I barely got the creature's genome to fit on three of them."

Drayson stared down at the objects in his hand. "This is one copy? I thought you were doing the triplicate thing."

"One copy. As near as I could tell, almost five percent of the creature's body weight is genetic material. That's unprecedented."

"What does it need with all that?"

"That's a good question," she said. "I don't know. I do know that it's far more than information theory says would be necessary to specify and construct a organism of the size and complexity of the one you brought me."

"How much more?"

She squinted as she thought. "Maybe two hundred times too much."

"Which means what?"

"I don't know," she said with a shrug. "The context is missing. Maybe when your team reports—"

"Speculate, please."

Eicroth frowned. "Well, there's a lot of old biological history in our chromosomes, in the form of inactive genes. Maybe this is something similar, but covering a much longer history or a more convoluted evolutionary path."

"Any other ideas?"

"One kind of weird one," she said, showing a self-effacing smile. "Maybe it's because I started off with the idea that these code capsules were parasites, but I keep wondering what good they are to the organism itself. The protein coat just about ensures that they're inert. I also wonder how they're passed on to offspring. The virus analogy is tempting—likewise for mitochondria."

"If you had to guess—"

"If I had to guess, I'd say it almost looks like this species carries a giant catalog of spare genetic blueprints around inside itself."

"Blueprints for what?"

"I don't know. There's a kinship in the genetic sequences—something recognizable as kin, anyway. Biochemically, there'd be a family resemblance."

"What about the analogy to the Fw'Sen?" Drayson asked. "Don't they mate only once, before they're sexually mature?"

"You mean, could these be retained fertilized eggs? I don't think so. The capsule tubules are completely separate from the somatic-cell reproductive anatomy." She shook her head. "It's very odd, and I don't pretend to understand it."

Nodding, Drayson stood. "I have to go do something with this," he said, holding up the datacards. "Will you stay?"

Her smile brightened. "If my boss is willing to wait a little longer for the results of the dissection."

"I'll have a word with him," Drayson said. "Look, I'll be downstairs for a little while with this—get yourself something to eat if you haven't had a chance."

"When's the last time *you* ate?"

He shook his head. "I've had no appetite."

Eicroth knew better than to ask the reason. "I'll see if I can find something for two," she said, reaching for his hand and giving it a squeeze. "Come on back up when you can."

The instant that *Lady Luck* left hyperspace, its slave circuits relinquished control.

"That isn't supposed to happen," Pakkpekatt said, showing teeth and hissing.

His companion on the yacht's flight deck was Bijo Hammax. "What's supposed to happen?"

Agent Pleck appeared at the hatchway. "The usual arrangement for a hyperspace beckon call is for the responding ship to ping the signaling unit when it jumps in," he said. "The beckon call sends a local reference signal, and the ship follows it to the location of the transmitter. If the beckon call sends a wave-off instead, the responding ship should jump out again immediately."

"And we're just sitting here?" said Hammax. "Maybe we were stood up."

"Contact sweep," said Pakkpekatt.

"Coming up," Hammax said, turning to the displays at his station. "Something out there."

"A more detailed analysis would be considerably more useful," Pakkpekatt said.

"Something big," said Hammax. "A lot bigger than we are. Look, this isn't where I work. Pleck, maybe you'd better take the number-two position."

Pleck slid into the seat as Hammax vacated it. "Contact is capital, type three," Pleck read off the board.

"Too small," said Pakkpekatt.

"Range to contact, two thousand meters."

"Two thousand—stang, we're right on top of it," Hammax said, whirling toward the viewport. "We ought to be able to see it bare-eyed. They can sure see us." He dug into a storage bin for the laser cannon controller.

"Contact is blacked out, cold, and adrift. No transponder," Pleck said, then frowned. "A scatter of little stuff out there, too, same neighborhood. One floater that might be a body."

"Nothing that might be the vagabond?"

Pleck shook his head. "If she was here, she's gone."

"The same is not necessarily true of General Calrissian," Pakkpekatt said. "We'll go in for a look. Agent Taisden, please stand ready with your recorders."

Lady Luck crept toward the wreck of *Gorath* as though wary of waking the dead. At five hundred meters, Pakkpekatt called for the bow lights, and a great metal corpse suddenly appeared before them.

"*Strike*-class," said Pakkpekatt.

"Or used to be," said Hammax. "She's all stove in."

"This doesn't match what we saw at Gmar Askilon," said Pleck, studying the spectral display. "This is not the same weapon the vagabond used against *D-Eighty-nine* and *Kauri*. It doesn't match anything in the database."

"I know," said Pakkpekatt. His expression was unreadable, and remained so as he flew *Lady Luck* around the derelict at a distance of a hundred meters.

Before the survey was complete, Hammax removed the targeting headset. "What would you expect to happen if the transmitter got toasted?" he asked, turning to the commander. "If Calrissian and his team were aboard—"

"We need confirmation, Colonel Hammax, not speculation."

"That's my job," Hammax said, nodding. "I'll go get suited up."

Taisden grunted in surprise. "Excuse me—Colonel Pakkpekatt, would you take a look at the comm queue, please?"

Pakkpekatt spun his couch back toward the controls. "When did that show up?"

"Just now," said Taisden. "Is that your personal comm code, sir?"

"No," said Pakkpekatt. "How very interesting."

"What?" asked Hammax, leaning forward between the couches with a hand on the back of each.

Taisden pointed. "A ready-to-transmit notice for a white-star dispatch, personal to the colonel."

"A notice that can be received only by a military-rated secure hypercomm," said Pakkpekatt.

"I thought we'd loaded one aboard," said Hammax.

"We did," said Taisden. "This didn't come over our gear. Calrissian apparently has a few more surprises tucked away under the service panels of this ship."

"There is something else," said Pakkpekatt. "Look at the message size."

Hammax squinted. "That's heavy lifting."

"It has to be a mistake. We should send back a verify request," said Taisden. "Confirm the originating station, packet size, router. Or request a redirect to our own hypercomm transceiver."

"There is a simpler way to satisfy our curiosity," said Pakkpekatt. "I would like the bridge to myself for a few moments. Colonel Hammax, I believe you were headed aft?"

Hammax nodded. "I'll be skinned up in five to ten," he said, turning away and ducking through the hatchway.

"I'll check in with Pleck," Taisden said, climbing out of his couch. "Page me on the observation deck."

Even though he was alone, Pakkpekatt covered his right hand with his left as he entered his authorization code and switched the viewer to privacy mode as he read the notice.

COLONEL PAKKPEKATT

ACTIVATION OF FAIR LADY'S P'W'ECK COMPLEMENT
RECORDED HERE. SINCERELY HOPE THIS PRESAGES
RESTORATION OF PEACEABLE RELATIONS WITH HOST
WORLD AND DIPLOMATIC RECOVERY OF EXPEDITION.
PENDING DISPATCH CONTAINS LETTERS OF
INTRODUCTION, RECENTLY ACQUIRED AT GREAT
EXPENSE. TRUST THEY WILL OPEN DOORS FOR YOU.

It bore an apparently authentic Fleet Intelligence watermark and seal but was unsigned.

General Calrissian's friends, Pakkpekatt thought. *They should not know that I am in this ship, but they do, and they are still looking after him.*

He drummed his thumb-claws on his temples as he considered his response. *'Letters of introduction' can only mean the Qella genetic code—assistance that I requested through proper channels, which was denied when the task force was recalled.*

There was no real choice before him. With a few light touches on the display, Pakkpekatt entered his send authorization and returned a clear-to-transmit message to his unknown benefactor, noting the ship time as he did. At their present distance, the transit lag for a round-trip to Coruscant should be something more than forty minutes. If the reply came back too soon or too late, he would know what meaning to give it.

"Colonel Hammax, are you ready?" Pakkpekatt called over the comm system.

"Going through my weapons check now, Colonel."

"Very well. Agent Taisden, please return to the bridge. Agent Pleck, please assist Colonel Hammax at the airlock. Colonel, during the flyaround, did you identify where you would like to make your entry?"

"Those open ports on the far side looked to be as good a place as any," Hammax said. "I'm going to use a ring charge to cut in, and I can put some hull between myself and the blowback."

"Very well," Pakkpekatt said, taking the yacht's maneuvering yoke in hand. "I'll notify you when we are in position."

Colonel Hammax did not stay aboard the hulk of the cruiser for long. A mere fifteen minutes after he disappeared into the maw of launching port eight, he reappeared at the opening of launching port four. Raising his right hand in a wave, Hammax squeezed the thruster controls with his left and started across the hundred meters separating *Gorath* and *Lady Luck* as they drifted together through space.

Though Hammax's foray suit had voice, holo, and biomedical comm systems in both open and conductive modes, Pakkpekatt had directed him to observe strict comm silence unless confronted by a threat, and Hammax had done so. So his early return was the object of sudden and intense curiosity. Pleck and Pakkpekatt watched from the flight deck and Taisden from the observation deck as Hammax jetted toward the yacht, knowing only that it was impossible under any conditions to thoroughly search a 450-meter-long warship so quickly.

"He looks okay," said Taisden. "Maybe he had some equipment problem. Or maybe he got lucky and found what he was looking for right off."

"If Colonel Hammax had found what he was looking for, he would be returning with two body bags," Pakkpekatt said, tracking the spacesuited figure with the laser cannon.

"You're going to make him nervous, doing that," Taisden observed.

"Good. That will help him understand that I am," said Pakkpekatt. "Go back to the airlock and hold Colonel Hammax there with the overrides until I have satisfied myself."

As soon as the outer lock closed, Hammax broke his silence, using his suit's conductive transmitter. "Colonel, she's well gutted. Definitely Prakith, though."

Taisden startled at that. "A long way out for a Prakith ship—a *long* way out. Are you sure?"

"I could still read the blazons on bulkheads here and there. Colonel, it's a derelict. Nothing's functional, and there are no signs of life—a lot of bodies, but none of 'em are going to get any more use."

"Was there any sign of Calrissian?"

"No," said Hammax. "I checked both brigs—there were five bodies between them, none of them human. I also checked the bridge and the maintenance shop—no droids of any kind in either location."

"Why did you terminate your search? A *Strike*-class cruiser has two hundred fifty-eight compartments."

"Colonel, with the conditions over there, I wasn't going to find out any more in an hour than I did in fifteen ticks," Hammax said. "I thought the best thing was to come back and leave it up to you whether to commit the time to take it further. If you want all two hundred fifty-eight compartments searched, I'll turn around and get started on it."

"Is it your report, then, that Calrissian's party is not aboard the cruiser?"

"I can't tell you with absolute certainty that the general wasn't aboard when the balloon went up," said Hammax. "But in my opinion, it'd take a forensic salvage team the better part of a week to be any more certain. Your call."

"Stand by, Colonel Hammax." Pakkpekatt rubbed his temple crests as he checked the comm queue. The "Fleet Intelligence" dispatch was still spooling into *Lady Luck*'s comm buffers, pouring in at 94 percent efficiency of the highest available error-checking transfer rate. But even at that rate, the counters predicted it would take another twenty-three minutes to complete the transfer.

"All stations, conference," Pakkpekatt said.

"Hammax here."

"Taisden here."

"Pleck ready."

"It is my belief that the most probably scenario to explain our findings is that this vessel was destroyed by the vagabond by means of a weapon not previously seen. The vagabond is likely to have been damaged in the confrontation, prompting Calrissian to recall his yacht. Concur or dispute."

"Concur," said Pleck.

"I concur," Hammax and Taisden said simultaneously.

"Proposition: The degree of damage sustained will dictate the current location of the vagabond. If not seriously damaged, she will have jumped out. If seriously damaged, she will have moved off in realspace, perhaps to make repairs. If mortally damaged, she may still be present as an undetected debris field."

Pleck and Hammax agreed.

"Or she may have tried to jump out and broken up in the process, in which case there might be very little debris to find," said Taisden.

"Yes," said Pakkpekatt. "Disposition: We will remain at this location while we conduct a maximum-aperture deep scan for the vagabond, and until we examine the debris field more closely. Colonel Hammax, stand by for possible debris recovery operations. Agent Taisden, please return to the second seat to supervise the deep scan."

As Taisden reached the flight deck Pakkpekatt was turning the bow of *Lady Luck* away from the cruiser. "You said there was a possible body?"

"Let me locate it for you," said Taisden, reconfiguring the displays. "Twelve hundred meters, bearing two-one-zero, plus four-four, relative. A lot of smaller stuff between us and it, though."

Pakkpekatt responded by reactivating the particle shields so that they could shoulder aside any debris in their path. "Please begin your scan."

"That'll scatter the field," Taisden said. "Standard recovery protocol calls for deflectors only, with particle shields at zero."

"I know that," said Pakkpekatt. "But this is not a junker, Agent Taisden, and we are not scavengers." He pushed the yoke forward, and *Lady Luck* eased away from the shattered cruiser. Within a minute, it had entered the cloud of debris.

The "body" proved to be a curious object—a rough-surfaced sphere two meters across, carbon-scorched over one third of its surface and encrusted with a thin layer of fragile, long-crystal ice.

Pleck had come forward to the flight deck for a closer look. "Could it be some sort of escape pod?" he asked. "I've heard that spaceliners used to be equipped with something like the ferry bags S-and-R units use—you know, not much more than a soft-sided ball with a rebreather, so you can move people off a disabled ship without having to try to get them into spacesuits."

Taisden shook his head. "I'm still on passive sensing only, but the thing looks solid to me. If the colonel will let me strobe it—"

"No," said Pakkpekatt.

"Colonel, if it's something interesting, let me go out and get it," said Hammax. "At two meters, I should be able to bring it in through the cargo airlock."

"No," said Pakkpekatt. "I do not want it inside this ship. But I do want to know what it is made of. If it is not part of the cruiser, it may be part of the vagabond."

"You say it's iced over?" asked Hammax.

"To a depth of approximately one centimeter," said Taisden, recalibrating his displays for fine detail.

"Sounds like draw-frost," said Hammax. "You only get that on biologicals, and only for a little while, until the remains are desiccated or deep-frozen. See, the pressure differential pulls the water in the epidermal layers toward the surface, but it starts freezing on the skin before it can evaporate. The residual body heat can keep things pumping for a while, but eventually the ice evaporates, too, one molecule at a time."

"Maybe it is a body, then," said Pleck. "Just not a human one. Colonel?"

Pakkpekatt glanced at the counter on the comm display. "Very well, Colonel Hammax. See if you can move it to the fantail observation deck. I believe there are cargo tie-downs there, and we will not have to concern ourselves with turning the cargo deck into a hypothermic cooler—"

"Hold everything," Taisden said, sitting forward sharply and frowning at the displays. "I have a deep-scan contact alarm. Colonel Pakkpekatt, there's something coming in fast."

"You are acquiring Colonel Hammax's bad habits," said Pakkpekatt with a hiss. "What sort of contact?"

Taisden shook his head. "She's bow-on to us and still a long way out—nine hundred thousand kilometers," he said. "It'll be a little while, even for this rig." He paused, tapping the console with his fingertips. "On the other hand, if she's related to the late Prakith cruiser behind us, she's probably coming in with her don't-shoot-me lights on."

"Combat transponder," Pleck said. "Yes. Scan for it in the high forties—that's pretty common for *Imperial*-class designs, and I don't think the Prakith are likely candidates for a lot of field modifications."

"I've got it—forty-four two, for future reference. Uncoded, but in Prak." Then he grunted. "Looks like General Calrissian went for *all* the options when he bought this yacht. The system's giving me an on-the-fly translation—ha!"

"What?"

Despite the seriousness of the moment, Taisden was briefly consumed by a spell of deep, closed-mouth chuckles. "We are heading for a rendezvous with, and I quote verbatim, 'The gallant and eternally vigilant patrol destroyer *Tobay* of the Grand Imperial Navy of the Constitutional Protectorate of Prakith, in grateful and loyal service to His Glory, the potent and courageous governor for life, Foga Brill.' "

"And you thought your section commander had unreasonable expectations," Pleck said, clapping Taisden on the shoulder. "Do you think the Prakith navy holds public fawning competitions?"

Pakkpekatt parsed the puffery for the one detail that mattered to him. "Patrol destroyer, Imperial *Adz*-class. Primary armament three class-D quad laser cannon batteries, three class-B dual ion cannon batteries."

"Sounds like we definitely don't want to be here when they arrive," said Hammax. "Colonel, do you still want me to go after the floater?"

Pakkpekatt looked to Taisden. "How long?"

"Not quite six minutes, though she'll have to start knocking her speed down pretty soon. Call it eight."

"Not enough time, Colonel Hammax," said Pakkpekatt. "Come back inside. I need you to take over weapons control."

"Pardon me, Colonel," Taisden said.

"What is it?"

"Colonel, this other ship coming in may not be ignorant enough to think that we're the ones who rearranged the furniture on the cruiser, but they're sure as sweat going to be curious about what we know. I strongly recommend we jump out before they get anywhere near here."

"Recommendation noted," said Pakkpekatt. "However, inasmuch as we are currently receiving a mission-critical dispatch from Fleet Intelligence, we will not be able to jump out for another"—he leaned forward to read the display—"ten minutes."

Pleck and Taisden exchanged glances. "Anyone know the top speed of an *Adz*-class patrol destroyer?"

"Point-five-five," said Pakkpekatt.

"And this yacht?"

"Unknown to me," said Pakkpekatt. "Agent Taisden, tell me when the contact's velocity changes."

"We could hide in the scan shadow of the cruiser," Pleck said.

"I intend to," said Pakkpekatt, handling the yoke with a light touch that nudged the yacht sideways to port. "But I won't be able to do so for long."

"They might come in more slowly if they see us," said Taisden. "We only need a couple of minutes."

Hammax appeared at the hatchway, finger-combing his helmet-matted hair. "Patrol destroyer carries six fighters," he pointed out. "They can have it both ways—send the fighters in hot after us, and take a nice safe, slow approach to the wreck."

"Anyone know what kind of fighters the Prakith have?" Pleck asked, frowning. No one answered him.

"Contact is decelerating," said Taisden. "Looks like she's spotted the wreck. Colonel, the wreck's going to eclipse the contact in a few seconds."

"Tell me when."

"Coming up—damn. Fighter launch, two birds."

"Excellent," said Pakkpekatt, pushing the yacht's throttles forward to the limit. The sudden acceleration knocked Hammax back into the companionway and sent Pleck tumbling against the flight deck's rear bulkhead. "I suggest you both find a flight couch and strap in. We may need to discover not only how fast General Calrissian's yacht is, but how agile she is as well."

Pleck picked himself up and squeezed past Hammax, heading aft. Hammax came forward and reached for the weapons controller.

"You may store that," said Pakkpekatt. "I have retracted the laser cannon. This is a race, not a fight. I will jump us out before I let us be caught—but I am willing to take some risks in order to receive the complete dispatch."

"What's in it that's so important?" Hammax asked.

"The code that allowed this ship to pass through the vagabond's shields at Gmar Askilon—"

"But we have that."

"—and the code that would have allowed *D-89* to follow it in," Pakkpekatt continued. "The next time the vagabond asks us a question, we should know the answer."

"If we ever see her again," Hammax said with a lopsided frown.

"We will."

"*Tobay* is hailing us," said Taisden.

"I have nothing to say to the Prakith," said Pakkpekatt.

"You might be able to get them to give away some information—like whether the vagabond was here."

"We do not need confirmation of that," said Pakkpekatt. "And I will not take the risk of giving some information away to them." He glanced down at the display. "General Calrissian has a very fast ship. Range to fighters?"

"One hundred thousand meters and opening quickly," Taisden said. "Someone on the *Tobay* forgot that TIEs have solar-electric ion boost engines. Not much out here for them to eat. They won't catch us. Someone else has figured that out, too—*Tobay* is accelerating now."

"Too late," Hammax said. "Their captain made the wrong choice."

"Yes," said Pakkpekatt, his pride teeth gleaming. "He did."

"Three more minutes," said Taisden. "I'll set up the jumps if you'll tell me where we're going next. Back to Carconth and Anomaly Ten-thirty-three?"

"No. I have been thinking about what happened to us, being brought here by an automated system override," said Pakkpekatt. "I find myself asking what the

Qella would have done if, once having launched this vessel, they found reason to recall her."

"Sounds like a card you'd want to keep in your hand," said Hammax. "What do you have in mind, Colonel?"

"I have in mind for us to go to Maltha Obex, the vagabond's point of origin," said Pakkpekatt. "We will set up a hyperspace beacon there and transmit the sequences we just received."

"You mean to call her home," said Hammax.

Taisden's face was lit with sudden optimism. "We can use the entire communications grid of the New Republic as a repeater to send out the signal in realspace, on the frequency the vagabond used to interrogate our ships at Gmar Askilon."

Pakkpekatt nodded, human fashion. "And then we will wait for her. Who knows? If this yacht is as well named as she is outfitted, perhaps the vagabond will hear our call and come to us. The odds of that can be no longer than the odds of our stumbling on her in the dark—and I am weary of chasing shadows and echoes across the light-years."

Lando Calrissian cursed under his breath as he dragged himself through the narrow inner passage toward where Artoo indicated Lobot could be found.

The cyborg had stubbornly refused to return to where the droids were waiting, forcing Lando to shed his contact suit and come in after him. But the passages were twisty and claustrophobic, and it was difficult to find enough elbow room and enough purchase on the surface for fingertips and toes to keep him moving. The maze would have been impassable in gravity, at least for a human.

"Lobot!" he called ahead. "How about a little help?"

"You sound close by," was the faraway-sounding answer. "Just keep coming."

"What are you doing in here? Are you stuck and too embarrassed to admit it?"

"I am occupied."

"Occupied with what?" When he was answered with what seemed a pointed silence, Lando changed the subject. "You know we jumped out."

"Yes."

"You didn't by any chance have anything to do with that?"

"No."

One more toe-push brought Lando to a point where two passages merged into one. "The jump didn't sound good," he said, pausing there. "Lot of shaking and rattling we haven't heard before."

"There was much damage."

Lando started again in the direction of the voice. "Yeah, I saw some of it. Are you feeling all right, pal?"

"Fine."

"Really? I gotta tell you, you sound a little flat."

"I am occupied."

"That again," said Lando. "Well, if everything's all right, it would have been nice if you'd answered the messages Artoo sent to you for me. You could have saved me what's turning into a long and annoying climb."

"Impossible."

"What's impossible?"

There was a long silence.

"Lobot?"

"Impossible to reply. The channel was in use."

Lobot's voice was at last starting to promise that Lando might see him around one more twisting turn. "If there's some reason why I shouldn't come up there, maybe you could tell me now."

"No reason. Come ahead. You are close now."

"You said that once before."

"I was not listening with my ears."

"Of course," said Lando. "I make that mistake all the time." Pausing, he pulled the cutting blaster from the slash pocket of his flight suit and slipped the stay loop over his wrist.

"You will not need that," said Lobot.

Lando's head jerked up. There was still no sign of Lobot in the passage ahead. "You spying on me, buddy?"

Again, Lobot did not answer right away. "We are aware of you."

Drawing a deep breath, Lando reached out and pressed his palms against the inside of the passage, resuming his awkward floating crawl with new determination. "You'll have to pardon me for intruding—I thought you were alone in here," he called as he scrambled along. "I hope I can count on you to make the introductions."

"Yes. A little farther, Lando."

Ahead, the passage turned sharply, hiding what lay beyond. Lando let the blaster come into his hand before going around the bend. Then he wedged himself into the passage, using one foot to press his back against the wall, as he deciphered what he was seeing.

The next section of passage had a gentle curve that limited his view to twenty meters or so. But in those twenty meters, no fewer than fifty smaller side passages joined it. The openings were puckered in appearance, and the side passages were dark—the pale light illuminating the main passage seemed to stop where they joined to it.

Pulling himself forward cautiously, Lando directed the beam of his hand torch down the first of the side passages. Barely two meters in, the branch was completely blocked by what appeared to be a rounded plug, lighter in color than the enclosing walls. The configuration put Lando in mind of concussion missiles in their launchers, or assault pods in their drop tubes.

Spinning in midair, Lando aimed his light into another side passage, and the next, and the next. They were all blocked—*no, not blocked,* he thought, *filled*— in just the same manner by ellipsoidal objects potentially large enough to enclose and imprison a human being.

"Lobot, where are you?" Lando said quietly.

"Molo nag aikan nag molo kron aikan sket . . ."

The dreamy, disassociated voice came from a side passage another few meters away. Lando pulled himself along one-handed until he reached it, then pointed the beam of his hand torch inside without warning.

Lobot was floating inside, his feet toward Lando, his head at the object filling the passage. When the intense light reached Lobot's face, he raised a hand, squeezed his eyes shut, and turned his head away. That was when Lando glimpsed a shocking sight. The right side of Lobot's head was bare—there was only an outline of white skin and a pattern of socket holes where the interface band had been.

"Lobot, what's happened?"

"—eida kron molo sket aikan sket tupa vol . . ."

Drawing himself closer, Lando grabbed Lobot by the foot and shook him. "Hey, come back to me, pal."

Lobot flinched from the touch, jerking his foot away, but ended his recitation.

"Talk to me, or I'm going to have to pull you out of there," Lando said. "Maybe I'd better do that anyway—"

"No!" The vehemence with which the word was launched was part passion and part fear. At the same time, Lobot's hands slammed outward against the sides of the passage, his fingers digging deep as the substance there yielded to provide him with secure handholds.

Only then, with Lobot's arms no longer obscuring his view, did Lando realize what was happening. Half of the interface band was still in place on Lobot's left side. The other half was attached to the curve of the object beyond. A network of fine wires, no longer than the span of Lando's hand, connected the two as a tether.

"Starfire—you found a way to talk to the vagabond."

A smile crept onto Lobot's face. "Yes."

"To the vagabond, or to these things?" Lando gestured with the light.

"There is no distinction."

"Is it conscious?"

"It is aware." Lobot opened his eyes and looked at Lando for the first time. "I will need to remember to discuss this with Threepio. I may have better answers for him now."

Lando wedged himself sideways in the opening of the side passage. "What kind of conversation are you having?"

"It is willing to give me information. It will not give me control."

"Ask it where we're going this time."

"It is hurting," Lobot said. "I think it is going home."

Lando contemplated that information for a moment, then gestured with the beam of light. "What are these—eggs?"

"No. These are Qella," said Lobot. "The ship is the egg."

Chapter 7

◆

Bathed in the brilliant fire of the cluster's many suns, three New Republic warships made their entry into star system ILC-905 in the formation known as triangle-high-forward.

On the point, a hundred kilometers ahead of the others, was the picket *Folna*, with all its sensitive antennae passively scanning in all directions to the limit of their range. Trailing in the flank position was another vessel of the same size, the gunship *Vanguard*. In the anchor position, flying parallel to *Vanguard*, was the command vessel for the patrol group—the cruiser *Indomitable*, under Commodore Brand.

Though *Folna*'s sensing officer was reporting all displays clear, both the cruiser's and the gunship's primary and secondary armaments were at combat readiness, with their accumulators half charged, their aiming coils warm, and their crews on two-hour rotations. In addition, three of *Indomitable*'s five squadrons, including Red Flight's K-wing bombers, were fully armed and lined up for deployment, with their pilots standing by.

It would take just twelve seconds to bring the gun batteries to full power. Thirty-five seconds after the klaxon sounded in the bays, the first E-wings would clear *Indomitable*'s flight deck.

Or if Brand didn't like the odds, a word from him—and ninety seconds to spin up the hyperdrives—would have all three ships wheeling about and jumping out to safety.

Despite those precautions, the tension aboard all three ships was palpable. On the bridge of *Indomitable*, it was excruciating. The patrol group was hunting for the enemy in the enemy's own territory, and it would be just their bad luck, thought Brand, if they should find them.

Or, worse still, be found.

In any space patrol, there was an irreducible risk of being seen by an enemy they could not see. That risk was multiplied many times over by the richness of Koornacht Cluster's starfields.

Even with the best available instruments, an *Imperial*-class Star Destroyer was undetectable against the background of a first-magnitude star at a range of only six thousand kilometers. A ship the size of *Vanguard* could creep within three hundred klicks without being spotted. Any inattention, any errors of assessment, any deficiencies in the systems, and those margins would narrow still further.

Active sensing—a laser pulse, a radar ping—could remove that vulnerability, separating a nearby ship from a distant star. But active sensing created a vulnerability of its own, announcing their presence like a shout in the night.

As they had been for the last nine system entries, the active sensors of the patrol group were silent. Brand was counting on the skill of the seven officers seated at the passive-sensing stations in *Folna*'s darkened elint compartment—the bug box, in ship slang.

Sharp eyes and clear minds, Brand thought as he restlessly paced *Indomitable*'s bridge. The debacle at Doornik 319 had been embarrassment enough to his command. *No more surprises. No more mistakes.*

"Look after your station, Lieutenant," he barked, stopping behind a Hrasskis officer and leaning in to jab a finger toward the console. "You've got a yellow on your check board."

"I'm on it, sir."

"Twelfth planet entering our scan radius in one minute," called out one of the cruiser's own elint specialists.

Brand straightened and turned toward the forward viewpanes. "Helmsman, how is our velocity?"

"Beginning to pick up some measurable stellar gravity assist now, Commodore. Base velocity is one-third formation standard."

"Let her roll," Brand said—altering, on a sudden impulse, the procedure they had used in the past. "I don't care what the engineers at Technical say—I don't believe that the braking thrusters don't light us up," he added. "Let's just be a rock this time."

"Infalling in formation, sir?"

"Loose formation—we'll let 'em drift. It won't amount to much at this point. Signal the patrol."

"Yes, sir."

By the time the patrol group was closing on the sixth planet, the gravity of the star ILC-905—with some minor assistance from the system's outer planets—had boosted the group's velocity to 41 percent of formation standard.

An angry and puzzled Colonel Foag had long since registered his displeasure, signaling Brand from *Folna*'s bug box by means of ship-to-ship laser. "You're shrinking our safety radius," he complained. "The faster we go, the more pressure there is on my people—with the analysis lag and their reaction time, we lose a thousand, two thousand kilometers at least. Why the impatience?"

"It's not impatience, Colonel Foag. I'm just adjusting the tradeoffs slightly," said Brand. "I'm well aware that if elint ran the show, we'd make entry at one-tenth formation standard with engines cold and ninety percent of the ship's systems shut down."

Later, recording his mission debriefing, Brand

could point to the fact that all the ships destroyed during the mass recon of the cluster were making constant-velocity passes through their target systems:

—*This suggests that the Yevethan sensor grids are capable of detecting even very small vessels when they are following a flight profile requiring the use of braking and maneuvering thrusters*—

But the truth was that in the moment before he ordered the change, Brand had experienced a sudden, inexplicable spike of fear. Coming from a tribe that respected instinct as much as reason, Brand treated that fear as information. And the only response available to him at that moment was to make the group's system entry as stealthy as possible, even if it hindered the work of Foag's crew.

Brand had done the same thing in combat many times before—taken risks to follow an impulse and found justification for it later. It had carried him to the rank of commodore and filled his service record with close calls and commendations. It also guaranteed that he would never rise any higher than that—"too high-strung" and "too erratic to command the confidence of other senior officers" were among the review board's disqualifying conclusions.

Even knowing that, Brand could not, would not, change his ways. Honoring his feelings had saved his life more than once—and he had donned his dress uniform for the funerals of a roomful of by-the-book officers, too many of them friends.

As the patrol group left the fifth planet behind, Brand left the bridge for a quick, unannounced tour of *Indomitable*'s ready stations.

By that time, the crew had been standing at conflict-yellow alert for fourteen hours straight, and the fine edge of their vigilance had been blunted by fatigue and boredom. As more and more crew members came to the conclusion on their own that ILC-905 was clean, personal chatter, laughter, and even friendly roughhousing crept in to change the atmosphere in the gun batteries and on the flight decks. Conflict-yellow was in danger of being treated just like any other watch—peaceful, routine, business as usual for a warship under way.

Brand's visit put an end to that. Sweeping through station after station like a cold shower, he infected them with his own restless apprehension.

"Asteroid belt coming up next," he said, peering through a gunsight. "You going to be ready, aren't you, son? Have to be more ready than they are."

Extracting a promise, Brand moved on.

"Asteroid belt coming up," he said, poking his head into a fighter cockpit. "You have everything you need to do your job, Lieutenant? You know one pilot can be the difference."

Collecting a vow, Brand continued down the line.

In less than an hour, he was back on the bridge. He left behind him as a residue of the lightning tour the conviction that the commander knew something—that something was going to happen.

Brand did not know what was going to happen. But he was not surprised when something did.

Like many single-star systems, ILC-905 had an asteroid ring between the outermost rocky planet and the innermost gas giant—the remnant of a planet that never was, torn asunder by the giant's massive gravitational field.

Like most asteroid rings, this one's density was low. It was only a minor obstacle to navigation, and a poor place to hide anything larger than a probot. Despite what he said on his tour, Brand did not expect to find an Imperial shipyard cached there.

Nor did he expect a Yevethan thrustship to drop out of hyperspace almost dead ahead of them, six million kilometers on the far side of the asteroid ring.

Like a giant strobe, the instantaneous flash known as Cronau radiation put the arriving ship not only on the screens in *Folna*'s elint center, but on the other

ships' screens as well. Alarms began to keen on every
deck as Brand upgraded the alert to conflict-orange.

"What was the phase shift?" he demanded, bound-
ing out of his chair.

"Phase shift is negative," said the tracking officer.
"She's heading away from us."

"Going where?"

The navigator turned his head to answer. "If I had
to guess—third planet, just like us."

"What are the chances they've spotted us?"

The tactical officer leaned over the plot table and
studied the geometries. "Very small, in my opinion. We
couldn't have spotted *them* at this distance if they'd just
been cruising along in realspace like we are. Having
them fall out of hyperspace like that was an incredible
break."

"Maybe not," said Brand. He turned toward the
viewpane and looked out at ILC-905, crossing his arms
over his chest. "If they did move one of the shipyards
here, they'll have created some long supply lines for
themselves. This could be a pretty popular spacelane."

"That could be, sir," the tactical officer agreed. "If
they're trying to use the yard, and not just hide it."

Brand nodded. "Comm—"

"Yes, sir?"

"Signal the *Intrepid* that we have a contact, one
Yevethan T-type, and give our coordinates. Advise them
that we're investigating further. Helmsman—"

"Yes, sir?"

"Let's close the gap a little. Give me ten percent
forward thrust until we clear the asteroid ring. Otherwise maintain course, hands off. We're going to follow
her in."

A little more than an hour later, the Yevethan ship
began a long braking maneuver that ended with it disappearing behind the limb of the third planet. By that
time, the patrol group had closed to within half a mil-

lion kilometers, bringing the planet within range of its full array of sensors.

"Any sign of anything in orbit?" Brand demanded.

"Negative," said the sensor chief. "But we haven't seen complete orbital tracks for anything above two thousand kilometers."

"Given its approach, the most probable orbit for the target is three-two-five-zero klicks," the tracking officer announced.

Brand walked to the forward viewscreens. "Show me," he said, and a three-dimensional tactical map appeared side by side with the forward view.

Indomitable's first officer, Captain Tobbra, had a career book that was unremarkable in every respect, the product of a long habit of erring on the side of caution. That caution had been freshly renewed by a new baby back on Trallan, Tobbra's homeworld.

Tobbra was keenly aware that but for a few months' seniority, the flag chair might have been his instead. As it was, he thought of it as a shared command, and saw it as his role to counterbalance Brand's excesses.

"Commodore, if we get any closer, that ship's sure to spot us when she comes around," he said in a guarded voice, joining Brand.

"I don't doubt it," said Brand.

"If we stand off here, even back off a bit, *Folna* should be able to get everything we need for Five-Tac," Tobbra pressed, using the slang term for the fleet commander's tactical staff.

"That's true as well," said Brand. "But right now, we have the advantage—we know where they are, and they don't know we're here. You'd have me surrender that advantage."

"We don't have to try to do this alone," said Tobbra. "If there's a shipyard here, Five-Tac will send us some thumpers the moment we send them confirmation."

"And if there's a shipyard here, the Yevetha will try to reinforce its defenses the moment we're detected," said Brand. "Can you promise me our ships will get here before theirs?"

Tobbra frowned in silence.

"I thought not," said Brand. "Detection and destruction of the shipyards is our priority mission, Captain. Let's get on with it. We're going to use our advantage and ambush that T-type. Then we'll take care of whatever it's here to visit."

"Commodore, we don't even know what it takes to knock out a T-type."

Brand shook his head. "Someone needs to find out. I like the odds."

"But, Commodore—"

"End of discussion, Captain." Brand turned away from the viewscreen and called out to the comm officer. "Let me speak to *Folna*."

"On your number one," came the smart reply.

Brand clicked his comlink on. "Captain Madis."

"Yes, Commodore."

"We're taking *Vanguard* in to engage. Break formation and hold station. I want you here to record and relay."

"Affirmative, Commodore," Madis said. "We'll get you some good pictures for the scrapbook."

"I know you will," said Brand. He switched his comlink so that his orders would be echoed to the gunship, then looked up into a score of expectant faces.

"Time to settle up for Doornik Three-nineteen," he said grimly. "Comm, upgrade the alert to conflict-red. Tac, launch the fighter screen. Stand by to launch bombers. Helm, give me eighty percent thrust and an intercept on the hostile's projected orbit. *Vanguard,* close up and stay with us. I don't want you to miss the first act."

The moment the siren began keening through the forward flight deck, Esege Tuketu threw down his tiles and jumped up from his seat. He had been in his flight suit for hours, and had loosened the closures at the neck, wrists, and waist. As he ran toward his bomber, he struggled to close them, giving him a clumsy dance of a gait.

Skids was already in the cockpit, strapping in, when Tuketu arrived. He had been triple-checking the releases for the armaments strapped to the K-wing's hard points.

"How's everything look?" Tuketu asked as he clambered up the short ladder.

"Everything looks clean. Shouldn't have to make any hand deliveries."

"They'd definitely have to pay extra for that," said Tuke. "Any change in the load-out?"

"No change. One egg, eight CM-five concussion missiles. Packing heavy."

"All right. Preflight checklist, from the top—"

As *Vanguard* and *Indomitable* accelerated toward their rendezvous with the Yevethan thrustship, a thin fighter screen—two dozen fighters altogether, half E-wings, half X-wings—fanned out around them. When the lead ships in the formation came into view on the cruiser's viewscreens, Tobbra was prompted to once again seek out Brand for a private conversation.

"You're breaking every rule of engagement in the command codex," he said bluntly. "The standard fighter screen for this ship alone is *three* squadrons, not two. The spacing is so loose out there that it won't take much for the enemy to break through."

"I'm holding back the other two fighter squadrons for escort duty. The bombers are going to need help punching through," Brand said.

"We don't even know for certain how many fighters a T-type carries," Tobbra protested, his voice rising. "It could be twice or three times what we saw at Doornik Three-nineteen."

Brand shot Tobbra a frosty look. "Mind your tone and your volume, Captain, or remove yourself from the bridge. I don't intend to carry on a running argument with you throughout the engagement."

Tobbra lowered his voice, but his tone was unchanged. "We shouldn't *be* engaging the enemy, sir—that's the issue. It's my duty to point out—"

"That we don't know everything we might? This is no revelation, Captain. I can count, and I can read an Intell report. Give me that much credit."

"I mean no insult, sir."

"That's not always obvious from your words," said Brand. "Captain, if a smaller force never defeated a superior one, we could just weigh the orders of battle and declare the winner, neatly avoiding all the messy parts. But war's not like that. Throw away your calculator. You can't use it to make the hard decisions."

Tobbra frowned, but nodded silently.

Brand moved closed and dropped his voice to a near whisper. "Theb, there's something else at issue, too. Something you won't find in the codex. Which is that if a perfectly hale New Republic cruiser and gunship can't handle a T-type one-on-one, Fleet needs to learn that sooner rather than later. Because all the reports I've been seeing say the Yevetha have a *lot* of T-types."

Exhaling sharply, Tobbra said, "That's why you had *Folna* stand off."

"Apart from the fact that she's too thin-skinned for this kind of roughhousing, yes."

Tobbra looked out at the planet, now a distinct disc with a mottled yellow-brown face. "I'd better get back to my station," he said. "It's time to poll the batteries."

Fifteen minutes before the projected reappearance of the Yevethan ship, Brand gave the order to launch the bombers and escort fighters. He did not want to risk being surprised with the flight decks full of fuel and high explosives if the Yevethan ship made an early appearance, thanks to settling into a lower-than-expected orbit.

The K-wings formed up in groups of three, each group sandwiched between a trio of fighters above and another below. Brand watched from the bridge as they moved out to their positions twenty kilometers ahead. Though the wings and other surfaces had been darkened for space operations, their engine exhausts glowed like candles in the night. The triple exhausts of the K-wings stood out among them.

"I just hope they actually drop their eggs this time," the tactical officer said quietly when Brand returned to the plot table.

"They will," Brand said without hesitation. "And not because we changed the combat frequencies and installed scramblers. Because it has to be done."

Five minutes before reacquisition, *Vanguard* detached from the cruiser. It moved out on a trajectory that would both give it a clear field of fire and allow it to spot the Yevethan ship while the rest of the attack formation was still below its horizon. That would provide Brand with a scant few seconds to react to what *Vanguard* saw and adjust his orders accordingly.

One minute and nine seconds earlier than expected, *Marauder* reported in.

"Contact, one—no, two—three—four. Four targets. Analyzing. Contacts are as follows—one, repeat, one, Imperial type two shipyard. Three, repeat, three, Yevethan T-types."

"Three!" Brand said in surprise, loudly enough to be heard at most of the bridge stations. "Three," he repeated to himself. "Well, that yanks the rancor's whiskers."

"*Indomitable,* this is *Vanguard*. We're now taking fire from two of the Yevethan vessels. Shield effectiveness approximately ninety-two percent. May we engage, sir?"

Tobbra rushed to the plot table. "Commodore, we have to break off. Order the bombers in so that we can get out of here."

"Twenty seconds to reacquisition," said the tactical officer, tracing the electronic lines with a fingertip.

"*Vanguard,* this is Brand," the commodore said,

glaring at Tobbra. "Can you say status of the type two?"

"*Indomitable,* she's full up. Looks like six ship-ways with complete or substantially complete vessels, three more at the keel-and-skeleton stage."

Brand shuddered involuntarily. "*Vanguard,* you are free to engage, counterforce protocol. Repeat, free fire—concentrate on the T-types—"

Tobbra reached out and grabbed Brand above the elbow. "What are you doing?"

With a violent jerk of his arm, Brand broke the first officer's grip. "What has to be done," he said. "Confine yourself to your quarters, Captain Tobbra. Lieutenant Threld, take the captain's station." He turned toward the comm officer. "Let me talk to the attack squadrons."

There was a faint crackle on the K-wing's battle comm as the scrambler went active.

"Here it comes," said Skids.

"*Indomitable* to all squadrons," said Brand's voice. "I have a revised target appraisal—confirming type two shipyard in orbit, with birds in the roost. Confirming three thrustships in orbit. The patrol *has* been fired upon. These are your revised targeting orders—your primary target is the shipyard. We'll keep the T-types busy—you're to ignore them unless they get in the way. Flight leaders, commence your attack." After a microscopic pause, he added, "Good luck."

"There they are," Tuketu said as the cockpit was lit up by the distant flare of blaster bolts striking ray shields.

Moments later, the tactical display in the cockpit showed him the geometry of the battle. One thrustship was preceding the shipyard in its orbit, another trailing behind. The third—most likely the one the patrol had first spotted—was docked at the cargo port on the side of the great structure.

" 'Good luck'—Tuke, this is crazy," Skids was saying. "How are we going to duck three Fat Men?"

"We'll try the low road," said Tuketu. "Red Flight, this is Red Leader. Follow me down to the planet. On the break—now!"

The Battle of ILC-905 lasted just eleven furious, confusing minutes.

In the first moments, *Vanguard* fell under a fearful fusillade from both the lead and trailing thrustships. Even after it began returning fire, it was clearly outmatched in such a pairing. The only thing that saved the gunship from a quick end was the fact that the individual T-type main batteries were medium-cruiser-class at best.

Nevertheless, each thrustship had eight main batteries, spaced in such a way that every approach was covered, and up to four batteries could concentrate their fire on a single target. It would not take long for the concentrated fire of two such vessels to batter down the gunship's shields, and then to destroy it.

Then *Indomitable* joined the fight, and the alignment suddenly changed.

"Let's see if we can divide their attention," Brand said. "*Vanguard,* concentrate your fire on the trailer. We'll take on the lead ship. All batteries, *fire.*"

Indomitable's first salvo drew an immediate response from the Yevethan vessel, drawing the fire of half a dozen gun batteries. But the interceptor screen paid the price—two of the forward interceptors exploded, one after the other, as one of the Yevethan batteries targeted the tiny escorts. The brilliant flare of light made Brand momentarily turn away.

"Pull the screen back," he snapped. "There's nothing out there they can help us with right now."

Before the fighters could respond, a third fighter exploded just off the starboard shield boundary. It was like having a bomb go off at close proximity—the cruiser shuddered, and its shields glowed a pale yellow under the assault, signifying a momentary softening at that spot. But the shield firmed up quickly, and the remaining interceptors survived to slip behind the cruiser and hide in its shield shadow.

"Commodore," the tactical officer said quietly.

Brand looked up. "What?"

"We're not getting through the Fat Man's shields. *Vanguard* isn't doing any better. We may have to redirect the bombers."

"No," Brand said, shaking his head. "The shipyard is the priority target."

"Commodore, *Vanguard*'s taking a beating. We have to get her some help *now*."

The cruiser shuddered around them. "Retarget Green Flight," Brand said reluctantly.

By that time, the lead Yevethan vessel had discovered the flights of bombers trying to slip past. As though contemptuous of the cruiser's ability to harm it, the thrustship diverted its attention to the smaller ships, picking off two X-wings and a K-wing almost immediately. Moments later, it began to launch its own fighters.

"Brand to all batteries—target those hostile fighters! Pick 'em up where they clear the shields."

"Target is launching missiles," the tactical officer said, drawing a deep breath. "Six—eight—ten articles, all tracking this way."

There were more than twenty fast-firing, fast-tracking antimissile octets arrayed around *Indomitable*'s hull, and those that had a firing solution immediately began filling the missiles' projected path with a cloud of high-velocity metal shrapnel. When the missiles and the cloud met, spectacular flowers of red and yellow fire blossomed silently in the vacuum. But four missiles burst through the bouquet like angry insects, and three survived to slam in close succession against the cruiser's shield perimeter.

The bridge lights dimmed as the ship rocked under Brand's feet. "Trading punches," Brand said. "Arm and fire six, count 'em, six CM-nines. All batteries stand by to target the points of impact. Helm, move us closer."

Within seconds, launchers on both flanks of the cruiser spat out the high-velocity concussion missiles. They looped toward the thrustship on individual, indirect flight profiles meant to make them harder to intercept.

"Number three particle-shield generator is offline—we now have zero reserve capacity," said the tactical officer. "I count eleven Yevethan fighters under way. Green Flight has lost five fighters and two bombers. Blue Flight has lost three fighters and one bomber. Red Flight—"

A brilliant flare of light flooded the bridge, drawing Brand's eyes to the forward viewscreen. "Was that an egg?"

"Yes," said the tac officer. "Negative on target. That was Green Two—he must have armed it early, and it blew up under him. Lost three fighter signals at the same time."

"Damn."

"Commodore, Blue Flight has broken through and is making an attack run on the shipyard." Pointing to the middle of the plot table, the tactical officer identified the two small blue triangles moving toward the red rectangle that was the yard.

Brand nodded grimly and studied the plot. "Good. We're running short of pieces," he said. "Send Black Flight to help *Vanguard*. We can't afford to lose that one."

The orbital shipyard the Imperial Navy had called Black Nine was unarmed but not unprotected. In addition to the collision shields needed by any space-based complex, it was equipped with ray and particle shields comparable to those of a Star Destroyer.

Its guardian thrustships, *Tholos* and *Rizaron*, more than made up for the yard's offensive deficiencies. In addition to eight main batteries, each also carried forty fighters in four bays along the ship's equator, and four ten-tube reloadable missile launchers. With their enhanced Imperial shields, they were formidable warships.

The greatest weakness of *Tholos* was the inexperience of its primate, Par Drann. Like virtually all of his crew, Par Drann had never been in combat—not even to the extent of taking part in the Cleansing. So when the New Republic ships appeared, Par Drann responded out of the old instincts that governed fighting among the *nitakka*.

Those instincts, as inherently contradictory as they were innately strong, said

the closest threat is the greatest threat—

in a fight of unequal numbers, dispatch your weakest opponent first—

to discourage others from joining a fight against you, charge a newcomer immediately—

hold nothing back when you go to kill—

So it was that Par Drann's orders to his gun crews kept changing—to attack the gunship that first appeared, then the cruiser that joined the fight, then the vulnerable interceptor screen, then the bombers as they flew past, then the cruiser again as the bombers retreated. The Yevethan fighter pilots obeyed the same dictums, each singling out the nearest target and attacking it fearlessly, but often breaking off an attack when a closer target appeared.

If *Tholos* and *Rizaron* had continued their combined attack on *Vanguard*, they could have destroyed it before the late-arriving cruiser could do either of them harm. If Par Drann had allowed for it, *Tholos* could have swept the battlefield clean of New Republic fighters and bombers before turning its attention to *Indomitable*.

And if the Yevethan fighters had pursued Blue Flight toward the shipyard or Black Flight toward *Rizaron*, the outcome of the battle might have been different. But his Yevethan perspective did not allow Par Drann to recognize the threat they posed—not with *Indomitable* bearing down on him.

"Thetan nitakka, ko nakaza!" he cried. "To the strongest of us, glory in the kill!"

There was fire aboard *Vanguard* by the time Black Flight attracted the notice of *Rizaron*. Battery number eight, a twin-barrel laser cannon, had misfired in a spectacular explosion that gouged the entire gun compartment out of the side of the gunship.

Worse, the snapback from a salvo of Yevethan missiles had left the particle-shield generators dead and burning. The next Yevethan missile would explode against the hull, not the shields, and the thrustship's ion cannon were playing havoc with power all over the ship.

Captain Inadi viewed the arrival of the bombers with more apprehension than relief. "They'll never get through," she said, shaking her head. "Weapons, keep up the counterfire. Let's help them all we can. Helm, show the enemy our minimum cross section. Systems, give priority to the forward antimissile stations—they *have* to have power."

With the help of telescopic holo and the electronic battle plot, Inadi and the bridge crew watched the bombers jinking at high speed through the rain of laser blasts and ion bolts. An E-wing accompanying Black Two took a direct hit and spun out, burning. Black Three disappeared in a sphere of white fire, its escorts peeling away and narrowly escaping the hurtling debris.

Just then, *Vanguard* shook as though it had been hit.

"Damage control is reporting that the fire in the generator compartment has blown through and ventilated to vacuum."

"Noted. Weapons, launch all remaining CM-nines," Inadi said with a frown. "Maybe we can set her up for the knockout."

Three missiles leaped from the bow launchers, another four from the stern tubes. An eighth, located in a launcher adjacent to the destroyed number eight battery, hung up in the tube, starting a third fire.

"Incoming!" shouted the tracking officer.

The Yevethan thrustship had answered *Vanguard*'s salvo with one of its own—a cluster of ten more of the swift, powerful missiles that had destroyed the particle-shield generators.

"Helm, get us out of here," Inadi said grimly.

"I'll do my best."

The 190-meter gunship was among the most agile of the New Republic capital vessels, but it could not come close to matching the acceleration of the enemy missiles. Inadi's hope was that running would give the octets at the stern enough time to swat away all of the pursuing missiles. As she watched the gap close she regretted not having turned the ship sooner.

"Our CM-nines should reach the target in eight seconds," the tracking officer reported. "Bomber escorts have broken off—bombers are launching *their* missiles now. Confirming release of an egg from Black One— confirming release of an egg from Black Two—"

Something struck *Vanguard* astern with so much force that the tactical officer was knocked to his hands and knees and Inadi was thrown hard against the plot table.

"Missile impact," the damage control officer called out.

"Everything's dead back of section forty," the systems officer reported.

"Engines two, four, and six are gone," said the helmsman. "Thrust now at one quarter and falling."

Inadi stared at the plot table as two more fast-moving blips closed on her vessel. "Get to the pods," she said hoarsely. "All stations, abandon ship—abandon ship—"

Her answer was a roaring sound, darkness, a fierce light, and, finally, silence.

*   *   *

Hovering five thousand meters above the barren, pitted surface of ILC-905's third planet, Esege Tuketu and the other members of Red Flight watched the flashes of light overhead as they waited impatiently for their chance.

The order to stand off had come just as they had begun climbing toward the shipyard for their attack run. "Hold your position until we have the results of the attacks underway," said the tactical officer. "I need something in reserve, and you're it."

"They'd better leave some for us," Skids said over the bomber's cockpit comm on hearing their instructions. "We come back with the racks full and no scratches on the paint, and we'll never hear the end of it."

Tuketu said nothing. His eye had been drawn by the first of several brilliant explosions, above and portside of them. "That was an egg," he said, marking the distinctive pure white color of the flash. "And another."

The third explosion was different—smaller and yellower at first, but longer-lived, and larger and redder at its peak. As it started to fade, there was another series of flashes at nearly the same spot in the sky—three small blue-white flashes, then a blood-red irregular billow.

When Tuketu looked back at his tracking display, both the trailing thrustship and *Vanguard* had disappeared.

"What was all that?" Skids demanded. "Did we get one, Tuke?"

"Yeah," said Tuketu. "And so did they."

Both the successful attack on the second thrustship and the loss of *Vanguard* went nearly ignored on the bridge of *Indomitable*. The focus was the last few seconds of Blue Flight's dive toward the shipyard.

"Two thousand meters to shield boundary," said the tactical officer. "Fighters are pulling out. Fifteen hundred. One thousand. Confirming release on Blue

One—oh, blast, where'd he come from? Negative release on Blue Three. Somebody got 'im."

A Yevethan fighter streaking across at right angles to the attack vector had fired on Blue Three, first crippling it and then colliding with the debris. That tiny explosion was swallowed moments later by the detonation of Blue One's egg.

"Find out if the shields are down," Brand said grimly.

"Battery four, give me three bursts on the secondary target."

The laser bolts expended themselves uselessly against nothingness. The shields were still intact.

"Commodore, maybe the thrustship that's docked there is protecting it."

"No ship that size produces a shield envelope that large," Brand argued. "How did we take out the other ship?"

"Battle analysis says that *Vanguard* and Black Flight hit that Fat Man with seven CM-nines and ten CM-fives in the seconds before the first egg cracked. That must have pushed the shields close to their limit."

"Close to their limit," Brand repeated, then stabbed a finger at the plot table, pointing at the thrustship attached to the shipyard. "What's the standard radius of an Imperial particle shield?"

"Two hundred meters."

"What's the diameter of a Fat Man?"

"Two hundred forty meters."

"So the one that's docked—it's not fully enclosed by the yard's shields."

"So what? It has its own shields. Which are sure to be back up by now, even if it did have them down for unloading."

"Exactly. Which means that there should be an interference zone between the two shield boundaries," said Brand. "If we can wedge something in there—"

"Then the shields will concentrate and focus the blast, multiplying the effective yield."

"Can a K-wing targeting computer find the interference zone?"

Still trading blows with the lead thrustship, *Indomitable* shook and groaned around them.

"No," said the tac officer, shaking his head. "But the E-wings ought to be able to light it up for them."

Brand nodded. "Signal Red Flight. Tell them what we need."

Tuketu found it eerily disconcerting to be climbing toward such a huge target and not be receiving any defensive fire. The thrustship docked at the shipyard was completely and inexplicably passive to their approach.

"Tactical," said Tuketu. "Has this Fat Man mixed it up at all yet?"

"Negative, Red One. We have not seen any activity."

"Ignoring us so far, too, Tac." He closed the link and called back to Skids, "Maybe it's just a freighter. Or a dormitory."

"Doesn't matter to me," said Skids. "You get us there, I'll dent it up the same no matter what it is."

They were not to go completely unmolested—that was too much to expect. Five Yevethan fighters screamed in from the starboard, sending one E-wing spinning down toward the planet on a plume of smoke and drawing two others away in pursuit. Tuketu increased both his speed and the rate of his evasive maneuvers, challenging his escort to keep up with him.

"Who is that over there, Cover Four?"

"They call me Dogo, sir."

"Well, Dogo, they tell me that somewhere about a hundred meters wide of that Fat Man there's a seam between two shields. You paint it up so I can see it, and Skids here will do his best to rip it open."

"Will do, sir."

The E-wing jumped ahead and shortly after began firing its laser cannon at the invisible wall ahead, neatly sweeping his aim back and forth across its face.

"There it is," called Dogo.

"I've got it—clear out," Tuketu said at the same moment, looking at the line revealed by the E-wing's laser fire. "Looks pretty tight, Skids. Hang on to the egg—see if you can get a CM-five in there."

"I don't need any flapping target practice," Skids grumbled, but complied. "Ready to fire."

"Clear to fire."

"Missile away."

Running up the big third engine, Tuketu began a dizzying pullout. "Red Two, what do you see?"

"Sorry, Red One—your bird exploded at the shield boundary. Repeat, did not get in. Let me have a run at it."

"Negative," Tuketu said, wheeling the bomber around for another pass. "There's something I want to try—"

There was a sudden crackle of static, then Red Two came back on, his voice suddenly tight with excitement. "Tuke, that lead Fat Man's coming back this way— Cover Eight just got toasted."

"Run for cover," Tuketu said. "Take my escort— I've got the target zeroed. Keep the yard between you and the Fat Man. If I don't get in this time, I want you and Flick to put your eggs right on the seam, one-two. Got it?"

"Got it. What are you up to?"

"Just get clear and be ready to scamper." Tuketu switched off the combat comm. "Skids?"

"Here as always."

"I want to take her in and park right on that seam, zero velocity, so you can line it up from ten meters away. If it goes in, I'll get us clear—their own shields will protect us long enough."

"You think so."

Tuketu glanced out the cockpit bubble at the shipyard. "This thing's full of Star Destroyers, Skids. It's got to go. Can you make the shot? It's up to you."

"Yeah, I can make the shot," he said. "Let's do it."

"What in the devil is he up to?" Brand demanded. "He didn't drop his egg on the first pass, and now he's just sitting there."

"I don't know—his combat comm's down," said the tactical officer. "It almost looks like he's trying to put himself right *in* the interference zone."

Brand looked away from the plot table and out at the shipyard just in time to see it enveloped in an enormous explosion that ripped the thrustship free and sent the yard into a slow, tumbling roll. Swallowing hard, he ordered the mains directed at the mortally wounded structure and watched as they tore through what was left, turning the jumble of vessels inside into a spreading cloud of burned and twisted debris.

While the dissection continued, the damaged thrustship slowly fell planetward in a graceful death dive. The lead thrustship followed it part of the way down, then climbed out and away under full thrust, leaving half a dozen of its fighters scattered behind it, abandoned.

Brand turned away and leaned heavily on the plot table with both hands, as though he needed support for shaky legs.

"Now we know what it takes to beat them," he whispered. "Begin recovery operations."

Three thousand kilometers above the plane of the star system, the thrustship *Tholos* slowed to a stop and turned end for end.

During the climb out from the third planet, a full load of gravity bombs had been racked in the central drop chute, and the main batteries had been shuttled along their internal tracks until all eight were located in the ship's upper hemisphere. From there, they could be directed at a single target during the attack dive.

Hold nothing back when you go to kill—

"*Ko nakaza!*" cried Par Drann, his fighting crests flushed and swollen. "*Soko darama*—for the honor of the viceroy, the Blessed, the All. Now, Proctor—there is our target. Speed! Before the vermin escape us—"

Nil Spaar gently caressed the *mara-nas* hanging in alcove five. In only three days it had more than doubled in size, and the surface had taken on a rich iridescent sheen that foretold a superior nesting. Wrapping his tongue around his finger, he drew in the complex scent and taste of the oily secretions.

Nitakka, he thought. *A strong young male to carry my blood.*

There was a noise behind him, and the viceroy turned to see Tal Fraan standing in the doorway of the cell. Behind him, Nil Spaar caught a blurred glimpse of the keeper as he hurried away, his errand completed.

"*Darama,*" Tal Fraan said, taking one step into the alcove and kneeling, his head lowered, his neck bared.

"My proctor cogent," said Nil Spaar. With a half stride forward, he reached out and lightly laid his hand on the back of Tal Fraan's head, keeping him in the posture of submission. "Tell me—when you warranted your knowledge of the vermin with your blood, was it sincere, or simply what was expected?"

"Most sincere, *darama.*"

"Good," said Nil Spaar, tightening his grip on the younger male's skull. His fighting crests were a purplish red and swelling quickly. "Now let us be certain of my memory. Did you promise me that the prospect of an alliance between myself and these Imperial vermin would fill Leia with such fear that she would not dare make war against the Blessed? This was a shadow they feared and would not dare enter—did you say that?"

"*Darama,* what has happened?"

Nil Spaar pushed Tal Fraan's head down sharply,

until his neck was bent to the breaking point. He made a
fist with his other hand, and the long, sharp dewclaw
slid out of its retractile casing. "The vermin destroyed
Black Nine, at Prildaz."

The resistance went out of Tal Fraan's body. "I give
you my blood as a gift to your child," he murmured.

"You gave me this gift once before," said Nil Spaar.
"But this time I will take it." He struck with such sudden violence that Tal Fraan's head was severed completely, coming free in his hand while the body dropped
to the floor. Discarding the head with casual contempt,
Nil Spaar stepped over the body and left the alcove as
the keeper came running.

"The sacrifice was unclean," Nil Spaar said. "None
of his blood is to go to my children. Make meal of his
carcass."

"Yes, Viceroy."

Taking no notice of the blood spattered on his armor and vestments, Nil Spaar strode through the corridors with long strides and a vengeful countenance,
driving those he encountered to flee before him. When
he reached his quarters, he shouted for Eri Palle.

"Yes, *darama,*" said the attaché, coming at a run.
One glance was enough to tell him the viceroy's state,
and Eri Palle took care to abase himself well out of the
viceroy's reach. "How can I serve you?"

"Send for Vor Duull. Tell Vor Duull to bring his
boxes," said Nil Spaar, plunging himself into the deep,
comforting folds of his own nesting. "And then bring
Han Solo to me—I have a message to send to the vermin
queen."

For once, there was no craft or subtlety in a transmission from Nil Spaar—and for once, there was absolute silence in the conference room. Leia watched it with
her arms wrapped tight against her body, one hand covering her mouth. When it was over, she left the room,
her face white, her eyes dead.

Ackbar was little better off, despite having looked

away through the worst of it. Alole was weeping silently, fat tears painting her round cheeks. Behn-Kihl-
Nahm wore a scowl of ultimate contempt.

Alone in his office, Drayson wore a mask of cold
rage.

They had seen Nil Spaar savagely beating a bound
Han for nearly twenty minutes—not just beating him,
but kicking and hurling him about an empty compartment in an animal rage. The beating went on until Han
was bleeding freely from his mouth, his nose, from
gashes on his face and arms, his chest, his calf. The
beating went on until Han's blood was smeared on the
bulkheads, the deck, and halfway up Nil Spaar's powerful forearms. The beating went on until Han could no
longer stand when the viceroy dragged him to his feet,
not even with a wall to support him.

For long seconds, Nil Spaar had stood in a half
crouch over Han's crumpled form. The viceroy was
partly turned away from the lens, and they could not see
his face. But they could see his thorax plates rise and
fall, and one hand flexing menacingly as a great claw
appeared, vanished, appeared, and vanished again.

Then Nil Spaar had straightened and turned to face
them. They saw that he was bleeding as well—tiny rivu-
lets running from the two enlarged scarlet crests at his
temples. Staring into the holocam, he had wiped at the
blood with the back of one hand, then sucked his hand
clean.

Finally, he had made his message explicit, though
with unusual economy of words—the only words spoken throughout the entire horror, delivered in a dark,
angry growl:

"Leave Koornacht now."

Chapter 8

◆

Akanah was the first to discover the Yevethan starship orbiting J't'p'tan.

As soon as *Mud Sloth* dropped out of hyperspace on the fringe of the Doornik 628 system, Akanah slipped away to the service compartment. There she entered a deep meditation, submerging herself in the Current and searching for the presence of the Circle.

Staying at the skiff's controls, Luke first performed a sweep with *Mud Sloth*'s feeble sensors, then closed his eyes and entered his own reverie, connecting to his new surroundings and searching for local disturbances in the Force.

Neither he nor the skiff found anything of note, but when Akanah rejoined him, she told him of her discovery.

"How do you know? Can you actually *see* this ship?" he asked skeptically.

"It is difficult to explain. Let me try to show you—"

"In a moment," Luke said. "Explain first."

"Is this important *now*? What does it matter how I know? I know."

"It matters if you expect us to base what we do on what you've told me," he said.

The unspoken tensions dating back to Utharis were fully awakened by then. "Have you become a skeptic, now?" she asked, her expression more hurt than angry. "You no longer trust my gifts?"

"Akanah, I know there's more than one source of knowledge and more than one kind of truth—"

"Is it that the Jedi are unwilling to share the Force, then?" she asked. "Are you uncomfortable knowing I have a path to knowledge that doesn't require you, that isn't yet open to you? At the same time that you ask me to teach you, you seem to need to doubt, even to discredit—"

Luke was shaking his head vigorously. "No—no, that's wrong. The Force is a river from which many can drink, and the training of the Jedi is not the only cup that can catch it," he said. "If we didn't know that before we met the witches of Dathomir, we surely know it now."

"That is something, at least."

"But the truth lives side by side with lies, and errors, and self-deceptions—with hopeful dreams, and baseless fears, and mistaken memories," Luke added gently. "And we have to try to know one from the other. All I ask is that you help me understand the source of your insight. That will help me know what weight to give it."

"Is the damage done at Utharis still with us?" she asked sadly. "I had hoped to receive your trust again."

"There's very little I trust in this life, Akanah— myself included."

"Too true," she agreed. "Very well—I will try to explain." Akanah frowned as she searched for the right words. "Where the Current touches self-awareness, there is a tiny ripple—as when you sense a presence with the Force. The metaphor is more different than the means."

"But I can't feel anything here—nothing more than the energy of the ecosystems on the fourth and fifth planets," Luke said. "Nothing of consciousness—nothing of will."

"It is not consciousness or will that matters—it is the profound essence of *being*, nothing more," she said. "I can perceive the crew just as you would perceive a handful of sand I scattered on the far side of a pool. From a distance, sometimes you can see only the effect, not the cause." She smiled. "But you must be very still to see even that, for you are also of the Current, surrounded by the ripples of *your* being."

"So what you sense is the crew of this ship?"

"Whether they are crew, or cargo, or captives, I can't say. I only know that there are many thousands there, orbiting J't'p'tan, and some smaller number on the surface below."

"Colonists," said Luke. "They must be here to settle the planet." At her questioning look, he added, "I heard some rumors in Taldaak that the Yevetha were expanding their territory by taking over the habitable worlds."

"And you trust these rumors because—"

He laughed grimly. "Because they came from the Fleet. I obtained a tactical briefing on the war."

"So you already knew that a ship was here," she said. "And said nothing to me of it."

"I knew that a ship *was* here at one time," Luke said. "I didn't say anything to you because I couldn't. I take seriously the oath that allows me access to secure data. I wouldn't tell *your* secrets to *them*, either," he added.

"Then you weren't testing me just now? To learn if I've spied on you?"

"No," Luke said. "I just needed to know how you knew. What about the Circle?"

She shook her head. "The essence of concealment is merging with what surrounds you. Not even the best among us could answer your question at this distance, and I am far from the best. I hear only silence—I do not know what the silence means."

*   *   *

Pushing *Mud Sloth* to its navigational limits, Luke began to contrive a spiraling approach that would keep the mass of the planet between the skiff and the Yevethan vessel.

"Best for everyone if they never see us at all," he said as he charted the course.

"Done," Akanah said, looking on from behind Luke's flight couch.

Luke looked up at her quizzically. "It can't be that easy."

"Why not?"

"Eh—don't you have to know who it is you're trying to hide from?"

"Why?" she asked.

"So you have a focus. So you know whose thoughts you're trying to deflect. It's done with precision, not brute force."

"That's coercive," she said. "And invasive. You reach into another mind and bind its thoughts, or place your own there."

"Well—yes," Luke said. "But the use of that power is constrained. The purpose must be important enough to justify the deed and the consequences."

"It seems the Jedi are always finding reasons to justify their violence," she said. "I wish you would try as hard to find ways to avoid it."

"Violence? What violence?" Luke protested. "More often than not, all that's required is to induce a moment's inattention, or reinforce a suspicion. No harm is involved. A sworn Jedi would never—oh, make someone walk off a cliff thinking there was a bridge there."

Akanah shook her head in earnest disagreement. "You, who're immune to your own tricks—who are you to judge the harm done? You do this in secret, to lead a suggestible mind, or compel an opposed one. Do you think that those you've coerced see the morality of it the same as you do? Besides," she sniffed, "it's inefficient."

"What?"

"Inefficient," she repeated. "It requires your constant attention and involvement."

"If you know an alternative, I'm your eager student."

"What about the way you concealed your hermitage?"

Luke frowned. "That's different. I created it from elemental substances to have that quality—to blend in with the coastline as though it were part of it."

"It was a powerful bit of work," she said. "When I saw it, I knew you had the gift of the Fallanassi. But you didn't go far enough and apply the principle to its ultimate conclusion."

"Which is—"

"To make it not merely resemble its surroundings, but merge with them," Akanah said. Closing her eyes, she drew a deep breath. She let the breath out slowly as she lowered her chin to her chest—and then she was not there.

"I'll be a—" Luke reached for her where she had been standing, but his hand grabbed only air. "Cute trick," he said, taking a step toward the refresher, away from the forward deck. "Handy for breaking into libraries, escaping arranged marriages—where are you?"

"Here," she said from behind him. He turned to find her sitting sideways in the right-hand seat, wearing a small proud smile. "Did I touch your mind?"

"No," he admitted. "Not that I could notice."

Akanah nodded. "A long time ago, one of the Circle discovered that when she achieved a particularly profound Meditation of Immersion, she would disappear from the view of others. Much later, we learned how to take an object in with us and leave it there."

"Where do you go when you disappear?"

"Where do you go when you dream? It's impossible to say. What does an answer from that context mean in this one?"

"Well—is it difficult?"

She shrugged. "Once mastered, it's no more difficult or mysterious than concealing a cup of water by pouring it in the sea." Then she smiled. "But achieving mastery is much like trying to remove that cup of water afterward."

"And you've merged this ship?"

"Yes. Some time ago, while I was in meditation."

"Will the engines still work?"

"Did the floors of your hermitage hold you, and the roof keep out the rain?"

Luke wrinkled up his face. "So we're completely undetectable now?"

"No," she said. "Nothing is absolute. But we're safe from eyes, and from the machines that are like eyes. Take us directly to J't'p'tan, Luke—as quickly as you can. Trust me in this, at least. I've depended on this art for my survival, virtually from the time I was taken from Ialtra. I promise you that we won't be discovered—not by the beings in that starship."

The stone ruins of the temple of J't'p'tan sprawled over more than two thousand hectares. Even scorched and smashed, what remained made the extent of the builders' ambition clear. The ruins filled the floor of a pocket valley with an intricate pattern and climbed the inner walls of the enclosing hills.

But it was also clear long before *Mud Sloth* landed in the middle of an open diamond that the ambitions of the H'kig had collided with the ambitions of the Yevetha, and the latter had triumphed.

Long walls of finely chiseled cutstone had been toppled and shattered. The slope of the hills had been undercut in several places, collapsing parts of the great structure onto itself. The quarries were half filled with water, the quarry sledges burned to charcoal, the quarry road blasted out of existence. And nowhere was there a hint of life.

Luke climbed down from the skiff slowly, wordlessly. The destruction assaulted his senses—there was a sick smell on the slight breeze, and before he had gone a dozen meters from the ship his eyes began to pick out the blackened lumps of corpses among the scattered stones.

"It's like Ialtra all over again, only worse," he whispered to himself. Then he turned back toward the skiff, looking for Akanah. He found her kneeling on the paving stones near the ship's front skid, bent forward with her head on her forearms.

"Akanah—"

When she made no response, gave no sign she even heard, he became concerned and moved toward her. But she rose to her feet before he reached her and moved away from him at an angle, climbing over a jumble of stones that had once been a wall and then breaking into a run.

Puzzled, Luke stopped and called after her. "Akanah—what is it? Where are you going?" Reaching out with his sense skill, Luke swept his surroundings for threats, but found none. "Akanah!"

When she did not even look back, he started after her. But in the next moment, she vanished—as thoroughly and effortlessly as she had aboard the ship. There was not even a tremble in the Force to mark her disappearance or betray her presence afterward.

Luke's first thought was of betrayal. *She got me here like she was supposed to, and now she's getting herself out of the way.* Crouching behind a jumble of broken cutstone, Luke swept the area again, concentrating on the ridgeline of the enclosing hills.

The ship's vulnerable—if I were them, I'd take it out first.

But there was no blaster fire from the hills, no sudden appearance by troops concealed in the rubble, no patrol flyer swooping up through the entrance to the valley. He found his failure to detect any other life presence—Imperial, Yevethan, H'kig, Fallanassi—puzzling.

"Akanah!" he called loudly.

There was no answer. Luke stood up slowly, letting his lightsaber fall from his hand to dangle at his hip. Still scanning warily, he walked to where Akanah had knelt, but there were no clues there.

Maybe she never was real, he thought. *Maybe someone's been playing with my mind.*

Whether he was alone or not, Luke did not intend to become stranded on J't'p'tan, with only a Yevethan colony eight thousand klicks away to look to for help. There was no place to hide or shelter *Mud Sloth,* but he knew that the skiff's navigation shields would provide some protection against hand blasters and other small weapons. Luke revisited the cockpit just long enough to activate them, then sealed the hatch and set off in the direction Akanah had been heading when she vanished.

When he reached the spot where he had last seen her—or as closely as he could fix it—he sat down on the edge of a giant building stone that was scorched black and cracked in half.

"No Yevetha. No Fallanassi. No Akanah," he said aloud. "No Imperial troopers. No Nashira. So why am I here? There's something missing from this picture. What's this all been about? There's something here still not seen."

Prodded by his own words, Luke turned his head slowly to one side, then the other. "Maybe a lot of somethings not seen," he said, more loudly. "Finding a cup of water in an ocean, was it? I can do that. All it takes is time, and knowing that it can be done."

When there was still no response, Luke stood. "If I have to pick between your being an illusion and your being real, Akanah, I think I have reason enough to know that you're real." He turned slowly in a circle, waiting. "So I know that you're still here—and I'd bet that you can hear me."

When waiting was not rewarded, Luke climbed atop the broken stone, making an easy target of himself. "At first I thought you were hiding from whoever did this," he called. "But they're long gone and far away, aren't they? And you didn't run away in fear, did you— no, you wouldn't need to. You told me over and over that you can protect yourself."

Jumping down, he began walking slowly in the direction Akanah had been going when she vanished.

"Which leaves only one conclusion, Akanah—that you were running *toward* something. That you *found* what you were looking for." He felt his throat tighten as envy washed over him, and his next words came out with a hoarse rasp. "That the Circle is here."

Ten meters away to Luke's right, three women suddenly appeared, as though they had stepped through an invisible curtain. One wore a sashed white gown with diagonal sky blue bands. Her silver hair tumbled down her shoulders to her waist. A second, copper-skinned and short-haired, wore very little at all—a dusty yellow wrap that started low on her hips and fell only to her knees. Akanah was standing between them, clinging to their hands with fierce possessiveness, her face streaked with tears and lit by a profound joy.

"This is Wialu, who marked the way for me," she said brightly, her voice thick with emotion. "And this is Nori—Norika, my friend of long ago." She looked from one to the other, first left, then right, with an almost disbelieving expression in her eyes. Then she smiled a giddy smile and looked toward Luke. "Yes, Luke—I am real, and they are real. And I am finally home."

Wialu released Akanah's hand and came forward to where a stunned Luke stood.

"You helped our child Akanah return to us," she said. "We are grateful to you for that. Akanah tells us the burden was taken freely, but the risk and sacrifice were substantial. Is there a debt owed?"

"What?" Luke searched Akanah's face. "Not a debt, no."

Wialu nodded. "You are the man of honor that she said you were," she said. "Your friendship to the Fallanassi will be remembered."

"Thank you," Luke said uncertainly.

"Your ship must be removed from here as soon as possible," she said. "It has already been a disruption, and its presence threatens what we do here."

"Of course," Luke said. "Just show me where you'd like me to move it to—"

"It must leave the planet," said Wialu. "Its presence in the temple is intolerable, but even elsewhere it would be a danger."

"It's Akanah's ship."

"She has given it to you, in gratitude," said Wialu. "But it is also simple pragmatism that she do so."

Luke squinted. "Are you telling me I have to leave?"

"I am grateful for your understanding."

Luke looked again to Akanah, expecting her to speak out. "I can't do that," he said. "Akanah isn't the only one who came here hoping for a reunion—I'm searching for someone, too. Her name is Nashira."

Wialu's expression did not change, but she inclined her head back almost imperceptibly, as though listening to something Luke could not hear.

"I am sorry," she said. "I do not say I know the name—I do not say that I do not know the name. I cannot help you."

"I can't accept that," Luke said. "If she's here, you have to at least tell her that I'm here. If she isn't—" He shook his head as though throwing off a thought. "I'm her son."

Wialu turned her head as though listening to someone behind her. "I'm sorry," she said at last. "My answer must be the same."

Luke stepped past her in the direction of Akanah, then stopped and turned back. "It's not a debt," he said, "but it *was* a promise. Akanah said that she would help me find Nashira. She thought we would find her here with you."

"Is this true?" Wialu asked, looking past him to Akanah.

"It is," she said. "His loss has been longer and more profound than mine. He has been separated from the Current and ignorant of the Creed. I had hoped to bring him to them."

"Reckless," said Wialu, shaking her head. "We will

speak of this later." She turned to Luke. "I am oath-bound. None of us can betray another to outsiders, by denial or by affirmation. Akanah cannot make such a promise, and such a promise cannot bind me."

"I'm not asking you to betray your oath. All you need to do is tell Nashira that Luke is here, and let her decide what to do." He looked past her, sweeping his gaze across the ruins. "Or let me tell her. Bring her here and let her see. She can choose."

"That is impossible," Wialu said. "You speak a name, and if I give that name meaning, I have given you power over she who carries it. I'm sorry. I cannot help an outsider."

"He's not an outsider," said Akanah, letting go of Norika's hand and advancing on Wialu. "He asked to learn the ways of the Current, and I have taken him as my student."

"This is also impossible," said Wialu, "for you are but an untrained child yourself."

Akanah's eyes flashed anger. Her hand shot out and grabbed Luke's wrist. "You do not understand the importance of his presence," she said darkly. "You do not understand the importance of his quest."

"Do not do this, Akanah." It was said with sadness rather than threat.

"What choice have you left me?" Closing her eyes, she threw her head back and drew a sharp breath.

The air trembled. The bodies, the ruins, began to shimmer and dissolve. Akanah let out a little cry of pain, or surprise. Standing beside her, Luke felt her anger drawing on the Force—controlling, not merging, hurling it against something he could scarcely perceive.

Then, in an eyeblink, everything before him, everything surrounding him, was transformed. The burned bodies vanished. The scorching was bleached from the cutstone, the shattered stones healed, the toppled walls and towers restored, the scarred hills painted and smoothed. The tragedy of the ruins was transformed into a glorious work in progress, filling the valley in every direction and filled with the vitality of thousands of solemnly industrious H'kig.

Akanah gazed defiantly at Wialu, whose answering look mixed gentle reproof and regret.

"My stars," Luke breathed. "It wasn't destroyed? You've been hiding this from the Yevetha—"

"Yes," said Wialu. "Akanah must have thought this important for you to know."

Luke shook his head in disbelief. "The Fleet memorandum called this a cult colony—they have no idea— *look* at what they've done! How long have the H'kig been here?"

"Not even fifty years," said Wialu. "Just in the time since we arrived, we have seen it grow almost beyond belief. It is a constant wonder."

A quartet of H'kig dragging a heavily laden sledge passed between Wialu and Luke. "They're doing this work by hand?" he asked. "No fusion cutters, no droids?"

"That is the meaning of it—the purpose in it. The building of it is a way of giving honor. That work cannot be given to a machine," Wialu said. "The temple embodies their vision of the universe, of the mystical essences—the immanent, the transcendent, the eternal, the conscious."

"How long until they finish?"

"They may never finish," she said. "It is the life's work of a community united by the purpose that defines them."

"Is this why you're here?"

"Yes," she said. "And it is why you must leave."

"You're protecting them. Protecting this."

She nodded. "It became necessary."

"How long are you prepared to keep doing it?"

"Until it is no longer necessary." Wialu stepped closer. "Please—your ship is resting in what will be the Inner Court of the Transcendent. It is distracting the H'kig, and disrupting the work. It is time for you to go."

"Wait," Luke said. "The day of the attack. The

bombardment, the planetary blasters—those weren't illusions."

"No."

"Then what happened here?"

"As I have already said. We protected ourselves, and these people, and the others where we could. I will not say more."

"Protected them with illusions," Luke said. "Wialu, you know that this isn't the only construction project under way on this planet. There's a Yevethan colony ship in sync orbit on the other side of this planet and a colony city being built on the surface. Akanah knew that, so I'm sure you do, too. The Yevetha think this is their world now."

"They are mistaken," said Wialu.

"Not necessarily," Luke said. "They claim all the stars in their sky, and all the worlds of those stars. What you were able to prevent from happening here happened on a dozen other planets where there was no Fallanassi Circle to provide a shield and deceive the Yevetha. The bodies on those worlds were real."

"We know what happened there," said Wialu.

"Then let me ask you what you know about what's about to happen," said Luke, a harder edge coming into his voice. "What the Yevetha did here has been challenged by my sister. Their claim to this planet and all the others will be contested—with force. Two opposing fleets are gathering up there—hundreds of ships, tens of thousands of soldiers. If this war comes, it will be long, brutal, and bloody. And it will come here."

He saw that his words had reached her fears. "I have seen it coming."

"Will you help me try to stop it?"

"We cannot allow ourselves to be used that way. Our loyalty is to the Light, and our way is of the Current. Nothing has changed."

"If nothing has changed, then you're divided among yourselves, as you were on Lucazec," Luke said, looking past Wialu, searching for other Fallanassi faces among the H'kig. "There must be at least some of you who believe that you *must* do what you *can* do, just as you protected these people."

"It is not our war. It is yours, and theirs."

"Neither was this your war," he said. "But you intervened, and saved these lives, and this treasure." Then he pointed at Akanah. "She challenged me to put down my weapon and try to find other ways to serve my conscience. What she asked isn't easy for me, but I've seen the worth in trying. Now I challenge you to give up your isolation, and be the water that quenches the flame."

At that moment another woman, slender and large-eyed, appeared beside Wialu, surrendering her concealment to take part in the colloquy. "Can this be done?" she asked.

"Of course it can," said a voice from another direction. Luke turned to find two more Fallanassi standing by the temple wall. "The Yevetha are vulnerable to us," said the shorter of them. "If we wished for the invaders to crash their ship into the city they are building, any one of us could accomplish it, at any time."

A young Duu'ranh female appeared nearly at Luke's elbow, startling him for a moment. "But can it be done without such violence?" she asked. "The goal is to prevent a war, not to join it, or decide the victor. We cannot choose sides."

"You must," Luke said. "It's not enough to simply prevent the fighting—there has to be a resolution to the conflict behind it. You must choose to frustrate the will of one side or the other—the Yevetha, or the New Republic."

"The difference between them is immaterial," said a new voice, behind Luke. He turned to see a round-bodied Ukanis woman holding a child. "To build a war fleet is to accept the morality of violence and coercion. They are equally guilty."

"When war comes, the price is paid by the guilty and the innocent alike," Luke said.

"And we are paying the price instead of the H'kig,"

said Akanah. "We will never be free to leave here so long as the Yevetha remain."

"Not unless you're prepared to see these people and this place destroyed," Luke said. "And the Yevetha will never leave of their own accord. They believe that they are the rightful inheritors of all the worlds they conquered—including J't'p'tan."

Turning in a slow circle, Luke found that more than twenty Fallanassi had revealed themselves. "You have to decide whether to affirm their belief or reject it," he said. "You must choose."

"And what would we be choosing if we chose to involve ourselves?" asked Wialu. "If they are as resolute as you say, how can the will of the Yevetha be frustrated without force?"

Luke turned quickly toward her. "I don't know for certain that it can," he said. "What I'm asking is, are you willing to try? Are you willing to use your gifts in an effort to prevent the war—a war that will surely come if you do nothing? There's very little time left. Once both fleets are committed to the fight, any chance there was will be gone. There'll be too much fire, and too little water."

"A chance to try what?" asked Norika. "What can we do?"

"You can deceive them, as you have here—but on a grander scale." He advanced a step toward Wialu, holding his open hands out before him. "I don't know the limits of your power to project illusions. But if the Fallanassi are capable of creating an illusion of a vast New Republic fleet, a projection with the same depth of reality as what I saw when we first arrived here—"

Wialu raised an eyebrow questioningly. "You believe that if the Yevetha face overwhelming odds, they may yield."

"I have to think that their lives mean something to them—more, I hope, than their claim to J't'p'tan does," said Luke. "Whether they surrender or just withdraw, many lives on both sides would be saved."

"Would the New Republic accept their surrender

or simply use it as an opportunity to exterminate the Yevetha?" asked Norika.

"Leia would never allow such a thing," Luke said. "I stake my honor on it."

"Perhaps we should first see if we can drive *one* Yevethan ship away with this trickery," said another woman.

Luke spun on his heel, searching for the face that belonged to the voice. "No—no, that would be a mistake. Not without at least one real warship available to back up the bluff," said Luke. "We have to give them every reason to believe—and only one chance to decide, with everything at stake."

"Then it will be necessary for the fleet commander to be part of this plan," said Wialu.

Turning back, Luke nodded hopefully. "Yes."

"Do you know where he is, or how to find him?"

"I can find the fleet," Luke said. "I can take you to General A'baht."

"Then I will go with you," said Wialu. "And we will see how great a fire is burning." She turned and directed a hard look at Akanah. "You will come, too."

There were no walls or guards at the perimeter of Mon Mothma's estate in Surtsey. Though she was still under the protection of Ministry Security, their presence on her property was limited to a sensor grid monitored by two fast-response teams based just off the grounds. A special traffic patrol kept the airspace near the estate swept clear of possible threats.

Even though Leia had been neither invited nor asked to visit, none of those precautions was any hindrance to her arrival. She landed her orbital jumper neatly on the smaller of the two landing pads in the northeast corner of the estate, then began the long walk through the outer gardens and the tree moat to the house itself.

The outer gardens had vivid patches of purple, cobalt blue, and pale orange—intybus, commelina, and anagallis were in bloom, and centaurea pods were everywhere, promising an eruption of pink in the next day or two. The air in the tree moat was cool, shadowed, and rich with complex scents. Leia felt the deep peacefulness of an old forest envelop her.

Inside the circle of the tree moat were the house and inner gardens, and both were more modest than what surrounded them might lead a visitor to expect. The low, squarish house had but three rooms, all with transparent walls and ceilings, and the inner gardens were little more than accents for patches of soft ground cover and walking paths.

Mon Mothma was inside, sitting in what she called her salon with her feet up and a datapad on her lap. She looked up as Leia neared the entry door, and motioned her inside.

"Leia," she said with a smile. "It's been months. Come in."

Leia was taken aback by Mon Mothma's appearance. Her short hair was now startlingly silver, and the fine lines around her eyes were visible from across the room. "Mon Mothma," she managed to say. "I hope you'll forgive my intruding—"

"It's hardly that," she said. "But you're staring," she added gently.

"I—"

"This is not the mark of Furgan's treachery you see lingering on me." The allusion was to the Caridan ambassador's nearly successful attempt to poison her—an attempt that had precipitated Mon Mothma's retirement. "I've earned every line and white hair, Leia. Just as you are starting to earn some of your own. Now, it's true—I refuse to paint my face and pretend to youth and inexperience. Do you think that vain of me?"

"I think you're still full of surprises, Mon Mothma—and still teaching little lessons at every opportunity."

A little laugh lit the older woman's eyes. "Get yourself a drink and come sit with me. The afternoon sun will have the thrann tree dripping sap before long, and then the barbary birds will come out to feed. They're so tiny and so swift—I can watch them for an hour and never be bored."

Mon Mothma's pantry contained a legendary array of potent and aromatic drinks collected from all over the galaxy, but Leia contented herself with a tall flask of cold fallix water.

"So tell me what's driven you away from Imperial City," Mon Mothma said when Leia had settled in the chair beside her. "I don't keep up with capital affairs these days, but I know it wasn't my gardens that drew you here."

"Do you know what's happened to Han?"

"That particular bit of bad news has been inescapable, I'm afraid," Mon Mothma said, resting her hand gently on Leia's. "How are the children coping?"

"Jaina is angry. Jacen is afraid," Leia said. "Anakin is mostly confused—he can't understand why anyone would want to hurt his daddy. We've managed to keep them from seeing the recording, but I had to tell them—too many other people know, and I didn't want them to hear talk."

"And you," Mon Mothma said, giving Leia's hand a squeeze. "How are you doing?"

"I'm having trouble seeing my way."

Nodding silently, Mon Mothma set her datapad on the floor beside her and sat back in her chair, waiting.

"Tomorrow afternoon, I have to go before the Senate to face a recall petition," Leia went on. "The Ruling Council thinks that with Han being held by the Yevetha, I can't be trusted with the power of the Presidency."

"How foolish of them."

Leia shook her head. "To tell the truth, after seeing that last transmission from N'zoth, I'm not sure they aren't right. My first impulse was to give Nil Spaar what he wants, to recall the fleet if only he'll send Han back to me alive. My next was to go ask Special Operations for the most horrible weapon they have, something I could send to N'zoth to kill every last one of them—preferably in lingering agony."

Mon Mothma's smile was full of affection and sympathy. "You would not be human if you were not feeling both of those things right now."

"But I can't let either of those feelings guide what I do," Leia said. "And I don't know that I can keep them from doing so. I only watched it once, but I can't stop seeing it."

"Leia, dear, surely you haven't told yourself that being President means that you can't listen to what you *feel*, that all your decisions must be guided solely by what you *think*. Leadership is more than calculation, or we would hand the whole messy business over to droids," Mon Mothma said. "Kings and presidents, emperors and potentates—the best of them are guided by honest passions as much as by a noble ethic or cool, incisive reason."

"Passion and power have always seemed to me to be a dangerous combination," said Leia.

"Without reason or ethics, they almost always are. But reason needs a passion for truth, and ethics a passion for justice. Without that, neither is really alive," said Mon Mothma. "What is it you're struggling with, Leia?"

"What to do," she said simply. "What to do tomorrow—to fight or to concede. What to do about Koornacht while I'm still here."

"What do you want?"

"Han, home safe," she said unhesitatingly. "The Yevetha held to account. And I want to keep this job, because there's still work to do."

"And if you cannot have them all, which of those would you surrender last?"

The barbary birds had put in their appearance as predicted, and Leia's eyes tracked the darting flight of a black and yellow male. "That's exactly where I have trouble seeing the way," she said. "Do I answer for principle? For myself and the children? For the good of the New Republic?"

"But you've been at this very crossroads before," Mon Mothma said. "When the enemy was Emperor

Palpatine, you were ready to risk all, and you sacrificed much, for principle and posterity. What mattered most to you was what you believed was right. So it was for all of us—both those who died for the Rebellion, and those of us who sent them to die."

"I have more to lose now," Leia realized. "And I am less willing to risk it than I was then."

"More proof that you are human, and still no reason for shame. The young think they are immortal," Mon Mothma said with an understanding smile. "Those who do not survive that mistake teach a harsh lesson to the rest of us. And twenty years of war provided enough harsh lessons for all. We cling more tightly to what we have—to life, and to love—knowing its impermanence."

Leia stood and walked to the transparency separating her from the darting barbary birds. "It *is* the same crossroads, isn't it? What will you risk for what you believe—and what is your belief worth if you will not risk anything in its defense?" She shook her head. "I have part of the answer to your question, at least."

"And what part is that?"

"I know which of those three things I want that I'm willing to give up first," she said. "The moment we begin to think about staying in power before we think of anything else, we betray the Rebellion. That's the heart of what we were rebelling against."

"It was, at the end, the only idea Palpatine stood for," Mon Mothma agreed.

Leia turned and looked back at her mentor. "But I still don't know how to choose between the other two."

"I think you do," said Mon Mothma. "What you don't know is how to live with the choice. And there I can be of no help to you. That secret escaped you when the clarity left you."

"When did that happen?" Leia asked, returning to sit on the edge of the stool at Mon Mothma's feet. "I didn't see it go—did you? Never before in my life have I struggled with decisions, or with accepting their consequences. It's been so strange, watching myself from the inside, wondering why this woman was speaking for me."

"Your clarity came from your certainty that our cause was just and our purpose worthy," Mon Mothma said. "But there is little certainty of that kind to be had in a place like the Senate, in a city like Imperial City. Certainty is eaten away by the thousand and one compromises that are the currency of democracy. Causes fall victim to the building of consensus. Accountability becomes so diffused that it vanishes, and agreement becomes so rare that it startles."

"I would have said that I understood that—that none of that was a surprise."

"Understanding it and dealing with it every day are separate problems," Mon Mothma said. "You have always drawn your map with straight lines, Leia, and in that respect, you were ill prepared for the arcane cartography of the Senate." She smiled gently, fondly. "You are welcome to blame me for that—privately or publicly."

Leia shook her head. "There's no need for such talk. You have nothing to apologize for." She stood and glanced over her shoulder toward the door. "I have to be going. I don't want to leave the children alone for too long."

Mon Mothma rose to her feet as well. "There is something your father told me a long time ago, when I was new to Coruscant and its ways were a mystery. It was valuable to me—perhaps you will find something in it as well. He said, do not expect to be applauded when you do the right thing, and do not expect to be forgiven when you err. But even your enemies will respect commitment—and a conscience at peace is worth more than a thousand tainted victories."

By the time the recitation was over, Leia's eyes had misted. "That sounds like Bail, all right."

Mon Mothma gathered the younger woman into a fond, comforting embrace that lasted fully half a minute. "Draw a straight line, Leia," she whispered as they separated. "You will see where it leads."

*   *   *

It was still an hour before the Senate was to dissolve into the New Republic Assembly to consider the
petition of recall against Leia, and the session itself
promised to last many hours under a rule of unrestricted
debate. But both the media and public levels of the Senate gallery were already filled, and the corridors outside
were choked with the overflow.

Some of those crowding the public areas held a
color-coded gallery pass for a later three-hour block.
Others had managed to wangle only a site pass and a
place in one of the overflow auditoriums. With demand
exceeding supply, the going price for a gallery pass had
already topped ten thousand credits—if you could find
someone willing to sell.

And despite the efforts of Palace security to discourage it, there was a brisk and animated swap meet
under way among those already holding passes, driven
by a series of contradictory rumors about when key
events might take place—most especially when Leia
would appear at the podium. Session Three passes, covering the period from seven to ten that evening, were
presently commanding a three-thousand-credit premium over Session Two and a five-thousand-credit premium over Four and later.

Both the commotion and anticipation were more
muted in the private back corridors and chambers, but
only by comparison to the public ones. The recall was
the signal event of the Third Electoral, and no one with
a claim to a seat in the great chamber meant to miss it.
Crowds and unfamiliar faces were everywhere, and the
normally tranquil Council caucus room was hosting a
heated shouting match between half a dozen senators
who couldn't wait for the session to begin.

In such an atmosphere, Leia's unheralded arrival in
the Senate anteroom went unnoticed at first. And the
first to spot Leia were among the last she wanted to
see—Engh's image analysts.

She had never troubled to learn or remember their
names—she called them the Ventriloquist and the Cos-

tumer. The Ventriloquist, who called her President Solo, was forever trying to put words in Leia's mouth, then critiquing the words that had come out of Leia's mouth. The Costumer, who called her Princess Leia, treated Leia like a dress-up doll, endlessly worrying about whether her clothes sent the right image for a particular public appearance.

They came rushing up to her together and greeted her with a rush of words.

"Princess! Where have you been?—"

"President Solo! I haven't seen your speech yet—"

"—I have your clothing in the diplomatic lounge. There's no immediate urgency, but I need to talk to you about your jewelry choices—"

"—thank goodness you won't be the first to the podium. Let's find a room where we can go over what you expect to say—"

"—I've opted for a very plain look, not quite widow-in-mourning but moving in that direction, and anything too gaudy would just be jarring—"

"—I've scheduled you for interviews with Global, Prime, and ING right after the session—"

"Stop," Leia said sharply. "Both of you—just stop."

Both stared at her with the same flavor of we're-just-trying-to-help surprise.

"Is there something wrong, President Solo—"

"I didn't mean to be insensitive, Princess Leia—"

"Not another word," she said, interrupting. "Not one more. As of this moment, you're both fired." With two quick movements, she collected their area passes from their clothing. "Report back to the ministry and resume doing whatever it is you used to do—which I can only hope is something more useful than what you've done here."

By then, everyone within ten meters was aware of her presence, and a curious crowd had begun to gather around her. Ignoring them, Leia brushed past the Ventriloquist and continued on through the anteroom until she found Behn-Kihl-Nahm. The chairman was with

Doman Beruss, huddled over what looked like a chalice of dark brew and a schedule of speakers at a table near the courtesy bar.

"Bennie," she said, turning her shoulder to Beruss and ignoring him completely. "Let's go upstairs. We need to talk."

There was a sudden murmur—a collective gasp, more truly—from the thousands packed into the Senate chamber when Behn-Kihl-Nahm and Leia entered together and ascended to the upper tier of the podium. When the murmur subsided, all that could be heard were the faint voices of newsgrid commentators echoing through a dozen or more active comlinks scattered across the floor of the chamber.

"—was not expected to appear until much later, until called on to make her own presentation. Her unexpected—"

"—fueling immediate speculation here of a surprise resignation—"

"—was considered unlikely that she would choose to be present during what promises to be a long and intense debate—"

But the Senate's protocol officers quickly hunted down the offending devices, and there was barely a rustle as Behn-Kihl-Nahm walked to the podium.

"Fellow senators," he said, then cleared his throat twice. "Fellow senators, there will be a change in the published schedule for today's session."

Innocuous as they were, his words caused an immediate stir in the audience. He ignored the stir and went on, leaning in toward the podium's audio scanner. "As provided for under the Senate rules of order, and in respect of the provisions of Article Five of the Common Charter, I yield the gavel to the President of the Senate, Leia Organa Solo, hereditary Princess of House Organa of Alderaan and elect senator of the restored Republic of Alderaan."

As Leia rose from the bench where she had been

waiting, something unexpected happened—a slow-growing, defiant-sounding ovation. In scattered twos and threes, then pockets of ten and twenty, seated senators rose to their feet clapping and calling out the traditional affirmation of "Ho, huzzah!" By the time Leia reached the podium, half of the left aisle and nearly all of the right had joined the impromptu demonstration.

There was less enthusiasm from the center aisle, where representatives from most of the human worlds were seated, but even there nearly half were on their feet, with stragglers still swelling that number. Noisiest of all was the public gallery, the occupants of which were ignoring the warnings of the protocol officers and the architects both and stamping in unison. Taken aback, Leia looked to Behn-Kihl-Nahm for a cue or an explanation, only to find him applauding her as well, with equal measures of determination and dignity.

Leia turned back to the chamber and raised her right hand, asking for silence. "Please," she said. "Please. I'm grateful for your support, so spontaneously and genuinely offered. I accept it as a deeply felt expression of your concern for Han—mirroring the concern that so many people from all over the New Republic have taken the trouble to share with our family. I am gratified to learn that his welfare matters to so many of you. We love him dearly, and it's unimaginably hard for us to see him suffering.

"But I did not come here today to speak of Han, or to presume on your sympathy," Leia said. "I have come here to make an announcement in a matter of great gravity. I'm glad that so many of you are here to hear it firsthand.

"At thirteen-thirty today, in the presence of the chairman of the Defense Council, the first administrator, the minister of state, the admiral of the fleet, and the director of the Intelligence Ministry, I invoked the emergency-powers provisions of Article Five with respect to the crisis in Farlax Sector."

A startled gasp from thousands of throats tore the silence. "That is the formal language required by the

Charter," Leia went on. "But it can be said more simply—we have declared war on the Duskhan League.

"I have taken this step for one reason, and one reason only—because it is the right thing to do.

"This is not a personal crusade or a political maneuver. It is a campaign for justice—justice for the victims, and justice for the criminals.

"The crimes of the Yevetha are not as well known to you as they should be, nor as they will be. You have seen the faces of two of Nil Spaar's victims: Han and Plat Mallar. But what the Yevetha have done to these two—as much as it hurts those who love them—is among the least of their offenses.

"The Duskhan League is led by an absolute dictator whose bloody amorality is the equal of any enemy the Republics have known. They have exterminated, without the slightest provocation, the populations of more than a dozen peaceful worlds. They have murdered innocents by the tens of thousands, without the slightest justification.

"Humans, Morath, H'kig, Kubaz, Brigians—no one who stood in their way was spared. Not the women. Not even the children. Their bodies were incinerated. Their homes were leveled. Their cities were bombed back to atoms.

"And the last memories of those children, those cities, are now held by the few who the Yevetha spared—spared so that the Yevetha could use their living bodies as shields in battle.

"The possibility that the Yevetha may not be finished with their murderous expansion, the prospect that they might next fall on Wehttam or Galantos or another more familiar world, is unnecessary to our response.

"If these horrors do not demand our answer, then shame on us. If these tragedies do not enrage your conscience, then shame on you. If we cannot stand together against such a predator, the New Republic stands for nothing of value."

Leia paused to drink in the utter silence that reigned in the great chamber.

"In consultation with Admiral Ackbar and the Fleet Office, I have ordered additional forces to Koornacht to strengthen our position there. I have charged General A'baht, the sector commander, with the task of eliminating the Yevethan threat and reclaiming the conquered worlds of Koornacht. He has the necessary command authority to do so, and he has my full confidence.

"We will take away the Yevetha's ability to make war on what they call the vermin. Not only because we, too, are vermin in their eyes, but because they have shown us an evil heart, and evil must be challenged, even though the cost may be great.

"Any government that objects to this decision is free to withdraw from this body. And this body is welcome to choose a new President—the day *after* Nil Spaar is defeated and the Yevetha disarmed."

Leia fully expected the silence to follow her away from the podium. But she had not gone two steps before a tumultuous roar of approval washed over her from the floor below and the galleries above. Turning, she saw virtually the entire Senate on its feet, affirming her decision by acclaim.

The acclaim was not unanimous—dozens of dissenting senators had remained in their seats or headed for the exits in disgust. But they were a startlingly tiny minority of the whole. Leia stared, barely comprehending the miracle she had wrought. Her words had reached them, and moved them, and united them—for a moment, at least, a moment of principle over politics.

She would have been moved to joy, but for the fact that at the end of the straight line she had drawn, Leia saw Han's death.

INTERLUDE IV:

Maltha Obex

It was a cold day on Maltha Obex, even by the standards of a planet locked in the grip of a century-long ice age. A brutal storm half a continent wide was scouring the northern latitudes with driving winds and sheets of tiny, hard snowflakes as coarse as sand. The storm had forced Team Alpha to abandon its excavation site on the ice field east of Ridge 80.

Team Alpha's cold shelters had been fighting their tie-downs all night, as though eager to take flight and tumble headlong across the wastes. When team leader Bogo Tragett suited up to check the status of the excavation dome, he found the rip-proof tunnel connecting his shelter to the dome torn lengthwise and shredded to tiny yellow flags whipping from the tension cables. Visibility fell to near whiteout with the gusts, hiding a bright blue work dome that was no more than five meters away from Tragett.

Inside the dome Tragett found an ice-cold heater, a massive drift of crystalline white, and a continuing swirl of snow particles blowing in from under the dome's partial floor. The heater had chewed through a three-day fuel supply in something less than ten hours and then quit, surrendering.

Tragett did likewise. Crossing to the supply shelter through a still intact connecting tunnel, he hailed *Penga Rift* and asked for a pickup, then paged the rest of the team and told them to pack whatever personal and team gear they could backpack or carry. Then it was a matter of waiting for conditions to ease enough for the expedition's weather-rated shuttle to fight its way through to them.

That wait stretched to three hours, in the course of which Tragett's shelter broke loose from its tie-downs and was thrown against the upwind side of the excavation dome. Before the shelter itself had collapsed and torn free, it had caved in a third of the dome and turned the faces of two team members as white as the landscape.

But Dr. Joto Eckels never gave as much as a passing thought to offering Team Alpha a respite aboard *Penga Rift*. He regretted the loss of equipment and the investment of time at N3, with no return on either—but there were many more sites, and far too little time. Trusting that Tragett would see to the motivational needs of his team, Eckels had dispatched the shuttle to the relatively balmy coastal site S9, where the dawn temperature had been twenty-six degrees below freezing under quiet skies.

"We preloaded the shuttle with the entire spare excavation kit, from domes to bits," Eckels informed Tragett as the shuttle turned south instead of skyward. "You can draw whatever replacements you need from there. I'd say you should have no trouble getting set up by nightfall—be ready to go again first thing in the morning."

Tragett, a veteran and a pragmatist, understood the issues driving the decision. "Affirmative, *Penga Rift*. But if that's the plan, I'd like to rotate Tuomis out, bring someone else down. He's been fighting shelter fever, and he's a little shaken right now."

"Site setup is half outside work," Eckels said. "Might turn him around, just being able to see that horizon. And hard work is a lot better for the disposi-

tion than lying there all night listening to the wind howl.
Let's wait twenty and review the options when we see
how he is in the morning."

With the Team Alpha crisis past, *Penga Rift* returned to its normal orbital pattern, and Eckels con-
tacted the other teams in turn for their daily updates.
Team Beta was conducting a deep-water survey from a
camp on a massive slab iceberg; Team Gamma was
working the ridges above Stopa-Krenn Glacier in search
of postcatastrophe Qella habitations and nomadic artifacts.

"You have one more day to wrap things up there,"
Eckels informed the Beta team leader. "Then I'm moving you to S-Eleven. With Alpha being driven out of
N-Three, we still haven't gotten into a city site—which
is why I'm making that our top priority for the time
remaining."

"Understood, Dr. Eckels. No objection here—
we're clearly into diminishing returns."

Eckels's news for Gamma, delivered half an orbit
later, had a similar flavor. "You have a hundred hours
to find a no-fooling, hip-deep-in-midden habitation before I pull you off and split you up so we can go double-
shifts at S-Nine and S-Eleven. We have all the skin
flakes, callus scrapings, scat sheddings, and ice-burned
limbs the Institute can use. We're not leaving here without at least a peek at how they lived—before if not after,
and both if at all possible."

"Acknowledged," said the Gamma leader. "Let me
talk to Tia about yesterday's side scans. There's a spot I
want her to get a second look at."

"Transferring you now."

Eckels studied the schedule on his datapad's display a moment longer, then stored it. He knew that he
was pushing the team hard, both those on the surface
and the analysts and catalogers in the lab. But he saw no
real alternative. They had custody of *Penga Rift* for
twenty-nine more days—after which Dr. Bromial's Ko-
gan 6 expedition, already postponed two months,
would take over. That broke down to thirteen produc-

tive days at Maltha Obex and sixteen wasted days in
transit back to Coruscant.

*All that time just to drag our hands and brains
from one side of the galaxy to another—the universe is
an offense to any reasonable concept of order.*

Eckels found himself envying his client for having a
ship like *Meridian* at his disposal. The black-hulled
sprint that had made the pickup had completed a round
trip to Coruscant in less than the time it would take the
elderly research vessel to complete one leg. But the
Obroan Institute would never invest its precious resources in something as ephemeral as speed.

"Archaeology is not a race," Director bel-dar-
Nolek would say. "It is a profession for the patient. We,
who think in centuries and millennia, can hardly notice
a handful of days."

But bel-dar-Nolek no longer did fieldwork. The
longest trip he regularly made was a twenty-minute
walk from his home to his office at the Institute.

Leaving the comm booth, Eckels started aft toward
the labs. But before he reached them, he found himself
paged over the shipcomm.

"Captain Barjas, to the bridge, please. Dr. Eckels,
to the bridge, please."

Eckels recognized the voice of the first officer, who
had been with the ship for nine years and uncounted
expeditions. Eckels also recognized the note of urgency
that made Manazar's words more than a polite request.
Turning, Eckels reversed his steps, adding a jot of haste
to them until he passed into the crew section and
climbed the triangular ladder to the bridge.

Barjas had arrived before him. "Doctor," he said
with an acknowledging nod.

"What is it?"

Barjas pointed at the navigation display, Manazar
out the forward viewport.

"Incoming ship," Barjas said.

Manazar added, "And they don't seem too happy
that we're here."

*　　*　　*

Wary of being followed, Pakkpekatt had guided *Lady Luck* through a series of three hyperspace jumps en route to Maltha Obex. The extra jumps added less than an hour to their travel time, but vastly increased the difficulty for anyone attempting to divine their destination.

Having taken those extra precautions to ensure that they would be undisturbed, Pakkpekatt was all the more concerned to discover that though the planet was dead, it was not deserted.

"Vessel answers as *Penga Rift,* registry Coruscant, ownership Obroan Institute for Archaeology, captain Dolk Barjas. Supplementary: Length one-twenty-six, beam thirty-two, no registered armament, rated speed—"

"Agent Taisden, can you suppress that vessel's comm ability?"

"Local," Taisden said. "Not hypercomm."

"Do nothing, then," said Pakkpekatt.

"Colonel, you weren't thinking about taking that ship out, were you?" Hammax asked, his face showing concern. "That's not only a civilian boat, but a friendly—and from the size of her, probably berthing upward of thirty."

"My concern is that we have sufficient privacy to do our work here," said Pakkpekatt, slowing *Lady Luck* to give them more time before being detected. "I will entertain all options."

"This entire expedition has been black ops from the start," said Pleck. "Why not just drop the curtain over the whole system, commandeer the ship under NRI authority, and lock in a comm blackout?"

"I do not think we have as much authority here as you would like to presume—either in fact or in appearance," Pakkpekatt said. "If you were her captain, would you surrender your command to the crew of a private yacht that showed up without its registered owner? Only the greenest captain would fail to suspect piracy in such circumstances."

"Okay, so when we blip in on their sensors, they're

not going to be intimidated," said Hammax. "But surely we could get General Rieekan or Brigadier Collomus to have them ordered out of the system. We could even wait out here, out of range, until they've been spanked and sent home."

Taisden was shaking his head. "Listen, I did a turn in the Senate liaison office. The colonel's right. Without a native population here, Maltha Obex is an open system, and Article Nineteen of the Charter applies. The Obroan Institute has as much right to be here as we do. The NRI doesn't have the authority to claim territory for itself—not even the Fleet has that power. They have to go to the Senate Defense Council for a presumptive finding of a security interest to support the claim, give public notice to the member nations—"

"So how do we get them to leave without telling them who we are and why we're here?" Hammax demanded.

"That's another question, isn't it?" asked Pleck. "What are *they* doing here?"

"They are here because we sent them here," said Pakkpekatt.

That drew puzzled looks. "*We* did?" Hammax asked.

"Effectively. Before the vagabond escaped our control at Gmar Askilon, I asked General Rieekan for Qella genetic material, and for reasons of expediency the agency enlisted the Obroan Institute to locate and retrieve it. But we now have what they came here to retrieve for us—they should be gone."

"Well, then, it's simple," said Hammax. "If we sent them here, we can order them to leave. We just have to tell them that we're here to take over the operation and their services are no longer required."

"I don't think so," Taisden said. "From the comm traffic, it sounds like they have at least three operations under way on the surface. They're not going to believe that this ship, and the four of us, are here to take over."

"Doesn't matter what they believe," said Hammax. "If we hired 'em, we can fire 'em. And maybe this yacht

isn't very intimidating, but everyone here knows that
the colonel can be. That could turn out to be all the
authority we need."

"And if they don't go for it?" Taisden asked.
"They're civilians, Colonel—even worse, scientists.
They don't herd well."

"Then there's one other option. Colonel, that's basically a Dobrutz liner," said Hammax. "I know something about the type, because I've spent some time in
one. The Alliance had a fistful of them, pressed into
service as small troop transports during the Rebellion."

"Go on," said Pakkpekatt.

"See, that ship down there has a single comm array, mounted outside the nav shields because of the interference from those miserable DZ-nine shield
generators," said Hammax. "It was a known vulnerability. I'm sure I could take it out without collateral
damage. Shouldn't require more than two shots. Might
get it in one."

"Thank you, Colonel," said Pakkpekatt, advancing
the throttles. "However, I believe I will hold that option
in deep reserve. There is something here that still eludes
me. Perhaps I can encourage these interlopers to reveal
it."

The inbound vessel had remained silent until it was
nearly on top of *Penga Rift*. Then the first signal had
come over the emergency comm channel, lighting up
several warning bars on the panels at Manazar's elbow.

"Penga Rift, this is a priority alert. You are operating in a restricted area, and your vessel is at risk. Please
verify your transponder identification profile."

Startled out of inattentiveness, Manazar nearly sent
the confirming data without questioning the request.
Only at the last moment did he recover his poise and
respond, "Unknown vessel, this is *Penga Rift.* Please
identify yourself—this ship is not equipped with an in-
terrogator module."

"I say again, *Penga Rift,* this is a priority alert. You

are operating in a restricted area, and your vessel is at
risk. Please verify your transponder identification profile." As though to underline the seriousness of the request, a concealed weapons bay had opened on the
underside of the new arrival's hull. The retractable laser
cannon that emerged cycled through its full range of
motion, then locked on *Penga Rift*.

That was the point at which Manazar called for the
captain and the expedition leader. Then he quickly
checked to see if the transponder had already been inter-
rogated, and sent the requested information when he
saw that it had.

"I thought since they already have the information
and we have nothing to hide, there was no harm in
complying," Manazar explained. "But the very next
thing, they wanted to talk to the master of the vessel,
with full holocomm. I've been putting them off until
you got here, but I don't think they like being put off."

Barjas nodded. "You did fine, Mazz. I'll take it
from here."

"No," said Eckels. "On the starlanes, this ship is
yours, Captain, but here in orbit, the expedition leader
is in command. I will deal with this."

He crossed the bridge to *Penga Rift*'s small
holocomm booth and settled himself inside it. "Monitor
to station one. Record to personal log Eckels. Begin
transmission." After a moment's pause, he said, "This is
Dr. Joto Eckels of the Obroan Institute, expedition
leader. Whom am I addressing?"

When the answering holo formed before him, Eckels felt his body trying to retreat deeper into the seat.
The face was not only intensely alien, but both inhu-
manly large and close enough to violate Eckels's psychological boundaries. It could have been no more than
that the other was leaning forward toward his holo lens,
but it made Eckels feel cornered in the booth.

"I am Colonel Ejagga Pakkpekatt of New Republic
Intelligence," said the other, showing teeth that were
distinctively those of a carnivore. "My mission in this
sector is under the direct authority of the director of

operations, and with the knowledge and consent of the Senate Intelligence Council. What is your business here?"

"We are conducting a contract survey and excavation of Maltha Obex."

"And what is the purpose of your survey and excavation?"

"This is an archaeological research vessel," said Eckels, recovering some measure of his equilibrium. "Not surprisingly, we're here to do the things archaeologists do—to retrieve biological samples and cultural artifacts related to the former inhabitants of this planet."

"Who contracted for this expedition?"

Eckels considered refusing to answer. There were nondisclosure clauses in the standard Institute contracts that offered not only a suitable pretext, but also a reasonable defense of his actions after the fact. But being difficult would not help move the conversation forward to what the visitors really wanted—though Eckels was already sure in his own mind what that was. He had had but one thought since the ship had arrived, only one explanation for this coincidence—this confrontation.

"Harkin Dyson, a private collector," said Eckels. "But come, you know all that already. Tell me, what did Dyson do? I should not have trusted him. Men with that much wealth do what they want and let the law try to catch up. Please tell me he didn't try selling the remains piecemeal."

Pakkpekatt did not seem interested in Eckels's confessions. "Was this contract the only basis for your interest in Maltha Obex?"

"No," said Eckels. The alien's unblinking gaze was becoming an annoyance. "We lost some people here, folks who were working another contract. But I would guess you know all about that, too. The rumor going around the Institute was that it was an NRI job."

"Dr. Eckels, I have not asked of you that you tell me only things I did not know already," said Pakkpekatt, somehow managing to loom even closer.

"Have you encountered any other vessels since your arrival here?"

"Just the other NRI ship—"

The holo display suddenly dissolved in a burst of snowy static. "What happened?"

"I broke the link," said Manazar. "Doctor, this Pakkpekatt—I just identified his species. He's a Hortek."

"And?"

"They're supposed to be telepathic. That's why he demanded the holo link. He's probably already found out everything he wanted from you."

"Well, I am *not* telepathic, and I have not found out everything I want," Eckels said frostily. "Restore the link."

"There you are, Doctor," said Pakkpekatt a moment later. "Your reply was garbled by the equipment malfunction."

Eckels nodded. "It was no malfunction, Colonel—just a bit of clumsiness."

Pakkpekatt fanned his fingers and gestured dismissively. "You were speaking of an NRI ship."

"When we reached Maltha Obex, there was a military vessel here. I presumed it was NRI, though nothing was ever said openly," Eckels said. "It was the ship that brought our late colleagues here. The pilot guided us to their bodies before he left. That was an unexpected courtesy, to have him wait—I do give you credit for that."

"It was no courtesy, Doctor," said Pakkpekatt. "Just a bit of bureaucratic paralysis."

"I see." Eckels sat forward in the booth. "It was impatience that killed Stopa and Krenn, Colonel—their own, and that of whoever dangled a bonus worth twice their annual research budget in front of them. It's curious that what was so urgent suddenly became unnecessary. Or did it? I was willing to accept Dyson at face value, as another of the artifact hunters who hover around the Institute. But your arrival here is one coincidence too many. Dyson is one of you, isn't he?"

"I don't know who he is, Doctor," said Pakkpekatt. "A meddler who's succeeded in manipulating both of us, it seems."

Eckels was taken aback by the unexpected answer, but quickly recovered his momentum. "What is *your* business here? And what's this about our vessel being at risk? Did you mean that as a warning or a threat, Colonel?"

"A warning," said Pakkpekatt. "A ship may be coming here—a ship that has already destroyed or crippled at least five warships from four different navies. Our business here is to intercept it. Your vessel will be at grave risk if you remain here. I suggest you wrap up your work and move on."

"That's not possible, Colonel," said Eckels. "We're scheduled for another thirteen days here, and we need every minute of every hour."

"It may be possible for you to return at another time," said Pakkpekatt. "But Maltha Obex is not a safe place to be now."

"That has been the case for quite some time, Colonel."

"Are your people willing to keep working on the surface knowing that you can't promise them you'll have time to come back for them? Are they willing to risk freezing to death with the memory of seeing *Penga Rift* turn into a very brief bright spot in the sky?"

"You are trying to frighten me, Colonel. That shows a disappointing lack of respect," said Eckels.

"I am trying to save your life, and the lives of those under your command."

"You are trying to protect your secrets," said Eckels. "What kind of ship is coming here, Colonel?"

"One that destroyed an Imperial-design cruiser with ease, just two days ago," said Pakkpekatt. "Perhaps you should consult with the captain of *Penga Rift* and ask him how he views the prospect of commanding it in battle."

"I will not cede Maltha Obex to the NRI," said Eckels. "The work is important—and a friend died here.

Both of those things matter to me, Colonel, even if they mean nothing to you. Do what you need to here. We won't interfere with your business if you grant us the same courtesy."

"It isn't *our* interference you need to be concerned with," said Pakkpekatt. "Doctor, I cannot offer you protection—"

"Oh, yes, from the mysterious ship that's no threat to your vessel, but a terrible threat to ours. The rampaging juggernaut that dispatches warships with ease, yet apparently will cower when confronted by your yacht. I don't believe a word of it. Really, Colonel, couldn't you have invented a more plausible lie? I thought spies were supposed to be good at that—"

Pakkpekatt hissed and lunged forward, his threat ruffles unfolding. Eckels startled, sitting straight up. Even Barjas, watching on the flatscreen display, flinched noticeably.

"I have spoken only the truth to you," Pakkpekatt said, his voice thick with anger. "The dead will wait for you. Leave this place before you join them."

This time, the threat was effective. Only simple stubbornness trumped the sudden flash of fear that showed in Eckels's eyes. "Perhaps you are telling the truth, as you say," he said. "But if you had the authority to order us to leave, you would have already done so. So let it just be understood between us that we're staying. We accept the risks. Others may return here in the future, but this is our time."

"You do not know what you risk by that decision, Dr. Eckels."

"You remain free to enlighten me," said Eckels. "What kind of ship is coming to Maltha Obex?"

Pakkpekatt sat back and folded his hands in his lap. "A Qella ship, Dr. Eckels."

Eckels stared, dumbfounded, then cast his gaze downward. Twice he opened his mouth as if to speak. Both times he momentarily closed his eyes and shook his head, as though disowning the thought trying to reach his lips. Finally he ran a hand back through his thinning hair and raised his head.

"Would you care to come aboard *Penga Rift,* Colonel?" Eckels said, his voice surprisingly steady. "I believe I owe you an apology, and then we need to talk."

"That's what you wanted from the start, isn't it?" Taisden said when the link was terminated, looking at Pakkpekatt in surprise.

"I never intended for them to leave," Pakkpekatt agreed. "That ship contains all of the New Republic's experts on the Qella. What they know—however little—may be the difference between success and failure."

"Sure—and if we can make use of them, better to keep them here than chase them away. But you played him like a kolo-fisher working a record catch," said Taisden. "Chances are you left him thinking he won that showdown, with a chance at the vagabond as his reward for hanging tough."

"I had the insuperable advantage of being able to tell the bait from the hook," Pakkpekatt said, rising. "Still, perhaps there's something about sitting in Calrissian's couch that brings such manipulations more readily to mind and tongue."

"What manipulations?" Taisden asked, his expression innocent of humor. "After all, Colonel, just as you said, all you told him was the truth."

But they both knew that Eckels had not yet heard all of the truth.

Pakkpekatt left Colonel Hammax in command of *Lady Luck*'s flight deck and charged Pleck with making the arrangements with Coruscant for the recall signal to be rebroadcast from NRI stations and vessels operating in the open. Then he and Taisden went across to *Penga Rift* in the research vessel's skiff.

They brought with them a selection of images from Gmar Askilon, a copy of the genetic catalog, and a request for one of *Penga Rift*'s orbital relay satellites. Standard equipment aboard research and exploration vessels—but not aboard *Lady Luck*—the generic helmet-sized units were ordinarily used in sets of three to give a single ship global comm coverage.

"We can and will originate the recall signal from *Lady Luck*," Taisden explained. "But for obvious reasons, we might not want to be right next to the antenna if and when the vagabond jumps in-system."

A profoundly distracted Joto Eckels agreed with a wave of his hand. "Yes, of course. We carry two spares—Mazz will make one available to you." The holos of the vagabond escaping from the armada, juxtaposed with selected views of the destroyed Prakith cruiser, had made a deep impression on Eckels.

But the major distraction was the dispatch containing the report on the Qella genome. "This is very good work," Eckels said, studying the sequences on his datapad. "These Eicroth bodies—what an extraordinary discovery. This report is based on the single example I delivered to Harkin Dyson, yes?"

"I assume so," said Pakkpekatt. "It appears to be the only Qella material to have left the system."

"Then we do not know if these Eicroth bodies are typical of the species, or indicate an abnormal condition, or represent a variant of the species," Eckels said. "With only a single example, no generalizations can be made."

"Presumably not."

Eckels closed his datapad. "Colonel, we have five additional Qella bodies in the specimen lab. They've all been fully scanned, but the scans haven't yet been reviewed in detail—"

"Why not?" Taisden interrupted.

"We scan them as soon as we receive them because of the risk of sample deterioration," Eckels said, turning toward the younger man. "Analysis is something we can do on the way home, or at the Institute." He looked back at Pakkpekatt. "Colonel, we did not know about this secondary genetic material. If I could take this data back to the lab for a few hours, I may be able to answer that question, and perhaps some others as well."

"That copy is for your use," said Pakkpekatt, "assuming that you will accept one restriction."

"Any reasonable one," said Eckels. "This really must be looked at right away."

"I ask only that the data not leave this vessel in any form, by any channel, until we better understand it. If what you hold there is in fact the key to stopping and controlling the vagabond—"

"I understand. An intact Qella vessel would be a treasure far too valuable to risk. This data will not leave my personal custody," Eckels vowed. "I will do this work myself, under isolation protocols. Will that be satisfactory?"

"Entirely satisfactory," said Pakkpekatt. "In the meantime, we will return to our vessel with the relay satellite and continue our preparations."

"I'll signal you when I have something," said Eckels, waggling the datacards. "Can you find your way back to the skiff by yourselves? I want to get started immediately."

"Of course."

"Thank you. I'll have First Officer Manazar meet you there with the relay satellite."

As they waited for Manazar at the skiff, Taisden asked quietly, "When are you going to tell him about the general being onboard?"

"When I know that Calrissian *is* still onboard," said Pakkpekatt. "By now even the most prudent rationing, the most severely restricted activity, will have exhausted their personal consumables. I have been wondering if that might be the explanation for the beckon call to *Lady Luck*—a last act of desperation by the last surviving member of Calrissian's team, in the last hours of his life."

The somber mood set by Pakkpekatt's words stayed with them all the way back to *Lady Luck*, and cast a long shadow on the work waiting for them there.

*　　*　　*

Instead of signaling, Dr. Eckels came calling. By the time the skiff came alongside *Lady Luck,* her entire complement had gathered to learn the reason for the change of plans.

"Colonel," Eckels said, ducking his head as he stepped through the inner airlock. "Agent Taisden. These other gentlemen I do not know—"

Pakkpekatt supplied perfunctory introductions. "Is something wrong, Doctor?"

"Wrong? No, quite the opposite. I think I have good news for you. Is there somewhere we can work?"

Pleck led them forward to the lounge of Lando's personal suite.

"You'll have to go slowly with us, Doctor," said Hammax as they filed in. "Combat medicine isn't long on theory, and I don't think the rest of them have had even that much."

"I understand. I'll try to make certain no one needs to be telepathic to keep up," Eckels said. His voice had the faintest hint of a playful lilt.

"An excellent policy," Pakkpekatt rumbled. "I follow it myself."

Taisden cleared his throat. Otherwise, there was silence as the five sorted themselves into the available seats.

"You checked the other cadavers for these Eicroth bodies?" asked Pakkpekatt.

"The first thing I did," Eckels said. He ran his hands over the soft leather covering of the padded arms, then looked around the cabin, taking in the luxury appointments. "Are all NRI ships outfitted this way?"

"Not generally," Pakkpekatt said.

"This is a, uh, special-use vessel," added Pleck.

"What use would that be—bordello?" asked Eckels. "Well, never mind. I've long suspected that I took the wrong career path. Yes, Eicroth bodies. They all had them."

"That confirms it then, right?" asked Taisden. "They're normal parts of Qella physiology."

"By itself, it would only be strongly indicative,"

said Eckels. "A common parasitic infestation would still
be a possibility. But I have other evidence."

Taisden looked to Pakkpekatt. "So we need to send
all three sections of the code."

"No, no," said Eckels, waving his hands in front of
him. "Sending a third of it should be sufficient. Here, I
will explain. In your cells, and mine, and even those of
the colonel here, there is a universal pattern—a chemical alphabet with four letters, a vocabulary of words
two letters long, a grammar of sentences three words
long."

"Nucleotides, base pairs, and codons," said
Pakkpekatt. "This is elementary biology."

Eckels's gaze narrowed as he looked toward the
colonel. "Yes," he said. "Every sentence specifies a component of a biochemical structure. The instructions for
building a particular structure may be hundreds or
thousands of paragraphs long."

Pleck sat forward. "So are the Qella part of this
pattern as well?"

"Yes—and no," Eckels said. "Most Qella cells, including reproductive cells, use the same alphabet, vocabulary, and grammar." He smiled and nodded to
himself. "But the Eicroth bodies do not. They use an
entirely different alphabet with *six* letters, and sentences
of five words. And they use these extraordinary extended proteins to build structures that seem to exist on
the dividing line between living and nonliving."

"Are you certain?" asked Pakkpekatt. "Why didn't
the people who discovered them know any of this?"

"Because I have something available to me that
they didn't—as do you." Eckels sat back and laced his
fingers together in his lap, clearly enjoying their rapt
attention. "They didn't have any examples of the finished product to compare with those instructions. I have
six hundred of them."

"Six hundred?" Hammax said. "Six hundred bodies?"

"Artifacts," Pakkpekatt said.

"Yes," Eckels said, raising an eyebrow. "Six hundred Qella artifacts—no, we will need a new word for them now. We recorded them as being fashioned from natural materials. Now I know that they were not fashioned but—grown. The Eicroth bodies contain their plans."

"You were able to match your artifacts with the sequences we gave you?"

"Every one of them," said Eckels. "Do you understand what I am saying, Colonel?"

"Yes," said Pakkpekatt.

"No," said Hammax.

Eckels turned toward the soldier. "Every sentient being inherits its species' memories through both body and mind—the ancient duality," he said, his tone fervent. "Humans found a way to extend our memories by recording our thoughts and collecting them in libraries. Somewhere a long time ago, the Qella found another way. They carried their libraries within their own bodies."

"And this helps us how?"

"I'm still missing something, too," said Taisden. "From what you've said, it seems to me that it's that much more important to send out the entire database."

Eckels's disappointment in their response to his revelations was evident on his face. He had proudly brought them a treasure, but they were too uncultured to appreciate its beauty.

"The database has three components," Eckels said with impatient annoyance. "The somatic cells, the lesser Eicroth bodies, and the greater Eicroth bodies. The match for every Qella artifact we recovered can be found in the lesser bodies. Then there's your piece of the puzzle—your dialog with the vagabond. You have two interrogatives and one successful reply."

"They appear in the greater Eicroth bodies," said Pakkpekatt.

"Yes," Eckels said, looking hopefully at the Hortek as he would at a student teetering on the verge of insight.

"That *is* what the greater bodies are," said

Pakkpekatt. "They are the instructions for building a starship from that which is more than inanimate and less than alive. The ship we are chasing was not designed or invented—it was remembered."

"Yes," Eckels said, relaxing into his chair and showing a relieved smile. "Yes, Colonel. However you came to it, at least *you* understand."

"Do you think that somewhere in those sequences is a code that will call the vagabond back to Qella?" asked Taisden.

"Do you want an expert opinion or a personal one?"

"I'll take two for the price of one, if I have a choice."

"The expert declines to opine, due to lack of supporting evidence," Eckels said. "But personally—since it has not gone somewhere *else* in all this time—I suspect that it was intended to come back here."

"What are the chances that what we propose to do will just confuse it—like throwing all the switches at once?"

Eckels shook his head. "You are asking for reassurances quite beyond my ability to offer—"

At that moment, shrill alarms began to sound both in the suite and the corridor beyond. Taisden was the first out of the lounge by two steps and the first to the bridge by five.

"Meeting's over," he called back to the others as he slipped into the number two seat. "You'd better get back to *Penga Rift* right away, Doctor. Colonel, mayhaps we should have been talking more about what to do *after* the quarry puts a leg in our snare."

"What are you talking about?" Eckels demanded. "Colonel, what's happening?"

Taisden sent the long-range image to the primary sensor display, then shook his head in amazement as he glanced up at it. "See for yourself," he said. "The vagabond's just jumped into the system—and she's headed this way."

Chapter 9

◆

The director of Alpha Blue was nodding off in his chair, his office lit only by the bluish glow of the primary status display. With his shoes off and the top two fasteners of his civilian blouse unbuttoned, he looked like an old bachelor who had fallen asleep in front of the holo.

"Admiral Drayson?"

Drayson's eyes snapped open and found the face of Major Aama, one of his senior facilitators. "Yes?"

"Admiral, you said you wanted to be notified immediately," she said. "We have a tracking update on *Millennium Falcon*."

"Go."

"She's reached the N'zoth system," Aama said, turning and pointing a controller at the display. "She's standing off at twelve hundred radii below the plane—the best guess is that they're scanning the system before jumping in."

"They'd have to, if they're going to try a close-intercept jump," said Drayson, leaning forward and rubbing his eyes. "Is *Pride of Yevetha* still in-system?"

"Still in-system and still in orbit around N'zoth. It's getting a bit crowded in that neighborhood, though—

four more Imperial types have shown up, and six more T-types have lifted off from the planet."

"Include that in the update packet and have it sent immediately."

"It's already been seen to."

Drayson rocked back in his chair. "So there are sixteen thumpers there now," he mused. "Not the best news for Chewbacca's people. What assets do we have in the area?"

"There are four stasis probes on station, and two more moving into position."

"Let's take a look," Drayson said, gesturing at the display. "We may have to think about sacrificing one or more of them if it'll give the *Falcon* a fighting chance to get the job done."

"Yes, sir—I think we can probably arrange a timely diversion or two. Sir, are you sure you want to continue the blackout where the Princess is concerned? It could give her a real lift to know—"

"Not at these odds," Drayson said firmly. "Even with what we've been able to pass to Chewbacca through Formayj, I don't think they have more than one chance in twenty of getting in and out in one piece. As for finding Han alive—" He sighed. "But that's still probably a better chance than any other rescue effort would have. Is Ackbar still talking about a battle group assault supporting a Jedi retrieval team?"

"Yes. They've got the lights on late over at Fleet tonight."

"The general will never agree to it," said Drayson. "And he'll be right not to. So let's be creative, Major, and figure out what else we can do from here to shift the odds."

Given an unobstructed view and the eight-kilometer length of the Yevethan flagship, the oversized and exceptionally sensitive sensor dish atop the *Millennium Falcon* had no difficulty picking out *Pride of Yevetha* from among the many ships orbiting N'zoth.

But fixing the orbit of the flagship with enough precision to jump within a thousand meters of it required more than a single snapshot. Chewbacca needed to know not only the flagship's orbital track, but also the tracks of any ships near it or en route to it. The task was complicated by the distances involved—when looking at the tracking data, Chewbacca was looking several minutes into the past. He could only guess about the present and the future, and a wrong guess would mean failure—even sudden death.

There was no perfect answer. The closer they were to N'zoth, the more current the tracking data would be, but the more likely it was that the *Falcon* would be spotted. The longer they waited, the more complete the tracking data would be, but, again, the more likely it was that *Falcon* would be spotted.

Chewbacca's natural impatience with anything other than a direct frontal assault only aggravated the matter. He had to keep reminding himself of the lessons of the Shadow Forest, and the difference between stalking and making the kill.

For the first few minutes after reaching the N'zoth system, Chewbacca was alone in the cockpit. Lumpawarrump was in the lower gun turret, Jowdrrl in the upper. Meanwhile, Shoran and Dryanta were checking the equipment that had been mounted in place of the escape pods at Esau's Ridge.

The starboard pod had been replaced by a mine launcher loaded with sixteen firecracker mines. The portside pod had been replaced by a hull-cutting ring, a traditional tool of both pirates and police. Both devices were critical—if not to the mission, then to their confidence that they could survive it.

When Dryanta was satisfied that the cutting ring was ready, he moved on to the crew quarters and began triple-checking the boarding party's weapons. Because they expected heavy resistance, bowcasters had given way to Draggis blaster rifles and fusion-cutter grenades.

When Shoran was finished arming the mines, he came forward and joined Chewbacca in the cockpit.

[Everything is ready,] he said.

Chewbacca's reply was interrupted by a double chirp from the comm board, signifying an incoming message. The encrypted transmission carried a priority flag and a short holo header.

[Formayj,] Chewbacca said. [Curious.]

"Chewbacca, hot-blooded friend," said the broker cheerfully. "Mining my archives, I found something else maybe you can use. No charge—tell Solo I will get it back from him at sabacc."

By the time the attached data had been downloaded, Dryanta had replaced Lumpawarrump in the lower gun turret, and the youth joined his father in the cockpit.

[What are you looking at?] he asked eagerly.

[A friend sent something interesting,] Chewbacca said.

[Can I see?]

Chewbacca waved a hand toward the data display and shifted to his left so that Lumpawarrump could lean in between him and Shoran.

What he saw was a Fleet Intelligence assault plan for a Super Star Destroyer—a complete three-dimensional technical drawing of the ship with the location of the cell blocks marked, the best breaching sites highlighted, and the shortest paths between them drawn in.

[We're sure to find him now, aren't we?] Lumpawarrump asked excitedly. [How does Formayj do it? Where does he get his information?]

[Exactly my question,] said Shoran. [Chewbacca, this gift worries me. Would you trust Formayj to guard your back?]

[That question does not trouble me,] said Chewbacca. [Formayj can make more money cheating his customers than killing them. Lumpawarrump, call the others down from the turrets—I am ready to make the jump. I want everyone to study this on the way in. Shoran, launch the first string of mines.]

[Yes, Father,] said the youth, hastening away.

[Yes, cousin,] said Shoran, leaning forward to the controls.

Chewbacca did not point out to either of them that, unlike the material Formayj had delivered to him at Esau's Ridge, the assault plan could not have come from any data mine or broker's archive—the timestamp on the document was less than forty hours old.

I wonder who this map was drawn for, Chewbacca thought as he set up the jump. *And I wonder what happened to them.*

[Mines are away.]

Chewbacca threw the throttles forward, opening up a gap between *Falcon* and the rocketing mines. When the gap had reached five hundred kilometers, he moved his large, furred hand to the hyperdrive controls.

[Set off the string,] he ordered.

Shoran sent the triggering signal, and as the first of the mines exploded spectacularly behind them, Chewbacca pushed the ship forward into hyperspace, racing the light of the explosion to N'zoth.

By necessity, the plan was simplicity itself: Hit fast and hit hard.

When the *Millennium Falcon* burst out of hyperspace eleven hundred meters off the starboard bow of *Pride of Yevetha,* the intense burst of light and radiation from the first of the firecracker mines had just flooded the sensors of the Yevethan defense grid, momentarily blinding the operators and scrambling the analyzers. The mines continued to explode at ten-second intervals, effectively masking the Cronau radiation from both ends of the *Falcon*'s microjump.

Meanwhile, Chewbacca whipped the transport into a smart half turn, standing it on its tail with the engines at maximum thrust. That maneuver quickly killed off the ship's velocity, at g-loads that tested the limits of even Wookiee physiology. For the gun crews aboard the Yevethan flagship, it was like looking up into the sub-atomic fury of a fusion reactor. For seconds afterward, the best-positioned batteries could not see to find their target.

Those were precious seconds to the *Falcon*. As quickly as the ship slowed, Chewbacca diverted engine power to the combat shields, reserving only enough to wheel the ship over on its back and match orbital velocities with the great Star Destroyer. By the time the first blaster bolts lanced out from the side of *Pride of Yevetha* and from the two trifoil fighters closing in, the *Falcon* was inside the shield radius, and Chewbacca had spotted his landing site.

Following their instructions, the moment the *Falcon* came under fire, Jowdrrl and Dryanta began a savage counterattack with the ship's quad turrets. Chewbacca roared with delight as a Yevethan fighter disappeared in a fireball, and growled at Shoran to launch the remaining mines. When the mines were away, he sent the *Falcon* diving edgewise toward the many-faceted hull of the Star Destroyer.

[Go stand by the cutter,] Chewbacca ordered Shoran as he guided the *Falcon* low across the face of the flagship.

By the time Shoran reached the port pod hatch where the hatch-cutting mechanism was attached, Chewbacca had gently nestled the *Falcon* against the enemy vessel's hull, allowing the cutting ring's magna grapples to grab hold. By the time Chewbacca rejoined Shoran at the hatch, the cutting ring had already burned halfway through the armored plasteel. Lumpawarrump was there as well, holding both Chewbacca's weapons and his own, ready to take up his assigned task of defending the entrance to the *Falcon*.

[Chewbacca!] Jowdrrl shouted down the access tunnel. <They've stopped firing on us—all of a sudden, just like that. I can see half a dozen fighters flying past, but they're ignoring us. Should I fire on them? Maybe they've lost us in the clutter down here.>

<Hold your fire—it just means they expect to handle us from the inside.> Chewbacca collected his blaster

rifle from Lumpawarrump, then placed a paw on his son's shoulder. [Go trade places with Jowdrrl.]

[Father—]

[Hurry.]

The nitrogen overpressure pumped into the space between the two ships before the final burn-through caused the metal disc cut from *Pride of Yevetha*'s hull to blow back into the enemy ship as a spectacular half-ton projectile.

Chewbacca and Shoran poured through the opening moments later, each wielding a heavy blaster in each hand. Standing back to back, they quickly cut down the half dozen Yevetha who came running at the sound of the breach.

As Chewbacca stepped over the bodies he saw that none of the Yevetha had been armed. [Ship's crew,] he said to Shoran. [Troops will be next.]

Still back-to-back, they hurried down corridor 278 toward detention block three.

Lin Prell, senior tender of the breederies of Viceroy Nil Spaar, paid no mind to the alarms sounding at the monitoring console. They concerned matters outside his realm, and the new hanging in alcove five needed its blood wash.

After that, he would check the temperature of all the active alcoves, record the growth of the other fertilized casks, and wet-sweep alcove seven for the *mara-nas* expected later that night. And when he could find no more work in this breedery, there were four others he could inspect—anything to keep his hands and mind busy, to keep his thoughts away from the castration knife that had been delivered to his quarters this morning, and the example he was expected to set.

In that frame of mind, Lin Prell almost welcomed the interruption when two hulking, shaggy-furred ver-

min blasted through the wall of the monitor room and
began shooting up the consoles.

There will be much work to do—much work, he
thought as he hurried down the narrow corridor toward
the commotion.

"What is it? What do you want?" he called ahead,
catching a glimpse of one of the invaders moving about
the outer compartment.

The only answer was a horrible growl and another
volley of blaster fire around the mouth of the corridor.
Lin Prell quickly reexamined his commitment to protecting Nil Spaar's progeny, and then began to back-
pedal down the metal walkway.

The monsters were apparently incapable of speech,
so Lin Prell made no further attempts to communicate
with them. When one of the creatures appeared at the
end of the corridor, roaring in savage fury, the senior
keeper hurled himself into the nearest unused alcove
and secured the door behind him. As he huddled in the
corner, waiting, he comforted himself with the thought
that he might never see the black-handled knife again.

[Where are they?] Chewbacca roared. [Where are
the prisoners? What are these repulsive things?] Raising
the rifle, he blasted the fleshy sac hanging from the cell
wall, causing a pulpy explosion. [Honor brother!] he
roared. [Call to me!]

There was no response, leading to a murderous
growl of frustration. With Shoran guarding his back,
Chewbacca picked his way down the corridor, peeking
into each cell in turn and then laying heavily on the
triggers of his weapons.

[Come on,] Shoran urged. [This is a hothouse—
they're holding him somewhere else. We have to keep
moving.]

Chewbacca peered through the grating of the cell
door at the Yevetha cowering within. He bared his teeth
and growled, low and ominously.

[Come on!] Shoran said, pulling Chewbacca away.

* * *

An eerie silence continued to surround the *Falcon*.

From the gun turrets, Lumpawarrump and Dryanta could count dozens of fighters cruising over the hull of the Star Destroyer—obviously searching for the intruder, and inexplicably unable to locate it. One fighter had passed within seventy meters of the ship, so close that Dryanta could see the pilot's face, so close that it was all Lumpawarrump could do to keep his hands off the triggers of the Dennia quad.

Even stranger were the comlink reports from Jowdrrl at her station guarding the hatch.

[Someone talk to me,] she said.

[We're here,] Dryanta assured her.

[I just had visitors,] she said. [Nine of them, almost as big as Shoran and armed like stormtroopers.]

[Help's coming,] said Lumpawarrump.

[No, stay where you are—they're gone now. But I don't know why,] Jowdrrl said. [They looked over the bodies in the corridor, stood around jabbering for a minute or two, then walked right past the cut-hatch on their way out.]

[That doesn't make any sense,] Lumpawarrump protested.

[I know. I was ready for them to rush me, but they never even glanced in my direction—as if they couldn't see that there was a hole in the bulkhead big enough to crawl through.]

[Just like our fighters up here,] said Dryanta, both wonder and worry evident in his voice. [Like we've become invisible. I don't understand it.]

Detention block two had been modified as well, though it was empty and deserted. But by the time Chewbacca and Shoran were ready to leave it, their noisy entrance had drawn a small crowd of Yevethan soldiers to the corridor outside.

With no more than a glance between them, the two Wookiees plunged through the destroyed entryway, turning back-to-back the moment they were clear of it. By the luck of the draw, Chewbacca had five targets in front of him, Shoran eight.

Roaring defiance, Chewbacca sprayed the corridor with crisscrossing blaster bolts. The last of his targets was tottering when he heard Shoran grunt, and felt him sag against his back. A whiff of burnt hair and fresh blood reached Chewbacca's nostrils.

Whirling, Chewbacca caught Shoran up with one hand before he could fall and dispatched the last two Yevetha with a flurry of shots from the blaster in the other hand.

Then he turned his attention to the limp weight cradled in the crook of his arm. And what he saw drove him to howl with fury and scatter a dozen more blaster bolts into the corpses littering the floor.

[Shoran has fallen,] he called over the comlink when the impulse was spent. [Dryanta, come for him.]

Lumpawarrump was the first to the cut-hatch, beating Dryanta by three steps. [I'm going,] he said to Jowdrrl. [I know the map. You don't need me in the gun turret. And Dryanta shouldn't go alone.]

Jowdrrl saw the determination in his eyes, the eagerness in his stance, and did not argue. [Go,] she said. [Just remember that the Yevetha can see *you* perfectly well.]

Glancing down at his hands, the youth clicked his blaster's lock to ACTIVE and checked the power level. [We'll remember,] he said. [Dryanta?]

She nudged him from behind. [Take the lead.]

They met Chewbacca halfway to detention block two. Dryanta took Shoran from him without a word and hurried away back toward the *Falcon,* leaving Lumpawarrump with his father.

The two stood looking into each other's eyes appraisingly, one searching for strength, the other for approval. Then Chewbacca grunted and turned away.

[Follow,] he said. [Protect my back.]

*   *   *

Detention block one was being guarded by half a dozen armed Yevetha, which raised Chewbacca's hopes. But when he and his son had blasted their way through the interference, all they found were more of the grossly distended fleshy sacs hanging in the cells.

[This is taking too long—there are too many places he could be,] Chewbacca fumed. [They will have killed him or moved him by now.]

[Father, when I think about Han, I do not see him in a place like this—]

[Be quiet—I have to think.]

[I keep seeing him in a room full of people—a large room, and all different species. I don't know where this picture comes from—]

[I do not believe this,] Chewbacca said. But Lumpawarrump's words had put the picture in his mind as well.

[And yet I see what I see, Father. It comes to me without imagining. Is it a deception?]

[When did this vision present itself to you?]

[While I was in the turret—and it will not leave me. It is most insistent.]

Chewbacca growled and blasted the ceiling at random. The thought of Han was now inextricably connected to an oddly detailed vision of a high-ceilinged compartment half filled with a zoo of species. The image would not leave his mind either, and he could not see Han in any other surroundings. [This is powerfully annoying—and I do not understand it.]

[Father, what if the enemy has taken many hostages? What if Han is just one of hundreds? Where would he be then?]

There were noises in the outer corridor, and Chewbacca moved to the ruined security door. [In your mind, as you see Han,] he called. [Are there any markings, any numbers or words?]

Lumpawarrump squeezed his eyes closed. [Yes. Yes, on the wall—D-two.]

It was the same as what Chewbacca saw—bold

black lettering high on the bulkhead above the prisoners: CARGO D2.

[The mass detention holds,] Chewbacca roared.
[Come!]

Back to back, Chewbacca and Lumpawarrump
fought their way forward to cargo hold D2. Strangely,
the resistance seemed to weaken rather than strengthen
as they went, almost as though they were moving too
fast for their pursuers to find them—or as though the
carnage they left in their wake discouraged other
Yevetha from getting in the way of a headlong Wookiee
charge.

But the guards and patrols they did encounter
fought tenaciously, never flinching or fleeing. Armed or
unarmed, alone or in groups, the Yevetha confronted
the intruders with a foolish courage that made them
easy targets and persistent threats. Chewbacca and
Lumpawarrump were forced to fire on anything that
moved and to keep firing until it stopped moving. By the
time their objective was in sight, the gauge on
Lumpawarrump's hand blaster was nearing the POWER
LOW mark, and the gauges on both of Chewbacca's were
closing in on POWER CRITICAL.

Ahead of them was one final hurdle. Unlike with
the detention blocks, blowing a hole in the bulkhead
with a grenade threatened the occupants of the cargo
hold. But the sectional doors of the hold were guarded
by half a dozen Yevetha deployed behind a pair of Imperial portable shields. The waist-high curved panels contained both ray-shield generators and energy absorbers,
and the Yevetha had nothing to fear from hand blasters
so long as they stayed behind the arc of the shields.

Worse, the doors to the hold were on the other side
of a hundred-meter wide flight deck—a deck that normally housed some of the fighters now searching for the
Falcon, and offered no cover whatever when they were
gone.

[Your bowcaster,] Chewbacca said as they crouched in the hatchway.

Lumpawarrump unslung the weapon and began to surrender it to his father, but found to his surprise there was no hand extended to take it from him. Instead, Chewbacca was offering him slug cores—the nuclei of the explosive quarrels.

[First, the shields,] Chewbacca said, gesturing with his blaster. [Then go for your enemies on the extreme left and right. That will likely freeze the others and keep them bunched up for you. You must fire as quickly as your bowcaster allows—as when trying to take *flarion* before the flock scatters into the cover.]

[Yes, Father.]

[I will divide their attention, as one gives the thar-riarr a morsel to distract it,] Chewbacca said. [Try to keep your quarrels out of my back, son.]

Lumpawarrump laughed easily. [Try not to run in front of my sights, Father.]

Chewbacca thumbed his comlink. [Jowdrrl.]

[Here, cousin.]

[Prepare to make a pickup from the flight deck which is directly forward of your position.]

[I will seal the hatch and be ready for your call.]

Chewbacca looked back at Lumpawarrump. [This is your *hrrtayyk*.]

[I am ready.]

Chewbacca gestured, and Lumpawarrump stood up into the hatchway, bringing the bowcaster up to chest height as he rose. The first explosive quarrel was away before he was fully erect, the second before Chewbacca had taken his first long stride out onto the flight deck.

The twin explosions that came an instant later were compact and focused. One shield was driven violently backward, knocking two of the Yevetha off their feet. The other shield simply shattered, pelting the deck, the bulkhead, and the guards with sharp-edged fragments.

Tracking his targets through the smoke as though

they were shadows in the underbrush, Lumpawarrump
kept firing. One quarrel burned out the thorax of a
Yevethan guard, and the next spun his nearest companion around like a ragdoll.

Just then, Chewbacca loosed a blood-chilling howl
and began spraying the flight deck with his blaster. The
howl contained all of Chewbacca's grief over Shoran
and his fury over Han, and it riveted the attention of the
surviving guards. With Chewbacca's hunger for vengeance driving his long legs, he crossed the open deck
with stunning speed. None of the few blaster bolts directed his way came anywhere near him.

By the time Chewbacca reached what was left of
the guard station, the return fire had ceased. Every one
of the guards had fallen victim to Lumpawarrump's
steady hand and hunter's eye. True, three guards still
had some fight left in them, despite massive bowcaster
wounds—but Chewbacca did not object to that.

He crushed the chest of one who was trying to rise
from the deck, then threw himself on the back of another and broke his neck with a savage twist. Spinning
away from the toppling corpse, Chewbacca found himself face-to-face with the last guard.

The Yevetha was bleeding profusely from gaping
shrapnel wounds in the shoulder and right cheek, and
his thorax plates were scorched and bubbled. He
slashed the air with his claws, and Chewbacca roared a
challenge. They charged each other, meeting in a collision that would have leveled lesser creatures.

Their short struggle ended with Chewbacca hoist-
ing his huge attacker overhead and hurling him against
a structural column. The Yevetha slid heavily to the
deck and never moved again, his back broken. Standing
over the body, Chewbacca tipped back his head and
made the Wookiee triumph-cry echo to the farthest corners of the flight deck.

Then he turned away and waved Lumpawarrump
across to join him.

Only then did Chewbacca see that his son was injured, dragging his right leg as he ran. When and how

seriously Lumpawarrump had been wounded, Chewbacca did not know—he only knew that his son had not uttered a sound in complaint, and that when the moment had come, he had faced the katarn without flinching, and his aim had been true.

The woman called Enara crouched beside where Han Solo lay dozing and lightly touched an unbruised spot on his forearm.

"There is fighting on the ship," she whispered. "Your friends have come for you."

Moving awakened a thousand pains and brought a sharp wince to Han's face, but he struggled to a sitting position nevertheless. "For me? How do you know?"

"I know," she said, her face drawn. "I have called them to us, and they have finally heard me. Come, we must move you. It is not safe to be close to the walls."

"I don't understand," Han said. But he allowed Enara to help him limp to the center of the hold. The effort left him weak, making it necessary for him to lay himself out once more on the uncomfortably hard surface. "I don't hear anything."

"They are a long way from here. I cannot hide them—it is too much for me. But I will try to help them find you." Enara sat down beside him, arranging the folds of her scorched brown caftan around her as though it were a fine gown and she was expecting to receive guests. Then she cupped her hands lightly around one of his and looked away toward the locked loading doors that sealed them in.

Han did not question her words. She was a puzzling woman, given to curious pronouncements and long periods of distraction marked by a faraway gaze and an aversion to company. But of all the prisoners in the hold, Enara was the only one to step beyond her own fears and needs to befriend him. She had been the first to speak to him when he had first arrived, and hers had been the only compassionate face he had seen when he awoke in agony after the beating at the hands of Nil Spaar.

But the tenuous promise of a rescue was not enough to keep Han from dozing. Pain quickly exhausted him, and his bruised organs, his torn and battered muscles, assailed him relentlessly when he was conscious. Sleep was his only relief.

"The fighting is close now," Enara said during one of Han's wakeful moments. "If you need to walk—"

"If those doors open, I can get to them. But I still don't hear anything."

"Soon," she said.

He saw that her face was pale, and he felt her hands trembling, the skin that was usually soothingly cool now hot against his. "Enara—what's wrong?"

"I cannot keep them apart. So many dying—your way is so hard, so much chaos," Enara whispered.

"Are you some kind of empath?"

"It is not hard to feel death," she said. "They are coming. They are almost here."

It was at that moment that Han began to believe that something truly was happening aboard the starship. He struggled to a seated position just as Enara pitched forward, whimpering loudly, her palms pressed to her forehead, her tousled hair hiding her face.

Moments later, there were noises from beyond the doors—cries, blaster fire, thumps against the bulkhead, and a grating, unnerving sound that Han was certain he knew but which his pain-drugged mind could not identify. Then the small hatch inset into the large loading doors was flung open, and a towering Wookiee frame filled the opening.

"Chewie!"

With a piteous wail, Chewbacca rushed across the deck and scooped Han up into his arms. Throwing back his head and roaring delight, he spun Han in circles—a dance of joy.

"Ow—not so rough. What kept you?" Han answered gleefully. "Where's my ship?"

Then Han yelped as Chewbacca juggled him in an

effort to reach his comlink. After barking into the device, Chewbacca slung Han over his shoulder and started back toward the hatch, now guarded by another giant.

"Wait—wait—the others—wait, Chewbacca, the others. We have to take them, too—Enara, Taratan, Noloth—*stop,* you thick-headed furball," Han bellowed. "Put me down, I'm not dead yet. Enara!"

As Chewbacca reluctantly complied, Han saw that Enara was still seated where she had been, though no longer doubled over. "Come on," he called to her. "There's room for you, too, isn't there, Chewie? How many of them can we get—"

His words trailed off as he looked around the hold. None of the other prisoners had reacted at all to what was happening—they were scattered in their usual haunts and gatherings, sleeping, talking, sucking water from the drip-pipes.

"What's happening?" he asked, taking two unsteady steps toward Enara. "Come on—our reservation here's expired."

"I cannot go," Enara said. "Go, please—I am at my limit."

"I don't understand."

Enara shook her head sharply. When she did, the rest of the prisoners vanished, leaving only Enara, Han, and Chewbacca. Chewbacca whined unhappily and tightened his grip on his blaster.

"Now you are inside," she said, "seeing as I do."

"Where are the others?"

"They were never here," she said. "They escaped at the transfer camp and were picked up by *Star Morning.* They are elsewhere now, safe. You can go."

Chewbacca whined again and tugged at Han's shoulder.

"That was—they were an illusion?" Han said, ignoring Chewbacca's urgings. "You were covering their escape? Never mind, it doesn't matter—you can leave now, too. There's no one here to protect."

"I must stay," she said softly. "Denied his prizes,

Nil Spaar would try to replace them. Denied the security of their protection, he would seek security through the death of his enemies. Go, Han—I am not a prisoner here. I have chosen this freely. Go now."

Turning away from them, Enara lowered her chin to her collarbone. An instant later, the hostages reappeared—including a crippled, dozing Han Solo, lying on the deck beside Enara.

There was a cry from the Wookiee at the door, and then the achingly familiar roar of the *Falcon*'s engines.

"Enara—" Han said plaintively.

Then his legs buckled under him. Chewbacca caught him cleanly before he hit the deck, and would not listen to his protests as he carried him away.

Enara never looked up. Han's last glimpse of her was of a tiny woman with tangled hair, sitting cross-legged beside the man whose life she had just helped preserve.

At just about the same time that the *Millennium Falcon* was roaring away from *Pride of Yevetha* behind a curtain of exploding firecracker mines, *Mud Sloth* was dropping out of hyperspace in front of the Fifth Fleet's flag group.

Even as the forward pickets were relaying the contact to *Intrepid,* the gunship *Warrior* surged ahead, breaking formation to place itself on an intercept course.

"Contact ahead," the tactical officer announced to the bridge. "Type not identified. Size class, F—possibly a probe of some sort. She came right out of the heart of the cluster."

On the other side of the room, a blank display at comm three suddenly lit up with a string of numbers. "Receiving transmission from the contact—they're attempting to authorize a link."

That drew *Warrior*'s captain over to peer at the screen. "Sender code is valid, but it's coming over the air, unsecured—that's not a military transmitter," said the comm specialist. "Same with the authorization code—checks as valid but not current. Someone's trying to get in the front door without a key."

"I'd like to know who," said the captain. "Identify the sender code."

"Sir, it returns as classified."

"Really," said the captain. "Take us to level two alert and authorize the link."

The numbers vanished from the display, to be replaced by Luke Skywalker's face.

"Captain," said Luke's holo. "Do you recognize me?"

"I recognize who you appear to be," said the captain. "I have no information that that person was known or expected to be in this sector."

"Very good, Captain. By now you should have an identification on this ship and an assessment of its threat potential."

The captain looked away toward the tactical officer. "Transponder says it's civilian, yacht, skiff class, unarmed—now confirming from direct scans. It's a Verpine Adventurer, sir."

There were several snorts and chuckles around the room.

"'Unarmed' is not confirmed, Lieutenant," the captain said, turning back. "A ship of that size could easily carry tactical munitions in its passenger compartment."

Luke nodded in agreement. "I'd appreciate it if you'd rendezvous with me and have your people inspect the ship. Once you've satisfied yourself that I am who I appear to be, and that we haven't replaced the refresher with a fusion bomb," he said lightly, "I trust you can arrange for a ride or an escort to the flagship. I am carrying some extremely important information for the fleet commander."

The captain was well disciplined or stubborn enough not to bend. "Continue on your present course," he said. "Keep this channel open. We will rendezvous with you shortly." But when the link was closed, he turned to comm one. "Signal *Intrepid*, secure. Notify the general that Luke Skywalker is inbound."

When the message had been sent, comm two craned his head around toward the captain. "This is *good* news, right, sir?"

"I hope so, Lieutenant," the captain said grimly. "I dearly hope so."

By the time *Mud Sloth* came to rest in slots thirty-nine and forty on *Intrepid*'s forward flight deck, everyone in that section of the ship—and many elsewhere, in every other section—knew that Luke Skywalker was coming aboard.

No official announcement had been made. The scuttlebutt spread among the officers and crew via two distinct chains of friendships and contacts—with equal rapidity, but slightly different flavors of meaning. Among the officers, it was styled as "Heard the big news?" To the crew, it was definitely good news.

Luke could see it in the grins of the deck crew as they tied down the skiff and in the jaunty thumbs-up they offered to him as he clambered down out of the ship. When he turned and helped first Wialu and then Akanah down, the mood around him changed for a time. But soon he felt the focus shifting back to him again—a focus for hope and reassurance, for belligerent pride, even chauvinism and xenophobia.

It's as though they think I'm here to win the war for them, Luke thought as he followed their escort off the flight deck. *But it's the people they're nearly ignoring who I'm hoping can do that.*

He had wanted and asked for a private meeting with A'baht, but that was perhaps too much to expect. Either he was too much of a magnet, even among the officers, or A'baht's idea of "private" automatically included two spare colonels and an extra captain.

Luke dealt with them by ignoring them. "What's the status of the conflict, General?" he asked, offering no introductions for his own companions.

"The President has declared war on the Yevetha," said A'baht. "As a first step, we're preparing to return to Doornik Three-nineteen and take it away from them. We've also gotten more aggressive in searching for the remaining shipyards. And planning's underway for deeper penetrations of the cluster, all the way to the Yevethan homeworlds."

"Are any of your forces currently engaged in hostilities?"

"No. This is the lull before the storm," A'baht said. "Now, can I ask you to explain your presence? I assume that if you had been sent here by the President, we would have been notified in advance."

"I've come here from J't'p'tan. On your charts, Doornik Six-twenty-eight-E. Before that—well, the full explanation would take too long, and I'm not prepared to share all of it in any case," Luke said. "But the part that matters is simple and straightforward. I'm here to offer you a chance to take that first step in a different direction."

Even for someone with Luke's status, Colonel Corgan, Colonel Mauit'ta, and Captain Morano were a tough audience—especially when what was being peddled had the look of magic.

"Do I need to defend the Jedi to you as well?" Luke snapped in response to the most recent expression of skepticism. "The nature of the universe transcends the definitions of science, and the possibilities of the universe exceed the limitations of technology."

"I am not eager to risk the lives of my crew on tricks and invisible forces that cannot be measured," said Morano.

"You're apparently not eager to *save* the lives of your crew, either."

"I prefer to trust what I know. We can win this war with the weapons we have."

Loose objects were scarce on a ship rigged for combat, so Luke found it necessary to create some. Reach-

ing out with the Force, he ripped the decorations from
the three officers' uniforms and deposited them in neat
rows on A'baht's desk.

"Now you know a little more about invisible
forces," Luke said.

"This is not helping," General A'baht said with a
sigh.

"I'm simply trying to remind them that the Force is
as real as anything in this room—it's a mystery, but not
a fantasy," Luke said. He pointed a finger in the direction of Morano, who was still staring wordlessly at the
naked fabric where his service bars had been. "His way
of winning this war means thousands, tens of thousands, of deaths on both sides—needless deaths."

"Needless only if your trick fools the Yevetha,"
said Corgan, gathering up his decorations with a cross
expression on his craggy face. "And you can't know if it
will fool them."

"What Wialu is offering us is no 'trick,' " Luke said
with studied patience. "Her instrumentality is older
than the technology of that blaster you wear, and more
powerful. But it's more *difficult*—it takes a life commitment, not just a squeeze of the trigger."

"Perhaps she could tell us more about how it
works," said Mauit'ta.

Luke turned away, raising his hands in the air in
disgust and frustration.

"Reflection," said Wialu, "from the surface of the
Current."

"I'm afraid that's not very useful to me," said
A'baht as Luke turned back. "You must realize that
you're asking us to mount a major military operation
around something we've never experienced. Would it be
possible to have a demonstration?"

Luke expected Wialu to refuse that imposition, but
she surprised him. "You are asking me to create a major
projection of something *I* have never experienced," she
said. "It seems it would be to the good of all if you
would demonstrate first, and then you can judge my
practice."

A'baht glanced at Corgan. "Colonel?"

"Well, there are about twenty ships from the Fourth due to join us in"—he glanced at his chrono—"about half an hour. Would that do?"

"I would like to be as close to the phenomenon as possible," said Wialu.

"There's an observation bubble on the maintenance rover," Marano offered. "I think we can probably squeeze the seven of us in there. If you don't object to the presence of skeptics, that is—"

"Your beliefs are irrelevant to me," Wialu said. "I am empowered by mine."

When the rover had reached the fifty-kilometer boundary of the arriving task force's jump target, General Etahn A'baht tapped the driver on the shoulder from behind.

"That's close enough, son," said A'baht. "And drop us a few kilometers below the entry track. I don't wish to have the command staff erased by a navigational error."

"I'm more worried about being erased by an error of enthusiasm by some gunnery lieutenant," said Corgan. "Those ships are jumping into a hot zone, and they're not going to be expecting us to be sitting here waiting for them."

"Akanah will address that," said Wialu. "The ships will not see us."

"What do you mean?" asked A'baht.

"General, just take her at her word," Luke said. "If I had wanted it that way, you wouldn't have known *Mud Sloth* was in the neighborhood until I'd parked it in your space."

Corgan shook his head disbelievingly, but there was no opportunity to pursue the issue.

"Here they come," said Maiut'ta.

One after another, the great ships emerged out of the center of overlapping white flashes of radiation, like new stars winking on in the night. Cruisers and attack carriers, Star Destroyers and gunships, all quickly closed the distance to the rover, roaring by overhead in a spectacular display.

"Are we allowed to talk?" asked Corgan.

"Patience," said A'baht, gazing up with his fingers laced together behind him. "Patience and attentiveness will both be rewarded, I suspect."

"I don't take your hint."

"How many ships were we expecting?"

"Twenty-two."

A'baht nodded. "I have counted thirty so far."

Corgan and Morano stared, gaping, as the broad hull of a fleet carrier sliced the vacuum above their heads. "That has to be a mistake."

Luke caught A'baht's faint smile. "I'm confident I can still count to thirty," he said. "I suggest you check with Tracking."

Maiut'ta was already reaching for his comlink. "Sweep the arriving ships," he ordered. "Give me a count."

"Thirty-eight—forty—forty-one—still clicking over."

"Are they all normal tracks?"

"Everything as expected—wait a minute, some of the IDs are duplicated. Colonel, do you want to tell me what's going on now?"

"No, Lieutenant. Stand by," Mauit'ta said, switching off the comlink.

A'baht turned to the other officers. "Well, gentlemen, we have our demonstration." He gestured with his hand as a gunship rumbled by just a kilometer away. "Which ones are real? That one? The next? I can't tell— I suspect even Tracking can't." He turned back to Akanah. "Thank you. I am quite satisfied."

In the next moment, half the battle group passing in review vanished. Wialu sagged noticeably and sought her seat immediately afterward. Akanah settled beside her protectively.

"General, what did I just see?" the rover driver asked in an awestruck voice.

"Nothing, son," said A'baht. "Officially and literally nothing."

"But—"

"Don't ask about it and don't think about it," the general said. "Just get us back to the barn as quickly as you can." He glanced at Luke. "We all have a lot to do."

They were on final approach to *Intrepid* when they were waved off for the launch of a flight of fighters. Morano's face immediately took on a worried expression. "What's that about? Patrol rotation isn't for another hour."

He got an answer from the flight controller after the rover landed.

"Outer patrol is moving out on an intercept," the controller advised them. "We've got a ship coming in from the interior, high speed, no proper ID, nothing but some kind of jammer or scrambler signal in response to our hail."

Morano wheeled around to face Wialu. "Is this part of your demonstration, too?"

"No," she said, shaking her head. "This one belongs to you."

"General, Commander Jarrou has taken the group back to a level two alert," the controller continued. "Captain, you and the general are wanted upstairs, flank speed."

Luke raced to the bridge at General A'baht's heels, then anchored himself in front of a tracking display. The image was still small and two-dimensional. His head cocked to the side, Luke studied the image as it slowly grew larger.

"Specialist, how fast is that ship moving?"

"Eight sublight, sir. She's cooking."

"Can you let me hear that jammer signal she was transmitting?"

"Still transmitting," said the specialist. "On the

headphones, sir. Watch the volume—it's an eardrum-killer."

Luke slipped the earpieces in place and listened. Almost at once, he laughed.

"Sir?"

"That's not a jammer. That's Shyriiwook. Wookiee-talk," he said, tearing off the headphones. "It's Chewbacca, and he's upset about something." Luke peered at the display again. "He wants those pilots to get out of the way. General A'baht!"

A'baht looked up from a huddle with the tactical officer. "What now?"

"Better tell those fighters they're on a rendezvous-and-escort, not an intercept," said Luke. "That's the *Millennium Falcon* coming in."

Shoran and Han were both carried off the *Falcon* on medevac stretchers.

By appearance alone, they looked to be in equally dire straits, but the indicator lights on the stretchers' monitor panels foretold their different destinations. The indicators on Shoran's stretcher were static and mostly red, and he was taken directly to *Intrepid*'s morgue. The indicators on Han's stretcher were jumpy and mostly yellow, and he was taken directly to a bacta tank in med ward one.

There was no chance for Luke or anyone else to talk to Han before he went into the tank. He had apparently been unconscious since before the *Falcon* jumped out from N'zoth, his already fragile state aggravated by the stresses of the rescue, particularly the high-g escape. And even if Han had been conscious, there was Chewbacca to contend with—the Wookiee hovered over Han so protectively that he got in the way of the doctor and the medical droid, and ultimately had to be dragged back from the triage table by two of his companions.

The four Wookiees made an impressive sight, and their presence in the med ward drew a great deal of curious attention. Luke thought he recognized the injured one as Lumpawarrump, a thought confirmed when Chewbacca made him the next object of his anxious hovering.

Lumpawarrump had limped off the ship under his own power, but the second-degree blaster burn on his right calf was ugly with leaking blisters and needed care as well. A translator droid arrived in time to assist K-1B to negotiate with his patient.

"Skin and hair cell damage is serious. Underlying fat and muscle damage is limited," said K-1B. "All damage is repairable. Prescribe immersion, one session, ten hours."

Both Chewbacca and his son looked at the prep table where Han was being fitted with his breather and monitors. Chewbacca drew his upper lip back over his teeth in an expression of disgust, and Lumpawarrump shook his head vigorously as he growled an answer.

The droid's translation was diplomatic. "The patient has expressed an unwillingness to be immersed."

K-1B's head swiveled in a distinctively mechanical fashion. "Topical treatments are of limited effectiveness. Grafts are contraindicated for species with body fur. Scarring is likely without immersion."

Both Lumpawarrump and Chewbacca answered at once, and their growls had sharply contrasting timbres.

"The patient says that he finds scarring socially desirable. The patient's guardian expresses his concern that if the injury is not effectively treated, K-1B will experience serious malfunctions and system disruptions."

Despite the shadow of concern for both Han and Chewbacca's son, Luke could not contain a chuckle at the droid's obvious paraphrase. The sound led Chewbacca to look up and in Luke's direction—the first time their eyes had met since the *Falcon* had docked. The Wookiee gestured angrily toward Han, and voiced a sharp-edged rebuke. No translation was necessary. The look said, *Where were you?*

"I didn't know, Chewie," Luke said. "It wasn't

even in the TBM. The General says there was a complete blackout on the news. I was away, and no one told me. Not even Leia." He looked across the room at Han, who was at that moment being transferred from the prep table to the bacta tank. "I just didn't know."

Technically, the camp on Pa'aal, the primary moon of the fifth planet of the N'zoth system, was not a prison. Slaves are not housed in prisons.

The camp was the permanent residence of the surviving members of the former Black Sword Command occupation force under Governor Crollick. At its peak, it had housed nearly three hundred thousand—mostly human, and mostly from the crews of the Star Destroyers *Intimidator* and *Valorous,* captured intact by Yevethan raiders on what was to have been the final day of the Imperial occupation.

The captives had purchased their lives with service to the viceroy, and in the beginning, that service had been essential. They had taught the Yevetha both the operation of a capital warship and the final secrets of their construction. They had served aboard their renamed vessels under new, alien captains and labored in the shipyards under new, alien overseers. The knowledge in their heads and the experience in their hands made them valuable enough to keep alive—at least until the Yevetha had wrung every last secret from them.

In the first and second year, only the uncooperative were removed from the population on Pa'aal. But in the third year, their keepers began to thin their holdings in earnest. By that time, the overseers had a clearer idea of who had specialized technical skills and who did not. The latter could be replaced in their duties by Yevetha, and were—many trained their replacements before being executed. The former were kept without regard to need, as spare parts for the war machine the Yevetha were building.

Half the population of Pa'aal disappeared during the third year—most at the hands of the Yevetha, but no small number through suicide. Conditions on Pa'aal were desperate and miserable, and hope of rescue had collapsed as the coldly calculated winnowing wore on.

Those who survived to see the fourth year were in many ways a select group—smart, tough-minded, inured to the privations of their existence, astute in the politics of their status. And they had found a replacement for hope, in the form of a leader and a plan.

In the long years since, every slave taken from Pa'aal for a day's, a week's, a month's service to the Yevetha had gone willingly, with a purpose and a mission beyond mere survival. The more useful they were, the more opportunities there would be to advance the plan. They needed access to the ships, to materials and tools, to unsupervised time—all of which could only be obtained through guiltless and systematic collaboration with the enemy.

Despite their efforts, there had come a time when the Yevetha seemed to no longer need them, and Pa'aal had become not a storehouse but a dumping ground. An entire year would pass with no measurable progress and no promise of change. Suicide and the carelessness that went with profound depression once more began to thin the numbers.

But seven months ago, the slavemasters had started coming to Pa'aal again. For the first time since the end of the winnowing, there were Yevetha in camp for more than a few hours, observing, questioning. The additional scrutiny was more than balanced by the additional opportunity, as more and more of the population was called to service and carried off in the parade of shuttles. Before long, Pa'aal seemed primarily populated by ghosts.

Word of the reasons for the change filtered back with returnees—new ships being launched, new crews being trained, new problems with cloned drives and weapons. Gradually the whole story was pieced together, until the prisoners on Pa'aal were more aware of the coming war than the Yevetha themselves.

And through it all, the work went on, at an intense—even dangerous—pace.

"There is a moment coming," Major Sil Sorannan had told his secret command, "a moment of opportunity that will never be repeated in our lifetimes. If we are not ready when that moment comes, we will all die on Pa'aal."

Sorannan remembered his words as he gazed at the four tiny pulse-transceiver chips that had just been delivered to him by a courier from a returning work party.

"Major Neff said to tell you that they'd passed all the tests with generous margins," said the courier. "He has very high confidence that they're good."

Nodding, Sorannan gestured to the other man in the room. "Have the controllers brought here."

From four different parts of the compound, four very different—yet commonplace—objects were rounded up and placed before Sorannan. Using an engineer's loupe, an improvised jig, and a handheld microwelder, Sorannan added one of the chips to the circuitry concealed inside each of the objects.

The chips were the last pieces missing from the controllers, and Sorannan irreversibly sealed the clever access slides and panels before handing each object over to a courier.

"Deliver this to Dobbatek.

"See that this reaches Jaratt on *Valorous*.

"This is for *Harramin*.

"I want this delivered to Eistern on *Intimidator*. Tell him I will be there soon. Tell him to pass the word that it is almost time."

Chapter 10

◆

While Han slept in the healing bath of the bacta solution, the command staff analyzed the latest data from the stasis probes deep inside the cluster, and the Wookiees prepared the *Falcon* for the battle ahead. Not included in any of those activities, Luke found himself alone and with time on his hands.

He went by Wialu and Akanah's cabin, intending to reopen the subject of Nashira. But Wialu was not there, and Akanah would not tell him where he could find her.

"She will be in deep meditation until the time comes, preparing herself," said Akanah. "This will be very difficult—she must be strong enough to hold the projection even if fighting begins."

"Will you be helping her?"

"She has not asked that of me."

"Do you think that I can?"

"Ask me, or help her?"

"Help," he said.

"No. You have great power, Luke, but this is not a work of power. When you lay your touch on the Current, it is still a thousand times too forceful."

He digested that in silence. "Did you know that there's a Fallanassi aboard *Pride of Yevetha*? At least, that's how I sort it out, going by Chewbacca's account. A woman named Enara." He shook his head. "They had to have *some* kind of help. Going in there like that was crazy. Wookiee-crazy, the kind that comes from an excess of courage and a shortage of patience."

"Yes, I know," Akanah said.

"Will *she* be able to help Wialu?"

"I do not think so."

Luke frowned. "You seem to have gotten a lot more reluctant to talk to me since we reached J't'p'tan."

"Circumstances have changed," Akanah said with a small, rueful smile.

"Because Wialu is watching and listening?"

"We have lost more than privacy," she said. "We are no longer moving in the same direction."

"If you know that, you know more than I do about where I'm headed," Luke said, pulling a chair toward him and sitting down on it backward. "I have more questions now than ever."

"You must be greatly tempted to try to force Wialu to answer them," Akanah said.

"An occasional, resistible temptation," Luke admitted. "I know better."

"It would be an immeasurable mistake."

"I know that, too," he said. "But you could answer some of my questions—as my teacher."

Eyes downcast, Akanah shook her head. "I don't think so, Luke."

"Because of what Wialu said about your not having the right to? She said you were a child yourself—"

"She was right," Akanah said. "I told you on the day we met that I was incomplete—that there was a weakness, an empty space, in me—that the loss of what my mother would have taught me had left me less than whole."

"I suppose you did," Luke said. "I guess at the time, I paid more attention to what you were saying about me."

"It was easy enough for me to forget myself," said Akanah. "But even a short time with Nori was enough to show me how far I have strayed without guidance. These days in Wialu's company have shown me how far I have to go to return to the path."

"Your mother—Talsava—is she with the Circle?"

"No," Akanah said. "When we are finished here, I will ask Norika to be my teacher."

Luke folded his arms on the back of the chair and rested his chin on them. "So *your* journey is over."

She shook her head. "It is just beginning. I know that I must go back and unlearn before I can move forward again. Do not envy me too much, Luke."

Luke answered with a tight-lipped smile. "A momentary self-indulgence," he said. "Well, I suppose I can't ask you to work with me on the skill of concealment."

"You will need another teacher if you choose to follow this path and become an adept of the Current," she said, her expression earnest. "I hope that you will. You have great strength, Luke, but you hunger for lightness. That is part of the gift that you have been denied."

Frowning, Luke straightened his back and caught the top edge of the chair in his hands. "Maybe you can answer this question, at least—if Enara could conceal the *Falcon* and create phantom hostages, why couldn't she protect Shoran?"

"I am sorry for your friend's loss," Akanah said, then paused. "I do not know the limits of Enara's skill. But creating a reflection from the surface of the Current and merging nearby objects with the Current are very different tasks. It is terribly difficult to do both at the same time. And there is something else—a person does not stay settled in the flow the way an object without volition will."

Luke's eyes lit up. "Is *that* why the Circle is still at J't'p'tan—what you meant when you said they couldn't leave?" he asked. "Because it sounds as if the Fallanassi could hide the temple from the Yevetha and go away, and it would stay hidden—"

"Yes. Objects which are at rest, or which follow the current without resisting it, will remain merged until they are disturbed," she said. "All of the effort comes at the beginning, and a single adept can manage it. But hiding the community of H'kig requires the constant attention of a great many adepts, and the effort is never-ending."

As he listened to her, Luke experienced a flash of intuitive insight. "Yes. Yes, that's the only way it could be. Do you—"

"I have already said too much," she said, shaking her head. "Please, Luke, ask me no more questions. Answering you and refusing you bring me equal burdens of guilt."

"I'm sorry," Luke said. "I understand."

"You understand, and you used it to get your answer," Akanah said sharply. Then she showed a quick smile, taking the sting out of the rebuke. "Please, Luke—go now."

"All right," he agreed, standing and replacing the chair where it had been. But when he reached the cabin door, he stopped and looked back. "I'm sorry. I have to ask one more."

She nodded wordlessly, as though she had expected it.

"Did you see Nashira on J't'p'tan?"

"No," Akanah said with regret. "I do not know where she is."

It was decided early that the "phantom fleet" bluff should be played where it would have the most impact—in the light of N'zoth's sun, over the capital of the Duskhan League and the home of Viceroy Nil Spaar.

"It's the strongest Yevethan fleet we've located—especially in the wake of the rescue of the commodore," Corgan explained at the strategy session where the assault plans were first disclosed. "If the Yevetha are still monitoring developments on Coruscant through their spy network, they know that the President's sending us reinforcements, and that'll help sell the bluff.

"We've planned a feint at Doornik Three-nineteen

for the day before, just to keep them jumpy and maybe draw off a ship or two from somewhere else. And on the big day, we'll turn out in strength at Wakiza, Tizon, and Z'fell, plus go after the shipyard that just turned up near Tholaz. But the big play is at N'zoth—that's where we have to break them, one way or another."

Taking *Intrepid* to N'zoth meant a transfer for Han, from the flagship's medical ward to a medical frigate delegated to stay behind with the other noncombatants. The transfer, in turn, meant the first conscious moments for Han since he had come aboard.

Both Chewbacca and Luke took advantage of the opportunity. The Wookiee had an emotional reunion with Han while the doctors and K-1B gave him a quick but thorough hands-on exam. Luke did not intrude on that time, waiting instead to hitch a ride with Han on the transfer shuttle.

"Hey," said Han, craning his head at the sound of Luke's voice. "I used to know a guy who looked just like you."

"Whatever happened to him, anyway?" Luke bantered back, finding a perch beside the stretcher and catching Han's right hand in his own. "How are you doing?"

"You know you're getting old when you start wondering about what it is that's finally going to kill you," Han said with a pained grin. "I guess I'm gonna have to sit this one out, eh?"

"Unless we have a sudden need for underwater commandos," Luke said. "They tell me you're due for another five days in the tank."

Han's countenance darkened with concern. "Say, do you think you could use your powers of persuasion to get 'em to let me talk to Leia before they dunk me back under? Has anyone told her—"

"Already set up for you, Commodore, as soon as we reach the frigate," said the doctor seated at the head of the stretcher, monitoring the readouts.

"Of course she was told," Luke said. "The general

sent a message as soon as you were aboard, and Chewie talked to her later."

Luke saw that Han noted the omission. "Well, when you talk to her, make sure you mention I was bothering the lady doctors—otherwise she'll worry," he said. "Say, how about Chewie's kid? He sure hit his growth, didn't he? Chewie said this was some sort of rite of passage, and he's taken a new name— Lumpawaroo, I think it was."

"With Waroo as the familiar," said Luke. "I think it means 'son of courage.'"

"Well, that fits—both ways," Han said. "They said back there that Waroo will be coming over to the frigate, too. I think that leaves the *Falcon* one hand short."

"I don't think I'm welcome to sign on," said Luke, squeezing and then releasing Han's hand. "Chewbacca seems to think I abandoned you to the Yevetha."

"Aw, he'll get over it. He's still wound up, that's all. I couldn't talk him out of going back to N'zoth with you—figures he owes it to Shoran."

"There's no arguing with a Wookiee," Luke said. "He'll be all right. There won't be enough shooting to worry about."

"Why's that?"

At that point, the doctor saw on his displays the same fatigue Luke was seeing on Han's face and ordered an end to the conversation. They completed the trip to the frigate in silence, save for the off-key humming of the shuttle pilot and the wheeze at the end each time Han exhaled. The last third of the run, it seemed as though Han was asleep.

But when the hatch had opened and the orderlies were unstrapping the stretcher to carry Han out, he opened his eyes and found Luke with a steady gaze.

"Hey—kid."

"What?"

"You'd have come for me if you knew, right?"

"You know I would," Luke said. Then he grinned crookedly. "It's a bad habit from the old days."

Han let his head loll back and his eyes close. "You

can keep that one," he said. "Give the bastards hell, kid. They've earned it."

The final tactical conference for Strong Hand included not only the commanders of all sixteen battle groups—by hypercomm holo link, as the groups were already staged to their jump points—but also Luke, Wialu, and A'baht's five senior aides.

"Here's the good news," said Colonel Corgan. "Not only did the feint at Doornik Three-nineteen go off without any losses, but we got a free shot at an outbound Fat Man in the bargain, and made the most of it. Primary credit for the kill goes to Captain Ssiew and *Thunderhead*, and I'd like to tip my hat to them for showing us the way."

"Here's the interesting news," said Colonel Mauit'ta. "Looking at the data from today's action together with the clash at ILC-Nine-oh-five, we now believe that the Yevetha have their own game of where's-the-candy under way. That is, we are now ninety percent convinced that there are two versions of the Yevethan T-type—one a capital warship, and the other an unarmed transport. At this point, we're still looking for tip-offs to provide to your sensor crews. But we believe the risks would justify following a simple rule of thumb: Don't bother firing on any targets that aren't firing on you."

"Here's the bad news," said General A'baht. "The last survey of the N'zoth and Z'fell systems show that the Yevethan fleets there continue to be reinforced by ships coming in from elsewhere in Koornacht Cluster. N'zoth is now at forty-six capital ships and Z'fell thirty-four. That means that if they call our bluff and we end up in a tussle, we'll have only about a six-to-five edge—which could go to even odds by the time we get there. We will get one more snapshot from our stasis probes just before the jump-out." He looked down the table at Wialu. "A lot's riding on you, madam. If there's any reason to think—"

"I am ready," she said quietly.

"Then we go at the times established in revision nine of the coordinated plan," said A'baht. "Good luck to us all—and if luck disappoints us, then good hunting to us all." As the holos began dissolving, one after another, A'baht leaned toward Luke. "Can I talk to you for a moment?"

This conversation truly was private—just Luke and the general, alone behind the closed door of A'baht's office.

"I've been holding off saying anything about this, thinking I'd let you come to me on your own and let me know what sort of role you wanted to have in this," said A'baht. "But we're getting close to the end of the talking, so I'll get right to the point. If this comes to a shooting war, I'd like to have the benefit of your experience and leadership.

"I know there are some strictly bureaucratic issues about your status, but I don't care about them. I'd like to offer you command of Red E Squadron. That's twelve of this ship's best E-wing pilots, and I know there won't be any hard feelings about your coming in at the top. You can use my personal fighter—the crews keep it zeroed in—"

"I'm sorry," Luke said. "I appreciate your confidence, but I have to say no."

A'baht frowned. "I'm not sure I understand. What, uh—what are your plans, then?"

Luke stood. "I intend to be with Wialu and Akanah on the observation deck. My obligations to them come first."

Squinting unhappily in Luke's direction, A'baht said, "If it's their security you're worried about, I can put as many armed men up there as you want, so you'd be free—"

"Armed men will not contribute to their sense of security," Luke said. "The answer is no. I'm sorry if that answer disappoints you."

"It confounds me," said A'baht. "The choice is

yours, of course—but I would appreciate an explanation, if there is one."

Luke felt the heavy weight of expectations settle on his shoulders. *If you don't let them make your choices for you, they demand that you justify yourself to them—ah, Ben, how did you ever learn to refuse them with a tranquil conscience?*

"The obligations I spoke of don't involve protecting the Fallanassi," said Luke. "I can't stand with one foot in their world and one foot in yours. I asked them to involve themselves in our conflict as a matter of principle. Now I have to show that I respect that same principle myself."

"Where exactly do your loyalties lie, then?"

"That's a deceptively simple question, General, and we haven't the time to explore it," Luke said. "It does need to be explored—I suspect it's the question that eventually led to Palpatine's purge of the Jedi."

"I did not intend to question your honor," said A'baht.

"I know that, General," Luke said. "In the end, it comes down to this—there's far more to be lost by my climbing into that cockpit than you could possibly gain from my doing so. You have good pilots, good crews, and leadership enough to offer them. I'll celebrate a victory with you no matter how it comes. But my part in it will not be as a warrior."

The heralds of the coming armada were stasis probes 203, 239, and 252.

They were the last remaining survivors from more than fifty such probes Alpha Blue and the Fleet had sent into the N'zoth system. The others had either been hunted down by Yevethan patrol ships, or had expired under the stress of their mission profile.

Undetectable in hyperspace, a stasis probe would drop into realspace only long enough to take a sensor snapshot, transmit the data to its controller, and receive the interval instruction for its next appearance—altogether, a matter of no more than twenty seconds. Only passive sensors were used. Stealthiness was essential to the probes' survival.

Ordinarily, the most severe challenge to stealthiness was the Cronau radiation from the entries and exits. But with the probes' zero space velocity, the Cronau radiation collapsed into a narrow wave cone, which was carefully directed away from enemy sensors.

But the last instructions received by the three probes were far from ordinary. They were unprecedentedly strange—strange enough that probes with more sophisticated system droids might well have refused them.

The probes were to orient themselves gyroscopically so that on their next entry, the Cronau wave cone was pointed at N'zoth like a spotlight. Next, they were to begin active sensing, sending out optical and radar pings at ten-second intervals. Finally, they were to remain in that mode for the next hundred minutes.

Taken together, the instructions guaranteed that the probes would be found and destroyed long before that hundred minutes had elapsed. The flow of new data would be cut off—the probes' missions would be cut short, in failure.

But the three probes were not meant to survive. The data they were transmitting was now considered inconsequential. They were being sacrificed to draw as many Yevethan eyes as possible upward and outward— to assemble the audience for the show that was to follow.

And as heralds, they succeeded marvelously well.

Nil Spaar's highest priority that day had been replenishing the breederies. Nearly all of the new *maranas* had been destroyed during the vermin's clumsy and unsuccessful attempt to rescue Han Solo. The losses left Nil Spaar both grieving and aggrieved, and he had closed himself away with the most select *marasi* in order that the alcoves of the undamaged breederies be filled with all haste.

But the news delivered to his quarters with great timidity by the second proctor of defense was urgent enough to excuse the interruption.

"*Darama*—ten thousand apologies. But alien vessels of an unknown type have appeared in defense zones nine and eleven," the proctor said, flinching. "Our fleet is being scanned. Primate Dar Bille has called the ship to readiness, and begs your counsel."

When Nil Spaar reached the bridge, he found a disagreeable amount of confusion. Multiple alarms were sounding, and the new proctor of defense for the spawnworld was engaged in a loud clash of dominance with the ship's primate. But the viceroy's arrival resolved the hierarchical crisis, as both Tho Voota and Dar Bille knelt before him and then pressed their cases on him.

"Show me what has happened," Nil Spaar said, waving away their words.

He watched earnestly as the logs of various monitors and pickets were replayed for him on the main viewscreen. Three alien probes had appeared within moments of each other—probes of the same size, perhaps even the same type, as those the outer patrols had been destroying with some regularity. They marked the corners of a lopsided triangle, the longest side of which spanned fifteen degrees of the sky. The probes were persistently hurling radionic and light energy in toward the fleet, accounting for most of the alarms on the bridge.

"Dar Bille's judgment is correct," said Nil Spaar. "The meaning of this is that more ships are coming. We will move toward these probes at once."

"But *darama*, please consider—if this proves another false showing, as there was at Preza yesterday—" the proctor said in protest.

"Then they will not pass close enough for us to engage them from this orbit," said Dar Bille.

"Their purpose could be to draw us away, and leave the spawnworld unprotected."

"There are ships enough for both duties," said Nil Spaar, cutting short the argument. "But the flagship of the Protectorate need fear no enemy. We will move to intercept."

Dar Bille spun away. "Signal our companion vessels that we are breaking orbit. Helmsman! Set course for the anomalies, and make quarter speed when the way is clear."

With a slow grace, the bow of the great Star Destroyer swung out and upward, bringing the triangle of enemy probes to the center of the main viewpane. As Nil Spaar settled into his command lounge, he settled his gaze on that triangle and thought heartening thoughts about revenge for his lost children.

It was night in Giat Nor—a night like most nights on N'zoth, of quiet air and clear skies under the splendor of the All.

But a sentry had called Ton Raalk to the courtyard of the city proctor's hall and quarters with a report of a curiosity: three bright flashes in the sky over N'zoth's northern latitudes.

"One after another they were, like one word following another," said the sentry. "And bright—brighter than any of the All. I only saw the third of them directly, but it left me half blind for minutes after."

There were others of Ton Raalk's family and staff in the courtyard as well, having glimpsed the sky or the ground lit up though a window or door. The proctor was well aware of them as he answered loudly, "I see nothing here, and no reason for concern. Most likely it was part of our glorious fleet, going hunting for the vermin."

The sentry would not relent. In his post, he had seen many ships jumping in and out of N'zoth's skies, and that light was only a flicker by comparison. "Could it be that there is fighting here, *etaias*? Perhaps for safety the families should be moved—"

Then someone cried out, pointing skyward. Ton Raalk turned at the sound, then craned his neck upward. He stared wonderingly with the others as a small area of the sky, barely larger than his hand at arm's length, began to roil and dance with light.

As warship after warship appeared within the triangle marked out by the alien probes, Nil Spaar edged forward in his chair with eager glee in his eyes. "Yes, come, come," he urged. "What a glorious victory you will give us. What a splendid sky, full of targets for our guns. There will be honor for every Yevetha today, and vengeance for every lost child."

But at that moment, both fleets were well out of the range of each other's weapons. There was time for the game masters on both sides to array their pieces for battle, jockeying for advantage in the clash to come. The slow grace of the ballet belied its murderous purpose.

Dar Bille ordered the interdictor *Splendor of Yevetha* forward into the lead spot, to protect the flagship from any sneak attacks from hyperspace. Tho Voota held the flagship and its companions at a crawl while the balance of the home fleet rose from orbit to catch and join them.

Meanwhile, the count of the approaching armada continued to climb, topping two hundred before the entry flashes finally ceased. Then the formation began to spread, breaking into squadron-sized units spaced in a one-deep array that brought every ship into view. Their slow, almost stately approach declared an arrogant confidence.

"*Darama*, there is a signal from the vermin," announced the proctor of communication.

"I will hear them, for my amusement," said Nil Spaar, rising from his couch. "Let *all* hear, Proctor— these words will confess our enemy's weakness and impotence. They will boast and threaten and then conceal their cowardice as mercy."

"This is General Etahn A'baht, commander of the New Republic combined forces in Farlax. This is my final warning to the citizens and worlds of the Duskhan

League. You are called to account for your crimes against the peaceful peoples of Koornacht. You must give up the territory you illegally seized by force. You must surrender all hostages unharmed—"

Sil Sorannan witnessed the arrival of the New Republic fleet on the three-dimensional monitors in the flagship's fire control center.

It was from that room that *Pride of Yevetha*'s individual batteries would be assigned targets. Those decisions were in the hands of the three Yevethan officers seated at the consoles in the pit. Sorannan's responsibility ended at maintaining the data server for the target registry and its electronic links throughout the ship.

Still, he studied the holographic image-map with as much intent devotion as did the fire control proctors. As the first warships appeared, his hand slipped into his pocket and found the hard-toothed comb. He rubbed its spine like a worry-stone as the New Republic fleet grew. His respect for the attackers grew as well as he listened to their commander's warning.

"—Your past aggressions will not be tolerated. Future aggression will not be permitted. I call on the captains of all Yevethan vessels: Stand down your weapons. Lower your shields. Maintain your current orbits—or be destroyed. I call on Viceroy Nil Spaar: Order the immediate surrender of all Yevethan forces everywhere. Yield your claim to authority and your post as viceroy, and your cities will be spared. Resist, and you invite the total destruction of both your fleet and your way of life."

A frontal assault with overwhelming force—that is the way war was meant to be fought, thought Sorannan admiringly. *Strength against strength—not the weak and cowardly tactics of the Rebel Alliance. You have grown some since I last knew you.*

As A'baht spoke, Sorannan slid toward the leftmost section of his station and opened one of the several small service panels in its instrumented face. But he did not yet pick up the hand-built blaster pistol resting inside atop the circuits. He was waiting for Nil Spaar's answer, even though he had little doubt what it would be.

Standing with arms crossed and feet set apart, Etahn A'baht frowned deeply as he watched the Yevethan fleet form up. The bridge of *Intrepid* had fallen under a suffocating silence as he sent his ultimatum, and the silence was growing more uncomfortable by the second.

"Anything?" he asked finally.

"Not unless you count continuing toward us as a reply."

"That may be all the reply we get," said A'baht. "Time to weapons lock?"

"Six minutes twenty."

A'baht nodded. "All right," he said with a sigh. "Get the pilots into their cockpits. Start locking down the shield doors. And let's have about twenty of our thumpers light up that *Super* with range-finder lasers. Let's remind the estimable viceroy that we know where he lives."

As the minutes dragged out and the distance between the fleets continued to shrink, Sil Sorannan brought the comb out of his pocket and ran it through his thinning red hair. He knew that Nil Spaar's silence was an expression of contempt for his adversaries, but he was also confident that the viceroy would not be able to resist expressing his contempt directly. Sorannan waited calmly for it to come.

But when the most powerful weapons on *Pride of Yevetha*—on *Intimidator*, Sorannan reminded himself— were only a minute away from being able to deliver an effective blow to the nearest of the New Republic vessels, he could wait no longer. Holding the comb before him in both hands, he twisted it sharply, and it came apart in his hands. One of the pieces was a thin wand with three small buttons—it had been hidden inside the comb's hollow spine.

Keeping his eye on both the proctors and the holo tracks, Sorannan moved the wand to his right hand and picked up the blaster in his left. As he did so, Nil Spaar began to broadcast his answer of defiance to both fleets.

"You are low and impure creatures, and your threats mean nothing to me," the viceroy said. "Your presence fouls the perfection of the All and offends the honor of the Blessed. I will rip the soft white bellies of your ships open and spill their disgusting entrails for all to see. Your lungs will thirst for air. Your vigorless blood will boil in your ears. Your pleas will go unanswered, and your screams will go unheard. Your bodies will fall into the sun and be consumed. You will be forgotten by your offspring, and your mates will bring new blood to their beds."

Fool, Sorannan thought. *They have your fleet outgunned three to one—soon to be five to one.* Without a flicker of change in his expression, he pressed the first two buttons on the wand with his thumb, then raised the blaster to shoulder level and began to fire.

A'baht listened to Nil Spaar's screed with his jaw set in a grim expression and the last flickers of hope dying in his eyes.

"That's that," he said. "Get those people down from the ob deck—it's not safe up there. Break the Showcase formation, and bring all the batteries up to full power."

"General!" called the tactical officer. "The Yevethan flagship is slowing."

A'baht nodded acknowledgment. "That's a small break for us, if he's decided to let the rest of his fleet do the fighting."

"Sir, *all* of the Imperial types are slowing—the Super, the interdictor, the SDs—all of 'em. They're stopping in a hurry, too—just sitting there. I can't figure this tactic—the T-types are hard for us to knock out, but the Imperial designs have more punch."

A'baht stared at the tactical display. "Signal the armada to slow to one eighth—let's give ourselves a little more time to sort this out. Are *any* of the T-types holding off?"

"No, not one of them—they're still coming on," said the tactical officer. Seconds passed. "General, the Imperial types are definitely veering off now. I don't know—maybe the viceroy's having an attack of good sense."

A'baht's thoughts leaped at once to the officially discounted claim of a treaty between the League and something called the Grand Imperial Union.

"Or someone else is," he said. "Maybe there's a falling-out between friends under way over there. Let's see if we can aggravate it. Task Forces Blackvine, Apex, Keyhole—the leashes are off. Pursue and engage."

There were 513 Black Sword Command veterans aboard *Pride of Yevetha* and more than 15,000 Yevetha. Those proportions did not trouble Major Sorannan. His contingent was armed with more than blasters and a profound motivation. The ship was already under their control; dealing with its last owners was a mere detail.

There was a precious irony, Sorannan thought, that the principle instrumentality of their freedom was something called a slave circuit.

Within three minutes of his pressing the button that turned the ships away from the New Republic fleet and toward Byss, he was joined in the fire control room by Captain Eistern and three other men whose former duty stations had been elsewhere in the engineering section.

"Looks as though you managed without us, sir," said Eistern, observing the carnage in the pit. Tendrils of smoke were still rising from the consoles where three blackened corpses were slumped.

"They gave me no trouble," Sorannan said with evident satisfaction.

Eistern glanced up at the targeting holo. "Wish you could say that about the Alliance," he said. "It looks like they're coming after us. We're not ready to fight this ship, you know."

"We will be gone before they catch up," said Sorannan.

"They don't know what's happening here. Maybe they wouldn't even bother with us if they did."

"I intend to tell them, but not for that reason," said Sorannan. "I want them to know who they owe their victory to."

He climbed back to his station, pulled out a pair of system boards, and replaced them upside down. The monitors flickered as the displays changed to reflect the new functions being controlled from that location.

"General A'baht, can you hear this transmission?"

"This is A'baht." There was curiosity in the tone. "Please identify yourself."

"Proudly, General. This is Major Sil Sorannan of the Black Sword Command, Imperial Navy—acting captain of the Star Destroyer *Intimidator* and commodore of the Camp Pa'aal Squadron."

"I am not familiar with your unit, Major."

Sorannan laughed stiffly. "It's newly commissioned, General—sorry you couldn't be here for the christening."

"If your intentions are not hostile—"

"It is not that we have any more love for you now than when we last faced you," said Sorannan. "But we won't fight to defend our enslavers."

"Heave to, and you won't be harmed."

"Oh, no," Sorannan said. "We've been here too long already—nearly thirteen years on a nine-month detail. No, General. This is good-bye. We are taking back what is ours, starting with our freedom and these ships. We leave the Yevetha to you."

He pressed the middle and third buttons on the wand, and an unjammable hypercomm signal leaped across the emptiness to slave circuits buried deep in the command architecture of every Imperial warship deployed at N'zoth and its daugher worlds across the cluster.

Autopilots calculated jump vectors, and hyperdrive motivators called on the immense power of solar ionization reactors. Space trembled, twisted, and yawned open around the accelerating warships.

Moments later, Black Sword Command's withdrawal from Koornacht Cluster was finally complete.

Cheering broke out on the bridge of *Intrepid* as the heart of the Yevethan fleet vanished from the tracking displays, but A'baht quickly put a stop to it.

"We have no way of verifying what we just heard. Those ships could jump out half a light-year and return on our flank," he said. "Moreover, there are still forty-four T-types out there, and none of them have broken off yet. This is not over."

There was very little time left before the fragmented Yevethan formation and the New Republic fleet met. A'baht used most of it to broadcast another appeal for surrender, directing it at the individual captains of the approaching vessels, emphasizing the superior numbers of his force.

But there was no reply, and no change in the Yevethan fleet's disposition. Whatever orders Nil Spaar had given before disappearing were apparently still in force. That, more than anything, convinced A'baht that they had not seen the last of the Imperial contingent.

"I cannot believe that a unit that has been decimated—no, worse than that—before the battle begins, which has lost its senior commanders before a shot has been fired, and which faces a vastly superior force, would not collapse," the general said. "By all manner of reason, those commanders should be thinking of surrender or retreat."

"Well, they're not," said Colonel Corgan. "Targets eighteen, twenty, and twenty-one just opened fire on the phantom elements of Task Force Token."

"So I am led to conclude that none of those things

has happened," said A'baht. "Their force has not been decimated, only divided. Their command structure remains intact—and they have other forces not yet committed to the battle zone. Therefore we can infer that these are low-value assets meant to occupy us, to disrupt our formations, and to soften us up for a planned counterstrike."

"I concur that the evidence can be read that way," said Colonel Corgan. "So how do we play it now, General?"

A'baht studied the tactical display. "We must neutralize this force without compromising our unit integrity or our mobility," he said at last. "Pass the word as follows: Hold back the bombers. Keep the patrol screens close, and launch the A-wing interceptors only in response to direct threat from other little birds. Our operational unit for this engagement is to be the fleet squadron, and squadron commanders now have operational autonomy. All units, pursue, engage, and destroy all targets of opportunity. Since they insist on a fight, we'll give 'em one."

"What about the hostages, sir?"

A'baht shook his head. "Pray for them, Colonel. That's all we can do."

A great conflict is nothing more than the aggregate of many small struggles, and so it was with the Battle of N'zoth. There was no single vantage point from which its entirety could be grasped—not even the observation deck of the New Republic flagship.

Luke and Akanah had turned away the lieutenant who came to remove them from that spot. The commencement of hostilities had not meant the end of Wialu's efforts—to Luke's surprise, she continued the illusion of the phantom warships even as ion and laser cannon began to light up space all around them.

"She told that she would maintain the projection as long as she could, even if the Yevetha did not surrender," Akanah whispered.

Luke nodded. "If the phantoms draw their share of the Yevethan fire—"

"She said that no one would die aboard a ship that wasn't there."

But it was obvious to both of them that the effort was taking a toll on Wialu. As the battle wore on and broken and burning warships began to dot the starry backdrop, Wialu began to sag visibly. Finally, moments after a New Republic light escort blew up spectacularly just a few kilometers away, Wialu slumped forward on the deck where she had been sitting, and the phantoms vanished from the New Republic formations.

Even then, she surprised Luke again by declining to be helped from the observation deck.

"I will watch to the end. No matter what path you follow, it is important to be reminded what war means," she said, letting Akanah guide her to one of the empty semireclined chairs.

Luke had been holding a question for hours, and the urgency of it had grown in the waiting. He crouched beside Wialu, his back to the fighting.

"Wialu, I have to know—are there Fallanassi aboard any of those vessels?"

"Yes," she said.

He drew a deep breath and released it slowly. "Is Nashira among them?"

"I cannot hear your question," Wialu said.

His frustration sharpened to the point of pain, Luke turned angrily away.

"I can tell you only that they are not hostages," she went on. "They chose this service for themselves, on the last morning that the Current scalded as it does now— the day the Yevetha came to make their claim. Many, many died that day. But some were saved by those who placed themselves between. I did not ask it of them, but I honor them and their sacrifice."

Staring out at a burning Yevethan thrustship, Luke found he had no choice but to respect that sacrifice with silence.

*   *   *

In reality, the outcome of the Battle of N'zoth had been foreordained from the moment Sil Sorannan departed with the Black Sword vessels.

But it was no less brutal or difficult for that. The Yevethan thrustship shields were superior to New Republic shields, and the spherical symmetry of the thrustship design made them even more effective. And though they were not heavily armed by Imperial standards—the combined output of the eight batteries was less than that of a gunship, to say nothing of an escort or a heavy cruiser—the ability to focus all of that energy on one small area gave them the knockout punch of a much larger ship.

Under attack by three and four New Republic vessels each, one after another of the Yevethan warships succumbed. But it was a war of attrition, with nearly as many losses as there were victories—*Thunderhead. Aboukir. Fulminant. Werra. Garland. Banshee.*

Nor were all of the losses among the smaller vessels. Commodore Farley Carson's *Yakez* was caught between two thrustships and broken in two by the detonation of the forward magazine after its bow shields collapsed. The fleet carrier *Ballarat* took a brace of Yevethan missiles just forward of the number four flight deck, and the chain of explosions that followed hurled three squadrons of shattered E- and X-wings out into space.

Ballarat's misfortune gave Plat Mallar his first chance to do something more than watch from the yawning maw of a flight deck. All of the fleet's launches, gigs, and shuttles had been outfitted for rescue and recovery work and distributed among the task forces. Mallar and his shuttle had been assigned to the cruiser *Mandjur,* which was part of *Ballarat*'s squadron and the closest vessel to it when the missiles struck. While *Mandjur* dueled with the Yevethan warship, Mallar brought back one live pilot and two dead ones in three trips through an intense field of fire.

But despite the painful losses scattered across the entire battle zone, the trend was clear.

There were only two points at which that trend threatened to reverse itself. The first was when the phantoms vanished, allowing the Yevethan ships to focus their fire on the real threats. The second came near the end, when the last eleven thrustships began launching their trifoil fighters—fighters that screamed toward the New Republic vessels, diving through shield gaps opened for them by the Yevethan batteries and hurling themselves against their targets as suicide missiles.

In a matter of only five minutes, half a dozen of the vessels engaging the remnant of the Yevethan fleet were either destroyed or forced to withdraw. *Mandjur* was among the ships that came to fill the gaps, but it was struck twice near the stern before it could launch even half of its interceptors. It began to drift, crippled and vulnerable, its engines dead and its aft shields gone.

In the moments after the twin impacts rattled the cruiser, Mallar ran to join a group of pilots, deck crew, and droids who were trying to clear a damaged E-wing from the mouth of the flight deck. Their chatter told him what was happening outside the ship and decided his course.

Ever since coming aboard *Mandjur,* he had been eyeing Captain Tegett's X-wing. Painted a vivid red, it sat in a reserved tie-down slot under the broad transparencies of the flight control office. And when the debris was finally cleared and the undamaged interceptors began to move forward to launch, Mallar ran to the red X-wing instead of back to his shuttle.

When the flight operations chief cleared him to start engines instead of trying to chase him away, Mallar knew just how dire the ship's plight was. Using the power of his ship's signature appearance, he edged into line between two E-wings, and not long after got the green ball to launch.

"Four coming in!" Mallar heard over his cockpit comm as *Mandjur* fell away behind him. "This is Blue Five—I need help back here!"

Hauling the X-wing around sharply toward the cruiser's stern, Mallar had a moment of dizziness. He heard Ackbar's voice echoing in his thoughts. *Don't try to turn with them—use your speed, know your strengths and your limits.* He saw Polneye burning before his eyes.

Thanks for the lessons, Admiral, he thought. *Thanks for the chance.* As Mallar thumbed the squawk button he saw an E-wing turning with him and another coming up from behind to settle on his starboard wing.

"This is Red Leader," he said with quiet confidence. "On my way, Blue Five, with company. Take the first one—we'll get the rest."

Then he pushed the throttles ahead, and the fighter leaped forward with an eagerness that matched his own.

The reports that came in from the intelligence sources scattered through the outer regions of the cluster all mirrored each other: The ships that had been orbiting the destroyed colonies were gone. Asset analysis would later show that those same ships were among those that had reinforced the fleets at N'zoth, Wakiza, Z'fell, and the other large-population worlds.

The reports that came in from the task forces sent to those worlds mirrored the experience at N'zoth: The Imperial ships turned and jumped out without apparent cause or explanation, but not a single Yevethan vessel surrendered or fled. Every last thrustship had fought relentlessly, taking the fight to the Fleet as the aggressor, until it was destroyed.

A'baht had never seen the like of it in thirty years of soldiering, and it left him shaken.

"It has always been enough, in the past, to defeat the enemy," he said to Morano in the privacy of the now-quiet situation room. "I've never known an enemy who forced me to utterly destroy him. By the end, I was looking for ways not to have to destroy those last few ships. If they had given me any chance to spare them, shown any hesitation, even just broken contact and fallen back—"

"They never gave us a chance," said Morano, shaking his head. "You can't show mercy to someone who's going for your throat."

"No," A'baht said.

Tapping a key slowly with his index finger. A'baht began paging through the casualty summaries. It took a long time. "This is an error," he said, pausing at one point. "Tegett never left *Mandjur*—it was someone else in his fighter. They still don't know who."

"Too bad. Spoils a grand heroic story for the newsgrids," said Morano. "Captain saves his ship by ramming a suicide bomber—"

"There's still a story there," said A'baht, tapping the key. "A lot of stories here, and they won't all get told."

Tap—tap—tap—

A'baht shook his head. "What a terrible price we paid for this one."

"Second thoughts, General?"

"No," he said firmly. "Oh, no. What I said earlier, about wanting to spare them at the end—I'm lucky I didn't have that chance. It would have been a mistake."

"I don't understand."

A'baht gestured at the screen before him. "Can you imagine if they'd had the patience to wait another ten years or so, studying us, building up their fleet? No, no regrets, Captain. I'm glad for what happened today, even though doing it made me sick at heart. I'm glad we did this before the Yevetha got any stronger, or any smarter about us." The general closed the casualty file and pushed his datapad away from him. "I just hope we're smart enough now to figure out a way to see that they never build a starship again."

Nil Spaar's arms were bound at his sides, his claws locked helplessly against the restraining bar. His ankles were manacled together with a short plasteel cable. Even so, he tried to lunge at Sil Sorannan when the Imperial officer appeared in the bridge's escape pod access tunnel.

The lunge did not carry him far. It was not even necessary for anyone to shoot the viceroy—Lieutenant Gar, one of the four witnesses, simply hooked Nil Spaar's ankle cable with his own foot, bringing the Yevetha down hard on the deck.

"For twelve years of torture, and too many friends, there isn't enough I can do to you," said Sorannan, stepping closer. "I already know that killing you won't be satisfying. No matter how I do it and how long it takes, I'll wake up tomorrow and see the face of someone who didn't get to go home with us, and I'll know in my gut that you got off too easy.

"But still, you deserve to die. And the only thing I can think of that will help me answer those faces that come into my mind is to make you wait for it—and make sure that my face stays in your mind while you wait.

"So here's something you should know about me. Before I joined Black Sword Command, I was detailed to the Research Section as a pilot for the experimental hyperphysics team. We were trying to learn how to drop bombs from hyperspace. We never learned how."

Sorannan crouched by Nil Spaar's head, and his voice grew soft. "You see, it turns out that no matter which way you go through the magic door, you need a hyperdrive to open it. Anything that we released in hyperspace just stayed there. We even took a drone and blew it up in hyperspace, to see if that might open the door. None of the wreckage ever appeared again in real-space."

As he stood up again, he gestured to Captain Eistern, who stepped to the hatch of escape pod 001 and unlatched it.

"It's really too bad the project didn't work out," Sorannan said, stepping back while Gar and another witness dragged Nil Spaar to his feet. "Because it turns out to be very easy to release an object in hyperspace. One good shove will do it—like the ejection charge of an escape pod, for example."

The viceroy stood tall and silent, his expression one of contempt and haughty pride.

Sorannan leaned his face close to Nil Spaar's, so that the breath of his whisper kissed the viceroy's cheeks. "I don't know how long you will survive there," he said. "I do know that you will die there."

Stepping back, the major watched as the others forced Nil Spaar into the escape pod and sealed him inside.

"Die slowly," Sorannan said hoarsely, and slammed his hand down on the firing switch.

With a roar, the escape pod hurtled away into oblivion.

INTERLUDE V:

Rendezvous

Joto Eckels stared at the sensor display with a degree of awe approaching the religious. In a lifetime of archaeological fieldwork, Eckels had never faced a moment like this one, when a functioning instrumentality of a dead race had appeared to bridge the centuries.

It was an event on a par with the greatest finds of the modern era—the Shadow Traproom on Liok, the Nojic Beanstalk, the Great Subcrustal Tubeway of the Pa Tho, the Foran Tutha star probe. But at first, there was no joy in it—only the sudden, numbing weight of responsibility. Dreiss and Mokem had died in the Shadow Traproom. Bartleton had watched helplessly as the Foran Tutha probe was gutted by a fire his own people inadvertently triggered.

But Pakkpekatt's team did not appear burdened by thoughts of either history or posterity. With matter-of-fact efficiency, they immediately began to deal with the surprise.

"What message should I send to HQ, Colonel?" asked Pleck.

"A contact report only," said Pakkpekatt. "Let us see what sort of greeting she has for us first. Is the satellite prepared for deployment?"

"I'm finished with it. It's set up on the fantail and ready to go," said Taisden.

"Recommendation?"

"*Penga Rift* needs to move to the far side, keep the planet between it and the vagabond until they've collected their people and cleared orbit. If we place ourselves and the satellite a hundred and eighty degrees apart in geosynch, we can get complete coverage of the approaches plus maximum separation."

"Deploy the satellite," said Pakkpekatt. "Doctor?"

Looking slightly bewildered, Eckels shouldered his way forward. "May I speak with *Penga Rift,* Colonel?"

"Of course. Colonel Hammax, get the doctor set up at station three."

Eckels gave the recall order, then apprised Captain Barjas of the situation. "Get everyone aboard and everything locked down," he said. "Have Mazz monitor everything that goes through our satellite. See what you can get on the incoming ship. But don't risk the artifacts—at the first sign of any direct threat, jump out."

Then he turned his attention back to the others, who seemed to have forgotten him for the moment.

"Let's do one more test cycle on the autoresponder," Pleck was saying. "When that interrogative comes—"

"No," said Pakkpekatt. "The earlier tests were satisfactory. The interrogative could come at any time. Bring it up and put it online."

"Yes, Colonel," Pleck said.

"Satellite is away, active, and moving to position," said Taisden. "Fourteen minutes to station. We can make our station six minutes after the skiff clears."

Pakkpekatt turned toward Eckels and eyed him curiously. "Doctor, shouldn't you be going?"

"Where?"

"Back to your ship—to *Penga Rift.*"

"To hide on the other side of Maltha Obex? I don't think so, Colonel. I think you can make more use of me than that."

Eckels expected and braced himself for an argument. But the only detectable dialog took place between his determinedly steady gaze and Pakkpekatt's sharply inquiring one. Against the possibility of an undetected dialog, Eckels held one thought in his mind: *I accept your authority. Let me help. Let me be there when the door is opened.*

Pakkpekatt grimaced in a manner reminiscent of a yawn. "If *Penga Rift* does not need you, then we will take advantage of your presence," he said. "Agent Pleck, take Dr. Eckels to the observation deck and familiarize him with the equipment."

Lobot found sharing his interface with the vagabond a seductive preoccupation. After as little as twenty minutes, he began to lose both the will and the ability to respond to Lando or the droids.

It was not that the link was so rich and easy that he experienced what cyborgs spoke of among themselves as "falling down a hole into heaven"—much the opposite, in fact. The link was so difficult, communication so painfully slow, and the data structures so alien that staying in contact with the vessel gradually absorbed all of his attention and resources.

Even switching to Basic to process aural input or formulate and voice a response gradually became an insuperable burden. For the first time in his memory, Lobot found himself single-tasking, surrendering his own internal processes and thinking in the base-six binary algorithms of the vagabond. The cyborg community called that loss of boundaries "turning inside out" and viewed it as a danger to systemic integration—one step away from dissociative collapse.

Lando knew only that Lobot was connected to a machine with the power to take him away and no apparent inclination to return him. After observing the phenomenon the first time, Lando set strict limits and appointed himself the enforcer of them. Throughout the duration of the hyperspace jump, Lobot spent no more

than an hour at a time linked, with at least two hours
between sessions.

Even allowing that much was a concession to
Lobot, who insisted that the most productive part of a
session was the part when he was insensible to anything
but the vagabond's data structures. That assertion was
one Lando had to take on faith. So far, Lando hadn't
seen enough in the way of useful results to justify risking
any contact at all. The insights Lobot was gleaning from
contact with the vagabond seemed far more meaningful
than the ones he was managing to communicate to
Lando.

"It doesn't know what it is," Lobot had explained.
"It only knows what it does." But even within those
parameters, what the vagabond "told" Lobot seemed all
too changeable, subject not only to interpretation but to
Lobot's errors of enthusiasm.

The ship was a protect-against-harm, a shelter-and-
nurture, a heal-and-succor, a flee-from-predators, a
maintain-and-preserve, and a welcome-and-teach—
which Lobot variously interpreted as egg, mother,
creche, repository, and chrysalis. The rounded bodies in
the inner tubules were sleepers, keepers, corpses, creep-
ers, sacrifices, and directors—with half of those designa-
tions suggesting they were part of the vessel and half
suggesting they were something apart.

"I don't think it knows any more," Lobot had said
at one point, responding to Lando's frustration. "Its
reflexes are complex and elegant, and it has great power
at its command. But it lacks even a child's self-awareness or sense of purpose. It does what it knows to do, by
stimulus and response, by instinct—it is conscious of
those processes but nothing beyond them. I don't think
it even realizes where it is, any more than a seed buried
in the ground does."

"If you and it make up your mind about anything,
make a point of sharing that with me," Lando had answered in disgust. "If it won't obey us, I don't see that
we're getting anything useful out of this. So if you're

going to keep communing with it, at least keep working on that point."

Even as Lobot had found a new focus, Lando seemed to have lost his. They had access to the entire ship now, but Lando had shown little interest in making use of it. He had powered down both droids, and spent most of his time floating in chamber 229. The near exhaustion of his propellant was only a pretext concealing his loss of heart.

Lobot made one attempt to talk to Lando about what he was seeing. "In our travels together, I have only seen you leave the table twice," he said. "Once when you found yourself in a rigged game, and once when that woman, Sarra Dolas, came and sat at Narka Tobb's side instead of yours. I have only seen you fold your hand in the face of a game that could not be won, and a game that you no longer cared about winning. Which is it this time?"

"Neither," said Lando. "I've done everything that I know how to do. None of it's done a thing to improve our position. Now you say it's headed home. I'm just waiting for the last hand to be played."

But the unprecedentedly violent shaking of the vagabond as it exited from hyperspace shook Lando out of his indifference. "Lobot, where are you?" he called over the suit comm.

"In the interspace, aft," Lobot replied.

"Did you hear what just almost didn't happen? On my worst mornings after my worst days, I don't sound that bad trying to get up," Lando said.

"Yes, Lando," said Lobot. "The exit growl was extraordinarily loud and extended here—I had the distinct impression of hearing it from behind, from the stern first, and then a fraction of a second later from the bow. And I could see an oscillation wave with an amplitude of at least a decimeter traveling along the outer hull."

"You're lucky there still is an outer hull," Lando said. "I've figured out why the jumps keep getting rockier. Come forward to two-twenty-nine—there's something I need you to check on. I'll explain while you're en route."

"Coming," Lobot said. "Please continue."

"I don't know why I didn't realize it sooner. The ship's power reserves—whatever it's been drawing on—must be way down. Either it's been out too long without topping off the tanks—just like you, me, and the droids—or the damage from the last attack affected either the reserves or the generators."

"The vagabond does not have generators."

"Whatever," said Lando. "Take it as a metaphor. The ship manages to store and transform energy somehow, for weapons, and motive power, and light, and all the little gadgets in the chambers."

"Granted."

"So whether the tanks are empty or the converters are below minimums, there isn't enough to go around. That's why it opened all the portals and left them open. That's why none of the gadgets have worked since the attack, and why the lights went out on us. We're in some sort of energy-conservation mode. It's not just hurting—it's tired."

"Yes. The ship and I have talked about that."

"You might have shared that part with me," Lando said with a touch of annoyance. "Lobot, the transitions have been getting rougher every time out because the ship's right at the edge—at least as far as opening a big enough hyperspace portal, and opening it fast enough to minimize the stresses. It's a matter of being able to focus enough energy in a small enough space in a short enough time. And one of these days, it's not going to be able to do it—and either the middle of the ship will jump out and leave the rest behind, or the portal will snap back and crush it."

In the middle of Lando's exposition, Lobot rejoined him in chamber 229. "That is something I would prefer to witness from a distance."

"Get in line behind me," said Lando. "That's why you have to link up with your friend. We need to know where we are and what's going to be happening—if its home is that planetary system depicted in the orrery instead of next-to-nowhere deep space, maybe we have a chance."

"What is it you want me to ask it?"

"I was thinking that maybe it could be persuaded to, say, let us have a viewport—under the general heading of being willing to provide us with information."

"I can try," Lobot said, and began stripping off his suit so he could enter the inner passages.

"Do you want me to go in with you?"

"No," Lobot said. "But come in after me if I have not returned in twenty minutes."

While he waited, Lando reactivated Artoo and, for the first time since the incident with the beckon call, Threepio.

"Good day, Master Lando," Threepio said brightly, with no apparent awareness of Lando's lingering grudge. "My word, but my circuits are clear this morning. I haven't felt this way since my last defragmentation diagnostic. I hope you are feeling well. Where is Master Lobot? He hasn't been harmed, has he? I see his contact suit, but I don't see him anywhere. Artoo, my dear friend and companion—how have you been? Please tell me everything. Master Lando, my system controller is still showing a low-power alarm. Have you located a power coupling yet? This ship has a distinctly droid-hostile design, not to have made them more readily available—"

"Threepio," Lando said sharply.

The droid's head swiveled toward him. "Yes, Master Lando?"

"Shut up."

"Of course, sir."

Artoo loosed a *wheep* that might have been an expression of relief. Lando turned to him and asked, "Artoo, will you scan local space for comm traffic? We just might be back somewhere near civilization."

"Oh, I do hope so, sir—" Threepio began, until Lando silenced him with a glare.

Before long, Lobot emerged from the forward inner portal and rejoined them.

"Any luck?"

"I am not certain," said Lobot. "It said we should go back to the auditorium. At least, I think that's where we're to go—as best as I can translate, it called that chamber the Reflection of the Essential Infinities."

"But the orrery was destroyed."

"Perhaps not rebuilding it was a choice, not a necessity."

"All right," Lando said, gesturing with both hands. "Let's go find out."

When all four members of the quartet were clinging somewhere on the auditorium's inner face, the chamber's outer face once again underwent the transformation to a great transparent panel. Once more they found themselves suspended in space, looking down on the sphere of a planet, and beyond it to the disc of a blue star.

"What's going on here?" Lando cried in dismay. "Lobot, what did you ask for? This is a different planetary system. I don't want a tour of the astrographic catalog."

"I believe your first impression has misled you," said Lobot. "This is the same system."

"The hell it is. Look, that planet is an iceball," Lando said. "It looks like Hoth." He shook his head. "Oh, blast—this must mean the vagabond didn't make it home."

"I think you are mistaken," said Lobot. "Artoo, scan and analyze. Compare with your recordings of our first visit to this chamber."

"Oh, come on—the other planet had two moons," Lando said. "I don't have to have an analysis module to see that there aren't any moons." Lando squinted at the orrery. "But there *is* something there, in orbit. Something tiny."

"The moons could both be eclipsed from our perspective."

The astromech droid squawked briefly. "Pardon me, Master Lobot," Threepio interrupted. "Artoo-Detoo says that the principal elements of this display are identical in both absolute and apparent size to the one we previously viewed."

"I told you," said Lobot. "Lando, what we saw the first time was Qella as it was when the vagabond last saw it. What we see now is Qella as it now appears."

Threepio resumed his report as soon as Lobot stopped speaking. "Artoo also says that there is no correspondence in size, number, or orbital configuration between the minor elements of this display and the earlier one—"

"That's what I was trying to tell you," said Lando. "If that's Qella, where are the moons? This isn't of any use to us. It's a one-size-fits-all planetarium show."

Artoo began chirping more urgently. "Artoo says, however, that he can identify four of the minor elements," Threepio reported. "The largest and closest of them is—"

"—is this ship," Lobot exulted. "Lando, it's a real-time tracking display—a scale model of the neighborhood, including this vessel."

"What? Artoo, illuminate this object you're talking about with your laser pointer."

"It's right there in front of your eyes," Lobot said. "It's just *small*—I said *scale* model. Threepio, what are the other objects Artoo can identify?"

Threepio nodded formally. "Of course, sir. The other objects are all orbiting the planet. In increasing order of size, they are a New Republic Engineering orbital relay satellite, a SoroSuub PLY-Three-thousand, and a Dobrutz DB-Four starliner—"

"Just a—SoroSuub Three thousand? That's *Lady Luck*!" Lando shouted, punching the air with a fist. "I can't believe it—we're going to get out of here! Where is she? Artoo, illuminate *Lady Luck*—show me where my lovely lady is—"

The request was lost in the sounds of exuberant rejoicing coming from the droids and reverberating off the faces of the chamber.

Only Lobot did not join in the celebration. "Lando, please—wait," he said. "There's still something very wrong."

"What are you talking about?" Lando said, letting go of his handhold and drifting down in front of Lobot. "Our ride is here. All we have to do is ask the vagabond to sheathe her claws and then call *Lady Luck* alongside. Food, a hot shower—*gravity*—"

Lobot shook his head. "Lando, please listen—you were right. If this *is* Qella—if this model is accurate enough to show us objects the size of an orbital relay satellite, in enough detail for Artoo to identify it—*where are the moons of Maltha Obex?*"

"What's our strategy?" asked Colonel Hammax, studying the tracking display over Pakkpekatt's right shoulder.

"Given that she's a hundred times as large as we are, and considerably more than a hundred times as powerful, it seems to me the real question on the table is, what's *her* strategy?"

"How close are you going to let her get?"

Pakkpekatt pawed his chest. "That, too, depends on her."

"The effective radius of the vagabond's defensive zone at Gmar Askilon was twelve kilometers," said Taisden. "Given the size of this orbit, we shouldn't have any trouble keeping a cushion of twelve *hundred* kilometers, which I hope would be more than sufficient."

"Shouldn't we at least *try* to contact General Calrissian?" asked Hammax.

"I don't want to spook the vagabond," said Pakkpekatt. "We got along very well with her at Gmar Askilon so long as we were sitting still and in a passive sensing mode. Let's stay that way until we have a better idea why she's here."

"Sure seems like it'd be nice to know if anyone's alive," said Hammax. "If I'm going to have to go inside—"

"There will be time for that," said Pakkpekatt. "For now, I want silence. Can you reach *Penga Rift* with a directional comm signal?"

"For another minute or so. She's about to go over the horizon to nightside."

"Notify them what we're doing—instruct them to observe a comm and sensor blackout, and to stand by." Pakkpekatt studied the tracking display. "Patience will serve us best now."

"Look, this isn't that complicated," Lando said impatiently, squeezing into the tubule beside Lobot. "Tell it we want to leave. Get it to promise not to fry my yacht when it tries to come alongside. That's all we want—that's all we're asking. Then we'll be gone, and it can go where it wants and do what it wants."

"If it tries to go anywhere, it might destroy itself," said Lobot. "I have to make it understand that first."

"As long as we're not on it when that happens, what do we care?" Lando demanded. "For all I know, those droids are back there plotting to duplicate the beckon call signal—I wouldn't put it past either of them to take things into their own hands."

"Your response to these developments seems to have an alarmingly narrow focus," said Lobot. "You are indifferent to the fate of this vessel, to the mystery concerning the planet's moons, to why *Lady Luck* is even here—"

"That's right. All I care about right now is getting out of here alive," said Lando. "And if you're worrying about anything else, I say you're the one with the problem. Come on, I can already taste the tranna nougat and doth brandy waiting for me in my suite. Say 'pardon me' and then palaver your persuasive head off until you have a docking permit for our lifeboat and exit passes for us."

"I will see what can be done," Lobot said with a frown. "But I don't know why you think anything has changed. The vagabond will not take instructions from me."

"If you care what happens to this ship, you'd better hope you're wrong," Calrissian said. "Because if *Lady Luck*'s here, the rest of the task force can't be far away. And if *Glorious* and *Marauder* have to break us out, it's not going to be gentle or pretty."

"I will try," said Lobot.

Lando clapped him on the thigh. "That's the fellow. I'll be nearby."

The vagabond made its approach to Maltha Obex at high speed, slowing only at the last to settle into a retrograde high equatorial orbit. Orbiting more slowly than the planet turned, the vagabond would linger on the dayside for nearly thirty hours while the planet seemed to slowly spin backward beneath it.

"What do you think this is about?" Pakkpekatt asked. "Anyone?"

"A very detailed surface scan," said Taisden. "She's looking for something."

"Or she's sunbathing," said Hammax. "It's cold where she's been," he added when the others looked at him quizzically. "Dr. Eckels said it's a biological, didn't he?"

"Let us be careful not to anthropomorphize," said Pakkpekatt. "Agent Taisden, it appears that the vessel's present orbit will bring her very close to us shortly before she crosses the terminator."

"Sixty kilometers," said Taisden. "And within sixty kilometers of *Penga Rift* nineteen hours after that. How comfortable are we with that spacing, Colonel?"

"I would prefer not to be that close."

"There's no way we can change our own orbit without calling attention to ourselves," said Taisden. "If she stays where she is—"

Pakkpekatt hissed and shook himself. It went

against both habit and nature for him to take the initiative in such a situation. "We may have no choice but to call attention to ourselves in one way or another," he said, sitting back in his couch. "And if we must do so, it is better done when the vagabond is still a generous distance away."

"She'll never be farther away than she is right now."

Pakkpekatt reached forward and cradled the flight controls lightly in his hands. "Notify the others what we are doing. Then page Calrissian on the frequency he was using for his suit comm at Gmar Askilon. Bounce the page through the satellite."

"Wait—what happens if the yacht's slave circuits are activated again?" asked Hammax. "We seem to be assuming they won't be. Even if the general and his aide are out of it, couldn't one of the droids send the signal?"

"We will have to trust that they will not do so if it is not safe to do so," said Pakkpekatt. "Send the page."

Moments later, they heard Lando Calrissian's voice, shaky, hoarse and impatient, saying, "Yes, what is it, Threepio? What's happening now?"

"Sir, I did not—"

"Calrissian!" Pakkpekatt roared. "What are you doing alive?"

"Pakkpekatt!" Calrissian answered in kind. "What are you doing on my ship? And why are you just sitting there?"

"Hey, General—we're still waiting for our invitation," said Hammax.

"Hammax? Is that you?"

"They kept telling me you were dead, but I told them they were being overly optimistic."

"Spoken like a man on the wrong end of a gambling debt," said Lando. "Tell you what, Colonel—I'll forgive half of it for a ride back to Imperial City."

"Better sweeten that offer—I can get clear of the whole thing if we take you back in a box."

Even though his own outburst had triggered the torrent of animated familiarity, Pakkpekatt made an effort to reclaim and restrain the conversation. "General Calrissian, please advise your status."

"Status? Let's see, what don't you know? The ship's empty—completely automated, bioengineered. No one else is aboard. We're all more or less well. Lobot, haven't you gotten anywhere yet? Are you hearing all of this? What's *your* status, Colonel? Where's the task force?"

"We *are* the task force now," said Pakkpekatt. "The rest were recalled to other duty, and you and your party were written off."

"That's not funny, Colonel," said Lando. "The admiral would never do that."

"Which admiral? Coruscant is overrun with them," said Hammax. "General Rieekan redlined the mission after you ran off with his date."

Pakkpekatt rebuked the colonel with a glance. "General Calrissian, we've been looking for you ever since your escape. We believe we have a complete Qella genetic sequence, and we have an autoresponder set up. Rather than force the issue, I'd like to wait and see—"

Laughing tiredly, Lando said, "Predictable. Isn't this where we started, Colonel?"

"—if we can't get, as Colonel Hammax said, an invitation," Pakkpekatt continued. "I understand you must be eager to get out. But can you hold out a few more hours so we have a chance to—as someone once suggested I might consider—pick a lock rather than blow one up?"

Lando sighed. "I bow to the indisputable wisdom of your advisor. We can hold out a bit longer."

Hour after hour, the vagabond searched the surface of Maltha Obex, listening for the sign it had been told to wait for, waiting for the cue that would tell it what to do next.

Five times before, it had come here, obediently following the plan built into its very substance, trying to keep an appointment with those who had shaped it and

sent it into the void. Five times it had lingered, searching, waiting, bathing in the rich energies of N'oka
Brath, the glowstone. Five times it had gone away again,
not aware enough to be disappointed, but knowing that
its purpose was unfulfilled.

Never before, though, had it arrived here crippled—burned and poisoned by the intense energies that
had poured in through the same aperture through which
N'oka Brath fed it. The burns had healed, but the poi-
sons lingered, and with them a memory of the form and
action of the attacker.

And never before had it found others waiting—tiny
creatures sharing the circles above Brath Qella, the
homestone, the place of beginning. They were unfamiliar in form and did not sing. But they did not move
toward the vagabond, or reach out to touch it, and so it
left them alone, no imperatives having been invoked.
Still, it noted them and watched them closely.

After the appointed time for waiting, the vagabond
began singing. And for the first time in all its journeys
home, an answer came.

But the answer did not come from Brath Qella—it
came from one of the tiny eggs sharing the circles. And
the answer was sung harshly, without the gentle
strength of Brath Qella. The vagabond searched its
memories and knew the answer to be form without substance, a deception, a predator's lure.

And there were imperatives concerning predators.

When the vagabond finally broke its silence and
broadcast a fourteen-second interrogative, only Taisden
was on the flight deck to hear it.

Hammax was napping in his cabin, wearing all but
the boots and gauntlets of a combat suit. Pleck was on
the observation deck trying to coax what he considered
a more realistic measure of the vagabond's displacement
from what he suspected was a faulty magnetometer.
Pakkpekatt and Eckels were behind closed doors in
Lando's suite, engaged in a heated discussion prompted

by Eckels's belated discovery that an NRI team was aboard the Qella vessel.

Taisden's alarm roused all of them from their other pursuits, and brought all but Pleck running forward to the flight deck.

"Don't know what the question was, but we are responding," Taisden told them. "And the target is changing orbit and accelerating."

"Toward us?"

"Toward the relay satellite."

"She sure can motor when she wants to," Hammax said, shaking his head.

"Is this good?" Eckels demanded. "Is this what you expected?"

"Maybe," Taisden said. "If she's going over there to make nice, next time we can transmit our reply directly from *Lady Luck*—"

At that moment a blue glow appeared at the vagabond's bow, making it suddenly bright both through the viewscreens and on the monitors.

"The scythe," said Pakkpekatt.

"Impossible," said Taisden. "The satellite's three thousand klicks away from it—"

Three slender but brilliant beams of energy slashed across the darkness and came together at a point 3,409 kilometers ahead of the vagabond. Where they converged, there was a small explosion intense enough to leave an afterimage in their eyes. Then the glow vanished, and the lances disappeared, leaving a spreading cloud of atomized plasteel and metal glittering in the light of N'oka Brath.

"She did not go there to make nice," Hammax said in awe. "What kind of weapon *is* that?"

Even before the vagabond turned back, Taisden had shut down the autoresponder. At the same time, Pakkpekatt pulled the throttles back, dropping them into a lower, faster orbit that would carry them away from the vagabond and over its horizon.

"She could have taken out the whole task force at

Gmar Askilon at any time," said Taisden, shaking his head.

"Give me voice to Calrissian," said Pakkpekatt. "Run it through one of *Penga Rift*'s regular satellites."

"Ready," said Taisden. "Comm two."

"General," said Pakkpekatt, "this is *Lady Luck*. Why are you firing on us?"

"It wasn't *our* doing," Lando said. "What did you say to it? Why are you running away?"

"If your yacht has a sensor cloak or a shield of invulnerability, General, this would be a very good time to inform us."

Lando's answer was lost in a blast of static as the vagabond reached across nearly eight thousand kilometers and vaporized *Penga Rift*'s ORS-2.

"Going over the horizon from that thing looks better all the time," said Pakkpekatt.

"Six minutes."

"Colonel—" Eckels's voice had a tremble. "Perhaps it is time to transmit it all while there is still an operational satellite that can be used to relay it. Whatever message we sent just now was not taken well. Perhaps we need to be more convincing—or more confusing."

Pakkpekatt looked to Taisden. "I have no better ideas, Colonel."

"Then do it," he said. "Doctor—"

"Yes. Let me speak to *Penga Rift*."

Captain Barjas's voice answered the hail. "Doctor—thank goodness. We're showing two satellites have suddenly gone dead, and we were concerned."

"The vagabond has turned hostile," Eckels said. "Is everyone back on board?"

"Except for you. We just got the last of them up."

"Good. I order you to leave orbit immediately, and jump out to the agreed coordinates for rendezvous one."

"Very well, Dr. Eckels. Good luck, sir."

"We'll be all right. Get out of here—take care of my people."

"Eight minutes to horizon," said Taisden.

"What? How are we losing ground?"

"The target is accelerating toward ORS-One, which is currently relaying the Qella database."

Hammax shook his head. "Keeping the rock between us and it might not be all that easy to do."

"*Penga Rift* is getting under way," said Taisden.

"Perhaps the reply should be coming from the surface—" Eckels began.

Pakkpekatt ignored him. "Is there any spare bandwidth on ORS-One?"

"I can make some," said Taisden.

"I want to talk to Calrissian."

The agent's fingertips danced over the controls. "Ready on two."

"General, this is Pakkpekatt."

"Colonel," said Lando. "Looks a little warm out there. Is this a good time to mention that my yacht's uninsured? Perhaps you might consider running away just a little faster—"

"General Calrissian, I don't know how long we'll be able to talk. Is there anything you can do to put a stop to this?"

"I don't think so," said Lando. "We just had a little mutiny over here—about ten minutes ago, my good friend Lobot drained the power cell on our only blaster into one of the droids. The droids are backing him up."

"Do you know of any weakness or vulnerability of the vagabond that we can exploit?"

"Yes. Blaster cannon, cruiser-weight and up. The hull's not armored, and there don't seem to be ray shields, at least not at those frequencies. You can hole it and hurt it. But you have to get in the first shot, and make it good."

They could hear a second voice saying, "Lando, it does not deserve this—"

Then Eckels found his voice in protest, drowning out Lobot. "This is completely unacceptable, Colonel. This artifact is unique, irreplaceable—"

"And deadly," said Pakkpekatt. "Acknowledged,

General. Stand by." He gestured to Taisden. "Hyper-comm, secure, to Rieekan and Collomus."

"Go."

"This is Colonel Pakkpekatt, commanding, Teljkon task force at Maltha Obex," he said. "Confirming: We've found the vagabond and made contact with the team aboard. But the target has turned hostile, and we can't get anywhere near—"

The flight deck was suddenly and momentarily flooded with light, marking the precipitous disappearance of the third satellite.

"—it. I believe we could jump out using the planet as our shield, but only at the cost of losing contact with the vessel. I am opting to try to maintain contact, and requesting immediate assistance and support to secure the target and recover our people." He paused as though listening, then added, "Don't bother with a cruiser—send a Star Destroyer, or two. We're going to need a heavyweight to stop her."

Chapter 11

◆

The morning after the Battle of N'zoth, the Kell Plath Corporation liner *Star Morning* entered the system and requested a rendezvous with *Intrepid* for the purpose of picking up passengers.

Since the news did not directly involve Luke, he knew nothing of it until Wialu sent him a message requesting that he come to the cabin she and Akanah had been sharing. He found the women putting the cabin in order, preparing to leave. Akanah greeted him with an eager embrace.

"Did you hear? Our ship will be here in about an hour."

Luke turned to Wialu. "You're going back to J't'p'tan?"

"We are going away," she said. "It is time for us to find a quieter place. We need to grieve, and heal—to absorb the lessons of J't'p'tan, and find a new focus."

His gaze narrowed. "Then the rest of the Circle—they're on the ship already?"

"We are no longer needed at J't'p'tan," she said.

"And so the Fallanassi disappear again."

"We do not require or desire the attention of outsiders," said Wialu. "And events have already cost us much privacy. We will go away long enough and far enough to earn it back."

"I don't suppose I was expecting an invitation to come along," Luke said, turning his gaze on Akanah.

"I wish there were more time," she said, showing a sad smile. "I wish that I could finish what I started. It was unfair to you for me to make that promise, not knowing if there would be a chance to keep it."

"Unfair," Luke repeated. "I'm not sure that's a strong enough word. Because when you made me another promise, the one that brought me on this journey, you must have known that you *couldn't* keep it—that I'd run into a wall of silence if we found the Circle." He looked back toward Wialu. "Unless you asked me here to tell me more than good-bye."

"You can't ask that of her, Luke—"

"Why not?" he said, his gaze hardening. "She went to the trouble of scattering signs and markers across five sectors so that one child could come home. But she won't even come to the door when another one's standing outside knocking. Can you explain *that* to me, at least—why Akanah is welcomed back, and I'm being turned away?"

"Akanah is of the Fallanassi, by blood and affinity both," said Wialu. "We do not claim you, Luke Skywalker."

"You do not claim—what are you saying? That Nashira isn't my mother? That my mother wasn't of the Circle?"

Wialu nodded toward Akanah. "This is the one who must provide your answers."

Blinking, Luke stared at Akanah questioningly. She looked away uncomfortably, then sank down onto the edge of the bunk as though it were something fragile.

"I know nothing about your mother, Luke," she said in a small voice. "And I have not told you the truth about mine."

All of Luke's emotions save for curiosity were numbed by her words. "What does your mother have to do with this?"

"You remember what I told you of how it was for me, living on the underside on Carratos, and how my caretaker took my money and left me there—"

"Talsava," Luke said. "I remember."

Akanah looked up and met his eyes. "Everything I told you about her is true, save one—her name was Isela Talsava Norand, and she was my real mother," she said in a whisper. "And she was the one who brought the Empire down on the Circle."

Wordlessly, Luke sank into a chair. Wialu took up the narrative.

"We could not allow Isela to remain with the Circle after her betrayal," she said. "We could not trust her to know where we were bound when we left Lucazec. She was banished from the Circle before that decision was made. But Akanah was not banished—we would have kept her with us, cared for her, continued her training. She would have been loved.

"But Isela refused our offer, and took Akanah away with her. Isela's decision distressed us all. She was punishing Akanah for her own transgression. There was much grief and anger in the Circle on the day they left. And in my own grief, I made Akanah a promise—that the way back to us would be marked for her, so that when the choice was hers, she could rejoin the Circle." She looked at Akanah with an affectionate smile. "So many years went by that I thought we would never see her again."

"And I thought I would never leave Carratos."

"Why didn't you?" Luke asked.

"What I told you of my life there was the truth. The war came, and then I was left alone, with nothing," Akanah said. "I had to learn the ways of a world run by different rules, with no one to guide me or protect me. I have already admitted to Wialu how I misused what they taught me, to survive. How I became like the ones who had what I needed."

Akanah looked down at her hands and smiled as though at a fond and tender reminiscence. "Then there was the miracle of Andras, who created a safe place for

me, and brought love back to me—and though I could
have left Carratos then, I did not want to."

"So why did you make me part of it when you
finally did leave?" Luke asked. "You didn't need me to
find the Fallanassi, or to get to them—though you tried
to make me think that you did. The Imperial agents on
Lucazec—they were another lie, weren't they? We were
never being hunted."

"No," she admitted. "They were never there. It
was a test. I had to know who you were—what I could
expect from you, where to begin."

"The blood," Luke remembered.

"A mistake," she said. "I felt your surprise and
thought I had betrayed myself. I had never seen a lightsaber strike flesh. I had to draw your attention to me, to
Nashira, or I would have lost you then."

"Lost me for what? I still don't understand. What
was the deception meant to gain you?"

Sad-eyed, Akanah shook her head slowly. "It was
not for me, Luke. What you gave me, what this has
meant to me—that just happened, unexpected—that
wasn't planned."

"Then why?"

"Because I have been afraid of you," she said simply.

"I don't understand."

"Luke, I have seen the underside of war, where
there are no heroes, only victims. I've seen what power
is about, how it's used, what it means not to have it in a
world where that's all that matters." The weight of her
words was echoed in her sad eyes. "I was ten years old
when the Emperor's stormtroopers swept across half the
galaxy—I had a childhood in paradise and an adolescence in hell. I have good reason to fear power."

"You thought—think—I'm the same kind of threat
the Emperor was, the same as the stormtroopers?"

"It is not just you," Akanah said. "You are training
others to follow your path. Where there was one, there
are now many, and there will be many more. I had to
know you. I had to see what inside you balances the

power you have—I had to see what I could give you of what the Circle had given me. I did not lie to you about my purpose. Something has been missing, something of the Light, something of peace, of acceptance. I tried to help you find it."

"By lying to me," Luke said, his restless emotions bringing him to his feet.

Akanah smiled ruefully. "As you have seen, the Fallanassi are not above using deception."

"So Nashira was nothing but your fantasy? A reflection of what I wanted her to be?"

"No," said Akanah. "She was more than that."

"Akanah—" Wialu said in a cautionary tone.

"I have to tell him," Akanah said with sudden anger. "A secret is too much like another lie." She stood and took a step toward Luke. "In the second year, a woman came to see Isela on Carratos. She was Fallanassi, but I did not know her—she had not been with the Circle on Lucazec. She stayed with us for five days, and spent hours alone with my mother, talking."

Then she turned toward Wialu. "I think that she was sent by the Circle to try to persuade my mother to let me go. Perhaps she would even have taken me away with her when she left, if my mother would have agreed to it. I've wondered if my mother got her to agree to something else—a sum of money to be sent later, perhaps, to buy a child's passage, and a child's freedom. Who would expect that she would take the money and leave the child?"

Wialu's impassive face offered neither confirmation or apology. After a long moment of staring expectantly into her eyes, Akanah turned back to Luke.

"This woman's Circle name was Nashira," she said. "She was beautiful, and kind to me—enough to remind me of everything that Isela was not. She talked to me as if I mattered, and she shared her heart with me. When I asked her why, she said that the Emperor had taken her children from her—a boy and a girl. And all she could do was try to love the children who were near her, and hope that someone was doing the same for

hers. When you asked me about your mother, I pictured
the woman I wished had been mine. I told you about
Nashira."

"But it was all about you," Luke said, shaking his
head. "Your pain—your fantasies—"

"Are they so different from yours?" she asked. "I
have seen inside your heart, too, Luke Skywalker. I
could only deceive you by knowing you. I could only
deceive you with the truth."

Luke backed slowly away from her, toward the
cabin door. "Enough," he said. "I've heard enough. I
can't believe anything you say. I can't believe anything
that's happened since Coruscant. There's more truth in
her silence than in your words."

He gestured toward Wialu as he spoke the last,
then looked to her. "You must think me a fool, chasing
after the phantom *she* created. Thank you for the wake-
up call. I wish you luck in coaxing her off Isela's path,
and onto yours."

Then Luke turned and left the cabin, missing
Akanah's honest tears.

"Is he coming?" Akanah asked anxiously.

Etahn A'baht frowned and looked across the loading bay to the open entryway. "Let me check with my
people again," he said, reaching for his comlink and
stepping away from the foot of the boarding ramp.

Akanah looked to Wialu as a *Star Morning* porter
passed between them, carrying their bags aboard. "I
have to talk to him. I can't leave like this."

"How long would you have us wait?" Wialu asked
gently. "The damage you have done—"

"I know," Akanah said. "But I have to make him
see that it wasn't all lies."

"There can be one star of deception in a galaxy of
stars, but if that is the star before you, you can see
nothing else—and if you stare at the deception, you will
be blinded by it," said Wialu. "It will take time,
Akanah—more time than we have."

Akanah sent an anxious glance toward A'baht, who was returning to them. "If you can't wait, then I'll have to stay here."

"Akanah, you cannot force the flow to come to you," said Wialu. "You can only ride it where it goes."

The general rejoined them then, his frown deeper than before. "Luke's not answering. No one seems to know where he is," said A'baht. "I don't understand it—he brought you here, and I'd think he'd want to see you off. We owe you a debt—"

"There is no debt," Wialu said firmly. "The choice was mine, and I ask for nothing."

A'baht grunted. "I still feel I should apologize—"

"He is here," said Wialu.

The others looked toward the entryway, but Wialu directed her gaze toward an empty corner of the compartment. A moment later, Luke appeared there, as though walking through a door no one could see.

"What the—" A'baht said, then shook his head in disgust. "Jedi."

Akanah ran to meet Luke, but stopped a step short of the embrace she wanted, and looked into his eyes for a cue.

"I came to say good-bye," Luke said.

"I'm not sure that I'm leaving."

Luke shook his head. "Your place is with them. Wialu is right. Even I can read that in the Current."

"There's something I have to say before I can go," she said fervently. "Please—don't judge us by my example. I beg you not to reject the truth because of the lie that preceded it. There is something gentle, and beautiful, and healing in the Fallanassi way—and if I failed to put it before you, the weakness was in me, not in the way of the Light, or the path of the White Current. There is depth there beyond what I've mastered, and worth there beyond what you've seen."

"I've seen deception, manipulation—"

Stepping forward bravely, she touched his breastbone lightly with the flat of one hand. "It is not a way of power, but a way of peace—and I dearly wish for you to have that peace within you. I wish for you to add that strength to the great strength you already possess. I always wanted that for you—I never wanted anything from you." A tremble entered her voice as she added in a near whisper, "I never wanted to add to your pain."

Luke covered her hand with his own and lowered his eyes. "It seems I must choose what to believe," he said at last. "I will try to believe that first, and perhaps it will guide me through the rest."

She looked up at him gratefully. "Then I can go now," she said, and kissed his cheek softly before backing away.

He stood and watched as she accepted a final word of thanks from the general, then moved up the boarding ramp past Wialu, who turned and followed.

Akanah hesitated for just a moment before vanishing through the inner airlock, looking back to him with a final apology in her eyes. Somewhere he found a forgiving smile for her, and then she was gone.

By then A'baht was approaching Luke. "Comm shack has some messages for you, Luke—a couple of priority flags that came in this morning—" he began.

"Luke Skywalker."

Looking up at Wialu's voice, he found her standing at the inner airlock. "Yes?"

"There is one small service I ask of you."

Luke cocked his head. "What's that?"

"Tell your sister," Wialu said, "that when she is ready to follow her own path, she would be welcome among us." Then she turned away, needing no reply and inviting no questions.

By the time a startled Luke could find his voice again, *Star Morning* was moving away from the dock, continuing its journey.

There was no message from Leia.

The chief librarian's office on Obroa-skai advised him that his pending request for a contract researcher had moved up to number five on the waiting list, and he

should be certain he had the research subject FALLANASSI
clearly defined and all supporting materials ready to
transmit.

The senior rehab therapist on board the medical
frigate *High Haven* passed on the word that Han was
being transferred again, this time back to the Fleet hospital on Coruscant.

"It's not that he's in any danger—he's doing pretty
well, better than a lot of the folks in here now. And it
opens a space up on our ward, which we can use," said
the therapist. "Given that the commodore had his own
transportation available, it seemed like the best course."
After a pause and a frown, he added, "Besides, the
Wookiees insisted."

The third message was from Streen, who had com-
piled an overly conscientious report on activity at the
academy on Yavin 4. In his present mood, Luke found
none of it of enough interest to read closely.

The final message was from Alpha Blue.

"Hello, Luke," said Admiral Drayson. "Now that
things are a little quieter where you are, I wanted to tell
you that I've located your missing droids. You can have
them back whenever you want, in fact. But, as you'll
see, I'm afraid you're going to need to pick them up
yourself."

"Are you sure about this?" asked the senior crew
chief, following at Luke's heels as he carried out his
preflight check of the exterior of *Mud Sloth*. "Even with
the losses, I'm sure Captain Morano would be more
than willing to put you in most anything else we
have—"

"I'm sure," Luke said, ducking under the tail plane.

"I mean, after all, you Jedi swung the fight our
way, driving off all those Star Destroyers with your
phantom fleet," the chief persisted. "It just doesn't seem
right to send you away in a low-budget—"

"That isn't what happened," Luke said as he

reached the boarding ladder. "And this ship serves my needs right now."

The chief scratched his head. "Well, if you say so." He stole a glance back over his shoulder. "I guess the general'll be down to see you off, eh?"

"He doesn't know I'm leaving," Luke said, throwing his bag up through the open access hatch. "I'd appreciate it if you weren't in a hurry to tell him."

"That's a bit of a problem," the chief said, frowning. "Nothing's supposed to leave the flight deck without authorization from the hot room."

"Not my problem," Luke said, climbing the ladder. "Civilian pilot, civilian ship. Shouldn't even be here. Clear me through the patrol screen, will you? She's not real strong on flash breaks or roll-and-run."

"Sure," said the chief dubiously. "Sure, for you, I can do that. But, look, I have to at least be able to tell the booth where you're going—you know, for the log."

"You've never heard of it," Luke said as he reached for the hatch closure. "Just log me out, Chief—and thank the gang for prepping her so quickly."

Not long after, Luke and *Mud Sloth* plunged into the welcome solitude of hyperspace for the long jump to Maltha Obex.

By the end of that journey, Luke could feel himself changing. The ship was like a tiny chrysalis, and it was his metamorphosis that was underway.

He had wanted time where he and Akanah had spent so much time. He had wanted to hear the echoes of their conversations, feel the residue of the emotions. Luke spent the journey in silence, alternately reflecting and playing with reflections. He inventoried his memories of the last months, discarding some, rewriting others. And he collected a set of drill objects, and spent hours honing the one Fallanassi skill he grasped in its wholeness.

The work was not yet finished when the galaxy reappeared around him and Maltha Obex appeared before him. He did not know at that moment quite who he was becoming, or what would presage the transformation. He only knew that he welcomed that moment of reconnection, and the possibilities that it offered.

For days, *Lady Luck* had been fleeing before the Teljkon vagabond, staying over the horizon from the powerful and unpredictable Qella artifact. Two tasks had occupied them during that time—keeping tabs on the vagabond by means of the equipment at the abandoned surface camps, and scanning for what they hoped would be a task-force-sized entry into the Maltha Obex system.

But the ship that did finally appear on the scanners was so small that Joto Eckels felt a rush of disappointment rather than relief. "Perhaps it's some sort of probe," he suggested at Pakkpekatt's shoulder. "Don't you usually send a probe in ahead of the main body?"

"It's a civilian skiff," said Taisden. "No military comm."

"Then we have to warn it away at once," Eckels said. "Colonel, once the vagabond spots it, half an orbit from now—"

A display screen above their heads flashed on as he spoke. "This is *Mud Sloth,* hailing the *Lady Luck.* Lando, report your status, please."

Eckels began to look more hopeful as he recognized Luke's face. "Lando's not here, Luke—"

But Pakkpekatt rose from his seat, blocking Eckels from the holocomm as he leaned forward to reply. "*Mud Sloth,* you are entering an NRI security zone, and you are at risk. Turn your ship about at once and leave this system."

"You'd be Colonel Pakkpekatt, I take it," said Luke. "And was that Dr. Eckels? Is Lando still aboard the vagabond, then? You haven't been able to get to him? I need an update covering the last five days."

"You are not authorized for that information,"

said Pakkpekatt. "You are not cleared for this security zone."

"Colonel, I'm all the assistance you're likely to get for a while, given the demands on the Fleet at the moment. And I know Dr. Eckels doesn't want to see this expedition end with a shoot-out, anyway—"

"Absolutely correct," Eckels said, pushing his way into the holocomm's field of view.

"—so let's see if we can't work together and make something better happen."

"Do you have any ideas about what that might be, Luke?" said Eckels. "The artifact has been notably uncooperative so far—even more so than the colonel."

"I know. I've reviewed your reports—yours and his both," Luke said.

At that news, Pakkpekatt threw his hands in the air in disgust and turned away from the flight console. "I will demand an investigation of this entire operation," he muttered. "The breaches of security—the complete disregard for the lines of authority—"

"I think I can get the team off the vagabond," Luke went on. "But I'm hoping for more than that. Why don't you tell me what you think happened here, Doctor?"

"May I ask first if you're planning to board the vagabond yourself?"

"Yes, I am, Dr. Eckels."

"Then would it be possible for you to collect me before you do? I will likely have better answers for you once I've seen it for myself."

"I was hoping you'd offer, Doctor," Luke said. "If you and the colonel would locate some power packs for the droids and put together a mercy basket for the men, I'll rendezvous with you on your next orbit."

"Very good," said Eckels. "We'll be ready."

As the vagabond grew outside *Mud Sloth*'s cockpit viewpanes, Eckels looked nervously from it to Luke's face.

"How will you know if it's working?"

"We'll know if it isn't," Luke said, closing his eyes.

"Shouldn't we at least alert General Calrissian that we're coming in?"

"No signals," Luke said. "No sounds. No thrusters. Nothing that will disturb the flow. Nothing that will announce our presence."

Eckels looked back toward the alien vessel. "But can't it see us just as easily as we can see it?"

Luke shook his head slowly. "You're aboard a submarine, Doctor, not a spaceship. We're five hundred meters under the surface and just floating with the current. They won't know we're there until we bump up alongside."

The scientist received Luke's reassurances with a dubious expression. "You've done this before, I trust?"

"No, never," Luke said.

"Oh, my—"

"But I saw it done, not too long ago."

Eckels swallowed. "I trust that you've been practicing since then, at least."

Eyes still closed, Luke smiled. "All the way here. Relax, Doctor. I learned this trick from people who were at the top of their class in the business of hiding." He paused. "But even so, you might want to let me concentrate."

Pressing his lips together in a line, Eckels slumped against the back of his seat and stared at the vagabond, which now filled half the sky ahead.

"Lando."

At the sound of his name, Lando stirred and reached slowly for his comlink.

"What is it, Lobot?"

"Someone is here."

"Where here?" Lando said, suddenly shaking off his sleepy lassitude.

"Outside, near the bow." Lobot paused. "We are

puzzled. There is a touch, and yet we cannot find the source."

"They're knocking on the door," Lando said impatiently. "Open it up and see what comes in."

There was a long silence. "The visitors are in the interspace," Lobot said at last.

"So who or what are they?"

"We do not recognize them."

"I'll check it out," Lando said gruffly. Fatigue and hunger had left him in a state of permanent annoyance. "Artoo, let's go—power up. Artoo—"

The droid remained inert—like Threepio days before, its power supply was finally exhausted.

"Sure," he grumbled. "Make me be the one to check out the noise in the dark. It'd serve you both right if I never came back."

"Ahoy the ship," a new voice crackled over the comlink. "Anyone home?"

Lando blinked, trying to force his mind to recognize what it was hearing. "Luke? Luke, is that you? What are you doing here?"

"I could leave, if it's not a good time—"

"You leave without me, and I'll hunt you down and kill you one cell at a time," Lando warned, with no trace of humor in his voice. "Stay where you are. I'm coming out."

"We're already in," Luke said. "The vagabond's hull opened up and swallowed us whole."

"Nooo—"

"It's all right. We're in some sort of zero-g hangar area between the outer and inner hulls—we even seem to be tethered. I'm suiting up to come to you," said Luke. "Stay put and talk us in."

Grabbing a liter of water from Dr. Eckels, Lando drained it so fast that his stomach balked and threatened to reject it.

"Luke," Lando said, flipping the container away. "Can you believe it? This whole monstrosity is nothing but a museum—" He stopped to swallow the bitterness climbing his throat, and started coughing when the taste reached his mouth.

"Go easy, Lando—"

Lando waved off the concern. "A museum! And when—*when* have you ever known me to go near a museum?" He laughed hoarsely. "And you don't even know the funny part—none of the treasures is real. It's all just modeling clay—nothing of any value."

"Do you know what he's talking about, Dr. Eckels?"

"Possibly," Eckels said, digging in the supply pouch for a FirstMeal food pack.

Lando continued to babble, his tone turning sorrowful, almost maudlin. "Can only look—can't take anything with you. No souvenirs. What a waste of time, Luke—what a miserable waste of time. Like picking flowers. Pretty today, dead tomorrow—" He suddenly noticed the food pack and snatched it away, turning his back on them as though protecting it against poaching.

"Lando, where's Lobot?"

The answer came after a long draw on the food pack's straw. "He has new friends." Lando shrugged. "He hardly talks to me anymore." He chortled abruptly. "He's lost his mind. You'll see."

"Take us to him," Luke said firmly. "We need to take care of him, too."

Somersaulting slowly, Lando waved a hand absently toward the interior. "In there. Left, left, right, right, center, right, center. Something like that." The food pack expired with a sucking sound. "You can't miss him. He's the one with legs."

Luke and Dr. Eckels found Lobot curled up in a side tubule, floating, his eyes closed, his hands cupped against the side of his head. The transparent leads of his split interface tethered him to the rounded mass at the far end of the tubule.

"Do you have any idea what we're looking at here, Doctor?"

Eckels peered into an adjacent tubule for an unobstructed view. "These are the size and geometry of the Qella remains we recovered from the ice," he said in hushed awe.

"These don't feel like remains to me," Luke said, entering the tubule where Lobot was floating. "Lobot—it's Luke. Wake up, fella—your relief's here."

"Are you saying that they're alive?" Eckels demanded. "I had discounted those reports as unreliable."

"Why?"

"Why, it's unprecedented—unthinkable—"

"This whole ship feels alive to me, Doctor," Luke said. "Though with a different quality than I'm used to."

"Different how?"

"Usually this much power is matched with much greater awareness. It's almost like—sleeping. Just like Lobot here seems to be sleeping." Frowning, Luke reached out and dug his fingernails into Lobot's elbow. "Hey—talk to me."

"But these bodies have no limbs," Eckels protested. "The creatures on the surface were quadrupeds."

"I'm not trying to tell you what they are, Doctor. I'm just telling you that what Lobot reported is true—these things are alive, and this ship is alive. I'll let you tell me the relationship between them."

Lobot was stirring by then. "Waiting," he murmured in a trancelike monotone.

"Waiting for what?" Luke asked. "What question is that an answer to?"

Behind him, Eckels was frowning. "Physically, the relationship mirrors one that exists *inside* the Qella, between the Eicroth bodies and—" His eyes widened in surprise. "Luke, I must see the rest of this vessel at once. I must see these exhibits Lando spoke of."

"Lobot, talk to me," Luke was saying. "What do you need from me?"

"We wait," Lobot said dreamily.

"What are 'we'?" Luke asked.

"Answers," said Lobot.

"Yes, I need answers," Luke said. "What are you waiting for? What do you need?"

The words came haltingly. "We wait . . . for . . . the thaw."

Luke looked questioningly back at Eckels.

"I must see the ship," he insisted. "I will not make wild guesses when there is evidence at hand."

Nodding agreement, Luke said, "I think we need to break up Lobot's new friendship, anyway—I can hardly find a boundary between his mind and everything else. Know anything about neural interfaces, Doctor, or should I just pull the plug?"

Eckels grimaced. "Do what you think best. I'll wait outside."

It was nearly an hour before either Lando or Lobot was fit for their final duties as host and guide. For Eckels, it was an hour of maddening impatience. For Luke, it was an opportunity to bring the droids back online and begin repairs to Threepio's damaged arm.

"I'm very glad to see you, Master Luke," the droid said. "You won't believe the stories I have to tell you. I don't know *why* I was sent on this mission in the first place. Why, I was nearly vaporized by the vagabond, and then we were attacked by an entire fleet of warships. Master Calrissian abandoned me to be captured by intruders—"

Luke grinned. "It's good to see you, too, Threepio. And I promise to let you tell me all the stories, later. Twice, even, if you need to."

"That's very kind of you, sir."

When the droids had been moved to the skiff, Luke went off to explore with Lando, while Lobot led Eckels on a separate tour. But before long Lando decided the familiar comforts of a starship, however humble, had greater appeal than Luke's company, and excused himself from sight-seeing.

By then Luke understood the geometry and instrumentality of the vagabond well enough to manage on his own. The "museum" rooms and the interspace gallery were equally astonishing, but Luke found himself drawn back to the interior, to the maze of tubules and the clusters of what Luke had begun calling Eckels bodies. They were the center of the vagabond's limited consciousness, the focus of the flow of energy through the ship. Four hours vanished in an eyeblink before Luke even thought of rejoining the others. Another hour and a half passed before he actually did.

They were all there—Lando asleep in the bunk, Lobot stretched out on the floor of the systems compartment, Threepio strapped into the right-hand seat, and Artoo contentedly plugged into both the data port and the power port at the interface board.

Eckels was in the pilot's seat, bending forward over the ship's small data displays with a frown while keying the datapad on his lap fluidly by touch alone.

"I believe I have an answer for you now," Eckels said without looking away from his work. "Shall we wake the others?"

"No," said Luke. "They've done their part—let them rest. Let's compare notes first. If we find we have questions for them, we can take care of that later."

"I was able to get the benefit of Lobot's thoughts while he showed me around," said Eckels. "He has an admirably disciplined mind."

"People have been underestimating him for as long as I've known him," Luke said. "So what do you have?"

Eckels sat back in his seat and pointed to the data display. "Lobot was right," he said. "The moons are the key."

"The moons they saw in the orrery."

"Yes," said Eckels. "With the assistance of Colonel Pakkpekatt, we've analyzed the recordings Artoo-Detoo made the first time the expedition reached the auditorium and viewed the diorama. The orbits depicted for the moons turn out to be unstable."

"Check me if I've missed something, Doctor, but Maltha Obex has no moons."

Eckels nodded. "But Qella did. Unremarkable moons—nothing to inspire a grand mythology. At least not until one of them fell from the sky."

"The ice age is the result of a moonstrike," Luke said, his expression gravely thoughtful.

"Yes, it would appear so," said Eckels. "The smaller moon was a capture moon, with an irregular orbit. Working backward from Artoo's recordings, we found that the gravity of the larger moon disturbed the capture moon into a decaying orbit—a hundred years, in round numbers, before the fall."

"And the Qella saw it happening. They knew what lay ahead for them," Luke said. "And they used the warning, and the time they had left, to build this vessel."

"The ultimate and supreme achievement of their species," said Eckels. "Judging from what I saw, they did not have the means to destroy or repulse a moon—even the small moon of Maltha Obex dwarfed this vessel and its power. Nor did they have the means to evacuate a populous planet—the culture depicted in these serographs numbered hundreds of millions, if not more."

"It would have taken thousands of vessels this size," Luke said. "An impossible task in the time they had."

"But they could build one, and send it away before the end came," Eckels said. "When the expedition looked at the orrery, they saw this system as it was when the vagabond had last seen it—before the moonstrike, the destruction of the Qella, and the death of their planet under a blanket of ice."

Eckels gazed out the front of the cockpit at the faces of the gallery. "Your friend Lando was wrong," he went on. "What's here is very real. This ship isn't a collection of objects—it's a collection of ideas. We may never know why, but the Qella valued these ideas more than their lives. And that which we value is that which gives meaning to our lives. What a grand gift they have given us—what a gloriously defiant futility."

"Futility?" Luke asked. "What about those things in the interior? Lobot keeps wanting to call them Qella. *You* said that they *looked* like the Qella. And now the ship has brought them home."

Frowning, Eckels looked down at his datapad. "But there are only a few thousand of them, on a vessel that could have held many more." Eckels shook his head. "No, it cannot be. This is not an ark, or even a lifeboat. Those bodies are the controllers and protectors of this vessel, not its treasure. The real treasure of this vessel is in ideas and memories—a thousand years of history, a thousand years of art, this splendid bio-mechanical science. No, this is no museum. This is a monument, Luke."

"No," Luke said stubbornly. "There's something more here." Turning away, he dropped gracefully through the open entry hatch. Catching a handhold on the hull, he catapulted himself forward, away from the skiff and into the silence and darkness of the interspace.

There, drifting slowly in front of the Qella gallery, Luke extended his senses to the planet below. He found only a great stillness. There was no halo of life energy, no reservoir of the Force. The ice-encased surface had the same profound quiescence as the mass of rock below it.

"What are you looking for?"

"A reason to wait for the thaw," Luke said.

"So it can finish its journey," Eckels said. "It meant nothing more than that."

"Shhh," Luke said. He had drifted close to the outer skin of the vagabond, and he reached out and drew himself to it. He listened to the complex rhythms of the ship and allowed them to resolve into the deep, fundamental pulse of its being. He listened only to that pulse until he had absorbed it completely, knew it utterly.

Then he extended himself toward the planet once more, this time quieting his own urgency and desire, seeking that most profound state of egoless connection in which everything could be heard without distraction or distortion.

And suddenly there they were, like millions of grains of sand falling slowly to the surface—a collective heartbeat so faint and so languid that the slightest whisper of impatience would obscure it. With an exultant cry, Luke pushed himself away from the wall in a backward somersault.

"What? What is it?" Eckels exclaimed. He jetted across the open space to intercept Luke, catching him just before he reached the gallery.

But Luke twisted away from Eckels's grasp, turning to trace the lines of a Qella face with both hands. "The bodies you found—the Qella who roamed the ice—those weren't the survivors," Luke said. "They were the *dissenters*."

"What do you mean?"

"Exactly what I said. We were *all* wrong. This ship isn't a museum, or a temple full of treasure, or a lifeboat—or a monument, either. It's a tool kit, Doctor—a tool kit for rebuilding a destroyed world."

Turning, Luke grabbed both of Eckels's hands in a fervent grip. Joy and wonder together animated his smile. "They had time to do more than prepare this ship, Doctor—they had time to prepare themselves. That planet is not dead—there are millions of Qella buried in the ground, awaiting the thaw. And we can give them that."

As soon as *Mud Sloth* cleared the opening the vagabond had created for it, Luke gave the thrusters one hard kick, then turned the skiff around so that all could watch the Qella vessel fall away behind them.

"Are you sure you don't want to cloak us, like you did before?" Eckels said worriedly to Luke. "I'd really rather not contribute personally to the warming of Maltha Obex."

"The vagabond will not harm us," Lobot said with quiet assurance.

"Don't worry, Dr. Eckels," said Lando. "Lobot here spent so much time in the tubules that he got promoted to honorary egg."

Luke chuckled. "If you want something to worry about, Doctor, worry that your friends back at the Institute reversed two digits and dropped a decimal."

"Our very best planetary climatologist personally supervised the modeling of the Qella glacial epoch," Eckels said with stiff professional pride. "If Lobot communicated his recommendations accurately—"

"It understands," said Lobot. "The task required the building of a new strand of memory code, but it understands."

"I'm still surprised at how small an energy input it's supposed to take," Luke said. "I thought at first we'd have to bring in half a dozen Star Destroyers and keep them here a month."

"Small inputs, and time," said Eckels. "This planet teetered on the edge—it would probably have recovered on its own, as the Qella must have expected it would, but for the orbital wobble caused by the loss of the second moon."

"Look," said Lando. "It's starting."

The hull of the vagabond had begun to glow, crawling blue snakes of energy snapping along its length as the capacitance charge built up to a cascade. Then triple beams of energy stabbed downward from each end of the ship, creating ionized tunnels through the atmosphere in which precious chemicals began to be renewed. The beams converged at the surface of the half-frozen ocean below, creating massive explosions of steam, with towering, scalding plumes rising amidst the ice floes.

"Pretty good light show," Lando said lightly. "Kind of a shame there's only the six of us to see it."

"Quite the contrary, General Calrissian," said Eckels. "That soup will have to simmer a long time, and it would be best for the Qella if it did so undisturbed."

The bombardment of the planet went on throughout *Mud Sloth*'s long climb toward its rendezvous with *Lady Luck*. When the two craft finally met and docked, Lando and Lobot both eagerly escaped the crowded skiff for the luxury accommodations of the yacht. Threepio went with them, chasing a promise of an oil bath.

But Luke and Eckels lingered, looking down on Maltha Obex as the vagabond, now a small thing in the distance, fell silent. Neither man spoke of his thoughts, but they shared a single mood of lingering awe and curiosity.

When Luke closed his eyes and began breathing in deep, slow waves, Eckels noted it without comment. But he was not wholly surprised when, a short time later, the vagabond disappeared completely from view.

"You *have* been practicing," Eckels said, clapping Luke's shoulder approvingly. "I confess I want to stay and document it all—most especially the day when the Qella begin to emerge. But this is best, to leave them alone. Tell me, what will you have done last?"

"I don't know how long it will last," Luke said, gazing down on the planet. "Maybe not long at all. The forces affecting the ship are complex, and my teacher said that my touch is still too heavy. I had to try, though—try to draw the curtain and give them back their privacy, give them some time to heal, to build." He looked toward Eckels. "But I *want* to come back, to meet them. I wonder how long we'll have to wait."

There was more than a touch of sorrow and regret in the archaeologist's answering smile.

"Give them a hundred years," Eckels said, knowing as he spoke that that meant he would never return to Maltha Obex. "Or a thousand. We will let this place stay on the charts as a dead, frozen world with nothing worth stealing or exploiting. The Qella will not miss us. Their lives will be full without us. You have given them a great gift, Luke—a future." He looked out toward the pale white disc of the planet. "Somehow I know they will make the most of it."

EPILOGUE:

Coruscant, Eight Days Later

A damp, cold wind blowing out of a broken sky buffeted Luke Skywalker as he stood on the cliff above his seacoast hermitage. He stood there a long time, thinking of all the reasons he had raised it from the rocky sands, of the work he had thought to do there.

He had taken the broken pieces of his father's fortress retreat and tried to remake them into something that could redeem them from their history. But he saw now that all he had managed to build was a prison, and that he had been fortunate to escape it.

Extending his hands and his will, Luke found the points of greatest stress within the structure and pressed upon them, found the points of greatest fragility and sundered them. With a roar that momentarily rivaled the wind, the hermitage collapsed in on itself, crushing the fighter still sealed within it.

But that was not enough to satisfy Luke, not enough to forever erase the temptation. One after another, he raised the pieces of the ruined hermitage, the broken ship, up out of the sand and into the air, crumbling them with the force of his thoughts, until it was a dense, swirling cloud of pebble-sized fragments and metal bits.

Then, with a final, explosive effort of will, he hurled the cloud of debris far out beyond the breakers, where it rained down on the churning water and vanished from sight.

"It's not time yet for me to go away," he said to the wind by way of explanation. "And when the time comes, there will be a better place for me than this."

Guiding her three children through the gate ahead of her, Leia nodded to S-EP1 as she passed by. "You can lock down the perimeter, Sleepy," she said. "We're in for the night, and everyone else can stay out till morning."

"Yes, Princess."

Jacen and Jaina ran on ahead along the flower-lined path, and unexpected laughter and delighted squeals came back to Leia moments after they were out of sight. Leaving Anakin ambling on alone, she hurried toward the house to see what the cause of the commotion might be. But after only a few long strides, she was brought up short by the sight of Luke carrying Jaina in one arm, with Jacen at his other elbow. The three of them were all smiles, though Luke's faded quickly when he saw Leia's expression.

"Been to the Fleet hospital, I hear," Luke said, making room on the other arm for Anakin. "How's Han doing?"

"Better," she said. "He's out of the tank now, and looking more like himself. This was the first time I took the children. What are you doing here?"

"Belatedly accepting an invitation," he said, showing a rueful smile.

"Help me get the children to bed," she said.

That took some time, for Luke's surprise appearance had swept away any hint of sleepiness. The children would literally not let go of him without a promise that they would see him in the morning.

"But right now, your mom and I need to talk," Luke said firmly. "So it's lights out and eyes closed for you. Think about your father and send him healing thoughts, so that he can come home as soon as possible."

Leia watched and listened with a passive curiosity. When she and Luke were finally alone in the warmly lit family room, she asked lightly, "Who are you, and what have you done with my brother?"

He laughed. "I haven't changed as much as you probably wish."

"Did you find what you were hoping to?"

The laugh faded from his eyes. "No," he said. "But as happens sometimes, I found something else. I don't know if I can explain what."

"I can feel a difference in you," Leia said. "You feel—calmer."

"A lot happened," he said. "I learned from some of it. Leia, I still want to know who our mother was, and what she gave to us. That still matters to me. Not knowing is an empty hole inside me, and some of what Akanah told me would fill it so well that I still want to believe it."

"But you came back."

"It's the one little piece that maybe I did find that brought me back," Luke said. "A lesson about love and family from a woman I never met, and probably never will. Leia, it's crazy for me to be chasing a hope from Core to Rim when you and these kids are right here, real as can be. And if you'd still let me be part of loving them, and teaching them, and sharing your delight at watching them grow—well, I'm the Jedi uncle you're looking for."

Her eyes misting, Leia went to him and gathered him into a long, fiercely glad embrace. "Welcome to my family, Luke," she whispered, both offering and accepting the familiar and comforting warmth of connection. "Welcome home."

About the Author

Michael P. Kube-McDowell* is the pen name of Philadelphia-born novelist Michael Paul McDowell. His highly praised prior works include the star-spanning 1985 Philip K. Dick Award finalist *Emprise* and the evocative 1991 Hugo Award nominee *The Quiet Pools*. Both of the preceding "Black Fleet Crisis" books were *New York Times*, *USA Today*, *Publishers Weekly*, and *Washington Post* bestsellers.

In addition to his ten previous novels, Michael has contributed more than two dozen short stories to leading magazines and anthologies, including *Analog*, *The Magazine of Fantasy & Science Fiction*, *After the Flames*, and *Alternate Warriors*. Three of his stories have been adapted as episodes of the horror-fantasy television series *Tales from the Darkside*. Outside of science fiction, he is the author of more than five hundred nonfiction articles on subjects ranging from "scientific creationism" to the U.S. space program.

A popular guest at SF conventions throughout the Midwest, Michael is also a member of the cheerfully amateur folk-rock group The Black Book Band, in

* "Kube" is pronounced "CUE-bee."

which he plays guitar, keyboards, and viola. A live album, *First Contact*, was released in 1995 by Dodeka Records.

Michael resides in central Michigan with artist and modelmaker Gwen Zak, children Matt, Amanda, and Gavin, cats Doc and Captain, and "entirely too much stuff." Passions he will admit to publicly include the Philadelphia Phillies, Michigan State University, New Jersey soul food (birch beer, pork roll, and Tastykakes), the Hammond B-3, and the Oregon coast. At various times he has called Fairview Village (Camden), New Jersey; East Lansing, Sturgis, and Lansing, Michigan; and Goshen, Indiana, home.

The World of
STAR WARS Novels

In May 1991, *Star Wars* caused a sensation in the publishing industry with the Bantam Spectra release of Timothy Zahn's novel *Heir to the Empire*. For the first time, Lucasfilm Ltd. had authorized new novels that *continued* the famous story told in George Lucas's three blockbuster motion pictures: *Star Wars, The Empire Strikes Back,* and *Return of the Jedi*. Reader reaction was immediate and tumultuous: *Heir* reached #1 on the *New York Times* bestseller list and demonstrated that *Star Wars* lovers were eager for exciting new stories set in this universe, written by leading science fiction authors who shared their passion. Since then, each Bantam *Star Wars* novel has been an instant national bestseller.

Lucasfilm and Bantam decided that future novels in the series would be interconnected: that is, events in one novel would have consequences in the others. You might say that each Bantam *Star Wars* novel, enjoyable on its own, is also part of a much larger tale.

Here is a special look at Bantam's *Star Wars* books, along with excerpts from the more recent novels. Each one is available now wherever Bantam Books are sold.

SHADOWS OF THE EMPIRE
by Steve Perry
Setting: Between *The Empire Strikes Back* and *Return of the Jedi*

Here is a very special STAR WARS story dealing with Black Sun, a galaxy-spanning criminal organization that is masterminded by one of the most interesting villains in the STAR WARS universe: Xizor, dark prince of the Falleen. Xizor's chief rival for the favor of Emperor Palpatine is none other than Darth Vader himself—alive and well, and a major character in this story, since it is set during the events of the STAR WARS film trilogy.

In the opening prologue, we revisit a familiar scene from The Empire Strikes Back, *and are introduced to our marvelous new bad guy:*

He looks like a walking corpse, Xizor thought. *Like a mummified body dead a thousand years. Amazing he is still alive, much less the most powerful man in the galaxy. He isn't even that old; it is more as if something is slowly eating him.*

Xizor stood four meters away from the Emperor, watching as the man who had long ago been Senator Palpatine moved to stand in the holocam field. He imagined he could smell the decay in the Emperor's worn body. Likely that was just some trick of the recycled air, run through dozens of filters to ensure that there was no chance of any poison gas being introduced into it. Filtered the life out of it, perhaps, giving it that dead smell.

The viewer on the other end of the holo-link would see a close-up of the Emperor's head and shoulders, of an age-ravaged face shrouded in the cowl of his dark zeyd-cloth robe. The man on the other end of the transmission, light-years away, would not see Xizor, though Xizor would be able to see him. It was a measure of the Emperor's trust that Xizor was allowed to be here while the conversation took place.

The man on the other end of the transmission—if he could still be called that—

The air swirled inside the Imperial chamber in front of the Emperor, coalesced, and blossomed into the image of a figure down on one knee. A caped humanoid biped dressed in jet black, face hidden under a full helmet and breathing mask:

Darth Vader.

Vader spoke: "What is thy bidding, my master?"

If Xizor could have hurled a power bolt through time and space to strike Vader dead, he would have done it without blinking. Wishful thinking: Vader was too powerful to attack directly.

"There is a great disturbance in the Force," the Emperor said.

"I have felt it," Vader said.

"We have a new enemy. Luke Skywalker."

Skywalker? That had been Vader's name, a long time ago. Who was this person with the same name, someone so powerful as to be worth a conversation between the Emperor and his most loathsome creation? More importantly, why had Xizor's agents not uncovered this before now? Xizor's ire was instant—but cold. No sign of his surprise or anger would show on his imperturbable features. The Falleen did not allow their emotions to burst forth as did many of the inferior species; no, the Falleen ancestry was not fur but scales, not mammalian but reptilian. Not wild but coolly calculating. Such was much better. Much safer.

"Yes, my master," Vader continued.

"He could destroy us," the Emperor said.

Xizor's attention was riveted upon the Emperor and the holographic image of Vader kneeling on the deck of a ship far away. Here was interesting news indeed. Something the Emperor perceived as a danger to himself? Something the Emperor feared?

"He's just a boy," Vader said. "Obi-Wan can no longer help him."

Obi-Wan. That name Xizor knew. He was among the last of the Jedi Knights, a general. But he'd been dead for decades, hadn't he?

Apparently Xizor's information was wrong if Obi-Wan had been helping someone who was still a boy. His agents were going to be sorry.

Even as Xizor took in the distant image of Vader and the nearness of the Emperor, even as he was aware of the luxury of the Emperor's private and protected chamber at the core of the giant pyramidal palace, he was also able to make a mental note to himself: Somebody's head would roll for the failure to make him aware of all this. Knowledge was power; lack of knowledge was weakness. This was something he could not permit.

The Emperor continued. "The Force is strong with him. The son of Skywalker must not become a Jedi."

Son of Skywalker?

Vader's son! Amazing!

"If he could be turned he would become a powerful ally," Vader said.

There was something in Vader's voice when he said this, something Xizor could not quite put his finger on. Longing? Worry? Hope?

"Yes . . . yes. He would be a great asset," the Emperor said. "Can it be done?"

There was the briefest of pauses. "He will join us or die, master."

Xizor felt the smile, though he did not allow it to show any more than he had allowed his anger play. Ah. Vader wanted Skywalker alive, *that* was what had been in his tone. Yes, he had said that the boy would join them or die, but this latter part was obviously meant only to placate the Emperor. Vader had no intention of killing Skywalker, his own son; that was obvious to one as skilled in reading voices as was Xizor. He had not gotten to be the Dark Prince, Underlord of Black Sun, the largest criminal organization in the galaxy, merely on his formidable good looks. Xizor didn't truly understand the Force that sustained the Emperor and made him and Vader so powerful, save to know that it certainly worked somehow. But he did know that it was something the extinct Jedi had supposedly mastered. And now, apparently, this new player had tapped into it. Vader wanted Skywalker alive, had practically promised the Emperor that he would deliver him alive—and converted.

This was most interesting.

Most interesting indeed.

The Emperor finished his communication and turned back to face him. "Now, where were we, Prince Xizor?"

The Dark Prince smiled. He would attend to the business at hand, but he would not forget the name of Luke Skywalker.

THE TRUCE AT BAKURA by Kathy Tyers
Setting: Immediately after *Return of the Jedi*

The day after his climactic battle with Emperor Palpatine and the sacrifice of his father, Darth Vader, who died saving his life, Luke Skywalker helps recover an Imperial drone ship bearing a startling message intended for the Emperor. It is a distress signal from the far-off Imperial outpost of Bakura, which is under attack by an alien invasion force, the Ssi-ruuk. Leia sees a rescue mission as an opportunity to achieve a diplomatic victory for the Rebel Alliance, even if it means fighting alongside former Imperials. But Luke receives a vision from Obi-Wan Kenobi revealing that the stakes are even higher: the invasion at Bakura threatens everything the Rebels have won at such great cost.

STAR WARS: X-WING
by Michael A. Stackpole
ROGUE SQUADRON
WEDGE'S GAMBLE
THE KRYTOS TRAP
THE BACTA WAR
Setting: Three years after *Return of the Jedi*

Inspired by X-wing, *the bestselling computer game from LucasArts Entertainment Co., this exciting series chronicles the further adventures of the most feared and fearless fighting force in the galaxy. A new generation of X-wing pilots, led by Commander Wedge Antilles, is combating the remnants of the Empire still left after the events of the STAR WARS movies. Here are novels full of explosive space action, nonstop adventure, and the special brand of wonder known as STAR WARS.*

In this very early scene, young Corellian pilot Corran Horn faces a tough challenge fast enough to get his heart pounding—and this is only a simulation! [P.S.: "Whistler" is Corran's R2 astromech droid]:

The Corellian brought his proton torpedo targeting program up and locked on to the TIE. It tried to break the lock, but turbolaser fire from the *Korolev* boxed it in. Corran's heads-up display went red and he triggered the torpedo. "Scratch one eyeball."

The missile shot straight in at the fighter, but the pilot broke hard to port and away, causing the missile to overshoot the target. *Nice flying!* Corran brought his X-wing over and started down to loop in behind the TIE, but as he did so, the TIE vanished from his forward screen and reappeared in his aft arc. Yanking the stick hard to the right and pulling it back, Corran wrestled the X-wing up and to starboard, then inverted and rolled out to the left.

A laser shot jolted a tremor through the simulator's couch. *Lucky thing I had all shields aft!* Corran reinforced them with energy from his lasers, then evened them out fore and aft. Jinking the fighter right and left, he avoided laser shots coming in from behind, but they all came in far closer than he liked.

He knew Jace had been in the bomber, and Jace was the only pilot in the unit who could have stayed with him. *Except for our leader.* Corran smiled broadly. *Coming to see how good I really am, Commander Antilles? Let me give you a clinic.* "Make sure you're in there solid, Whistler, because we're going for a little ride."

Corran refused to let the R2's moan slow him down. A snap-roll brought the X-wing up on its port wing. Pulling back on the stick yanked the fighter's nose up away from the original line of flight. The TIE stayed with him, then tightened up on the arc to close distance. Corran then rolled another ninety degrees and continued the turn into a dive. Throttling back, Corran hung in the dive for three seconds, then hauled back hard on the stick and cruised up into the TIE fighter's aft.

The X-wing's laser fire missed wide to the right as the TIE cut to the left. Corran kicked his speed up to full and broke with the TIE. He let the X-wing rise above the plane of the break, then put the fighter through a twisting roll that ate up enough time to bring him again into the TIE's rear. The TIE snapped to the right and Corran looped out left.

He watched the tracking display as the distance between them grew to be a kilometer and a half, then slowed. *Fine, you want to go nose to nose? I've got shields and you don't.* If Commander Antilles wanted to commit virtual suicide, Corran was happy to oblige him. He tugged the stick back to his sternum and rolled out in an inversion loop. *Coming at you!*

The two starfighters closed swiftly. Corran centered his foe in the crosshairs and waited for a dead shot. Without shields the TIE fighter would die with one burst, and Corran wanted the kill to be clean. His HUD flicked green as the TIE juked in and out of the center, then locked green as they closed.

The TIE started firing at maximum range and scored hits. At that distance the lasers did no real damage against the shields, prompting Corran to wonder why Wedge was wasting the energy. Then, as the HUD's green color started to flicker, realization dawned. *The bright bursts on the shields are a distraction to my targeting! I better kill him now!*

Corran tightened down on the trigger button, sending red laser needles stabbing out at the closing TIE fighter. He couldn't tell if he had hit anything. Lights flashed in the cockpit and Whistler started screeching furiously. Corran's main monitor went black, his shields were down, and his weapons controls were dead.

The pilot looked left and right. "Where is he, Whistler?"

The monitor in front of him flickered to life and a diagnostic report began to scroll by. Bloodred bordered the damage reports. "Scanners, out; lasers, out; shields, out; engine, out! I'm a wallowing Hutt just hanging here in space."

THE COURTSHIP OF PRINCESS LEIA
by Dave Wolverton
Setting: Four years after *Return of the Jedi*

One of the most interesting developments in Bantam's Star Wars *novels is that in their storyline, Han Solo and Princess Leia start a family. This tale reveals how the couple originally got together. Wishing to strengthen the fledgling New Republic by bringing in powerful allies, Leia opens talks with the Hapes consortium of more than sixty worlds. But the consortium is ruled by the Queen Mother, who, to Han's dismay, wants Leia to marry her son, Prince Isolder. Before this action-packed story is over, Luke will join forces with Isolder against a group of Force-trained "witches" and face a deadly foe.*

HEIR TO THE EMPIRE
DARK FORCE RISING
THE LAST COMMAND
by Timothy Zahn
Setting: Five years after *Return of the Jedi*

This #1 bestselling trilogy introduces two legendary forces of evil into the Star Wars *literary pantheon. Grand Admiral Thrawn has taken control of the Imperial fleet in the years since the destruction of the Death Star, and the mysterious Joruus C'baoth is a fearsome Jedi Master who has been seduced by the dark side. Han and Leia have now been married for about a year, and as the story begins, she is pregnant with twins. Thrawn's plan is to crush the Rebellion and resurrect the Empire's New Order with C'baoth's help—and in return, the Dark Master will get Han and Leia's Jedi children to mold as he wishes. For as readers of this magnificent trilogy will see, Luke Skywalker is not the last of the old Jedi. He is the first of the new.*

The Jedi Academy Trilogy:
JEDI SEARCH
DARK APPRENTICE
CHAMPIONS OF THE FORCE
by Kevin J. Anderson
Setting: Seven years after *Return of the Jedi*

In order to assure the continuation of the Jedi Knights, Luke Skywalker has decided to start a training facility: a Jedi Academy. He will gather Force-sensitive students who show potential as prospective Jedi and serve as their mentor, as Jedi Masters Obi-Wan Kenobi and Yoda did for him. Han and Leia's twins are now toddlers, and there is a third Jedi child: the infant Anakin, named after Luke and Leia's father. In this trilogy, we discover the existence of a powerful Imperial doomsday weapon, the horrifying Sun Crusher—which will soon become the centerpiece of a titanic struggle between Luke Skywalker and his most brilliant Jedi Academy student, who is delving dangerously into the dark side.

CHILDREN OF THE JEDI
by Barbara Hambly
Setting: Eight years after *Return of the Jedi*

The Star Wars *characters face a menace from the glory days of the Empire when a thirty-year-old automated Imperial Dreadnaught comes to life and begins its grim mission: to gather forces and annihilate a long-forgotten stronghold of Jedi children. When Luke is whisked onboard, he begins to communicate with the brave Jedi Knight who paralyzed the ship decades ago, and gave her life in the process. Now she is part of the vessel, existing in its artificial intelligence core, and guiding Luke through one of the most unusual adventures he has ever had.*

In this scene, Luke discovers that an evil presence is gathering, one that will force him to join the battle:

Like See-Threepio, Nichos Marr sat in the outer room of the suite to which Cray had been assigned, in the power-down mode that was the droid equivalent of rest. Like Threepio, at the sound of Luke's almost noiseless tread he turned his head, aware of his presence.

"Luke?" Cray had equipped him with the most sensitive vocal modulators, and the word was calibrated to a whisper no louder than the rustle of the blueleaves massed outside the windows. He rose, and crossed to where Luke stood, the dull silver of his arms and shoulders a phantom gleam in the stray flickers of light. "What is it?"

"I don't know." They retreated to the small dining area where Luke had earlier probed his mind, and Luke stretched up to pin back a corner of the lamp-sheath, letting a slim triangle of butter-colored light fall on the purple of the vulwood tabletop. "A dream. A premonition, maybe." It was on his lips to ask, *Do you dream?* but he remembered the ghastly, imageless darkness in Nichos's mind, and didn't. He wasn't sure if his pupil was aware of the difference from his human perception and knowledge, aware of just exactly what he'd lost when his consciousness, his self, had been transferred.

In the morning Luke excused himself from the expedition Tomla El had organized with Nichos and Cray to the Falls of Dessiar, one of the places on Ithor most renowned for its beauty and peace. When they left he sought out Umwaw Moolis, and the tall herd leader listened gravely to his less than logical request and promised to put matters in train to fulfill it. Then Luke descended to the House of the Healers, where Drub McKumb lay, sedated far beyond pain but with all the perceptions of agony and nightmare still howling in his mind.

"Kill you!" He heaved himself at the restraints, blue eyes glaring furiously as he groped and scrabbled at Luke with his clawed hands. "It's all poison! I see you! I see the dark light all around you! You're him! You're him!" His back bent like a bow; the sound of his shrieking was like something being ground out of him by an infernal mangle.

Luke had been through the darkest places of the universe and of his own mind, had done and experienced greater evil than perhaps any man had known on the road the Force had dragged him . . . Still, it was hard not to turn away.

"We even tried yarrock on him last night," explained the Healer in charge, a slightly built Ithorian beautifully tabby-striped green and yellow under her simple tabard of purple linen. "But apparently the earlier doses that brought him enough lucidity to reach here from his point of origin oversensitized his system. We'll try again in four or five days."

Luke gazed down into the contorted, grimacing face.

"As you can see," the Healer said, "the internal perception of pain and fear is slowly lessening. It's down to ninety-three percent of what it was when he was first brought in. Not much, I know, but something."

"Him! *Him! HIM!*" Foam spattered the old man's stained gray beard.

Who?

"I wouldn't advise attempting any kind of mindlink until it's at least down to fifty percent, Master Skywalker."

"No," said Luke softly.

Kill you all. And, *They are gathering . . .*

"Do you have recordings of everything he's said?"

"Oh, yes." The big coppery eyes blinked assent. "The transcript is available through the monitor cubicle down the hall. We could make nothing of them. Perhaps they will mean something to you."

They didn't. Luke listened to them all, the incoherent groans and screams, the chewed fragments of words that could be only guessed at, and now and again the clear disjointed cries: "Solo! Solo! Can you hear me? Children . . . Evil . . . Gathering here . . . Kill you all!"

DARKSABER by Kevin J. Anderson
Setting: Immediately thereafter

Not long after Children of the Jedi, *Luke and Han learn that evil Hutts
are building a reconstruction of the original Death Star—and that the
Empire is still alive, in the form of Daala, who has joined forces with
Pellaeon, former second in command to the feared Grand Admiral
Thrawn. In this early scene, Luke has returned to the home of Obi-
Wan Kenobi on Tatooine to try and consult a long-gone mentor:*

He stood anxious and alone, feeling like a prodigal son outside the
ramshackle, collapsed hut that had once been the home of Obi-Wan
Kenobi.

Luke swallowed and stepped forward, his footsteps crunching in the
silence. He had not been here in many years. The door had fallen off
its hinges; part of the clay front wall had fallen in. Boulders and
crumbled adobe jammed the entrance. A pair of small, screeching
desert rodents snapped at him and fled for cover; Luke ignored them.

Gingerly, he ducked low and stepped into the home of his first
mentor.

Luke stood in the middle of the room breathing deeply, turning
around, trying to sense the presence he desperately needed to see. This
was the place where Obi-Wan Kenobi had told Luke of the Force.
Here, the old man had first given Luke his lightsaber and hinted at the
truth about his father, "from a certain point of view," dispelling the
diversionary story that Uncle Owen had told, at the same time planting seeds of his own deceptions.

"Ben," he said and closed his eyes, calling out with his mind as
well as his voice. He tried to penetrate the invisible walls of the Force
and reach to the luminous being of Obi-Wan Kenobi who had visited
him numerous times, before saying he could never speak with Luke
again.

"Ben, I need you," Luke said. Circumstances had changed. He
could think of no other way past the obstacles he faced. Obi-Wan had
to answer. It wouldn't take long, but it could give him the key he
needed with all his heart.

Luke paused and listened and sensed—

But felt nothing. If he could not summon Obi-Wan's spirit here in
the empty dwelling where the old man had lived in exile for so many
years, Luke didn't believe he could find his former teacher ever again.

He echoed the words Leia had used more than a decade earlier, beseeching him, "Help me, Obi-Wan Kenobi," Luke whispered, "you're my only hope."

THE CRYSTAL STAR
by Vonda N. McIntyre
Setting: Ten years after _Return of the Jedi_

Leia's three children have been kidnapped. That horrible fact is made worse by Leia's realization that she can no longer sense her children through the Force! While she, Artoo-Detoo, and Chewbacca trail the kidnappers, Luke and Han discover a planet that is suffering strange quantum effects from a nearby star. Slowly freezing into a perfect crystal and disrupting the Force, the star is blunting Luke's power and crippling the Millennium Falcon. _These strands converge in an apocalyptic threat not only to the fate of the New Republic, but to the universe itself._

The Black Fleet Crisis
BEFORE THE STORM
SHIELD OF LIES
TYRANT'S TEST
by Michael P. Kube-McDowell
Setting: Twelve years after _Return of the Jedi_

Long after setting up the hard-won New Republic, yesterday's Rebels have become today's administrators and diplomats. But the peace is not to last for long. A restless Luke must journey to his mother's homeworld in a desperate quest to find her people; Lando seizes a mysterious spacecraft with unimaginable weapons of destruction; and waiting in the wings is an horrific battle fleet under the control of a ruthless leader bent on a genocidal war.

Here is an opening scene from Before the Storm:

In the pristine silence of space, the Fifth Battle Group of the New Republic Defense Fleet blossomed over the planet Bessimir like a beautiful, deadly flower.

The formation of capital ships sprang into view with startling suddenness, trailing fire-white wakes of twisted space and bristling with weapons. Angular Star Destroyers guarded fat-hulled fleet carriers, while the assault cruisers, their mirror finishes gleaming, took the point.

A halo of smaller ships appeared at the same time. The fighters among them quickly deployed in a spherical defensive screen. As the Star Destroyers firmed up their formation, their flight decks quickly spawned scores of additional fighters.

At the same time, the carriers and cruisers began to disgorge the bombers, transports, and gunboats they had ferried to the battle. There was no reason to risk the loss of one fully loaded—a lesson the Republic had learned in pain. At Orinda, the commander of the fleet carrier *Endurance* had kept his pilots waiting in the launch bays, to protect the smaller craft from Imperial fire as long as possible. They were still there when *Endurance* took the brunt of a Super Star Destroyer attack and vanished in a ball of metal fire.

Before long more than two hundred warships, large and small, were bearing down on Bessimir and its twin moons. But the terrible, restless power of the armada could be heard and felt only by the ships' crews. The silence of the approach was broken only on the fleet comm channels, which had crackled to life in the first moments with encoded bursts of noise and cryptic ship-to-ship chatter.

At the center of the formation of great vessels was the flagship of the Fifth Battle Group, the fleet carrier *Intrepid*. She was so new from the yards at Hakassi that her corridors still reeked of sealing compound and cleaning solvent. Her huge realspace thruster engines still sang with the high-pitched squeal that the engine crews called "the baby's cry."

It would take more than a year for the mingled scents of the crew to displace the chemical smells from the first impressions of visitors. But after a hundred more hours under way, her engines' vibrations would drop two octaves, to the reassuring thrum of a seasoned thruster bank.

On *Intrepid*'s bridge, a tall Dornean in general's uniform paced along an arc of command stations equipped with large monitors. His eye-folds were swollen and fanned by an unconscious Dornean defensive reflex, and his leathery face was flushed purple by concern. Before the deployment was even a minute old, Etahn A'baht's first command had been bloodied.

The fleet tender *Ahazi* had overshot its jump, coming out of hyperspace too close to Bessimir and too late for its crew to recover from the error. Etahn A'baht watched the bright flare of light in the upper atmosphere from *Intrepid*'s forward viewstation, knowing that it meant six young men were dead.

THE NEW REBELLION
by Kristine Kathryn Rusch
Setting: Thirteen years after *Return of the Jedi*

*Victorious though the New Republic may be, there is still no end to the
threats to its continuing existence—this novel explores the price of
keeping the peace. First, somewhere in the galaxy, millions suddenly
perish in a blinding instant of pain. Then, as Leia prepares to address
the Senate on Coruscant, a horrifying event changes the governmental
equation in a flash.*

Here is that latter calamity, in an early scene from The New Rebellion:

An explosion rocked the Chamber, flinging Leia into the air. She
flew backward and slammed onto a desk, her entire body shuddering
with the power of her hit. Blood and shrapnel rained around her.
Smoke and dust rose, filling the room with a grainy darkness. She
could hear nothing. With a shaking hand, she touched the side of her
face. Warmth stained her cheeks and her earlobes. The ringing would
start soon. The explosion was loud enough to affect her eardrums.

Emergency glow panels seared the gloom. She could feel rather
than hear pieces of the crystal ceiling fall to the ground. A guard had
landed beside her, his head tilted at an unnatural angle. She grabbed
his blaster. She had to get out. She wasn't certain if the attack had
come from within or from without. Wherever it had come from, she
had to make certain no other bombs would go off.

The force of the explosion had affected her balance. She crawled
over bodies, some still moving, as she made her way to the stairs. The
slightest movement made her dizzy and nauseous, but she ignored the
feelings. She had to.

A face loomed before hers. Streaked with dirt and blood, helmet
askew, she recognized him as one of the guards who had been with
her since Alderaan. *Your Highness*, he mouthed, and she couldn't read
the rest. She shook her head at him, gasping at the increased dizziness,
and kept going.

Finally she reached the stairs. She used the remains of a desk to get
to her feet. Her gown was soaked in blood, sticky, and clinging to her
legs. She held the blaster in front of her, wishing that she could hear.
If she could hear, she could defend herself.

A hand reached out of the rubble beside her. She whirled, faced it,
watched as Meido pulled himself out. His slender features were covered with dirt, but he appeared unharmed. He saw her blaster and

cringed. She nodded once to acknowledge him, and kept moving. The guard was flanking her.

More rubble dropped from the ceiling. She crouched, hands over her head to protect herself. Small pebbles pelted her, and the floor shivered as large chunks of tile fell. Dust rose, choking her. She coughed, feeling it, but not able to hear it. Within an instant, the Hall had gone from a place of ceremonial comfort to a place of death.

The image of the death's-head mask rose in front of her again, this time from memory. She had known this was going to happen. Somewhere, from some part of her Force-sensitive brain, she had seen this. Luke said that Jedi were sometimes able to see the future. But she had never completed her training. She wasn't a Jedi.

But she was close enough.

The Corellian Trilogy:
AMBUSH AT CORELLIA
ASSAULT AT SELONIA
SHOWDOWN AT CENTERPOINT
by Roger MacBride Allen
Setting: Fourteen years after *Return of the Jedi*

This trilogy takes us to Corellia, Han Solo's homeworld, which Han has not visited in quite some time. A trade summit brings Han, Leia, and the children—now developing their own clear personalities and instinctively learning more about their innate skills in the Force—into the middle of a situation that most closely resembles a burning fuse. The Corellian system is on the brink of civil war, there are New Republic intelligence agents on a mysterious mission which even Han does not understand, and worst of all, a fanatical rebel leader has his hands on a superweapon of unimaginable power—and just wait until you find out who that leader is!

Here is an early scene from Ambush *that gives you a wonderful look at the growing Solo children (the twins are Jacen and Jaina, and their little brother is Anakin):*

Anakin plugged the board into the innards of the droid and pressed a button. The droid's black, boxy body shuddered awake, it drew in its wheels to stand up a bit taller, its status lights lit, and it made a sort of triple beep. "That's good," he said, and pushed the button again. The droid's status lights went out, and its body slumped down again. Anakin picked up the next piece, a motivation actuator. He frowned at it as he turned it over in his hands. He shook his head. "That's *not* good," he announced.

"What's not good?" Jaina asked.

"This thing," Anakin said, handing her the actuator. "Can't you *tell*? The insides part is all melty."

Jaina and Jacen exchanged a look. "The outside looks okay," Jaina said, giving the part to her brother. "How can he tell what the *inside* of it looks like? It's sealed shut when they make it."

Anakin, still sitting on the floor, took the device from his brother and frowned at it again. He turned it over and over in his hands, and then held it over his head and looked at it as if he were holding it up to the light. "There," he said, pointing a chubby finger at one point on the unmarked surface. "In there is the bad part." He rearranged himself to sit cross-legged, put the actuator in his lap, and put his right index finger over the "bad" part. "Fix," he said. "Fix." The dark brown outer case of the actuator seemed to glow for a second with an odd blue-red light, but then the glow sputtered out and Anakin pulled his finger away quickly and stuck it in his mouth, as if he had burned it on something.

"Better now?" Jaina asked.

"*Some* better," Anakin said, pulling his finger out of his mouth. "Not *all* better." He took the actuator in his hand and stood up. He opened the access panel on the broken droid and plugged in the actuator. He closed the door and looked expectantly at his older brother and sister.

"Done?" Jaina asked.

"Done," Anakin agreed. "But *I'm* not going to push the button." He backed well away from the droid, sat down on the floor, and folded his arms.

Jacen looked at his sister.

"Not me," she said. "This was your idea."

Jacen stepped forward to the droid, reached out to push the power button from as far away as he could, and then stepped hurriedly back.

Once again, the droid shuddered awake, rattling a bit this time as it did so. It pulled its wheels in, lit its panel lights, and made the same triple beep. But then its holocam eye viewlens wobbled back and forth, and its panel lights dimmed and flared. It rolled backward just a bit, and then recovered itself.

"Good morning, young mistress and masters," it said. "How may I surge you?"

Well, one word wrong, but so what? Jacen grinned and clapped his hands and rubbed them together eagerly. "Good day, droid," he said. They had done it! But what to ask for first? "First tidy up this room," he said. A simple task, and one that ought to serve as a good test of what this droid could do.

Suddenly the droid's overhead access door blew off and there was a flash of light from its interior. A thin plume of smoke drifted out of the droid. Its panel lights flared again, and then the work arm sagged downward. The droid's body, softened by heat, sagged in on itself and drooped to the floor. The floor and walls and ceiling of the playroom were supposed to be fireproof, but nonetheless the floor under the droid darkened a bit, and the ceiling turned black. The ventilators kicked on high automatically, and drew the smoke out of the room. After a moment they shut themselves off, and the room was silent.

The three children stood, every bit as frozen to the spot as the droid was, absolutely stunned. It was Anakin who recovered first. He walked cautiously toward the droid and looked at it carefully, being sure not to get too close or touch it. "*Really* melty now," he announced, and then wandered off to the other side of the room to play with his blocks.

The twins looked at the droid, and then at each other.

"We're dead," Jacen announced, surveying the wreckage.